THE AMERICANS

John Jakes was born in Chicago, graduated from De Pauw University, and gained his MA in Literature at Ohio State. He worked for fifteen years at various creative posts in advertising before deciding to write full-time.

John Jakes is the author of short stories, plays and novels, including the ambitious and brilliantly researched international bestseller, the *North and South* trilogy – *North and South*, *Love and War* and *Heaven and Hell*. The first two volumes were made into a highly successful television mini-series.

The Kent Family Chronicles, the eight-volume, bestselling epic saga, was first published between 1974 and 1980.

by the same author

The Kent Family Chronicles

THE BASTARD
THE REBELS
THE SEEKERS
THE FURIES
THE TITANS
THE WARRIORS
THE LAWLESS

The North and South Trilogy

NORTH AND SOUTH
LOVE AND WAR
HEAVEN AND HELL

JOHN JAKES

THE AMERICANS

THE KENT FAMILY CHRONICLES
VOLUME VIII

FONTANA/Collins

First published by Jove Publications 1980
First published in Fontana Paperbacks 1989

Copyright © 1980 by John Jakes and Book Creations, Inc.

Printed and bound in Great Britain by
William Collins Sons & Co. Ltd, Glasgow

For Nina

'But as you already know your rights and privileges so well, I am going to ask you to excuse me if I say a few words to you about your duties. Much has been given to us . . . and we must take heed to use aright the gifts entrusted to our care. It is not what we have that will make us a great nation; it is the way in which we use it. I do not undervalue for a moment our material prosperity; like all Americans, I like big things; big prairies, big forests and mountains, big wheat fields, railroads . . . big factories, steamboats, and everything else. But we must keep steadfastly in mind that no people were ever yet benefited by riches if their prosperity corrupted their virtue.'

July 4, 1886:
Hon. Theodore Roosevelt,
addressing the first
Independence Day celebration
in Dickinson,
Dakota Territory.

A Note to the Reader

This novel is one of a cycle of eight dealing with
several generations of a single family,
against the background of American history.
Each novel is independent and can be read
on its own, without reference to the others.
It is the author's suggestion, however,
that they be read in the order written.

J. J.

CONTENTS

BOOK SIX

The Education of Will Kent

PROLOGUE

Lost

Forty, Gideon Kent thought. *Before the year's over, I'll be that old. The country – and the Kents – have survived a great many disasters in that time. So have I, for that matter. But what about the next forty years? Will I live that long?*

Of late he'd begun to wonder. He'd been experiencing some pains that alarmed him; pains about which he said nothing to anyone else. His father had died at a relatively young age. And he was already edging close to the limit of an average man's life expectancy – forty-seven years and a few months. The approach of his fortieth birthday merely emphasized that fact.

I may have only a few years left to set things in order. And once I'm gone, who will bear the burden of leading this family?

Above all other worries, that one beset him almost constantly. During the day it ruined his concentration, and during the night it ruined his sleep. Again this evening – the close of the first day of January, 1883 – it made him uneasy and restless.

A half hour after the evening meal was over, he looked in at the door of the sitting-room belonging to his wife Julia. He told her he needed a bit of air. Her concerned expression and wordless nod said she understood some of the turmoil he was going through.

Downstairs again, he flung a long muffler around his neck and set an old top hat on his head. In recent years he'd taken to wearing a full beard. Along with the leather patch on his blind eye and the grey streaks in his tawny hair, the beard lent him a piratical air. He

17

looked as if he belonged in some deadfall near the docks rather than in the splendid, brick-fronted residence on Beacon Street from which he emerged into swirling fog.

The night was damp and exceptionally warm for January. He turned eastward without a conscious thought. His solitary walks always took him to the same destination; a place which usually brought him solace, and the answers to whatever questions had driven him to walk in the first place.

Lately, there seemed to be no answers anywhere. He was upset about the country's drift toward materialism and sharp dealing. The worst excesses of the Grant years were growing pale by comparison. Only success mattered, not the means by which a man achieved it. Appearances counted for more than substance, which seemed not to count at all. Newspapers, including his, were guilty of paying more attention to the guest lists for opulent dinner parties than to the plight of the poor starving in urban slums. It seemed that in America, a man's highest ambition was no longer to live in liberty, at peace with his conscience, but rather to be accepted by, and live in the thrall of, a few elderly women who ruled what everyone called Society.

Gideon realized he might be cynical about Society because he would never be admitted to it no matter how long he lived. It was human to dislike what was denied you. But even if Mrs Astor had kissed his foot and begged him to attend one of her fancy balls, he still would have loathed Society and all it represented. He might have gone to the ball, though. Just to smoke a few cigars, sing a few old cavalry songs, and ruffle the hostess.

But his most pressing concern these days was a drift he saw in the family. A drift that might well presage the decline of the Kents.

He was far from young. The pains were a telling

18

reminder of that. He was beginning to fear that when his mortality finally caught up with him, no one would be ready to take over the leadership of the family. And he feared no one had the desire.

He strode up the sloping street toward Charles Bulfinch's magnificent State House. Its great dome dominated Beacon Hill and the city's skyline. The building was one of those which led people to call Boston the Athens of America. But tonight Gideon was oblivious to the attractions of the local architecture and all but unaware of the emptiness of the streets. Last night, they'd been thronged with noisy revellers welcoming the new year.

As he approached a hack standing at the kerb, he reached into his coat for a cigar. The hack driver sat motionless on the high seat, an indistinct figure in the fog. Gideon struck a match. By its light, the cabman recognized him.

'Why, hello, Mr Kent. Foul evening for a stroll.'

'Oh, it isn't too bad, Sandy. Looks like business is slow.'

The driver surveyed the empty sidewalk and chuckled. 'You might say. But last night I did double my usual, so it all works out. Thank the Lord I didn't forget my best friend when I left home in Roxbury.'

From his lap robe he pulled a pottery bottle shaped like a coachman complete with whip, greatcoat, and top hat. When he tugged on the hat, it came away from the neck of the bottle with a pop. The cabman tilted the bottle and swigged. Then he held it out to Gideon:

'Care for a tot, Mr Kent? I short myself on a lot of things, but never on bourbon.'

'Don't mind if I do.'

He reached up for the bottle. The picture he must have presented – a Beacon Street Bostonian tippling on the kerbstone – amused him. Such behaviour was one reason the Kents would never be welcome in

Society. One reason, but not the main reason; he thought as fragments of the McAllister Incident of two years ago flickered in his mind.

The whiskey slid down smoothly, but was still powerful enough to make him blink and catch his breath. 'Very fine stuff, Sandy.'

'It's Kentucky, Mr Kent. The best.'

'Easy to tell that. Thanks for sharing it.'

'Don't mention it, sir. Just send me a fare if you come across one.'

Gideon waved and walked on. The bourbon made him feel a bit better, and he felt ashamed of his own pessimism. Why couldn't he be content? he wondered as he continued eastward. He had a wife he loved deeply, and who loved him. He had a thriving publishing house, a successful newspaper, a very large fortune which continued to increase thanks to rising profits and prudent investment. And he was lucky enough to live in what he considered to be one of the world's finest cities – the first American city his ancestor, Philip Kent, had seen when he stepped off the ship from Bristol.

The Kents had been back in Boston since 1878. Gideon loved the place as much as he loved New York. From the Common and the adjacent Public Garden to the new neighbourhoods of the expanding South End, it was a bustling blend of the traditional and the modern. The city had a healthy economy produced by foundries, rubber and shoe factories, and the commerce of a harbour always filled with ocean vessels, coastal packets, ferries, barges, and the new steam tugs. In such a prosperous setting, culture flourished.

Boston was a fine book town, for example. One bit of evidence was just ahead, at the intersection of School and Washington Streets. William Ticknor's famous Old Corner Book Store. Gideon paused to look at several titles from Kent and Son displayed in a window. One of the volumes was an expensive fifteenth anniversary edition of Louisa May Alcott's *Little Women*, a favourite ever since its publication. Miss Alcott wrote fiction appropriate for the whole family under her own name, and more lurid material under pseudonyms. She was one of Gideon's neighbours on Beacon Hill. Others included elderly Mr Whittier, the Quaker poet; Dr Holmes, the physician and author of popular light verse; and Mr Howells, the editor, critic, and novelist.

Boston was a good theatre town, too. Top touring companies regularly played the Tremont, where Dickens had lectured on his second American tour in '67, and the Boston, said to be New England's largest playhouse. There was vaudeville to be seen at the Howard Athenaeum, and fine music to be heard at the Music Hall opposite Park Street Church.

Gideon loved music; all sorts of music, familiar or new. Just a little over a year ago he and Julia had been among those at the Music Hall when George Henschel conducted the Boston Symphony Number Two by Henschel's friend, Johannes Brahms.

Gideon thought it a splendid, stirring work. Yet many people had walked out during and immediately after the *allegro non troppo*. The Kents had stayed through the remaining three movements, and later some of their friends had teased them about their taste for modern music; had jokingly called them 'brahmins' because they'd liked the symphony.

Gideon also shared the city's affinity for sports. He liked nothing better than to stroll along the shore of the Charles at twilight and watch the Harvard rowing team working out in swift-moving sculls. He'd become a strong partisan of the college football team, especially in its intense rivalry with Yale. The first game between the schools had been played in '75, Harvard emerging the winner. Since then, Yale had won every game. But hope still drew Gideon to Holmes Field on Saturday afternoons in the autumn.

Though he seldom brought up the subject with Julia, he enjoyed less respectable forms of athletics as well. Like most Bostonians, he'd become a bare-knuckle prize fight addict in the past year or so; the country's reigning champion, twenty-three-year old John Lawrence Sullivan, had been born in nearby Roxbury, and had knocked out his first opponent on the stage of a Boston variety theatre when he was nineteen. The preceding February, Gideon had ridden a succession of trains to reach Mississippi City, Mississippi, to see Sullivan take the crown from Paddy Ryan in nine rounds. Gideon didn't think much of Sullivan's often-stated contempt for foreign fighters. But there was no doubt that the handsome, hazel-eyed Irishman could indeed punch hard enough to fell a horse – even when he was half drunk or hung over, which was often. The Boston Strong Boy had a notorious passion for spiritous liquors and barroom brawling.

At the intersection, Gideon crossed brick-paved Washington Street and walked north. At State he turned east again. He could smell the waterfront now, the salt of the sea penetrating the fog. How he'd miss Boston if he were ever forced to leave!

He could hardly count all the things he'd long for. The great metal tea kettle, big enough to hold over two hundred gallons of water, that hung in front of the Oriental Tea Company on Court Street. The convivial meetings of his two literary clubs, the Saturday Club and St Botolph's. The animated conversation of the members of the Ladies' Visiting Committee who frequently met at the Kent house; Julia was on the charitable society's board of managers.

He'd miss the equestrian statue of Washington at the entrance to the Public Garden. The tower clock, and the noise of trains shuttling in and out of Providence

Station. The sight of the glowing beacon atop the Custom House; the smells of the flower and vegetable shows at Horticultural Hall; the taste of the hot rolls at the Parker House hotel—

Of course he'd have to give it all up one of these days. The months kept racing by. Much faster than they had when he was young, it seemed. There would come a moment – perhaps sooner than expected – when he would have no more time.

And who would lead the family?

Gideon Kent loved his daughter, his son, and his stepson. That didn't prevent him from recognizing the problems each one faced. Problems which might well prevent them from carrying on the family's tradition.

Eleanor, for example, was preoccupied by the demands of her profession. She was an actress – which automatically barred her from full respectability for the rest of her life. She was currently being courted by a member of her troupe, a young Jewish actor whom she'd known for some years. If she wanted to fall in love with a Jew, that was her business. But Gideon understood the temperament of a good number of Americans. Should Eleanor's liaison become a permanent one, it could lead to difficulties. Perhaps heartbreaking ones.

There was something else about Eleanor that disturbed Gideon. A secret hurt he believed she'd suffered on the night in 1877 when his New York mansion had been invaded by a mob of roughnecks. His first wife, Margaret, had died that night. And something had happened to his daughter. Something about which she never spoke. But it had scarred her, of that he was positive.

Then there was his younger child, Will. A vigorous boy, Will would be fourteen this year. He had an innate decency and a trusting nature, but he thought

23

poorly of himself. Gideon saw evidence of that almost every day.

Will's lack of confidence left Gideon feeling inadequate as a father. Inadequate and guilty. The guilt was heightened every time he tried to bolster his son's faith in himself. He never succeeded. Gideon feared that, left uncorrected, Will's feeling of inferiority could blight his life.

Will's relationship with Julia's son, Carter, bothered Gideon, too. Carter had been a companion for Will at a time when Will most needed one. But now the younger boy had become dependent on the older. And Carter wasn't exactly an ideal model for anyone's character.

Oh, he had good qualities. He was intelligent, and certainly not without courage. But he tended to glibness, he was headstrong, and he had a calculating streak. His father, Louis Kent, had been a Civil War profiteer, an unashamed opportunist all his life. Gideon detected signs of a similar disposition in Louis's son.

Furthermore, Carter's tendency to resist authority made his school career a disaster. Only repeated intervention on Gideon's part had prevented his dismissal from preparatory school, the exclusive Adams Academy out in Quincy. Now Carter was barely hanging on at Harvard. He hadn't survived the social winnowing which traditionally took place during the sophomore year; he hadn't been chosen for the first of the clubs by means of which a student made his way up the school's invisible social ladder. Of course the fault was in part Gideon's; all the prominent families that sent sons to Harvard knew of what Gideon mentally referred to as the McAllister Incident.

Academically, things were even worse for Carter. He was having particular trouble with a professor of German, a bad-tempered fellow whose dictatorial manner clashed with Carter's dislike of any and all rules. The professor was determined to see him dismissed from the college – or so Carter claimed.

In his own way, Gideon loved Eleanor, and Will, and Carter. But that love hadn't prevented him from losing faith in the ability of the three young people to hold the family together in the years ahead. None of the three showed the slightest interest in the ideals by which several generations of Kents had tried to live. Eleanor was too busy. Carter was too reckless and irresponsible. And Will – the one among them who might offer the best hope of leadership – Will's character was being warped by his low self-esteem, and his worship of his stepbrother.

How shameful of me to think so poorly of them.

Yet Gideon was powerless to do anything else. And he couldn't explain away his loss of faith by reminding himself that as people grew older, they always developed a scepticism of the young, thus acting out one of the eternally recurring patterns of human life.

With a start, he realized he'd reached the waterfront. Down a dark lane, a concertina squeaked faintly. To his right, he heard petticoats rustling but couldn't see the whore because of the fog. Ahead, men bellowed a shanty behind sulphurous-looking windows of bottle glass. The singing came from a notorious dive called the Red Cod. Every week or so, someone got knifed or beaten there.

He walked out along a pier. There were at least two hundred such piers in Boston now. But many of the oldest ones were gone, including Griffin's Wharf where Philip Kent had gathered the tea which was kept in the small green bottle that stood on a mantel at home. Griffin's had been buried by the landfill that had expanded the city along the waterfront and the Back Bay.

A steam tug chugged out on the water, its engines at dead slow and its bell ringing a constant warning. Its

25

running lights were barely visible in the heavy fog. Amid the reek of fish and cordage, Gideon stood shivering in the dank air. Europe, the family's homeland, lay out there somewhere. But it was hidden.

Just like the tug—

Just like the future.

Fear surged through him. Fear that the family traditions would wither, the family's dedication to principle evaporate in the climate of materialism settling over America—

He shivered again. Despite the mildness of the evening, his hands and legs had grown cold and stiff. He rubbed his upper arms and stamped his feet. The pilings of the pier creaked.

Could he somehow change things? He wasn't sure. He feared there were already forces at work too powerful for him to overcome.

But he *had* to overcome them; struggle against them until he set each of the younger Kents on the right road—

Tonight, it was hard for him to feel any confidence in his ability to do that. In this cold forlorn place, his spirits had sunk to their lowest point in a long time.

Suddenly a dart of pain pierced the centre of his chest. Pierced and spread outward, towards the edge of his breastbone. The pain quickly became a tight constriction; a heavy weight pushing against him. He had trouble getting his breath. For the ten or fifteen seconds in which the pain persisted, he was terrified.

When it passed, his cheeks were bathed with sweat. What was the cause of the pain? Was he going to be struck down by the same kind of heart seizure that had killed his father, Jephtha Kent, at a relatively young age?

He couldn't permit that to happen. Not with the family in its present state of disarray. Upset and anxious, he gazed to the east. What would Philip have done? Old Philip, that self-assured, faintly truculent man who stared out from the ornate picture frame in Gideon's study.

From the dark and the fog hiding the Atlantic, no answer came.

God forgive him for having lost faith in the younger Kents and their ability to take command of the future, instead of letting it take command of them. The hopelessness was growing in him like a disease. He knew the real reason for it. The childen weren't to blame; he was. He had lost faith in himself. He had lost faith in his own ability to stop or redirect forces already in motion—

Sudden footsteps. He turned and saw an old seaman outlined against the light of a tavern door; the Red Cod again. The door had been opened so that two men could throw a third out into the fog. His chin struck the cobbles and Gideon heard the snap of a bone breaking. The men inside shut the door with a muffled bang. The darkness hid the man lying motionless, and the old seaman too. But Gideon heard the latter's drink-slurred voice address him:

'Ye don't look like ye belong in this part of town, mate. Are ye lost?'

Gideon chuckled; a hard, humourless sound. 'Completely.'

'Can I help ye out?'

'By God I wish you could. Thank you anyway.'

Gideon walked by the old man and headed back in the direction of the city. His words, spoken quietly but with the fervour of desperation, made the old seaman scratch his head and stare after him long after Gideon's form was lost in the fog.

BOOK ONE

The Chains of the Past

CHAPTER 1

At the Red Cod

Of all the waterfront dives in Boston, none looked meaner or dingier inside than the Red Cod – and none was more dangerous.

The place catered to the rough men who worked the fishing boats, and to others who cleaned, cut up, and packed ice around the fish the boats brought back. There was also a smaller group of patrons even more reckless and amoral than the first two. These were the men and women who lived off the fishermen and the packing house workers.

It was a female in this smaller group whom Carter Kent had decided to visit tonight. The visit was possible only because Carter had hoarded his allowance for several weeks. Like many parents of young men at Harvard, Gideon was generous with his stepson; perhaps overly generous. Carter often thought with great amusement that if his stepfather knew how the so-called pocket money was being spent, there would be no more of it.

Unlike Gideon, Carter did not go to the docks for peace and contemplation. He liked the Red Cod because it was so distinctly different from his college surroundings. There was an air of casual disregard of the law, a refreshing contrast to the discipline under which he suffered as a student. He found the atmosphere of barely suppressed violence exciting, though he was well aware that it was risky for Harvard men to set foot in the tavern. Few did. Even his friend Willie Hearst, who also had a liking for excitement, didn't come down to this part of the city.

Tonight – Washington's birthday, 1883 – the Red Cod seemed unusually crowded. The stench of sweat, beer, gin and fish hit Carter like a bludgeon as he stepped inside, feeling, as always, the quickening of his pulse that accompanied a visit here.

The tavern was noisy and the constant calls for service almost uniformly profane. The landlord, a greying runt named Phipps, looked annoyed by the commotion. When he recognized Carter, his gaze grew even more sullen.

Carter slid past a table of rowdies to an old deacon's bench that had just been vacated near the smoky fireplace. At a table behind the bench and close to a little-used side door sat Tillman, an obese fisherman who worked for Carter's sometime drinking companion, Captain Eben Royce. Tillman waved his battered pewter mug. Carter grinned and returned the greeting. Phipps, meantime, came out from behind his serving counter with three tankards in each hand. 'One side, one side, you damned lazy louts.'

Carter spied the serving girl he hoped to engage for a few minutes later on to relieve the tension that had built up recently. Josie was illiterate, and rather stout, but still in her twenties, and good-natured. She had breasts of positively amazing dimensions. She was displaying them by leaning over while she served a table in back. Carter saw the redness of a nipple showing above the line of her none too clean blouse.

She in turn saw Carter watching, and smiled. Phipps gave his girls time to make a quick dollar or two, and in return for his generosity he collected a portion of their earnings.

A number of patrons gave Carter surly, even hostile looks. At twenty-one, he was a broad-shouldered, handsome young man with jet black hair and eyes. His skin had a swarthy cast – a heritage from his paternal grandfather, an officer in the Mexican army. His colouring might have induced some to take him for one of the Portuguese fishermen who frequented the tavern, except that he didn't move or speak like a sailor; his upbringing in a wealthy household gave him a certain polish and grace he couldn't entirely disguise. And although he always wore old clothes to the Red Cod, they were cleaner and neater than those of the other patrons.

He reached the high-backed bench and dragged it across the dirty floor to a place immediately next to the fire. He was chilled. It had been a long walk down from Beacon Street, through streets wet with the melting of last night's heavy snow. Phipps, on his way back to the serving area, passed close to Carter just as he moved the bench. The landlord reacted with a loud exclamation.

'Leave the damn furniture where I put it, boy.'

Carter's faced darkened. He knew Phipps wouldn't have picked on him if he were one of the regulars. Phipps despised Harvard students. Last fall, several of them had come in, ostensibly for ale, and had uncorked bottles of bugs especially collected for the occasion. Even the patrons of the Cod, who were familiar with vermin of all sorts, still talked of the prank. The bugs had numbered in the hundreds – the count depended on the source – and Phipps had been violently antagonistic toward the college crowd ever since.

Still, Carter automatically resented the order. Then he remembered what sort of place he was in, and smiled the bright, charming smile that was one of his few assets:

'Mr Phipps, I'm damn near numb from the trip down here. Can't hurt to let me sit by your fire a min—'

'*Leave it where I put it!*' Phipps shoved him aside and then pushed the bench back to its original position.

33

Chairs scraped, heads turned, and men snickered at Carter's expense.

Anger consumed him then. But instead of giving in to it, as he wanted to do, he had the good sense to call on his only real talent, one he'd discovered years before. He had a certain quickness of mind and facility with words which made it easy for him to speak persuasively. And he had that charming smile, which somehow gave credibility to even his most outrageous statements.

'What a thing to do to a frozen patron – especially in this city and on this day!' he said with a grin, quite aware of the splintered bung starter Phipps kept in his belt. The landlord was resting his hand on it, as if hoping to find an excuse to use it on his young customer. But Carter's remark confused him.

'This day?' Phipps repeated, blinking.

'The first president's birthday! Old George fought for freedom, and on his birthday, in the town that was the very cradle of liberty, I should think a man would be free to move a bench a few inches when he's frozen his ass to come here and give you his money. Seems to me you're not a very proper, liberty-loving American, Mr Phipps.'

The glibness of the words caught the fancy of the previously hostile patrons, who laughed and applauded:

'He's got you there, Phippsy!'

'Let Harvard put his bench where he wants it.'

Phipps eyed the crowd, and Carter, with disgust.

'Ah, do it, then.' He pivoted away. Carter kept that glowing smile in place and executed a mock bow to the man:

'President Washington thanks you, and so do I—' He was bent over at the bottom of the bow, and thus his face was hidden from the landlord as he added in a whisper, '*You ignorant jackass.*'

34

Suddenly he blinked. That was it. The solution he'd been seeking for weeks – ever since it had become clear that his nemesis, Eisler, would give him failing marks this year, too. In this distinctly unlikely setting, old Phipps had inadvertently triggered the answer to Carter's problem.

Royce's fat cohort, Tillman, congratulated him on winning the battle of the bench. Carter grinned again, thanked him and sat down, barely able to contain a new kind of excitement. The scheme for revenge had jumped full-blown into his mind. His friend Willie, one year his junior but already a connoisseur of pranks, would love it. The only question was – did Carter have the money and the nerve to carry it off?

2

He'd completely forgotten Josie. He realized it when he felt her big breast pressing against his right shoulder; she had come up beside him at the end of the bench, feigning a pout:

'Hello, Carter my sweet. I thought you'd come to see me, an' then all at once, you looked a hundred miles off.'

He grinned and pulled her down on his knees. He ran his hand up beneath her skirt – she never wore drawers – and fondled her.

'Ah, that feels lovely,' she laughed, wiggling. 'But you know Phippsy don't allow samplin' of the goods.'

'He doesn't allow much of anything,' Carter grumbled, withdrawing his hand.

She giggled again. 'You showed him up good. That tongue of yours is a wicked instrument.'

'Of course you speak from experience—'

She batted at his nose in feigned anger. In an age in

which the stern and upright British queen set the moral tone for the entire Western world, tavern sluts liked to mock their upper-class counterparts; this Josie proceeded to do with elaborate gestures, sniffs, and grimaces. But she hadn't the talent to carry it off more than a few seconds, and Carter soon grew bored:

'I mustn't be too annoyed with Phippsy. He gave me a splendid idea for getting back at Eisler.'

'That German still giving you fits, is he?'

'He's out for my balls – academically speaking, of course.'

Again she laughed. 'Trouble with you, sweet – you can't stand to have anybody tell you what to do.'

'You've discovered that, eh?' He bussed her cheek. 'Well that may be. On the other hand, Eisler can't do anything *but* tell people what to do—' Suddenly dejection overcame him. 'I really don't belong in that damn college, Josie. I don't know whether I'm more inept scholastically or socially.'

'My, my,' she sighed, 'what a lot of big words. You act like they're all mighty important. You'll feel a lot better as soon as you decide they aren't.'

He gave her a long, thoughtful look. 'I think you may be right. There's one thing I'm going to do well at Harvard, at least. I'm talking about paying that bastard back.'

'I know something you do very well,' she said, leaning over to kiss his ear. His cheek itched from contact with a piece of false hair. The hair was made of tow, he suspected. On occasion his mother wore expensive natural hair imported from France, but tavern harlots couldn't spend that kind of money just to enhance a hairdo.

Phipps banged his palm on the counter. 'Josie! Get back to work. He don't get to feel till he pays up.'

'Told you,' Josie whispered with a resentful glare at her employer. She slid off Carter's lap causing him to lose the pleasurable stiffness he'd been enjoying ever since she plumped her hefty buttocks into his lap. What a pity that stiffness was all he'd enjoy this evening. He had decided to dispense with Josie's services. He'd need every cent to rent the equipment necessary for carrying out his splendid scheme.

'Be ready for me soon?' Josie asked as she started off.

'I imagine so,' he replied in a vague way. 'Right now bring me a pot of beer, will you? And tell Phippsy to go to hell.'

While another patron grabbed Josie's wrist and engaged her in conversation, Carter noticed the leather-faced Phipps watching him through the slow-moving smoke. Carter would have liked to smash the landlord's face for him, but he was determined to avoid trouble tonight. He wanted to concentrate on planning his revenge against the man he loathed above all others.

3

Associate Professor Edmund Eisler taught German. He had given Carter failing marks twice the preceding year, had failed him again at the end of the first term this year, and had made it clear that he intended to fail him a fourth time in the spring. Carter had asked university officials why, when he was required to repeat the introductory German course, he was put back into Eisler's section. The answer was blunt: Eisler had requested it.

In Carter's opinion the man belonged in the Prussian army, not in a classroom. His curly blond hair lay over his forehead in damp, effeminate ringlets. He had protruding blue eyes, and a superior manner, and loved to strut in front of his classes with a gold-knobbed cane in hand. He issued study instructions as if they were military orders, emphasizing them by whacking the cane on the desk.

What had really precipitated the trouble between them was a tea Eisler and his dumpy wife had given for the professor's students during Carter's first term at Harvard. There Carter had met the Eislers' daugher, a yellow-haired, dumpling-shaped girl whom some of Carter's fellow students said would take on any boy who asked. Over hot tea and lemon snaps, Carter asked – but not softly enough; the professor was standing just a step behind him.

Eisler's daughter protected herself by pretending moral outrage. And from then on, Eisler was the foe.

He missed no chance to demean Carter. It was widely known in Cambridge that Eisler's wife had social pretensions, and curried the favour of women considered to be leaders of Boston society. Once, after a particularly heated exchange, Eisler sneered:

'Why should I expect anything but boorishness from you, *Herr* Kent? I know, after all, what your stepfather did to McAllister.'

The more Eisler bore down on Carter's deficiencies as a student of languages – 'You speak German as if you were an immigrant from the moon. And a rather dim-witted immigrant, at that.' – the more Carter resisted. When Eisler assigned homework due the next day, Carter finished a day late. When Eisler doubled the assigned work as a means of reprisal, Carter handed the assignment in a week late – or not at all.

In class, they argued over everything; Carter had a talent for that. They went round and round on subjects as diverse as the pronunciation of the umlaut and the worth of the campus humour magazine, the *Lampoon*, the efficiency of Boston's Metropolitan Horse Railroad and, not many weeks earlier, the music of Richard Wagner, which Eisler adored. Knowing absolutely nothing about it, Carter classified Wagner's work as turgid and bizarre, two words he'd read in a newspaper article about the composer. This last, supreme insult had provoked an outburst from Eisler which reminded Carter of where he stood:

'You are an idiot, Herr Kent.' He *always* said *Herr* Kent – the pompous ass. 'You speak with the experience of an infant and the intelligence of a flea. You don't care what you say as long as you can bully and wheedle others into believing it – ' That was true enough. ' – and you are not fit to be a Harvard student. I shall not rest until I see your repulsive presence removed from this campus.'

So there they stood, clear enemies. For weeks, Carter had been hunting for a way to avenge himself against the unremitting abuse. The encounter with old Phippsy had done the trick.

'Jackass,' he whispered again, savouring the word as much as he savoured the beer Josie brought him a moment later – just before the real trouble began.

CHAPTER II

Brawl

By the time Carter finished a second pot of beer, the chill had left him. Josie was sending questioning looks his way, as if to ask whether he'd forgotten about going upstairs. He was spared the need to invent an excuse by a flurry of cheerful greetings at the front door. When he saw who had come in, he smiled too.

Captain Eben Royce was a small, trim man who

made his living with his own fishing smack. Boston-born and raised, he was fifty or more, but only his lined face and greying hair gave away that fact; he had the energy of someone half his age.

Royce and Carter had struck up a conversation the first time Carter had visited the Cod. They'd got along well, becoming occasional drinking companions. Royce was a tolerant man. Hearing that Carter attended Harvard, he'd smiled and shrugged:

'If you prove yourself worthy in other ways, we'll not hold that against you.'

Royce had a good many friends in the tavern and each wanted a bit of his time. This proved a little awkward for his companion – a stunning dark-haired woman about ten years Carter's senior, and four inches taller than Royce.

The woman had high cheekbones, a full mouth, smooth skin, and shining dark hair that fell across the shoulders of her threadbare cloak. The cloak emphasized rather than concealed the lines of the large breasts which heightened her aura of robust sexuality.

Carter had never seen the woman before. But he knew her name was Helen Stavros, and that she was Greek. Royce had formed a liaison with her about six months before. He bragged about her constantly: 'A beautiful, angelic face – and a disposition to match.' From a man toughened to the ways of the world and the disappointing weaknesses found in most human beings, it was a compliment indeed. Gazing at the woman now, Carter understood what his friend meant. He envied Royce.

Royce socialized with acquaintances a moment longer, then took the woman's arm and guided her to a table at the very back of the tavern. He ordered bowls of chowder and pots of beer, then began to circulate again. Soon he reached the fireplace. He shook Carter's hand with great warmth:

'Didn't expect you here. Thought you'd be celebrating Georgie's birthday up at Harvard Square.'

'The girls up there aren't my kind,' Carter shrugged. 'I must say, Eben, your lady is all you said she was.'

Royce beamed. 'Aye, she's a beauty, ain't she? Never thought a female could persuade me to think about changin' my bachelor status.'

'I wouldn't expect a woman that handsome to be unmarried.'

'She wasn't till her husband died. Two years ago it was. She and Stavros came from a little village called Poros, on an island near Athens. Her husband sickened in our climate and died pretty quick. But their town was a fishing town – which is why she don't mind the way I smell.'

He cast an almost worshipful look toward the woman, who sat calmly surveying the rafters of the room. Carter surmised she was intentionally avoiding the gaze of the other men. Many were watching her closely.

'She says she's right fond of me, Carter. Right fond – and I guess that makes me the luckiest man in Boston.'

'I agree with you that she's beautiful,' Carter told him, meaning it.

'G'wan, now – she's taken,' the fisherman laughed, knuckling Carter's shoulder in a good-natured way. 'How you getting along with all those perfessors?'

'Worse than ever.'

'Well, my offer stands. If that stuff gets too disagreeable, I'll put you to work on the *Atlantic Anne*. Hard work keeps a man out o' trouble.'

'I can find other ways to stay out of trouble, Eben.' Carter said it with a smile, but he wasn't entirely joking.

Royce shrugged, and walked behind the bench to speak to his employee, Tillman. Helen Stavros was spooning chowder from a cracked bowl. The Cod wasn't the sort of place a decent woman would dare enter alone. But with Eben present, no one molested her – and Carter's estimate of the woman's character increased even more when he saw that she did absolutely nothing to give the captain cause for jealousy.

Carter frowned suddenly. The noise level had dropped all at once. Heads again turned toward the front door. Carter looked that way and saw a man enter. He had never seen him before, but obviously many of the other patrons had.

2

The man was stouter than Eben Royce, thicker of waist and arm. Carter reckoned him to be about forty. His clothes were old, drab and dirty. A small gold ring, badly tarnished, pierced the lobe of his left ear. Shiny black hair curled out from under a woollen cap. He had a curving nose and a petulant mouth. From the stranger's clothes as well as from his expression, Carter formed an immediate impression. This was a man who cared about neither his appearance nor the feelings of anyone else.

Never had Carter seen a crowd so instantly divided as when the man swaggered toward the bar. Phipps and many others sent dark looks at the new arrival. But friends greeted him, and Carter heard one call:

'Hello, Ortega. Where's your brother tonight?'

'Stoking a boiler somewhere between here and Liverpool,' the man answered in heavily accented English. 'Be back in a month or so.'

Ortega, eh, Spanish, Carter guessd. Later he discovered his guess was wrong, and that Ortega was the Portuguese version of the name; in Spain it would have been Ortegas.

The man stepped up to the serving counter. Carter saw no sign of a weapon, but the patrons on either side of the stranger made room – clear indication that they feared him. The new arrival smiled at Phipps in an insincere way:

'A mug of your usual. *É una porcaria.*'

When Phipps shook his head to show he didn't understand, the swarthy man grinned all the wider. 'Your usual. Swill. Pig slop. That's all you serve in this place. I wouldn't have come here except that some of the company is interesting.'

He pivoted, leaned on his elbow and let his eyes rest on the Greek woman. Evidently he'd spotted her as he was coming in. There was no mistaking his interest. Above him a sperm-oil lantern hanging from a beam cast the sharp shadow of his nose across the upper part of his cheek. Just below the shadow-line, Carter noticed what he hadn't noticed before – a small white scar in the shape of a fishhook.

The man's eyes raked the Greek woman's face and torso. He paid no attention to the pewter mug Phipps slid to him, calling out:

'*Eh, puta, trabalhas aqui?*'

She avoided his eyes and kept silent.

'Can't speak Portugee? I asked if you work here.'

'Leave her be, Ortega,' Phipps said, though his voice was none too strong. 'She came here with with Eben Royce.'

Phipps turned, as if to point out the fisherman. The startled expression that appeared on his face made Carter lean out past the end of the deacon's bench and look behind him, where he expected to find Royce talking to a crony.

The fisherman was nowhere in sight. For the first time, the Greek woman saw that too.

43

'Where the hell'd he go?' Carter whispered to the man at the table nearest the bench. The man hooked a thumb at the side door:

'Slipped out a couple of minutes ago. Tillman had some'pin to show him.'

Carter turned back, saw Ortega scrutinizing the area round and behind the bench. Seeing no one he recognized, the Portugee smiled in a smug way and walked toward the table where the Greek woman sat rigid with tension. Carter decided Ortega wasn't a sailor like the brother someone had mentioned; he didn't have the recognizable gait of a man accustomed to tilting decks.

The woman looked past the Portugee and searched the room, fear showing clearly on her face now. Her eyes touched Carter's. *Oh, no*, he thought. *I'll have no part in this quarrel*.

But those eyes held him – begged him – and he knew that if he looked away, she'd think him a coward. Besides, Royce was a friend, she was Royce's woman, and she was in trouble. If he could just delay any trouble for a few moments, surely Royce would return.

He waited another few seconds to see whether anyone else would get up. No one did. He swallowed hard, tried to ignore his suddenly tight stomach and stood.

4

Phipps's eyes warned him not to interfere. So did a patron who plucked his sleeve as he passed and whispered, 'Leave him alone, lad. He's half crazy.'

Carter heard, but he was committed. Ortega reached

the Greek woman's table and stopped there. Behind him, Carter walked past goggle-eyed men at the serving counter. The Portugee heard Carter's footsteps. He turned and gave him a quizzical smile, as if he couldn't believe anyone could be so stupid as to challenge him.

With contemptuous politeness, the Portugee asked, 'Do you want to get through here? Do you want me to step aside so you can reach the place you obviously belong? The outhouse, I mean.'

Someone snickered. Carter tried to keep his voice steady:

'I just want you to leave that woman alone.'

Again that raking scrutiny. The man scratched the fish-hook scar with one grime-crusted fingernail. 'Your name Royce?'

Desperate, Carter called on the talent that had sometimes served him well before:

'I'm Eben Royce's cousin.' He heard murmurs of surprise; hoped the reaction of the crowd wouldn't give him away immediately. The Greek woman was staring at him. He hurried on, 'There are a lot of Eben's first and second cousins in the neighbourhood, so if you bother this woman, you'll have a lot of people down on your—'

'*Mentiroso*,' Ortega interrupted, his crooked white teeth shining when he grinned. 'In case you don't understand Portugee, I said you're a damn fucking liar. Captain Royce is a man with no relatives, that much I know.'

He leaned forward, resting his hands on the back of a heavy chair. 'But I don't know who you are – except a very stupid young man.'

Still grinning, he whipped the chair up so fast Carter had no time to react before the Portugee smashed it against the side of his head.

Carter crashed backwards, and would have cracked his skull on the serving counter except for the men

45

standing close by, who pushed him away. He struggled upright, rage and fright warring within him as Ortega's hand slid under his tattered coat. Someone gasped when the Portugee's hand flashed into sight again, a short length of metal glinting in it.

Ortega's face looked unhealthy in the lantern light. He licked his lips, anticipating his pleasure as he began to move the knife's blade in a small, provocative circle:

'Come on, *meu amigo*. Let's show the lady what you're made of, eh? I'll cut your insides out and strew them all over the floor.'

Ortega lunged then, and Carter heard shouting – most of it directed against the Portugee, but some in support of him. Carter dived to the floor to avoid the slashing blade. He landed on his belly and Ortega checked his lunge. The Portugee raised his right heel and brought it driving down toward Carter's neck.

At the last instant, Carter rolled, escaping the blow that might have crushed his neck. It glanced off his collar bone. '*Bastardo!*' Ortega yelled, and raised the knife in preparation for a downward slash at Carter's exposed throat. Carter was trying to roll again when he saw a chair sail into sight, smash a hanging lantern, then strike the Portugee on the side of the head.

The impact staggered Ortega. He would have fallen on top of Carter – impaling him with the knife – if Carter hadn't twisted onto his back and rammed his boot hard into Ortega's groin. The Portugee let out an involuntary cry. Men laughed. One or two clapped. Ortega turned red from humiliation as he lurched away. Carter saw blood oozing in the man's curly black hair. The chair had struck harder than Carter had thought.

The Portugee was still off balance. He fell, and Carter rolled wildly to avoid the knife. He got out of the way just as the other man crashed to the floor, the point of his blade penetrating the pegged boards where Carter's head had been a moment earlier.

Above him, vengeful and powerful-looking despite his small frame. Eben Royce – who had evidently flung the chair – attacked Ortega from behind with an ash-blackened poker. Ortega was groggy but he saw the weapon, and frantically crawled under a nearby table. Down came the poker, so hard that the flimsy table broke in the centre. Ortega covered his head as wood rained down.

Carter struggled to his feet. Fights had broken out all over the tavern. Pro-Ortega patrons were punching and kicking those who were against him; Carter saw paunchy Tillman grab two men by their collars and ram them head-first into the fireplace. Only when they screamed did he let go and seek someone else to punch.

Phipps rushed back and forth, vainly trying to break up the fights. He protested once too often, and someone broke an oak trencher over his head. Wailing obscenities, he folded and hit the floor.

Royce turned his attention to Carter. 'I shouldn't have gone outside with Tillman an' left her alone. 'Preciate your steppin' in when you did, I owe you for that. Now get out of here 'fore the coppers show up.'

Queasy all at once, Carter nodded. He was beginning to realize what had almost happened to him.

Under the broken table, Ortega was floundering as he tried to raise himself. Suddenly his bleary eyes fixed on Carter.

'*Cagão!*' he said through clenched teeth. 'I'll see you again, that I swear.'

A tankard came flying from the back of the room, where the Greek woman hd pressed herself against the wall. Royce raised the poker and batted the tankard aside like a ball player. In the distance Carter heard clattering hoofs and shrill whistles – a police wagon on the way.

'Get out of here and don't come back for a while,' Royce urged. Carter needed no more prodding. He turned – and in dismay saw half a dozen men fighting between him and the door. He turned sideways, slipped between two of the men, absorbed a glancing blow from a third, gut-punched a fourth, and finally made it into the damp darkness as the police wagon came charging toward the head of the pier, the manes of its two heavy horses standing out behind them.

Carter ran the other way, miscalculated, and plunged off the edge of the pier.

He dropped into the icy water with a great splash, went numb as the water closed over him, and in panic, fought his way to the surface.

He broke into the air, sputtering and splashing loudly until he realized how much noise he was making and strove to keep quiet. Fortunately the commotion up at the Cod – cursing, shouting, whistles blasting – smothered his own sounds. He paddled to a slimy piling directly under the edge of the pier and clung there, out of breath. He shut his eyes and shuddered. He'd almost lost his life in that damn place. *How in God's name did I get into this?*

He knew very well. He'd got into it by being a failure at Harvard, and by coming to a dive like the Red Cod. Before, he had always enjoyed observing the some-times violent doings at the tavern. Tonight he'd involved himself in them to help a friend – and quite suddenly, the Red Cod's atmosphere of violence was not titillating, but terrifying. He'd never go back to the place. Especially not after the Portugee's warning.

Carter pulled himself up out of the water and slipped away, shivering. He was too soaked to go home to Beacon Street. Trying to put the frightening memory of Ortega out of his mind, he headed instead for the

dormitory room of his best friend, Willie Hearst. He
could get a drink there. And Willie was always happy
to hear about his escapades. And Carter was sure that
when he described the scheme for vengeance which
he'd conceived, Willie would be delighted by it.

Of course, the prank was risky. But Carter hated
Eisler so much, he no longer gave a damn.

CHAPTER III

Caught

Carter was right. Willie Hearst had loved the scheme.
But he'd bet his friend twenty-five dollars that he would
never go through with it.

Now, sixty days later, Carter was finally ready to
undertake his revenge against Eisler. By this time
Willie was accusing him of cowardice, and demanding
his twenty-five dollars. Carter assured him he had no
intention of paying. Eisler would get his comeuppance,
and precisely according to plan.

All the elements had to be right, though. That took
time. First he had to hire equipment for a particular
night. A bakery was willing to rent its delivery wagon
and the horse that pulled it, but because Carter was a
student, and told the bakery owner he wanted the
wagon so his social club could take an excursion in the
country, the price was double what the bakery man
first quoted him. Harvard students were not famous for
respecting property – their own or others'.

Carter found it a bitter experience to have to pretend
he was a member of a Harvard club. He hadn't been
chosen for the Institute, the quasi-literary organization

49

which dated from 1770, and which inducted about thirty-five per cent of the sophomore class every year. The chosen ones were grouped into tens, and the tens were ranked. This ranking was posted at the college, and also published in the Boston papers. The social elite at Harvard were not destined to remain anonymous.

Rejection by the Institute meant there was no chance for Carter to be taken into DKE, the secret society which represented the next step up the social ladder; all the members of Deeks, as it was sometimes called, came from the Institute list.

Willie was a member of DKE, of course. He would advance from there to one of the waiting clubs – most of which were chapters of national fraternities – and then to the pinnacle: one of the two final clubs, AD or Porcellian. Willie wanted Porcellian. And here Carter was – only able to pretend that he was a member of that elite. He played the role well enough to convince the bakery man, which only enhanced his bitter feelings of isolation. But those feelings made him more determined than ever to pull off his prank.

Obtaining the animal to be hidden away inside the wagon was more difficult. Carter canvassed the stables in the area and thus learned of a drayage firm that used mules for some of its wagons. He was eventually able to buy an old, spiritless donkey that had almost outlived his usefulness. Cost of the donkey and a stable stall for him – $22.

Carter's financial reserves were at this point exhausted. He was forced to ask Willie for a loan. Again complaining about stalling tactics, Willie nevertheless gave him the money.

The final necessary element was a faculty meeting which would keep Eisler away from home most of the evening. After Carter had made all his other arrangements, he waited for such a meeting. Finally one was scheduled for late April.

The morning of the meeting Carter left home in a state of excitement, having told Gideon and Julia that he'd probably be playing cards with Willie and some other students until very late.

He skipped all his classes that day except Eisler's. His hopes plummeted when the professor was even more ill-tempered than usual thanks to an aching tooth. Carter asked him about it. The teacher was instantly suspicious:

'What's this, *Herr* Kent? Sympathy? For me? How unusual. You'll pardon me if I don't take you seriously. Are you trying to delay class recitation because you're unprepared again?'

The professor threw his shoulder back and sniffed. 'Be assured, *Herr* Kent, a little thing like a toothache will not incapacitate me in the least. Nor prevent me from asking to see the exercises you were to prepare for today—'

Without warning, he whipped his cane down on the desk, inches from Carter's hand. 'I'll see them now, if you please.'

Hate in his eyes, Carter growled, 'I don't have them.'

Eisler's smile was more of a sneer. 'I thought not.' He pivoted away. Silently, Carter cursed him. But he had the answer he wanted. Eisler was well enough to attend the faculty meeting. So tonight was the night.

2

At a few minutes past nine, tense and perspiring, Carter turned the hired wagon into the mouth of the alley which ran behind Eisler's modest residence on Berkeley Street, in Cambridge. The horse was docile, easy to control. The donkey inside the wagon was another matter. From time to time Carter heard hoofs slam against the rear doors. Old as the donkey was, he resented confinement.

Slowly, making as little noise as possible, Carter drove the wagon down the alley, which was quite dark. The only illuminations in the vicinity came from gas lamps burning in the back rooms of houses.

The balmy spring night smelled of earth still wet from an earlier shower. Through a break in the trees, Carter discerned Eisler's house not far ahead. Lamps glowed in the kitchen, front parlour, and two rooms upstairs. Of course the Professor's wife would be home – and his bitch of a daughter, too. Carter knew the latter for a certainty when badly played pianoforte music drifted from an open parlour window. The wretched music was a blessing of sorts. If he were careful, and the donkey gave him no trouble, no one in Eisler's house would hear him.

He held his breath as he approached the small outbuilding at the rear of Eisler's large lot. Carter had surreptitiously inspected the building by daylight some weeks earlier. He knew the professor kept his horse and ancient buggy inside, and that the main doors opened onto the alley.

Just as Carter was reining the horse to a walk, the donkey kicked again, harder than before. The noise seemed to resound through the spring darkness like a gunshot.

'Sssh, damn it!' he whispered. As if the donkey could actually understand him, the animal kicked the inside of the wagon again. Carter winced and begged whatever unseen forces controlled the universe to stop the donkey from being so cantankerous. Carter had accomplished nothing worthwhile in nearly two years at Harvard. He felt that if he didn't succeed tonight, his presence at the school would have left no mark at all.

When he was honest with himself, he had to admit that his whole life up until this moment was eminently forgettable. He had been living in Boston since 1878 with his mother, his stepfather, and his stepbrother Will – the only human being besides his mother that he truly cared about. His stepfather was a rich and successful businessman. He operated a local book publishing house as well as a daily newspaper in New York, the *Union*. Carter's mother also had a career. The name of Julia Sedgwick Kent was also known in the nation's lecture halls. She spoke and wrote on behalf of the American Woman Suffrage Association.

Thus Carter had grown up among people who amounted to something. True, the Kents would never be admitted to so-called Society. But they were accomplished and successful in their own way. Carter's repeated failures were a galling contrast – and one of which he was very aware.

As far as he could tell, he had only one talent: his facility for persuading others. He thought part of that talent was inherited, and part acquired from his surroundings. Gideon enjoyed his ability to sway opinion by means of the *Union*, and of the books he published. Julia did the same thing from the platform; several times, Carter had watched admiringly as his mother converted a hostile audience to an attentive one, and then to one which was noisily enthusiastic about female suffrage – and about her.

Equally important, Carter knew he was descended from a woman who had always got her way. His paternal grandmother, Amanda Kent, was revered in the family as driving and dominant – someone who didn't know the meaning of failure. So perhaps he came by his talent naturally.

He often daydreamed about finding a career in which he could wield power and influence as the elder Kents did. Realistically, he knew it to be a hopeless ambition. He couldn't stand discipline, and his Harvard experience had taught him that he didn't have a very good mind, at least in the formal sense. He could work hard if necessary, but he hated doing that. All he had was a certain canny understanding of what motivated people, and an instinctive, though as yet undeveloped sense of how best to play on those motivations with a word, a look, a smile—

So success tonight was crucially important. If he couldn't succeed in the classrooms of Cambridge, he could at least create a legend Harvard students might talk about for years to come.

Sweating again, he braked the wagon, then tied the reins and climbed down. He crept toward the double doors of the stable. They were closed. Did that mean Eisler hadn't gone to the faculty meeting? Carter's heart pounded as he slid one of the doors aside. He winced when its rollers squeaked.

He held his breath and looked into the dark interior. Finally his eyes adjusted. He grinned—

Empty! The horse and buggy were gone. With his passion for order, Eisler had shut the doors after driving out, that was all.

Carter allowed himself a moment of congratulations, then started toward the rear of the wagon, and the hard part of the night's work.

3

Before opening the wagon doors he listened to be sure Eisler's daughter was still assaulting the pianoforte. She was. If he made no unusual noise, he could pull it off. Suddenly soaring confidence told him that.

When he opened one of the wagon doors, the donkey stamped and brayed. Not loudly, thank God. Murmuring soothing words, Carter reached in and removed the planks down which the donkey would have to walk.

Then he lifted out the cardboard sign. With that in hand, he shut the wagon door again.

He carried the sign into the stable, whose interior he could discern now that his eyes were accustomed to the darkness. The place was far too tidy for its function – Eisler's German temperament again. There was a single stall. The only light was a weak glow from under the narrow door leading to Eisler's back lawn.

He was surprised that he didn't have to struggle to get the donkey out of the wagon. The animal didn't balk or even bray. Perhaps he was glad to escape his confinement. Carter led him down the planks to the stable door and got him inside with so little fuss and noise that he began to think the gods were smiling on him at long last.

He left one of the alley doors standing open. Carefully he tied the donkey's rope to a post at the end of the stall. He felt sure this would precipitate more kicking and braying, and when it didn't, he was almost beside himself with jubilation. All he had to do was hang the sign over the donkey's neck and get away, and the thing was done.

'Gently. Gently now,' Carter whispered as he lifted the rope over the donkey's head and long, floppy ears, admiring the Gothic lettering it had taken him so long to ink on the cardboard. But the final effect – the size and clarity of the message – was well worth it. Wait till Eisler opened the stable door and read it:

Ich bin ein deutscher Esel.
Jetzt gibt's zwei unseresgleichen.

'You certainly are a German jackass, my friend,' Carter whispered. 'And now there are indeed two of you – here, hold still,' he grumbled as the rope slipped down over the donkey's neck and the sign swayed under his muzzle. Unexpectedly, it was the touch of the rope – the feel of the sign – that ruined everything.

The donkey began to shy and pull against the rope. Carter tried to calm him, to no avail. Within seconds, the donkey was braying. Then he turned and kicked out against the side of the stall – *bang*! It sounded like a mortar going off.

'Don't do that,' Carter pleaded, his euphoria gone, replaced by desperation. The donkey replied with three more swift kicks – *bang, bang, bang*.

'Oh, God,' Carter groaned. He heard another, more distant bang – a door – then someone's voice: 'Who is there? What is that noise?'

Eisler! Surely that couldn't be. Carter inched the backyard door open and then his heart seemed to hit the bottom of his stomach. The familiar haughty figure was silhouetted against the lamplit windows of the house. Eisler was storming toward the stable with his gold-knobbed cane in one hand and an ice bag in the other. He was holding the bag against his swollen jaw, and instantly, Carter knew that a foolish assumption had undone him. It was Eisler's wife who was using the buggy – contrary to the professor's assertion, the bad tooth had kept him home.

He turned to run to the alley. The donkey lunged forward so hard his rope broke. Carter stumbled against the frantic animal. Without thinking, he shouted, 'Get out of my way!'

Eisler, coming fast, heard him:

'I recognize that voice. What are you doing on my property, Kent? What are you—?'

The thunderous question broke off as Eisler yanked the door open. He loomed in the opening, a huge, frightening figure, somehow. Carter, frozen in place by fright, darted a look over his shoulder. Eisler's pop eyes popped even more. He saw the donkey. He saw and instantly understood the sign – a moment before the donkey brayed one last time and ran away into the alley and the darkness beyond.

'You damned arrogant whelp!' Eisler shouted, dropping the ice bag as he leaped inside. Holding his cane by the ferrule end, he whipped it into a hissing arc. The huge gold knob would have struck Carter's temple if he hadn't broken his terrible paralysis and stumbled backwards. The knob hit the side of the stall and wood splintered.

He's crazy, Carter thought. *He's liable to kill me if I let him*. The cane was swinging in another murderous arc. Carter ducked away, and out the door. He was halfway to the bakery wagon when Eisler emerged from the building and, with his long arm helping to extend his reach, smashed the knob of the cane against the back of Carter's right leg.

Carter cried out, falling against the bakery horse. The frightened animal leaped forward. Carter slid to the ground and the horse's right front hoof nicked his forehead. He covered his head to prevent further injury as the horse tore away down the alley. Panting, Eisler reached for Carter's shirt to drag him up—

He was trapped – caught – an unbearable feeling. Like a man escaping a jailor, Carter pushed Eisler violently, and thus sent him spilling into a hedge bordering the alley. Eisler ranted and cursed – in German now.

Carter struggled to his feet. He saw a sickening sight at the far end of the alley. The bolting horse turned left into the street but now there was no guiding hand to control the wagon. The traces broke. The wagon tilted on its side, crashing over and splintering apart as the horse ran away.

Carter fled toward the wrecked wagon while Eisler's bellowed threats filled the dark behind him. In nearby houses, windows were raised and people called out anxious questions.

Carter's chest began to hurt as he passed the wagon. It was in ruins. Everything was in ruins now. What the consequences of this night's disaster would be, he didn't dare contemplate.

CHAPTER IV

Hearst

Carter ran to the left along the darkened street connecting Berkeley and Garden. At Garden he turned right, dashing across to Cambridge Common. Ahead, old red brick buildings rose in the darkness, most of them partially concealed by the huge trees of the College Yard. A mongrel yapped in the April night.

Clouds were scurrying across the moon. A hack hurtled by, crowded with noisy undergraduates who had no doubt been over in Boston, gorging themselves on wine and lobster; Willie Hearst did that often. In the north, there was a brief peal of thunder.

Dishevelled and badly shaken, Carter paused at the east side of the Common, listening. He heard no sounds of pursuit – no outcries from that hateful voice, either in English or German. For a moment he experienced a delicious relief.

Then he grimaced. He was not only a bungler, he was a fool. Of course Eisler wouldn't come rampaging after him. The professor would collect his wits and realize he had other, more effective and certain means of punishment at his disposal.

Carter wiped his sweaty forehead with his sleeve. The night was a failure. The whole scheme, planned for so long, was a failure. He didn't want to face that, and he didn't want to go home to face the family – particularly Will, who looked up to him. He knew he had to start thinking about the defence he must mount against Eisler, but before that he wanted a drink.

Where to get it? The Red Cod? Too far – and too risky. Heeding Captain Eben Royce's warning, he hadn't been back since the night of the trouble.

He glanced at the trees rustling in the Yard. Maybe Willie was in his room, instead of taking supper with some little shopgirl over in the city or sitting with cronies in a box at the Howard, awaiting the right moment to begin pitching custard pies at the actors. He'd welcome Willie's company right about now, even though he would be forced to tell his friend that he'd failed.

Carter limped across the brick avenue, through the gates, and turned right after he passed the end of Massachusetts Hall, the oldest building on the campus. He fervently wished he were anywhere in creation except Boston.

2

Light showed beneath the door of Willie's dormitory room. Willie still lived in Matthews, in the Yard, but he was talking about moving next term to one of the more fashionable dormitories on Mount Auburn Street – Dunster, Fairfax, Apley, or one of the others that were starting to comprise a so-called Gold Coast that attracted the elite of the student body.

To judge from the tangy smell of cheese in the hall, Carter's friend was cooking an evening snack. He knocked. A high-pitched, almost girlish voice invited him in.

Willie was stirring a pot on a gas ring. He waved and grinned at his visitor in that ingenuous way Carter liked so much. There were some things about Willie which the older boy didn't like at all. His pranks that took innocent and unsuspecting people as their victims, for example. Still, Willie was always diverting, and a stout comrade once you breached his initial shyness.

William Randolph Hearst hailed from California. He had spent almost a full academic year in Cambridge, yet he didn't have many close friends. Carter suspected one reason was his peculiar appearance. Quite tall and skinny, he had unusually large hands and feet and a startling, baby-pink complexion. He parted his long yellow hair in the middle and sported a silky moustache. Neither feature could offset his awkward-looking physique, or the oddness of his eyes. Blue-grey irises were all but lost in immense whites.

'You're just in time, Carter. The Welsh rabbit's almost done.' Willie pointed a dripping spoon at an armoire. 'The beer's in there.'

Carter slumped in a brocaded armchair. All the furnishings including the books on the shelves had been chosen by Willie's mother, Phoebe Hearst. She'd accompanied him to Cambridge for the opening of the school year. Willie liked his mother, yet he'd once spoken unenthusiastically to Carter about being an only child.

'As a sprout, I was dragged all over Europe with a tutor and my friend Gene Lent. I wouldn't be so stinking spoiled if my parents had produced more than one youngster. Mother wanted more but somehow it never worked out. There are times when I wish it had.'

Now Willie took two mugs from behind a stack of textbooks. He handed one to his friend.

'What's wrong, Carter? I thought you'd be buoyant after your triumph. And impatient to collect twenty-five dollars.'

Carter glanced up. His black eyes caught and held tiny reflections of the room's gaslights. With sarcasm, he said:

'The triumph, Willie, ended in a rout. Mine.'

Twenty-year-old Willie Hearst blinked, his delicate lashes momentarily hiding those peculiar yet curiously compelling eyes. Then he sprawled in another chair and draped a stork-like leg over the arm. He looked totally relaxed, as if he worried about nothing and wanted for nothing – which in fact, he did not.

When he'd arrived at Harvard, Willie's reputation – and especially the names of his father's various mines – had preceded him. George Hearst had started life as a Missouri dirt farmer. But in the last two decades, he and an assortment of partners had wrested several fortunes from the American earth, just as Amanda Kent had taken the bulk of the Kent family fortune from the California gold fields. Hearst hadn't struck it rich until he was forty. After that, bonanza had followed bonanza. He owned the Ophir in Virginia City, a silver mine that was part of the fabulous Comstock Lode. He owned the Homestake in the Dakota Territory – gold. He owned a small Montana silver mine, the Anaconda, which had ultimately revealed its true riches – an incredible vein of copper.

'Have a cigar and tell me what happened,' Willie said in a sympathetic way. This evening he was, as always, well dressed: checked trousers, a plain but obviously expensive linen shirt, and one of the large, garish cravats he fancied.

Carter reached for a costly rosewood cigar box. He lit up and said through a blue haze, 'Things went fine at first. I got the jackass into the stable with no trouble. But then there was some noise, and Eisler came storming out to see about it.'

'You mean he was still at home?'

'That's right. He had a toothache and didn't go to the faculty meeting.'

'Did he see the sign?'

'Yes, right before the donkey ran off.'

'Then technically you won the bet,' Willie said with

61

a delighted expression. 'By God, I'd have loved to have seen that Dutchman's face.'

'No you wouldn't. He recognized me before I got away.'

Willie's smile vanished. 'My stars. No wonder you look so glum.'

'He'll have me hung up by the balls,' Carter said. The words made Willie look uncomfortable; he never swore or used offensive language.

Carter carried his mug toward the armoire, speaking around the cigar in his teeth:

'At the very least I'll be in trouble with the college. At worst Eisler will haul me into court on some charge or other. If he doesn't, the bakery owner will. I wrecked the wagon I hired for the night. And the horse ran off – God knows where.'

Willie whistled softly. Carter went on:

'I'll have to deal with my mother and stepfather, too. And I don't make a habit of lying to them. It bothered me a lot when I had to tell them I'd be playing cards tonight. I don't know what the hell I can tell them about Eisler, except the truth.'

He paused, a hand on one of the armoire door handles. The gaslight accentuated the olive cast of his skin. Even bedraggled, he was a handsome young man. Thick arms and a slim waist testified to his fine physical condition.

'I'll take my winnings whenever you care to pay me,' Carter added. 'That wagon will cost a small fortune – and while I get a pretty decent allowance, it isn't the same as getting a nugget as big as a baseball shipped from California once a month.'

Willie smiled an obligatory smile, although the campus joke which had been invented to explain his large and constant supply of money was growing stale. Carter jerked open the door of the armoire. He leaned down toward the zinc tub containing a pail of beer sitting on a block of ice. He was too preoccupied to really see the tub until something beside it stirred.

'*Jesus Christ!*' he cried as a three-foot alligator roused and opened its tooth-studded jaws not six inches from his hand.

3

That brought another laugh from Willie. 'Oh, the devil. I forgot Charlie was asleep in there.'

Carter quickly stepped away. 'Like hell you did.'

Willie walked back to the gas ring. 'Go ahead, get your beer. Charlie won't bother you. I got him drunk again tonight.'

Warily, Carter leaned down and dipped his mug in the pail. Champagne Charlie, as Hearst's pet alligator was officially named, regarded Carter with a sinister eye for a moment. Then he lowered his head lethargically. Carter slammed the door.

He sat down and sipped the beer. It didn't do much to raise his spirits. Nor did the hot, zesty cheese dish Willie served. The young Californian folded himself into a chair again. He spooned up some of the rabbit. Tapped a napkin against his lips, then said:

'I don't blame you for feeling rotten. I knew right after we met that we were peas from the same pod. Must be why we get along so well. We both hate the unexpected – unless, of course, we engineer it to surprise somebody else. And we like to hold the reins. Can't stand to let another person control things, am I right?'

An emphatic nod from Carter. Willie continued:

'I'll tell you something else. Personally, I can't take much more of the regimentation around here. Chapel. Roll calls. Lesson recitation – I doubt I'll ever get my degree. I wanted to go into the theatre like your

63

stepsister Eleanor. Mother wouldn't hear of it. But it's the theatre's loss—'

To cheer his friend, he jumped up, threw his head back and yodelled. Then he executed one of the quick, deft minstrel show dance steps he admired. With his beer mug raised and his other fist cocked on his hip, Willie grinned at Carter:

'It's the theatre's loss. I'm pretty good, don't you think?'

'Wonderful.'

'Don't strain yourself with enthusiasm.' Willie faced the wall, as if an audience sat there. He bowed from the waist several times. 'I love applause—'

'It isn't the applause you like, Willie, it's being around actresses.'

'Well, that too,' Willie admitted, smiling again. He flopped back into the chair. 'You know, maybe we're both simpletons for wasting our time here. I know Harvard's the finest school in America. But I've already dropped more courses than I'll finish this year, and there isn't a blasted thing in the curriculum I give two hoots about.'

He hunched forward. 'The only thing that interests me is a problem Gene's going to inherit next year.' Eugene Lent was the son of one of George Hearst's business associates. He was the friend with whom Willie had travelled in Europe when both were younger.

'What problem?'

'The poor chump has agreed to be business manager of the *Lampoon*. Thankless job! Humour doesn't sell very well at this pious institution. And the business manager has to make up any operating losses out of his own pocket.'

Carter whistled. 'I didn't know that.'

'It's true. I'd like to help Gene. I don't mean with loans. I mean by thinking up schemes to get people to read the magazine. Stunts, contests, maybe a parade – I'd enjoy that.'

'Because you'd be controlling things.'

'Things and people.' Willie grinned. 'Without letting 'em know I was doing it. That's part of the game, too.'

He ambled to the armoire. Helped himself to beer. Champagne Charlie again raised his deadly-looking head and scrutinized his owner for a few seconds before returning to sleep.

Willie knocked foam from his moustache after he drank. 'That's the real charm in life, Carter. Holding the reins. That and a good joke. Pa isn't much for joking, but he surely likes the other. I expect that's why he's so eager to go to the Senate.'

Carter had heard a good deal about George Hearst's political ambitions. A loyal Democrat, Hearst had bought the foundering *San Francisco Examiner*, the unofficial newspaper of the local party organization. He'd pumped money into it in the hope of furthering his political career. But the effort hadn't been enough to earn him the 1882 Democratic endorsement as the candidate for governor. He'd lost the primary by a narrow margin. Undiscouraged, he was searching for a stepping-stone to Washington.

All at once, Willie fixed his friend with one of his disconcerting stares:

'Pa's going to make it some day. Then he'll handle the reins smartly. That's what politics is all about. Maybe you should try it. You could start by passing out handbills, or running errands for a boss. You might enjoy it, and that silver tongue of yours would take you a long way, I think.'

Carter momentarily forgot Professor Eisler. 'In which party?' he asked.

'Why, the Democracy, I suppose.'

'The Kents are Republicans.'

Willie waved his mug. 'A sinner can always reform.

I tell you, for a fellow who likes to be in charge, politics is a natural.'

'Then why don't you try it?'

'With this voice?' Willie let out a loud yodel. 'I'd be laughed off the platform. Even my looks are against me.'

He swigged beer, then finished with what sounded like perfect confidence. 'I'll find some other way. But I'll pull the reins, too, you can count on that.'

The more Carter thought about Willie's suggestion, the more it intrigued him. Politicians wielded immense influence. Disbursed huge sums of patronage money and collected rewards in turn. Sometimes those rewards took the form of bank drafts or stock certificates. A great many important Americans were constantly in need of favours from Washington, which helped explain why most top-level politicians could afford large wardrobes, lavish homes, and frequent European vacations.

Of course there were risks in politics. Look at what had happened to poor Garfield two years earlier. But he could handle the risks, he decided.

The conclusion came easily because of the beer. He investigated and found there was plenty left in the armoire. This time Champagne Charlie didn't even raise his head. Carter helped himself, anxious to let the beer ease him into forgetting he'd been unable to control anything or anyone tonight.

He lurched back to his chair, his confidence ebbing rapidly. If he couldn't carry off a student prank, how the devil could he ever hope to manoeuvre his way into political office? He couldn't buy his way, obviously. He stood to inherit only a token sum from the Kent fortune; his mother had already informed him that the bulk of Gideon's estate would go to Eleanor and Will.

Well, he'd get around those obstacles somehow.

He and Willie finished the food and then guzzled

more beer, talking non-stop between drinks. The drunker they got the more fanciful became the careers they spun for themselves. Carter rose from dispenser of political leaflets to big-city machine boss. Willie graduated from circulation manager of a humour magazine to newspaper reporter. In a final step, he became a publisher more influential than Gideon Kent of the *Union*, and more ambitious than Joe Pulitzer, the St Louis newpaperman who was in the process of buying Jay Gould's moribund *New York World*. Willie was, at the end, a publisher whose impact was felt far beyond San Francisco; a publisher who shaped national opinion and influenced national policy – and knowing his friend, Carter believed that was exactly what Willie would be one of these days.

Carter lost track of time. He put Eisler, the aborted prank, and the wrecked wagon completely out of his mind. Sometime after midnight a thunderstorm broke. By then he was asleep in the armchair. When he awoke, grey light showed outside the rain-speckled window. He was brutally sober.

He sat up and groaned. Willie raised his head. He'd been asleep on the couch, a full-sized coverlet barely reaching from his neck to the mid-point of his calves. He yawned, then scrutinized his friend:

'You sick?'

'Yes. I just remembered what happened last night.' His bones creaked as he pushed against the arms of the chair. 'I have to go home.'

Carter grew dizzy suddenly. Speech was difficult:

'I – need some air. Thanks for the hospitality, Willie. I like your idea about politics. But first I have to get by the old professor.'

'Use that silver tongue,' Willie advised in a sleepy voice. 'Talk your way out.'

'Just the ticket,' Carter nodded as he stumbled to the door. 'Why didn't I think of that—?'

Then he told a lie:
'It'll be easy.'

4

Carter trudged toward the Charles River in a dawn
that smelled of the rain that had already moved out to
sea. A pebble in his shoe bedevilled him. When he
reached the Cambridge Street bridge, he took off the
shoe, inverted it and held it out beyond the rail to
shake the pebble loose. The shoe slipped from his
grasp and fell to the water.

He bellowed an obscenity that brought a reproving
shake of the finger from the driver of an early horse
car just travelling into Cambridge. For a moment
Carter watched the shoe go bobbing downstream. Then
he limped on toward Charles Street.

What was he going to tell his mother and stepfather?
He thought of several unbelievable stories, and
rejected them all because they were ludicrous, and
because they were lies. He loved his mother, but he
also respected her. She was too intelligent to be fooled
by invented stories. And as he'd told Willie, he didn't
lie to Julia or Gideon. Not often, anyway. That was
just about his only remaining point of honour.

'Just swallow the medicine,' he muttered to himself
as he walked slowly and wearily eastward along Beacon
Street, through a dawn awash with familiar smells of
fish, cordage tar, and the lump coal smoke plumed
from scores of household chimneys.

The morning was chilly. His teeth began to chatter.
He clenched them, then raised his head and squared
his shoulders. He could take the worst that Edmund
Eisler had to offer. The very worst. Didn't Gideon
alway say the Kents were, above all, survivors?

But unconsciously, he began whistling 'Pop Goes the Weasel' to keep his courage up.

CHAPTER V

At Home on Beacon Street

More than fifty million people inhabited the United States in 1883. Only a few hundred belonged to what was termed Society. The Kents did not. Although they were one of the richest families in the nation, wealth alone had not been enough to get them an invitation to the social event of the year – Mrs William K. Vanderbilt's costume ball. The ball had been held on the night of March 26. By any standard, it exceeded anything yet offered for the approval of those who comprised Society.

In prior years Mrs Astor's annual ball in January had always been considered the season's paramount event. The Vanderbilt affair changed that. Conservative estimates said it cost the hostess a quarter of a million dollars to stage her little party. The opulence of the costumes of the guests was matched only by the cleverness of some of them. Another Vanderbilt, Mrs Cornelius, had come arrayed in white satin and diamonds, representing the electric light. And although elaborately costumed and choreographed quadrilles were no novelty at formal balls, Mrs Vanderbilt's quadrilles – especially the Hobby Horse Quadrille featuring realistic life-size representations of horses which were attached to the dancers' waists – had been talked of for days afterward.

No wonder the established leader of Society, Caroline Astor – *the* Mrs Astor, as she preferred to be known – had been forced to recognize Mrs Vanderbilt at long last. Before the ball, Mrs Astor had discovered that her daughter was rehearsing for the Star Quadrille but had not received a card of invitation. The significance of the omission was clear. There would be no invitation unless Mrs Astor paid her respects to Mrs Vanderbilt, even though the latter was theoretically inferior in the social ranking.

Putting her daughter above her pride, Mrs Astor ordered up her carriage and drove to the Vanderbilt chateau at 660 Fifth Avenue in New York. She sent one of her blue-liveried footmen inside with her card. In recognition of her eminence, it bore only the words *Mrs Astor*. She didn't personally enter the mansion, or even leave the carriage. But she had humbled herself sufficiently. The invitation was in her daughter's hands soon afterward.

No symbolic act of reverence could have secured an invitation for Gideon and Julia. The list of reasons was an extremely long one.

Julia's family credentials – she had been born a Sedgwick – might once have entitled her to consideration, but they no longer did. Not since she had divorced one Kent – Amanda's son – and married another. The women who ruled New York Society did not divorce. Not even if their husbands slept with other women, which most of them did. Julia was also on the disapproved list because she had publicly espoused the cause of female suffrage.

Gideon had even more against him. First, he'd served on the Confederate side during the war. After Appomattox he'd associated himself for a time with the labour movement. His newspaper and his publishing house were considered scandalously liberal. And he was 'in trade,' the contemptuous term for anyone

70

who wasn't a gentleman of leisure, living off a business income but doing nothing to earn it. Gideon actively involved himself in his business, and had even been known to repair a broken book press if the schedules of Kent and Son demanded it.

His recent history was cloudy, too. His first wife had died in a fall from a window of the mansion he'd formerly owned on upper Fifth Avenue. His daughter was in a disreputable profession, and his younger brother had a reputation for outrageous behaviour. In Europe, Matthew Kent's paintings were making him famous, but his escapades had long ago made him notorious in his native land. Added to this was Gideon's murky role in the 1877 shooting death of the Chicago railroad magnate Thomas Courtleigh. All in all, the head of the Kent family had a reputation as a radical and a roughneck. Definitely not good social material.

There was one other event which absolutely assured the Kents' ostracism. This was what Gideon privately referred to as the McAllister Incident. Two years earlier he'd had a sharp encounter with the man who served as Society's unofficial prime minister, responsible for drawing up the guest lists for the balls which the great ladies gave, and for planning the themes and costumes of the quadrilles performed at those balls. Mentally – and sometimes openly – Gideon called that gentleman the little toad.

In Gideon's estimation, Mr Samuel Ward McAllister was undistinguished in intellect as well as appearance. He was remarkable only in that he managed to prosper by being no more than a parasite. It disgusted Gideon that a born Southerner would thus debase himself. Perhaps that was why, during a chance meeting at Gideon's club in New York, things had gone badly.

After introductions, someone had happened to mention Gideon's war record. This brought a sniff from McAllister.

'I'm from Savannah, as you may know. But at least I was never a traitor.' He eyed Gideon's chin. 'Your beard led me to briefly mistake you for a member of the Grand Army of the Republic.'

'I don't know what led me to briefly mistake you for a man, Mr Make-A-Lister.'

Society's prime minister turned purple when Gideon applied the scornful name the newspapers had given him. But he had no time to utter a protest because Gideon immediately knocked him down with one punch.

2

Gideon usually rose before sunup. His work day seldom ended until nine or ten at night. This evening was no exception. After a light supper, he retired to the library of the splendid three-story Federal brick house that he'd purchased when he and Julia returned to Boston in 1878. He had paid the exorbitant asking price solely because Philip and Amanda Kent had both owned the residence during their lifetimes. Gideon intended to see that the house never slipped out of the family again.

On Beacon Street below the library window, gas lamps glimmered, as they did above Gideon's large desk. Immediately after moving in, he'd taken over the library and converted it to an office.

Wires hung from several holes in the plaster. The house would presently be electrified with some of Mr Edison's lamps. And Gideon planned to install a telephone as soon as long distance lines were available between Boston and New York. At present he could only phone long distance to Lowell. Who the hell wanted to call Lowell?

Puffing on a cigar, he settled down to work just

about the time Carter was leading the donkey into Eisler's stable. Gideon's own son was upstairs in his room, studying, Gideon presumed. Will attended the excellent Boston Latin School; Carter's wayward behaviour at the Adams Academy had put the name Kent in such disfavour, Will could not possibly have gone there. Gideon reminded himself to look in on his son later.

Over the library mantel hung the sword and rifle Philip Kent had collected in the early years of the Revolution. The rifle was the kind commonly called a Kentucky; the sword, a French grenadier's briquet. On the mantel itself stood the original glass bottle of tea Philip had brought home from Mr Adams's tea party.

All the other family mementoes were displayed in the library as well. A glass case contained the medallion struck by Gilbert Kent, Philip's second son, as well as the bracelet of tarred cordage from Old Ironsides, on which Philip's grandson Jared – Gideon's grandfather – had served. Nearby hung the oil portrait of Philip himself, painted when he was an affluent, middle-aged Boston printer. On the wall opposite, Gideon had put the framed Auguste Renoir cartoon depicting Matt and his wife, Dolly, dancing at a Paris cabaret before their permanent separation. Dolly was now teaching school at an army post in India, and raising her son, Tom.

Next to the cartoon hung Gideon's contribution – a decidedly inferior one, in his opinion. Strictly speaking, he had contributed nothing, merely rediscovered a memento left by another. When he'd moved in, he had come across it in a packing crate that had evidently been abandoned in the cellar years ago. Now it was displayed as befitted a treasure – nestled in a velvet background under glass contained by a thick walnut frame. It was a splinter of wood, four inches long.

He had found the splinter wrapped in oilskin and shoved in among rotted garments in the packing case.

One mouldering coat bore a legible label. *G. Kent.* From that, Gideon knew he'd found the lost piece of the mast of Old Ironsides which Jared had brought home to Gilbert from the War of 1812. Gilbert's correspondence had referred to the sliver of wood, but no Kent had seen it until Gideon chanced upon the crate.

For a moment he felt tired, reluctant to attack the papers piled on his desk. Very little had changed since New Year's night. He'd made no progress in solving the problems which had sent him wandering the docks that evening and many evenings since. If anything, one of the problems had grown worse. Carter had taken to roistering more and studying even less.

Gideon hadn't suffered a recurrence of the chest pain, though. That was only part of the situation which had improved.

With a sigh, he picked up the first paper. It was a detailed cost estimate from the Herreshoff Company in Bristol, Rhode Island. John Herreshoff and his younger brother, Captain Nat, built steam launches for the United States and torpedo boats for other countries. Lately they'd introduced a new kind of pleasure boat – a small steam yacht noteworthy for its speed and economy. Gideon was negotiating for construction for an eighty-five foot vessel that would incorporate one of the Herreshoffs' innovative triple-expansion engines. He could easily have afforded one of the much larger floating palaces of the kind skippered by Astor, Gould, and Bennett. A Herreshoff yacht was more to his taste. He intended to christen it *Auvergne*, after the region in France where Philip had been born.

He studied the estimate for ten minutes, wrote several questions on the margin and approved the total, appending a note to the Herreshoffs asking them to proceed with all speed.

Next he read a memorandum from his banker,

Joshua Rothman. It informed him that the New England Telephone and Telegraph Company could now make service available between his home and the Rothman Bank. Except for communication between cities, Gideon considered Mr Bell's telephones an impractical novelty. But he liked to surround himself with the latest gadgets, so he scribbled a note to the bank officer who handled details of his account. The note authorized installation of a line. To the first note he pinned a second one approving a new roof for the family home at Long Branch, New Jersey, where his father's widow, Molly, a near-invalid now, lived the year round.

He turned to a belated letter of appreciation from the young Irishman, Oscar Wilde, with whom Gideon and his Beacon Hill neighbour, William Dean Howells, had shared a delightful evening at the Kent dinner table the preceding year.

Boston had been one of the stops on Wilde's American lecture tour. Gideon and Howells – both of whom favoured the new, more realistic approach to literature which Howells practised in his novels – had jumped at the chance to entertain the young aesthete. The country's chief defender of old-fashioned literary virtue, Edmund Clarence Stedman of New York – 'The Mrs Astor of poesy,' Gideon called him with great sarcasm – had been outraged by some of Wilde's earlier pronouncements, and had written the Boston newspapers in an effort to persuade the literary community to ignore him when he came to town. In response, Gideon invited Wilde to dine. He'd asked Howells to join them to make sure Stedman was properly affronted.

Oscar Wilde had turned out to be a moon-faced, brown-eyed chap. He had lank, dark hair which hung around his ears, and a manner that was languid and faintly decadent. But there was something delightful about him, too. Entering the United States, he'd told them at the dinner table, he had been questioned by customs officials. 'I replied that I had nothing to declare except my genius.'

After reading Wilde's letter, Gideon put it aside to save. Then he turned to the competitive newspapers delivered every day by special messenger from New York. He spent an hour with the papers. Buried in a back column of the *Times* he found an item about a new type of outdoor pageant being tried out in Omaha by Buffalo Bill Cody. Something called a Wild West show. The *Times* was too dignified to give it more than a paragraph, but Gideon quickly got on the telegraph transmitter which served in lieu of a telephone. The private wire linked the house with the editorial rooms of the *Union* down on Park Row.

Gideon had taught himself telegraphy so he wouldn't have to rely on intermediaries to transmit confidential instructions. He clicked off his message. Five minutes later, he received a confirmation that a reporter would be dispatched to Omaha to see the outdoor show and write an article about it.

The *Union* needed a steady supply of colourful copy. Theo Payne, the paper's superb editor, was nearing seventy, but his judgement was as keen as ever. He constantly reminded his employer that competition among New York dailies was intensifying every day. Neither Payne nor Gideon was as smug as some newspapermen about the arrival of Joe Pulitzer, who was taking over the *World*. Like Gideon, Pulitzer was something of a crusader. But Pulitzer also had fewer scruples about printing items of a sensational or sordid nature. He knew how to get a newspaper read by those who counted most – ordinary people. Now Gideon proceeded to write down some thoughts for a long, long letter to Payne on the subject of trying to enliven all sections of the paper.

A last glance at the *Times* brought a smile to

Gideon's face. Eleanor was mentioned in the column headed *Theatrical Gossip*. In fact she was referred to as 'one of the country's most talented young actresses.' In the next line, her name was linked romantically with one of her fellow players, 'the handsome Mr Leo Goldman.'

Leo Goldman had pursued Eleanor ever since they were young members of an amateur theatre club in New York City. Leo would marry Eleanor eventually, Gideon supposed. He admired Leo, who was talented, ambitious and bright. But he hated to think of Eleanor being forced to deal with bigotry all her life, as she surely would be if she became the wife of someone of the Jewish faith.

And of course, the more deeply she involved herself in the theatre, the less interested she would be in the affairs of the Kents.

His last task was to write a special editorial for the *Union*. It had been stewing in his head for weeks. In three quick paragraphs, he reiterated the *Union*'s endorsement of the Pendleton Act, which had become law over President Arthur's signature in January. The act removed about twelve per cent of Federal jobs from the realm of patronage and made them subject to competitive examinations. It also established a commission to oversee the civil service. The snivel service, as one of the act's disgruntled opponents, Senator Roscoe Conkling, called it.

The act had been passed as a direct result of President Garfield's assassination in '81. The president had been shot by a man named Charles Guiteau, who had expected a Federal patronage job and failed to get it. Gideon's editorial lashed the Congress for waiting for a tragedy before passing needed legislation. He headed the editorial *Must Someone Always Die?* He feared he knew the answer to the question. Congress seldom acted swiftly or decisively until jolted by some disaster.

On a scrap of paper he scribbled a reminder about another editorial he ought to compose soon. Something had to be done to set up better machinery for presidential succession. The Constitution was vague on the procedure, and while Garfield lay dying with a bullet in him, the country had in effect been leaderless for three months.

A small clock showed Gideon the hour. Almost eleven. He hadn't heard Carter come in yet. No wonder the young man was failing most of his courses.

A frown on his face, Gideon climbed the stairs to the second floor, passed the door to his wife's sitting room and looked in on Will, who was under the sheet devouring a paper-covered ten cent novel about Bill Cody.

3

'Time to put out the light,' Gideon said. His voice still bore traces of the soft, rhythmic speech of his native Virginia.

Will yawned. He was a stocky boy of fourteen with brown eyes, brown hair, and features that favoured his late mother. When he lost the adolescent fat still showing in his cheeks, he'd be good looking – though never as handsome as Carter, of course.

'All right, Papa.'

'Did you finish your school work before you turned to great literature?' Gideon asked with a smile.

'Yes, sir. Barely. The math gets me down. I can't do it.'

'Of course you can! A person can do anything if he puts his mind to it.'

Will looked doubtful. Gideon was sorry he'd snapped. 'Did you ride today?'

'For an hour. The mare almost threw me, though.'

'Ask them to rent you a different horse next time.'

'All right.' From the boy's expression, Gideon knew he probably wouldn't have the nerve to make the request.

'You have the makings of a fine horseman, Will. Maybe you'd like to drive four-in-hand.'

Will's face lit up. 'Yes, sir, I surely would.' Hesitancy then. 'At least, I'd like to try to learn it—'

Gideon pretended he hadn't heard the last sentence. 'Good. We'll do something about that. Coaching's a coming sport.'

'That's what Carter said a few days ago.'

Gideon scowled. No statement was ever true unless it bore Carter's imprimatur.

'Is Carter back yet?' Will asked.

In spite of Gideon's good intentions, the scowl deepened. 'No. Why?'

'I need to ask him a question.'

'What about?'

'Oh, just something.'

'Could I answer it?'

'I'd rather ask him. It's something to do with fellows our age.'

'And a greybeard like me wouldn't understand?'

Will smiled back. 'Your beard isn't grey. Well, not very.'

'What about your question?'

Again the boy's eyes shifted elsewhere. 'It can wait until I see Carter.'

'All right. Good night.'

Gideon leaned down and squeezed his son's arm. The boy had grown self-conscious about being kissed by his parents.

As Gideon left the bedroom, he tried not to be annoyed by Will's blind affection for his stepbrother. Perhaps Will owed that to Carter. After all, it was

Carter who had moved in with the Kents after Margaret's death and given Will the comradeship the younger boy so desperately needed. Carter had done what no adult could. By serving as a brother and surrogate father combined, he'd restored a little of the zest for living which Margaret's crazed behaviour had driven out of her son.

But it was disturbing to Gideon that Will had becomed dependent on Carter for the answer to virtually every question. He ought to discuss the situation with Julia, and soon.

Will's lack of confidence was a problem already beyond solution, Gideon feared. It was also a mystery he suspected he'd never solve. Will absolutely refused to discuss it. What on God's earth had caused the boy to think so poorly of himself?

CHAPTER VI

Midnight Visitor

The answer to Gideon's question lay hidden in the past. Not all of Margaret Kent's cruelties had died with her on that July night in 1877 when the mansion at Fifth Avenue and Sixty-first Street, New York, had been invaded and ransacked by men sent by one of Gideon's enemies.

Just before Margaret fled from the men and accidentally plunged through a second floor window in a fall that took her life, her mind had cleared. For a moment or so she was blessedly free of the all but ungovernable madness which, combined with the effects of her alcoholism, had made her concoct schemes to drive a wedge between her husband and Eleanor.

In that brief period of clarity, Margaret's long-suppressed maternal love reasserted itself. She warned Will to remain in his room with the door bolted.

Seconds later, the invaders appeared at the end of the hall. Margaret ran from them, and died—

Leaving a frightened and bewildered boy of eight crouching behind a locked door. His mother's last lucid act had been totally unlike the behaviour she'd exhibited toward him for the past several months.

It had become a game, her tormenting him. No, worse than a game, for in each of their encounters she managed to convey a loathing for her son. She reinforced that loathing with an instrument that filled Will Kent with utter terror – a rod cut from a stout hickory limb she had somehow secured from Central Park.

Margaret beat him with the rod whenever he displeased her. And she arranged situations to insure that he would displease her. On each occasion, she warned Will that the slightest mention of the rod would be punishable by even worse reprisals. Over a period of a year or so, the boy suffered beating after beating because of a misguided and desperate hope: by putting up with pain – by enduring Margaret's abuse – he thought he could win the approval and the love he seemed unable to win merely by being her son. Will took what his mother gave, and said nothing to anyone.

There had been one final encounter with her on the afternoon of the day she died. Of all the encounters, it was the one he remembered most vividly, and with the greatest pain.

About three-fifteen, Margaret rang for a pot of tea. Everyone on the household staff knew she never drank tea, only the liquor she kept hidden in her room. But the staff members always humoured her rather than risk her irrational fury.

Through the speaking tube to the butler's pantry,

Margaret said she wanted Will to bring the tea up to her. By now the boy was accustomed to the harrowing routine. But knowing what was going to happen seldom made it any easier to bear.

He walked upstairs, not like an eight-year-old going to greet his mother for the first time that day, but like a grown man shuffling stoically to his own execution. Margaret's bedroom was dark and fetid, as always. Will could barely stand the smells of airless corners, soiled bedding, whiskey, unwashed flesh.

He set the tea tray on a small marble table, then immediately turned to leave. Margaret pointed to the tea cup's rim:

'There's a smudge on the cup, young man.'

He looked at her sadly. Her hair was unkempt. Her eyes lacked focus. 'Mama—' he began.

'Do you expect me to drink out of a filthy cup?'

The cup was spotless. He was sick with despair. 'Mama, there isn't any smudge on—'

'There is. There is! Are you blind?'

Now her eyes had that irrational glint. She was starting the cruel game again. But much as he loved her – much as he feared and pitied her – today something in him rebelled:

'Mama, the cup is clean. If you'll just look, you'll see.'

'Don't tell me what I see and what I don't!' She pushed him. He fell against the table, upsetting the tea pot and shattering the cup.

'Oh!' Her mouth curved down in disgust. Her gleeful eyes made him cringe. 'See what you've done, you stupid child.'

She was sometimes quite graceful when she'd been drinking; this was such a time. With a smooth, supple motion, she bent and snatched the hickory rod from its hiding place beneath the bed:

'Turn around and lean over.'

82

'Mama—'

'Lean over, I say!'

'Mama, don't.' He fought back tears. She never struck him on bare skin; she didn't want any marks to show. The worst blows weren't delivered by the rod, in any case. 'Mama, it was an accident. And you punished me only yester—'

'You were clumsy yesterday,' she interrupted. 'That's why I punished you. Again today you were clumsy, so you must be punished again. *Lean over.*'

He bit his lower lip until he tasted blood. He couldn't stand to cry in front of her. His eyes were dry as he bent forward at the waist. The rod rose above her right shoulder. Her forearm brushed against a spiky strand of her unwashed hair. He heard the beginning of the litany which by now had become familiar:

'Perhaps one of these days you'll show me you can do something right, Will Kent.'

Her timing was exquisite. The rod came down as she spoke, and it struck him precisely as she uttered the word *right*. Then it flashed upward again.

'You'll be a bungler all your life!'

She struck.

'You'll never—'

Struck.

' – amount to anything!'

She beat him faster then. Faster and harder, her words becoming thick and running together. Her mouth filled with saliva as she cried:

'Never! NEVER!'

In a minute or so the orgiastic frenzy passed. She flung the rod under the bed and collapsed onto the mussed covers, weeping and moaning. He stole out.

He was still too young to understand why she behaved as she did; that it was her loathing of herself which, in her misery and delirium, she transformed into a loathing of him. As he cowered in his room, a whipped animal, he returned to a conclusion he'd reached long before. His mother might be disturbed, but she couldn't be wholly irrational. She was his *mother*. In his scheme of things, that made her well nigh omnipotent. Thus, he concluded, she must have a very good reason for everything she said and did. The reason could only be that he was, indeed, worthless.

That night, she died.

2

In the aftermath of the attack on the house, Margaret's diary was discovered. In the book she'd kept a secret account of her deception of her husband. The disjointed, sometimes almost incoherent, narrative revealed the way she'd deliberately played father against daughter so that Eleanor came to hate Gideon for a time. Margaret's mistreatment of her son was nowhere written down – except on the tablet of the boy's mind.

With the findings of the diary on the day Margaret's things were removed from her bedroom and consigned to a bonfire, Eleanor and her father were set on the road to reconciliation. But nothing could undo the damage done to Will.

Suffering silently, he concluded that the memory of his mother, already badly tarnished, could stand no further staining. He decided he must say nothing about the beatings.

Someone had certainly found the hickory rod and tossed it on that bonfire without guessing the purpose to which it had been put. There was no point in accusing his poor mother after she was gone. She'd suffered enough. And she could no longer hurt him.

Or so he thought.

You'll be a bungler all your life.

Months later, he still heard it in nightmares, or in waking daydreams in which he watched the rise and fall of the terrible rod.

You'll never amount to anything.

NEVER.

As the years passed, he continued to hear that voice and never let on. Sometimes the voice was faint, sometimes it was quite loud. But either way, he never misunderstood what it was saying.

3

Gideon walked into Julia's sitting room. The two of them kept separate quarters for working, but not separate beds. They were ideally matched, and found that the approach of middle age had in no way diminished their ardour. Gideon's only regret about their marriage was that they'd been unable to have a child of their own. One had been born – a girl; a sad, blue-faced little creature who had gone to a nameless death in forty minutes. On the advice of doctors, Julia had never risked pregnancy again.

She was writing at her desk by gaslight. Notes for another lecture, he supposed.

The sitting room was jammed with furniture and all sorts of ornamentation. That was perfectly in keeping with current fashion, but Gideon had to be observant to navigate. Reaching Julia's desk was like running a maze, in and out among the matching pieces of the rosewood set finished in gold brocade. Other areas were occupied by a tall grandfather clock, assorted whatnots, two pedestals bearing marble busts of elderly Romans, a rubber plant, two Boston ferns in expensive jardinières, and a pair of large cabinets holding Julia's collection of cut glass.

Almost every other horizontal surface in the room

was equally cluttered. A cloth-of-gold lambrequin draped the mantel of the small fireplace. Several tables were almost completely concealed by long fringed cloths. The cloths in turn were nearly hidden by books, picture albums, vases, figurines and even a jar full of dried rose petals.

Nor did the walls escape. Julia had chosen all the decorations either because she liked them, or because they had some family significance. They included two Audubon prints, a large sketch of couples strolling in the garden of the Tuileries which Matt had done in 1879, two smaller prints based on his etchings for the Kent and Son book, *100 Years*, and the stuffed head of a fierce owl with yellow eyes. The owl's head jutted from the wall near three brown-toned photographs showing the Parthenon on the Acropolis, the Colosseum in Rome, and Westminster Abbey. Photographs were becoming quite popular as household art.

A memento which the Kents especially prized had come into the family at Christmas, 1880. One of Gideon's favourite hymns was 'O Little Town of Bethlehem,' which had been written and set to music in 1868. The author of the lyric was the Kents' friend Philip Brooks, currently head of the Episcopal Theological School in Cambridge and former rector of Trinity Church in Copley Square. Julia had gone to Brooks and asked him to copy the first stanza of the song, then sign it. She'd presented the manuscript to her husband as a surprise gift, and he in turn had insisted she frame it and hang it in an honoured place in this room.

Julia put her work aside and stood on tiptoe to greet her husband. Even so, she barely reached his shoulder. She was just five feet, with a perfectly proportioned figure, lustrous dark hair, and flawless pale skin that heightened the vivid blue of her eyes. She planted a kiss on his mouth.

'Finished?'

He pulled another cigar from the pocket of his velvet smoking jacket. 'Who's ever finished these days? The world gets busier and busier.'

'Or could it be that we get older and slower?'

They laughed. Julia was forty-three, older than her husband by three years. As she sat down, she noted his expression:

'Darling, you're worrying again.'

He perched on a brocaded footstool beside the desk. He described the little scene with Will. When he was through, she shook her head:

'I don't quite see why you're worried. The boys have been close for a long time. That's natural for brothers. To have secrets is natural too.'

'It's a matter of degree. I feel Will relies entirely too much on Carter. Your son's a strong young man – temperamentally as well as physically. Maybe Will needs—'

A gesture with the cigar. He groped for the words:

'Independence. Independence and toughening. So that when he's on his own as a man, he can think and act for himself, not run to someone else for suggestions about everything from clothes to girls.'

In silence, Julia considered that. After a moment she nodded. 'Very well. If you feel there's a problem, we must try to find some way to solve it.' She sighed. 'There seems to be problems everywhere. Carter's going to be dismissed from Harvard at the end of this term unless a miracle takes place at examination time.' Her tone said she didn't anticipate a miracle. 'I've failed to direct him properly, Gideon.'

He reached for her hand. 'Nonsense. All boys his age assert themselves. I did.'

'Did you always try to impose your opinions and your wishes on other people?'

'Sometimes,' he said, though he couldn't remember having been so single-minded about it.

'And did you absolutely refuse to accept authority?'

He grinned. 'Unfailingly.'

'Gideon Kent, you're just trying to make me feel better. You could never have served even one week in the cavalry if you acted the way Carter does.'

She shook her head. 'Sometimes I see so much of Louis in him. Louis's disposition. Selfish. Wilful—'

'He's a good boy, Julia. You mustn't start believing otherwise, because he'll feel it.' The reminder was for himself as much as for her.

'He's also a man. Twenty-one years old. I can't control him any longer. But it's evident that I did a wretched job of raising him. In some ways I fear he's still Louis's son.'

'The past is gone. We ought to work on channelling the talents he's got.'

'What talents?' she replied in a melancholy way. 'A talent for smiling? For charming people? Shall we encourage him to be another Ward NcAllister?'

Gideon frowned. Julia took her hand from his, covering her eyes. 'I'm sorry. I don't mean to say unkind things about my own son. But lately I've been very downcast about his future.'

'That makes two of us. I've been downcast about Will's.'

She nodded. 'Sometimes I fear Carter hasn't any future, unless it's one like his poor father's – ' She patted her husband's hand. 'But it's good we got all of this into the open. It may be that we each need the other's objectivity. You think about Carter and I'll think about Will. Perhaps between us—'

A knock interrupted. The Kents looked up to see their tall, rather austere butler, Crawford:

'Beg pardon, madam – beg pardon, sir. I tried to

discourage the visitor, but he was insistent. He demands to see both of you.'

Gideon jumped up. 'He's got a hell of a nerve demanding anything at this hour. Who is this fellow, Crawford?'

'The gentleman claims to be from the college, Mr Kent. He says he's driven all the way from Cambridge, and he's in a perfect rage about something. His name,' Crawford added, 'is Eisler.'

CHAPTER VII

Defiance

Edmund Eisler departed forty minutes later. But as a result of his visit, the Kents were in no mood for sleep.

The servants went to their beds down on the ground floor. Gideon and Julia had the first floor all to themselves. Around three-thirty, a heavy storm broke, drenching the house and the Common. The rain quickly slacked off, then stopped.

There was little conversation between husband and wife. Gideon could tell how upset Julia was by the way she made frequent trips to the front parlour window. The rain-glistening slope of Beacon Street remained silent; empty. Four o'clock came.

Four-thirty.

Five.

Finally, just as daylight was breaking and Julia was urging Gideon to go to the police, a soggy and tired-looking Carter hove into view. It was Gideon who spied him. He quickly dropped the drapery and stepped away from the window.

'He's coming. Minus a shoe, but there's no other visible damage.'

Julia murmured relief, then smoothed her features and stood beside her husband, ready to deal with her son.

Carter let himself in with his key and came to the parlour door, where light spilled out. Gideon had to admire the young man's brass. His smile was confident and guileless.

'Still up? Hope I didn't worry you. The card game lasted until just a while ago.'

Julia fisted her hands at her sides. 'Please don't make matters worse by lying.'

For an instant Carter's confidence cracked. Then the all but irresistible smile slipped back in place:

'Lying? I don't understand. I've been in Willie Hearst's room all evening, playing poker – only not for ten thousand a hand, the way his father does—'

Gideon stepped forward. 'Young man, you've caused your mother no end of anxiety tonight. As she said – don't compound it by making up half truths. We know where you were, at least during the early part of the evening. Around midnight, we had a caller.' He paused to let that sink in, then added, 'Professor Eisler.'

Carter sagged against the door frame. 'Oh Jesus.'

'Kindly do not use that sort of language in front of me,' Julia said. 'This is not a saloon or a bordello.' Then, in spite of everything, a plaintive note crept into her voice. 'Why did you deliberately set out to humiliate that man?'

Jaw thrust out, Carter retorted, 'He had it coming. He humiliates me every time I go to class.'

'Apparently,' Gideon said, 'that is due in large part to your failure to turn in the assigned work.'

Carter refused to answer the charge, exclaiming

instead, 'He's made my life miserable for almost two years!'

Julia's eyes filled with angry tears. 'What kind of son have I raised?

'Mother, don't make such a damn to-do—'

'I should say we will make a to-do, as you call it!' Gideon roared.

'But it was just a prank!'

'And a very costly one for you,' Gideon retorted. 'Eisler said you drove a wagon to his house. A wagon which was totally demolished. How in God's name did you get hold of a wagon?'

Carter shrugged. 'It was easy. I paid good money, and I told the owner a good story about needing it for my club.'

Gideon seethed: 'Just another little test of your powers of persuasion? The ingenuity you've developed in lieu of intelligence—?'

Nervous and defensive, Carter smiled. The smile struck Gideon as utterly insolent. He could barely keep from storming across the Oriental carpet and hitting his stepson.

'You might call it that,' Carter answered finally. 'Do you mind if I say goodnight?'

'Not until we've finished with you. Stand up straight!'

The younger man glared. But he stopped leaning against the door frame. Fuming, Gideon went on:

'You act as though rules are made for everyone but you. As though life consists of nothing but challenges to your cleverness. Apparently you never trouble to consider the propriety or the consequences of your behaviour. What's become of the Carter Kent who helped his stepbrother get into baseball games in Central Park? When you persuaded those slum rough-necks to let Will join in, you were doing something with a worthy purpose!'

Carter looked baffled. 'I helped Will because I like

him. And because I enjoyed wrapping those clods around my little finger – ' A glance at Julia. 'Just the way you wrap up an audience.'

'It isn't the same!' she cried. 'I'm not playing some – some intellectual game. I mean every word.'

'I wish I knew what you were getting at, Mother.'

'At being *responsible*, not merely successful,' Gideon broke in. 'Somehow we've failed to make the distinction clear.'

Julia caught his arm. Red-faced, he turned away, struggling to draw another breath. Carter did his best to act nonchalant.

'May I go to bed now?'

'You might as well,' Julia said. 'And there's no point in getting up for your classes. Eisler told us he's going to the administration first thing this morning. I'm afraid you're finsished at Harvard.'

Gideon recovered and was breathing evenly again. There was iron in his voice as he said, 'Nevertheless, Julia, I shall expect Carter at the breakfast table one hour from now.' He turned an implacable eye on his stepson. 'We will discuss the reparations you must and will make to the owner of the wagon.'

It was no satisfaction to Gideon that Carter finally looked stunned by the news of his dismissal from Harvard. He limped toward the staircase without another word. His wet shoe squeaked in the silence.

When he was gone, Julia leaned against her husband and held onto him. 'I really have failed to teach him anything.'

'The responsibility is mine too.'

'What can we do with him?'

Gideon told her the truth. 'I don't know.' He feared it was already too late to change Carter's amoral approach to life. But he was obliged to try.

Associate Professor Edmund Eisler hadn't been uttering idle threats. The next afternoon at four o'clock, a
special messenger delivered a notice from Harvard
College stating that Mr Carter Kent, Beacon Street,
had been dismissed from the second year class and
could not under any circumstances be reinstated.

It came as no surprise. In fact, Gideon had already
planned his stepson's future on the basis of an impending dismissal. At breakfast he had presented Carter
with a series of ultimatums. He would take a job at
Kent and Son, and from his salary, repay the fair price
of the wagon in weekly instalments. He would pay for
the horse too if it failed to turn up. Carter was required
to call on the bakery owner, admit his deception, and
handle all the arrangements.

On every point, Carter quickly murmured an agreement. But Gideon feared the young man was secretly
unrepentant and was only making a show to mollify his
mother.

No matter. He *would* pay for the damage he had
done. Early the next day, he was put to work carrying
paper from the warehouse to the pressroom of the
publishing house. The paper was heavy, the work
tiring. Carter didn't complain. At least not within
Gideon's hearing. And although Carter did face the
bakery owner and work out details of the repayment,
Gideon was still suspicious that the change in his
stepson's attitude was merely temporary.

He was right. It lasted just two weeks.

On Tuesday, shortly after the noon break, Gideon
summoned Carter to his office on the top floor of the
building. Near the desk littered with ledgers, bills, and
galleys stood Mr Verity Pleasant, the stout, grey-haired

superintendent of the pressroom. Pleasant was the great-grandson of Supply Pleasant, the editor of Philip Kent's first newspaper, the *Bay State Federalist*. Verity Pleasant had begun his working career as an apprentice at Kent and Son, and had quickly advanced to his present position of responsibility. He had come to Gideon with a complaint which Gideon now presented to his stepson:

'Your work isn't satisfactory to Mr Pleasant.'

Carter wiped an inky hand on his apron and resorted to a dazzling smile.

'I'm sorry to hear that, Mr Pleasant. I thought I'd done everything you asked.' For an instant his dark eyes flickered with resentment. 'Everything you ordered.'

'Oh, yes, you've done everything that was asked,' Pleasant rumbled. 'And quite a few things you were not.' He stabbed a thick finger at a folded sheet lying on the corner of the desk. 'I have shown that petition to Mr Kent.

'Oh.' Carter eyed the sheet, pondered a moment, then shrugged. 'I'm sorry if the petition offends you, Mr Pleasant. Or you, sir. But I definitely feel that fifteen minutes is not long enough for a midday meal. Most of the other men share my opinion, as their signatures on that paper should prove.'

Pleasant couldn't hide his contempt. Even Gideon's relationship to the offender made no difference.

'They share your opinion because you've palavered and wheedled and talked 'em dizzy. Half of them probably signed just to shut you up.'

'No sir, that's not true,' Carter said. 'They agree with me. In fifteen minutes there isn't even time to step out for a growler of beer.'

Gideon laced his hands together. 'Nor is it allowed. I remind you that I set the rules in this business, young man. I set them after a meeting with the craft union once a year. At that meeting, the men have an opportunity to air every complaint, whether large or small. My employees are paid and treated fairly. Better, in fact, than in most printing houses. I admit the noon meal period is short. But the men also get to leave forty-five minutes early because of it. A year ago, they agreed they wanted it that way.'

'Oh, we want to keep that early quitting time,' Carter nodded. 'But we also believe the noon interval should be stretched to half an hour.'

The floor vibrated from the rhythm of the presses and binding equipment. Gideon sighed and shook his head:

'Why do you do this, Carter? You don't really care about working conditions at Kent and Son. Why do you always have to try to take charge of a situation? Is it because deep down you're doubtful of your own ability?'

Carter glared. 'I don't know what the hell you're talking about – sir.'

'Nor do I,' Pleasant declared. 'All I know is, I won't have troublemakers in my pressroom. He cares for naught but the sound of his own voice, Mr Kent. Since he's your adopted son – ' He reached behind him to the strings of his apron. ' – I suppose you'll be wanting my resignation.'

Gideon stayed Pleasant's hand. 'Absolutely not. When I brought Carter in here, his mother and I agreed he'd get no special treatment.'

Handsome as a marble statue, Carter stood motionless in a beam of sunlight falling through the grimy window. His defiant eyes seemed to be testing the older man's determination. *How much of his lack of morality is my fault*? Gideon wondered. *And how much comes out of the past, from Louis?*

Gideon rose behind his desk. 'No special treatment,'

he repeated, to make sure Carter understood. 'You're discharged.'

For a moment, Carter looked hurt. Then he stiffened:

'Sir—'

'You heard me. Go find a job on your own.'

'What if I don't choose to find a job?'

'Then you go to jail. I won't pay a penny of what you owe for that wagon. Now get out of here.'

'With pleasure!' Carter untied his apron and flung it on the floor. Then he stomped down the stairs.

Verity Pleasant started to offer an apology for disrupting relationships in Gideon's household. With a slashing gesture, Gideon waved him to silence. Pleasant left. Only then did Gideon raise one hand to cover his eye. He trembled with impotent fury.

And he's to be one of the stewards of the Kent family in the next century? If that's the best we can offer, we're finished.

CHAPTER VIII

Eben's Fate

Carter was miserable about being fired from Kent and Son. But he was damned if he'd let anyone know, even though the firing created all but unbearable tension at home. It was a source of bitter amusement to him that he really loved his mother and, in his own way, admired Gideon. But neither of them suspected.

Gideon had said one thing that was completely true. Carter did have a compulsion to control things, whether it was the way Eisler conducted his classes, or

96

the way Gideon conducted his business. He wanted to be in charge of whatever he did, whether the realities of the situation made that feasible or not. He didn't know why he felt such a compulsion, but he'd long ago accepted it. The sooner Gideon and Julia accepted it too, the happier they'd all be.

He toyed with the idea of ignoring his stepfather's latest warning. But if he refused to look for work, he might indeed be jailed for failure to pay a debt which he'd already agreed was his. The alternative was to run away – something he was not yet prepared to do. Still the idea had a certain appeal. If others kept trying to control his future – well, who could say what would happen?

Reluctantly he set out to find work. He hd no luck. Jobs were scarce that spring and a slight weakening of the economy was being felt most keenly among the unskilled. After being turned away from the hiring offices of several mills on the outskirts of Boston, he reluctantly returned to the one area where he thought he might be successful – the docks. He hadn't been back since the night of the trouble, and he was still a little fearful about the possibility of encountering Ortega. The man *had* promised to repay him for his interference—

But necessity, and the memory of something Eben Royce had said, overcame his fear. Late one sunny afternoon, he went down to the pier where Royce would anchor when he returned with the day's catch. Instead of an empty slip, Carter found Royce's boat tied up, her sails furled. She looked as though she hadn't put out into the ocean for days.

'Captain Royce? Tillman? Hello, anybody aboard?'

Gulls swooped over the bright water of the harbour, wheeling and crying. An old seaman mending nets further down the pier shouted to him:

'Ain't anybody about. Read the sign.'

He pointed to a notice board at the head of the pier. Carter had passed it, but paid no attention. Now he hurried back to it, and in seconds found the hand-printed advertisement to which the old man had referred:

To be sold at
PUBLIC AUCTION
at her berth on Purdy's Wharf
the excellent & widely-known
FISHING SLOOP
'ATLANTIC ANNE'
Sale by order of the owner,
Capt. E. Royce

Carter stared at the notice for a long time; the date of the auction was the very next week. An ominous feeling came over him. What had forced the sale of the vessel that was Royce's whole life? For an answer, he turned back toward the end of the pier. The old seaman, net slung over his shoulder, was just stepping over the gunwale of a ramshackle barge.

'Ahoy there,' Carter called, waving. 'I see the sign – but where's Captain Royce? Is he all right?'

'Some say he's lucky to be alive,' the old man replied. 'Others – me among 'em – think maybe he'd be better off if they done the whole job, 'stead of leavin' him like he is.'

And with a final suspicious stare at Carter, the man disappeared into the barge's wheelhouse.

What the old man said unexpectedly brought an image to Carter's mind. He saw the vicious eyes of the man with the fishhook scar, and there in the bright sunshine beside the familiar, sail-dotted harbour, he shuddered.

He walked a while before making up his mind to go to the Red Cod. After all, how much harm could come to him in the daylight? He knew from experience that there would be few if any patrons in the Cod at this hour. And he wouldn't be forced to explain his absence to Josie; the serving girls didn't start work until six o'clock or later.

A bell was tolling in a nearby church as Carter opened the tavern door. For a moment he could see little in the dark interior. Then an unpleasantly familiar voice hailed him.

'Well, if it isn't Kent. Thought the rough crowd in here had scared you off.'

Carter leaned on the serving counter and thumped down one of his last coins. 'I'll have a beer, Phippsy – without the insults.'

While the wizened landlord filled the pewter pot, Carter overcame his embarrassment and forced out the next sentence:

'And if anybody in the neighbourhood is looking for help, I'd be glad to know that too.'

Phipps served the beer, clawed up the coin and deposited it in his grimy apron. From the rear of the tavern floated the smell of the day's batch of chowder. Phipps blinked and licked his lips.

'You mean you're hunting a job?'

'Correct.'

'What happened to your fancy education?'

'I decided I had enough of Harvard.'

'Or they decided they had enough of you?'

'Look, dammit—'

'All right, all right!' Phipps broke in, obviously

relishing Carter's plight. 'I've got nothing to offer you here—'

And I wouldn't work for you if you did.

'—but I hear the Northeast Fishery Company's hiring. They're always hiring. It's dirty work.'

'Where is it?' Carter asked. Phipps gestured:

'The big building three squares north. Right at the head of the wharf. Can't miss it.'

'I'm in your debt,' Carter said, offering a mocking salute with the pot. He drank, then added, 'I'd hoped maybe Eben Royce would take me on but I see the *Atlantic Anne*'s up for sale. What happened?'

Phipps frowned. 'It's too sorrowful to talk about. You better ask him.' He gestured past Carter.

Carter turned and for the first time saw Tillman. The fat fisherman was seated at the same table he'd occupied on the night of the trouble with Ortega. He regarded Carter with watering eyes. He was drunk.

Carter carried his beer toward the man, who stirred in a slow, slothful way and drained what was left in his own pewter mug. Most of it ran down his chin and dripped on the stained table. Tillman looked defeated and miserable – and Carter wasn't sure he wanted to hear the answer to the question about Royce. Something grim had happened, that much was certain.

3

Tillman wasn't too drunk to take advantage of Carter's curiosity. Of course he'd relate the sad story of Eben Royce – if Carter refilled his mug. Carter sat down, signalled Phipps and wrinkled his nose at the fat man's sour smell. Presently, drink in hand, Tillman unburdened himself:

'Goddamn shame, it is – fine man like Eben. Happened eight, nine days after the last time you was in here. Eben had his supper – that very table – and he was heading back to the boat when three men jumped him and dragged him up Hampshire Alley. They put a rag in his mouth to keep him quiet, then they went to work on him. They broke his legs, both wrists, and all his fingers. His hands are like this – ' Tillman formed a claw. 'And they'll never be right again. Takes him two, three minutes just to pick up a spoon now.'

Dry mouthed, Carter swallowed and managed to say, 'Good God. Who did it?'

'Eben says it was Ortega and his brother, who was in port a few days. Dunno the third man.'

'What's anyone done about it?'

Tillman shrugged. 'Nothin', lad. Down here we don't have much truck with the damn crooks on the police force. We settle things amongst ourselves. But Ortega left town right after it happened, an' no one's set eyes on him since. His brother shipped out again. Round the world this time. Least that's the story. They say Ortega is down in New York, but figures to come back when he thinks it's safe. So you ought to be careful, too.'

Carter shivered again. 'Did Eben really have to sell the boat?'

'He says he did, which amounts to the same thing. With what they did to his hands, he surely can't handle lines or the wheel or a net any more. And you know Eben – a working skipper, and not content to be any other kind. I'll tell you, Kent – he only seems to care about one thing these days.'

'What's that?'

Tillman made smacking sounds as he drank, then squinted into the empty mug. Carter said he had no more money with him. It was a lie but Tillman accepted it with a sigh, then answered the question:

'Gettin' even. He's just waiting for Ortega to show up. Oh, it's bad business – ' Tillman shook his head and gave Carter a melancholy look. 'It put the whole crew on shore, but what's worse, it's did something terrible to a good man. It broke more than Eben's bones. It broke his spirit. He's always been sound and healthy – but since they hurt him, he's acted queer. We asked him to stay on as the owner of the *Anne*, and let us do all the skippering, but he wouldn't hear of it. He just sits in his rocker in his little room, talking wild talk about getting even with that Portugee.'

Back in the kitchen, Phipps querulously called for more potatoes in the chowder. Carter heard a scurrying along the wall on the other side of the fireplace, but refused to look to see what kind of creature was at large. The fading daylight through the bottle glass window cast a deep yellow glow on sections of the tavern floor.

Tillman roused again: 'I think Eben would be mighty glad to see you, if you'd care to drop in. He doesn't get many visitors.'

'Sure, of course.' Carter nodded with a quick, uneasy smile. 'I'll try to get to his place first moment I can. But I'm in a tight spot, Tillman. I need money. I'm trying to find a job.'

'You take a job, you'll have to dance to somebody else's hornpipe,' Tillman said. 'That isn't your style, is it?'

'I'll make it my style – ' Carter quickly controlled the sarcasm, adding, 'I'm certainly sorry to hear about Eben. At least he has that woman to care for him. She's beautiful, and she loves him – that counts for something.'

Tillman gave him another strange stare.

'Not as much as you might think.'

'What do you mean?'

'Nothing.' Tillman heaved his huge body out of the chair and lumbered toward the door. Carter asked another question but the man wouldn't elaborate on his remark. The door opened. Tillman looked like a great black balloon against the brassy light of the sky.

'Bear in mind what I told you,' he called. 'They do say Ortega isn't gone for good. And those who were around after the fracas that night said he spoke your name nigh as often as he spoke Eben's. Have a care where you walk.'

The door closed, leaving Carter in the amber-tinged shadows, the palms of his hands suddenly much too cold for the spring day.

4

He was soon on his way back to Beacon Street. He glanced over his shoulder every block or so, and walked wide of the mouths of unfamiliar alleys en route. Tomorrow was time enough to look into the job at the processing plant; tonight he was glad to be going home.

He knew Gideon and Julia would be gone by six o'clock; some civic banquet or other. He spent his last few cents for a large tin pail of beer, entered the house by the rear entrance and took the back stairs up to Will's room.

His relationship with his stepbrother was the one bright spot left in his life. The younger boy continued to take Carter just as he was, faults and all. He never mentioned the recent troubles which were common knowledge even amongst the servants.

'Greetings, little brother,' Carter said as he entered Will's room. 'Look what I brought.'

He displayed the pail. Grinning, Will jumped up from his desk.

'Beer?'

'Right you are. Lock the door. Some of the servants are too blasted nosey to suit me.'

Carter had given Will his first taste of beer only a

couple of months earlier. The younger boy didn't care for the stuff, but he was anxious to make Carter think he was grown up and worldly. And he was more than happy to put his geometry text aside. He liked his courses at the Boston Latin School about as much as he liked beer. Still, good marks were necessary for admission to Harvard. Carter continually encouraged him to go there, even after his own dismissal. So Will studied hard. Without being fully aware of it he was already trying to disprove what the voice from the past said about him.

He bolted the door. Carter propped a couple of cushions against the black haircloth sofa and sat down with his back against them. He swigged from the pail, then handed it to the younger boy.

'Where have you been all day?' Will asked. 'Still hunting for a job?'

Carter nodded. Then, sounding almost irritable, he said, 'Go on. Drink up or let me have it back.'

Will frowned. He lifted the pail to his lips. Carter watched his stepbrother drink, wince, and stifle a cough. But he didn't laugh. He wouldn't have embarrassed Will for the world.

'That's good,' Will declared without conviction. Carter reclaimed the pail and gulped as the younger boy went on, 'I'm sorry you're having a hard time finding work. I'm sorry you decided to quit the publishing house.'

'It was either that or be fired.' He'd told Will that the decision had been his. Gideon had never said anything to the contrary in Will's presence. 'I hate to say anything against your father, but he acts pretty high and mighty around that place. I got tired of him ordering me around.'

'Don't apologize. I'm starting to feel the same way myself.'

'Well, don't let me influence you.'

Carter took another long drink. Will observed the older boy's every move, admiration in his eyes. 'Gideon and Mother still have confidence in you,' Carter went on. 'They've given up on me. Mother thinks I'm too much like my real father to amount to anything.'

Will looked shocked. 'She doesn't say that, does she?'

Carter's answer was a truthful one: 'No, never in so many words.'

'Then why do you feel it?'

Carter's dark eyes seemed to search past the younger boy into some lost time or place. 'I don't really know. But I'm positive she and Gideon believe I'm a good-for-nothing – exactly like the late Mr Louis Kent.'

'Maybe you feel that way because too many people have told you how bad your father was.'

A shrug. 'Like father, like son. There must be something to an old saying like that. Else why is it a saying in the first place?' He gulped from the pail again.

Carter's dour mood upset the younger boy. Will sat down beside his stepbrother and changed the subject:

'What are you going to do now that you don't have to go to Harvard?'

'I hear there's a fish processing plant looking for men. I'm going to inquire there tomorrow. What a comedown for a member of the Kent family – smelling like hake or market cod twenty-four hours a day.'

'I didn't mean what are you going to do about working,' Will said. 'I mean what are you going to do for the rest of your life?'

'It's easy to answer that.' He smiled in a humourless way. 'I'm damned if I know.'

Then he thought of Willie Hearst. The smile grew cynical. 'I'll probably wind up a politician, or go to hell by some other, equally direct route. I've finally realized

I'm stuck with talking my way through life because I don't know how to do anything else.' He held out the pail. 'Want any more?'

Will shook his head, his expression unhappy. Carter noticed. Instantly, a smile spread over his swarthy face:

'But don't fret about me, little brother. If I'm headed for hell, I promise you I'll have a fine time getting there.'

Will refused to smile. He continued to stare at his stepbrother for a long moment. Then he said very softly:

'Well, you'd better not leave Boston.'

'What's that? Why not?'

'Because – ' Avoiding Carter's eyes, he forced out the rest. ' – because I couldn't get along without you. You're the only one I can ask for advice about important things.'

'Such as cigars and girls, eh?' Carter said. He was secretly touched by the younger boy's words.

'I'm serious. Having you here is like having a real brother.'

'But you could get along without me. It's nice to hear you say otherwise, though. One thing's for sure – ' He squeezed his stepbrother's arm affectionately. 'You don't want to follow my example. You need to attend to your studies and behave yourself. If you do, you'll get somewhere.'

Carter scrambled to his feet. There was pain showing in his eyes. Will saw it, but he didn't know what to do.

'Back to your lessons, little brother,' Carter admonished as he left. 'Mother and Gideon deserve at least one son who turns out right.'

CHAPTER IX

The Greek Woman

Carter lied to the man doing the hiring at the Northeast Fishery Company. He said he was experienced, and because he could say it with a show of conviction, he got the job. He was scheduled to start work the following evening, on the twelve-hour shift which began at six, after the fishing boats returned.

So that he wouldn't be fired the very first day, he began a search through the taverns in the neighbourhood as soon as he left the hiring office. Around ten that night he located whiskey-sodden derelict who was pointed out as a former processing plant worker discharged for constant malingering. Carter approached the old man and gave him some money he'd borrowed from Will. The man called for a knife and a rancid gray scrod from the kitchen. He showed Carter how to chop off the head and tail and clean and bone the fish – all that he needed to know to keep his inexperience from being detected.

The effort – and the money – turned out to be wasted. Carter was assigned to the bottom of the chute down which the catches were dumped. The head of the chute opened onto a dock at street level. The bottom was one flight below ground level – where the principal work area of the packing house was located. Carter was one of half a dozen men who hacked off the heads and tails of the incoming fish, then threw the fish on to a large, slimy table where four other workers sorted them on to moving belts powered by steam. By midnight of his first shift, Carter was ankle-deep in stinking fish parts.

He hated the sight of the eyes in the lifeless heads; the dead fish seemed to be watching him in an accusing way, as if he were the one who had deprived them of life. He hated the smell even more. It was so persuasive, he couldn't eat the supper he'd brought wrapped in a piece of butcher paper. By the time he went home, spent and nauseous, right after sunrise, he was almost deliriously anxious for his first whiff of fresh air. A long hot bath somehow failed to cleanse the fish odour from his hands or hair, though. Even Will made a face when Carter saw him later that day.

He didn't think he could stand to go back to the Northeast Fishery Company, but somehow he did. He didn't encourage the other workers when they attempted to strike up a conversation. They were an illiterate, foul-mouthed lot. But they did impart one useful piece of information. They told him he'd stay cleaner if he wore gloves, a black rubber apron, and high rubber boots, as they did. He'd have to buy them for himself, though. That was company policy.

On that subject, he had his first dispute with the foreman.

To those around him, he began arguing that boots, aprons, and gloves should be provided for every worker. A man shouldn't have to pay out part of his already low salary in order to have the proper work outfit. The men needed to stand up together and make their demand known to the owners.

He had little trouble persuading the other men to accept that viewpoint – or so he thought. Then, on the first night of his second week, the foreman, a long-jawed lout named Kimpton, marched into the work area and sarcastically called him down in front of the others:

'Hear you been tellin' everybody they should make some *demands* of the company.'

'How'd you find out about that?' Carter exclaimed,

108

gesturing with his serrated knife without thinking. The foreman grabbed his wrist and shoved it aside.

'Don't wave that damn thing at me, college boy.' Kimpton growled the words. 'And listen close. You're here to work, not think. You obey the company rules as written, or go back to Harvard.'

He gave Carter's wrist a second shove, pivoted, and left. Carter looked around and saw a couple of his fellow workers snickering as they bent their heads over the fish coming down the chute in a glistening silver avalanche.

Someone had talked behind his back, that much was certain. It gave him an eerie feeling to know there were company spies within the work force – and that information evidently flowed both ways. He'd told no one, not even the hiring manager, that he was a former Harvard student. But Kimpton knew, and now the others did too. What else did they know?

The foreman's harsh words made him want to quit on the spot. But he kept working – *chop the head, chop the tail, throw the fish* – because of the large debt he still owed for the wagon. He despised being treated like a slave, and forced to put up with it, but reluctantly decided he'd have to until he could work his way out of his present difficulties. If the company didn't pay for the boots, apron and gloves, then he'd have to ask his stepfather for a loan. Stifling his frustrated fury, he plied the knife with savage single-mindedness. *Chop the head, chop the tail, throw the fish—*

At the end of the second week he discovered that someone knew much more about him than he liked. Each worker at the plant had an old, wooden locker in a dingy room near the employees' entrance. None of the lockers could be secured against entry by unauthorized persons; you stored your things and took your chances. When he got off work early on a Saturday morning he opened his locker and blinked. A folded scrap of paper lay on the locker shelf.

He unfolded the paper, and read it, and hastily folded it again. He leaned against the adjacent locker, sick with fright.

He looked to the right and left. Men were stripping off aprons, tugging off boots, chattering sleepily about going home to their beds or their women or a morning meal. Who had put the note in his locker? A friend of Ortega's certainly – but who was it?

On the way to Beacon Street, he stopped and studied the scrap of paper again. The message was scrawled in pencil; the handwriting was terrible – perhaps on purpose, to disguise it.

> *Ortega wil be glad to know wher*
> *to find you*

Any anonymity he'd possessed when he started work at the processing plant was gone. Someone – perhaps more than one person – knew who he was.

Should he quit? Try to find another job in a different part of town? It was the sensible thing to do, perhaps, and yet he equated such a move with cowardice. He didn't want to flee the docks unless it became absolutely necessary.

Which it very well might, he realized as he limped wearily on toward home, and sleep, while the city woke around him.

2

At the end of a month – four weeks of hard work and constant watchfulness – Carter concluded that the note might have been nothing more than a malicious joke perpetrated by one of the clods at the packing plant; someone who knew of his trouble with Ortega, but had no personal stake in it; someone who just wanted to make him squirm because he'd gone to college.

Reassured, he started venturing into the taverns again. He even returned to the Red Cod. No one had seen Ortega or heard a word about him. Carter began to think Tillman had been wrong, and that the Portugee had left Boston for good.

Soon he no longer hesitated to go anywhere after dark. And although he was repaying the bakery owner, and working twelve hours a night, six nights a week, he had enough time and money left over so that he could occasionally enjoy a beer and the favours of a whore such as Josie.

On one of his free nights, he was ambling toward the Cod when he spied a familiar figure half a block ahead. Even at a distance, Carter could see the cruel malformation of Captain Eben Royce's hands. The fisherman hobbled along on a heavily padded crutch braced beneath his left arm.

Carter stopped near a chandler's side door to watch Royce. He made good progress, yet Carter couldn't help rubbing his stubbled chin, and swallowing hard. Royce's left foot was unmistakably twisted. It scraped the ground, useless.

Royce was coming toward him. Carter stepped out from the doorway, waved and called, 'Eben? It's me – Carter. I haven't seen you for—'

He stopped. With a strange, almost humiliated look, Royce turned and hobbled out of sight down a passageway. Carter ran to the passage and peered into it. But it was so dark, he could see nothing, only hear the dragging of Royce's foot.

The sound grew softer, then died. Carter shook his head and turned back on his original course. Later that week he ran into Tillman who had a new job as a mate on another fishing boat. When Carter mentioned the encounter with Royce, Tillman told him Royce had

111

become almost a complete recluse. He lived near the Red Cod, but he no longer went there or to any other tavern. He only left his room to get food or tobacco:

'He makes do with the money he got from the sloop. All he talks about – all he lives for – is the chance of seeing Ortega again.'

Carter didn't say so, but he fervently hoped poor Eben Royce never got his wish.

3

Shortly after starting at the processing plant, he'd learned why Tillman, during their first conversation about Royce's misfortune, had given him an odd look when Carter mentioned the Greek woman. It was Phipps who told him the woman had moved out of the quarters she shared with Royce, shortly after Royce sold his boat.

Carter supposed her action was understandable. Royce was no longer a whole man. At least she'd helped nurse him back from the worst of his injuries.

When he said as much to Phipps, the landlord replied, 'Oh yes, she's a regular Nightingale, that one.'

Carter resented the sneering tone. He assumed the landlord had some grudge against the woman, whose beautiful dark eyes were often in Carter's thoughts, and whose face he sometimes imagined when he was making love to a whore. The Greek woman remained an ideal; perfect – someone he wished he could see again.

Eventually he did. It happened on another Sunday evening late in June. He had left the tavern where he'd eaten supper and was bound for the Red Cod, planning to take Josie over the jumps. It had been three weeks since he'd been able to afford her – the tension in his groin testified to that.

He was just passing an old man playing his concertina while a trained monkey jigged at the end of a rope. Suddenly, on the far side of the small crowd, he saw Helen Stavros turning the corner into a dark, narrow lane. He ran to catch up:

'Mrs Stavros – wait.' Excited about his good fortune, he ran after her in the lane. He came up beside her where she'd paused near the lamplit doorway of an oyster house. He raked a hand through his dark hair, wishing he were better dressed.

'Perhaps you don't remember me—'

It was a warm evening. Above the scoop neckline of her blouse, her cleavage was visible, shiny with sweat. After one covert glance at it, he was rigid.

She smiled. 'Of course I do. You're the one who helped Eben that night at the Red Cod. You helped me too.'

Her voice was low and pleasant, her English smooth and only slightly accented. She gave him a smile whose unmistakable sexuality bothered him. She was too beautiful to behave that way with someone she hardly knew.

She touched his cheek, then, adding, 'I am grateful.'

He waved that aside awkwardly. 'I haven't seen much of Eben lately.'

A remote tone came into her voice: 'But you know what happened to him.'

'Yes. I can understand why you might not want to stay with him for good. But I heard that you stayed for several weeks after he was hurt. I'd say that was very kind.'

She shrugged. 'No kindness about it. I stayed until he sold the boat. He promised me part of the money and I didn't want to leave without it.'

He blinked, uneasy. 'That's pretty cold-blooded, Mrs Stavros.'

'Cold-blooded? What are you talking about?'

'I thought you liked Eben.'

'Hah!' Her dark eyes glinted, without warmth, and Carter began to wish he hadn't chased her. The face in the lantern light was as lovely as ever, and yet he was beginning to notice wrinkles in it, and the cratering of the pores in her skin. He supposed those flaws had always been there. But now he *saw* them – just as he saw other things that surprised and upset him.

'If that's how you feel, why did you stay with him at all?'

'Because he earned a good income before he got hurt. I want to go home to Poros. I've wanted to go home ever since Stavros died. Eben and I made an arrangement whereby each week, he gave me what I needed – money – and I give him what he wanted. Just ten dollars more and I'll have enough for passage to Greece. I feel sorry for Eben, but he wasn't an attractive man. He was old and he stank of fish. So do you – but you're young and good-looking.'

Her words shocked and saddened him. Poor, lonely Eben had talked so proudly about her angelic disposition – assuming no one would ever discover he had willingly paid for her companionship, and that she had just as willingly sold it. A business transaction. Christ. Were all women as mercenary as she was? For the first time, he wondered.

Languorously, she relaxed against the dirty brick wall, drawing her shoulders back and pushing her belly forward so that her skirt touched his trousers. She moved her hips and laid her left arm over his right shoulder, then crooked it around his neck and pulled his head closers to hers:

'Aha, that teases you a little, doesn't it? Feeling me excites you—'

With her right hand she reached down and touched him. He wanted to tear the hand away and run.

'I despise America, but I don't despise American

114

men. Not all of them, anyhow. Just the pious ones who pray on Sunday and try to put their hand up your dress the other six days of the week. I've met plenty of those. Tell them to stop and they call you a dirty foreigner – which is what their wives call you all of the time. But with ten more dollars – just a little bit – I can go home to the place I love. Would you give me ten dollars? For five dollars, I'll take you to my room and let you love me any way you wish. Ten dollars – you can have me all night. I did business with old Eben, surely I can do busines with—'

Carter flung off her arm. 'Get away from me before I break your damn neck.'

'What's the matter with you?' she whispered. 'What kind of self-righteous, cockless little wart are you? Maybe you're more Greek than I. Maybe you like little boys—'

'Whore!' he shouted, and shoved her so hard she fell. Lithe as a cat, she caught herself on hands and knees and glared from under a fall of dark, gleaming hair. Three longshoremen walked by, their box hooks hanging from their belts. One called:

'What d'you think she'd be if not a whore, my lad? Ain't any other kind of woman walkin' around here this time o'night.'

Helen Stavros scrambled to her feet, gave Carter a withering look and poured out profanity, English and Greek, so filthy and violent it was almost like a physical blow. Then she turned and strode away, haughty and injured.

Bewildered, he watched her go. A huge, sick ache filled his middle. He'd thought she was a beautiful woman who loved poor Royce. But she wasn't beautiful, she was a slut. She'd deceived him. There was, apparently, nothing to believe in and no one to trust, save yourself.

Carter slouched on toward the Red Cod, the mood

of profound disillusionment refusing to lift. He was by turns shocked and angry the rest of the night. When he flung Josie on her pallet in her cubicle upstairs at the Cod, she complained afterwards that he had never treated her so roughly – as if he were revenging himself on her rather than loving her.

CHAPTER X

Campaign Year

Business pressures forced Gideon to neglect Carter and his problems during the next few months. Carter had managed to hang onto his menial job at the fish processing plant. And he'd repaid about a third of what he owed for the wagon. He still lived with the family, but they saw less and less of him; he worked nights and slept days – when he wasn't off carousing. With increasing frequency, he was away from home several days at a time. Gideon decided to assign a man from Kent and Son to make occasional inquiries. He didn't prettify this action with some high-sounding description that absolved him of guilt. In his thoughts he called it what it was – spying. But he justified the measure on the grounds that he might learn something with which to reassure Julia.

His hope was a vain one. The information brought back to him was so disturbing, he didn't dare pass it along to his wife. Gideon's informant repeatedly said the young man was mixing with a bad crowd. Tavern idlers; harlots; people prone to resolve trivial quarrels by violence. His favourite haunt was the notorious Red Cod.

Something would have to be done to put the young man's life back on a better course. But what? The answer continued to elude Gideon.

The end of the year brought the prospect of a presidential election campaign and a new employee to the publishing house. In offices all around the country, typewriting machines were bringing a new neatness, speed and efficiency to the preparation of letters, records and memoranda. A Wisconsin inventor named Sholes had designed the prototype in 1867. After several modifications, it was being manufactured by Remington and Sons, and meeting wide acceptance.

Of course it required an operator, who was called a typewriter. Many firms put men in the jobs until the men complained the work was demeaning and not sufficiently masculine. When Gideon expressed his interest in obtaining one of the machines, Julia urged him to hire a woman to run it. She said that because of the new machine, women were being taken into offices for the very first time. Julia's suffragist group saw the Sholes typewriter and Sir Isaac Pitman's shorthand system as weapons of economic liberation for the female sex.

Gideon recognized the familiar signs of determination in Julia and bowed to them. After interviewing four obviously inexperienced women, he found one who favourably impressed him – a prim spinster named Helene Vail. Miss Vail was somewhere in her forties. She had lively hazel eyes and the prettiest contralto voice he'd ever heard. She was also monumentally ugly.

Using his new office machine, Miss Vail demonstrated her skill. She was fast and accurate. She was equally good with dictation. They were soon discussing wages. Gideon mentioned a very high figure – eighty dollars per month. That was the amount he'd put into a preliminary yacht budget for both his captain-pilot and his engineer. He assumed Miss Vail would be as important to him as either of them.

'Would eighty be satisfactory?' he asked.

Miss Vail pursed her lips, the closest she was ever to come to smiling, he would discover.

'Very satisfactory, sir. If each of us remains content with our arrangement in the months to come, you may be sure nothing will distract me from my duties, or induce me to leave for another post. My parents are gone, I have neither brothers nor sisters, and I have been in the world of commerce most of my adult life. I have no emotional attachments. At an early age, I was disappointed in love.'

'I see.' Gideon suppressed a grin. 'Are you always so candid, Miss Vail?'

'Yes. It is the only way to accomplish things quickly and without misunderstanding.'

She surveyed his desk. 'As soon as I become familiar with my other duties, I will undertake the sorting and arranging of that material. This office is a disgrace. I'm sure you'll work more happily and efficiently when I take charge of it.'

Open-mouthed, he recovered sufficiently to say, 'I'm sure I will.'

And so it proved.

2

Gideon was a Republican, though not a fanatical one. In less than two decades the party foundation of crusading idealism had eroded. More and more, it was becoming the captive of private interests. He disliked many of its positions and practices, and wondered how much longer he could support its candidates in good conscience.

Of course it was not only the Republicans with whom

he found fault. There were plenty of trimmers among the Democrats, too. As a newspaper publisher – a professional malcontent – there were some days when he despised the whole damn population.

He continued to be deeply concerned about the growing self-indulgence of the American people. Wealth was worshipped above all else. To many, admission to Society had become more important than eventual admission to Heaven. It seemed to him that the desire for personal comfort, the pursuit of prestige and the fulfilment of selfish ambition had replaced an earlier ideal of earning one's livelihood in some occupation which bettered the lot of mankind. As 1883 closed, he reluctantly concluded that the country's ruling passion was greed.

Greed in the form of the patronage issue had all but split the Republican party in 1880, when Senator Conkling's so-called Stalwart wing had fought with the reform-minded Half-breed faction. The Half-breeds had succeeded in nominating and electing Garfield. The president's assassin had publicly identified himself as a Stalwart. That had dimmed the movement's star forever.

The split in the Republican ranks was still very much in evidence, however. Early in 1884, Gideon began to hear rumours that at the convention the Republicans might finally turn to James Blaine. Twice before, Blaine had been denied the presidential nomination because of impropriety.

Years ago, Blaine had been dubbed the Plumed Knight. But now the plume was dirty and broken. After the war, Blaine had been caught profiteering. He'd peddled his influence and his Congressional vote, and taken payment in cash, stocks and bonds. A bookkeeper named Mulligan had got hold of evidence in the form of a packet of letters. Blaine was able to recapture the letters, which he took to the floor of the House in a bold move to vindicate himself. After he'd read some of the letters aloud for the record, his fellow Congressmen had cheered and shouted for his vindication. But there was no doubt that he was guilty. And so, in '76 and again in '80, the Republicans had denied his bid for the nomination.

Now one faction of the party was talking him up again. Another group, which included men such as Carl Schurz and Charles Francis Adams, Junior, was saying Blaine could never win – especially if the Democrats nominated the vigorous reform governor of New York, Stephen Grover Cleveland.

Among some Republicans, sentiment for and against Blaine was even stronger than Gideon had suspected. He found this out during one of his regular visits to New York City during the winter. At a party function, he met numerous outspoken foes of the candidacy. But he met some fierce partisans, too, and got into a shouting match with one of them – a paunchy and garrulous real estate millionaire named Thurman Pennel.

Pennel maintained that Blaine had merely done what dozens of other Congressmen of both parties had done before and since. The Plumed Knight's only crime had been to get caught, Pennel declared. Gideon considered that specious excuse the mark of a confused mind. He told Pennel he didn't believe in pardoning a murderer merely because an unknown number of other people in the world had committed the same crime and got away with it.

From that point, their words grew hotter. He and Pennel almost exchanged blows before others dragged them apart and pushed Pennel out of the room with a demand that he sober up. For a few minutes, Gideon regretted what he'd done; it was the McAllister Incident all over again. Then he shrugged off the regret. He believed every word he'd said, and it didn't matter that some bloated plutocrat disliked him. It was too late for Gideon Kent to polish his reputation. Besides, a ruined reputation was often the price of choosing to tell the truth.

Sometimes, Carter thought one more day at the processing plant would make him lose his sanity. Yet each night he forced himself to walk through the old, warped door at the employees' entrance, and hack and chop with the serrated knife until the sun came up again.

He often played mental games to help pass the time. A fish which he decapitated was Eisler, or Phipps, or the Portugee who had ruined Eben Royce's life. At other times, he considered ways to escape the trap in which he found himself. He couldn't think of any that were realistic. The wagon was about two-thirds paid for, and he convinced himself that he didn't really have to think about his situation until the debt was completely erased. It was a convenient means of postponing the admission that he didn't know what the devil he was going to do with his life.

He saw Royce occasionally – always from a distance. After that first time, he never approached him again. The men who frequented the taverns, most of them whole of body and mind, spoke sadly, even uneasily of the pathetic man who hobbled around the docks on his padded crutch. As for Helen Stavros, she was gone – back to Greece, Carter presumed. Sometimes he thought of taking a horse-car to Cambridge to see Willie Hearst, but he was too ashamed.

The monotonous routine at the foot of the delivery chute did drive one thought deeper and deeper into his being. Somehow, *somehow*, he would find a way to be the one who gave the orders, instead of just another one of the millions who took them. He clung to that certainty, and by means of it, his sanity.

He heard no further word of Ortega. The man might have stepped into a crevice in the earth and fallen to China. Then, after a particularly lively four-day stretch of roistering, he came to work one bitter winter night nursing a ferocious headache and a queasy stomach and there, folded on his locker shelf, he found another note.

Don't think he will forget
– Frend of O.

That did it. Carter could no longer control the spasms in his gut. He managed to lurch outside before he threw up what little his stomach contained. He closed his eyes, gulping the piercing winter air that had dried his lips and cracked them open. He kept seeing Ortega's vicious eyes, and the fishhook scar. He wished to God the Portugee would come back from wherever he was hiding, so they could get it over with and he could live in peace again, not forced to study every shadow and analyse every sound when he roamed the docks by night.

4

The Republican group which expressed aversion to Blaine included one New York State assemblyman of whom Gideon had been hearing good things lately – especially in his own newspaper. Theo Payne was a confirmed cynic, yet he'd been lavish in his praise of this particular assemblyman, whom his colleagues in Albany had dubbed the Young Reformer. The name was applied admiringly or sarcastically, depending on party affiliation or the amount of graft being taken by the speaker.

There was no doubt the young man had made quite a mark during two terms in the state capital. Payne claimed he'd done well because he was rich, and therefore incorruptible. Gideon was anxious to meet him, and when he did, found him to possess an interesting and complex personality.

Of average height, the young man had blond hair parted in the middle, and English side whiskers. He wore his eyeglasses on a black silk cord. He was ruggedly built, yet affected a languid drawl. Perhaps he thought an aristocrat was supposed to talk that way, Gideon reflected. But his voice – quite high-pitched – was already disconcerting enough.

At twenty-six, he had already written his first book, a study of naval operations in the War of 1812. Gideon quickly realized he was intelligent, but a bit priggish, too. Still the young man didn't equivocate as so many politicians did:

'I am a Republican through and through, Mr Kent. Through and through! I shall support the party's candidate no matter who it turns out to be. But I cannot give any credence to those who say it must and will be Blaine. He's a talented man. And contrary to what some drunken scoudrels like that Thurman Pennel claim, the Mulligan letters have *not* been forgotten. I shall expend every effort to block Mr Blaine's nomination.'

'May we quote you on that in the *Union*?' Gideon asked, reaching for the pad and pencil he always kept in a pocket.

'By godfrey, indeed you may. You my also say this. Mr Blaine is unacceptable because he is too intimately connected with the class represented by Mr Gould – which is, in my opinion, the most dangerous of all

123

classes. Far more dangerous than the so-called radicals—'

Bright, unblinking eyes met Gideon's through heavy lenses.

'I refer, sir, to the wealthy criminal class.'

Right after the war, Gideon had had a run-in with Mr Jay Gould, the notorious financier. So the remarks he'd just heard helped him decide that he liked young Mr Theodore Roosevelt of the West fifty-seventh Street Roosevelts, Harvard, and New York's Twenty-first Congressional District. The two men corresponded during what turned out to be a tragic winter for Roosevelt, and they promised to meet again at the Republican convention.

5

The Republicans convened in Chicago on the third of June. Gideon took a train from Boston, entering the convention city for the first time in seven years. He was astonished at how completely the downtown area had been rebuilt. Hardly a trace of the effects of the fire of 1871 remained.

He had been caught in the midst of that fire, and there were many reasons why he could never forget it. Making love to Julia on the night the fire broke out was perhaps the most important.

Chicago reminded him of Tom Courtleigh, too; Courtleigh who for four years had tried to destroy him. It reminded him of his youngest brother, Jeremiah, whom everyone had thought lost in the war. Jeremiah had turned up in Chicago, as one of Courtleigh's bodyguards. He'd sacrificed himself in Courtleigh's offices to save Gideon from being killed.

This summer, Chicago produced another unexpected link with the past. Gazing up from the press area of the convention floor, Gideon thought he recognized a face in the gallery. He climbed the gallery stairs and sure enough, he was right. There sat Michael Boyle.

The Irishman was in his early to mid fifties. With hardly a grey hair, Gideon thought enviously. Boyle had not yet seen him standing at the head of the stairs. Gideon pondered whether he ought to push on through the crowd and make his presence known.

Michael Boyle was the man to whom Gideon's father had willed the one-third interest in the Kent fortune that would have gone to Gideon's brother Jeremiah. Jephtha had made the decision during the years in which everyone presumed Jeremiah was dead. Boyle had borrowed against some of the money which was to come to him at Jephtha's death. He'd used the loan to start a chain of general stores along the Union Pacific right-of-way. The stores had earned him his first million dollars.

Gideon had always regarded Boyle as an opportunist who'd exploited his position as Amanda Kent's clerk and confidante in order to get some of the Kent money. Julia insisted the judgment was unfair. For someone who'd only met the Irishman a couple of times, she seemed curiously vehement in her defence of him.

Still, perhaps he was guilty of misjudgment, Gideon thought now. Boyle hadn't squandered the fortune Jephtha had left him. On the contrary; he'd preserved and increased it. From his home in the Wyoming territorial capital; Cheyenne, he'd made fortunes of his own in retailing and in cattle.

He'd also taken Kent as his legal middle name. He was evidently a Republican, something Gideon hadn't known before. The political tie overcame Gideon's habitual suspicion. He walked along the packed aisle to Michael's box. There he stopped, and extended his hand:

'Boyle? Gideon Kent.'

Michael stood up, a graceful man with gold eyes. He wore an expensive coat of bottle-green velvet, fawn trousers and spotless linen. He was taller than Gideon by several inches. His handshake was firm.

'Yes, I saw you down there on the floor. I was debating whether to make myself known.'

'I'm surprised you recognized me. We only met on that one occasion in New York.'

Michael nodded. 'But I remember it quite distinctly. Hannah and I called on you at your mansion. You were about to sell it and move to Boston. You and your wife were extremely gracious. Besides, it isn't easy to forget a relative who's a public figure. Even in my part of the world, you're famous.'

Gideon shrugged to brush the compliment aside. 'What brings you to Chicago?'

'An attempt to get more favourable freight rates for the cattle we ship from our ranch. And of course this convention. I work for the Republican party in the territory.'

'Look, this place is damnably noisy. Why don't we have supper tonight? I'm at the new Palmer House.'

'So am I. Suite eight hundred.'

That rankled. Gideon had only booked a single room.

'Shall we say eight o'clock in the dining room?'

'Fine,' Boyle said. 'I'll look forward to it. We may have been on opposite sides in the late war, but we *are* members of the same family.'

Presumptuous bastard, Gideon thought. Then he silently chastised himself. Michael Boyle was fully entitled to think of himself as a Kent. Gideon's father had decreed that. The trouble was, Gideon still hadn't completely accepted the decree.

On the way back to the convention floor, he passed a man who gave him a venomous scowl. He'd gone another half dozen steps before he rememberd who the

126

man was. Thurman Pennel, the real estate millionaire from New York. Pennel clearly hadn't forgotten the quarrel about Blaine. The animosity didn't bother Gideon. As a newspaperman, he was accustomed to being hated.

6

That evening in the crowded dining room of the Palmer House, Gideon and Michael engaged in a verbal sparring match for the first ten or fifteen minutes. They tested each other's political positions and explored each other's recent history, but superficially, and without great warmth. A certain unsmiling stiffness remained as the waiter brought the first course.

When they were about halfway through the meal, a harried Theodore Roosevelt bustled in. He seemed to run everywhere, never walk. He was on his way to a table for one, a sheaf of papers in his hand. He paused to greet Gideon and be introduced to Michael.

'You're welcome to join us, Theodore,' Gideon said.

The young man held out the papers, which were covered with names and figures. 'Thank you, but I must do another analysis of delegate strength while I'm dining. This convention must choose a reform candidate such as Senator Edmunds of Vermont. Blaine isn't electable and neither is Chester Arthur.'

Gideon puffed his cigar. 'I agree. If Blaine's the candidate, the party won't have my support. Nor my paper's endorsement.'

'Oh?' Michael raised an eyebrow. 'I think a man's duty-bound to stick with his party whether he approves of the candidate or not. Otherwise, how can a man consider himself a true member of that party?'

'Afraid I feel the same way, Mr Boyle,' Roosevelt said in that squeaking voice. 'That's why I'm working so vigorously to see Blaine defeated. The Democrats will choose Grover Cleveland, I imagine. His reform record will be a powerful asset. It might even overcome the scandal connected with his personal life.'

'What scandal?' Michael wanted to know.

Gideon answered. 'There have been rumours that Cleveland fathered a bastard when he was in law school or shortly after he got out. It's never been proved. But I fear some of our party loyalists won't let that stop them from spreading the story.'

Michael scowled. 'I don't like that kind of tactic.'

'Nor do I, sir. Nor do I!' Roosevelt exclaimed, and hurried off.

The Irishman stared after him, then shook his head:
'He's one of the strangest ducks I've ever met.'

'We need more like him. He's a comer in the party,' Gideon said. 'Got quite a remarkable history, too. Family's old New York aristocracy. Lot of money. As a boy, he was almost incapacitated by asthma. His father built a gymnasium in their townhouse, and Theodore exercised for hours every day to overcome his physical weakness.'

'He's done it, obviously. He looks strong as a bull.'

Gideon nodded. 'He whipped everything except his bad eyesight. That doesn't keep him from going hunting in Dakota. He's been out there quite a lot this year. In February, his wife and his mother died in circumstances no editor would ever find credible in a story.' In response to Michael's quizzical look, he went on. 'They died on the very same day, of unrelated illnesses. It was quite a blow to him. But he pulled through. He doesn't give up. That's one of the reasons I like him.'

'You know him well?'

'I met him just this past winter. But I'd say we've become good friends. We exchange letters from time to time. I like the way he thinks. For instance, he can't stand what he calls fireside moralists. You know – the sort of people who are forever crying about bad government, but who sit home and do nothing to correct the flaws. Theodore isn't that kind.'

Michael glanced at a nearby table where Roosevelt was scribbling on one of his papers. 'I liked him because he's willing to support the Republican candidate. Without reservation.'

The remark was pointed. So was Gideon's reply:

'That's certainly more than you can say for me.'

'We disagree, then.'

'On that and a few other things, from tariffs to the money policy, I should imagine.' Gideon fought down his annoyance; he managed a wry look. 'But politics should be barred from the conversation when relatives eat together. How do you feel about the buffalo steak?'

Michael sampled another morsel with his fork. He dabbed his moustache with a stiffly starched napkin.

'Damn good. Some of the best I've ever tasted.'

'Well, there's a common ground.'

For the first time since their meeting at the convention, both men smiled.

7

The chance meeting in Chicago touched off an occasional correspondence that extended throughout the summer and into the fall.

Blaine had taken the nomination on the fourth ballot. And as predicted, Cleveland was the choice of the Democrats. Independent Republicans were faced with the question of whether to support the candidate or bolt. Gideon joined the so-called Mugwumps who bolted. Young Roosevelt, who was trying to embark on a second career as a Dakota ranchman, did not. A letter mailed from the town of Medora, Dakota Territory, told Gideon the decision hadn't been a happy one.

Never had Gideon witnessed a more vicious national campaign. In late July, the Buffalo *Evening Telegraph* confirmed that Cleveland had indeed fathered a illegitimate child. The mother was a woman named Maria Halpin. The candidate quickly admitted his culpability, and supplied evidence that he'd provided for the child's care. His candour turned a liability into an advantage. But the Republicans were soon singing a derisive song in every one of their torchlight parades:

> *Ma! Ma! Where's my pa?*
> *Gone to the White House—*
> *Ha! ha! ha!*

The Democrats were no more scrupulous. They sang lustily about 'Blaine, Blaine, James G. Blaine! The continental liar from the state of Maine!' In letters Michael and Gideon wrote during September and October, they twitted one another about supporting a lecher and a swindler.

The letters grew more and more cordial. Politics gave way to chatty news of their prospective families. Michael and his wife Hannah had two children – a son Lincoln, named after the president, and a daughter Erin. Gideon soon found himself enjoying the correspondence immensely. He and Michael might never be warm friends, but at least he regarded the Irishman with less suspicion now. He still considered Boyle an idiot for remaining loyal to Blaine.

On election night, Gideon was at Democratic headquarters in Boston. In the fine baritone voice he'd once used to sing in the saddle with Stuart's cavalry, he joined the rest of the revellers as they praised the victorious Cleveland:

> *Hurrah for Maria,*
> *Hurrah for the kid!*
> *We voted for Grover,*
> *And we're damned glad we did!*

130

When Gideon arrived at Kent and Son the next day, Helen Vail was waiting for him with a paper in her hand:

'I think you'd better read this at once, Mr Kent.'

He held his head and slumped into his chair. 'I can't read anything this morning.'

'Please make an effort, sir. This is a telegraph message from your daughter.'

Giving him a severe look, she laid the paper on the desk. Then she brought a damp cloth from the wash stand concealed behind a screen in the corner.

'Here, sir. Put this on your forehead. I fail to understand how you can be so debilitated from a night of celebration.'

'Then you've never celebrated with Democrats.' He laid the cloth over his eyes and put his head back. The throbbing persisted. After a moment, she cleared her throat.

'Mr Kent—'

He groaned. 'Miss Vail, can't the message wait?'

'Not long, sir. It's November already. Your daughter wants to be married here in Boston before the year is out.'

On the thirtieth of November, the coastal steamer MS *Prince of Fundy* docked at Boston on her way northward from New York to Halifax and St John's. Among the third class passengers was a man with a red bandana tied around his curly black hair, his few worldly possessions packed in a stolen carpet bag, and a knife hidden under an expensive sheep-lined coat he'd killed to get.

Deck lights whitened the facial scar shaped like a fishhook. A gale wind had begun blowing off the dark Atlantic, and he had to struggle down the gangway against its buffeting fury. He was glad to return. But in order to resume his life, and have people again treat him with respect, there were matters to which he must attend. One involved the young student who had humiliated him at the Red Cod, the night all his trouble had started. Ortega would accept many things that life or other men dealt out, but humiliation was not one of them.

Fortunately, thanks to a friend in Boston, he knew where to find the student any time he chose. He wanted to settle that particular score, and several others, very soon. Then he could celebrate the holy Christmas season in good spirits.

CHAPTER XI

The Secret Door

Eleanor Kent arrived home during the first week of December. She was glad to be back in Boston. Glad to see the familiar rooms and furniture of Beacon Street. Glad to be reunited with Julia and her father and brother. And yet, from the moment she stepped off the train and ran into her father's embrace, the visit was marred by uneasiness. She hoped there would be no overly frank discussion of her decision to marry Leo Goldman. Such a discussion could lead into areas she must avoid. It could lead to the dark door kept closed for so many years—

Still Eleanor was in a cheerful mood when she got home. She'd spent a few days visiting at Mrs Louisa Drew's Arch Street Theatre in Philadelphia and found it an enjoyable experience. The Christmas season was just getting underway, with decorations greening the windows of homes and shops, and the lovely old hymns pealing from choir lofts on Sunday – and from the throats of carollers the rest of the week.

To heighten the excitement, there was the wedding. A one-hour family meeting on her first night home produced a mutual agreement on the date; the wedding would be held during the week after Christmas. Leo would be bringing his father up from New York. Mr Goldman, a widower, had finally consented to come even though he disapproved of his son marrying outside the faith.

Eleanor had a great many anecdotes to relate to her family during the first days at home. She preferred talking about the theatre rather than the forthcoming marriage, simply because she was of two minds about the latter. She loved Leo Goldman, and she wanted to marry him. Yet a small part of her held back, and it was that part she feared for Julia and her father to see.

There was no danger of Will seeing it – he was too young. And Carter – well, he worked nights, and when he reeled home the morning after her arrival, he bussed her sleepily and went staggering upstairs to bed. He smelled of fish and – shockingly – beer. She quickly sensed that there was trouble in the house, tension between Gideon and Carter. But no one mentioned it. Nor was she critical of her stepbrother. If Carter had flaws, so did she. One of the worst was her confused reaction to the prospect of marriage. On one hand, she wanted to be Leo's wife, and make him happy, and enjoy a normal existence. But against that, there was the door. The hidden door she kept closed almost constantly. Surely it would be opened at least a little commencing with her wedding night—

As best she could, she avoided giving any hint of this turmoil to her parents.

At twenty-two, Eleanor was not only a stunning dark-haired beauty, but also a veteran actress. She'd embarked on a career as a touring performer at fifteen, looking mature enough to convince audiences she was three to five years older. She and her father hadn't been getting along at the time she left home – due to her poor, demented mother's schemes to divide the family. But Gideon had had nothing to say about her decision to go on the road with J. J. Bascom's third-rate troupe of players who travelled the country performing *Uncle Tom's Cabin*.

Some years later, long after Margaret's plotting had been exposed and Eleanor and Gideon were friendly again, her father told her that one factor had lessened his worry when she joined the Tom show. That was the presence of young Leo Goldman in the same company. Leo had been in love with Eleanor even then; the two had met at one of the amateur theatrical clubs which had flourished in New York in the seventies.

For years, Leo had pursued Eleanor in a good-humoured but persistent way, frequently stating his intention of marrying her. And then one day, she realized she had indeed fallen in love with him. Soon after, she told him so.

It took her a couple of years beyond that to accustom herself to the idea of marriage. Leo talked of it constantly. She joked and fended off his pleas that they visit a justice of the peace in some town where they were appearing. She invented reasons why she couldn't do that.

Many women in her situation would have worried about marrying Leo because he was a Jew. They'd have fretted about being exposed to the insults and the irrational hatred Jews seemed to inspire. She'd confronted that sort of thing with Leo before, and learned a method of coping with it. And it was nothing – *nothing* – compared to the fright she felt in connection with her own inadequacy as a woman.

The inadequacy made her hesitate. She wanted to marry him, she would say, but the time wasn't right. The frequently repeated excuse had finally provoked an argument during the recent theatrical fiasco in Fort Wayne. Leo was growing impatient; Eleanor realized that she'd better say yes or she might lose him. Only that danger enabled her at last to overcome her fear. She flung her arms around Leo and whispered, 'Oh, yes, dearest, I'm tired of waiting too. Let's go to Boston and get married before the year's over.'

Thus Eleanor crossed a kind of emotional Rubicon. But even then, the image of the door persisted. Perhaps now it was more important than ever.

The image was vivid because she had made it so. She had created it. It was of a single door, made of reddish-brown wood heavily decorated with intricate carvings whose subject matter she never got close enough to examine, but which gave her a faintly unclean feeling, somehow. The door hung in a vast, gloomy limbo without a visible source of light. Yet when she approached the door in her imagination, she could see it with a fair degree of clarity. The door was not unlike the one leading into the room where Margaret Kent had hidden from reality during the last years of her life, concealing her alcoholism, her deteriorating mental condition, and the diary in which she recorded all the deceptions she had used to drive a wedge between Gideon and his daughter.

Eleanor never wanted to be like her mother. But she found the imaginary door useful for blocking out a part of the past she didn't want to remember because the memories produced overpowering feelings of guilt and self-hate. She learned to control those emotions by picturing the memories as being safely locked behind the imaginary door.

Yet the influence of those memories remained profound. They were responsible for her reluctance to agree to marry Leo, despite her love for him. They were responsible for feelings of apprehension that were with her almost constantly now that a wedding date had been chosen.

For although Eleanor would come to her marriage bed never having made love to any man, she was not a virgin.

2

Gideon Kent's New York City mansion had been invaded in 1877, just a few months before Eleanor's departure with the Tom show troupe. Enemies of her father had hired hoodlums to wreck his property and injure his family. The men had done their work well. During the attack, two of them had cornered her, and she had been raped. She was fifteen years old at the time.

The experience had left an emotional wound that had never healed. It had left a feeling that she had been permanently soiled by the experience, and could never cleanse herself, no matter how she tried. For years afterward, it was necessary to prepare herself mentally before she could let a man touch her, even a man she liked. A sudden, unexpected contact would thrust her back to the night of terror. To the feel of the hard floor beneath her naked hips, and all the raw, punishing pain.

She never told anyone of the experience, of course. What woman would willingly announce to the world that she had been raped? Eleanor's mother had had a strongly Puritanical view of sex, particularly toward the end of her life. She considered it a filthy act, and those who indulged in it equally filthy. Eleanor would not consciously go that far; she wanted a healthy relationship with a husband – someday. But there was no question that the rape had sullied her permanently. Hence she never mentioned the despicable event to Julia, and certainly not to her father or her younger brother. It was her secret, and would always remain so.

But it still had the power to bring cold sweat to her palms and dryness to her throat when she recalled it. The reaction was far worse than stage fright; that she could control. This she could not. And so she created the imaginary door, and pictured herself gliding toward it along a corridor of vast space. She pictured herself checking the door to be certain it was securely closed; pictured herself turning the filigreed key, and listening to the bolt tick over in place, and dropping the key into the pocket of her skirt.

Thus she tamed and contained her *bête noire*, black beast as it was called in translations of the novels of Zola. She enjoyed his writing because it was realistic, just like the best of the new plays. But realism, while commendable in literature, was ruinous in her personal life. Thank God for the imaginary door.

She hoped it would enable her to do what she wanted to do so badly:

Be a good wife to the handsome young actor she had come to love, and had now decided to marry, whatever the risks.

'So we rang down the curtain at the end of the second act,' Eleanor said at the dinner table on her third night home. 'It was either that or get hit by all the things the audience was throwing.'

Julia shook her head. 'I know how you must have felt. I've been in similar situations.'

Eleanor laughed. 'The difference is, we deserved every last cabbage and tomato.'

'Why?' her father asked.

'The script was perfectly dreadful, Papa. Mr Todd, the company manager, wrote it himself. It couldn't have taken him longer than three hours. There hasn't been a first-rate Indian play since Forrest did *Metamora* over fifty years ago. But *Arrow of the Heart* by J. Pulsifer Todd established a new low for bad dialogue. Just before the second act curtain, I was actually required to rush on stage and make a tearful inquiry about—'

She pressed her fisted hand to her bosom and lowered her voice. 'My brave Algonquin brave.'

That made Will laugh for the first time since the meal had started. He was such a sad, sober child, Eleanor thought. Was that Margaret's legacy? Sometimes it seemed to her that all the Kents were encumbered with invisible shackles, put on them in the past and forever preventing them from living in peace and happiness.

Gideon chuckled as he hunted through his pockets for a cigar and matches.

'I'm afraid even your considerable abilities can't redeem a line like that. I can see why your troupe had problems.'

Seated across the dinner table, Will continued to

smile at his sister, admiration at last bringing some animation to his face. Outside the window, fat snowflakes drifted down. Eleanor nodded in reply to her father's remark:

'Mr Todd thought audiences in the hinterlands wouldn't be overly critical, but he was very wrong. Even in Fort Wayne, they recognize a turkey.'

'A what, dear?' Julia asked.

'Turkey. It's slang for colossal failure.'

'How on earth did they come up with a name like that?' Gideon asked through a cloud of smoke.

'The *Union*'s theatre critic could tell you, Papa. Turkey actors are hopeful performers – generally a lot more optimistic than they are talented. They get together, hire a hall, and perform a play on Thanksgiving Day.'

'I still don't see—'

'Audiences are always in a good mood on Thanksgiving. Stuffed with turkey and chestnuts and easy to please. The actors in these shows were usually so bad, though, that turkey became synonymous with a flop. Such as the late, unlamented wilderness drama by J. Pulsifer Todd, Esquire. In Fort Wayne, Mr Todd rushed out on stage to control the crowd and got hit with a melon. A very large, rotten melon. I think that's when he realized there was no hope. He cancelled the rest of the tour, paid us off, and disbanded the company.'

'Well, I've never gotten used to seeing missiles fly out of the audience,' Julia said. 'I'm sure your experience must have been terribly unsettling.'

Eleanor smiled. 'Oh, I've been through it with four or five other shows. And it could have been worse. We could have been performing one of those Ibsen dramas all the bluenoses consider so filthy. We could have been pelted with garbage *and* put in jail.'

'I don't think Mr Ibsen's work is filthy,' Julia

declared. 'In fact, I read a translation of *A Doll's House* and found it quite moving. To my way of thinking, it's a suffragist play.'

'I agree. I intend to do the leading role one day.' It was an ambition she and Leo talked about often. 'Anyway, being let go in Fort Wayne really wasn't that bad.'

'Is that when Leo asked you to set a date?' Gideon wanted to know.

It was no more than a casual question, yet it set her nerves on edge and destroyed the mood of good cheer which had been with her during the meal. Gideon's inquiry reminded her of how long she'd held Leo off – and why. For the space of a second or two, she concentrated on an image of the closed door. Soon she felt calmer. But the earlier mood was indeed broken.

'That's right,' she said. Calling on all her acting skill, she leaned back in her chair, and forced a smile and a sigh of contentment. 'And it's wonderful to be home again, even for a little while.'

'It's wonderful to have you here,' Gideon said, though she noticed uneasily that he was watching her more closely than he had a few minutes ago. He gestured with his cigar, tracing a blue line in the air. 'You've hardly touched your sherbet, though.'

Julia leaned forward. 'You ate very little of anything. Are you feeling all right?'

She smiled as best she could:

'Perfect. I guess I'm too excited to eat, that's all.'

'Understandable,' Julia said. 'You must be very happy to be marrying such a handsome young man.'

I'm terrified, she thought as she nervously pushed aside the plate holding the silver sherbet dish. She laced her fingers together in front of her, thinking of the door with desperate concentration. The door was closed. Closed and *locked*—

140

'Leo's a dear, kind person,' she forced herself to say finally. 'I love him very much.'

And then she noticed her father scrutinizing her again, his good eye like a bright blue light that somehow seemed to transfix her and melt away her artifice, until he saw the unhappy truth. Was that why his expression had become more sober, and why he sat straighter than before? His scrutiny made her uncomfortable. She wanted to break off the dinner conversation and leave.

Gideon, unfortunately, had different ideas.

CHAPTER XII

A Father's Fear

Leo's a dear, kind person. I love him very much.

For several minutes after Eleanor said that, Gideon turned the response over and over in his mind. Julia had asked about happiness. And Eleanor hadn't said she was happy. Glad to be home, yes. But not happy to be marrying Leo.

He'd noticed a definite hesitation before she had given her reply. He thought he also noticed something else. A marked change in her mood when Julia asked the question. Before that point in the conversation, Eleanor had seemed to be talking cheerfully. A less charitable person might even have said she was running on; breathlessly cramming every moment full of ideas and anecdotes as if, by means of that distraction, she could avoid—

What?

He didn't know. The whole notion was probably

silly. Yet he continued to study his daughter through a veil of smoke. Her evasive answer disturbed him.

He and Julia had long suspected Eleanor of harbouring some deep inner hurt which she refused to discuss. The origin of the hurt was hidden in the past, but the two agreed that the incident had probably taken place during the ransacking of the New York mansion. A female servant had been raped that night, and it was logical to assume Eleanor had been threatened with a similar fate, if not actually subjected to it.

He thought that might explain why his daughter sometimes reacted with shock and alarm when a man touched her unexpectedly. Once, during some horseplay connected with a family game of croquet, Gideon had seen that kind of shock, and the man had been Leo Goldman. In the split second before Eleanor recognized him, there was fright in her eyes – as if the sudden hand on her forearm triggered memories of someone else who had taken hold of her for a less friendly purpose.

Several times, Julia had tried to question her stepdaughter in a tactful way. She'd learned exactly nothing, but the failure was not surprising. Sexual assaults took place in Victorian society, but they were never discussed afterward. A girl who went through such an ordeal was thought to be soiled for life. Beyond that, it was to be expected that Eleanor might not confide in a woman who was not her real mother.

It was also important to remember the time at which the destruction of the mansion had taken place. It was toward the end of a long period in which Eleanor had been dominated, not to say manipulated, by poor Margaret – and without fully realizing that her mother was unbalanced. In Margaret's last years, her ideas about romance and marital love had become negative and warped, to say the least. Could that too have a bearing on Eleanor's odd response to Julia's question?

Or was he – typical father! – fearing all sorts of imaginary troubles just because he so very much wanted his daughter's life to be free of them?

Hard to say. Harder still to unravel the mystery of that night in 1877 – at least the part that pertained to Eleanor. He should stop bothering with questions that could never be resolved, and deal with those which could. One such question – and a rather delicate one – remained to be discussed. Perhaps this was as good a time as any to get it out of the way. For whatever the reason, the jolly mood which had persisted for most of the meal had completely dissipated.

2

'Do you think Carter will be able to come to the wedding, Papa?'

Eleanor's question interrupted his thoughts. He tried to laugh. It was more of a snort. 'If we ever see him again, we'll certainly ask him.'

Will exclaimed, 'He's only been gone two days, Papa.'

'Oh, yes – a mere two days. Nothing unusual in that.'

Julia looked troubled. 'Must you be so caustic, dear? It isn't the least bit funny.'

'Of course it isn't. I'm sorry.' He meant it. Carter's prolonged absences upset Julia terribly. The boy usually dragged home looking much the worse for wear.

With a frown, Eleanor asked, 'He's working again tonight, isn't he?'

'No,' Gideon said. 'On Sunday, he said he would have tonight off. We expected him for dinner.'

Julia flashed him another sorrowing look. Eleanor asked, 'What does he do when he stays away so long?'

Gideon shrugged. 'God only knows.' He didn't dare

reveal what he'd learned about his stepson's fondness for waterfront dens.

Will sat with downcast eyes and fidgeted on his chair. His expression showed that he didn't like to hear his stepbrother being picked apart. Julia reached out to tap his arm:

'Come, young man. Not so glum. No one's insulting Carter. But we do worry about him.'

'Carter can take care of himself! He's old enough to stay away as long as he wants to – and he can talk his way out of any mess he gets into.'

Let's hope your confidence is warranted, Gideon thought. What he said was:

'Quite right. I only wish he wouldn't test our faith so frequently.'

So saying, he smiled at his son. That mollified Will a little. 'Now, young man, we have wedding details to discuss. I'm sure you'd find that very boring.' Will nodded in an emphatic way.

'Then you may be excused,' his father said. The boy hurried out. A frown creased Eleanor's forehead:

'What details, Papa? I thought we'd covered everything.'

'Yes, we've taken care of all the arrangements for the ceremony and reception,' Julia said with a nod. 'But there's one point which your father and I felt we would be remiss not to mention.'

Silence. Eleanor's frown deepened. The window glass whined under the thrust of the December wind. From the floor below rose the sweet smell of pine logs and branches. Some of the servants were readying the Yuletide house decorations.

'There really isn't much preparation required for a civil ceremony—' Eleanor began.

Watching her closely, Gideon said, 'It isn't what happens before the wedding that we want to discuss. It's what might happen afterward.'

144

She stiffened. It was almost as though a mask had been clapped onto her lovely face:

'Papa, I find that a rather personal subject. And an inappropriate one, I might add. For this occasion or any other.'

The tone and tenor of her words disturbed him. She sounded angry and inflexible to the point of shrillness. For a moment, he'd heard an eerie echo of Margaret in her voice. It was the very first time he'd ever noticed such a thing.

Julia intervened to lessen the tension:

'He isn't referring to matters that are solely the province of a husband and wife. He's referring to what's involved when you marry someone of Leo's faith.'

'Oh.' The moment Eleanor understood, she relaxed and was herself again. 'You mean the kind of bullying he sometimes gets because of his name? Or the other ways people show how much they dislike Jews?'

'Exactly,' Julia said.

'Something poisonous is happening in this country,' Gideon said. 'A hundred years ago, Jewish families such as the Rothmans were welcome here, and easily assimilated. About ten years ago, things began to change. An important New York banker like Joseph Seligman could be turned away from the Grand Union Hotel in Saratoga Springs, and now that sort of incident is repeated a thousand times a month. Just last week, Theo Payne told me one Saratoga hotel has put up a sign which says "No Jews and no dogs admitted."'

Eleanor gave a sad little shake of her head. 'You forget, Papa – Leo and I have been on the road seven years. I'm familiar with that sort of thing.'

'You may have encountered it,' Julia agreed. 'But have you actually felt that kind of viciousness directed against yourself?'

'Of course. I've usually been right there at Leo's

145

side. He takes it in his stride. Well – most of the time.' She gave a small sigh. 'I can't understand why people harbour such an intense dislike of the Jews. In school we were taught that any man is welcome in this country, no matter who he is or where he comes from.'

'That's the theory,' Gideon agreed. 'And it's a splendid one. Sometimes, though, reality falls far short. Some human beings can't explain their own failures except by finding scapegoats. And some are threatened by the economic competition a minority usually represents. That's why the Irish were the favourite scapegoats for so long. These days the Italians and all the Jews arriving from Eastern Europe are the fancied threat to people who've been here for a couple of generations.'

'Your father and I want you to marry a man you love,' Julia added. 'But we also want you to do so with your eyes open. You'll almost certainly encounter a great deal of ugliness when you're Leo's wife. Can you deal with it?'

Eleanor smiled a radiant smile. 'Easily. Together Leo and I can do anything.'

The answer bothered Gideon. He suspected that youth and romance had coloured Eleanor's perceptions. He felt that she was being highly unrealistic. He hoped she wouldn't receive a sudden and disillusioning jolt one of these days – which was precisely why he'd raised the whole question. Paradoxically, though, he found himself envying the cheerful optimism of what she'd just said – and wondering whether he had completely misinterpreted her earlier response to Julia's question about happiness.

'Besides, Papa,' she went on, 'I think you're painting too gloomy a picture. People in this country are basically quite decent. And if things do get nasty once in a while, Leo and I can always escape.'

'Escape?' Gideon repeated, jolted again. Her word unexpectedly conjured an image of Margaret's room;

Margaret's locked door; the fearful barrier behind which she'd hidden her madness, and her pain—

Nonsense. He was carrying the comparison too far.

'Certainly,' Eleanor was saying. 'That's what the theatre is, after all. A place of escape. A fantasy world. It's true for the actors as much as for an audience.'

And is that how you've dealt with your hurts all these years? By hiding from them the way your mother did? Is that why you became an actress in the first place – because it was a way to hide?

The insight left him shaken, though he didn't yet know whether it was a valid insight, or fatherly foolishness. Now it was his turn to be nervous – and annoyed. He puffed his cigar, toyed with a spoon and said:

'Eleanor, forgive me, but – do you mean to say you feel no obligation to stand up to bigots?'

'Leo's more militant than I. He feels that obligation. I try to talk him out of it.'

'I find that incredible in a member of this family.'

'Oh, Papa – why? Arguing with a bigot is futile. Why should anyone struggle to change minds that can't be changed?'

'Because if you don't, your silence sanctions the behaviour of such people. Encourages them to spread their hateful ideas—'

She shook her head. 'I'm sorry, Papa. I don't think it's my fight.'

'It will be the moment you become Mrs Goldman.'

'Then you must let us deal with it our own way. I tell you we can overcome any problems we encounter.'

'And you'll overcome them by pretending they don't exist? By running from them?' Gideon kept his voice calm but firm. 'I'll tell you this much. If you don't stand up for your rights, someone will take them away.'

Julia's eyes pleaded for forbearance. She reached out to touch his sleeve:

'Dear, haven't we strayed from the main subject?'

'Indeed we have,' Eleanor answered, smiling again. 'I repeat – Leo and I must deal with things in our own way. I know we can. All that matters to either of us is getting ahead in our profession.'

At that, an image of the tea bottle flashed into Gideon's mind. His flare of anger was moderated by a sudden melancholy. With her present attitude, Eleanor would be incapable of providing any leadership for the family in the years ahead; she was uninterested.

The father within him pushed the preacher aside. He had no wish to prolong the argument. But he now had two things to fret about: her willingness to ignore questions of principle, and some deeper problem of which he'd become aware during the course of this distressing evening. He couldn't reconcile the coming wedding with her refusal to make a simple statement that she was happy. Something was wrong in her relationship with young Goldman. Something she was keeping locked away inside herself—

But he wouldn't discover it tonight. So he might as well try to end the evening on a more positive note. He summoned a smile and said:

'All right, Eleanor. You're a grown woman. I can't live your life for you. And perhaps Julia's right. Perhaps we've ventured into areas that are none of our affair. Let me turn to something a bit more cheerful. Let me wish you well by giving you this.'

From an inner pocket he took an envelope which he handed to her.

'Inside, you'll find our wedding gift to you and Leo. Round trip steamer tickets to Europe – a first class suite – plus reservations for the boat train to Paris and the Continental Hotel on the Right bank. Finally, there's a bank draft to cover a month's honeymoon. As you know, old Philip's mother was an actress in the French theatre. Good enough to have had a couple of her performances praised by the popular gazettes, too.

That's especially noteworthy when you recall the low esteem in which actresses were held in the eighteenth century.'

Trying to banish all the upsetting thoughts the table conversation had raised, he reached for Julia's hand. 'We wanted you and Leo to see the theatres where Marie Charboneau appeared. That's as much a part of this family's heritage as those weapons of war we treasure.'

Gideon's words had quite smoothed away any anger Eleanor had felt. The tears in her eyes were tears of joy:

'Wait till Leo hears! Oh, Papa – Julia – thank you. Thank you both.'

She rushed to her stepmother's side and flung her arms around Julia's neck. A moment later she gave her father a similar hug. Julia sipped her tea, painfully aware of the artificiality of Gideon's smile, and of the worried look which Eleanor couldn't see as she pressed her cheek to his.

CHAPTER XIII

Reprisal

A week later, just past midnight, Carter climbed the stairs to the second floor of the Red Cod with Josie.

Her plain, cramped room at the end of the corridor had a slanting ceiling – the underside of the roof – and a large round window in a gable at one end. The window overlooked the water; the back of the tavern perched on the pier directly above the harbour.

Carter had spent the first part of the evening at the

processing plant. But he'd been out of sorts, and resentful of his situation, too much so to stay until the end of the shift. He'd gone to Kimpton and spun a story about feeling sick. It only took a few words to overcome the objections of the witless foreman, who really didn't care whether Carter worked or walked out. If he did the latter, his pay would be docked, Kimpton said with a shrug.

Although the night air was chilly and damp, Carter roamed the streets for an hour, wondering why he was unable to put up with the work routine tonight. He always hated it, but this evening was the first time he'd been incapable of lasting to the end of the shift.

Maybe it was the season. At Christmastime people felt happy – or pretended they did. The mood at home was doubly cheerful because of the forthcoming wedding of his stepsister.

Carter, by contrast, felt miserable. Gideon was bullyragging him again. Last week they'd had a ferocious argument, just because Carter had promised to be home for dinner on his night off and hadn't showed up. An all night card game at a tavern called the Gloucester Arms had kept him occupied.

The game had cost him nearly twenty dollars, too. When Carter played poker, he won an occasional hand but generally came out the poorer at the end of the evening. He liked cards but had no true card sense. He often wished he did, because gambling was one relatively effortless method of making your way in life – *if* you were good. Since he wasn't, he had to keep searching for something else.

Cross and tense, at the end of this hour of roaming, he drifted to the Red Cod. He'd decided that what he needed was a woman. He was right. Not long after paying Phipps, he lay with his arm around Josie in the darkness of her mean room and felt far more relaxed than he had when he first flung her on the pallet and began pawing at her clothes. He felt peaceful; almost happy. Josie, too, was in a warm, reflective mood, in part because he'd paid to be with her until morning.

She leaned her cheek against his bare shoulder, sighing in a contended way. Downstairs, a couple of raucous voices were raised above the murmur of conversation. The men began to bellow 'On the Banks of the Sacramento.' In the harbour, a deep horn sounded once, then again. In the last hour, a heavy fog had blown in.

'Ah,' Josie said softly. 'Times like this, I wish I could get out of the North End an' marry a young man like yourself.'

Carter laughed and tugged the coverlet high over both of them. 'Don't be fooled, Josie my love. If you married the likes of me, you'd be disappointed.'

'Oh, no!' She tapped the end of his nose with an index finger. 'Why d'you think so poorly of yourself?'

'Usually I don't. Tonight, though—' His voice trailed off.

'Well, I think a lot of you, love. You're handsome. Clever. You can be generous if you're feeling like it. An' you speak so beautifully. At least when you have a mind to—'

'Lot of good that does me in the plant,' he grumbled.

'You'll find a place where it'll do you good, Carter. I know you will.'

Her faith touched him – though for a moment, he wondered whether she was another Helen, who would now want extra payment in return for all the compliments.

But she didn't ask for that; just for his nearness, warm flesh against flesh, and sometime later, for renewed intimacy. Her hands reached down to caress him and he kissed her, glad to forget the world's deficiencies – and his own – for another brief interval.

Afterward, he yawned, glanced out the moisture-speckled window at the thick fog, then fell asleep on her shoulder.

2

At a few minutes past four, Phipps bid the last of his serving girls goodnight, sleepily rubbed his eyes and opened a drawer beneath the serving counter, preparing to count his receipts for the evening.

The Cod was still, and empty save for one last customer who slept the night on the high-backed deacon's bench before the fire. The man was a regular, so Phipps permitted that. The sleeping form was invisible except for the man's boots, which jutted past the end of the bench to the hearth, where the embers brightened, faded, and sent up showers of sparks when gusts of air whipped down the chimney.

Except for the sleeping patron, Phipps was alone. Of his girls, only Josie was employed for the night. He dumped the coins from the drawer on the counter and began separating them into piles. But his eyes blurred from exhaustion, and he was forced to close them and put his head down on his forearm.

The quick, soft opening of the front door brought Phipps's head up again. A thin, shabbily dressed man scanned the interior of the Cod. Phipps recognized him, and was not too sleeping to realize the man should have been somewhere else:

'What are you doing here, Sancosa? Did the plant let you off early, or—'

The words died in a welter of saliva that suddenly filled Phipps's mouth. Sancosa had merely been scouting the tavern for another man who now appeared behind him. The little ring in Ortega's ear glinted as he stepped in, shut the door, and leaned against it.

152

'I heard you were back,' Phipps said with a nervous smile.

'Right you are, *mamão*.'

Phipps didn't know what the last word meant. But from the contemptuous way Ortega said it, he knew it wasn't complimentary. Phipps was rigid with terror. The sound of voices had roused the sleeper by the fire. Phipps could hear small noises from the other side of the deacon's bench, but he didn't dare look that way.

Ortega walked – or more properly, swaggered – toward the serving counter. His companion, who was also Portuguese, followed. Sancosa's frayed coat was unbuttoned. Beneath it, tucked into the man's belt, Phipps glimpsed a fish knfe.

What the devil did these two want here? he wondered. Not a drink, certainly. Not this late. His legs began to wobble. He gripped the counter for support, trying to smile in an ingratiating way.

'That's a handsome coat, Ortega. New York must have agreed with you.'

Ortega shrugged. 'I was married for a while. I thought I was going to stay in New York, and let her sell hats in a hat shop to support me. But I found she couldn't get enough cock – not even from me – so I had to kill the man she was fooling with.'

He fingered the woolly yellow lining of his lapel. 'I took this coat from him. And I fixed her so no one would ever again think she was pretty. After that, I decided it was time to come home.'

Abruptly, the deacon's bench fell over. The three at the counter stared at the fat man who had risen suddenly and clumsily and was now staring at Ortega with disbelieving eyes. It was Tillman.

Sancosa jerked the knife from his belt and started toward the fat man, who bolted for the side door with surprising speed. The door banged. Sancosa started to chase Tillman into the fog but Ortega called:

153

'*Deixa que êle vá!*'

Sancosa halted, frowned, then turned back. But he didn't return his knife to his belt.

'But that man is—' Phipps began, then choked off the words. He would volunteer no information. He smelled liquor on Ortega, and from the way the Portugee blinked and smiled, Phipps knew he was dangerously drunk. Not so drunk that he couldn't make his intentions clear, however:

'I hear he's on the premises tonight. The college boy. Sancosa works at the Northeast too. He saw the boy leave earlier and followed him. Sancosa knows of my interest in the young man.'

Without thinking, Phipps exclaimed, 'It's a hell of a long time to hold a grudge, Ortega.'

The Portugee fixed him with a murderous stare, though he still smiled. 'That's right, *mamão*. But I can hold a grudge for years. I have a fine memory. That boy and Royce – they made me look less than a man. They made me give up a good life in this town.'

'Because of what you did to Royce afterward!'

Ortega's smile widened. Suddenly his hands flew – one beneath his coat, one to the bib of Phipps's leather apron. He dragged Phipps halfway across the serving counter and with his other hand brought the point of his fish knife to a spot half an inch below Phipps's left eye.

Then, slowly, he drew the point down Phipps's cheek a distance of three inches, very lightly yet with sufficient pressure to produce blood. Behind the counter, unseen by the others, Phipps urinated in his breeches.

'Are you going to argue with me?' Ortega purred. 'Or are you going to tell me where he is?'

The landlord detested the boy who had been a friend of Eben Royce. But disliking someone and consigning him to death were two different things. If he told, there was no doubt that—

Ortega's smile disappeared. He tugged the bib of the apron:

'Come on, *mamão*. Else I'll cut you in parts and cook you in your own stove.'

Phipps swallowed. The only responsibility he had was to save himself. The only one! Besides, the college boy was arrogant. He deserved whatever he got. The landlord whispered:

'Upstairs. Last room at the end.'

'Thank you.' Ortega bobbed his head and released Phipps. 'You stay here and don't interfere or I'll come back down and kill you.'

'Ortega, I – I can't afford any trouble in my—'

'Don't worry,' Ortega cut in, smiling and squeezing his shoulder as if they were the warmest of friends. 'I won't hurt him the way I hurt Royce. I'll just scare him. If he dies of fright, it won't be my fault – eh, *mamão*?'

With a jaunty wave of his knife, he strolled toward the stairs, Sancosa right behind.

3

Josie's scream wakened him. Her scream and the rough hand that ripped the coverlet away and left him shivering and groggy.

'Wake up. Wake up, *filho de puta*.'

He reached for his eyes to knuckle them. Why was the voice so familiar?

There were shadows in the room. The silhouettes of two men etched against the feeble lantern light from the corridor. Josie cried out: 'Carter, don't you see who it—?' Then a fist smacked her cheek and she tumbled out of bed, striking the floor hard and whimpering. The shorter of the two men – the one with the familiar voice – grabbed Carter's bare shoulder and hauled him to his feet.

Suddenly Carter saw yellow-tinted light flash on the serrated blade of a knife. A second knife gleamed in the hand of the taller man. Recognition flooded over Carter then. The tall Portugee guarding the door was a worker at the plant; Carter didn't know his name. The shorter, thicker man with the ring in his ear—

'Ah.' A dazzling smile. 'I see you remember me. I don't forget either. I trust you got messages to remind you of that. Now—'

Ortega began to draw small circles in the air with the knife point. Carter backed up a half step. Felt his bare heel come down on the edge of Josie's pallet. He heard her breathing loudly where she'd fallen, but didn't dare take his eyes from the slow-moving knife.

He was naked. It made him feel even more vulnerable. He was trapped – the slanting ceiling behind him, the door blocked, and only the round window offering escape – but it was a two-story drop to the icy water.

And where was Phipps? The son of a bitch had probably helped the Portugee trap him!

Tormenting him, Ortega moved the knife two inches closer, still drawing circles. The Portugee glanced at Carter's groin; snickered.

'A big man. Maybe I fix it so you won't be so big any more. What do you think? Should I? You made me mad enough, that night you helped Royce – the two of you made me look foolish and weak in front of many others—'

His face wrenched suddenly. *'Cagão!'* he spat, jabbing the knife at Carter's belly. Carter cried out in surprise and jumped back, smacking his head on the ceiling and almost losing his balance on the skidding pallet.

His reaction made Ortega laugh. Again Ortega jabbed the knife towards him; again Carter had to dodge to keep from being slashed. Ortega enjoyed the game, feinting left and forcing Carter to move that way, then lunging in from the other direction. Carter's throat quickly grew dry. His heart pounded so hard it hurt. He was terrified of the moving, taunting knife. He could actually smell the blade each time it slid by him at the end of one of Ortega's lunges. The blade reeked of fish.

How long could the game go on? He was numb with cold and with fear, and Ortega was relentless – jabbing at him, then drawing back. Almost cutting him each time; almost but not quite. Forcing Carter to jump and enjoying the sport of it while Sancosa stood behind him, a smiling observer, the knife still in his hands but his arms folded over his coat.

The game went on.

Two minutes.

Three.

The Red Cod was silent except for Ortega's occasional sly chuckle, and the creak of the floor when the Portugee lunged and Carter jumped. He thought he heard a door slam somewhere, but he wasn't sure. In the shadows, Josie's face was a white oval dotted by her huge, dark eyes, watching the awful contest—

Finally, out of breath, Carter could stand no more:

'For God's sake get it over if that's what you're going to do!'

'Watch him,' Sancosa warned his friend. 'He's getting mad.'

And so he was. Carter's fear, consuming at first, had begun to lessen, because he could be no more frightened than he already was. He guessed he was going to die. If he did, he might as well make the death worthwhile. He wasn't brave, but there was a kind of desperate, half-crazed courage pumping through him, and it wrenched his face into a pattern of rage and turned him from passive victim to aggressor. Ortega recognized the change in Carter's eyes and stance. The change made him hesitate.

In the stillness, they all heard a thumping at the far end of the hall. Sancosa's face blanched:

'Blood of the Mother! Someone's coming.'

Ortega half turned. 'The landlord?'

'No, it's two men.'

Sancosa stepped through the door into the corridor just as a man appeared – a man who was no more than a round, black silhouette. Carter saw a knife tear through Sancosa's coat and sink into his belly. Sancosa dropped to his knees, dying, and Josie screamed.

CHAPTER XIV

A Violent Lesson

Carter clamped both hands on Ortega's wrist, more to defend himself than out of any impulse towards heroics. Ortega spewed curses in Portuguese, hammering his free hand into Carter's ribs while trying to wrench his knife hand from the younger man's grip.

Sancosa slumped over in the hall. Carter heard a rapid *thump-thump*, as of a cane striking wood. Ortega threw his weight forward. The attack rammed Carter backwards, forcing him under the slope of the roof. He hit his head again, dizzyingly hard.

Ortega forced his knife hand over so that the blade penetrated the back of Carter's left hand. Sudden pain made his fingers fly open, and Ortega tore free.

Josie saw Ortega balance himself on the slippery pallet, ready for one last lunge at Carter's belly. Because of hitting his head, Carter was dazed; slow to react. Josie screamed again, just as Carter realized the nature of the tapping sound. A crutch, moving rapidly over the floor—

A sick terror filled Carter as Ortega drew his arm all the way back, preparing for the killing stroke. Simultaneously, a hobbling figure entered the room. Against the light, Carter saw something with a fishhook shape. It was a longshoreman's box hook, clutched in Captain Eben Royce's right hand.

Somehow, despite his grotesquely crippled fingers, Royce managed to keep his grip on the handle of the hook. Just as Ortega started to drive the knife into Carter's stomach, Royce whipped his arm forward. The curved point of the steel hook shot past Ortega's jaw from behind. Royce jerked backwards and the point of the hook sank into the Portugee's throat.

Royce pulled hard. Ortega was dragged off his feet. 'Jesus!' Carter cried, almost out of his mind with fright. Ortega's throat opened and an artery pumped blood that spurted over him, and stained the ceiling and the pallet with big dark splotches.

Carter staggered away, turning his head as Ortega went down. In the corner, he covered his mouth with both hands and somehow managed to keep from throwing up.

'Carter?' he heard Eben Royce say behind him. 'You all right?'

'Yes, yes – God.' He was choking. 'Is he—?'

There was no emotion in Royce's voice as he answered, 'I hope so. It's what he deserved. Tillman came to find me. I've been waiting a long time.'

Before the night's work was finished, the fog was whitened by an unseen sunrise.

Carter had regained a measure of composure, but he doubted he could ever forget the images of those last moments.

Ortega's face.

The knife turning in tormenting circles.

The smell of fish on the blade.

The blood pumping from the cut artery—

Tillman and Eben Royce were much calmer than either Carter or Josie. Tillman had given the girl a stiff drink of rum to keep her from crying hysterically. She had never stopped since Sancosa fell back into the room, Tillman's knife in his belly.

The older men displayed no remorse about the two bodies, and methodically went about the jobs that had to be done.

Tillman left the room just as Phipps came upstairs. The landlord peered into Josie's room before Royce could prevent it, and promptly vomited in the hall. When he had recovered a little, Royce pressed the box hook against his chest and talked to him softly. Carter couldn't hear what was said, except that Phipps kept nodding and repeating, 'Yes, yes, yes.'

Phipps located some old bedding. Tillman returned with a long coil of ship's line. He looked at Carter, who by then was dressed.

'Are you steady enough to help me truss 'em? We have to get rid of both bodies or we're all in dutch.'

'I – I know,' Carter said, nodding. The images persisted. Ortega's face. Ortega's stinking knife. Ortega's throat spouting great dark blots of blood onto the ceiling. He wanted to run and hide.

Royce was still talking to Phipps. Carter heard him say, 'You'll never be able to get the wood clean. Lock the room. Board it up. Never use it again. Understand me?'

'Yes. Yes. Yes.'

Somehow, Carter pulled himself together and helped Tillman wrap the bodies in the bedding, then tie each with pieces of line. They carried the bundles down to the main room. Carter was thankful that Tillman took Ortega's body; he didn't think he could have managed that.

'I found two big stones,' Tillman gasped as he lurched toward the side door with his burden. 'We'll lash one to each and drop 'em into the water. I don't know a better way – 'specially with morning coming soon.'

Tillman reconnoitred the fog to be sure no one was about. Then he motioned Carter outside. In the clammy darkness, they weighted the feet of the dead men and slipped the corpses into the water. Tillman stood up and wiped his palms on his trousers, murmuring:

'If we're lucky, the tide will take 'em a long way out after they rot a while.'

Carter could only nod and stare into the heavy fog which hid the water lapping just a couple of feet below the ramshackle pier. He saw Ortega. He saw the knife. He squeezed his eyes shut but still he saw them.

Inside, Eben Royce poured rum for Phipps and the others. Then, still in an emotionless voice, he spoke so there would be no misunderstanding:

'It had to be done, but it's still against the law. So the safety of all of us depends on the silence of each of us.'

'I'll keep quiet,' Phipps exclaimed, bringing the dented pot of rum to his lips with both hands. Even

161

grasping it that way, he could barely hold it still enough to drink.

Royce looked at Carter with a strange, forbidding gaze. The crippled man was not the man Carter remembered. He was a little wild-eyed, yet chillingly calm as he nodded and said:

'I know you will.'

'So will I,' Josie said in a faltering voice. She sat limply at a table, wrapped in an old flannel robe. The rum had taken the edge off her hysteria, and she was watching the others in an almost childlike way, as if she still couldn't believe the events of the past hour had taken place there in her room. They belonged in dark, late-night dreams.

'We all have to watch what we say,' she added after a moment. 'I guess that man – the little one, Ortega – still has friends on the docks.'

'And the other one—' Carter began.

'Sancosa,' Phipps said.

Carter gave him a hard stare. 'He has friends at the plant, I suppose.'

'Nothing will happen if we all trust one another and keep our mouths shut,' Royce said. 'Even if the bodies are found in the harbour in a few months, no one will connect them with this place so long as *we* don't say anything.'

'Someone told those two I was upstairs,' Carter said with another ferocious look at Phipps.

'I had to!' Phipps cried. 'They were going to kill me.'

Carter didn't believe that, but it no longer mattered. He just wanted to get out of this godforsaken place and go home and sleep for a year. He turned to Royce.

'You can be sure about me, Eben. I won't say anything.'

Royce gave him a stare that made his spine crawl. 'If you do, I'm done for.'

'I won't. I owe you my life.'

'Pay the debt with your silence. And stay away from here from now on.'

'But if I disappear from the plant, they'll suspect something immediately.'

Royce thought that over. 'You're right. Just stay away from this place, then.'

Without looking at Josie, Carter nodded.

There was silence again. Phipps drank noisily from the pewter pot. Josie put her hands to her face and began to weep, long, racking sobs, like those of a scared child. Carter blinked and rubbed his eyes and noticed that the bottle-glass windows looked pale.

Morning was coming. He wanted to forget this night. He knew he never would.

'Well—' he began, extending his hand and realizing too late that he couldn't shake Royce's splayed fingers without embarrassing the man. Tillman bent over the serving counter, refusing to watch.

Royce looked at him, though, and in those old, hurt eyes, Carter saw no one he recognized; only a faintly maniacal stranger.

'Goodbye,' he whispered as he bolted for the door, never realizing how foolish and unnecessary the utterance was.

3

He stood a few moments on the edge of the pier, facing the ocean.

He could hear marine traffic out there. Engines; bells; foghorns. But he saw nothing except the white veil of fog, and, due east above the unseen horizon, the hot white disc of the risen sun with its edge clearly defined. He was alone in an eerie white world, and he didn't know how he could get through the next few days and weeks.

But he *would* get through them. He had to in order to survive.

The immediacy of the night's events was lessening. The images were softening – blurring in memory like recollected nightmares. But he was still shaken to the marrow by what had happened, and while he stood silhouetted against the sun floating in the fog, the simple, stark meaning of what had happened came home to him: when you resorted to violence, you invited terror, and you took the most foolish of all chances. You exposed yourself to death. Young as he was, he had in one night come to an understanding of his own mortality; the kind of understanding most human beings didn't reach until they were in their middle years. He understood the fragility of his own life – all life – and he knew how stupid he'd been ever to imagine that the violent atmosphere of the Red Cod was exciting.

He wiped his mouth and stared into the strange glowing whiteness as if searching for the sunken bodies. He couldn't see them, of course. He could barely see the water. But he would see them as long as he lived.

As long as he lived.

A sickening smell of fish surrounded him. He realized it was only imagination. Putting his stiff hands in his pockets and lowering his head so as not to be recognized, he turned and disappeared in the direction of the city, chastened, and changed forever.

CHAPTER XV

A Detective Calls

The wedding took place as scheduled.

Leo's father, Efrem Goldman, had come with his son from his home in the ghetto of New York's lower East Side. The Goldmans were met at the depot by Gideon's largest and handsomest coach, a Brewster pulled by four matched bays. As Gideon had told Will, coaching was becoming a popular avocation among the well-to-do. It was also one of the few conspicuous displays of wealth that Gideon truly enjoyed – probably because he'd liked being around horses ever since his boyhood in Virginia's Shenandoah Valley.

Carter was present for the ceremony, having just come home from another three-day absence without offering a word of explanation. He wore a sober black suit which accentuated his pallor. The whole family noticed how haggard and tense he looked. He'd looked that way for the last couple of weeks in fact, but he had resisted all his step-father's attempts to question him.

Will attended the ceremony, too, of course. So fascinated was he by Mr Goldman's black skull cap, fringed prayer shawl, and phylacteries, he paid hardly any attention to the words intoned by the justice of the peace. Earlier, Gideon had told his son that the pair of little leather cases, one worn on Mr Goldman's arm and one on his forehead, contained slips of paper inscribed with religious texts. The phylacteries were meant to remind the wearer to observe the laws of his faith – something that was particularly important to Mr Goldman today, surrounded as he was by Protestants.

He looked uncomfortable about that. But his daughter didn't. Berthe Goldman, a fat, cheery spinster from Chicago, was the only one of Leo's nine sisters to attend the wedding. The only one, apparently, who was willing to acknowledge that her brother was marrying one of the *goyim*. Will liked her. With her good humour, she seemed determined to make up for the absence of the other eight Goldmans.

Leo looked fine in a new suit of dark wool, a white shirt, and black cravat. Eleanor had chosen an emerald silk travel dress with the requisite bustle, an item of feminine apparel Gideon found ridiculous, if not downright inhuman. Eleanor already had her valises packed. A buffet supper with champagne was to be served after the ceremony, and then the Brewster coach would whisk the newlyweds to the piers and a coastal ship for New York. By tomorrow evening they'd be steaming toward Europe and enjoying Cunard's finest accommodations.

The justice was droning:

' – *and so, by the authority vested in me by the Commonwealth*—'

Gideon's eyes wandered to the bridegroom. Leo was handsome almost to the point of prettiness. With massive shoulders, a slim waist, and hair and eyes nearly as dark as Carter's, he definitely had the look of a leading man. He had a beautiful speaking voice, too; rich and deep. Eleanor said he could reach the highest gallery of any theatre without strain.

' – *pronounce you husband and wife.*'

Efrem Goldman sniffed and rubbed his patched brown sleeve across his nose. Gideon was unexpectedly touched by the sight of his daughter enfolded in Leo's arms there between the immense floral baskets Julia had ordered for the occasion. He started to wipe a tear from his good eye. Suddenly he felt Julia tug at his arm.

166

'What is it?' he asked in a whisper.

She pointed. He turned around to see Crawford standing at the parlour door. He was summoning Gideon with sharp, urgent gestures. Irked, Gideon stepped behind his wife's chair and hurried out.

In the foyer, the butler presented him to a pair of unexpected guests – a stocky man who identified himself as Detective Dennis O'Goff of the Boston police, and a burly uniformed officer whom O'Goff introduced as Sgt Mulvihill. O'Goff looked to be in his late thirties, with a ruddy face, blue eyes so pale as to be almost colourless, and heavy inlays of gold in several front teeth. His suit was neat but of poor quality. He had a tough, hostile air about him.

Gideon frowned at the intruders. 'What can I do for you gentlemen?'

'Sorry to interrupt the festivities,' O'Goff said, turning the brim of his derby in his fingers. 'But there's a mistake here. Evidently this man didn't listen – ' The detective's tone betrayed a bitter envy of the sumptuous surroundings in which he found himself; or so Gideon thought, anyway. O'Goff added:

'I said I wanted to speak with Mr Kent.'

'But I'm—'

'Mr *Carter* Kent.'

Gideon's palms turned cold. 'Yes, Crawford did misunderstand. Carter Kent is inside. What do you want with him?'

O'Goff scowled, but he answered:

'To ask him some questions.'

'Can't it wait a few hours?'

'I'm afraid not,' the detective replied with a self-importance which annoyed Gideon even more. He signalled Crawford to close the parlour doors, then snapped:

'I demand to know what all this is about.'

A smug smile curved the detective's mouth. His pale

167

eyes danced in anticipation of the blow he was about to deliver to the highfalutin' owner of this fancy Beacon Street house.

'Happy to tell you, Mr Kent. It's about a dead body which was found floating in the harbour two nights ago. A Portugee chap. A bad actor. We've discovered that your son—'

'Carter is my stepson, but go on.'

O'Goff didn't like being interrupted. 'We've discovered that he knew the deceased. We think he may be able to shed some light on how he died. I don't make this inquiry lightly, sir. Not lightly at all. It's clear that the dead man came to a very violent end.'

He obviously hoped to intimidate Gideon with the last remark. He succeeded.

2

When Carter was pulled aside at the end of the wedding ceremony, he knew something disastrous had happened. He soon found out what it was. The blankets in which Ortega had been wrapped had loosened much more quickly than Royce or the rest of them had counted on. The lines holding the stone had obviously loosened too, because the floating body had been found by the captain of a fishing smack returning to harbour from the Georges Bank.

Because of Gideon's name and position in the community, O'Goff didn't take Carter to headquarters. But he did insist that other members of the family be absent during the interrogation. He closed the door of Gideon's study and the uniformed officer placed himself in front of it, as if to make sure Carter understood he was a temporary prisoner.

Carter understood all too clearly.

Crossing the foyer with the policemen, he'd watched

Eleanor's face, and his mother's; he'd seen the surprise and the uneasy suspicion there. He hadn't been able to bring himself to look at Will. Inwardly, he was aching from tension.

After the bloody night at the Cod, he'd gone back to his job without exciting any suspicion. Since Sancosa worked in another section of the plant, his disappearance wasn't even mentioned by those with whom Carter worked. He had started to believe the whole matter had sunk from view just as those two hideous bodies had. And now this.

'Well, now,' O'Goff said, dry-washing his hands as he stood before the chair in which he'd ordered Carter to be seated. A fire roared in the grate, and in seconds Carter's face was shiny with perspiration. 'Well,' O'Goff said again, keeping up that damnable, school-teacherish washing motion. 'Where shall we begin?'

'You could begin by opening the window.'

'No, I don't think so,' O'Goff said with a smile that showed the gold in his mouth. 'I'm comfortable. But you say you're warm. Interesting. Quite interesting.'

O'Goff locked his hands at the small of his back and paced back and forth, almost like an officer reviewing his troops. 'Handsome room, this. Handsome house. I couldn't afford to be here unless it was on business.' The blue eyes pierced him, humourless. The smile was gone. 'Which it is.'

He's stalling intentionally, Carter thought. *Working on my nerves. Trying to break me before he even asks the first question. But he hasn't explained why he's here, other than that they found Ortega. If I admit nothing, I'm in no danger.*

He didn't quite believe it. The shabby, stocky man, who had carelessly draped his derby over an expensive china vase, terrified him because he represented a threat. A threat to Eben Royce, who had saved Carter's life, and a threat to Carter's freedom and safety.

He'd heard all about Boston city jail from the men who gathered at the Red Cod. Quite a few of them had been locked up for varying lengths of time, and every one of those men testified to the filth and the violence of the place. Prisoners were beaten by turnkeys as well as by other prisoners. There were even less savoury assualts committed in the dark of night – sometimes for the amusement of an audience of leering inmates.

'Shall we begin, Mr Kent?' O'Goff said, consulting a small pocket notebook for a moment. He flipped the notebook closed and put it away, as if to show he was confident of his mastery of all the facts in the matter. 'The subject under discussion is one Silvera Ortega. You know who I mean?'

Carter had already established what he would admit to and what he wouldn't. He intended to scrupulously observe the boundary between the two. But to do it, he would need all the conviction and persuasive ability he could muster.

'Yes, I do,' he answered.

'When was the last time you saw him?'

He paused a second or so, as if thinking carefully. Then:

'A year and a half ago. No, more than that. April, I think it was. April of last year.'

'The two of you had trouble—'

'That's no secret.'

'No, it certainly isn't,' O'Goff said with a quick little smile that was almost prissy. 'Your friend Captain Royce, Eben Royce – he had trouble too. He had trouble with Ortega.'

The sweat was pouring off Carter's cheeks now. He took some satisfaction in noting that it was also pouring off the cheeks of Sgt Mulvihill. Outside the bolted doors, a murmur of cheerful voices told him the wedding was over and the reception underway. Out there was freedom. In here – the total lack of it. He

170

would never surrender that freedom for any length of time. Never. *Run others or they'll run you*. It applied to this moment as much as to any in his entire life.

'I say, Mr Kent – he had trouble with Ortega, too?'

Carter wiped the sleeve of his heavy black coat across his chin. 'Also no secret.'

'But you fought with Ortega.'

'Yes. So did Royce.'

'When did that happen?'

'I told you. April. Last year.'

'Tell me again.'

'April! Last year!'

Calm down. *Calm down*. He wants you to lose control.

'Let's talk about this year. This month. Where were you the night that Silvera Ortega died?'

'What night did he die? You didn't tell me.'

O'Goff frowned for a second, angry that his little ruse had been detected. With a slightly more respectful look in his pitiless eyes, he said:

'Early morning on the ninth of December, as far as we can tell. He and one José Sancosa were seen together around midnight, but not after that.'

Carter was edging close to the limit of what was admissible.

'I think that was the night I left work early. I felt sick.'

'You think? Don't you know? Surely you recollect the night Ortega died, Mr Kent.'

'No, I don't, there was nothing special about it. I didn't kill him.'

Bastard, he thought. What made the interrogation so much worse was the accusing look in O'Goff's pale eyes. The detective knew Carter was lying, and Carter knew his own face must suggest that, but the questions and answers just skirted the truth. O'Goff was desperately trying to catch Carter off guard; punch through

171

his defences and let the truth come spilling up into the open. Just one ill-advised admission – one fact too many – one slip and it would all be over. Carter knew it just as he knew that was the reason O'Goff talked in staccato fashion, and gave each question such a hard edge:

'Oh, I see. We'll let that pass. For the moment. You said you left work early—'

'I said I thought I did. I was sick.'

'Did you go home?'

'No, I stopped for a drink. I thought it would help.'

'Did it?'

'Yes, and I drank a lot more. I stayed out all night.'

'Where?'

'Several places.'

'Name them!'

'The first was the Gloucester Arms. After that, I can't remember. I was drinking. I was drunk.'

O'Goff took a quick, threatening step toward Carter – perhaps to throw him off guard by startling him:

'At which place did you see Ortega?'

The strategy didn't work. O'Goff looked furious when Carter said calmly, 'None of them.'

'But you fought with Ortega.'

'A year ago April! I told you that. What the hell are you trying to do, trick me into a confession?'

O'Goff's eyes flickered; he'd been caught.

'I didn't do it!'

But O'Goff refused to let go:

'Did Royce? He says he was in that sleazy room where he holes up, playing cards with a friend of his, a fat pig named Tillman. The two of them are obviously thick as thieves. Lying. Just like you.'

Carter fought to keep his face impassive; he shrugged. 'I don't know anything about Royce. We used to be friends but I haven't seen much of him lately.'

'He's a wreck. Hands like an old woman's.' O'Goff raised his to demonstrate. 'They say Ortega did that.'

'So I've heard.'

'So he has a motive for doing murder. When Ortega was pulled out of the harbour, his neck looked like the gill slits of a fish that's been on a hook too long. His throat was torn open. By some sharp instrument.'

'I wouldn't know.'

'About that or about Royce?'

'Both.'

'But we've been told you might.'

Try as he would, Carter couldn't keep a nervous quaver out of his voice.

'Who told you?'

'Acquaintances of Ortega. You had a fight with him after midnight on the morning of the ninth.'

'God damn it, I did not.'

'Did Royce?'

'I don't know. Ask him!'

'I'm asking you.'

'*I DON'T KNOW!*'

It went on for another half hour, but that half hour was largely an exercise. O'Goff knew he was beaten, and his demeanour showed it. By the time he jammed his derby on his head, he was in an ugly mood:

'Do you have any plans to travel?'

Carter was slouched down in his chair, limp, drained by the questioning. He didn't even have the energy to congratulate himself on using his one talent to its maximum – successfully. He could only look at the detective in a blank way and say:

'Travel? What do you mean?'

'I wouldn't stay in Boston indefinitely.'

'Why not?'

'Because I don't like a double standard. One kind of justice for a poor man's son, another for a rich man's. I'd get the truth out of you if your stepfather wasn't so

173

prominent. I'd have had you in a little room we keep at headquarters just for questioning suspects. In four, five, six hours at the most, I'd have the information I want. But I wasn't allowed to take you to headquarters. I was ordered not to in fact. But if you stay in town, my arrogant friend, you're going to stumble one of these days. Murderers always do. And someone will be there to catch you. I'll give you this – you're pretty good at holding to your story – even if it is a fucking lie from start to finish. So don't think you've gotten away with anything. If the friends of the dead man don't get you, I will.'

He tipped his derby and went out with Mulvihill.

3

After they'd gone, Carter sat with his head in his hands and gave in to the shuddering of his arms and shoulders. Gradually the tremors ceased. When they did, he got up – still shakily – intending to return to the party that he could hear in progress outside. He stepped before a small, gilt-framed mirror on the wall. Gazing into the oval, he smoothed his hair and straightened his cravat. He was almost starting to feel decent again when he remembered one thing he'd forgotten.

He might have beaten O'Goff. But he still had to face his stepfather.

4

'Once more, if you please!' Gideon shouted.

'God,' Carter groaned. 'You'd think you were the police. I satisfied them. Why can't I satisfy you?'

It was several hours later. The festivities were over; the guests gone. Gideon's office was dark save for one dim lamp and the glow of embers in the hearth. Julia watched from a chair in the corner.

Gideon was still outraged that the detective and his assistant had interrupted the wedding and cast a pall on the festivities afterward. Eleanor and Leo had left on schedule, but without the family giving them what Gideon considered a proper sendoff. He'd barely had time to kiss the bride's cheek and shake the hand of the groom before rushing back to corner O'Goff on his way out, and discover the reason for his visit. The servants and the other guests had lined up and thrown rice, but the merriment was halfhearted.

'Because I want to know what induced the police to come here in the first place!' Gideon exclaimed to his stepson. 'Why do they suspect you of being involved in some wharf rat's death?'

Sweat on Carter's face glistened in the firelight. He was resentful of the accusing look in his stepfather's eye. To eradicate it, he could admit the whole thing – but the truth would compromise Royce, who'd saved his life. His only choice was to lie.

'Well,' he began, thinking ahead to each word. 'I did know the man. From the Red Cod. It's a pretty unsavoury tavern—'

'An understatement! Continue.'

It was hard; Gideon's hectoring unnerved him. Once again he needed all his verbal skill:

'Last year – right before the stunt with the donkey – I helped this friend of mine, a fisherman named Captain Royce, deal with a man who was bullying him.'

'The man named Ortega? The one who was found dead?'

Carter nodded. He told the rest of the story, up to and including the finding of the two notes in his locker. Julia looked stunned to hear that her son was associating with such violent people, but Gideon, curiously, didn't act at all surprised.

175

'That's as much as I know,' Carter concluded. 'I haven't seen the Portugee for over a year and a half. I don't know how he died, and I don't know what happened to his friend – the man the copper thinks I know from the packing plant.'

He found he couldn't look at his mother. His stepfather loomed over him like some Old Testament figure, immense in his wrath:

'Go on.'

He wiped his face with a pocket handkerchief. 'There – isn't anything more to tell except what you've already heard. I don't know how or when the Portugee died. I only know what the detective told me.'

Gideon's gaze was unforgiving. 'At least that's your story.'

Hurt and resentful, Carter shouted, 'So you think all I do is lie to you?'

'We never thought so until the night you went to Eisler's,' Julia said, her voice quiet yet somehow stinging. 'That night, you told us you would be playing cards. Why is this occasion so different? You can't blame either of us if we distrust what you tell us.'

No, I can't blame you. And since you expect lies from me, lies are what you're getting.

But he hid his bitterness as he said:

'Look, that copper came here grabbing for straws. I'll say it again. He doesn't even know when Ortega died!'

And he won't find out if Josie and Phipps keep quiet. The trollop was trustworthy; Phipps much less so. Pretending confidence he didn't feel, he went on:

'They can't charge me with anything, and they won't.'

'For the time being.'

'Listen, Gideon!' That jolted the older man. Carter never called his stepfather by his Christian name. 'The man had a lot of enemies, that much I know. Any one of them could have done away with him.' *And one did.*

'That's all I know, except this. I didn't kill him. Now will you permit me to go upstairs?'

'Yes,' Julia put in. 'So long as you promise not to go near those dives again.'

'Mother, I work right in the middle of them.' Suddenly it was impossible for him to contain his anger. 'Besides, I think I'm old enough to do whatever I—'

'You'll do as you're told while you're living in this house!' Gideon roared. 'Get to your room!'

'If I choose to do it—'

Gideon started for him. Carter pivoted hastily and fled.

5

Once the doors were closed, Gideon leaned against them, spent.

'Is he telling the truth, Julia?'

She wasn't offended by the question. 'I'm not sure. I used to think I knew him pretty well, but now—'

Sounding bewildered, she let the words trail off.

In a moment she collected herself. 'I'm sure Carter wouldn't coldbloodedly kill anyone. That much I know about him. What frightens me most is his involvement with that waterfront crowd. How are we going to stop it?'

'God only knows. Obviously I should have taken action months ago. But he was keeping his job, and paying for the wagon, so I let everything slide.'

'How much does he owe on the wagon now?'

'Just a few dollars. I was the one who insisted he get a job. Pay for the damage he did—'

'And I agreed. Don't score yourself.'

'But I have to! You see – I knew Carter was running with a bad crowd.'

He explained. When her surprise passed, she whispered, 'Why didn't you tell me?'

'Because I didn't want to alarm you. Because I thought he could handle himself.'

And because I got busy, and let things drift.

'So you think it's possible he might have some information about the murder? Information he's holding back?'

Gideon looked away, the answer torn out of him:

'It's possible, yes.'

'Oh, Gideon—'

Shuddering and starting to cry, she came into his arms. They held one another in the firelit shadows. The wedding might never have taken place, so gloomy was the atmosphere created by the detective's visit. He stroked her hair:

'I'm sorry for keeping you in the dark. I thought it was best. But there's no point in looking back. What matters now is the boy's safety.'

'He's so headstrong. Almost uncontrollable—'

'And we won't have many more chances to set him straight. We've got to do it before he gets himself killed.'

She raised her head to gaze at him. 'How?'

His anguished answer was a familiar one:

'I just don't know.'

CHAPTER XVI

The Note

Twenty-four hours later, with the problem of Carter still unsolved, Gideon was stricken with a bad case of grippe. For five days he lay delirious in bed. When his fever broke, he was too weak to return to the office. Julia suggested moving Helene Vail into a spare bedroom next to Carter's. Gideon was enthusiastic.

With Miss Vail at his bedside every morning, he was able to answer his mail and deal with bills, cost summaries, circulation figures, and dozens of other matters. Then Miss Vail would go off to Kent and Son to implement his decisions. When they affected the *Union* she composed and dispatched long but very precise telegraph messages to Theo Payne. She was quickly establishing herself as much more than a typewriter. She was making it her business to learn every phase of Gideon's work, and quietly taking on new responsibilities one after another. Gideon didn't complain; he was glad to have the help.

Pale January sunlight streamed into his bedroom on the ninth day of his illness. He lay there under three blankets, his beard overlapping the topmost one. The night cap which Julia repeatedly tried to force on him lay discarded beside the bed.

Perched on a stool in a rigid pose, Miss Vail was saying:

'I have made reservations for you and Mrs Kent at Willard's in March.' She removed the pince-nez she wore for reading. 'Personally, I would not care to witness the inauguration of any president who practises bastardy.'

'For heaven's sake, Miss Vail. Cleveland doesn't *practise it*. He made one mistake.'

'That we know of,' she replied. 'That concludes the morning's agenda, sir. Except for one more matter which I hesitate to mention.' She said it so firmly, it was evident she wasn't at all hesitant, and indeed thought it her duty to speak up.

From a pocket of her capacious skirt, she pulled a scrap of paper. 'I confess to have read this, Mr Kent. When I came to breakfast this morning, I saw it lying on the carpet between my door and that of your stepson's room. I only opened it to see whether it was important. It makes no sense to me, yet it sounds serious.'

He took the paper, which smelled of fish. It was coarse brown stuff used for wrapping. On it, someone had scrawled in an unsteady hand:

Ortega is dead but his bro. will be back in spring, your fathers money wont help you then
— Frends of Ortega

'Obviously someone dropped it by accident,' Miss Vail said.

Gideon nodded. He seemed to ache again, as he had during the worst of the fever. Did he dare treat the note as an idle threat? He thought not.

He stared at the signature. A crude little skull and crossbones had been linked beneath it. The note only confirmed what he had suspected; Carter did know something about the death O'Goff had been investigating.

Exactly how much did he know? Rightly or wrongly, Gideon didn't want the answer to that question. The truth might devastate Julia. What mattered now was protecting Carter from danger—

His protracted silence brought a keen look from Miss

Vail. Trying to act unconcerned, he folded the paper and tucked it into the pocket of his nightshirt.

'I'll have to ask the boys if they know what it means,' he said.

Miss Vail continued to scrutinize him. 'Could it have something to do with the visit of those policemen the day Miss Eleanor was married? I was under the impression they were only making a routine inquiry.'

How easily they had all become enmeshed in Carter's lies – if lies they were, Gideon thought sadly. He was almost brusque as he said:

'Yes, that's all it was, a routine inquiry. Is Carter at home?'

'No, sir. The plant closed down for two days. Something to do with repairs on its conveyor system.'

'Oh yes, he did say something about that.'

'Master Carter took Master Will to watch the indoor foot races over at Harvard.'

'Well, I doubt the note's anything other than a joke. But I'll check into it.'

His response didn't satisfy her. 'It strikes me as sinister, Mr Kent. I wouldn't take it so lightly.'

'Leave it to me, please,' he said more sharply than he intended. 'Just leave it to me.'

2

During the following week, Gideon was obsessed with worry about his stepson – both his wayward behaviour and the possible threat to his safety posed by the note.

It galled Gideon not to know whatever his stepson knew about the death of the man found floating in the harbour. Gideon's whole background as a newspaperman rebelled at a self-enforced state of ignorance. And yet he remained convinced that it was useless, even dangerous, to pursue the inquiry. He felt certain Carter couldn't be personally involved in a murder; that was just too incomprehensible. But any further investigation might lead to relevations that could only hurt Julia – and Carter's future.

No, the solution to the problem didn't lie in pushing and pushing until the truth came out. It lay in another direction. Gideon needed to get his stepson out of the city for a while – and before the return of Ortega's brother, mentioned in the note. That gave him a month or so.

He pondered and rejected various plans. Military service, for example. But the lot of enlisted men in the peacetime army was little better than that of a prison inmate, at least in terms of food and living conditions. And Carter certainly wasn't suited to taking orders.

Gideon knew he could get his stepson a job in New York. But his conscience rebelled at foisting Carter off on some unsuspecting business acquaintance. Besides, he couldn't give Carter a good recommendation without lying.

The failure to find any satisfactory answer made Gideon testy and gave him several sleepness nights.

A week after he returned to work, a January blizzard struck Boston. Gideon sent his employees home early that day. When he arrived at Beacon Street, he found a letter from Michael Boyle waiting.

With his numbed legs stretched on an ottoman in front of the parlour hearth, and a long drink of brandy at his elbow, he began to read the letter. One passage toward the middle was of particular interest:

> *During the trip which Hannah and I took to California to escape the winter storms, I ran into an old family friend. You may not be acquainted with him – his name is Israel Hope – but he knows of you, and holds great affection for the entire family.*

'Hope, Hope,' Gideon repeated aloud. Yes, he'd heard about Israel Hope from his father. Hope was a mulatto; a runaway slave who had met Amanda Kent – Mrs A, as Boyle always called her – in California in the 1840s. He had been her friend and companion, helping her operate a little restaurant in San Francisco. When she had finally moved east, Hope had remained behind to manage the gold mine she'd inherited from her cousin Jared. Hope had held that post for nearly ten years after Amanda's death, quitting it at the outbreak of war between the states. His resignation was a protest against Louis Kent's scheme to make money from the war. Louis had planned to sell supplies secretly – and illegally – to the South. Hope, of course, had wanted the rebels defeated and humbled, not helped.

Gideon resumed reading:

I had met Mr Hope in person only once before, on the occasion of his split with Louis, but I had heard about him long before, when I clerked for Mrs A. I recognized him instantly in San Francisco, for he is distinctly tall, with skin the shade of a well-worn yellow glove. He inquired about the health of Mrs A's son, not realizing Louis was dead. He was most interested to hear that Carter strongly resembled his father.

Hope is married to an octoroon, Clotilde, and they have one daughter. Though well up in years, he is vigorous, and active in the management of an enterprise by means of which he has prospered greatly in San Fransicso – the Hope House Hotel, one of the city's finest. Hannah and I stopped there without realizing the identity of the man who owned it. The staff is entirely white save for the porters. Hope told me that in order to secure white trade, he must, so to speak, remain invisible. He is seldom if ever seen in the establishment's public rooms.

183

And, of course, he is required to live in the negro section west of Montgomery Street and north of Jackson, though I am told his home in that district is among the finest in the entire city, excluding of course the palaces on Nob Hill – or Snob Hill, as some call it.

Hope wishes to be remembered to all the Kents. Never having met you personally, he still hopes you or anyone in your family will stop at his hotel, on a complimentary basis, should travel bring you westward. And if he can be of service to you in any way, he would be most happy to hear from you.

'Happy to hear from you,' Gideon repeated, shifting his leg on the ottoman and squinting at the paragraph he'd just read. 'Happy to hear from one of Jeb Stuart's own?'

Suddenly he had a flash of inspiration. 'Let's see about that!'

3

Gideon had shown Julia the crumpled note sent to her son – but only after his plans for Carter were complete. At dinner on a rainy evening in mid-March, they presented the idea to Carter. The moment he heard it, he erupted:

'San Fracisco? Why the devil should I go there?'

Gideon put his napkin aside. 'Because I'm asking you to do so. Because I've already made arrangements for you to take a job at Israel Hope's hotel. He's written to say he'll be pleased to have you. I've even bought your railroad ticket. I want you on your way by the first of April.'

Will was gazing at Gideon with a stunned expression. Carter leaped to his feet.

'I don't care what you want. I don't give a goddamn about what you've bought or arranged. I'm not going.'

'Don't send him away,' Will said. It startled Gideon to hear that kind of plea from his son. Will was even more dependent on his stepbrother than he had imagined.

'Will, this is none of your affair,' he said. 'Kindly excuse yoursel—'

'It is my affair! Carter and I are as close as real brothers.'

Above his beard, Gideon's cheeks were red. 'You'll see him again. He'll only be spending a year with Mr Hope. It's not as if we're sending him to China – or into permanent exile. Israel Hope strikes me as an exceptionally fine man. He's even accepted the fact that I served in the Confederate Army.'

Julia didn't like to see Gideon so upset. She tried to calm things:

'Will, please do as your father asks and leave the room. Do it for me.'

The boy hesitated. Julia's gentle smile of entreaty at last overcame his resistance. He walked out. Looking almost destitute, Gideon observed.

Carter stepped behind the chair in which he'd been seated. With both hands he gripped the high walnut back upholstered in golden damask. 'I've finally discovered how things are done in this household. When I'm ninety, I'll still be having everything arranged for me. I'll still be asking permission to fart.'

With a bellow, Gideon leaped to his feet. His chair toppled over as he reached across the table and seized Carter's arms:

'I will not permit such language in front of—'

Carter wrenched free. 'Don't shout at me. I'm not your son. I won't be ordered about by you or anyone else.'

'Oh, Carter, Carter,' Julia cried, hurrying to his side

while he glared at Gideon across the silver and crystal and china. Carter's swarthy face had lost most of its colour. His black eyes blazed.

'You've made too much of this,' Julia said to him. 'Caused too much commotion—'

'You're damn right I'll cause a commotion! You just announced that you're shipping me halfway around the world.'

'San Francisco is not halfway around the world,' Gideon said. 'It's a splendid, cosmopolitan city. And much more suited to your free and easy disposition than Boston, I suspect.' He was struggling to hold his temper in check. 'Most young men your age would be thankful for an opportunity to see the West. Furthermore—'

Carter interrupted: 'I don't consider being packed off like a remittance man any great favour, thank you very much.'

He pulled out a cheap metal cigar case. Took out a dark green cheroot which he proceeded to sniff, then roll between his fingers. Angry as Gideon was, he couldn't help admiring his stepson's cockiness.

'You can donate the railroad ticket to some bohunk just off the immigrant boat at Castle Garden,' the younger man said with a wave of the cigar. 'And you can send that nigger my regrets.'

Seething again, Gideon said, 'You won't even take this suggestion for your mother's sake?'

Carter threw the cigar down beside his plate. 'No. And kindly don't trot out that sentimental family bullshit, Gideon.'

Livid, Gideon started for him again. Julia's right hand pressed the tablecloth, her skin almost as white as the fabric. Carter forestalled Gideon's attack by pivoting toward his mother:

'I'm sorry to speak that way in your presence—'

What disconcerted Gideon was a realization that, for

186

the moment anyway, Carter was sincere. He did have feelings for Julia. The trouble was, those feelings never controlled him for very long.

'I guess I lapse into bad language out of desperation. Maybe if I swear enough, someone – ' He threw a swift glance at Gideon. ' – will realize I'm not a schoolboy who can be rapped on the knuckles and told what to do every minute of the day.'

Growing a little calmer, he ran a hand through his thick black hair. 'I admit it might be entertaining to see the West. In other circumstances, I'd probably jump at the opportunity.'

Gideon reached into the pocket of his waistcoat. 'You didn't allow me to finish. In your case, I don't think the right word is opportunity. The right word is necessity.'

He gave his stepson the folded paper. 'Miss Vail found this outside your room one day back in January. I assume you dropped it.'

Carter recognized the threatening note; his face showed that. He handled the paper with nervous fingers, tossed it next to his cigar, then gestured at it in a tense way:

'I thought I'd lost it on the street.'

'Where did you get it in the first place? The same place you got the others?'

Carter nodded. 'The locker. I don't know who put it there—'

The end of the sentence faded away. Gideon detected anxiety in Carter's eyes.

'Does that fellow Ortega really have a brother?' Julia asked.

'Yes,' Carter said. 'A rough sort, they say. A seaman. Away for long periods of time—'

Trying to be patient, Gideon said, 'You told us you knew nothing about the death of that Portugee. Someone obviously thinks otherwise.' Carter avoided his stepfather's eye as Gideon went on. 'I have never liked to run from a quarrel. But neither do I think it's very intelligent to court one. The trip would do you good. You'd have both independence and a means of support out West, and your absence for a year would permit this local situation to cool down and be forgotten.'

Carter's dark eyes returned to the folded paper. Either someone in the plant had made a lucky guess about Sancosa's disappearance and Ortega's corpse, or – much more likely – Phipps had been bribed or frightened into saying something.

Twice before, he'd received notes warning him of Ortega's eventual return – and then Ortega had showed up. This latest note therefore could not be ignored. When he coupled the note with O'Goff's promise to bring him to justice one way or another, he was confronting a double danger.

Well, what did it matter if he stayed in Boston? Will could manage without him, and if he left, it would further reduce the chance of his stepbrother finding out why the police had questioned him. Carter had so far got by with a story about witnessing a dockside robbery. Will had accepted it without question.

As for Gideon and Julia, they'd be glad to get rid of him, he thought with momentary bitterness. Both of them considered him a liar and a troublemaker, and he was caught in the trap of being unable to tell them *why* he'd lied about events at the Red Cod. To keep his vow to Eben Royce, he had to keep silent for the rest of his life.

Slowly the hostility, the studied bravado, disappeared. His shoulders sagged, and for a few seconds he looked much more a boy than a man. Gideon knew he and Julia had won out when Carter shrugged and said in a surprisingly mild tone:

'San Francisco – well, maybe I can at least think it over.'

CHAPTER XVII

The Promise

'WATCH OUT!'

Carter crashed into Will, knocking him out of the path of the boneshaker – one of the newfangled bicycles that nearly shook a rider to pieces on a rough road.

The embarrassed wheelman called an apology from his high seat. Then he realized he was out of control. While Carter helped his stepbrother to his feet, the bicycle careened down Beacon Street and tipped over right in front of the house belonging to Dolores Wertman. The wheelman took a terrific spill.

Will stayed on the kerbing in the hope the Wertmans would come outside. Sure enough, they did. First the choleric-looking father; then the mousy mother; and finally Dolores, a red-haired, full-bosomed girl of seventeen. Will had noticed Dolores as she practised croquet on the Common the first warm weekend of spring. He'd hardly been able to think of anything else since.

'Damn fool deserves a broken neck if he can't drive any better than that,' Carter said. The wheelman was still lying motionless in the street. He got up groggily as Carter tugged out his silver pocket watch. 'My train leaves in two hours, little brother. We'd better take our stroll.'

He tilted his straw hat so the brim shielded his eyes from the March sun. It was the last Saturday of the month, a beautiful afternoon, cloudless and unseasonably warm. Already the Common and the Public Garden were swarming with people who didn't have to work. Games of bowls and lawn tennis were in progress, but for every such game, there were five groups playing croquet. It was still the national craze.

Carter turned and gazed across Beacon to the Kent house. 'I wanted one last look at it. All of a sudden, I think I'll miss – oh-oh!' He saw the object of Will's rapt stare. 'I see what *you're* missing.' He gave his stepbrother a nudge. 'Don't worry, you'll get your share soon enough. But here's a tip. If you want a girl, you have to make her think you care for her more than anyone else in the world. You mustn't actually come out and *say* that, though. If anything happened – I mean if she got a little something in her belly later – she might hold you to it.'

From her front step, Dolores Wertman noticed Will watching her. He started to wave but didn't have the nerve. Dolores tossed her red hair, took her father's arm and vanished among the people who were either trying to assist the wrecked wheelman, or jeering at him.

'Ah, Carter, I'll never get close enough to a girl to follow your advice. Besides, if you – if—'

Blandly, Carter asked, 'Are you trying to say fuck?'

Will turned red and nodded. But he still couldn't repeat the word:

'If you do that with a girl, you're duty-bound to marry her.'

The older boy looked thunderstruck. 'Who says so?'

'Ma, for one. That's one of the things she harped about.'

Up shot Carter's eyebrows. 'She harped about that to you? How old were you?'

'No, not to me – I was little. To Eleanor. I heard her give Eleanor a big long lecture about it in her room one day. Ma thought the door was closed, but it was open this much.' He measured half an inch between thumb and index finger. 'I listened outside.'

190

'I hate to say it, but it sounds like your mother spouted a lot of nonsense. You don't have to marry a girl just because you sleep with her. You'd better get rid of the notion that you do, or one of these days some woman will use it to trap you.'

The Greek woman's face flashed into Carter's thoughts just then. He had begun to think no woman could be trusted.

'Sometimes, Will,' he finished with a shake of his head, 'I think you're just too decent for your own good.'

'Do you mean dumb?'

With an affectionate chuckle, Carter replied, 'I don't believe I'll answer that one.'

Will shrugged. 'Doesn't make much difference what I am or how I act. Dolores Wertman would never be interested in me. She wouldn't let me within ten feet of her.'

Carter put his arm round Will's shoulder as they strolled along a sun-dappled path leading through the Common to Charles Street and the elaborate wrought-iron gates of the Public Garden beyond. 'Wish I knew who made you feel so damn worthless, little brother. Was that your mother's doing, too?'

Will studied the ground. 'Doesn't matter.'

'It surely does. Someone did a job on you. Hold your head up, for God's sake! Otherwise you're absolutely right – that girl won't look at you.'

Ironic, Carter thought. He was encouraging his stepbrother to appreciate his own worth even when he felt worthless himself. He would never have let on to Will, but lately that feeling all but overwhelmed him. When he'd given his notice at the Northeast Fishery Company, no one had said they were sorry to see him go. And he'd thought it prudent to refrain from saying goodbye to Josie or Eben. He'd made a botch of everything in Boston.

There was one reason he wasn't altogether sorry that note had fallen out of his pocket when he'd come reeling home one night. Despite his protests, he was secretly grateful to get away from Boston. Even now, he could smell the fishy odour of the knife with which Ortega had tormented him. Once, Carter had liked to eat fish. Since that night, he couldn't bring himself to touch it. The mere smell brought cold sweat to his palms and forehead.

Yes, he was definitely glad to escape from Boston. He wanted no meeting with Ortega's brother. But he didn't know what he *did* want. He was determined not to let Will see his confusion, though. He resorted to a prop that always made him feel jaunty and self-assured – a cigar.

As he stopped to light up, he got disapproving stares from three men standing in a small tent beside the path. On a counter in the tent were two dozen glasses and six large pitchers of clear liquid. Above the tent's front awning hung a neatly lettered sign:

FREE! FREE! FREE!
Greater Boston Businessmen's Association
COLD WATER PAVILION
*'It's Never Too Late or Too Early
For Temperance'*

Irked by the way the men eyed his cigar and his plaid jacket, Carter sauntered over and started to pour himself a glass of water. 'Hope you gents don't mind if I help myself—'

One of the businessmen snatched the glass from his hand. 'This pavilion is for the encouragement of abstinence in slum children, not race-track loafers.'

Carter smiled. 'Then why don't you set up shop in the slums? Don't bother to answer, I know why. The slum boys would run your fat asses out of their neighbourhood in thirty seconds.'

192

He plucked the glass from the fingers of the outraged man, tossed off half the contents, then threw the glass away. Another man jumped and caught it, but he soaked his expensive waistcoat in the process. By then Carter was laughing and hurrying down the path, Will right behind.

When they were safely out of sight of the cold-water soldiers, they slowed down. Will leaned against a tree, gasping with mirth:

'Oh, Carter, you – you've got more nerve than any ten people.'

'That's right, little brother. Because I've got confidence in myself,' he lied.

They crossed Charles Street to the gates of the twenty-four-acre Public Garden. On the garden's four-acre pond, several of the swan boats designed and operated by the Paget family carried young couples in a leisurely fashion. The boats were barges with several rows of seats and a large wooden figure of a swan at the stern. From a seat inside this figure, a man operated pedals to propel the boat. In less than ten years, the swan boats had become an institution.

'Remember how I marched you over to Central Park?' Carter went on. 'How I told those roughnecks I was the nephew of the Grand Duke Whoozis, and that we were going to join their baseball game? They didn't fuss once, did they?'

'No.'

'I knew they wouldn't.'

'I'll never forget that. Before you came along, they always ran me off.'

'You didn't have any confidence in yourself. They spotted it. No matter what you said, the look on your face talked louder. With confidence, little brother, you can do anything.'

'Even get around Dolores Wertman?'

Carter rested his foot on the rim of a wooden tub at

the edge of the walk; palms would be set in the tubs for the summer months. Nearby were moist beds of black dirt in which pansies, dahlias, and cannas would soon grow to brighten the garden.

'Will, my boy—'

Carter puffed his cigar, and the smoke drifted away in the warm breeze. He had his stepbrother hanging on every word. Children chasing a cocker spaniel went noisily past on the path. Only when they were out of earshot did he continue:

' – with confidence, you can fuck Miss Wertman and as many others as your stamina permits. But you have to *believe* you can. You have to believe in yourself. That's what I've been trying to pound into your head for years.'

Will was humiliated by the emotion he felt then. He was supposed to be grown up. Almost a man. And yet he was ready to bawl. Carter noticed.

'What the devil's wrong now?'

'I hate to see you leave. You know everything.'

'Brace up. I'll write you a letter now and then. When I'm not busy getting in the bloomers of the belles of the Barbary Coast. I've been reading about San Francisco. They say it's the wickedest city on the face of the – hey! You've got to cut this out, little brother!'

Ashamed, Will turned away. He squeezed his eyes shut and hoped the tears didn't show. He wanted to die on the spot.

'I'm sorry, Carter,' he said a moment later. 'I just don't know how I'll get along without you.'

'Oh, you will. Very easily. You'll be surprised.'

'I don't think so.'

Carter's jet-black eyes softened. There was an edge in his voice as he said, 'I surely do wish I could get my hands on whoever whipped the starch out of you. It wasn't Gideon, was it?'

Will shook his head. 'Let's not talk about it.'

Carter bucked him up with another punch on the shoulder. 'Whatever you say. Just remember one thing. You're important. Not because you're Gideon Kent's son. Because you're you.'

Will didn't believe it.

'And when you're my age,' Carter went on, 'you've got to do one more thing. You've got to let the world know you're somebody. You can be the richest man in creation, but if no one realizes it, every dollar you've got is only worth fifty cents.'

All at once, from the lesson he was trying to impart to Will, Carter drew strength of his own. So far he'd failed to follow the advice he dispensed so freely. In San Francisco, he'd change that. Start over. Use his talent and become the kind of person he told Will to be—

Maybe he'd try politics, as Willie Hearst had suggested. Two nights ago, Carter had overcome his embarrassment and gone to Cambridge to bid his friend goodbye. Willie was the only person outside his family who might miss him. Of course he hadn't said a word about his troubles at the Red Cod and the processing plant. It had been a grand evening, and Willie had written out a list of fine San Francisco restaurants and saloons he ought to visit. Carter was sure all of them would be well beyond his means, but he thanked Willie warmly and promised to go to every one.

Willie was doing splendidly at Harvard in everything but his studies. He'd taken over the post of *Lampoon* business manager, had thought up a number of stunts which had generated a lot of new advertising, and had put the publication in the black within a very few months. He'd been elected to Hasty Pudding and played a role in the club's annual musical – another ambition fulfilled.

But Willie still liked class work too little and pranks too much. He admitted that his fondness for practical jokes would probably get him tossed out of Harvard as Carter had been. But Carter had faith in his friend. He knew Willie's bent for the sensational would help him make a mark—

'Carter?'

'Oh.' He smiled at Will. 'Guess my mind was wandering.'

'What were you thinking?'

'That it's time I followed my own advice and amounted to something.'

'You will, I know it.'

'So will you, little brother. But to make sure, I want you to give me a promise.'

He faced Will. Laid his hands on the younger boy's shoulders. Brothers enjoyed a special relationship a mother could never participate in, or fully understand. No matter what the facts of their births, he and Will Kent were brothers. He felt that as the two of them stood looking at one another in the spring sunshine.

'Promise me you'll be somebody,' Carter said.

Will heard the voice then.

You'll be a bungler all your life.

Only with great effort was he able to whisper, 'I promise.'

'And promise me you'll make sure everybody knows it. That's every bit as important. Maybe more.'

You'll never amount to anything. BUNGLER—

'Will?'

'I promise that too, Carter.'

Carter smiled. 'Good enough.'

They started along the path again. Presently Carter had a last thought:

'You'd better not break that promise, either. Not if you want me to stay your friend.'

So lightly, even carelessly said, those words. Carter never knew the force with which they struck Will Kent. Struck him, and marked him for life.

That night, Will lay in his darkened room and listened to the dying echo of a great steamer's whistle from the harbour. It reminded him of the train Carter had boarded. The train would carry him to Cleveland, then Chicago. At Chicago he'd change to the westbound transcontinental cars. He was *gone*. The mournful sound reverberating over the midnight rooftops only emphasized that fact, that loss.

Will kept seeing Carter's grin. And his dark eyes shining as he extracted the promise:

'Promise me you'll be somebody.'

'I promise, Carter.'

'And promise you'll make sure everybody knows it.'

'I PROMISE.'

He'd meant it. He knew he'd never made a more important pledge to anyone.

The void created by Carter's departure would hurt for a long time. But in leaving, he'd given Will a new determination to try to overcome the worthless feeling Margaret had whipped into him. Carter had literally created that determination by extracting a promise Will didn't dare break.

Not if you want me to stay your friend.

Although Will was restless, he soon drifted to sleep. He woke about an hour later. Moonlight was flooding through the window, and one part of his body was as stiff as a piece of steel.

He reached down by his hip. The bedclothes were damp. He'd had a dream. The kind of dream whose aftermath had frightened him until Carter assured him it was perfectly normal for young men.

Now, along with the lingering tumidity came shameful yet thoroughly enjoyable thoughts of Dolores Wertman. He imagined her in some featureless place where she could safely shed her clothes and romp naked without fear of observation or disapproval.

He was there, too. He put his head back and let his imagination carry him into incredibly wicked acts involving a Dolores who *liked* him, and showed it with every response she made with her mouth, her hands, her round breasts, her—

He awoke again, warmer than ever. He was humiliated to discover he'd had a second dream. Was he some kind of pervert?

No, no. Carter – far away in the darkness to the west – Carter had taught him not to fear the natural responses his body made during its passage to adulthood. Carter had taught him that, and so much more—

Now Carter expected him to put his knowledge to use. He would, no matter how timid or unsure he felt at first. He'd made a promise and he'd keep it.

A week later, he worked up nerve to ask Dolores Wertman to go walking on the Common at dusk. He nearly fainted when she said yes.

They strolled in the spring twilight, their conversation halting and inconsequential. After ten minutes of fear-wracked hesitation, he forced himself to grope for Dolores' hand and squeeze it. The moment he did, he experienced an embarrassing physical reaction. He turned sideways to hide it.

Several minutes later they found themselves on a deserted portion of a path. He turned to face her. He saw her smiling at him in a strange, puzzling way. His heart was thundering in his chest. His ears rang. His palms were slick with sweat.

Without a word of preamble, he darted forward and planted a kiss on her cheek.

The instant his lips touched her soft skin, he was transfixed with terror. He was sure she'd shriek for her parents, or the police.

She did neither. She stepped closer to him, cocking her head and continuing to smile at him in that soft, strange way. The sinking sun struck fire from her red hair.

'I didn't think you knew how to kiss a girl, Will Kent. Or had the gumption.' Suddenly she brought her mouth to his. 'I'm glad I was wrong.'

She flung one arm round his neck, closed her eyes and pressed against him, without embarrassment, for a wondrous moment.

'Oh, that was grand,' she whispered when they resumed their walk. Will was still so full of astonishment and joy, he was speechless. 'I've watched you for days. I thought you'd never come near my house, or speak to me. Will you take me walking again?' She squeezed his hand in hers. 'Please?'

He managed to say in a strangled voice, 'Whenever you want, Dolores.'

Margaret was all but forgotten. But she was still there in the darkness of his mind.

Watching.

Waiting.

Biding her time.

CHAPTER XVIII

Carter's Choice

On the trip west, Carter lacked neither spending money nor creature comforts. Gideon, perhaps conscience-stricken over sending his stepson into a kind of exile, had not only paid off the last few dollars of Carter's debt, but had bought him a first-class ticket from Boston. That meant Carter was permitted in all the cars, including the parlour car with its rosewood paneling and deep, comfortable seats of turkey red plush.

Mr Pullman, builder and operator of the cars, did things in style. At least for first-class passengers. Carter slept in one of Pullman's convertible berths, and ordered his meals from a menu rivalling that of a fine restaurant. On his first full day of travelling, he started with a breakfast of shirred eggs and champagne. Shortly after noon he sat down to a heavy full-course dinner which included oxtail soup, mutton with a caper sauce, fresh fruit, and coconut pudding in wine. The main dish of his light supper was a tasty rabbit pie.

On a first-class ticket, Carter was allowed in the second-class cars, where he could gawk at the poorer passengers crowded on hard, narrow wooden seats. Those travelling second class weren't permitted in the first-class cars, of course. Porters rigidly enforced the rule.

Carter rather enjoyed trolling through second class, a book under his arm and a cigar in his hand. The farmers, the immigrants – all the drab, weary-looking men and woman packed on the benches – gazed at him with sullen envy. They knew he had money. To be on top – recognized as important and special – that was a wonderful feeling.

The apple orchards of upstate New York slipped by, and the lake shores of Ohio, then the rich farmlands of Indiana. Gideon had provided Carter with a number of current books, including an advance copy of the ailing President Grant's *Memoirs*; a dull novel about a businessman named Lapham; and the only volume Carter really enjoyed dipping into, *The Adventures of Huckleberry Finn*. The Mark Twain novel had been sold on subscription, before publication. It was already being damned as trash. In Concord, where old Philip had stood and fought at the bridge, the Library Committee had banned the book, terming it 'suitable only for the slums.'

The man behind the Mark Twain pseudonym liked to think of himself as a businessman as well as a famous writer, Gideon often said. Twain was heavily involved in financing the publication of his own books on a subscription basis. But he'd licensed Kent and Son to print inexpensive reprint editions of some of his earlier work. Hence Gideon had gone out to Concord to protest the ban on Twain's behalf. Unsuccessfully, as it turned out. The author wasn't upset. The last time he'd come to dinner at the Kent house, he'd said to Gideon, 'Don't push too hard to get the ban lifted. I calculate it'll sell at least twenty-five thousand extra copies for me.'

At major station stops every hundred miles or so, a new conductor would tear off a perforated section of Carter's long ticket. Just before he reached Chicago, he found himself studying the ticket with resentment he couldn't explain.

In Chicago, he had half a day to himself. He used it to shop for a plaid travelling jacket at Marshall Field's. Then the Union Pacific bore him west out of Illinois.

At Council Bluffs, he saw two old men with seamed

brown faces dozing in the sun on the depot platform. He stoody studying the men while second-class passengers dashed for seats at the counter in the flyblown dining room. Curious decorations hung from rope belts the old men wore. Long hanks of dark hair, intertwined with what appeared to be bleached animal skin. While the Indians dozed, they fondled the decorations occasionally.

Carter asked a trainman about the objects. 'Scalps,' the old man said. 'I see those same two red bastards hanging around this station 'most every trip. I think they're Sioux. I dunno why the local citizens permit 'em in public places – 'specially since they sit there flaunting the fact that they killed white people. They ought to be put on a reservation, them and the rest of their murdering kin. Ought to put ninety-nine per cent of the niggers in with 'em.'

Cynically, Carter wondered just how gullible the man's bigoted views made him. He decided to find out. On the spot, he made up a story about a vast conspiracy involving French and German anarchists. In a hushed voice, he told the trainman the anarchists were slipping into America to gather recruits among the disgruntled Indians.

'By God I can believe it!' the trainman declared. 'This country's being taken over by Jew radicals. Every one of them who criticizes our government ought to be put in front of a firing squad.'

'Mmmm,' Carter murmured, meaning to be noncommital. He didn't agree, but the trainman thought he did. That was the purpose of the murmur. If he ever ran for public office, he'd know how to lock up the trainman's vote. Just scream that nigras, Jews, Indians, and anarchists were making plans to run amok and desecrate the flag. Interesting how even the stupidest people could teach you something.

Billowing smoke and sparks behind it, the Union

Pacific express sped across the darkness of Nebraska. More stars than Carter had ever seen illuminated the sky above the prairie. Soon, though, the stars paled, and anxious passengers crowded the platforms between the cars, pointing to the northern horizon. It glowed like a furnace.

The brilliant red light seemed to be sweeping toward the train. The whistle blared. The train picked up speed. At Carter's elbow, a conductor said:

'Prairie fire. We've got to go like blazes so it doesn't catch us. You can see the wind fanning it. Moving it this way.'

And in front of the wall of fire, dark specks leaped and darted. Deer? Bison? Carter watched in awe.

The danger was short-lived. The express outran the fire, which dwindled to a scarlet smudge in the north-east, then vanished. Once more the conductor tore off a section of Carter's ticket.

He stared at the remaining sections, trying to fathom why the sight of them bothered him so much. All at once he understood. The excitement of the journey and the novelty of the sights had diverted him from the answer for a while. He might be escaping to a new city, but he certainly wasn't escaping to a new way of life. The ticket didn't represent fresh opportunity, but a variation of all he'd rebelled against for years.

Other people restricting his freedom. *Telling him what to do.*

The ticket wasn't a symbol of fresh opportunity. It was a symbol of Gideon's will. Gideon's wishes. Gideon's plan for his life—

'Well, by God, it's *my* life!'

He hadn't meant to speak aloud. The Pullman porter, a sad, slope-shouldered old black man, thought Carter was calling him, and came hurrying along the aisle.

'Beg pardon, sir? Did you want me to make up your bed?'

The accumulated resentment boiled over. He jumped up. 'Yes! Get to it!'

'I will, sir. Right this minute.'

The man was cringing, almost servile. That pleased Carter. It wasn't that he felt as the trainman did about blacks; the porter's skin had nothing to do with Carter's reaction. What he liked was being in control of another human being – black, brown, red, white, it didn't matter. Only the control mattered. The control achieved by some method that would not get you killed; Ortega and the Red Cod had taught him to set that limit.

Control of others was what he wanted from life. Instead, he had the ticket.

When the lower berth was ready, he climbed in. Thus far on the trip, he'd slept soundly. Tonight he was restless. He cursed volubly whenever the train swayed or jerked. Hour after hour, all he could think of was the ticket.

'Sleep well, sir?' the porter asked in a hopeful tone when Carter climbed out between the green curtains the next morning.

'No. I had a miserable rest.' He knuckled his eyes; noticed the respectful look on the porter's face. How could he make everyone treat him that way? He knew. By following the advice he'd given Will. By being *somebody*.

He couldn't do it by going on to San Francisco, though. He couldn't do it by swamping floors or cleaning toilets in some nigger-owned hotel, that was for damned sure. He had to strike out in a new direction.

'I'm not spending another night on this rattletrap,' he announced.

'I thought you were going all the way to California with us, sir.'

'I changed my mind. What's the next stop?'

The porter consulted his watch. 'North Platte, Nebraska.'

'When will we be there?'

'About ten.'

'That's where I'm getting off.'

The porter bobbed his head. 'Yes, sir. Whatever you say, sir.'

The only other passenger to leave the train at North Platte was an old farmer from second class. Carter stood on the platform in the sun as the locomotive drivers began to shunt back and forth and the whistle blew. The moment the train pulled out, he knew he'd made a dreadful mistake. North Platte seemed to be nothing more than a collection of railroad sidings, unpainted commercial buildings and small, mean houses set down beside a dirty river in the middle of a sea of prairie grass. A stiff breeze filled the air with dust. It was only April but the sun was scorching. Sweat turned his linen shirt sodden beneath his new Marshall Field jacket.

He hoisted his two cowhide valises and trudged toward the main street. He felt hot, tired, and overcome with guilt. By bolting from the train, he'd betrayed Julia's trust.

He stopped a man emerging from a general store whose elaborately painted sign read:

H. & M. K. BOYLE OF NORTH PLATTE
—General Merchandise—

'Mister, is there a clean, inexpensive hotel in town?'

The plainly dressed townsman eyed Carter's fancy jacket and dusty button shoes. 'Try the Platte Palace.' He jerked a thumb into the sun's glare. 'Two blocks down. The widow Butts runs it.'

'Obliged.'

Carter touched two fingers to his forehead, picked up his valises and walked on. What he saw around him was discouraging. Shimmering heat devils on the horizon. Blowing dust. A godforsaken little town whose loftiest building seemed to be its grain elevator.

But he was free of all the ticket represented. *Free.* He had to remember that.

2

The Platte Palace Hotel was two stories high, half a block wide across the front, and deserted. He entered and saw a woman dusting the lobby counter. The woman was plain, heavy-breasted, in her early forties. She looked uncomfortable in her worn, high-necked dress of black silk.

She gave him a hard look. Her grey-green eyes had a curious intensity. He endured the stare without a sign of annoyance, then put on his most charming smile.

'I just got off the train.' He pointed to a chipped writing desk near the large and dusty front window through which the sunlight streamed. 'Do you mind if I sit and write a note?'

'I suppose not.' The tone of the reply said she wished he wouldn't.

Carter set his valises on the rug. The movement stirred motes of dust and set them whirling faster in the sunshine. He sank down in the chair. It creaked. He opened the desk drawer. It contained nothing but Union and Central Pacific timetables.

'You'll have to get your own stationery,' the woman called. 'I quit supplying it after my husband died. Too many people steal it, and it's expensive. My husband was always giving things away. That's why we were always broke.'

Carter nodded. Why was the woman staring at him so intently? Was she angry because he intended to use the desk? Well, the hell with her. He found his unused ticket; held it up:

'I have paper.'

She sniffed and gave him another oblique look. She tugged nervously at the waist of her dress, tightening the material over her breasts. He noticed that as she did so, she stood in profile. He was beginning to catch onto her game.

The woman disappeared behind the partition which contained the pigeonholes for mail. All the pigeonholes were empty.

A train whistle sounded in the distance. Carter bent his head over the desk whose top was illuminated by the blazing sunlight. He began to feel confused and depressed. Where could he go? How could he support himself after his money was gone? He only had fifteen dollars left. He was in the middle of a vast, unfamiliar country. Friendless. Alone—

He pulled an old steel pen from the inkwell. On the back of the ticket, he began a letter to Julia.

In brief sentences, he told her he'd left the train in Nebraska. He told her he couldn't go on to the Hope House and the menial job waiting there. He told her he had to do what he wanted, not what someone ordered him to do.

He stuck the end of the pen in his mouth and chewed on it. With a start, he realized the woman had come back and was watching him gnaw hotel property. He stopped. Smiled. She returned and slowly leaned her elbows and her pendulous breasts on the counter.

The pen scratched in the silence:

I don't want you to worry, which is why I am sending this. And I don't want you to be hurt, or fret, if you don't hear from me for a while. I must

*sort things out and make my way on my own. I'm
grown now, I can do it. I will write you from
wherever I land in a few months, and am sure I will
have good news about what I have decided to do in
the future.*

What lies, he thought, his face glum and his belly
beginning to hurt as he realized the enormity of the
step he'd taken. He had no idea where he'd go, or how
he'd get along when his travelling cash ran out. All his
thoughts about freedom – all his plans to control his
own destiny – seemed ludicrous in view of his situation.

But his mother mustn't know that. She'd be upset
enough when she learned what he'd done. Despite her
low opinion of him, he loved her, and he owed her at
least a little peace of mind. He finished the letter by
saying:

*Above all, please do not worry. I will be fine. Say
hello to Will.*

*Yr. Affectionate son,
Carter.*

3

He scratched a horizontal line under his name and
added a few ornamentations to it. He started to chew
the pen again. He heard a floorboard squeak. He
jerked the pen out of his mouth, getting a small splinter
in his lip as he did so.

A shadow fell across the desk. He spat the splinter
away and tucked the letter in his pocket, then glanced
up. The stocky widow was standing there, her arms
folded beneath her breasts as if to emphasize their size.

'Done?'

'Yes. Just now.'

'That's good. I can't stay here all day to see that you don't steal anything. I have rooms to clean upstairs.'

'All right.'

He pushed the chair back; accidentally brushed against her as he stood up. With a startled breath, she stepped away. He couldn't reconcile her scowl with her strange, searching gaze. Her eyes moved quickly across his shoulders, down to his waist, back to his face.

'I'll buy an envelope at the store,' he said. 'Thanks very much for letting me—'

'How old are you?'

'What's that?'

'How old?'

'In another few days I'll be twenty-two.'

'Why did you stop in North Platte? Do you know anyone here?'

He shook his head; smiled that charming smile. 'It seemed as good a place as any.' That was better than telling the truth – that North Platte looked like a hellhole.

'What's your name?'

'Kent. Carter Kent.'

'I'm Mrs Olga Butts.'

She extended her hand. They shook. Her palm was moist and warm. She gripped his fingers longer than necessary.

Continuing to smile, he felt an ache spread through his midsection. He was *alone*. He had no way to get along except by using his wits and his one talent. The talent that had come to him from his grandmother, and his father.

It was such an ephemeral thing to pin his hopes on, that talent. But he had nothing else. And because of his own impulsive actions, he was desperate.

He strugged to make sure the desperation didn't show. 'Happy to make your acquaintance, Mrs Butts. It's a pleasure to see anything resembling a friendly face. I haven't run into many lately—' He sighed, hoping he wasn't overdoing it.'

He was. She became suspicious:

'What kind have you run into? Are you in trouble with the law?'

'Mrs Butts—'

'You're old enough to be a thief. A bank robber, a train robber – a man who takes advantage of women.'

But she didn't move away from him. Her breathing had grown rapid. 'Tell me the truth, Mr Kent. Are you evading the authorities? Is someone chasing you?'

'No one would chase me, Mrs Butts. I'm not worth anything. Nobody'd want me.'

She denied that with an admiring glance, he noted from a corner of his eye.

'Where are you from, Mr Kent?'

'St Louis.'

He began to feel exhilarated then. The exhilaration was tinged with danger as he started to spin out a tale, not knowing what was coming until he said it:

'I'm an only child. When my father died five years ago, my mother inherited a prosperous livery business. She mourned for a year, then married a man from Minnesota. He ran the business into the ground. He was a drunkard. What's worse, he – infected her with a foul disease he had been carrying for years. For some reason the disease took its toll on my mother more quickly than it did on him. It affected her mind. My stepfather shut her away in an asylum for the insane, intending to let her die there while he spent the rest of her money. When I tried to get her out of the asylum, he bribed the sheriff to trump up charges against me. I had to leave St Louis at night, on a freight car – in a hurry.'

She seemed close to weeping:

'Oh, God, Mr Kent, that's a terrible story.'

He thought so too, but not for the same reasons she did. He looked mournful.

'Indeed it is. And it was a terrible choice – leaving my poor mother behind in order to save my own skin. But they'd have locked me up, maybe for years, and my stepfather had already ruined her. So I figured I'd make my fortune out west, then go back and settle with him. Provided the disease doesn't get him first. I hope to God it doesn't.'

It was straight out of a Beadle novel. But the emotions of the widow Butts were so stirred, the absurdity eluded her. She shook her head and dabbed an eye:

'It isn't an easy world, is it?'

'No, ma'am.'

'I lost my husband to influenza last winter. I miss his – comforting presence more than I can say. Since his passing, the hotel has deteriorated even further. He had no head for business, but I'm even more inadequate. Very lonely, too—'

She was struggling for worlds that suddenly burst forth:

'I'd be happy to fix you a meal if you're hungry.'

'That would be wonderful, ma'am. I'm starved.'

Now, he thought, *now*. He'd told the tale for one reason – so he wouldn't have to spend anything for a room in North Platte. All at once, he knew he was going to be successful. She said to him:

'And if you – if you care to stay overnight, you can have any bed in the hotel.'

She glanced past him to see whether anyone was watching from the street. Her sun-flecked eyes pierced him as she added in a whisper:

'Including mine.'

Despite her age, the widow Butts proved as frisky as a mare in heat. She nearly wore Carter out that night. Finally, around three-thirty, she fell asleep and snored.

He lay beside her, exhausted but too jubilant to rest. The experience with the affection-starved woman had renewed his confidence, vindicated the rightness of his decision to leave the westbound train and restored his faith in the future. Olga Butts had accepted his lies. Of course he didn't think of himself as a liar. Prompted by necessity, he'd merely used the one talent at his disposal.

The more he thought about the events of the day, the more delighted he was. His talent would help him survive. His talent would take him anywhere he wanted to go.

Out on the prairie, a locomotive hooted. Not a lonesome sound, but an exciting one, symbolic of the world that suddenly lay open to him.

Closer at hand, Mrs Butts let out a loud snore. He chuckled and snuggled down in the warm bed. The past no longer had any hold on him. And the future had never looked brighter.

BOOK TWO

The Journey of Will Kent

CHAPTER I

Unhappy Homecoming

On a dismal morning early in March 1886, the Cunard steamship *Excalibur* entered New York harbour.

Cold wind whipped the water to white foam. Rain threatened to become sleet as tugboats guided the liner toward her berth on the North River. The passengers had withstood gale winds and mountainous waves on the late winter crossing, so the inclement weather didn't prevent hundreds of them from rushing on deck to see the scaffolding and the great blocks of stone already in place on Bedloe's Island. Among the observers, perhaps the most envious was Gideon Kent.

He'd been abroad with Julia and Will most of the winter. They'd toured the museums of London and Paris, Rome and Madrid with Gideon's brother Matthew – and Matt's latest blonde and blue-eyed mistress – as their guides and companions. But he'd kept in touch with business affairs by cable. Thus he knew work was once more going forward on the pedestal for Bartholdi's great Statue of Liberty.

Before the resumption of work, the project had languished for months. While the crated sections of the statue remained in storage, Congress had debated and ultimately decided against funding construction of the pedestal. Then Joe Pulitzer had jumped in. The New York *World* had lashed Congress for failing to do its duty and for insulting the French people, whose donations had paid for the statue. A five-month campaign supported by articles and editorials had generated the necessary one hundred thousand dollars. School children had contributed their pennies, ordinary people their dollars, tycoons their thousands. It was an incredible outpouring that testified to the immense power of the press.

Or was it merely testimony to the power of Pulitzer's sensational brand of journalism? Gideon asked himself as he watched Bedloe's Island glide past in the murk.

Gideon knew Pulitzer, of course. He admired the publisher's insistence that his paper never become the captive of any group or political party. 'Indegoddampendent,' was Pulitzer's unique way of putting it. On the other hand, setting aside the worthiness of many of the causes Pulitzer embraced, Gideon didn't like the way the publisher manipulated the public, and pandered to low tastes by packing the *World* with accounts of crime and Society scandal. Gideon refused to employ such tactics on the *Union*, even though the *World*'s circulation was climbing dramatically at the expense of every other daily – including his own.

Standing at the rail with the sleet beginning to collect in his beard, he shivered and asked himself whether Pulitzer might one day drive him out of business.

Almost at once, he scowled and shook his head. It was wrong for a man to blame anyone else for failure. If the *Union* was ever forced to suspend publication, it would be the result of his bad judgement. His mistakes.

Still, it wouldn't hurt to have a conference with Theo Payne and once again urge him to enliven the paper's news columns.

The scaffolding on Bedloe's Island slid astern. Gideon's mood remained as gloomy as the day. On every front, the Kents seemed to be suffering setbacks.

Eleanor had abdicated any responsibility for the family's future. She and Leo were only interested in their profession. This winter they were working as members of Mrs Drew's troupe at the Arch Street Theatre, Philadelphia.

Carter was roaming the West. Since bolting from the

216

train in North Platte the preceding year, he had communicated with Julia just three times. He'd written the first letter on the unused portion of his train ticket. The other two letters, equally short, had been mailed from small towns in Texas. All summer long, Julia had kept telling her husband that Carter could take care of himself. He knew she didn't quite believe it.

Will had taken the news about Carter badly. Gideon believed that the abrupt changes in Will's behaviour last year had come about partly because of Carter and partly because of Dolores Wertman, the red-haired girl who lived farther down Beacon Street.

In the spring, right after Carter's departure, Will had seemed to come out of himself. To grow more cheerful; gain new confidence; throw off his dependence on his step-brother. Not coincidentally, he'd been calling on Dolores Wertman at the time.

Gideon and Julia had been pleased to see Will taking interest in a girl. Even the arrival of the letter on the rail ticket hadn't appeared to hit Will very hard; Dolores Wertman occupied all his attention.

Then, during a July heat wave, the girl's father had been felled by a stroke. He died two days later. The death immediately plunged the family into a financial crisis; Wertman had mortgaged himself heavily to expand his ice business. The Beacon Street house and its furnishings were the first things sold to settle the dead man's debts.

Impoverished overnight and ashamed of it, Dolores Wertman had moved away without giving Will a forwarding address. Within a few days, the boy reverted to his old self, hesitant and humourless. He began to talk about nothing but Carter's absence. To speculate endlessly about Carter's whereabouts or state of mind. The summer of '85 had not been a good one for Julia, but it had been even worse for Will. Gideon had

217

suggested the European tour as an antidote. But it had done nothing to restore Will's spirits.

Now the family was home. Matters held in suspension during the trip had to be taken up again. Will's future, for one. But perhaps discussion of that subject might be just the thing to prod the boy out of his despondency, Gideon thought. Certainly he didn't know where else to begin.

Despondent himself, he left the rainy deck in answer to the gong signalling the last breakfast sitting.

2

In the first-class dining saloon, Will sat by himself, fiddling with an untasted croissant. At sixteen, he was growing taller, slimming down.

He wasn't happy about much these days, but he supposed he was happy to be home. He'd found the European trip a bore. Except, of course, for the periods when Uncle Matt travelled with them. Uncle Matt was full of racy stories about his colleagues, their misadventures and their mistresses. Many of Uncle Matt's closest friends had been christened 'impressionists' after an 1884 exhibition of their work. Will's uncle had gone to some pains to explain that term to his nephew. He drew small, quick sketches to show how a human shoulder – or a cathedral such as Sacré-Coeur on Montmartre – never looked the same from season to season, or even hour to hour. To the eye of the trained observer, different kinds of sunlight – summer and winter, morning and afternoon – created distinctly different visual impressions of any subject.

It was this observed reality which was the true reality, Uncle Matt insisted. Reality was not the skeleton and muscle structure, or the architectural design, which your brain told you was always there and always constant beneath the shifting light. In their paintings, he and his friends attempted to capture not a textbook reality, but a higher, purer one – the impression of a sunlit moment forever caught on canvas.

But even artistic theory painlessly presented by a laughing, raffish and wondrously likable uncle was no substitute for the things that were suddenly missing from Will Kent's life. First Dolores had moved away and then the fact of Carter's disappearance had hit home. He lost the girl he loved and then he lost the confidence Carter had instilled in him for a time. When he was courting Dolores, he seldom heard Margaret Kent's voice hectoring him from the past. Now he heard it often.

And he fretted constantly about the promise he'd made to Carter. He loved his stepbrother and wanted to keep the promise. But he was listening to Margaret's voice again. He didn't know whether he'd ever amount to—

'Good morning, Will.'

Will glanced up. Gideon slipped into the chair opposite him. 'Morning, sir.'

The two table stewards appeared and hovered, all smiles at this last meal. Before the morning was over, they'd receive their tips for service on the crossing.

The senior steward inquired about Julia. Gideon said, 'She won't be joining us, Guy. She's a bit under the weather.'

'Very sorry to hear that, sir. May I suggest our kippers this morning?'

After Gideon had ordered a large breakfast and sipped some hot tea, he said to Will, 'Did they take the trunks out of the stateroom yet?'

Will nodded. Drizzly fog pressed against the huge saloon windows. The Cunarder was backing and turning in preparation for entering her slip. Will glanced at his father apprehensively. What was on Gideon's mind? Something of importance, certainly. He recognized the set of his father's mouth, and a certain purposeful glint in his eye.

The senior steward served Gideon a thick golden crescent of melon. The dining room was unusually noisy. Buzzing with the conversation of people about to arrive home.

Finely dressed people, too, Will observed. The kind of people you saw only in the first class section. In contrast to the splendid morning outfits of the men seated at nearby tables, Gideon's suit struck Will as plain and drab.

Gideon finished another bit of melon. 'When we're back in Boston, we must give some thought to your future. As young as you are, you can still enter Harvard if you can pass the entrance examinations.' Will grimaced at the reference to his age. He liked to be taken for older than he was.

Gideon went on. 'I'm sure you can do that. The Latin School's given you excellent preparation. Besides – you're a smart young man.'

Will said nothing. Gideon's smile quickly faded. Once more he grew businesslike:

'Naturally you'd take a general course of study at first. But it isn't too soon to consider the various careers open to you.'

Silence again. Perhaps it was that rebuff which goaded Gideon into going farther than he'd intended:

'I *do* expect you to choose a career, you know. A life's work—'

Will looked at his father. 'Somehow I thought managing the family financial interests might be enough.'

'Absolutely not. Our money is managed by the Rothman Bank. I'll permit no son of mine to live off an inheritance and do nothing else.'

Gideon's anger brought a resentful look to Will's

220

face. 'Do you suppose there'll be any news of Carter waiting for us?'

Gideon whacked the tablecloth. 'Don't change the subject, young man.' The hovering stewards exchanged looks. 'I know you're upset about your stepbrother dropping out of sight. But it does no good to mention it half a dozen times a day. I'm sure Carter's all right.'

'I'm not.'

'You won't help him by worrying. Stop it, if you please!'

Instantly, he was sorry he'd been so sharp. He apologized. Will sat motionless. Gideon drew a long breath:

'I suppose I should explain why I reacted so strongly to your suggestion of a moment ago. I mean about making a career of managing the family's affairs. As I'm sure you realize, there is a long-standing tradition among the Kents. A tradition of serving others in some way. Managing family assets doesn't qualify. Many other things do, however. Being a journalist, for example.'

'I don't want to work for your newspaper, Papa. Or for Kent and Son, either.'

Gideon's lips compressed. He was clearly restraining his temper:

'I can understand your wanting to strike out on your own. Read the law, perhaps—'

'That doesn't interest me either.'

'Then what does?'

'Nothing I can think of.' Will rose. 'Excuse me, sir.'

He left the table and hurried from the saloon. Gideon shook his head and swore softly. The years were passing. In another forty-eight months, he'd reach that symbolic age which had by now become an obsession with him. He was rapidly approaching the end of an average lifetime, and he was no closer to finding someone to whom he could give the mantle of family leadership. Will, his best hope, was rejecting all appeals that he think constructively about the future.

It made Gideon sad and furious at the same time. He would have run after his son and forced him to finish the conversation except for one factor – the dislike he'd seen in Will's eyes as they spoke.

All sons resented their fathers to a degree. But Gideon feared Will's animosity had somehow gone beyond normal bounds.

3

During the debarkation into the customs shed, Will deliberately separated himself from his parents. They were waiting a hundred feet farther down the boat deck.

He planted his elbows on the damp rail and gazed at the pier below. Rather than leaving the vessel en masse, passengers were summoned to customs in groups. The first group of men and women were moving down the gangway into the shed where each of them presented a passport – a large, unwieldy sheet of parchment covered with official seals and bearing a few descriptive phrases inked in an elaborate hand.

Will was some distance above the pier, but even so, he was able to see the great profusion of diamonds and others gems worn by the women leaving the liner. First-class passengers, obviously. How insignificant, even dull, Gideon and Julia looked by contrast. Julia wore no jewellery except her rings. Her clothes were colourful, but in good taste. Her gored skirt of burnt orange velvet, seven feet in breadth, was conservative in comparison with some of the styles and hues visible to him.

And Gideon's wardrobe was nothing short of drab, today and every day. Of course Will knew his parents were rich. But they didn't show it in an unmistakable way. They weren't interested in letting the world *know* they were important, as Carter said you must.

Will still hadn't figured out how he'd fulfil the promise to Carter. But he was positive of one thing. Being as unassuming as Gideon and Julia was not the way to go about it. The people he must emulate were the more typical first-class passengers – gaudy, rich, and proud to have others know it.

He cupped his chin in his hands and gazed down at those splendid people with undiluted admiration. When the signal sounded for the boat deck passengers to disembark, Gideon had to call his son three times.

4

After selling his upper Fifth Avenue mansion, Gideon had never entertained another thought of owning property in New York. Yet business often required his presence there. His answer to it was to rent a large suite in the old, prestigious Fifth Avenue Hotel. The hotel was located on the west side of Madison Square, which was still the cultural and commercial hub of the city that was rapidly expanding to accommodate new waves of immigrants from Southern and Eastern Europe.

Gideon kept the suite year round. The cost was exorbitant; two thousand a month. But having the suite gave the Kents a comfortable, homelike base when they were in town. Gideon also liked the suite because he could look across Madison Square and see the mansion Amanda Kent had occupied during the last years of her life. The original dimensions of the residence had been remodelled out of existence. But there *was* a house, large and neo-Gothic, on the site. In this decade of swift change, with America losing its rural orientation and becoming an industrial colossus, Gideon found it reassuring to have a sense of his own family's past. Of course, when he dwelled on that past these days, it prompted thoughts of the future – and he was face to face with his problems again.

After leaving Julia, Will, and their small pyramid of luggage at the hotel, Gideon proceeded downtown to the *Union*'s offices on Printing House Square. There he spent an hour sorting through a couple of hundred letters that had arrived during his long absence. Many went unopened but not the one from Theodore Roosevelt, which spoke enthusiastically of Roosevelt's ranching activities out West.

Next Gideon went into a meeting with Theo Payne, his senior editorial men, and the heads of the related departments such as production and circulation. Gideon listened to a summary of the *Union*'s financial position over the last few months; to several complaints about rising costs; and to pleas for a new Hoe press as well as a retail price increase of a cent a copy. He promised to consider acquisition of a press, but refused to raise the price of the paper.

'You don't charge more when you're in a circulation war with Joe Pulitzer. I'd lower the price if I could. Since we can't afford that, we'll hold the line.'

There were disgruntled looks but no arguments. Payne then took over, highlighting for his employer several foreign and domestic stories which in his opinion bore watching. In May, Pierre Lorillard would be opening Tuxedo Park, his 600,000-acre planned community for the rich. Gideon reacted with scepticism:

'You think a walled compound where the rich can hide constitutes news, Theo? I don't.'

'Then you don't understand the significance of Tuxedo.'

'Oh? Enlighten me.'

224

'In my opinion Tuxedo is the first concrete manifestation of a trend which has been developing for a number of years. The well-to-do have sustained the cities in the past, but they are no longer willing to do it. They're starting to pull out. Flee to the suburbs. They're tired of rubbing elbows with all the Italians and Hungarians and Greeks and Russians and Poles pouring off the boats. If the trend continues for any length of time, our cities will be in a hell of a fix.'

A moment's reflection convinced Gideon that his editor might be on to something. The wealthy *were* developing private vacation enclaves all along the Eastern seaboard. More and more of their sons were attending exclusive private preparatory schools, and living in privately maintained dormitories at Harvard, Yale, and Princeton. Older American families, conveniently forgetting that they too were the children of immigrants, no longer wanted to associate with newcomers.

Gideon urged Payne to send his best men to cover the official opening of Tuxedo, scheduled for Memorial Day.

Payne touched on several other topics, saving until last the one which might be the most explosive. In May, American labour unions were planning nationwide demonstrations on behalf of an eight-hour day. The editor wanted a special appropriation to send teams of writers and artists to several major cities, in case the demonstrations led to violence:

'If we get one gusher as it were, it will more than compensate for the entire cost of the drilling programme.' Payne covered his mouth and emitted a gentle belch which suggested he'd fortified himself with more than facts before the meeting.

Gideon wasn't enthusiastic about the suggestion:

'In other words, we'll be banking on trouble. Hoping

for it in the same way we did in '77, when I went to Pittsburgh and got shot.'

'You got shot because Tom Courtleigh was after you,' Payne replied. 'Besides, anticipating trouble is less opprobrious than creating it, don't you think? Joe Pulitzer isn't above the latter. Your trouble, Gideon, is that you've never stopped being disappointed over one fact.'

'Which is—?'

'Peace and morality don't sell newspapers. Do I get my special appropriation for the teams?'

Gideon sighed. 'All right.'

The meeting broke up at eight-thirty. Gideon caught a hack on Park Row and reached the hotel a few minutes later. He'd had no dinner but he had no appetite. He discovered his son sprawled in front of the parlour fireplace reading a letter.

Will barely nodded to his father. Gideon's return greeting was equally brusque. He threw off his overcoat and went to find his wife.

The sound of splashing led him to the suite's imposing bathroom. In a large marble tub, Julia lay up to her neck in perfumed suds.

He peeled off his jacket, threw it aside and knelt beside the tub. He received a damp kiss from Julia as he rolled up one sleeve, then picked up a sponge floating on the surface and began to scrub her back with slow, languid motions. It was one of their companionable rituals; she scrubbed his back when he bathed.

'You don't have to do that, dear,' she said. 'You look exhausted.'

He finished scrubbing and rested on his haunches. 'The meeting was tedious. The *World* is steadily whittling away at our circulation.'

'A challenge like that used to spur you to work twice

as hard.' She touched his wrist. 'Not that I'm urging you, mind. It's time you relaxed a little.'

'Relaxed?' He uttered a humourless laugh. 'I just came home from a European vacation. I've got to deal with my son, Julia. I've got to take him in hand. After Carter left, I decided the boy needed more attention. Now I think I was wrong. I'm afraid I've been guilty of coddling him. He needs toughening.'

'You used that very word a couple of years ago.'

'I remember. I'm sorry I didn't pursue the idea. Will needs to stand on his own feet a while. Find out what the world's really like. Maybe then he'll accept his own lot with more enthusiasm. He's an intelligent boy, but so far as I can tell, absolutely without ambition. He can shoot passable golf out at Brookline. He can ride a horse and play a good game of lawn tennis. He can read a chart aboard *Auvergne*, and he's even learned to be a pretty fair four-in-hand driver. We've given him all the social graces and somehow failed to give him much substance.'

Gently, she said, 'You're being very hard on your own son.'

'On myself! I've raised him. Or rather, I stood by and let Carter serve in my place. Will acts more and more like a swell every day. Let him start debauching shopgirls and he'll be a perfect candidate for society with a capital S.'

At the end of the vehement speech, Julia nodded. 'I agree, we don't want that. But do you really think you can jolt him out of this phase merely by finding some way to – toughen him, as you put it?'

'I think it's worth trying. I have an idea about the way to do it, too.' Bitterness crept in: 'Naturally I can't guarantee the results, having made a botch of fatherhood most of my life.'

Again she patted his hand. 'Stop feeling sorry for

yourself, dear. Sometimes your expectations are much too high.'

He pulled a face. 'Theo said the same thing a couple of hours ago.' He snatched a heavy towel from a solid brass ring in the wall. He was drying his hands when Julia said, 'I got a letter from Carter. It was in the batch Miss Vail forwarded here from Boston.'

Gideon looked hopeful until he saw her expression. She climbed from the tub, her diminutive body still firm and trim. He wrapped the towel around her. 'Where is Carter?'

'Someplace called Texarkana, on the Texas border.'

'Do you have the letter in here?'

'Will has it.'

'So that's why he looked so glum when I walked in.'

Gideon pivoted and returned to the fireside. Will had laid the letter down and was staring into the flames. *I musn't be angry with him*, Gideon thought. *I'm responsible for this. I sent his best friend away.*

He picked up the letter and read its three short paragraphs. Carter was working as a swamper in an establishment he euphemistically termed a parlour house. He didn't care for Texarkana, and had made no friends save for *an agreeable young nigra who plays the piano and composes lively tunes. His name's Joplin.*

Like the piano player, Carter was thinking of quitting and moving on again:

I can't seem to find a place I want to stay, or anything I'm happy doing. But I am in good health and earning my own keep, so that should set your mind at rest. I will write again if I ever have something worthwhile to report – which by now I am beginning to doubt. My regards to Gideon, and a special hello to little brother.

C.

Gideon shook his head, speaking half aloud: 'He sounds miserable.'

'He isn't the only one,' Will said. He rose and walked out.

An hour later, Gideon finished a long letter to Theodore Roosevelt.

CHAPTER II

Eleanor and Leo

Leo Goldman's index finger moved across the purple bruise under his left eye. He said to Gideon, Julia and Will:

'By some wondrous chemistry which only a mob possesses, my father – a hapless, harmless little Jew who'd done nothing but travel to Philadelphia to see his son and daughter-in-law perform – was transformed into an anarchist. Those four hooligans looked at him and saw some invisible brand that said, *I was in Chicago. I threw the bomb.*'

Leo's shoulder lifted in weary disdain. Eleanor, seated next to him, laid her hand on top of his. The gesture did little to alleviate the bitterness in Leo's dark eyes.

From all around the dining saloon of *Auvergne*, lamps cast a rich light on the dinner table, and burnished the half-inch bands of gold which decorated the edges of each piece of the china service. In the centre of the plates and saucers, there was an additional decoration, also in gold. The Kent and Son emblem: the stoppered, partially filled tea bottle.

Auvergne's triple-expansion engine throbbed softly. She was making about eight knots, Gideon reckoned. Her top speed was fifteen. It was late May; a peaceful,

229

moonlit evening with only a light chop on the Atlantic. Eleanor and Leo had come up to Boston for a short holiday between shows, and the family had embarked on a cruise around Cape Cod and down through Muskeget Channel into the open sea east of the village of Slaconset on Nantucket Island.

Eleanor squeezed Leo's hand again, then took up the story:

'Papa Goldman had just stepped into the alley for some air after the performance. That's where the hooligans saw him, and attacked. Leo heard him yell, charged into all four and drove them off.'

Again Leo's finger ticked against the bruise. 'And earned in the process this decoration for valour. Plus a few others which politeness prohibits me from showing you. Maybe they're decorations for stupidity. Only a thin-skinned Jew would take on a quartet of bully-boys from the Delaware River docks. Eleanor didn't approve.'

'No, but it was necessary.' She sounded dubious.

Gideon said, 'Damned unfortunate business.' In more ways than one. Evidently his daughter wasn't finding it as easy to avoid anti-Semitism as she'd expected. 'Your father wasn't hurt, was he?'

Leo shook his head. 'Just ruffled a little.'

'Feeling has been running high in Boston, too. Just last week, on the Common, a Jewish woman was mauled and pelted with rocks.'

'It's no wonder, Papa,' Will blurted. 'I don't mean to insult you, Leo. But everyone knows the Jews caused the strike at the McCormick plant. And started the riot.'

Leo's hand clenched around his napkin. Gideon was growing pale. He saw Julia's glance of warning and did his best to check his temper. It was hard. Lately his son's behaviour had become intolerable. Thank heaven

Roosevelt had finally sent an affirmative reply to the letter Gideon had written in March.

Julia tried to reprove her stepson gently:

'I don't believe you have your facts in order, young man. The *Union* reporters who were in Chicago said no one knows who threw the bomb in Haymarket Square. It's likely no one will ever know. The situation was extremely confused.'

Undaunted by the correction, Will said, 'Yes, but eight men were arrested and charged. Some of them are Jews, aren't they?'

'May I ask what that proves?' Eleanor asked.

Gideon's voice was heavy with irony. 'Why, it proves the Jews are responsible, just as he said. Everyone *knows* that if a man worships at a synagogue, *ipso facto*, he's an anarchist.' Will began sulking as his father went on, 'These days, Eleanor, your brother has the answers to everything. I'm sure the professors at Harvard can't wait to partake of his vast knowledge when he enrolls this fall.'

Julia tried to change the subject.

'Will's already passed the examinations, did we tell you?'

'No, you didn't,' Eleanor said. A distinct lack of enthusiasm was evident when she added, 'That's very nice.'

Anderson, the blond young steward, came in to clear the dishes and serve lemon ice and macaroons for dessert. Gideon kept glowering at his son. He'd hoped Leo and Eleanor's brief vacation between plays at the Arch Street Theatre would be a pleasant one. Will was doing his best to see it turned out otherwise.

Desperate for advice – or perhaps just sympathy – Gideon had discussed his son with Verity Pleasant only a couple of days earlier. Pleasant had a boy about Will's age. He reassured Gideon that his son, too,

231

often made outrageous statements which he expected everyone to accept without question.

'And he gets mad as a hornet if I don't. Arguing is one of the major sporting activities of young fellows that age. It's part of a lad's pulling away from his parents and discovering who he is and what he thinks.'

'Well,' Gideon grumbled in reply, 'I wish to hell my son would make the discovery, because the exploration's driving us crazy. Were you and I that obnoxious when we were his age?'

'Undoubtedly.'

Gideon shook his head. 'I don't remember.'

Pleasant smiled at that. 'Neither will he.'

Will's attitude – and the mention of the Haymarket – had destroyed the good mood which had prevailed during most of the dinner. These days the nation was talking of little besides the Haymarket. On the first of May, nearly four hundred thousand working men across the country had begun demonstrating for the eight-hour day. On May 3, police guarding Cyrus McCormick's reaper plant in Chicago had fired on men demonstrating there. One picket had been killed, several others wounded.

The following night, May 4, trade unionists had staged a protest rally in Haymarket Square. Socialists and anarchists were known to be among the organizers of the affair. As soon as the speechmaking was over, two hundred policemen had moved in to disperse the crowd. Someone had flung a cast-iron dynamite bomb.

After the explosion, guns appeared on both sides. When the shooting ended, seven Chicago policemen were dead from the bomb blast, ten or eleven civilians from the gunfire, and dozens on both sides were injured.

Thanks to Theo Payne's planning, the *Union* had been able to print dispatches describing the riot a few hours after it took place. Gideon still squirmed at capitalizing on mayhem to sell papers, though.

As Will had stated, eight men had been charged with being ringleaders of the riot. Gideon's reporters said there was no concrete evidence against them. Still, the eight were behind bars. And even the most responsible public officials were calling for them to be swiftly tried and hanged.

At the bar of public opinion, they had already been convicted. More irresponsible elements were demanding the arrest of union leaders, as well as mass deportation of all 'Jews and Socialists' within the labour movement. Because anarchists, some of them European Jews, did operate behind the cover of the movement, and attempt to direct it, all of the movement's members – but especially the Jewish ones – had been tarred with the Haymarket brush. Gideon wasn't surprised his son had picked up the misinformation he'd stated as fact.

He simply didn't know how to deal with Will any longer. Despite the boy's one concession – listless acceptance of his parents' wish that he enter Harvard – disharmony ruled their relationship. Will alternated between arrogance and timidity. The former was probably a device to conceal the latter, Gideon suspected. Understanding Will's turmoil didn't make it any easier to endure, though. Gideon was desperate. Roosevelt was his only hope.

Anderson brought in coffee and a dish of peppermints. The steward was one of four Scandinavians who constituted *Auvergne*'s permanent crew. The others were Captain Erickson, Mr Wennersten the engineer, and the deck hand Nyquist. Yachtsmen had the pick of available seamen because they paid top wages. Scandinavian sailors were generally considered the best in the world.

The smiling steward poured the coffee from a silver

pot Gideon had purchased from a descendant of Philip Kent's friend Paul Revere. Julia, meantime, drew Eleanor and her husband into conversation about Mrs Drew's theatre. Over the rim of his cup Gideon studied his daughter. She professed to be happy with Leo. Undoubtedly she was – in some ways, but he'd detected certain signs suggesting that happiness wasn't total.

She looked fatigued. Shadows showed beneath her lovely brown eyes. She never looked that tired simply from working on a role – a personation, as some actors called it. He must speak to her, father to daughter, and find out what was troubling her.

Leo spooned up lemon ice. Slowly the strain left his face, replaced by that wonderfully impudent grin Gideon remembered from the first night they'd met. Leo had been a street boy then, running newspapers from Park Row in order to earn a few pennies for his family. Somehow he found it within himself to forgive Will's wild pronouncements, and speak to him in a friendly way:

'Apart from being purveyor of the truth about the Jews—'

Julia stiffened slightly. Will eyed his brother-in-law, ready to defend himself. But Leo leaned back in his chair, relaxed and cheerful:

' – what's your ambition? Business? The law?'

'Papa's mentioned law,' Will said. The cocksure pose vanished in an instant. 'I don't think I have the head for it.'

His favourite reply, Gideon thought. '*I can't*. He fervently hoped the coming summer might change that.

Leo lit one of the relatively new cigarettes which Gideon disliked. Eleanor said to her brother, 'But what do you want to do after you finish at Harvard?'

Will's answer was a shrug. Still irked by his earlier remarks, Eleanor flared:

234

'You can't be serious. Isn't there anything you want out of life?'

'Oh, absolutely,' Will shot back, smiling in a cold way. For a moment he looked years older than his years. 'I want to have a lot of money – and I want people to know it.'

Eleanor looked stunned. 'Good Lord,' she breathed. 'How idealistic.'

'Now, sweet, don't be cutting,' Leo said. 'That's my ambition too.' He spoke with increasing cynicism. 'Let me give you one bit of advice, Will. If you want to realize your ambition, never become an actor. Your sister and I work like the very devil. We perform every night of the week. But we're still thought of as *luftmenschen*. That means people without an apparent means of support. Once, I was sure I'd be out of that category by this stage in my life. I was counting on making my fortune in America. I'm sorry to say the goal has thus far eluded me. If you can make a lot of money on your own, do it and don't apologize.'

Eleanor's fatigue-shadowed eyes searched her husband's face, sharing his disappointment. Gideon had heard the same sort of remarks from Leo before. Leo had failed to realize the ambition he'd set for himself when he was a young immigrant boy carrying newspapers. Perhaps the ambition was an unrealistic one, especially after he decided to be an actor. Yet all the rational explanations in the world couldn't prevent him from occasionally becoming embittered.

With a pointed glance at her brother, Eleanor said to Leo:

'But at least you aren't so – hard about what you want.' Will ignored her, gazing at a brass porthole surrounded by polished mahogany panelling.

'You have to be hard about certain things in this world, my dear,' Leo replied. 'Standing up for yourself, for one.'

235

He turned toward Gideon and Julia. 'Eleanor and I have frequent disagreements on that subject—'

Gideon glanced at his daughter; she avoided his eye. Leo went on:

'For a while she convinced me to ignore the slights. Turn away from people who do or say things to show they don't like Jews. I went along. But when someone attacks your own father, you change your thinking. I refuse to turn away any longer.'

He patted Eleanor's hand to show he harboured no ill feelings. But there was no mistaking the anger in his eyes.

Or the sadness in hers.

2

While Anderson cleared the table, Julia took Leo to the piano to choose some music. Leo enjoyed singing almost as much as Gideon did.

Without bothering to excuse himself, Will disappeared, presumably headed for his stateroom. Eleanor and her father strolled out to the starboard rail. Leo went on deck only when necessary. He had never learned to swim. Deep water terrified him.

Smoke streamed from *Auvergne*'s rakish stack amidships. Astern, a wake was faintly visible in the black sea. A canopy of stars spread overhead, and off the bow, a few lights twinkled in Slaconset.

Gideon leaned on the rail next to Eleanor. He lit a cigar, savouring a moment of silent companionship. He was calmed and renewed by the sea and the yacht's soothing rumble.

He loved *Auvergne*. Of course the New York Yacht Club didn't consider the eighty-five foot vessel to be a yacht at all. That prestigious club pretended that boats under a hundred and fifty feet didn't exist.

Gideon berthed *Auvergne* at a public slip in Boston. He'd been told privately that he stood no chance of being admitted to the New York Yacht Club because of what he'd done to Ward McAllister. So he'd applied for membership in the American Yacht Club when it was organized at Milton Point on Long Island Sound in 1883. He wanted to be able to dock at the club when he steamed down to the city on business.

He'd received one blackball, which denied him membership. He was sure the blackball had been dropped by his old acquaintance Jay Gould who had himself been blackballed at the NYYC. Gould had found the AYC to retaliate.

For all the attendant social difficulties, Gideon had never regretted purchasing the yacht. He could have afforded a much larger and grander vessel; something close to Gordon Bennett's *Namouna* with its 50-man crew, $2500 a month payroll and annual maintenance burden of at least $150,000. But this small, fast Herreshoff boat was perfectly adequate. It had three staterooms, a saloon, and a well-equipped galley. It took him wherever he wanted to go, in comfort.

He broke the silence by saying:

'I've been anxious to speak to you a moment, Eleanor.'

She rapped her fist on the smooth teak rail. 'I wish you'd speak to Will instead.'

'I don't blame you for being angry with him. He insulted Leo. If he weren't so blasted big, I'd turn him over my knee. I will say this in his defence, though. I think he's just going through a phase. One he'll grow out of, I hope. He sustained a great loss when Carter vanished. He depended on Carter for most of his opinions – and for encouragement in almost everything he did. Adolescence is a wrenching experience in its own right – as you perhaps remember.'

Eleanor managed to smile.

'I'm working on a solution to your brother's problem. But that isn't why I wanted to talk with you.'

From the galley came the muted sounds of dishes being stacked, crystal clinking in a washtub, the black iron griddle of the wood stove being scraped down. The deck hand, Nyquist, and perhaps even Mr Wennersten would be helping Anderson clean up. *Auvergne* had that kind of crew.

Through an open porthole they heard Leo say, 'That one! It's one of my favourites.'

'Mine too,' Julia said. She began to play. Leo's strong baritone rang out:

The young folks play by the little cabin door—
All happy, all merry, all bright—

The sound of Leo's voice brought another smile to Eleanor's face. Then she asked:

'Talk to me about what, Papa?'

By and by hard times come a-knockin' at the door—
Then my old Kentucky home, good night.

Leo and Julia sang the chorus. Overlapping the music, Gideon said, 'I'm not trying to pry into your affairs. But Julia and I worry about how you and Leo are getting along.'

She kept her eyes fixed on the stars; she answered softly:

'We love what we're doing. But acting has never been an easy profession. It wasn't when Philip's mother was excommunicated for going on the stage in Paris, and it isn't today. Sometimes Leo gets discouraged because we aren't making faster progress.'

'So I gathered from his remarks at dinner.'

Gideon's voice was calm. Inwardly, he was churning. What on earth had happened to his daughter's romantic enthusiasm? What had gone wrong?

'Does marriage agree with you, Eleanor?'

238

'Yes, Papa. Sometimes I do feel I'm horridly inadequate for the role of a wife, though.'

'Why do you say that?'

A too-studied shrug. 'Oh – various reasons. Working in a theatre, there isn't much time for me to do all the conventional things a wife is supposed to do. Cook. Sew—'

'You never particularly cared for them as a girl. I can't believe you've suddenly become interested in them.'

A dazzling smile. 'I loathe them. But I supposed I feel guilty for neglecting that side of married life.'

'Leo doesn't mind, does he?'

'No, he's a perfect dear about it.' The smile faded. 'But I feel inadequate in other ways, too.'

He clearly heard the embarrassment in her voice, and in a moment of uncomfortable insight, he thought he understood. Eleanor was not merely a child of the Victorian age; she was the child of Margaret Kent. Toward the end of Margaret's life, her view of the physical side of marriage had been a warped one. That unhealthy view had finally driven Gideon to Julia. Was his daughter now struggling against the same kind of negative attitude?

Gideon fixed his eye on a distant star. He asked gently, 'Do you want to say any more?'

'I can't, Papa. It's the sort of thing – well, no, I'd rather not discuss it.'

'Would you feel more comfortable talking with Julia?'

Vehemently: 'She isn't my mother.'

'But she'd be happy to listen.'

'*No!* I shouldn't have brought it up.'

Her uncharacteristic sharpness upset him. He couldn't tell whether she'd been angry about the drift of the conversation, or frightened, or a little of both.

Eleanor was gazing over the sea, a set, closed

expression on her face. Fruitless to press her on the subject, he thought. It could only lead to bad feelings between them. He tried another tack:

'I'm curious about something else. Do you often have to deal with incidents like the one in Philadelphia?'

'More often than I'd like.'

'Are you finding they aren't so easy to walk away from as you once thought?'

Her quick frown, clearly discernible in the starlight, told him he'd hit the mark.

'We manage.'

'It doesn't sound as if Leo will turn the other cheek any longer.'

'No.'

'I can't say that I blame him.'

'I just wish people would leave us alone! I hoped Philadelphia would be different. You'd think that in a big, supposedly cultured city a Jew wouldn't have so many problems. But look what happened to Papa Goldman. We even get a few people in the Arch Street galleries who see Leo's name in the programme and throw things.'

'Good God. What does he do?'

'He stops the play until they quiet down. It terrifies me. Last week, a coin came this close to his eye.' Her thumb and index finger measured a narrow space in the air. 'Leo gets so angry—'

'He should.'

'It isn't our fight!'

'Yes, it is, Eleanor. It's Leo's fight, and it became yours when you married him. But we'll never agree on that, I fear. I do understand how Leo feels. No man wants to be forced to deny what he is. I'm sorry there have been problems. I want your marriage to be a happy one.'

'Mostly it is, Papa.'

She sounded completely convincing. Then he recalled that she made her living by acting. He studied her; thought he detected a fleeting look of pain on her face.

What's wrong? What is it that she can't talk about? The bigotry? Or something else?

She was conscious of his scrutiny. Quickly, she linked her arm with his. They walked along the moonlit deck toward the open door of the saloon. 'Every marriage has its problems, Papa. I appreciate your worrying about us, but you mustn't.'

Her timing was superb. Precisely at the moment they entered the saloon, she finished by saying:

'Leo and I are very happy. I love him and I'm proud to be his wife.'

Leaning on the piano, Leo gave her a look of such intensity and sadness that Gideon's last doubt was banished. Despite Eleanor's protestations of happiness, something was seriously amiss.

3

Three days later, *Auvergne* docked in Boston and the Goldmans boarded the train for Philadelphia. Gideon and Julia saw them off with a silent hope that the marriage could survive the stresses to which it was obviously being subjected:

Sometimes I'm terrified. A coin came this close to his eye—

As the carriage bore them back to Beacon Street, Gideon's mind was a muddle of worries about his daughter and his son. Quite without realizing it, he began to sing softly:

'*By and by hard times come a-knockin' at the door—*'

241

'That song seems to be a favourite of yours lately, dear. You hum or sing it a dozen times a day.'

'Do you blame me? Eleanor's hiding some unhappiness – and Will was insufferable on the cruise – never a syllable of apology to anyone—'

'Remember what Mr Pleasant told you. It's typical of boys his age.'

'That's an explanation. It isn't an excuse. He needs a more competent hand than mine.'

'No, darling,' she said gently. 'Just a different one for a while.'

'That's why I asked Theodore to take him for the summer. Now that he's agreed, it's time I informed Will. I'll send him west and hope to God I'm not making the same mistake twice.'

CHAPTER III

Welcome to the Bad Lands

Will took the Northern Pacific west during the last week in May.

In his valise was a note of introduction to the Hon. T. Roosevelt, the Elkhorn Ranch, Billings County, Dakota Territory. Packed with it was Roosevelt's reply to Gideon's first letter. In it, Roosevelt said he thought it would be *grand* to have his good friend's son on the Elkhorn Ranch for the summer:

Have him hasten here quickly, so that he may ride with us in the spring roundup of District No. 6, Montana Stockgrower's Association, of whose Dakota Branch I am pleased to be president. If

your son is any kind of horseman, the roundup is
an experience he will enjoy and will not soon forget.
We shall be pleased as Punch to have him share it,
and I shall personally see to his welfare.

Did that kind of language sound like a cowboy's?
Definitely not, Will thought. But Gideon had assured
him that Roosevelt had readily adapted himself to the
rugged life of the Dakota Bad Lands, and had been
fully accepted by the less-than-refined inhabitants of
the district.

He recalled his father saying that Roosevelt had first
visited the Bad Lands on a hunting trip. He'd fallen in
love with the country, and had returned there after the
deaths of his wife and mother in 1884. He now made
several trips a year to the Territory. A sister cared for
his infant daughter, Alice, during his absence.

Settlers in the Bad Lands were trying to develop a
cattle industry there, even though conditions were not
as favourable as they were in Montana or Wyoming.
Roosevelt had joined enthusiastically in this effort.
Gideon said Roosevelt now owned about 3,500 head of
cattle, divided between his two ranches. The first, in
which he had a partnership, was called the Maltese
Cross. It was located not far from the rail stop on the
Little Missouri River. Roosevelt's own spread, the
Elkhorn, lay about forty miles north.

Roosevelt wasn't the only gentleman-rancher in the
district. A few years earlier, an authentic French
nobleman had settled on the Little Missouri with his
wife, the wealthy daughter of a Wall Street banker
named Von Hoffman. Using the wife's money, the
Marquis de Mores – full name Antoine Amédée Marie
Vincent Manca de Vallombrosa – had founded a new
town on the river's east bank. He'd named the town
after his wife, Medora.

The Marquis's stated intention was to create a beef

packing empire to match that of Mr Armour in Chicago. In rapid order, he had organized the Northern Pacific Refrigerator Car Company, build a thirty-room mansion, persuaded the railroad to move its depot from the original settlement on the west bank of the river and developed a reputation for lording it over the local citizens.

'Theodore's letters make it clear he and the Frenchman don't get along,' Gideon had observed to his son. 'At first that might seem strange, since they're both aristocrats—'

'There are no aristocrats in America, Papa.'

'Yes, there are. They don't have titles, that's all. The Roosevelts trace their ancestry back to the Knickerbocker era in early Manhattan. But that's where the resemblance ends. Theodore believes in democracy. He says the Marquis favours the old system of privilege. Oddly enough, their personal lives don't seem to fit with their philosophies. I gather the Marquis hangs out with the riffraff of Medora. Theodore's morals are like those of a grandee. He doesn't drink, smoke, or swear. If you've taken up any of those habits – ' At that point, Gideon had managed a tolerant smile. ' – better get rid of them before you reach the Territory.'

From the first, the prospect of a summer in the West had appealed to Will – much to his father's relief. Will was a competent driver and rider, although he realized Eastern coach and saddle horses weren't the same as cow ponies. He hoped he could hold his own out there, not disappoint his father's friend, or become a burden. He meant to do his best. But as the train left Minnesota, he began to hear a voice whispering in the clicking wheels. The voice disparaged his hope, and spoke scathingly of his certain failure.

He tried not to listen.

The train was in western Dakota now, the rolling prairie with its long Indian grass dropping behind, replaced by a flatter, more barren terrain. Trees became increasingly sparse. What few there were – cottonwoods, cedars, some yellow pine – had a stunted look.

The eastern part of the Territory had been blessed with vegetation: chokeberries, wild grapes, blue-grey pasque-flowers nodding in the spring breeze; even water lilies floating near the banks of sparkling creeks. Here little or nothing grew except the short grey gamma grass. Even that began to vanish as the train moved farther into the arid emptiness of the Missouri Slope.

Mesas spread along the horizon. Buttes jutted into the sky, their wind-scraped faces revealing distinct layers of brick red lava and blue, grey, and yellow clay. There were only a few streams, small, sluggish, and dirty. Obviously he was coming into the Bad Lands. They had been explored by French-Canadian voyageurs who had christened them *mauvaises terres pour traverser*. Will's destination, Medora, was right in the heart of the area.

Face close to the window, he again changed position on the hard bench. Gideon had learned a lesson from Carter's trip; Will was travelling on a second-class ticket. The car in which he was riding was nearly empty.

The vista outside was spectacular, even forbidding. But the country was far from devoid of life. In the space of an hour, he saw huge jackrabbits jumping, whitetailed deer running, flocks of magpies circling in the blue sky – and prairie dog villages beyond counting. He felt a fresh burst of excitement. The excitement had consumed him for days now, and helped ease the tension of living in Boston.

He knew the tension was partly of his own making. He honestly couldn't explain why he sometimes acted the way he did; lashed out at his parents with arrogance or scorn. At the moment he did it, he seemed to want to, but he always regretted it later. Of course he never admitted that to Julia or his father.

Things had been topsy-turvy ever since Carter had left and Dolores Wertman had moved away. His self confidence, never great to begin with, had been utterly destroyed by those two events. Even now, he was gazing out the coach window with an anxious expression, worrying about the weeks ahead. Could he handle his duties on a working ranch? He was in fine physical condition, but was that enough? Could he hold his own among experienced cowhands?

He was determined to try. Determined to silence the voice whispering to him through the clicking wheels:

You'll fail. You'll fail.

2

It was a brilliant sunny day. Two antelope bounded along beside the train, then veered away. By leaning against the window, Will could glimpse startling new rock formations rising ahead. Formations of lavender, olive, chalk grey. The conductor walked through to announce that Medora would be the next stop in half an hour. Will's heart began to beat faster.

The conductor went all the way to the head end of the train, then returned. When he reached Will's seat, he paused and gave the young man an amused look:

'Medora's your station, isn't it?'

'That's correct.'

'Plan to stay awhile?'

'I'll be working there all summer.'

'Better get yourself some new clothes. If you don't you'll be bullyragged all over the place. I wouldn't hang around the depot too long, either. Not dressed that way. Just a friendly suggestion,' the conductor added in a superior way, moving on.

For travel, Will had picked out a plaid suit, button shoes and a snappy derby. *I should have bought chaps and a sombrero in Minneapolis.*

Why did he always do everything wrong? The voice in the wheels chuckled:

Bungler.

He took a deep breath; composed himself. If he wanted people at the Elkhorn Ranch to believe he'd come to Dakota eager for adventure, he had to act like it. No matter how he felt inside.

He thought of the portrait of old Philip back home in Boston. In conscious imitation of his ancestor, he raised his chin and jutted it forward slightly. All at once he felt better; more confident. He sat in that pugnacious, if awkward, pose all the way to Medora.

3

Two expressionless Indians squatted on a low embankment beside the track, puffing on corncob pipes and watching the train arrive. The end of the platform slipped into sight. Beyond it, Will saw a number of new-looking brick and wooden buildings. Colourful signs identified the merchandise they sold. Clothing. Drugs. Hardware. Liquor.

He noticed a small white schoolhouse and then, to his astonishment, a sizable structure whose sign announced an unexpectedly civilized function:

ROLLER SKATING PAVILION

Out of sight at the head end of the car, the conductor was chanting the name of the stop. Will stood up; reached over his head to the metal rack holding his valise. The conductor's voice broke off abruptly. He burst into the car:

'Get up on the seats!'

The half-dozen passengers exchanged surprised looks. The train lurched once more, then stopped. The conductor had just started to repeat his warning when a shot exploded under the floor of the car. Instantly, all the passengers scrambled up to places of safety, some more nimbly than others. Will got onto a bench just as a second shot rang out.

Someone moaned in fright. Two more shots followed. Will saw smoke drifting upward between two benches three rows ahead. He heard men clambering around beneath the car, then muffled laughter. One of the passengers – a drummer, to judge from his sample cases – started to climb down from his bench. Cowering against the wall at the head end, the conductor yelled:

'Stay where you are! They aren't finished.'

'Who in tarnation is it?' the drummer called back.

'Yoo-hoo in there, you eastern punkin lilies!' someone bellowed from below. 'This here's rough country. Better skedaddle back where you come from.'

'The usual reception committee,' the conductor answered. 'Cletus Maunders and his friends. Town drunks. Mean. They meet damn near every train.'

More catcalls. The conductor continued, 'Sometimes they shoot out the windows. That's worse. They'll probably fire a few more rounds to scare the coon waiters in the dining car. Then if we're lucky, they'll go awa—'

'*Hal-ooo, you punkin lilies! What you got to say in there?*'

Will was growing tired of standing on the seat. He resented a bunch of drunkards keeping him imprisoned. If he was ever going to prove he could get along on his own, maybe now was the time to start. He drew

248

another deep breath, took a firm grip on his bag and stepped down in the aisle.

The conductor goggled. 'You damn fool, didn't I tell you to stay put?'

'Someone's supposed to be meeting me. Those men may be playing their game for an hour. I'm getting off.'

His heart hammered as he took a step toward the vestibule; then a second one. The drummer's eyes grew round. He didn't budge from his bench. Neither did any of the others.

Will kept moving. Another step. Another—

Under the car, someone said, 'I think one of 'em's moving around.'

'You're right. What say we put one up into his privates?'

'How you know it's a him, Cletus?'

'Hell, I never thought of that.'

'Never thought of it? Don't you like women no more?'

Laughter.

Will's palms were slick with sweat. Common sense told him to pull back, but something else within him refused. He jerked the door open and stepped onto the platform.

The air was hot and dry. For a moment the midday sun dazzled him. He heard men scrambling around under the car, laughing and whispering to one another. Then a voice he recognized – the man called Cletus – said:

'Let's go see this brave punkin lily. Let's give him a Bad Lands welcome he ain't gonna forget.'

CHAPTER IV

A Tilt with Mr Maunders

From alongside the car there appeared a middle-aged man with several missing teeth and mangy hair that straggled over his collar. He wore a greasy-black buckskin hunting outfit. A huge paunch pushed out the front of the shirt. Two equally disreputable types followed him. All three men were armed with huge revolvers.

Will swallowed, a metallic taste filling his mouth suddenly. The men snickered and nudged one another as they formed a semicircle near the steps of the car. The ringleader was clearly the man with missing teeth. One of his companions said to him:

'Hell, Cletus, he's nothin' but a youngster.'

'All the better sport, boys.' The wind brought Will a whiff of the speaker; he smelled like a distillery.

He swaggered closer to the steps and gazed up at Will with a bleary grin. 'You wasn't thinkin' of gettin' off this train, was you, punkin lily?'

'Yes.' Will tugged his derby down over his forehead, then shifted his weight, ready to move down one step. Somehow his foot slipped; slid off the edge. He lurched forward, then caught the handrail and recovered his balance. The three men whooped and waved their guns:

'Watch out, punkin lily! Don't fall an' spoil that fancy suit!'

'Lord God, ain't he the clumsy one!'

'Now boys, hold on,' Cletus broke in. 'Maybe it ain't his fault that he nearly busted his ass. Maybe it's his shoes causin' the trouble.' Cletus extended a grimy hand and wiggled his fingers. 'Lemme see if something's wrong with that shoe, punkin lily.'

Behind the trio, a frail station agent cleared his throat. 'There are passengers waiting to leave and board that train. You three have no right—'

One of Maunders' cronies cocked his revolver, aimed at the agent's forehead and smiled. 'Shut your mouth, Perkins. Else your two little boys'll be wearin' black armbands.'

The station agent backed away. A couple of male passengers on the platform protested the delay. The agent shoved them and whispered, 'Keep quiet. I won't be responsible for any injuries in my station. That's Cletus Maunders and his friends.'

Evidently the name meant something to the travellers. They too retreated toward the far edge of the platform. Somewhere to the left, hidden from Will by the corner of the car, a buggy rattled to a stop. A man exclaimed, 'There, sir. That must be him.'

Will was busy watching Maunders. Again the grimy hand moved toward his left foot:

'Take them shoes off, punkin lily. Then we'll get you down here an' have you dance proper for us.'

The hand changed direction suddenly; shot for Will's ankle. He reacted without thought. Lifted his foot and stamped down, hard.

His heel struck flesh and bone. The paunchy man screamed; reeled back. He dropped his revolver from his other hand; put the injured one in his mouth and sucked the fingers.

'Shoot the bastard,' he said in a muffled voice. Will brought his valise up to chest level, ready to hurl it. *Why the hell did I get into this?*

Maunders' companions aimed their revolvers at Will. Suddenly, down the platform, boots thumped and spurs clinked. One of the men looked in that direction, gulped and tugged the arm of the other:

'Chad, watch out.'

Maunders jerked his fingers out of his mouth. 'Shoot him, goddamn you!' His saliva-slimed hand groped toward the gun held by the man addressed as Chad. 'Shoot him or let me do it—'

'No, Cletus. Look out behind you. It's Four Eyes.'

Maunders ignored him, fixing all his fury on Will:

'This is all your fault, you son of a bitch.'

Will managed to keep his voice steady. 'I'd say it's yours. I just wanted to get off the train.'

'And by godfrey, Maunders,' exclaimed a high, thin voice belonging to one of the new arrivals, 'if you don't permit him to do so, you and your ruffian friends will regret it.'

The voice had a comical quality. But none of the three men laughed. One bent and snatched Maunders' revolver, shoving it into his own cartridge belt for safe keeping. Will walked down the steps to the platform. His heart was still beating at a frantic pace.

'This tilt ain't none of your business – ' Maunders began, blustering.

'Any quarrel involving one of my ranch hands is my business.'

'Four-eyed fucker!' Maunders snarled.

'If you use one more obscenity in my presence, Maunders, I'll thrash you to within an inch of your life. You know I can do it. Your behaviour will make it a distinct pleasure.'

Maunders seethed. But he didn't move. One of his companions tugged at his filthy hunting shirt:

'Come on, Cletus. Let's light out and find someone to take care of that hand.'

Cletus Maunders gave Will another venomous look. 'You damn near broke it, you little shit.'

The man with the high-pitched voice collared him. 'I warned you—'

252

Maunders flung off his hand. 'I'm leaving, I'm leaving!' Once more he fixed Will with a stare. Will held his ground. A sly light kindled in Maunders' eyes:

'You work for Four Eyes, do you? That means you'll be around Medora for a while.' He tried to flex the injured hand; winced. 'I'll see you again, punkin lily. I'll see you and settle up. Bank on it.'

He and his friends turned and walked past the two anxious passengers and the station agent hiding behind them.

2

Finally, Will had a chance to study the two men who'd come to his aid.

The first was about forty, very tall, with a heavy brown beard and taciturn face. He had wide shoulders and a pronounced stoop, as though he was continually bending to avoid doorways. His shirt and shotgun chaps were plain, even drab in contrast to those of the man who'd done all the talking.

Four Eyes was an absolute model of a cowboy. He was a slender, medium-sized fellow with a fair moustache. Somewhere in his late twenties, Will guessed. He was turned out in a giant white sombrero, scarlet silk neckerchief, spotless buckskin shirt with ornamental beadwork and long fringing, batwing chaps faced with glossy sealskin, and alligator-hide boots adorned with silver dress spurs. Two pearl-handled revolvers jutted from tooled holsters. To complete his outfit, he had a Winchester rifle cradled in his right arm, and eyeglasses on a black ribbon that dangled beside his nose.

'I saw you operate on that blackguard's hand,' the man said with a grin. 'Smartly done, sir. Smartly done.'

Will relished the compliment. 'Thank you.'

'Obviously you are Will Kent.'

'That's right.'

The young man beamed, transferred the rifle to his left hand and shot the right one forward. 'I'm Roosevelt. Delighted to meet you. Absolutely delighted.'

'Yes, sir. Same here.'

Roosevelt's grip was incredibly strong. Will wasn't the least put off by the rancher's glasses or his high voice. The sun-browned young man gave an impression of vigour, determination, and principle so high, it was almost intimidating.

'Sorry we didn't arrive sooner,' Roosevelt went on. 'We might have prevented that bit of nastiness.' Other passengers were getting off the train now; things were returning to normal. 'But you handled those bullies splendidly. Showed plenty of sand, as they say out here. Ah, but I'm neglecting the formalities—'

He gestured to the older man who was watching with a friendly smile. 'This is Mr Bill Sewall. Bill hails from Island Falls, Maine. He's my foreman at the Elkhorn Ranch.'

Sewall and Will shook hands. 'We're pleased to have you with us, Kent.' He sounded sincere.

'I'm glad to be here,' Will replied, meaning it.

'Wagon's down this way,' Sewall said. He had a distinct New England accent. He reached for the handle of Will's valise. Will protested. Roosevelt said:

'Might as well let him, Kent. It's the last time you'll get that sort of service this summer.' They started down the platform. Roosevelt went on. 'Mustn't judge the citizens of the Bad Lands by what just happened. Dakota people are grand. The Maunders clan's the exception. Troublemakers, every one of them. Jake Maunders has had a shady reputation for years. His son Archie was a holy terror and got himself killed sometime back. Cletus, who's a second or third cousin, has the worst temper of the lot. He imbibes freely and,

as you discovered, loses all restraint when he does. His
cronies, Sweeney and Chadburn, do whatever he tells
them. You'd be prudent to avoid all three, but
especially Maunders. Even man to man, he wouldn't
fight fairly.'

'I'll take your advice, Mr Roosevelt.'

The euphoria produced by Roosevelt's compliments
was quickly wearing off. Will began calling himself a
fool for what he'd done.

To be sure he'd got satisfaction from it. More,
perhaps, than he'd ever got from anything except his
brief conquest of Dolores Wertman. But he'd also
gained an enemy.

As he and Roosevelt and Sewall approached the
wagon standing at the end of the platform, Will studied
the sun-drenched fronts of nearby buildings. Maunders
and his friends had disappeared. Yet Will had an
uneasy feeling that he was being watched.

CHAPTER V

'Hasten Forward Quickly There!'

They headed south along the river Sewall referred to
as the Little Misery. Roosevelt said they would stay
the night at the Maltese Cross, the ranch in which he
owned a third interest.

Roosevelt was mounted on his favourite horse, a
high-spirited animal named Manitou. Will rode with
Sewall in the wagon, which was loaded with supplies
and mail picked up in town. Sewall said he'd be taking
Will up to the Elkhorn ranch while Roosevelt went
south to join the roundup already in progress.

255

The Maltese Cross consisted of a story-and-a-half log cabin with a shingle roof, and a smaller dirt-roofed shack built stockade style and used as a stable. Will would bunk there, Sewall informed him.

Will said that would be fine, and carried his valise inside. Several blankets had already been stacked on the dirt floor. He'd have company while he slept, he discovered. Three cow ponies snorted and stamped in their stalls.

Outside, Roosevelt introduced him to the men who owned the other two-thirds of the spread. They were a pair of sunburned and likable Canadians, Sylvanus Ferris and Bill Merrifield. Ferris was in his late twenties, Merrifield a few years older.

The job of showing Will around the place fell to Ferris. The others went inside as Ferris led the visitor past the kitchen garden to the circular horse corral with its snubbing post in the centre.

Beyond the corral was a much larger one filled with lowing cattle that had already been rounded up and tallied according to their brands, Ferris explained.

'That about takes care of the real estate,' he said with a smile. 'Hungry?'

'Starved,' Will said. He was worn out from the journey and the trouble at the depot. The tiredness began to erode his new-found confidence.

They started back toward the main building. The air was cool; the spring sun was almost down in the west. At the horse corral, Ferris stopped and rested one of his low-heeled boots on the bottom rail.

'In case the boss didn't tell you, you'll be working in this kind of corral up at the Elkhorn. Green hands always start out as wranglers. It's the meanest, dirtiest job on a ranch. But it's also very important, and fairly easy to learn. One of the boys will show you the fundamentals. Then they'll take you out on the roundup. By the way—'

He turned his back toward the ranch house. 'Even though most of the hands are a lot older than the boss, nobody calls him Theodore. Or Teddy, either. He hates Teddy. It's always Mr Roosevelt.'

'I'll remember that. But if he's your partner, why do you call him the boss?'

'Guess it just seems to fit. He's the smartest one of the bunch.' Ferris's tone grew wry. 'And you'll notice he has a way of taking charge.'

Will smiled. 'Yes, I noticed that already.'

'One more thing. Occasionally, one of us drinks a wee bit too much and calls him Old Four Eyes. Wouldn't advise you to do it until you know him a little better.'

'I heard someone in town call him that.'

'Maunders? Bill Sewall told me about your run-in with him. Bet a dollar he just said Four Eyes.'

Will looked puzzled. 'What's the difference?'

'A mighty big one. When the boss first came out here, he took a lot of ragging because of his voice and his fancy clothes and his glasses. One day in town, a drunk got pushy and really took after him. Kept calling him Four Eyes. The boss was patient for as long as he could stand it, but pretty soon he couldn't stand it any more. He put that drunken bully on the ground with two punches. Ever since, his friends have taken to calling him Old Four Eyes. It's meant kindly, and I think he sort of likes it. He's a hell of a fine fellow,' Ferris concluded.

Bill Sewall appeared at the ranch house door. Squinting into the copper light of the sunset, he called, 'Come and get it!' Ferris clapped a hand on Will's shoulder:

'You heard him. Hasten forward quickly there.'

'What'd you say, Mr Ferris?'

'Oh – ' A chuckle. 'That's another local joke. Goes back to the first summer Mr Roosevelt was out here.

257

He went on his first roundup, and a couple of yearlings bolted. He thought it was the start of a stampede. That's the most dangerous thing any of us has got to contend with, a stampede at roundup time. Anyway, the boss got all excited and started waving his arms and hollering at some riders who were coming his way. But instead of hollering for help so any cowhand would understand, he yelled, "Hasten forward quickly there!" It's the same as Old Four Eyes – something folks say because they like the boss and know he's got a sense of humour. So hasten forward – !' Ferris hooked a thumb toward the house. 'You need to eat your fill, every chance you get. Wrangling's hard work.'

'I've ridden a lot, but I don't know a thing about handling work horses. I hope I can do it.'

Ferris gave him a swift, questioning look. His smile was less cordial all at once:

'Let me give you one last piece of advice. Like I said, the boss is a damn fine man. But he can't stand anyone who's timid or unsure of himself. If you got any doubts that you're big enough for the job, don't let on to him. Now come on, let's eat.'

2

The evening meal was a hearty one – venison, beans, fried potatoes, sourdough bread, and strong black coffee. Roosevelt told Will how he'd met Bill Sewall. When he was a student at Harvard, he'd gone to Maine to hunt, and Sewall had been his guide.

The young rancher spoke with zest and enthusiasm. He laughed frequently and made abrupt verbal leaps from subject to subject, as if he were interested in everything, and couldn't begin to satisfy that interest in a normal lifetime. He discoursed on the weather, the roundup, national politics, the Marquis de Mores and his seamy friends, a prairie fire which had recently destroyed valuable grazing land, the plummeting price of beef in Chicago, his admiration of Tolstoy's novels, and the book he planned to finish writing over the summer. It was a life of Senator Thomas Hart Benton, for the well-known American Statesman Series.

Even though Roosevelt talked and talked, Will never got the impression that he insisted on dominating the conversation. From time to time his partners broke in with a comment or a story, and he listened attentively. When he asked a question, his direct gaze made it evident that he was vitally interested in the answer.

After the meal, Roosevelt drew Will off to a corner of the main room. He offered the young man a comfortable chair and took a rocker for himself. Full of food and close to falling asleep, Will fought a yawn as the rancher said:

'Well, sir – how do you feel about the Bad Lands so far?'

'It's beautiful country, Mr Roosevelt.'

'Right you are. Hard country, too. But if a man gives it everything he has, the country gives back satisfaction in full measure. It's my plan to start you out as a horse wrangler, by the way.'

'Mr Ferris mentioned that.'

The flames of a wall lamp flashed off his glasses. 'Think you can handle the task?'

Ferris's advice instantly came to mind. Will hid his true feelings:

'Yes.'

Roosevelt slapped both hands on his knees. 'Delighted to hear it. Thought that's how you'd answer. In ten days to two weeks, I'll stop at the Elkhorn, pick you up and take you out to the roundup with me.'

'That sounds exciting, sir.'

'It is, believe me. I suppose I ought to say something about the rules at the ranch. I never ask any more of a man than I'm willing to give myself. And it isn't my style to be bossy. But I insist on hard work, discipline, and regular habits. I can't tolerate malingering, half-finished jobs or hard luck stories. I demand complete integrity, too. That's what any Westerner expects of a man. I made my first business agreement with Ferris and Merrifield sitting on a log at Cannonball Creek. I handed them a cheque for fourteen thousand dollars and didn't want a receipt. Their word and their hand-shakes were good.'

Will nodded to signify that he understood. Roosevelt went on:

'One other, absolutely crucial point. On a ranch or a roundup, orders must be obeyed instantly, without pause or question. A man's life may be in the balance. Quick action may be the only way to save him. If you have questions, save them until afterward.' His stern-ness moderated. 'I don't expect you'll have any trouble. Provided you avoid Mr Maunders and the Medora saloons.'

Despite his doubts, Will murmured agreement. Then Roosevelt grinned that infectious grin and added, 'You may have trouble in one area. Getting enough sleep. We work late and rise early. I'd suggest you turn in.'

Will climbed to his feet. 'Gladly.'

'Do you need a lamp to light the way?'

'No.'

The promptness of the reply brought another pleased look to Roosevelt's face. Will was thankful the ranch-man didn't follow him outside to see how confused he became in the darkness. He really hadn't paid much attention to the precise layout of the Maltese Cross. He found the stable only by following sounds and smells.

Good smells, he decided as he approached the little building. Sweet hay and horseflesh mingling in the clean, cold air. But he doubted he'd sleep well on a hard dirt floor with cow ponies fretting next to him all night long.

He spread the blankets, crawled between them and put his head on his valise. He yawned. No pillow had ever felt softer.

Surprisingly, it took him only a minute or so to drift off. He was stiff when he woke. But he couldn't remember ever having slept so soundly.

3

Roosevelt rode out before daylight. After breakfast, Sewall drove Will back into Medora so he could spend some of his pocket money for work clothes – blue denim pants, flannel shirts, a sturdy pair of batwing chaps, mule-ear boots, and work spurs. Sewall's ranching experience was useful when Will was tempted to choose items more fancy than practical. The New Englander did approve the purchase of an expensive Montana-peak hat:

'You'll drink out of it, fan a fire with it, hide from hailstones under it – so it pays to get a good one. Next to a horse, a hat's a cowboy's most important possession.'

Will gathered up the purchases and prepared to pay for them. Sewall tapped his arm.

'Want one of those?'

He was pointing to a dusty showcase containing several revolvers – one S&W .45-calibre six-shot model; four of the famous and dependable 1873 Colt Frontier .45 Peacemakers, one with a silver-plate finish, an extra-cost option; and one immaculate and expensive Buntline Special, which was basically the Peacemaker with an extra-long barrel and detachable rifle stock added.

Will studied the weapons a moment. 'Don't think so,

Mr Sewall. I know how to shoot. My father taught me when I was eleven. We used to drive into the country west of Boston, find some woods and plink away at bottles. But I haven't fired a gun since then. I'm not anxious to take it up again.'

'Smart,' Sewall said with a brief smile. 'Sometimes a gun's nothing but an invitation for some drunken pup to pick a fight.' Sewall wore no side-arm, though while travelling from the ranch to town, Will had noticed that he kept a rifle in the wagon.

By noon they were headed north along the river in the wagon. All day they travelled through wild, spectacular country; a country of twisting gullies, huge rocky outcrops, and looming buttes. The only living creatures they saw were a few mule deer, some trilling larks, and pickerel and sunfish in a stream. Gnarled trees creaked in a wind that grew steadily colder as the day progressed.

High above, sunlight painted the summits of the buttes. Down where the wagon rumbled along there was only deepening blue shadow. It was late at night before they reached the Elkhorn.

The ranch was twelve miles from the nearest human habitation. It was situated on a low bluff near the broad, shallow river. The place had been named for a pair of wapiti skulls found on the site. The two bull elk had apparently got their horns locked during combat and had never been able to pull them apart. They'd died that way.

The main building, long and low, was constructed of hewn logs. Its veranda faced the Little Missouri and some intervening cottonwoods where mourning doves cooed. As the wagon pulled in, Will heard an owl hoot.

On the veranda he met Sewall's nephew Wilmot Dow, another New England Yankee of about the same age as Roosevelt. Together, Sewall and Dow ran the ranch for their boss, Dow told him. Will managed to murmur something. He was numb from the cold. But he refused to let on.

Inside, he was introduced to two other residents of the ranch about whom he'd heard nothing up till now – the wives of the two men. Both Mrs Sewall and Mrs Dow were visibly pregnant, and sleepy from awaiting Sewall's arrival with the new hand. But the women insisted Will have something to eat before he bedded down in the stable. He didn't argue.

While he wolfed freshly warmed biscuits and drank milk, he studied the interior of the ranch house. It had some unusual features, including three long shelves crowded with books. The spines of a few of them bore the gold tea-bottle colophon of Kent and Son, he was pleased to see.

There was also a rocking chair, and a large pan-like object whose composition and function he didn't immediately understand. Amused by Will's expression, Sewall enlightened him:

'That's Mr Roosevelt's bathtub. It's rubber. Came all the way from Minneapolis. You don't usually find such on a working ranch. But the boss is a stickler for keeping clean.'

'Wish some others would follow his example,' Mrs Sewall said with a teasing smile.

Sewall's nephew Dow showed Will to quarters like those he'd occupied the night before. Even before Dow wished him good night and carried his lantern away, Will was arranging blankets. He sank down on the hard ground with a sigh of satisfaction, as if he were resting in a plush hotel. After what seemed a very short sleep, he was awakened by the prodding boot of a sinister-looking fellow with bad teeth and a stubbled chin:

'Rise an' shine, Kent, if that's your name.'

He sat up, rubbing his frozen arms and yawning. It was still pitch dark.

'What time is it? Feels like the middle of the night.'

'Just about,' the man agreed. He gave off a strong odour of horse. He wiped his nose with the sleeve of a huge sheepskin-lined coat that made him look even smaller than he was. The lantern in his hand threw a grotesque shadow of his head – mostly big ears and untrimmed hair – on the stable ceiling.

Will had never seen so many wrinkles on one human face. He couldn't tell whether they'd been put there by age, weather, misery, or all three. The man went on:

'But I got half a dozen wild jugheads to bust 'fore noontime. Guess you're the one they give me for a helper. Christ on the mount, the things a man's reduced to doin' to survive in this world. I got to be a teacher – as if wrangling ain't bad enough. Y'know these ranchers around here won't pay more'n five bones for gentling a cow pony?'

'Bones—?'

'Dollars.'

'Oh.' He reached toward the nail on which he'd hung his hat. The man studied him with an increasingly sceptical eye:

'Say, where you from, anyway?'

'Boston.'

'Boston.' A pause. 'That anywhere near Illinois?'

Will decided it would be foolish to antagonize a man with whom he had to work. 'It's in the same general direction.'

'I was in Chicago once. A year after the big fire. Couldn't stand the goddamn crowds. Let me ask you somepin', Kent. You ever rode a wild mustang before?'

'I've never even seen one.'

The man gnawed his lip. Then:

'Ever handled a lariat?'

'No.'

'Jesus on the road on Easter morning. May my dear mother forgive my language. Might as well tell me the worst. Are you a complete dude?'

'I guess that's what you'd call it. But I'm here to learn, Mister—'

'Tompkins. Christopher P. Tompkins. My pals call me Chris.' His tone and expression suggested Will was not so privileged.

The young man felt a flare of resentment, but he struggled to remain friendly. Unconsciously, he imitated Roosevelt's smile and greeting:

'Delighted to meet you, Mr Tompkins.'

'Wish I could say the same. Don't try actin' like the boss. There's only one of him, thank the Lord. Human race ain't ready for two. And get this. You ever tell Mr Roosevelt you heard me cussin', I'll rip your gizzard out with my bare hands. The boss and I don't see eye to eye when it comes to profane language. I say a wrangler's entitled to all he wants, seein' as how his job's so dangerous. I 'spect you'll come to share my view pretty quick.'

Despite Tompkins' irascibility, Will sensed a good-humored streak in the man. Tompkins snatched his lantern from the empty nail keg on which he'd set it.

'Well, come on, Kent, come on. Hasten forward quickly there! Let's see whether you can stay alive in a horse corral long enough to learn a little something.'

CHAPTER VI

The Horse Corral

The next week had an unreal quality for Will.

To be sure, the days were essentially the same as all days; darkness gave way to light, and light to darkness again. But on the Elkhorn – especially if you worked for the head wrangler – the rising and setting of the sun had little impact on your routine. Will quickly began to think of his existence as divided among three main functions, and only three. The first involved working in the corral, in the midst of the dust and noise and sudden danger that accompanied the process of breaking wild horses for the Elkhorn herd. If not working, Will was eating. At a single sitting, he was soon consuming enough beefsteak, potatoes, beans, and coffee to equal three or four full-sized meals. When not working or eating, he was asleep, desperately trying to renew his energy and rest the strained muscles that filled him with pain from his boots to his neckerchief – and sometimes higher.

The wild mustangs chosen for the cavvy – the horse herd – averaged seven hundred pounds and twelve hands. What they lacked in weight and height, they made up in orneriness. Tompkins earned five dollars for each one he gentled – though given the techniques he used, gentling was hardly an appropriate term, Will thought. Literally, Tompkins broke their spirits. His tools included spurs, a quirt, a lariat, some lengths of grass rope for cross hobbling, an old saddle and bridle, and generous quantities of physical strength, profanity, and nerve. The pay was low because the wild, range-bred strays could never be sold for more than thirty or forty dollars, even if perfectly trained. But the work was important because, on a roundup, there was a constant demand for horses that were obedient and didn't spook too easily. Every working cowboy needed not just one mount like that, but a whole string.

All the Elkhorn mustangs had been rounded up on the open range. A structure such as a corral, which curtailed their freedom, was frightening to them. Attempts to further limit that freedom by means of riding gear brought instantaneous and terrified rebellion. Bucking; biting; kicking. In essence, Chris Tompkins' job consisted of demonstrating to the mustangs that rebellion – disobedience – brought an instantaneous penalty in the form of pain.

He first taught the lesson with a bridle, slipped on while the mustang was tied to the snubbing post. Next, while cross hobbled, the animal received saddleblanket and saddle. The first time Will helped Tompkins sling a blanket, he didn't dodge fast enough. The horse took a bite out of his wrist.

Will leaped away. Tompkins quirted the animal till blood showed on the leather. For a harrowing moment, the whip reminded Will of Margaret. It took effort to drive the memory out of his mind.

Mrs Dow applied a bandage to Will's wrist. Then he went right back to work.

It took him a little while to get used to the noise in the corral, to the sight of the lathered mustangs bucking and kicking, their huge eyes glaring from within clouds of tan dust. Soon, though, necessity taught him to ignore the extraneous; to move swiftly, as Tompkins did; and to keep alert.

Gradually, too, his concerns about mistreatment of the horses were pushed to the back of his mind by the need to do whatever was necessary to survive in the corral. It was quickly evident that the horses would gladly mistreat him, given half a chance.

Tompkins heaped scorn on Will for his clumsiness and inexperience. On several occasions the younger man was tempted to punch the wrangler, or just walk away from the whole business. He didn't walk away because he meant to succeed on the Elkhorn. He didn't hit Tompkins because he knew there was nothing personal in the criticism. The wrangler would have said the same thing to anyone he was teaching, Will suspected. And contrary to what Tompkins did with the horses, he wasn't out to teach Will by destroying his capacity for anger. Just the reverse. Tompkins' technique was to sneer and criticize until his pupil was in such a rage, he'd have died rather than fail again.

Sometimes the process seemed reminiscent of Will's experience with his mother. There were significant differences, though. He knew he deserved the condemnation he was receiving. And if he occasionally did something right, Tompkins never failed to mention that, too.

2

It was his seventh morning on the Elkhorn. Somewhere in the preceding six, there'd been a Sabbath, but he couldn't recall when. Tompkins observed no religious holidays. Shortly after first light, they put a saddle on a blaze-faced pony Tompkins identified as a cross between a *mesteño* – cowboys sometimes called a wild stray by the Spanish name – and a Cavalry thoroughbred.

The horse clearly hated the saddle; began to pull and roll its eyes and whinny in the cool air. At this stage, Tompkins usually passed the bridle to Will. This morning he hung onto it.

'Pick up the quirt, Will. Then get up on him like I showed you.'

'*Me?*'

'Jesus Christ walking on the water. You see anybody else out here?'

'No, but I don't think—'

'I don't give a damn for what you *think*. Pick up the quirt and ride him. Mr Roosevelt's gonna be back here inside of three days. He'll want to see you've made some progress. If he don't, he'll find a new wrangler. This job ain't as bad as some I've had. I aim to keep it. Pick up the quirt.'

Will wiped sweaty hands on his shirt. His mouth was dry all at once. He leaned down for the quirt, then sidled toward the mustang.

The horse turned its head and started to nip him. Will dodged the wicked yellow teeth. He grabbed the mustang's left ear and twisted.

Feeling the pain, the horse whinnied and shied. Will hung on. The horse stood still.

Holding his breath, Will swung up. He could feel the animal's pent-up fury beneath him. He squeezed his legs together. Still holding the horse's ear, he raised the quirt in his other hand. He let go of the ear and snatched the bridle—

Five seconds later he was sitting on his rump in the dirt.

His back felt broken. Tompkins chased the mustang, which had run off after throwing his rider. With much cursing and quirting, Tompkins got the horse under control. He brought him back to the centre of the corral, jerking savagely so the bit hurt.

Then, with great sarcasm, Tompkins said:

'Next time try to stay aboard long enough to give him at least one whack of the quirt, huh, boy?'

Through clenched teeth, Will said, 'Yes, *sir*. I'll surely try.'

'You don't sound as if you like this much, boy.'

'No, sir. Not much.'

The mustang looked wilder than ever. With steam rising off its flanks and its rolling eyes full of hate, it resembled some hell-born demon. Tompkins spat and scratched his groin.

'Well, boy, then your choice is easy. Get your ass in the saddle an' keep there or drag it back to Boston or Ohio or wherever it is they raise punkin lilies.'

The last words stirred memories of the Medora depot. Will's face, brown from a week's exposure to sun and wind, wrenched into lines of rage. 'You son of a bitch—'

'What'd you say, boy? Don't mumble.'

Will jerked his head up. 'I said hold the son of a bitch so I can mount.'

The wrangler grinned. 'Yessir, that's what I thought you said. All set? Here we go.'

3

This time Will stayed on long enough to apply the quirt twice. When the mustang bucked him off, he fell hard. A half-buried rock gashed his forehead. Blood began to drip into his eyebrows.

He said he wanted to find something to tie around his head. Tompkins apparently didn't hear:

'Get on him again.'

Enraged, Will suddenly noticed Sewall and Dow leaning on the corral fence, motionless figures against the ruddy light in the east. On top of everything else he had to have an audience!

'I said get on, Kent. We ain't got all day.'

Five more times he mounted and was thrown. On the sixth try, without any warning whatsoever, the mustang gave up and quit bucking.

Will almost couldn't believe it. He started to laugh and whoop, half blinded by blood and half crazy with pain. He heard Sewall call congratulations. Dow applauded.

He slid out of the saddle. His boots hit the dirt with a thump. He weaved toward Tompkins, grinning as broadly as the wrangler:

'I made it!'

'Damn if you didn't. I knew you would. Hell – ' He shrugged. 'It was either that or perish.'

Will untied his neckerchief and used it to swab blood out of his eyebrows. Meantime, Tompkins fetched a slicker that had been hanging on a rail of the corral.

'We spent enough time on congratulations, boy.' He

handed Will the slicker. 'Get back up there an' wave this around. Haze him good, so he gets accustomed to bein' spooked. That way, he won't throw the poor dumbbell who has to ride him in a gully-washer, when it's thunderin' and lightning to beat hell—'

'Mr Tompkins, you're a slave driver.' But he was still grinning. And despite the blood and pain, he felt wonderful. Wonderful and proud.

'Just doin' my job, boy. Just doin' what I'm grievously underpaid to do.'

Unsmiling, he stared at his young pupil for a moment.

'I s'pose it's all right if you call me Chris now. You're comin' along okay. I'm not gonna run you off the spread. Well – not for at least the next day or so.'

4

The wrangler was evidently lavish with his praise when Roosevelt returned. The first thing the Elkhorn's owner said to Will was, 'Your friend Tompkins says you have the makings of a passable wrangler.'

The term *friend* startled Will. He hadn't quite thought about the profane old bachelor that way before. To do so was gratifying.

'Well – ' He bobbed his head in what he hoped was a modest way. 'That's nice to hear.'

The words were restrained. But Will was happier than he'd been in years.

CHAPTER VII

Ambition

Next evening, just at sunset, Will walked out on the ranch house veranda for some air. Supper had been unusually good. He was well fed and content. The seat of his jeans pants sagged noticeably as he walked. Despite all he ate, he'd lost several pounds. His muscles were firming up, too. There was a pink patch on his nose where the skin had darkened, then peeled away.

He discovered Roosevelt already outside, seated in his favourite rocker, reading a letter. He murmured that he'd be done in a moment.

Will sat down on the steps and began fooling with a twig. Thrushes flitted in the cottonwoods overlooking the river. Above the treetops, a prairie falcon wheeled. The sinking sun turned the slow-moving Little Missouri brilliant orange. Out in the middle, a wild steer was wandering on a sandbar. One of the hands would probably rope the stray before dark.

Roosevelt finished the letter and dropped it into his lap. He told Will the letter came from a young woman named Edith; a childhood friend with whom he kept in touch. From the way spots of colour appeared briefly in Roosevelt's already ruddy cheeks, Will suspected there was more than friendship involved. Roosevelt had been a widower for a couple of years, after all.

The rancher's unforgettable smile returned. 'Been meaning for us to have a chat, Will. I'm curious to know your ambitions. What sort of future you want.'

Will's contentment vanished. 'To tell the truth, sir, I

don't have any plans. Beyond going to Harvard, I mean. I've been admitted for the fall term.'

'I believe your father did write me to that effect. Fine school, Harvard. I enjoyed myself there. My principal activities were working on the literary magazine and driving a dog cart all over Cambridge.' His smile grew rueful. 'I was a passable student, but a terrible snob. Sam Gompers drummed that out of me.'

'I've met Mr Gompers. Sometimes my father invites labour leaders to the house for dinner. Sometimes he even invites important businessmen on the same evening. Then the fur really flies.'

Both of them smiled. Roosevelt said, 'Your father was a trade unionist for a time, as I recall.'

'That's right. He tried to organize the Erie railroad yards when he worked there after the war.'

'I used to believe the union movement would bring this country to ruin. I still refuse to tolerate the sort of anarchy some trade unionists advocate. But I also think the doctrine of *laissez faire*, carried to its extreme, is equally repugnant. Too many capitalists use *laissez faire* as an excuse to gouge the public and exploit the poor.'

Settling into his rocker, he went on. 'I didn't hold these opinions four years ago. During my first ever year in the New York Assembly, I even voted against the bill to put a reasonable limit on the number of hours per day that a municipal streetcar company could demand from its employees. I called the bill sheer socialism, as I recall—'

He shook his head; chuckled with chagrin. 'Well, it's to be expected that young men will make mistakes. They aren't notoriously intelligent. They merely think they are.'

The good-humoured remark had a sting Roosevelt couldn't have imagined. With time and distance to add perspective, Will recalled some of his behaviour at home and saw it for what it was. Callow and boorish.

'What changed your thinking about unions?' he asked.

'Acquaintance with Sam Gompers,' Roosevelt said promptly, starting to rock back and forth. 'I'd never met anyone like him – a Dutch Jew – a cigar-maker and all that. At first, because of his union affiliation, I distrusted him. I soon learned that was wrong. Sam had plenty of lessons to teach a young man who'd lived in New York City most of his life but never really seen it. Sam took me into the tenements. Showed me the sweat shops. Six, eight, ten people – entire families – rolling cigars in a one-room flat. Sweating fourteen, sixteen hours a day just to earn a few pennies. We have laws regulating most of the work performed in factories. But no laws govern labour that's sub-contracted to private individuals in their homes. Factory owners find the situation most advantageous. I learned this much from Sam. The poor are usually too hungry and often too ignorant to protect themselves. And some of the rich, if permitted, will exploit those weaknesses without mercy.'

'I've never been in the slums—' Will began.

'The tenements are beyond belief. Dirty – lightless – Sam and his associates are trying to do what they can. Raise wages. Improve working conditions. But progress is so slow! Our laws are so antiquated—'

He began rocking faster, the chair's squeak growing steadily louder.

'Do you know that until a few years ago, dogs had more rights than children? A little girl of eight or nine, beaten and nearly starved to death, was brought into New York municipal court and legally declared an animal, just so she could get assistance under the law protecting mistreated dogs. Only then did someone start work on a new law to protect abused youngsters.'

Still rocking he sighed and smiled again. 'I know I'm the butt of a great many jokes. I've been accused of wanting to reform everything in creation between sunrise and sunset of a single day. By godfrey I'm not ashamed to plead guilty. There's so much necessary, constructive work to be done.'

He gazed out across the Little Missouri, a contemplative expression settling on his face. 'And it's because of that single compelling fact that I can't stay here the rest of my life. I love this ranch. I love the West. But personal gratification isn't life's highest goal. A man has obligations—'

The words struck a familiar chord. Will had heard Gideon express similar sentiments. When such things were said by a father, they could be ignored. When he heard them from a man he admired, he paid attention.

Roosevelt continued. 'To be honest, I've started to think about selling my interest in the two ranches. Not solely for altruistic reasons, I confess. I'd like to spend more time with Edith.'

His hand strayed to the letter in his lap. 'Miss Carow is a fine person. I'd like to show her the home I've built at Sagamore Hill on Long Island. Still, I sometimes wish I could stay out here forever. I like the active life as much as my father apparently detested it.'

A strained note had come into Roosevelt's voice. He added softly:

'My father paid for a substitute to take his place in the war between the states. I have heard hints that he was not a brave man. I loved him. But there are still aspects of his character that—'

Abruptly, he shook his head. Will sat motionless, aware that he'd been admitted to a very private place. Had he inadvertently been given an explanation for Roosevelt's almost fanatic devotion to physical activity – and for the value he placed on bravery? One of the ranch hands had used the word reckless to describe the boss. Was that recklessness a reaction to his father's lack of courage?

Odours of yeast dough and woodsmoke tinged the air now. Inside, Mrs Sewall and Mrs Dow laughed as they began the evening baking. Dow appeared at one corner of the ranch house, mounted on a nag called Old Mouse. With a wave, he rode toward the sand bar in the fading light.

The wild steer saw him coming and bolted into the shallows, kicking up a spray of sunlit water. Horseman and quarry disappeared in a patch of blue shadow alongside a bluff. Roosevelt's familiar smile returned:

'I've rattled on about myself far too much. I want to hear about you. You said you hadn't thought beyond college—'

'That's right.'

'Mmm, well – you're a bright lad. It would be a pity if you wasted your brainpower. You're more fortunate than most, you know. Your family's well situated. You can do more than choose between different methods of making a living. You can do almost anthing you wish, with no worries about earning your next meal. People in that fortunate position have a responsibility to serve others, it seems to me.'

'So my father always says.'

'That's one reason I took to him the first time we met. I know what the Kents stand for – and he's a Kent through and through.' He thought for a moment. 'Perhaps you'll gravitate to government, the way I did.'

'Politics doesn't appeal to me very much. Nor do any of the other fields my father's suggested.'

'What are those?'

'The law. Journalism—'

'I'm fond of writing. I'll never be a professional, but I can hold my own in the amateur ranks.'

'I read your latest book before I came out here. I enjoyed it.'

'Delighted to hear that. *Hunting Trips of a Ranchman* was well received. Publishers are a peculiar lot, though. They want an author to participate in all sorts of bizarre stunts in the name of publicity. My publisher insisted I have my photograph taken in a buckskin hunting suit—'

Stiffly, he posed with an imaginary rifle. 'Do I look like an authentic Westerner?'

'Absolutely.'

Roosevelt grinned. 'Then I continue to be in the minority. I thought I looked like an idiot.'

He dropped the pose and relaxed again. 'As to the legal profession, I share your aversion. After Harvard, I enrolled at Columbia law school. Couldn't finish. Too musty and stale, the whole business. I like to be in the middle of the action. In the arena, so to speak. Besides, these days the legal profession is a disgrace. Lawyers use their knowledge to evade justice for their clients more often than to promote it.'

Silence then. In that sunlit moment, while the two of them sat on the Elkhorn porch in the dying light of a long day, Will found Roosevelt's whole approach to life intensely appealing.

He leaned back against the post at the side of the steps and gazed at the river. Far away to the south, he heard splashing as Dow hallooed the steer through the shallows.

'Like you, Mr Roosevelt, I think I could spend the rest of my life here.'

'If you tried to make a living from ranching, you'd lose your shirt. I'm going to urge my partners to get out, just as I plan to do.'

'Why's that, sir?'

'The Dakota cattle trade is in a precarious state. That arrogant peacock de Mores strung his refrigerator plants and abattoirs from hell to Bismarck, but he didn't trouble to learn the realities of the business.

277

People back East simply don't like the grass fed beef we're forced to raise here. It's too stringy. The market wants beef that's been fattened on corn. On top of that, the first time widespread fires or severe winter storms do excessive damage to what little grass we have, the local cattle industry will go belly up. Ranching in Dakota may be pleasant, but it's no way to get rich.'

'Well, whatever I do, I want to be well off. Not from inherited money. From money I make myself.'

Roosevelt stopped rocking and gave him a sharp look:

'If that's how you feel, let me suggest you decide one thing right now. Which do you consider more important? Principles or personal wealth? The answer to that, and nothing else, determines the course of a man's life. Not to mention the worth of it.'

Frowning, Will asked, 'You mean it's impossible to have principles and be rich?'

The rocking chair remained motionless. 'Not at all. But it *is* nearly impossible to keep the two in perfect balance. The odds are reduced every time you take a stand on an issue of substance. Ask your father. Did he prosper while trying to organize the Erie yards?'

'No, he almost starved. He was nearly killed, too.'

'You see? Life constantly presents you with choices. Besides that, it's capricious. Just when you think you're secure, you're dealt a blow you never expected. Sometimes that too forces a choice. And the easiest choice is seldom the best one. If you decide when you're young that come what may, you will always favour principle above profit, life takes an altogether different direction. A better one, in my view. Better for you and ultimately better for your fellow man.'

The sermonizing angered Will. Politeness kept him silent, but the mood of a few moments earlier was spoiled. He stood up. Roosevelt could tell something was wrong.

'Off to bed?' he asked.

'Soon,' Will nodded. 'Tomorrow will be another busy day.'

'That's the only kind we have out here. I didn't mean to be unduly blunt with you.'

'I'm glad to know your opinions, Mr Roosevelt.'

'But you don't share them.'

'I didn't say that, sir.'

'Not in words—'

'Goodnight, Mr Roosevelt.'

'Goodnight, Will.'

Will walked out of sight around the corner of the ranch house. Ten minutes later, he was headed north along the river bank. He walked fast, kicking dirt and grumbling an occasional curse. He didn't like the choice with which the young ranchman had confronted him. He didn't like it, and he couldn't push it out of his mind.

Uneasily, he wondered if he was upset because Roosevelt's statements were in direct conflict with the promise to Carter. There was no doubt about the kind of choice Carter would make in a crisis.

Will vowed he'd never permit himself to be pushed that far. Henceforward, every decision would be made so as to protect him from the necessity of such a choice. Much as he admired the young ranchman, he believed Roosevelt was wrong. You could grow rich and at the same time live a decent, honourable life. The trick was to avoid crusades and lost causes; something Roosevelt – and Will's father – clearly refused to do.

Let Theodore Roosevelt be a conscience for someone else. He'd do things his own way.

And keep the promise to Carter in the bargain.

2

'Come on, boy, wake up. Wake up!'

'Chris? Is that you—?'

'It ain't the risen Lord.'

'It can't be morning already.'

'No, it's only ha'past three.'

'Good God.' Yawning and groaning, Will sat up.

'*Sssh!*' Tompkins put a finger to his lips. 'Watch that cussin'. The boss is right outside. Frettin' like a bull pup in heat, too. He's anxious to be away. Been up half an hour.'

All at once Will recalled what day it was. His resentment faded.

He reached for his pants, pulling them over his long flannel underwear. The night air was frigid. Tompkins' lantern provided no discernible warmth.

Will's breath plumed in the night air as he dressed. 'Almost ready.' He fastened his chaps on and reached for his hat. Outside the stable, he heard the creak and jingle of a saddle and gear. Manitou snorted. Roosevelt said something to Bill Sewall, who answered in a sleepy voice. Roosevelt's laugh boomed as another horseman arrived. All three men laughed and talked excitedly.

After the conversation on the veranda, Will and Roosevelt had continued to treat one another politely. But some of the friendliness had faded from their relationship. Now Will put the disagreement at the back of his mind and let himself share the excitement of the day. Before sunrise, the Elkhorn men would be on their way to the roundup.

CHAPTER VIII

Night Thunder

After an overnight stop at the Maltese Cross, the men from the Elkhorn pushed south again. They reached the roundup at noon on their second day of travel.

The June sky was cloudless, the air warm but not hot. Yet Will was soaked in sweat, and layered with dust that turned to mud in the creases of his skin. He was tired, too. Even Tompkins admitted to being worn out from pushing the cavvy of twenty-four horses so far so quickly. Luckily Will had ridden the whole way on a gentle, dependable mount, a little grey cow pony he called Boston.

He forgot his tiredness and discomfort as he gazed at the panorama of the roundup camp. Cowboys who had ridden the long circle all morning were coming in, driving strays and newborns ahead of them. Other hands were already at the chuck wagon, eating their noon meal in the midst of dust, smoke from branding fires, and a continual din created by profane men, high-spirited horses, angry steers, and forlorn cows bawling for their lost calves. It was a thrilling sight; Will could hardly get enough of it.

All the ranches taking part in the roundup contributed men to the work force. The cowboys, in turn, elected a foreman – in this case a well-respected man named John Goodall. The Elkhorn was supplying three experienced hands: Roosevelt; Sewall's nephew Dow; and Chris Tompkins, who preferred working on the range to busting horses, but did the latter because his skill was in demand.

A few minutes after Will and the others arrived, they

located the day wrangler, who would tally the Elk-horn's contribution to the roundup cavvy: six newly broken mustangs for each of the three men riding for the ranch, plus six more ponies available for use by any of the trio, as needed. This last half-dozen consisted of cow ponies trained for the more difficult work of cutting and roping.

The day wrangler was a muscular, friendly man with skin the colour of black coffee. He introduced himself as Robert Beaufort; the first syllable of his last name rhymed with dew. 'Most folks call me Bob,' he said.

When the wrangler met Will, who would be helping him, he shook Will's hand and said with a grave smile, 'You're in plenty of time for hard work, but you missed all the fun.' He was referring to the festivities that took place at the start of a roundup. The cowboys from the various ranches gathered a day or so early for horse racing, shooting contests, bareback riding, mock trials, marathon gambling, and just plain socializing.

The black cowboy spoke to Roosevelt. 'We just pulled in. The main cavvy's on the way. If you'll keep your horses close by for a few minutes, we'll get the afternoon corral up. You can help me string it, Kent. You know how, don't you?'

Will glanced at Roosevelt. Luckily the ranchman was saying something to Wilmot Dow. Will shook his head. To which Bob Beaufort replied:

'You will soon. Follow me. And shake a leg.'

Long, heavy ropes were quickly tied to the rear wheels of the wrangler's wagon. The ropes were laid out in the dirt to form a large circle. Jumping to obey Beaufort's orders, Will scrambled into the wagon and located half a dozen strong, well-worn tree limbs, each about three feet long. They had been cut to preserve a natural fork.

Beaufort showed Will how to set each limb vertically so the fork supported the rope, and how to brace the limbs in the ground. Then the cowboy untied the end of a rope attached to one of the wagon wheels and handed the rope to Will:

'This is your gate. Swing 'er open. Jump to it! Here comes the night man with the herd.'

Will had been too busy to pay much heed to a rumbling behind him. Now he turned, and his jaw dropped. A yelling rider was barely visible in a cloud of dust billowing behind sixty or seventy ponies. The four leaders of the horse herd were within a dozen yards of Will, and coming lickety-split.

He ran to the right, carrying the rope and thus opening the gate – the side of the corral nearest the horses. Beaufort, meantime, started uncoiling a second rope to be strung below the first. He tossed the end of that rope to Will, who had to leap for it, his left hand outstretched. He stumbled.

Down he went, tangled in rope. From the ground he had a distorted view of manes streaming, hooves pounding, white eyes rolling. Then he himself rolled, frantically churning the dust. He escaped the trampling hoofs of the first horses with only inches to spare.

As he lay on his belly, blinking and coughing in the dust, he realized something had nicked his forehead as he rolled to safety. A hoof, most likely. He touched the site of the nick. No blood. But the narrowness of his escape hit home, and his heart began to thump.

He scrambled up and ran to help Beaufort, who was attempting to close and re-tie the gate rope Will had dropped. The mounted wrangler who'd come in with the horses was driving them into a circle within the enclosure while loudly cursing them, Will, and the situation in general.

The black wrangler moved fast and expertly. He kept his eye on the rope he was swiftly re-tying to the wagon, saying to Will at the same time:

'You in one piece?'

'Yes, sir. I'm sorry I dropped that rope.'

'No harm done this time. You're the one who almost got the worst of it.'

Beaufort straightened up and wiped calloused palms on his jeans. Twisting his bandana up to his jaw, he mopped perspiration from his face. 'Five seconds more and you wouldn't have been alive to apologize.'

With a shiver, Will nodded. Cowboys were starting to emerge from the chuck wagon to pick their horses for the afternoon's work. Beaufort climbed under the top rope, which was now strung taut to form the perimeter of the large circular corral. The horses were milling and, to Will's surprise, staying inside the enclosure. Beaufort picked up the second rope and began to loop it around the tree limbs. As Will moved to help him, the black wrangler closed the conversation in terse fashion:

'Just don't make the same mistake again. We need more help 'round here, not less.'

2

It seemed to Will that never again would he be allowed to sleep past sunrise. In fact, the hour for rising seemed to get steadily earlier. On his second day at the roundup, he was wakened in the dark by the cook's hoarse cry:

'Get up, get up an' greet the little birds an' other signs and symbols of the Good Lord's handiwork!'

He asked the time of Bob Beaufort, who was just climbing out of his wagon. Will had slept on the ground beneath.

Beaufort tugged out his pocket watch. 'Quarter to three.'

It was freezing cold. Will pulled his top blanket off the lower one and rolled them together. He was about to complain about the early hour when he spied Roosevelt at a nearby fire. With the aid of a scrap of mirror and a tin cup of water, the Elkhorn's owner was shaving.

Beaufort noticed Will watching, and chuckled:

'He's just about the only man in the crew who shaves and uses a toothbrush.'

Will didn't have a toothbrush, so he had to settle for a leafy twig. For a toilet, there was a bush to step behind. Beaufort gave him ten minutes to prepare for the day. Then they began stringing the morning corral. Since the roundup was constantly on the move, the corral had to be put up and taken down twice a day.

Soon the night wrangler and another young hand brought in the cavvy. The two men had stood guard as the animals grazed and rested during the last four hours. Before that, Will and Beaufort had taken their turn on watch.

The night wrangler and his helper saw the horses safely inside the corral, then went off for their breakfast. After eating, both would sleep a while, then help bring the wagon and the cavvy forward to the noon campsite.

The roundup proceeded along a route which had been agreed upon ahead of time. Every morning a line was mapped out, along which the chuck wagon and horse herd would travel until midday. The riders, meantime, fanned out through the countryside on either side of the line, scouring every creek bed and hidden gulch for strays and newborn calves. The methodical search was called covering the dog. About noon the cowboys circled back toward the rendezvous point, herding the animals they'd found.

While the cowboys rode the long circle during the mornings, Will helped Beaufort and the other wranglers drive the cavvy forward. The horses raised great clouds of dust, and he soon learned to keep his water-soaked bandana tied tightly over his nose and mouth. Little more than his grimy eyesockets showed beneath his hatbrim.

He noticed that Roosevelt rode the long circle, wrestled calves to the ground at the branding fire, and took his turn standing night guard over the growing herd. But he never slung a rope or attempted to cut a cow from the herd for branding. One noontime he asked Chris Tompkins about this. Tompkins told him Roosevelt knew his limits – the ones imposed by bad eyesight:

'He don't like 'em, but he lives with 'em. Does a right smart job of it, too. First time he come out on the roundup, a lot of the boys snickered and called him a damn dude. They don't no more.'

In the afternoons, Will usually had some time to watch the activity at the branding fires. There the air rapidly clogged with smoke and the stench of seared hair and hide. The first time he observed the afternoon routine, Bob Beaufort was with him. The black man took notice of the calm way Will studied the contents of the work bucket next to the tallyman – the cowhand who kept the official count of the recovered strays, a list of their brands, and notes on the disposition of all unbranded calves and mavericks. In addition to the tallyman's work sheets, an informal second count was provided by the contents of the bucket. There was one bucket at each fire. Into it went a bit of ear from every branded animal, and bloody scrotums cut from the steers with metal loppers.

'Doesn't it make you sick to look at that stuff?' Beaufort asked, and his lips tightened in queasiness.

'Not particularly,' Will said. 'I've never been bothered by the sight of blood. Guess a lot of people are, though.'

A cowboy grunted and snapped the loppers shut.

The castrated steer howled. Beaufort pressed his fingertips to his mouth for a few seconds. 'Yes, indeed. First time they spy what's in one of those buckets, most new hands puke up a stream big as a geyser. Ever thought about being a sawbones?'

'A doctor?' Will shook his head.

'Well, it certainly appears you've got the stomach for it, if nothing else.'

3

Toward the end of each afternoon, the chuck wagon and the cavvy once again moved forward to the site chosen for the night camp. There, after nearly sixteen hours of work, Will could finally eat a solid meal and spend an hour talking to the black wrangler before exhaustion, their bedrolls, and then more guard duty claimed them.

Bob Beaufort was older than he looked. He'd been sixteen when horsemen in Union blue galloped up the lane of his owner's South Carolina rice plantation. The horsemen of Old Linkum – come to set him free:

'They came too late for my papa, Robert Senior. He died six months before Old Gray Fox Lee surrendered. All at once I had my liberty and no family left to share it with—'

Beaufort's owner had been a relatively benevolent one. He'd permitted a few of his best house slaves to learn to read, write, and cipher. In long night sessions before his death, Robert Senior had re-taught each lesson to his only son. Neither of them knew where young Bob's mother was. Eight years before the war, the fluctuations of a dwindling rice economy had made it necessary for the master to sell her off:

'No matter what else the master did for my daddy

287

and me, it never made up for that. I hated him and I prayed he'd burn in hell when he died.'

Lonely but hopeful, Beaufort had gone North right after the war. He'd had no last name, so he'd picked one he liked – the name of a small but fashionable seacoast town in the Carolina low country near the plantation.

The industrial North had proved a mighty disappointment to Robert Beaufort, freed man. He'd spent eight months tramping the streets of Pittsburgh, finding no work and sometimes sleeping in snowy alleys. On three occasions he'd been beaten by gangs of white steelworkers who resented all the blacks pouring in from the South in search of jobs.

The experience convinced Beaufort he wanted no part of the North. But what could he do? It was his ability to read that led to the answer. In a discarded newspaper he chanced upon an article about the rapid postwar development taking place in the Western beef cattle industry. War-ravaged Texas was pulling itself up by its bootstraps.

He'd travelled all the way to Texas on foot, with only determination and his wits to help him make the journey. The effort had been worth it. After a number of setbacks, he'd got a ranch job and settled down to learn cow, as the saying went. Eventually he'd worked his way north to Kansas with a trail drive, and pushed on alone to the Dakota Territory. He meant to spend the rest of his days as a cowboy:

'Can't think of a finer existence. 'Specially for a man of my colour. That's why you see quite a few black cowboys. I wouldn't say they love nigras out West. But most white men leave you alone if you pull your weight.' With a teasing smile, he added, 'Why, sometimes they even break down and act friendly for as long as five or ten minutes. Only time I don't like being a cowboy—'

288

Slowly he raised his right hand toward his neck.

' – is when it gets this warm—'

Smack.

He studied a smudge on his fingertips. 'My Lord, the skeeters look big this year.'

The weather had turned sultry during the day. A south wind blew intermittently. Will started to wrap himself up in his tarp – which was like consigning himself to an oven, but was the only decent protection against the attacks of the mosquitoes.

Suddenly he felt the wind begin to change. He looked at Beaufort. Firelight glinted in the cowboy's eyes as he turned his head and gazed into the northwest. He watched a moment. Then:

'I saw lightning, Will.'

'Storm coming?'

'I think so.'

Neither of them needed to say more. Will lay down and shut his eyes, but tension kept him awake. Soon he could hear Beaufort's shallow breathing up in the wagon. He was awake too.

After a while, Will heard a rumble of thunder. A silver flickering filled the northwest quadrant of the sky. Beaufort jumped down from the tailgate of the wagon:

'I'm going to saddle my pony. Yours, too.'

'I'll help.'

'No need for two of us to get up. Stay put.'

He vanished in the dark. Will's mouth grew dry. His stomach began to hurt. He knew stampedes were dreaded above all else. He also knew that if one started, every man had to be in the saddle to help stop it.

He lay rigid, listening as Beaufort saddled his own horse, then Boston. Far out in the darkness, beyond the campfires beginning to stream sparks in the rising wind, a man started to sing.

It was a wordless, nearly tuneless song. More of a chant than anything else. A second singer began somewhere else, with a little more melody.

'Are those the night herders?' Will whispered as Beaufort returned.

'Yes, indeed. When they start Texas lullabies, you know they're getting worried.'

Will rolled on his belly. A third man began singing to the cattle, trying to distract and soothe them. A fourth voice joined the others. Will saw men damping the blowing fires. The last thing anyone wanted now was a sudden eruption of flame in the prairie grass.

Behind a low sentinel butte in the northwest, another white glare lit the sky. Will held his breath. There was thunder, but muffled. After it died away, you could almost hear the silence; an eerie, oppressive kind of silence in which the only sounds were the herders' voices. The herders matched their chants to the slow rhythm of their walking ponies.

Dust blew against Will's cheek. He started to speak to Beaufort again, but there was a new burst of lightning followed by a deafening roll of thunder. Oddly, the thunder didn't die away as it had before. It continued. Will heard rather than saw Beaufort grab his hat and scramble to his feet. All at once Will realized the thunder wasn't coming from the sky.

The earth began to vibrate. 'They're up,' Beaufort said in a hoarse voice. '*Move!*'

The thunder of running cattle grew louder, interrupted all at once by a cow's bellow. Then another. A night herder yelled the warning that was already unnecessary:

'Stampede! *Stam-peeede!*'

The sky roared and the ground shook. Lightning flashed almost continuously as the storm came scything out of the northwest at incredible speed, whipping the grass all around Will's galloping pony. He and Beaufort were part of a group of riders racing along the left flank of the charging herd – two or three hundred animals strung out over a distance of a half mile.

The herd was stampeding south, along a dry, shallow watercourse. Once the stampede was on, the night herders had immediately ridden to the left side of the herd. Will and the other men had fallen in behind. Now, up ahead, cowboys began firing their revolvers into the air. As they shot, they hallooed and edged their racing ponies toward the leaders of the stampede, hoping to turn them to the right and keep turning them, until the leaders were into a spiral that would wind in upon itself and thus spend the stampede's force.

But turning the leaders was no easy trick. Especially when the cattle were aware of the men riding alongside. The presence of the cowboys only heightened the animals' fear and fury. Long horns shiny with lightning, a big steer came lunging out of the herd at Will and his pony.

One horn pricked Boston's right haunch. The pony leaped. Had the watercourse not been fairly level, horse and rider might have fallen. But Boston came down with a jolt, and barely broke stride.

The charging steer had already turned away and been absorbed back into the herd. Will tore his hat off, slapped it against his right leg, and yelled himself hoarse. Boston was moving so fast, he could only trust to the pony's instincts and hope they didn't chance onto some unexpected gully or unseen animal burrow. He kept yelling. Ahead, spurts of flame showed in the darkness. The gunfire was continuing. But the herd refused to turn.

Lightning again.

Thunder.

More lightning—

Will felt as though he were aboard a train hurtling out of control. In the next flash of lightning, he saw a cowboy lying on the ground ahead of him. The man's pony had broken a leg and was sprawled on its side, bellowing. The man's leg was pinned beneath the animal. Will reined Boston to the left to avoid a collision.

Before the lightning faded, the man saw Will coming and redoubled his efforts to pull his leg free. Thunder pealed. Will and Boston bore down on the cowboy at incredible speed.

Boston wasn't a cutting horse. Will had to rein him very sharply to signal that the fallen rider was the object of his attention. Once the little pony understood, he dug in his front hooves so suddenly, he nearly pitched his rider off.

Will clung to the saddle and mane as Boston rocked to a stop, stiff-legged. He shot his right hand down, shouting over the bellow of the injured horse:

'Grab hold and pull yourself up!'

The other cowhand freed his leg at last. But all the commotion attracted some of the charging cattle. Two steers and six or seven big cows left the main body of the herd, lumbering straight at Will and the man he was attempting to help.

Will leaned down further, his hat falling off and getting lost. He touched the man's fingers. Boston was shying away from the charging cattle, making contact difficult.

'*Hurry up!*' Will shouted. 'Grab on!'

The man seized his arm as if it were a tree limb. For a moment Will's back felt as though it might break. But he stayed in the saddle.

He jerked his right leg back to permit the fallen man to use the stirrup. With a grateful cry, the cowboy swung up behind him. Will yanked the rein to the left, to get them out of the way of the cattle bearing down on them.

Boston answered the rein and spurs, and bolted. They'd have made it safely away but for one of those burrows Will had fretted about. The pony's left foot went straight down into the hole. Bone snapped. With a shriek of pain, Boston fell, spilling both the cowboy and his rescuer directly into the path of the charging animals.

CHAPTER IX

The Victim

Will landed on his side and took a severe jolt – perhaps the only thing that saved him.

The pain goaded him to his feet. Without a conscious thought, he twisted his hands in the fallen cowboy's collar. The man was stunned; groaning. Will groaned too, from exertion, as he pulled.

Fortunately the cowboy wasn't too heavy. And there was desperate strength in Will Kent at that moment. The snorting steers were only fifteen or twenty feet away, coming fast.

He dragged the cowhand one more yard, dropped him and jumped in front of him, waving his arms and yelling at the top of his lungs.

On came the lead steer, head dipping, horns glinting as lightning streaked down the sky. Will's insides turned to water. But he stood his ground, shouting himself raw in the throat and waving his arms like a madman—

At the last instant, the steer veered away from the noise and motion.

Once the leader changed direction, the other animals followed. In seconds, Will and the other cowboy were safe.

As he knelt beside the man he'd rescued, he began to tremble from the shock of what had just happened. The other cowhand was a towhead not much older than Will himself. He came back to his senses slowly – a blessing, since it took Will a minute or so to get himself under control.

It wasn't easy. A few feet away, poor Boston was thrashing and screaming, a goner. The cowhand's pony was no better off.

The wind dried some of the sweat on Will's face. In the northwest, the horizon had disappeared in pouring rain. Pushing his hair off his forehead, he peered through a sudden puff of dust. Unless the lightning was tricking him, the leaders of the stampede had swung to the right. The forward momentum was slowing. If that was true, the danger was over. Once the leaders began milling, herd instinct would end the stampede just as herd instinct had begun it.

The injured horses kept bellowing. Will had never heard such cries of pain.

Something cold jabbed against his palm. Lightning reflected on metal. The groggy cowboy was trying to press his Colt into Will's hand:

'Use it, for God's sake,' the cowboy gasped. 'Don't let the poor things suffer that way.'

With a stricken look, Will staggered to his feet. He tried to tell himself it was an act of mercy, not an act of murder. He stumbled to the cowboy's horse; waited for a thunderclap so he wouldn't spook the herd again. While the lightning flickered out, he raised the Colt with both hands—

The thunder muffled the sound of the shot, but not the pony's scream. As the animal went into its final agonies, he bit down on his lower lip and turned toward Boston.

The pony held his head still a moment. He seemed to be looking at Will with his left eye—

I can't do it.

Boston slammed his head against the earth, bellowing. And Will knew he could and would do anything to prevent an animal, or a human being, from enduring that kind of terrible pain.

Tears running down his face, he killed Boston with a single shot.

2

The other cowhand mumbled half-coherent words of thanks. Will asked the cowhand his name. Frank Hixson, the young man said. He'd twisted his leg when he fell and was unable to walk. Will had to lift him, prop him up, and carry him back to the night camp.

By the time he reached it, the rain arrived. He barely had time to slide Hixson under the wrangler's wagon before the rain poured out of lightning-lit clouds, soaking him. All the fires were instantly drowned. Soon the area was swimming in a foul smoke. Out of the smoke a bedraggled Bob Beaufort came riding.

Will was on his knees in the mud next to the wagon, watching over the groggy Hixson. 'Got a man hurt here, Bob,' he called as the tired cowboy dismounted.

Beaufort limped toward him through the downpour.

'We got more than one, Will. I heard one of the boys was really torn up when his pony took a tumble.'

'Do you know who it is?'

Beaufort shook his head. 'What happened to you?'

'Same thing. My pony fell. So did his. Had to shoot both of 'em.'

' – saved me – I'd been killed,' Frank Hixson was muttering. Beaufort knelt next to Will, resting a forearm on the wagon wheel. Little waterfalls of rain water poured off the hub and spokes. Beaufort bobbed his head at the half-conscious cowboy:

'Does he mean you?'

' – *saved me, he surely did.*'

Will shrugged. 'I just pulled him out of the way of some beeves that were chasing him. I did it mainly because they were chasing me too.'

But it was one time I didn't bungle.

'Umm.' Beaufort studied Hixson for a moment longer. 'Maybe we can find some help for this fellow.'

Will knuckled rain from his eyes. Exhaustion and shock were beginning to make him tremble again. He fought the shuddering.

'I didn't know there were any doctors in these parts,' he said.

Beaufort laughed wearily. 'There aren't. The only sawbones within miles of here is Doc Stickney in Dickinson, and he isn't home but three or four nights a month. Someone told me he has patients strung out across a territory as big as all the New England states put together. We have to rely on somebody with a lot less book learning than Stickney.'

'Who are you talking about?'

'Ever seen that lanky cowhand with the black sugar-loaf hat?'

Will had seen a lot of cowboys at the roundup; it took him a while to remember this one. He finally did:

'The one who looks like an Indian?'

'That's right. He's one quarter Cherokee. He works for Murtry of the Slash Bar. When Murtry can keep him sober. Name's Lon Adam. Doc Adam, some call him, though he's got neither licence nor formal education. All he's got is a flannel bag full of dried-out plants, and plenty of experience. They say he's a good cowboy when he isn't drunk. I expect they've got him working on that man who's hurt bad. You might hunt around till you find him, and ask him to come by when he has a chance.'

'Lon Adam,' Will said, to fix the name in mind. He found a dry shirt, donned a slicker from the wagon and set off through the rain.

3

It took him twenty minutes to locate the man he wanted. Lon Adam was working beside a newly kindled fire that generated more smoke than light. He'd supplemented the fire with a lantern, and was busy bandaging a cowhand's swollen ankle.

Lon Adam struck Will as a nondescript man except for his immense black hat, his huge sharp nose, and his hands. Despite weather-roughened skin and calloused palms, they moved with the grace of a woman's.

Will watched a moment or so, then he approached and asked whether he'd located Mr Lon Adam.

Adam nodded, a trickle of rainwater falling off the front of his hatbrim. 'What do you want?'

Will told him.

'I'll come as soon as I finish here. This appears to be our worst casualty so far—'

'No, Mr Adam. I'm afraid we have a much more serious one.'

At the sound of the familiar high-pitched voice, Will spun round. Roosevelt walked into the dim circle of

297

the firelight. His eyeglasses were canted on his nose, the lenses fogged with condensation. Raindrops gleamed on his cheeks. Almost like tears, Will thought.

Roosevelt gestured behind him in an uncharacteristically vague way. 'It's my man Tompkins—'

'Oh my God,' Will whispered. Was he the one Bob Beaufort had talked about?

Roosevelt confirmed it:

'His horse went down near our campsite. I've ordered that he not be moved. I fear his back's broken.'

CHAPTER X

Old Doc Death

Quickly, Lon Adam tied a knot in the flannel strip with which he'd wrapped the cowhand's ankle. He gave the bandage a pat, then stood up. At his left hip hung a bulging bag made of worn material that had once been bright with madder dye. The bag was tied to his belt by a piece of frayed rope.

'Let's look at him,' Adam said to Roosevelt. 'You have whiskey?'

'I don't think it would be advisable for you to drink any—'

'Not for me, Roosevelt.' The man's dark eyes shone with rage. 'For him.'

'I'm sorry, I misunderstood. I'm afraid I don't keep that sort of thing in my kit.'

'I know you don't. But there are men around here who do. Find them. Find me some whiskey.'

'Yes, of course,' Roosevelt said as they hurried away

through the rain. Will had never heard the ranchman
speak so meekly.

2

The storm blew itself out within two hours. The sky
cleared, revealing a brilliant moon. The dry watercourse down which the cattle had stampeded contained
a half inch of water now; water that looked like flawed
onyx in the moonlight.

No one in the roundup crew slept much that night.
The men were still keyed up over the stampede, and
worried about Chris Tompkins. Quite a few of the
hands drifted to the place where the Elkhorn men had
been sleeping before the alarm sounded. There, beside
a cottonwood fire, Lon Adam bent over the injured
Tompkins.

The cowhands stood or sat in silent vigil on the other
side of the fire. Will took his place among them. Every
eye was fixed on Adam's patient. He lay under a
blanket, his head thrown back, his cheeks and forehead
sweat-covered despite the breeze. He was breathing
through his mouth in a loud, laboured way, as if to
draw something from the air that would put an end to
the agony visible on his face.

Adam crouched down beside him. Close by stood a
bottle containing three inches of whiskey. From the
bag at his hip, Adam took a gnarled root the length of
a little finger. He placed the root on a flat stone one of
the cowboys had washed and dried, and chopped the
root into small pieces with his sheath knife. Then, using
the flat of the blade, he crushed each piece into
powder. Will was fascinated by Adam's supple brown
hands.

Again he reached for the faded bag. When he
opened it, Will saw that the bag had a buckskin lining.

Adam pulled out something resembling dried grass. He crumbled this into an old tin cup, carefully added the powdered root, and poured in the whiskey. He stirred the concoction with the tip of his knife, smelling it, and seemed satisfied.

Tompkins' eyes had a glazed look. Every minute or so, pain contorted his face, and he groaned. The sight brought tears to Will's eyes. He sniffed and blinked, not daring to look at the cowboys standing next to him.

Adam wiped his palms on his jeans and slowly slipped his left hand under Tompkins' neck. Tompkins moaned. When Adam had his hand in position, he held his breath and exerted gentle upward pressure. Tompkins screamed as if he'd been seared with a branding iron. Will dug his nails into his palms.

'I know it hurts,' Adam murmured. 'But I've got to raise you so you won't gag when you drink the medicine I fixed.'

Comprehension and panic showed in the eyes of the injured cowboy. He tried to speak, but the only sound he could produce was a kind of rattle.

'I've got to go ahead, Tompkins,' Adam said. After a moment, Tompkins blinked. Adam took that as a sign of permission. With a grimace, he exerted more pressure. Tompkins screamed again.

Several of the hands turned away. Will heard one walk into the dark and retch. Even Roosevelt looked ill as he said:

'In the name of God, be merciful to him.'

Adam fixed Roosevelt with a ferocious stare. 'I'm trying. I can't save his life, but if he'll drink what's in the cup, the dying will be a mite easier.'

'*Dying?*' Roosevelt swallowed. 'I thought—'

'That I knew how to mend a broken back? No, sir. I have a certificate from a Chicago diploma mill, and a bag of remedies I've gathered in my travels. I've got some tricks I learned from my mother, who was an

300

Ozark granny woman, and I know from first-hand experience how much the human body and the human soul can hurt. I also know how many charlatans sport the title doctor, and I know I deserve it as much or more than they do. In other words, Roosevelt, I know what I am and what I'm not. The main thing I'm not is a magician. This man's dying. Now if it's all right with you, I'll get on with helping him the best I can.'

Roosevelt gestured again, for once at a loss for words.

3

It took Adam five minutes to elevate Tompkins' head far enough so that the contents of the tin cup could be administered. Will found those five minutes almost unendurable. No matter how gently Adam lifted him, Tompkins experienced excruciating pain. He screamed repeatedly. And after he drunk the potion, he screamed again while Adam lowered his head to the ground.

By then all but the hardiest had left. Those who lingered did so because they wanted to pay their respects to a man they had known and liked. Will, too, had ultimately come to like Christopher P. Tompkins, hard and profane though he was. That bond held him at the hissing fire with five other cowboys; that bond, and the fascination of watching Adam at work. He gently stroked Tompkins' cheek until the man's eyes closed and he began to breathe in a more relaxed and regular way.

Will had already been in the presence of great suffering once tonight. Now he was in its presence again. This time it wasn't the suffering of an animal, but of a human being. What a detestable thing that was, he thought while he watched Adam's hand. How terrible that it should exist at all.

The sight of Tompkins brought Margaret to mind. Could a man like Adam have helped her? Given her some powder or elixir to relieve the anguish she'd suffered almost daily during her last years? Adam might be a drunkard, as Bob Beaufort said, but that hardly mattered in the light of his talent. The slow, caressing movement of Adam's hand on Tompkins' face became for Will the symbol of the most meaningful skill a man could possess.

Awed and moved, he watched for another hour. By then he was among the last three lingering at the low fire. Roosevelt sat on a log to his right. Abruptly, the motion of Adam's hand stopped. He frowned, then moved his hand so that the palm was almost touching Tompkins' mouth.

The fire sputtered. Smoke streamed out. Adam looked from face to face, his gaze coming to Will last of all. Softly, he said:

'He isn't breathing.'

'God pity the poor fellow,' Roosevelt said. 'At least he was in much less pain at the end. You helped him immeasurably.'

Adam snorted. 'But not enough. You can never help anyone *enough*. They always end up taking their business to old Doc Death. Sometimes I wonder why we bother trying to outfox him.'

There was an almost feverish glare in his eyes. He gazed down at the dead man, who was beginning to give off an odour that was familiar and unpleasant. 'Someone clean him up and cover him, for Christ's sake.' Venomous, Adam looked at Roosevelt. 'And even if it offends your morals, I'm going to have a drink now.'

'Of – of course, Doctor Adam,' Roosevelt murmured. 'I'll find you one myself.'

302

Lon Adam stood with his head down, his great black hat in his left hand and his right moving back and forth across his eyes, as if he were trying to rub away a bad memory. Day was breaking. The cattle were becoming visible. They were lying down, spent after their run during the storm.

Will wrenched his gaze from the dead man who had been his teacher to the other man who had succoured him. In his cast-off clothing, Adam was a queer-looking sort. Obviously not a white man, nor a full-blooded red one either. He was unlike any human being Will had ever met.

'Mr Adam?'

The man pulled his hand down. Focused his eyes on Will. Finally remembered:

'Oh, yes. You had someone for me to see.'

'He wasn't very badly hurt. I suppose he's sleeping by now.'

'Let me come have a look anyway.'

They started to walk toward Bob Beaufort's wagon. The grass was wet and slippery. Adam momentarily lost his balance. To keep from falling, he grabbed Will's shoulder, then apologized.

'I'm worn out,' he said. 'I feel like my legs are about to give out.'

'You worked hard,' Will said. 'Go ahead and lean on me.'

Adam accepted the offer. Tired though he was, he didn't miss the worshipful look in the younger man's eyes.

5

Christopher P. Tompkins, address and origins unknown, was buried in the buffalo grass that morning. A crude wooden cross was pounded into the ground to mark his resting place. At noon the roundup moved on, behind schedule but having lost only eighteen head in the stampede – a surprisingly low figure, Beaufort said.

When they reached camp that night, Roosevelt appeared. He drew Will aside and complimented him on his bravery. Frank Hixson had wakened and was repeating the story of Will's quick action to anyone who'd listen.

'I appreciate your telling me, Mr Roosevelt,' Will said. And he did. For the first time in years, he'd done more than shout silent denials of Margaret's accusations. He'd done something to prove them wrong.

Roosevelt started to say something else. Will spied a familiar figure and spoke first:

'I wonder if you'd excuse me, sir.'

Before the rancher could answer, Will was off to catch up with Lon Adam.

CHAPTER XI

A Plan for the Future

The roundup moved on to Gardiner Creek, Bullion's Creek, and Chimney Butte with no further mishaps or interruptions. Will enjoyed each one of the warm June days, and found the work exhilarating. He understood the routine of the wranglers now, and could handle all that was expected of him.

Each evening he managed to find a few minutes to wander by the fires of the Slash Bar and talk with Lon Adam. More often than not, Adam could be found sitting by himself, a clay bottle not far from his hand. The first time he offered Will a drink, the young man hesitated. Adam laughed:

'You won't be breaking any rules, Kent. This is my pokeroot tonic. There's hundred proof whiskey in it, all right. But since the purpose of the beverage is wholly medicinal, the boys can all take a dollop after a day's work and there isn't a blessed thing Boss Murtry can do about it.'

Will took the bottle. One drink taught him that if swallowed too fast, the tonic had an effect similar to a blow on the skull. But it was flavourful. And it certainly relaxed a body.

It also loosened the tongue. On his fourth visit with Adam, he took two long swigs and then mentioned his new-found ambition.

Adam laid his sugarloaf sombrero on his knee. By day he always looked undistinguished, even pitiable in his shabbiness. At night, with the fire chiselling his face into planes of light and dark, he acquired a kind of regal aura. Now that aura was heightened by the cool, almost contemptuous way he responded to what Will had just told him:

'You mean to tell me you're seriously considering a career in medicine?'

Will was disappointed by the reaction but tried not to show it:

'Yes, indeed.'

'When did you come to this momentous decision?'

'The night I watched you help Chris Tompkins through his last hours.'

'That a fact. Sorry I'm the one responsible.' He took another pull from the clay bottle. 'Doctoring's fine if all you care about is feeling like a saint. If you like a roof over your head and three square meals a day, I recommend carpentry.'

'If doctoring's so bad, why'd you take it up, Mr Adam?'

A shrug. 'Runs in the family. My mother was a granny woman. Winter or summer, she'd ride miles and miles on her mule to help birth a baby. All she had with her were her little black bags of muslin and camphor, cornstarch, and goose grease. That and the things she learned from her mama, and her mama's mama before her.'

He brushed at a fly devilling his veined nose. 'Mama was a small woman. No more than ninety-five pounds. Tough as a she-wolf, though. Pretty as a daisy. A cancer took her when she was only in her forties.'

His eyes looked beyond Will, full of hurt. 'The cancer ate her prettiness an inch at a time, and there wasn't a goddamn thing anyone could do except fill her full of tonic to kill the pain.'

Like an animal shaking off rain, he stirred his shoulders. A melancholy smile stole over his face, a smile of remembrance:

'I grew up with dirt and disease. They're staples of life in the Ozarks. I watched old Doc Death take over the treatment of anyone he pleased, any time he pleased. Seemed to me there should be a way to put a stop to that. When my mother died, I decided to hunt for the way – which was my number one mistake. My life's been nothing but poverty and ruin ever since. In case I haven't made it clear by now, doctoring isn't a good way to make a living – not even for people who can afford to go into it with a proper education, which I couldn't.'

'That's all new to me,' Will said. 'I don't know anything about the way doctors live.'

'They live miserably. Most of 'em have another business to put food on the table. Medicine's just their sideline. I ran a farm implement store in Sedalia, then an apothecary shop in Colorado Springs, then a greasy spoon down near the Rio Grande where I went to study with the Mexican *curanderos*. All three of the businesses went bust. My three marriages broke up, too. My first wife was a poor crazy squaw who couldn't stand white men's ways. One night when I was off delivering a calf, she put a rifle bullet in her head. Second wife got weary of being poor and left me for a travelling preacher. Not much improvement that I could see. Third one disappeared too. To this day I don't know why, or where she went. She never even left a note. Amongst those three women, I fathered seven children. Before age five, every one of them died of measles, typhoid, grippe, or some damn thing. Always figured most of the fault was mine.'

'How could that be, Mr Adam?'

The older man shrugged. 'I paid too much attention to doctoring and not enough to keeping the accounts, or making a woman happy, or putting shoes on the wee one's feet. Irresponsible, that's the word my second wife used. If I had to put a description to it, I'd say it was being too interested in death. Interested in trying to stop some of it because it's such a goddamn, dirty, disgraceful waste—'

Once more he swigged from the clay bottle. Will didn't quite know what to make of this unkempt, sometimes wild-eyed man with the immense nose and gentle hands. Was he a lunatic or, to use Adam's own words from a while ago, a saint?

'Had another problem since I was twelve or thirteen,' Adam went on, waggling the bottle. 'After I got married, it was worse. My drinking didn't contribute to the peace of mind of any of my wives. Sure helped mine, though. Say – you care for another sip?'

'No thanks. You were saying doctors don't live very comfortable lives—'

An emphatic nod. 'I've been told only a few at the very top in the big cities make anything at all. If I were you, I'd avoid the profession like the plague. 'Less, of course, you find you can't do anything else. That's the real cause of all my problems. I can't do anything else. If there aren't any humans who need help, I can treat a horse or cow and be damn near as happy. Yes, sir, Kent—'

He drank again, finishing in a grave way:

'I'd think twice about doctoring.'

Whenever Will visited the Slash Bar campsite and prodded Adam to talk of his favourite subject, the older man never struck anything but that same half-bitter, half-proud note. He repeatedly said it was doctoring that had destroyed all his chances for a normal existence. Yet he admitted he probably would have remained illiterate if his thirst for a knowledge of medicine hadn't driven him to learn to read. And if someone needed his help, he was always ready, no matter what the hour.

On the roundup the demand for his services was fairly steady. One night one of the hands shot himself in the foot while cleaning his Navy Colt. Adam had an item in his bag to fit the problem. He worked up a paste from a kind of thistle called *contra yerba*. The paste kept the wound clean and free of infection.

Two days later, Bob Beaufort complained of cramps and a bowel stoppage. Adam powdered a little of his preciously hoarded mandrake root, mixed it with whiskey, and next morning Beaufort was good as new.

A third cowboy came down with the sniffles, then a high fever. Adam brewed a strong tea with something he called a fever plant. The tea brought the temperature down within twelve hours.

Adam's activities continued to make a profound impression on Will, to the point where his worship of the raffish cowhand became a kind of joke. Other cowboys teased him about wanting to play medicine man. He surprised them by saying they were absolutely right.

The roundup ended in late June. On the final day, Will went to say goodbye to Adam, who was already packed up and ready to ride out. He leaned down from his saddle to shake Will's hand:

'If you're serious, and doctoring's still your choice, so be it.' A smile, almost ugly in its mockery, twisted his mouth. 'Just don't hold me responsible for what happens later.'

Will wished he could smash that smile to pieces. Adam was making light of his own gift. 'You don't mean that, Mr Adam.'

'Hell I don't. So long, Kent.'

Adam turned his pony to join the amused Slash Bar hands who were watching the exchange. Will started to run after Adam; felt foolish; stopped and called:

'We never had time to talk about the plants and herbs you use. I'd like to write you—'

'Do that. Be happy to hear from you,' Adam called back, waving. His other hand was reaching for the clay bottle tied to his saddle by a thong. He was drinking as he rode out of sight.

Eventually Will wrote three letters to the Slash Bar ranch. None was ever answered.

2

On the first night back at the Elkhorn, Roosevelt came in after dark to find Will examining the book shelves.

'Hunting anything special, Will?'

'I wondered whether you might have a book on medicine.'

'I'm afraid not.' Roosevelt eased himself into his rocker and plucked off his eyeglasses. 'That Indian made a profound impression on you, didn't he?'

'Yes, sir. For the first time, I saw a man doing something I'd like to do myself. Something worthwhile.'

Dubious, Roosevelt countered, 'Medicine isn't exactly a highly paid profession, you know.'

'So Mr Adam told me.'

'Still, I applaud your humanitarian impulse. Even if it was prompted by someone as bizarre as Lon Adam. His boss, Dick Murtry, thinks the fellow's only half there. Dick wouldn't put up with him, but for the fact that Adam has a fine way with sick cows and horses.' Roosevelt paused. 'May I ask you a candid question?'

Will grew apprehensive. 'Of course.'

'Lon Adam was absolutely right. Most doctors can't earn a living wage. The night we talked on the veranda, you said you wanted to be well off – and achieve success on your own, not by inheriting your father's wealth. Have you suddenly abandoned those objectives?'

Softly, almost heatedly, Will said, 'No.'

310

'Then how do you reconcile them with this new ambition?'

'Why do I have to, Mr Roosevelt? I should be able to be a doctor and earn a good living at the same time.'

'Given the state of the profession, it's doubtful.'

'I'll find a way.'

'You'll be a very clever fellow if you do. It's more likely that at some point, you'll be required to make a choice.' Roosevelt rose and started for the door. There he turned and looked at the younger man. 'We discussed what kind of choice it will be. I'm sure you haven't forgotten.' With a wave, he walked out, calling goodnight as he went.

Will was so angry, he barely remembered to respond with a goodnight of his own. He glared at the doorway.

You're wrong. I'll have it all. Without a choice. Without sacrificing any of it.

Somehow, I'll find a way to have it all.

3

It almost seemed that events conspired to allow Roosevelt to keep reminding Will of the need to make a choice. The young rancher was invited to be one of two featured speakers at the Fourth of July celebration over in Dickinson, the county seat of Stark County which adjoined Billings County on the east. Roosevelt was flattered by the invitation, and immediately accepted. But as the Fourth approached, everyone on the Elkhorn saw the boss grow increasingly nervous. He'd often said he was no orator. With his high voice, he was handicapped the moment he stepped on a platform.

Nevertheless, he worked hard on the speech, staying up till two and three in the morning several nights in a row. On Sunday, the third of July, a group which included Will left the Elkhorn and rode to the Maltese Cross, where they stopped overnight. Roosevelt was up long before dawn the next day. Shortly after first light, the group rode into Medora to hop an eastbound freight. It was less than fifty miles to Dickinson; they would arrive in plenty of time to see the big parade at ten o'clock.

The weather was perfect for a holiday; cloudless and cool. While they waited for the train, Will found himself glancing up and down the platform. He hadn't been in Medora since the day after he'd arrived. The depot brought back unpleasant memories.

Abruptly, he saw the skinny station agent looking his way and whispering to Wilmot Dow. When they were aboard the caboose of the freight rolling toward Dickinson, Dow took him aside:

'I'm not trying to alarm you, but I think you should be forewarned. Back at the station, Perkins told me Cletus Maunders is still talking about getting even with you. Guess it hurt his pride pretty badly when you stomped on his hand and the boss ran him off.'

The caboose swayed and rattled round a curve. Will tried to shrug as if he wasn't concerned. 'Mr Roosevelt said Maunders was that kind. I'm not surprised he's holding a grudge.'

'Thing is,' Dow went on, 'Perkins said Maunders and his two pals jumped on a freight for Dickinson late last night. They were already drunk as ticks in a vat of beer. I'd keep my eye peeled today.'

Will's stomach started to hurt. 'Thanks very much for the warning,' he said.

The county seat of Stark County had been laid out on a hillside overlooking the Heart River, which cut across the prairie south of town. Dickinson had never before celebrated the Fourth in an official way, so that made the day doubly festive. People from miles around had driven, ridden, or walked to the celebration. A big crowd lined the main streets as the Dickinson Silver Cornet Band struck up a march and stepped off to start the parade at one minute past ten.

Next in line came a corps of mounted horsewomen, their riding habits as elaborate as the trappings of their mounts. On a float created from a draped wagon rode thirty-eight little girls in white, each representing a state. The float drew heavy applause. So did the local Union Army veterans, who marched with tipsy enthusiasm but not much precision.

Farm machinery went by, and dignitaries in buggies. The parade proceeded to the town square, where it disbanded. Will kept searching the crowd for Cletus Maunders and his friends but didn't see them. Perhaps the three men had already drunk too much and passed out in one of Dickinson's dingy alleys.

A free picnic dinner was served on trestle tables in the square. Afterward the crowd was called to order for the programme. It began with a lengthy invocation. Then the first orator, a politician named John Rae, was introduced. He delivered a typical Independence Day speech – too long and too bombastic. The crowd grew restless.

Roosevelt followed Rae. The boss of the Elkhorn looked ill at ease as the master of ceremonies introduced him. He got very little applause from the bored spectators. When he acknowledged his introduction, soft laughter rippled through the crowd. Someone behind Will made a caustic remark about Roosevelt's voice. Will turned round but couldn't identify the offender.

Roosevelt launched into his address, speaking loudly enough so that even the men and boys clinging to nearby roofpeaks could hear him:

'I am particularly glad to have an opportunity of addressing you, my fellow citizens of Dakota, on the Fourth of July, because it always seems to me that those who dwell in a new territory, and whose actions therefore are peculiarly fruitful, for good and bad alike, in shaping the future, have in consequence peculiar responsibilities—'

The beginning didn't sound promising to Will. It was as flowery as Rae's, if not more so. The bright sun glared on Roosevelt's glasses. Someone in the front row interrupted to point this out. Pink-faced with embarrassment, he removed the glasses and said in an aside, 'There. I'm surprised anyone would want to see more of this phiz of mine. I'd expect it to be the other way around.'

The little joke provoked laughter, friendly this time. Roosevelt capitalized on it:

'Without my glasses, I can't see my text. That should improve the speech a hundred per cent.'

More laughter, loud and prolonged. With just a few sentences, Roosevelt had overcome the crowd's hostility. He smiled that dazzling smile and took a more confident stance at the podium. Wind snapped the tricolor bunting nailed all around the edge of the speaker's platform.

Will was watching from halfway back in the crowd. He was standing beside young A. T. Packard, the owner and editor of the *Bad Lands Cowboy*. The newspaperman had also ridden the freight train from Medora. But Will was hardly aware of him, or of the

314

rattle of firecrackers a block away – or of anything except the speech. Roosevelt seemed to be talking directly to him:

'But as you already know your rights and privileges so well, I am going to ask you to excuse me if I say a few words to you about your duties.'

Sentence by sentence, the address stung Will with its relevance to his own situation. There was nothing wrong with enjoying the material prosperity which the country had achieved, Roosevelt said. But that prosperity could become a destructive force if it took precedence over principle.

It was clear Roosevelt had committed most of his text to memory. He used his eyeglasses only a few times to remind himself of a word or phrase. He expanded and restated his theme – wealth must never be allowed to corrupt national or individual virtue.

I am going to ask you to excuse me if I say a few words to you about your duties—

Will knew what Roosevelt was really talking about. Choices. Choices between responsibility and the lack of it; between personal success and personal morality. He resented having to listen to one more discussion of the subject.

The crowd listened in silence, completely won over by the speaker and his idealistic message. When Roosevelt finished, there was another moment of quiet, then an eruption of applause punctuated by cheering.

Editor Packard said, 'Fine speech, eh?'

Will didn't answer. Packard gave him a puzzled look. 'Nothing to get angry about, is it?'

Again Will was silent. The editor didn't press the issue, saying instead, 'I've never heard Theodore speak before.'

'I have.'

'What? I thought you told me you met him only a few weeks ago.'

'That's right. But he sounds exactly like my father.'
And I'll be hanged if I'll listen to either of them.

5

Several people from Medora had gathered around Roosevelt at the foot of the platform steps. They were shaking his hand and slapping him on the back. The young newspaper editor went to join them. Will knew he should add his congratulations but he couldn't. He was still seething.

He turned away and walked swiftly toward the back of the crowd and across the square to a plank sidewalk. Head down, a frown on his face, he paced toward the next corner. He was completely unaware of his surroundings until the door of a saloon swung outward and whacked his right arm.

'Christ sake, boy, get outa the – thunderation!'

Will stopped short, turned toward the speaker – and froze. He'd forgotten to stay alert. Now he'd paid the price.

'Cletus? Cletus, hurry up an' come out here,' said the man called Sweeney. The second man from the depot, Chadburn, appeared behind the first in the saloon entrance. Will took a step. Sweeney grabbed his forearm with fingers that dug in and hurt.

Panicky, Will saw that no one in the street was paying attention to what must have struck them as just another saloon altercation.

'Caught us a fish, Cletus,' Sweeney said. 'A Medora minnow. You been hopin' to get this one on your hook for quite a spell.'

Cletus Maunders came shuffling through the sawdust spread on the saloon floor. He was unsteady on his feet, but he wasn't so drunk that he failed to recognize the prisoner. He licked his lips and smiled.

'I have,' he said. 'I surely have.'

CHAPTER XII

Maunders Again

Cletus Maunders was as filthy as Will remembered. He reeked of whiskey and other, less appetizing things. So did his cronies. They stepped from the saloon door and crowded Will on both sides. The younger of the two, Sweeney, kept a hand fastened on Will's arm. A few pedestrians were struck by the group's odd tension. But no one interfered.

Maunders squeezed his nose with his thumb and index finger. Then he held out the hand, fingers spread.

"Member this, punkin lily? 'Member the harm you done to it? Damn thing was stiff for nigh onto a month. Gonna have to chastise you for that.'

Chadburn faced away from the street. 'Not out here, Cletus.'

A withering look from Maunders. 'Why, sure. We'll sashay into the square and invite the whole town.' Chadburn reddened. Maunders' eyes slid back to Will. 'No, we want someplace real private. Alley, maybe—'

Will was watching for a chance to pull free of the grip of the emaciated, pop-eyed man called Sweeney. His stomach ached ferociously now. He stiffened when Maunders reached toward his cheek. Grinning, Maunders slapped him lightly and whispered:

'This time you'll be on your own, punkin lily. You won't have Four Eyes to come along and save your hash – *look out!*'

Will lunged away from Sweeney, then rammed his elbow in the man's midsection. As Sweeney staggered, Will spun round. A father, mother, and three little girls from the state float blocked the sidewalk on his left. He whirled and ran the other way.

A short distance down the block, an alley opened on his right. Will ran down the alley, toward the point where it intersected a second one which formed the crossbar of a T. He glanced over his shoulder. None of the three had appeared at the alley mouth. Maybe they hesitated to chase him in broad daylight with the town so crowded. He ran on.

Damn you for not keeping your eyes open! an inner voice raged. Margaret's face flickered in his mind. Smiling a smug smile, as if he'd done exactly what she expected of him.

At the junction of the alleys, Will headed left. He was into the turn when he heard a crash and a thump. Panicked, he looked back. Sweeney ran out of the saloon's rear door followed by Chadburn, then Maunders. They'd seen him flee into the alley and taken a shortcut.

'Catch the little bastard!' Maunders panted, already out of breath. Sweeney sprinted past Chadburn. Will ran only four or five steps before Sweeney tackled him and knocked him down.

Tears of fury filled his eyes as he struck the cinders and sand of the alley. *A back door. Why didn't you stay out in front? Why didn't you think?*

Bungler.

Sweeney grunted, climbed off Will and rolled him over. Will pulled his right knee against his belly and kicked. Sweeney jumped out of the way. He caught hold of Will's boot and twisted until Will slammed his palms against the dirt, his face wrenched by pain.

Maunders pulled his little finger out of one of his nostrils, flicked something off the tip and waved:

''Nuff, Sweeney.'

Sweeney let go. Will gasped and shook his head. Now that it was getting on toward midafternoon, no sunlight reached the alley. The shadows were cold. Will's teeth began to chatter.

'Get him up,' Maunders ordered, shutting the saloon's back door. Sweeney took one arm, Chadburn the other. Will was jerked to his feet.

He could barely stand on the twisted ankle. But he quickly forgot the pain. Chadburn was subjecting him to a strange kind of scrutiny. It wasn't quite a bullying look; Chadburn was almost smiling.

Will really hadn't paid much attention to Chadburn until now. He was a powerfully built man about Maunders' age. White hair hung down beneath his hat, half concealing his ears. White stubble showed all over his chin. He had plump, sun-reddened cheeks, a pink mouth, and eyes so large and softly blue, they were almost girlish. With no warning at all, he reached out and pinched Will's buttocks.

'Don't make trouble, now, punkin lily.' His faintly moist eyes darted to Will's lips. 'Wouldn't want to hurt a fine lookin' boy like you.'

'Just your type, huh?' Sweeney asked with a grin.

'Anything in pants is Chadburn's type,' Maunders said.

A vile taste filled Will's mouth all at once. He was scared to death. He knew that unless he got out of the alley under his own power, he might wind up being carried out. Wounded, dead, or – or God knew what, he thought with a glance at Chadburn. Godamighty! The man didn't even bother to deny what Maunders said about him.

Still staring at the prisoner, Chadburn ran the tip of his tongue across his upper lip. Maunders walked around a brimming rain barrel, and leaned back, his knee bent and his boot braced against the saloon wall. He leaned there, relaxing. His helpers had dragged Will out of the alley intersection. They were safe from observation by those on the street.

319

Maunders fingered his groin. 'Chadburn gave me an idea, punkin lily. The three of us spent every last cent on whiskey. Been drinkin' since sundown last night. All that liquor made us mighty randy. But we can't afford no whores.'

His gaze slid down Will's legs, then back to his face. 'Maybe we got us a passable substitute.'

'Say, maybe we do,' Sweeney said with a grin. 'Way I been feelin', anything short of a sheep'd be fine.'

Chadburn's breathing quickened. His fingers began to drum a little tattoo on Will's forearm. With unmistakable eagerness, he said:

'The storeroom of the saloon was empty, Cletus. Shall we take him in there?'

'Jesus, Chad. Sometimes I think all you got for brains are your balls. We gotta take him someplace where it won't make no difference if he hollers. South of town, maybe. Out past that river—'

Maunders sauntered forward, his revolver bobbing on his hip. He squeezed Will's cheeks between his palms:

'Ought to be a real nice walk for you, punkin lily. You can think about all the sweet stuff that's in store for you when—'

Will brought his right knee up into Maunders' groin. Maunders staggered and gasped. Will reached across Maunder's right hip and yanked an old Smith and Wesson from the worn leather holster. Chadburn and Sweeney were yelling and starting to pummel him. He shoved the muzzle against Maunders' belly and cocked the hammer.

'Let go,' he said to the men on either side of him. 'Turn me loose or I'll kill him.'

320

A cloud passed in front of the sun, darkening the alley even more. Sweeney swore and reached for the revolver. Maunders whispered, '*No*.'

Sweeney pulled back. Maunders eyed Will, trying to judge the extent of his nerve. Angry, Chadburn said:

'Shit, I'll bet he don't know how to use it, Cletus.'

'I do,' Will said.

'We ain't gonna wager on it and find out we was wrong,' Maunders said. He glanced at the gun barrel digging a crater in the stained front of his hunting shirt. 'What happens now, punkin lily?'

'You and your friends leave. I keep the gun and that's the end of it.'

'Until you send the Elkhorn crew after us?'

'No, I won't do that.'

Sweeney snorted. 'Don't trust the little son of a bitch, Cletus. It's three on one. We can dig his ditch for good.'

'Shut your damn mouth!' Maunders cried in a hoarse voice. Nervous, he peered at Will. 'You mean to say that if we let you go, you won't try to get even?'

'Not unless you make trouble for me in Medora.'

'We call it a draw, that it?'

Chadburn was furious: 'Cletus, you don't have to call it a draw with some weak-livered city boy who—'

'Shut *up*. The gun's in *my* gut, not yours.' For a second Will thought he detected a foxy glint in Maunders' eye. Then it was gone. Blowing rancid breath in Will's face, the older man said:

'All right, punkin lily. It's a draw. I'll put both my hands in the air. At the same time, Chad and Sweeney will let go of you. Then I'll back away from that pistol and walk toward my friends and we'll light out. There'll

321

be no trouble for you in Medora long as we don't get none either. Bargain?'

Will's right arm was aching with tension. The revolver felt heavy and sweat-slippery in his hand. His hand and forearm started to tremble. So did his right leg. He held steady by force of will and said:

'Bargain.'

'Okay, then. Let him go, lads.'

Grumbling, Sweeney and Chadburn released Will. He heard their boots scuff as they moved behind him. He concentrated his attention on Maunders, who had raised his dirt-encrusted hands over his head and was stepping backwards slowly.

Maunders put his weight on his right foot and winced.

'Got a pebble in my boot. I'm gonna try to shake it into another position. Don't get spooked and shoot me.'

Sweat shone like grease on Maunders' face. He lifted his right boot eight inches off the ground. In the process, he executed a turn, so that his left leg partially blocked Will's view of the right one. Maunders grasped the top of his right boot with both hands, a peculiar manoeuvre for loosening a pebble way down at the bottom of—

'Duck, Chad!' Sweeney shouted as Maunders yanked a hideout knife from his boot top.

Maunders pivoted back toward Will, his hand streaking upward for the throw. The hand started forward. Will levelled the Smith and Wesson and fired.

The badly aimed bullet tore through the outside of Maunders' right thigh. The impact of the shot staggered him. His knife hand flew open. The blade dropped and hit the ground.

Will hurled himself against the saloon wall. He bumped the rain barrel. Water sloshed on his sleeve.

Chadburn and Sweeney were too stupefied to draw

their revolvers. They stared at their friend, who was clutching his right leg with both hands. Blood leaked through a powder-blackened tear in his buckskin trousers, then oozed between his fingers.

'Oh Jesus it hurts, *Jesus*—'

From the direction of the street came a rising clamour:

'Was that a shot or a firecracker?'

'A shot.'

'Where'd it come from?'

'The alley behind the saloon.'

'We got to get out of here,' Maunders whimpered. Tears were trickling down his cheeks.

'Got to kill him first, Cletus.' Chadburn pulled his revolver.

The voices were growing louder. Maunders shook his head, weeping as he squeezed his wounded leg:

'We got to get away or they'll lock us up. You want to get locked up, you stay. You want to get chased and lynched, go ahead an' shoot him.' He turned and started hobbling.

Chadburn looked at Will and raised his revolver. Sweeney seized his arm. Will waited, knowing that if Chadburn decided to fire, he probably wasn't fast enough to beat him now that they both had guns in their hands. Sweeney heard the men approaching in the other alley around the corner. He shook Chadburn's arm:

'Don't do it. You're liable to hang. The satisfaction ain't worth the cost.'

Chadburn glared at Will a moment longer. Then he rammed his revolver back in the holster.

He and Sweeney raced forward to Maunders. They propped his arms over their shoulders. Maunders beat a fist on Chadburn's back. 'Come on. Hurry it up!'

The three of them turned left at the mouth of the alley beyond the saloon's back door. The instant they were gone, Will started to close his eyes. Then he saw the knife shining just a yard away. He sprang toward it, groaning when he put sudden weight on the ankle Sweeney had twisted. He snatched up the knife and flung it in the rain barrel, and Maunders' revolver after it. He wanted no questions. No more trouble. He just wanted the whole business over with, because he hadn't acquitted himself well. Out in front of the saloon, at the very moment he'd needed to think clearly, his ineptitude had undone him.

Men turned the corner from the other alley and then they were milling around him. He seemed to hear a dozen voices, all shouting the same questions:

'What happened, boy? Who fired a shot?'

In fascination, Will watched the last of a stream of small bubbles rise and burst on the surface of the rain barrel. The bubbles had streamed upward from the sinking gun.

The men kept shouting at him. He wiped his sweating face to gain time. Over the back of his hand he scanned the alley for signs of Maunders' blood. He saw none. The final bubbles popped in the rain barrel.

'I don't know who fired the shot,' he said finally. 'I heard it too. Must have come from the next street.'

In moments they were gone, pursuing the gunman. Will hurried toward the square to find the Elkhorn men. When he was asked why he was limping, he said a drunk had lurched into him and he'd twisted his ankle, that was all.

3

Leaner, browner and more fit than ever before, Will boarded an eastbound Northern Pacific express in mid-August.

He'd planned to stay on the Elkhorn until September first. But Gideon had written to suggest that he come back before that. They had to arrange plans for schooling, Gideon said. Since Roosevelt had no objection to the early departure, Will didn't argue.

He had said nothing about the encounter with Maunders and his friends. For weeks after the celebration, Maunders' name hadn't even been mentioned on the ranch. Will finally assumed the secret was safe.

Then, two days before he was to leave, Bill Sewall had returned from a trip to Medora with some startling news. One of Maunders' kin was saying Maunders had died in a sleazy hotel in Bismarck.

According to what Sewall had heard, Maunders and his friends had shown up in Bismarck about the middle of July, intending to drink and gamble for a few days. Obviously they'd got money somewhere; stolen it, most likely. Maunders had been wearing a dirty bandage on one leg, and limping. Soon pain drove him to a doctor. The wound had become infected. Mephitic gangrene had already set in. Maunders had lasted only a couple of weeks after that. His friends had buried him in a pauper's grave, then telegraphed the news to relatives. Neither Chadburn nor Sweeney had come back to Medora.

Expressionless, Will had listened to Sewall finish the story. The whole business left him with a bad taste. He felt neither glad that Maunders was dead nor, God help him, more than fleetingly sorry. What he felt most of all was a renewed sense of his own inferiority. His penchant for doing things wrong had precipitated the tilt in Dickinson.

Now he was at the depot, ready to board the train. In many ways he hated to leave. The weeks he'd spent in the Bad Lands were among the happiest and most rewarding he'd ever known. He had learned a few things about himself, some not very pleasant.

Roosevelt had come into town to see him off. So had some of the hands. Wilmot Dow was there, and Ferris, and Bob Beaufort. Roosevelt himself had just returned from a trip East. Gossip among the cowboys said he was tiring of a widower's existence, and spoke often of his old friend, Edith Carow.

Dow shook Will's hand and wished him good luck. Then Beaufort stepped up. Will especially valued the black cowboy's handshake, and the moment when Beaufort smiled and said, 'Come back next summer and we'll make you into a first-class wrangler. You already turned into a pretty good one.'

'Thank you, Bob. Look me up in Boston sometime. You've got the address—'

'Right here,' Beaufort patted his pocket.

Sylvanus Ferris of the Maltese Cross took his turn shaking hands. In a voice pitched so only Will could hear, he said:

'See? The summer turned out a lot better than you thought. And I'll bet you did a lot more than you thought you could.'

Will remembered how unsure of himself he'd been the first time he spoke with Ferris. Much of that uncertainty had indeed been unwarranted. He'd found that if he pushed himself, he could do many things he'd thought were beyond his capabilities. He'd even saved a man's life on the roundup. A good feeling.

But the confidence he'd built up had been severely undercut by his experience in Dickinson. There, he'd learned that the past hadn't really been laid to rest, and would continue to undo him when he least expected it. That was the final, discouraging lesson of the summer. Some things had changed, but not the most fundamental one.

He refused to show Ferris how he felt. He smiled and said, 'You're right, it did turn out a lot better.'

'Glad you feel that way.' Ferris clapped him on the shoulder. 'Safe journey to you.'

Roosevelt joined them. Ferris touched his hat brim

and sauntered off. Will was happy to have a moment alone with the ranchman. For weeks, his conscience had been bothering him.

'Mr Roosevelt, I made a mistake on Independence Day. I never told how well you spoke.'

Roosevelt looked at Will in a sober way. 'Generous of you to say that. I didn't compose that address with you in mind. I was stating what I believe. But when I spotted you in the crowd, frowning and looking ready to explode, I realized that perhaps I'd unconsciously included some phrases and some thinking that came right out of our discussion. I was speaking to an issue on which we disagreed and still do, I suppose. I'd have been thunderstruck if you'd been among my well-wishers afterward.'

'But I was rude not to tell you that you did a fine job.'

Roosevelt's eyes grew merry then. 'An apology along with a compliment! There's no need for the former – but it makes the latter doubly important. Thank you very much.'

The conductor called all aboard. The whistle shrilled. Plumes of steam shot from under the locomotive. Roosevelt added, 'You've been an asset to the ranch. I hope the summer's been to your liking also.'

He thought of Lon Adam and nodded. 'I'll never forget it.'

A few words about your duties—

Why did that damned speech nag him day in, day out? It had no application to him. He had no *duties* in connection with anyone but himself; and he'd already decided on the direction his life was going to take.

Oddly, Roosevelt thought of the same thing just then. Sunlight flashed on his glasses as he said, 'And medicine still captures your fancy, does it?'

'Yes, sir. Definitely.'

'That's fine if it's what you really want. However,

I'm sure your father will have strong opinions about its suitability as a career. Write and tell me whether there's an argument. And who wins.'

The train began to move. Will jumped up on the steps of the coach. He clung to the hand rail, frowning. The ranchman had just articulated a fear he'd been trying to ignore ever since it popped into his head some days ago. Gideon *would* have something to say. But what?

Roosevelt whipped off his big sombrero and wig-wagged it in farewell. The other cowboys waved their hats too. Roosevelt's voice boomed as the train pulled away:

'Delighted to have had you with us! Deeee—'

The rest was lost in the howl of the whistle.

CHAPTER XIII

What Gideon Said

Gideon liked to install the latest conveniences in his suite at the Fifth Avenue Hotel. He felt it was his duty as a newspaper publisher to stay abreast of the inventions that were appearing at a dizzying rate, and he had the money to buy anything when it was new and hence at its most expensive. Some of the conveniences didn't always prove to be convenient, however.

He was on the telephone, approving a long list of stock purchases one by one. The voice at the other end of the connection began to fade. Then, in a burst of crackling, it died altogether. A moment later the crackling was replaced by silence.

'Daniel? Can you hear me, Daniel?'

The instrument emitted a low buzz.

Gideon cursed. He'd been speaking with Daniel Rothman, the eldest son of his Boston banker, Joshua Rothman. The Wall Street firm of Rothman Freres had been started by Daniel and his younger brother Micah just five years ago. It was already one of the most successful brokerage houses in New York.

Now Gideon's attention – and his wrath – were fixed on the telephone. Timing was essential to the success of a large-scale manoeuvre in the stock market, and the telephone had just caused his timing to misfire. He tore the instrument from its mounting, yanked the wires out of the wall and hurled the whole clanging mess on the floor.

'Good heavens,' Julia cried. 'What on earth are you doing?' She was just coming through the foyer, her arms full of Lord and Taylor parcels.

'Destroying Mr Bell's infernal machine.' Gideon pointed to the wreckage. 'That's the fourth time in two days it's betrayed me. The last time, too.'

He wrenched the crank of another recently installed device, the telegraph call box. Then he snatched a Western Union blank from a desk pigeonhole and scribbled on it:

D. ROTHMAN, ROTHMAN FRERES, WALL ST CITY. BUY ALL ON LIST AT PRICES QUOTED. TELEPHONE NO LONGER OPERATING. USE MESSENGER HENCEFORTH.

He signed his initials, cursing under his breath.

'Calm down, dear,' Julia said. 'Surely something can be done to protest such bad service—'

Gideon's face lit with inspiration. 'You're absolutely right.' He grabbed another blank and wrote a message to the telephone company:

TAKE OUT YOUR DAMNABLE MACHINE.

To that one he signed his full name.

Julia bent over his shoulder, watching. The touch of

her breast stirred him in a familiar but pleasurable way. She tapped a finger on the second telegram.

'I don't believe they'll transmit profanity, dear.'

'I know. But it will get their attention.'

Julia suppressed a smile and walked to the window. The late summer sunshine lent a golden cast to Madison Square, and to the suite's large sitting room. As she let the curtain fall, she asked:

'Is Will home yet?'

'No. He promised to be here by five.' Gideon indicated a book on the floor next to his favourite chair. 'I'm ready for him.'

'Dear – ' she faced him, her dark eyes luminous in the muted light. ' – I'm sorry to say this, but I can't see the sense of what you're planning to do.'

'You can't see the sense?' he exclaimed. 'Julia, his chosen profession is one which is in complete disarray!'

'Even so, we both feel—'

'Please, Julia,' he interrupted, almost testily. 'Let me handle it my way. Will's decision is extremely important to all of us.'

That, she understood. Gideon was constantly worrying about who would head the family when he was gone, and Will was his father's brightest hope. She supposed that explained all the reading and research Gideon had done in preparation for the forthcoming talk – and his nervousness now.

'By the way, you should read this.' He showed her a letter. 'It arrived in the afternoon delivery. It's from Theodore. He's back at Sagamore Hill and may go to Europe. To see Miss Carow, I suspect.'

She read the letter, her face brightening:

'Oh, Gideon, how grand. He's absolutely glowing in his praise of Will's work this summer.'

Gideon nodded. Will had been home for a couple of weeks; two days earlier, the family had steamed down to New York aboard *Auvergne*.

330

'The trip worked miracles on his attitude,' Julia went on.

'More than I could have hoped for,' Gideon agreed. 'I never imagined Dakota would give a direction to his life, but it did. That's why I'm so anxious for him not only to make the right decision, but to stick with it. A wrong choice now could ruin everything.'

He strode to the window; whipped the curtain aside. 'Where the devil is he, anyway?'

'It's a long way to the Annexed District, remember.' She was referring to the section of the city which lay beyond the Harlem River in Westchester County. It was open country for the most part, popular with young sportsmen. Gideon kept one of his carriages, the expensive Brewster, at the city stables of the Coaching Club. Will had taken the carriage for the day, hired four horses at a livery stable, and gone to the Annexed District to practise four-in-hand driving.

'And coaches do break down,' Julia added.

'Yes, but—'

He started at the sound of knocking. Of course it wouldn't be Will; he'd have walked right in.

It was the messenger boy from the neighbourhood telegraph office, responding to Gideon's signal on the call box. The boy took the two printed messages. He was all smiles until he saw the second one:

'Oh, sir, it isn't permissible to send—'

'Just make sure you give it to your supervisor. I wish to have this thing removed as soon as possible.' He kicked the wreckage of the phone, producing a feeble *ping* from the bell.

A tip pacified the shocked boy. Just as the messenger was leaving, Will walked out of the elevator and into the foyer. Julia spied him and gasped.

Will's suntanned face was filthy. There were big black stains on his bottle green coat, gold waistcoat, and white trousers. His boots were dirty, and a fine rust-coloured powder had sifted through his hair. The messenger boy gaped as Will said:

'Those damned elevated railways will kill us all.'

'What happened to you?' Julia asked.

'Nothing happened to me. Oh, I got shaken up a little, but otherwise I'm fine.'

Gideon shut the door in the messenger's face. 'You didn't have an accident with the carriage—?'

Glum, Will nodded. 'The Third Avenue Railroad's the culprit. I made the mistake of returning that way. The usual deluge of cinders, oil, and sparks came down. The off leader took a hot coal on his neck and bolted. The horses are all right – ' He dropped into a chair, sighing. ' – but the Brewster's a total wreck. I seem to make a botch of everything.'

2

At first Gideon was upset that one of his best carriages had been overturned and wrecked. Will was apologetic, and repeatedly promised to earn the money for a new vehicle. Somewhat testily, Gideon replied that a Brewster wasn't the same as the bakery wagon Carter had destroyed, and that unless his son had an income comparable to Jay Gould's, he might be a long time paying off the debt.

A moment after he'd made the remark, he apologized. He knew Will was a first-class whip, a fast driver but not a reckless one. And runaway horses were a frequent sight on the streets beneath the Third, Sixth, and Ninth Avenue Elevated Railroads. Once Gideon calmed down, he was inclined not to blame his son for the accident. He finally said so.

Will was grateful. He told his father that immediately after the wreck, he'd sent a bootblack to fetch the stable owner. From that individual he'd obtained a written statement acknowledging the horses were returned unhurt. He passed the paper to his father. 'Now he won't try to sue you for trumped up injuries to his animals.'

Next Will had squared matters with a policeman from the patrol district in which the accident had occurred. The policeman had been sympathetic, and had helped Will find and hire some men with a wagon to remove the wreckage of the coach from Third Avenue.

Gideon was pleased by the presence of mind his son had displayed. It was a characteristic new to Will's personality; surely one of the beneficial results of his summer with Roosevelt. Another result of that summer remained to be discussed.

'I'm thankful you weren't injured,' Julia was saying.

Gideon nodded. 'So am I. Do you want some whiskey?'

'No thanks.'

'Care to get rid of that coat? I'd like to have a talk with you.'

'A talk? What about?'

'Your plans.'

Will stuck his scuffed boots out in front of him. 'As far as I'm concerned they're settled. I don't want to enter Harvard as a regular undergraduate. I want to take the fall entrance exams for the Medical School.'

'You mean it isn't too late?' Julia asked.

'No,' Will answered. 'They're given just before the term starts at the end of September. If I pass and the school still has an opening, I can enrol right away. I want to.'

Gideon sat in his chair, facing his son. He laced his fingers between his knees as he leaned forward.

'I appreciate the sincerity of your wish. I appreciate that you met a man out West whose work you thought important, and worthy of emulation. I had a high regard for the one doctor I knew well – Cincinnatus Lemon, the man who took care of me when my eye was put out at Fort Delaware. But the worthiness of the work doesn't change the nature of the medical profession – or the way the public perceives it. Medicine has never been an altogether respectable calling. Have you ever read the apocryphal books of the Bible?'

'No, sir.'

'In Ecclesiasticus, the author says, "He that sinneth before his Maker – let him falleth into the hands of the physician."'

Julia smiled. But Will didn't. He dropped his elbow on the chair arm and put his chin on the heel of his palm, watching his father warily.

'Since that uncomplimentary statement was made centuries ago,' Gideon went on, 'there's been very little reason for anyone to amend it. Medicine has always been a haven for idiots and charlatans. It still is. This sterling work – ' He picked up the book at his side. ' – is *Dr Paul's Remedy Compendium*. It was published just last year.'

He opened the book. 'I quote. *Sleeplessness. Take half a pound of fresh hops and put into a small pillow case and use for a pillow*.'

He turned the page. '*Moles – to remove. Apply nitric acid with a pointed quill toothpick*. I'm sure that will remove moles, all right. Half your skin, too.' Another page. '*Baldness – to cure. One pound pressed hemlock bark – *'

He snapped the book shut. 'I needn't go on. The point's obvious. Here we are in the modern world, and someone who styles himself a doctor is writing prescriptions that are mostly nonsense, and in some cases downright harmful.' He waved the book. 'Unfortunately, this is all too typical of the profession.'

'I admit the truth of what you say, Papa. I just don't know why you're saying it.'

'I should think that would be obvious.'

Ignoring Gideon's sharp tone. Will shook his head. 'I watched Lon Adam cure sickness and help people who were suffering. When I saw that, I saw something I admired. I also discovered I could do it. I mean I have the stomach for the grisly part. The sight of blood doesn't bother me. I want to go to medical school and I'm not going to change my mind.'

'But you must have all the facts before you commit yourself,' Gideon insisted, jumping up and beginning to pace. 'Medical education in this country is a joke. Anyone who apprentices for a few weeks can obtain an impressive-looking degree from a diploma mill.'

Will nodded. 'Adam had one of those.'

'The medical schools aren't much better than the apprentice programmes. Charles Eliot has made some improvements at Harvard since he took over as president, but professors of the calibre of Oliver Holmes are rare.'

'Then if Harvard isn't all that good, I should have no trouble getting in. I can enter without regular college training so long as I pass the tests.'

'But you have to be twenty-one to graduate,' Gideon countered. 'I know that for a fact.'

'Harvard has a four-year programme. If I enrol in that, I'll get more thorough training than I would in their three-year programme, and I'll be just the right age at graduation.'

Grudging admiration showed on Gideon's face for an instant. 'All right – let's grant that you can earn your degree. What can you look forward to then? Damned little except gruelling work. Most doctors have to turn to something else to earn a living.'

Will was growing exasperated with Gideon's negative thinking. 'I know that.'

'As for earning the respect of society in general – you might as well hope to have Lillian Russell fly through that window in the next thirty seconds. A few, a very few doctors are lucky enough – or well-connected enough – to have a practice that gives them both a good income and some social standing. Such practices don't aid and comfort the suffering masses, however. Far from it. In a profitable practice, the doctor only treats a few wealthy households – servants included. All his work is performed in the mansions of his clients. Open an office for anything besides scheduling your time or handling your accounts and you're telling the world you're second rate. To use an office to treat ordinary folk – or to work in a hospital or free clinic – either one's an outright admission of failure.'

'Papa, let me ask you something. Whatever happened to the idea of people in this family helping others – regardless of the economic consequences?'

'That idea is very much alive.'

'How can that be? You obviously don't want me to go to medical school—'

'On the contrary, sir!' Gideon retorted. 'I said no such thing!'

Their voices had risen, and now a fist hammered the wall of one of the adjoining bedrooms. 'Quiet down or we'll call the manager!'

Ignoring the complaint, Will scowled at his father. 'By God, sir, you've got me confused. Just what the hell is it you want of me?'

3

Gideon drew a long breath. He avoided Julia's eyes; her face showed her disapproval of the way he'd allowed the discussion to become a shouting match. He resumed his pacing, but more slowly, and said:

'I apologize for raising my voice. I had no intention of starting a quarrel. I simply don't want you to decide to go into medicine, then belatedly recognize its negative aspects and quit.'

'I recognize every one of them right now,' Will declared. Gideon didn't believe him. Still, he was greatly encouraged by the conviction in his son's voice. When he spoke, his warm tone showed it:

'Just one final word, then. Your stepmother and I really don't want to discourage you. The fact is, if you do go ahead, it will make us extremely proud. Despite all the drawbacks, a career as a doctor would be in the best tradition of this family.'

Will's jaw had fallen. 'If you'll forgive my saying so, Papa, you have a damned strange way of encouraging someone.'

Smiling again, Julia said, 'Your father felt it was his duty to make certain you understood what you were undertaking.'

'I do,' Will told her. 'I know it won't be easy to make a handsome living as a doctor. But I think I can do it. In any case, I'll bear all the risks involved in the decision.'

In fact, some of his father's remarks had come as a happy revelation. Gideon had mentioned the very kind of doctor he wanted to be; one who served a select group of affluent patients and grew rich and renowned in the process.

I'll keep the promise. You'll see, Carter.

Gideon strode forward and clasped his son's arm. 'I know you can handle the course work at Harvard, no matter how diffi – oh good God.'

He drew his hand away from Will's sleeve. His fingers were sticky with a dark brown substance.

'Axle grease,' Will said with a rueful smile. 'That's about all that's left of the Brewster.'

'It makes no difference. None!'

Father and son embraced. Julia could see her husband's face over Will's shoulder. Gideon looked happy for the first time in months.

CHAPTER XIV

A Successful Man

At first Will was ecstatic over his father's endorsement of the decision to go to medical school. Then memories of some of Gideon's statements about the security of a medical career began to erode that enthusiasm. Forty-eight hours after the discussion, he was again in a doubtful frame of mind.

Despite a steady rain, he set out to walk and think. From Madison Square he headed up Broadway – the Rialto, New Yorkers called it. Here you found all the best theatres, some with their marquees already electrified.

One day Eleanor's name might appear on the gaudy posters pasted up in front of a New York playhouse. She might even have her name listed above the title of the show – a sign of true eminence. His sister, at least, was sure of the rewards that her profession offered.

Of course she'd never be respectable. The best people considered actors and actresses no better than those who earned a living in trade. If a Society hostess invited the cast of a hit play to perform for her guests, the cast members were never allowed to dine or mingle with the regular guests.

I want more than that, he thought as he passed the Standard Theatre at Thirty-third Street. *I don't want just the sufferance of the best people. I want acceptance.*

A roast chestnut vendor was closing up his little cart at the corner of Thirty-fourth. The vendor gave Will a puzzled stare as he hurried by, a faraway look on his face. To the vendor it seemed as if Will was trying to

338

gaze all the way to the rocky ledges of Central Park, where wild goats wandered.

Will was actually trying to plan his future. Certain things about it were already evident. For one, he knew that if he were to find a place in society, he'd have to do it on his own. Even if he wanted to live off the Kent fortune – which he didn't – the money would never provide an entrée to the best circles; it was too new.

The Kent name wouldn't help, either. Might be a hindrance, in fact. Besides the notorious Ward McAllister encounter, there was something else cloudy, even sinister, about Gideon's past, something to do with the death of a man named Thomas Courtleigh.

No one ever said Gideon was responsible for Courtleigh's death. But Will's father had been in Courtleigh's office when Courtleigh was killed in mysterious circumstances. Will had also got strong hints at home that Courtleigh was the person responsible for his stepmother's stabbing at the same time. He remembered that part vividly. For days, he and Carter had kept a vigil at Julia's beside, expecting her to die. Gideon had gone to Chicago, beside himself with anger and grief. And while he was in Chicago, Thomas Courtleigh had been shot to death—

Whatever else was unclear about the whole affair, one thing was certain. It had left the Kent name permanently tainted.

The rain pelted Will's face. He blinked and looked around. He'd walked all the way to the fifties in Fifth Avenue. Fifty-second Street was just ahead. On his left rose the huge, fortress-like triple brownstone built by William Henry Vanderbilt. Both Vanderbilt and his father, the old Commodore, had been immensely wealthy. Neither had been accepted into Society. Yet one of William Henry's sons, William K. Vanderbilt, was now one of Society's leaders. His wife was the woman who had humbled Mrs Astor.

339

He crossed Fifty-second to the northwest corner, and the house Mrs William K. Vanderbilt had commissioned Richard Morris Hunt to design. Depending on your views about mixing the architecture of a French chateau and a Renaissance palace and erecting the result on Fifth Avenue at a cost of three million, the mansion was a masterpiece or a monstrosity.

For Will the house had special significance. With luck and diligence, you *could* climb higher than your parents had been able to climb. You could escape the limitations they had placed on themselves – and you – by reason of their birth, occupation, and behaviour. To most Americans, that sort of highly visible accomplishment was epitomized by admission to Society.

Will genuinely wanted to help others. That was why medicine held such a strong appeal for him. But he also wanted to fulfil his promise – and, not incidentally, disprove his dead mother's accusations. This morning, in the rain, he was overwhelmed by a conviction that there was only one way for him to realize both ambitions, and that was to live on a footing equal with the country's elite.

It was a thoroughly American goal, he reminded himself. The half-French, half-English bastard who'd founded the Kent family had shipped to the colonies for precisely the same reasons – to escape the limitations of his past and better himself.

William K. Vanderbilt's mansion perfectly summed up Will's new, sharply focused ambition. It was the kind of house he wanted to own someday. It was inhabited by the kind of people with whom he wanted to associate. He leaned against the stone stoop of the mansion, studying the roofline with an envious expression. Suddenly the front door flew open.

A man in the maroon livery of the Vanderbilts appeared, gazing down through the rain to where Will stood on the sidewalk.

'No loitering on these premises. Move along!'

By God he *would* find a way to make his chosen career bring him all this. Abruptly, then, he knew he must take an important precaution before the family returned to Boston – and certainly before he tackled the medical school entrance examinations. He had to speak with a doctor of the kind Gideon had described. A wealthy, successful city practitioner. Before he invested four years in a hard programme of study, it would be wise to verify that there were doctors who lived well from their profession.

'I said move along!' the footman called. 'If you don't, we'll flash a message to the precinct house.'

Will grinned and held up his hands in a peacemaking gesture:

'All right, I'm going.' He started to walk backwards. 'But I'll be coming to visit one of these days. I'll be invited.'

The footman stood gaping from his shelter under the massive stonework blazoned with acorns and oak leaves, the emblems of the family. Will did a kind of impromptu jig on the sidewalk, paying no attention when a hack rolled through a puddle and sprayed him with muddy water.

'Invited *here?*' the footman said to himself, closing the massive door. 'He's utterly mad. What is happening to New York?'

2

The staff of the *Union* included a reporter who specialized in scientific subjects. Will went to see him at Gideon's suggestion, though he didn't tell his father the precise reason for the visit. He merely said he wanted to do some investigation of the medical field. Gideon seemed to approve.

The reporter was cordial when Will dropped in, and agreed to help him contact one of the town's better doctors:

'I suppose you want to speak with the most skilful man you can find?'

'Skilful? Not necessarily. I want to meet a successful one.'

'There's a difference?'

'To me there is.'

The reporter frowned, less friendly now. The next day he sent a list of names to the hotel. One name was underlined, with a marginal notation:

Said to have a net worth in excess of one million. This would make him most 'successful' of those listed.

Will fumed over the cynicism. But he soon pushed aside his annoyance. All that mattered was locating a prosperous doctor who would answer some candid questions. That, the reporter had done:

Cyrus Coates Vlandingham, M.D.

Even the name had the ring of success.

3

Dr Cyrus Coates Vlandingham conducted his practice in a number of large homes in and adjacent to Stuyvesant Square. Here dwelled what was called the Faubourg Saint-Germain Set – New York's oldest and most prestigious families, aristocrats who refused to follow the 'new swells' who were moving uptown to Fifth Avenue.

Vlandingham maintained a tiny office near Madison Square, but this was solely for handling his books. He had no consulting rooms. Will sent his note to the bookkeeping office. After two days he received a reply.

Dr Vlandingham agreed to meet him, but it would have to be at Sherry's, where the doctor always lunched when in the city. Vlandingham's note then made gratuitous mention of summering in Newport, a small resort town on an island in Narragansett Bay. Forty or fifty years earlier Newport had been a popular warm-weather retreat for Southern rice and cotton planters. Now it was beginning to attract some of the better New York families.

Will put on his best outfit and took a hack to Sherry's at the appointed time. A pompous head waiter with gleaming patent leather pumps and waxed moustache points bowed him to Dr Vlandingham's regular table in a quiet alcove.

The doctor was in his late fifties. A husky man; broad-shouldered, with a midsection resembling a prize pear. Large dark eyes and a deep, hearty voice instantly inspired confidence. He wore expensive clothes.

Will marvelled at the nonchalance with which Vlandingham ordered luncheon and wine for both of them – in French. As the waiter glided away, Vlandingham said:

'I am of course familiar with your family, Mr Kent. And with your father's newspaper. A socialist rag, if you don't mind my saying so. The *Union*'s soft position on the Haymarket bombers is particularly dangerous to American institutions. Men like those anarchists waste the time of our judiciary. They're animals and they've proved it. They deserve lynching, not due process.'

From the pocket of his waistcoat the doctor took a small gold box. Out of the box came a gold toothpick.

'But your note said you were contemplating a medical career, not one in journalism.'

'That's right, sir.'

'Happy to hear you've chosen something respectable.' An unctuous smile. Then Vlandingham began to work the gold toothpick between two lower front teeth.

Will resented Vlandingham's remarks about the *Union*, although he'd heard similar criticism many times before. He supposed it was a tribute to the power of his father's newspaper that the doctor had agreed to this meeting in spite of his disgust with the *Union*'s editorial viewpoint.

Presently the doctor finished probing between his teeth and laid the toothpick aside. An obsequious sommelier served the wine. There was an elaborate ritual involving the drawing of the cork, Vlandingham sniffing it, the waiter pouring a little into Vlandingham's glass, and the doctor sipping. After ten seconds of frowning reflection, he gave a nod of approval. At that point the waiter filled both glasses.

'I believe you'll enjoy the wine,' Vlandingham remarked as he took another sip. 'It's an unpretentious but frolicsome little Vouvray.' To Will it tasted like a cold, faintly sweet white wine, nothing more. He knew the fault was with himself, not the wine. He was increasingly in awe of the doctor.

'By the way, Mr Kent. Lest we conduct this interview on the basis of mistaken assumptions, I must inform you that my practice does not lend itself to apprentices. I have never had one, in fact.'

'I'm not looking for an apprenticeship, sir. If I can pass the entrance tests next month, I plan to study at Harvard.'

'Oh, do you. Well, university training seems to be the preferred method these days. I was educated under the apprentice system, and I remain partial to it.' A purse of the lips, quick and self-satisfied. 'It *is* the method advocated in the Hippocratic oath.'

They drank more wine.

'Have you decided to undertake any specialized training at Harvard, Mr Kent?'

Will smiled. 'No, Doctor, I hadn't thought that far. I'm just starting to cram for the entrance tests.'

'A specialty is no laughing matter, sir! It can be highly lucrative. I'd suggest you consider one in particular. The treatment of female diseases.'

He leaned back, twirling his wine glass. 'It's a specialty which neither taxes the practitioner's intelligence nor unduly dominates his time. That's because all female complaints, from *prolapsus uteri* to nervous headaches to various cancers, have but one source – the uterus. And one cause – some deficiency therein. Despite the claims of a few crackpots, the old, familiar treatments are still the best. I refer to application of leeches – injections – cauterization. Do consider it, sir. It can be worth a great deal of money to you. Especially in a well-to-do neighbourhood.'

At that, Vlandingham allowed himself a smile. Will was impressed.

Primed by the wine, the doctor grew less formal. He draped an arm over the plush banquette and said:

'Harvard's supposed to have a good medical school. The trouble is, too many universities are employing professors who teach radical rot. Listerism—'

He gave the word a dirty sound. Will had done some reading about Joseph Lister. The English surgeon believed in using carbolic acid to prevent transmission of infection. Lister had stated the idea more than twenty years before, but it still was not universally accepted. Even some of the Harvard medical faculty violently opposed it. Vlandingham wanted to be sure Will had no doubt about his opinion:

'Listerism is nonsense. Only last week, I treated a young female patient afflicted with a mild case of puerperal fever. One hour later I supervised the delivery of another patient's fine infant son, and I saw no need to perform foolish, ritualistic hand-washings in between. Of course it might be a sensible precaution for doctors who must work in the public almshouses, and in general hospitals. There the air is usually foul, and consequently a carrier of disease.'

The disdainful expression on Vlandingham's face said that of course he never found it necessary to enter such low establishments. Still, a hand-washing might have been in order, Will thought. The doctor's fingernails looked none too clean.

After pouring more wine, Vlandingham raised his glass.

'Here's to your ambition, Mr Kent. Now in what specific way may I be of assistance?'

Will began his carefully planned appeal:

'I need advice, Dr Vlandingham. Can I look forward to a decent future if I study medicine? I believe it's a doctor's duty to help as many people as he can. It's that aspect that started me thinking about medical school in the first place—'

'Laudable, very laudable.' But Vlandingham had lost interest. Even as he spoke, he was shifting his attention to three fashionably dressed young women at a nearby table. His eyes grew moist as he watched them. Will went on:

'On the other hand, I don't want to become a doctor and starve.'

Vlandingham's chuckle had an arch sound; Will had recaptured his interest:

'Do I appear to be starving, Mr Kent?'

'No, but – maybe you're an exception.'

'Quite right. I am an exception because I have chosen to be. You can make the very same choice.'

Will shook his head, dubious. 'A lot of people, my own father among them, tell me that being a doctor means being a pauper too.'

346

'People who say that are thinking solely of run-of-the-mill physicians. Short-sighted mediocrities who permit their altruism to override their common sense. I was born amid the rocks of New Hampshire. Early on, I decided I would never tolerate the sort of poverty my father endured in a lifetime of farming. When I finished my apprenticeship I married a young woman of poor health but impeccable family connections. She's long dead now, God rest her—'

Again his eyes slid across the rim of his glass to the breasts of one of the young women. A sip; a delicate belch. Then he dabbed his lips with the back of a veined hand and continued:

'The various entrées my wife provided before her untimely death enabled me to establish a practice which now earns in excess of one hundred thousand dollars per year. How much in excess we shall leave to your imagination. But I assure you, Mr Kent – it is entirely possible to practise the healing arts without wearing the hair shirt. Does that answer your question?'

'Yes, Doctor. It does.'

'Excellent! Believe me, doctors who go hungry have *chosen* to go hungry. They regard their oath as more important than the contents of an investment portfolio – an error I do not make, I assure you. Then, having engineered their own failure, they point an accusatory finger at any physician who is successful.'

Vlandingham noted a flicker of uncertainty in Will's eyes. He leaned forward:

'One must not, of course, leave the impression that nothing matters except profit. The practice of medicine is important in and of itself. But I make no apology for plying my skills among those who can best afford to pay. Each physician serves a certain segment of humanity either by chance or by choice. Some choices, however, are incomprehensible. My older brother is also a doctor. Growing up in New Hampshire together, we were quite close. He had one queer streak in his makeup, however. He seemed to consider our father's toil on the farm acceptable. Even ennobling, somehow. Ridiculous, eh? My brother and I started on the same road. Our paths soon parted, however. Clement married the daughter of the man under whom he served his apprenticeship. An old country practitioner. A misguided dodderer who believed his first obligation was to his patients, not himself. My foolish brother caught that disease and hied himself to the worst slum in this city—'

'He practises in New York?'

Vlandingham nodded. 'The need was keenest in the slums, he said with that superior air I quickly came to loathe. Perhaps he likes the slums because he had no competition. Everyone wants to practise in my part of town. Only a madman or a hack would choose his. But he's stayed there to this day, surviving God knows how. His wife died eighteen months ago, worn out by helping him eke out a pathetic living. We never see one another. I can't stand his odour of failure. Or his stupidity.'

Vlandingham finished his wine. 'Why should a doctor choose to serve any segment of humanity except the best? The answer is, he shouldn't. Not if he possesses an iota of intelligence or self-esteem. No, Mr Kent,' he concluded in a reflective way, 'be neither ashamed of your desire to make money in medicine, nor doubtful of your ability to do so.'

Will watched his host with admiring eyes. Overwhelmed by Vlandingham's worldliness and hence persuaded by his arguments, he silently agreed with everything the doctor said. Cyrus Coates Vlandingham was obviously a successful man, and one worth emulating. When Will went into practice, his hands might be cleaner, but his style of life would be comparable. And by means of his skill, he'd rise to the topmost level of

348

society and leave the other Kents and their questionable reputation far behind.

The waiter arrived with plates bearing silver dishes.
In each dish, raw oysters on the half shell rested on a
bed of rock salt. Vlandingham made an appreciative
murmur, then added a final thought:

'The splendid thing about medicine is that it *can*
serve the practitioner as well as the patient. One must
only remember to put first things first—'

His brown eyes slid past Will to one of the young
women at the nearby table. She had raised her arm.
Now she lowered it, concealing the lush curve of her
breast. Vlandingham sighed, then noticed Will
watching.

He broke into a big smile. Winked and said:

'First things first – eh, Mr Kent?'

Will smiled too. 'Absolutely.'

'I believe you'll make a very intelligent doctor.' So
saying, Vlandingham attacked his first oyster with a
small silver fork. Part of the oyster refused to come
free of the shell. With no hesitation, the doctor laid his
fork aside and resorted to his fingers. He popped the
remaining bit of oyster into his mouth, ate it with lip-
smacking gusto, then licked his fingers one by one.

CHAPTER XV

Journey's End

The late September day carried a bitter foretaste of
winter. The sky was grey, the wind gusty, the intermit-
tent rain unusually cold. The rain grew heavier just as
Will reached the foot of the massive marble staircase.

It had a set of steps on each side, leading up to a landing and the main entrance of the Harvard Medical School.

The school building stood on Boylston Street at Exeter, in Boston. After having been located near Massachusetts General Hospital for nearly forty years, the school had moved to this new, more modern structure in 1883.

Will shivered as he hurried up the steps. Rain dripped from his hat, and despite kidskin gloves, his hands were growing numb. He carried a small, cheap satchel. The satchel contained his admission papers, including one which verified that he'd passed the examinations in English, Latin, physics, chemistry, and one elective – he'd picked botany – and had therefore been admitted to the medical school.

The steps were slippery. Will kept his eye on them as he rushed to the top. Consequently he failed to see another young man coming up the stairs on the opposite side. On the landing, the two of them collided.

Will's left shoe slid out from under him. If he hadn't grabbed the balustrade with his left hand, he'd have taken a bad fall. As it was, his flailing loosened his grip on the satchel. It shot away, flung into a high arc that ended a few seconds later on the pavement of busy Boylston Street.

He clutched the stone railing and watched a team pulling a brewery wagon clip-clop over the satchel, knocking it back and forth under their hooves. When the wagon passed, he saw that the satchel's clasp had broken open. He started to run down the steps. Suddenly the wind scooped the papers from inside the satchel and scattered them in all directions.

'Oh my God,' he said in disgust, stopping.

From the landing, the other young man said, 'I'm really sorry, old fellow. My fault, I'm afraid.'

Will turned and forced himself to say, 'Just an accident. No one's fault.'

The other young man looked relieved. He was a year or two older than Will. And fat – Lord above, he was fat. If Vlandingham was a pear, this chap was a giant melon, with a smaller melon perched on top. Curly red-gold hair, soaked now, lay close to his head. His face and ungloved hands were white and soft as bread dough. His plain muffler and dark, tent-like overcoat looked homemade.

The rain slacked off abruptly. Will was nervous about walking through the doors of Harvard Medical School for the first time. The building had a forbidding quality. So he was almost grateful for a distraction, although he'd have preferred some other kind. There was no point in rushing to collect his papers. They were ruined; soaked by muddy water and torn by the traffic. Even as he looked down, a sway-backed hack horse paused and made a steaming deposit on one of them.

Will's mouth dropped open. Students were coming up both sides of the staircase. Some – upperclassmen, to judge from their studied air of boredom – laughed at his bad luck. Others, inexperience clearly written on their faces, did not. But he quickly saw the humour in the situation and broke out laughing. The fat boy joined in.

'New student, are you?' he said to Will. In marked contrast to his appearance, his voice was forceful, even a trifle bullying. He pronounced *are* as if it were spelled *ah*.

'That's right. My name's Will Kent.'

'Drew Hastings.'

They shook hands in a solemn way. Hastings' hand was much stronger than it looked.

'From Boston?' Will asked.

'Born in Bangor, Maine. I live in Hartford, Connecticut now.' It came out *Hahtford*.

351

'Are you taking the four year programme?'

A shake of the head. 'Three. You?'

'Four – if I can survive that long.'

'Well, the addition of *cum laude* after my degree is a luxury the Hastings family can't afford. That's the only substantial difference between the programmes, you know. After four years, you graduate doctor of medicine *cum laude*.'

He sounded defensive. And what he'd said about the programmes was oversimplified. Will saw no point in arguing, though.

Hastings wiped a stubby nose that had developed a drip.

'By George, I truly am sorry I didn't see you.'

Will laughed again and pointed to the paper on which the horse had relieved himself.

'That's a hell of a way to start, isn't it? There's one consolation. Things surely can't get worse.'

'Oh, I don't know,' Hastings countered in a teasing tone. 'Because of the local laws, the school is always short of cadavers. I hear underclassmen are sometimes sent out to dig up one or two.'

'*Dig—?*'

'Figuratively or otherwise. No questions asked.' Hastings glanced at the papers littering the street. 'I wouldn't even bother to pick those up. Come on, let's get out of this wretched weather.'

Will didn't move. 'What's the matter?' Hastings asked. 'Haven't changed your mind, have you?'

Will's chin came up a little. 'Not on your life.'

'Then let's go in.'

'You go ahead. I'll get my satchel. The papers are ruined but maybe the satchel isn't.'

'Suit yourself,' Hastings said with an amiable shrug. He turned and marched through the doors.

Students continued to stream up both stairways. They paid no attention to Will as he returned to the street and rescued the mud-spattered satchel. Doing that gave him a few minutes to gather his nerve and reflect on the remarkable events that had brought him here, to this place, at this moment.

He had learned a great deal on the long journey that had taken him to Theodore Roosevelt's ranch in the Dakota Bad Lands; to Lon Adam's side at the campfire; to Vlandingham's table at Sherry's Restaurant, and then to Harvard. At last he could see the continuity of the journey. He hadn't realized it at the time, but each step had led inevitably to the next. And from here, he knew exactly where he wanted to go:

To possession of a mansion like William K. Vanderbilt's.

To prominence as a member of Society.

To a good marriage with someone who could help him establish a practice among the best people, as Vlandingham's wife had done.

And most important of all, to fulfilment of his promise to his stepbrother.

Slowly, he started up the steps again. Halfway to the landing, he quickened his pace. Started taking the steps two at a time. One journey was over, another beginning. Roosevelt was wrong, he thought as he strode to the doors. There was no need to make a choice. But if there ever were such a need, he was sure about which way he'd go.

He would go Vlandingham's way.

2

That same night, Gideon turned over in bed and punched his pillow. Julia murmured in the dark:

'Can't sleep, darling?'

'No.'

'Are you upset about something?'

'On the contrary, I feel wonderful. I've been thinking of Will, that's all. He said his first day at Harvard was just fine.'

'I'm glad. But I'm terribly sleepy.'

'All right, I'll be quiet.'

He kissed her cheek, then slipped his arm round her and held her close. A sudden painful pressure at the mid-point of his chest reminded him of time hurrying on. But now it no longer mattered quite so much. Idealism had finally won out over less laudable characteristics. Gideon's son – his best hope for leadership of the family – was on the right path at last.

BOOK THREE

The Upward Path

CHAPTER I

In Galveston

That autumn, as Will was starting the long climb to the goal he'd set for himself, Carter was wandering with no goal, and a doubt in his mind as to whether he would ever find any work that suited him. He'd left Texarkana in the spring, drifting south. He'd tried cattle ranching and a number of other jobs. All had proved unsatisfactory. He spent no more than a week at any of them, always moving on. As a golden October began, he reached the Gulf Coast of Texas with just a few dollars in his pocket.

From Galveston Bay he took a ferry out to the thriving port city at the east end of Galveston Island. A man in Houston had told him there was always cargo to be handled at the harbourside, and strong backs needed to handle it. Perhaps he was drawn to the long, flat island with its subtropical vegetation because it was a shipping centre. It smelled of the sea. It reminded him of home.

The bad memories of his last months in Boston were fading; some of them, anyway. He missed the bustle of the docks, and the carefree life of people who made their living from fishing and maritime commerce. He felt at ease as he wandered by the piers and saw the baled cotton, the barrels of flour, the drums of rope, and the crates of cigars waiting to be shipped.

He spent the afternoon of his first day in Galveston strolling residential side streets near the centre of town. He passed low adobe walls with luxuriant gardens on the other side. The heavily-shaded houses, mostly with a Spanish flavour, looked substantial and not inexpensive. Palmetto leaves rattled their spear-like foliage in the warm sea wind. He could imagine how sweet and soft the air must smell in the springtime, when the magnolias and azaleas were blooming.

As the sun began to drop over the coast Jean Lafitte had sailed some seventy years earlier, he ambled back to the main section, admiring the city's Custom House, its solid-looking theatre, its Cotton Exchange. Across from the last, he saw a clean-looking saloon whose gaudy sign announced it as the *Sam Houston Rest*. He fished in his pocket, counted his money, realized he was hungry, and with his bedroll over his shoulder and his second-hand Montana peak hat shading his face, crossed the dusty street and pushed through the saloon doors.

It was his first mistake.

2

The place was popular, and noisy. Seamen and stevedores lined the bar. Carter had finished a tough piece of steak and was mopping up the gravy with a slab of bread when a round-faced stranger in a derby approached his table. The man had bland brown eyes, a stubby nose, and a short beard fringing his chin. He was about thirty-five; conventionally dressed. A merchant, Carter guessed.

'You look like a stranger in Galveston,' the man said with soft Southern speech and a friendly smile.

Wary, Carter returned his bread to his plate. 'You're right.'

'Mighty nice town. Mighty nice weather most of the year. About one more month and we'll see the end of hurricane season. Then we'll rest a lot easier.'

The man took off his derby and offered an apologetic

358

smile. 'Don't mean to intrude. It's just that the barkeep pointed you out as a newcomer and my brother-in-law, he's lookin' to hire a young man like you.'

The man's apology reassured Carter. He relaxed and prepared to finish his bread and gravy. But first he said, 'To do what?'

'Porter in a boarding house. Out on the edge of town.'

A porter? Carter rebelled at the idea. There should be better work available. Of course no work was very attractive to him. But he was nearly broke. He supposed it wouldn't hurt to explore this opportunity; maybe even take the job for a few days. That would give him time to look for something better.

His distrust of the stranger was quickly disappearing. The man was holding his derby in his hands, and with those round cheeks and that fringe of beard, he looked like a slightly overweight saint.

'I might be interested in talking to your brother-in-law,' Carter said. To make sure the man knew who was in charge, he added, 'As soon as I finish my meal and my beer. Meantime, why don't you sit down?'

'Thanks kindly.'

The man bobbed his head, took a chair and held out his hand. 'Name's Olaf. James Olaf. I'm a Kentucky Scotsman on my mother's side, and immigrant Swede on my father's. Care for a cigar?'

Carter pushed his plate away and hesitated only a moment. A cigar would taste fine with the last of his beer. He accepted, bent to the match Olaf extended, then leaned back his chair and introduced himself.

The meal had been his first solid one in a couple of days. He'd eaten so fast, he felt uncomfortable; a little dizzy. The cigar seemed to enhance the feeling. But he was so used to being tired and light-headed from lack of food and exposure to the elements, he didn't think much about it.

Sunshine slanted through a dusty window a few feet away. A ship's horn sounded in the harbour. Gulls cried in the fading autumn day. A sad season. A lonesome season. But they were all lonesome when you were wandering far from home.

'Shall we go?' Olaf asked presently, a touch of impatience in his voice.

A little glassy-eyed, Carter leaned back. 'I'll be ready soon.'

'Yes, of course, didn't mean to rush you,' Olaf murmured. Carter tilted his stein and drained it, thus missing the quick flash of hostility in his benefactor's deceptive eyes.

3

He should have been warned by the men loitering on the steps of the boarding house that sat on the Gulf side of the island, just outside of town. It was a large place – three stories – built on rotting pilings sunk in the sand. There was a palmetto thicket to the west, but no vegetation around the house itself except for a couple of patches of sea oats bending in the sunset breeze. Several miles out on the white-capped Gulf, a side-wheeler spewed black smoke from its funnels as it ploughed in the direction of New Orleans.

Carter's attention was focused on the two men, emaciated and dirty, who were lounging on the steps. One had a ring in his ear – an unpleasant reminder of Ortega. The other was whittling. Carter couldn't bring himself to look at the knife. He knew both men looked shady, yet at the same time he didn't care. He was still pleasantly tipsy from the beer – unusual for just one stein to do that to him – and so he wasn't as cautious as he should have been.

'Come on in,' Olaf said, a comradely arm across Carter's shoulder; yet there was pressure in Olaf's hand, as if he were hurrying Carter past the loungers. One said something Carter couldn't hear. The other snickered.

Inside, there was little light, and a heavy smell of cigar smoke and beer. In a minuscule room to the right of the frowsy entrance hall, Carter saw two more roughnecks leaning on a bar made of a plank and two ship's kegs. In a chair in a corner sat a yellow-haired girl in a chemise. Skinny, yet touchingly pretty. Twenty or so, Carter figured, smiling at her. She smiled in return, smoothing the front of her chemise so that her small breasts stood out.

'We like to make our boarders comfortable,' Olaf said with an understanding chuckle. 'Seamen expect certain amenities any place they stay—' He had led Carter to the back of the hall, and now pushed open a door to a kitchen. A heavy black woman was frying potatoes at an iron stove.

'Horace here?'

'Gone to Houston overnight, Mist' Olaf. Business. Your sister went too.'

Olaf looked upset. 'Horace didn't tell me he'd be away.'

'Came up sudden like.'

'Yes, but I brought this young man here to talk about the porter's job.'

The black woman studied Carter through the smoke rising from her skillet. Quickly she lifted the pan from the stove top and cooled it, hissing, in a bucket of water. 'Mist' Horace say he be back on the first morning ferry. We ain't full tonight. The young gen'-man could have a bed, I s'pose.'

'Capital idea,' Olaf said, beaming. 'We'll even give him a drink on the house. Thank you, Maum Charlene,' he added with great politeness.

In the makeshift barroom, only the girl remained. Olaf introduced her as a distant cousin of Horace's, from up San Antonio way. Her name was Lu Ann. 'You're welcome to chat with her, Mr Kent, but I'm afraid the largesse of the house doesn't include her favours. Any arrangement you make with her is strictly a cash transaction.'

Carter nodded blearily, still feeling the effect of the beer. 'Fair enough,' he mumbled. Olaf poured him a drink of surprisingly good bourbon, and left.

He sat down and began to chat with Lu Ann. She offered him another cigar, and after a few puffs he grew foggier still – drunkenly dizzy – and before long found himself toasting the little yellow-haired whore:

'To you, Miss Lu Ann. The most beautiful girl in Texas. The world, maybe.'

She laughed, showing bad teeth. 'My, my, Mr Kent. You have a charming way of talkin', indeed you do.'

'You inspire it, ma'am,' he said with a grin, knowing that he shouldn't let down so completely, yet too tired and drunk to care. 'I do believe I've fallen in love with you.' In his state, it was almost true.

She reached out, dropped her hand between his legs and began to stroke slowly:

'I declare, Mr Kent – you just take a girl's breath away. I 'spose we could do somethin' about the way you feel, though I hate to bring up such a thing as the price of our enjoyin' ourselves in my room.'

He told her he still had two dollars. It was enough.

He finished the cigar, which he had decided smelled curiously sweet – or was that Miss Lu Ann's scent? He followed her up to her quarters – the door had a tin numeral on it – where she disposed of her chemise, and he was soon floundering on top of her. Of the rest he remembered very little.

In the middle of the night he rolled on top of Lu Ann for a second romp, gushing out a lot of silly words about her beauty, and when it was finished, he slept long and hard. He roused in response to someone shaking him.

'Lu Ann?' he mumbled, his eyes not yet open.

'Wake up,' said a familiar voice. 'Wake up and pay your bill.'

Carter sat up and reached for his drawers, befuddled by the sight of James Olaf with a marlin spike stuck in his belt, a piece of paper in his hand, and a decidedly ugly expression on his face.

4

'Pay—?' Carter repeated.

Olaf thrust the paper at him. 'Four hundred and six dollars.'

He didn't think he'd heard correctly. 'For what?'

'Read, for Christ's sake!' Olaf shook the paper.

Sure enough, there it was – itemized. *Lodging*. *Liquor*. *Extra*. The extra amounted to a hundred and fifty dollars.

Dumbfounded, Carter pointed to the last item. 'What's this?'

Olaf sniggered. 'You mean you forgot little Miss Lu Ann already?'

For the first time, he realized she was gone. 'She told me – she told me it cost two dollars!'

Another laugh; harsh this time. 'What the hell does she know? She's only been here a week. The customers pay me.'

Carter raked fingers through his hair as he peered at the bill, noting that it was soiled and wrinkled, as if it had been used many times. There was no name at the top, merely a notation. *Charges, Room 6*. The tin numeral on the open door was 6, he saw.

'Where's the girl—?' he began.

'She doesn't want to talk to you.'

'But I thought—'

'That she liked you? She does what she's told, friend.'

'Let me speak to the man who runs this place. Your brother-in-law.'

'Horace?' He smirked. 'No such fellow. I run this place.'

Carter began to realize how stupidly he'd behaved. Hunger, tiredness, and the need for a little companionship had lulled him out of his usual wariness. In his hand he held the result.

He thought of the girl, and of his foolish babbling. How she must be laughing. She'd put one over on him. Put one over on the glib Mr Carter Kent, who always fancied himself *in charge of things*. Somehow, being cheated by this – this—

He couldn't finish. He didn't know the word he wanted. What was this place? The answer came suddenly from the past; from his memories of the docks of Boston:

'This is a damn crimping operation. You're all in cahoots.'

'Smart boy for a Yankee,' Olaf said with a chilly smile. 'Guess you're quick enough to figure what comes next, then. A choice. You can go to jail for refusal to pay my fair and lawful charges, or you can sign on as an ordinary seaman on the *Gulf Empress*, leaving day after tomorrow.'

'For where?'

'Liverpool, Marseilles – you'll only be gone half a year or thereabouts. Don't think you can go to the law about this. They're friends of mine.'

Carter shivered under the coverlet he was still clutching against his middle. He thought he heard someone tread on a board in the hall. Had the crimp brought help, just in case?

He eyed the room. No windows, but he seemed to

recall one in the corridor. Desperate, he knew he had to choose an option he detested.

'All right,' he said, feigning defeat. 'Guess I don't want to go to jail.'

'You Yankees have some brains after all,' Olaf chortled, weaving the paper. 'Pull your britches on. Maum Charlene will feed you a plate of grits, and then I'll introduce you to the master of the *Empress*.'

Carter nodded, rubbed his stubbled jaw, lurched from bed, and got dressed. Just as he was buttoning up his denim pants, Olaf turned and stepped through the door to say something to whoever was waiting outside. Seeing his chance, Carter lunged and hit him in the back.

CHAPTER II

Behind Bars

James Olaf was hurled across the hall so violently, his chin tore a hole in the flimsy wall. He hung there a second or so, his right hand clawing for the spike in his belt. 'Help, help up here!' he bellowed.

A man leaped at Carter from the left; one of the loungers he'd seen on the front steps the night before. Carter ducked as the man hacked the air with his whittling knife. Suddenly he smelled fish. His stomach ached so badly, he wanted to double over.

The knife shaved past Carter's left arm. He drove two hard but clumsy punches into the man's midsection. The man reeled backward, off balance. Not far behind him, there was a landing where the stairs went down to the left. At the far side of the landing was the window Carter remembered. Beyond it, calm water glittered in the morning sun.

Terror drying his mouth, he charged the staggering man and hit him with his shoulder, driving him toward the glass. The man realized he was falling, and fought for balance. That gave Carter a chance to rush in beneath the man's knife hand, seize his old blue seaman's shirt and fling him sideways down the stairs. Halfway to the bottom, he crashed into the black woman, Maum Charlene, who was coming up with a shotgun in her big hands.

Arms and legs flew, the gun discharged, and shot punched scores of small holes in the ceiling directly over the stairs. Carter had other things on his mind – chiefly Olaf, who was running toward him full tilt, swinging the marlin spike in a murderous arc.

Carter backed toward the window but miscalculated the distance. He struck the glass too quickly and forcefully. It gave way. He flung his arm over his face and tumbled through with a strangled oath. Because of his fall, the spike missed his face by three inches, burying its tip in the window frame instead.

Amid a shower of glass, he rolled down the sloping roof below the window. The roof saved him from a serious injury; when he tumbled off the eave, he fell only six feet to the sand. He fought to get his wind back as he scrambled to his feet. He ran toward Galveston in fear of his life.

2

When he reached the centre of Galveston with no sign of pursuit, he calmed down and tried to reassure himself that the incident was over. He'd hear no more from Olaf – the man was obviously a crook, and couldn't afford to draw attention to his crimping operation.

He was famished. But he had no money for a meal; his trousers had been searched while he slept in Lu Ann's bed. His Montana peak hat and his bedroll had been left behind, so he had nothing to sell, either. He'd have to steal the price of the ferry to the mainland, or sneak aboard. But that could wait until he filled his growling belly.

That decision was his second mistake.

Carter was foraging for food in the garbage cans of a large hotel when two uniformed men suddenly appeared at the mouth of the alley, billy clubs in hand.

'There he is!' the taller policeman shouted, charging.

Carter turned to run, bumped against one of the garbage barrels and overturned it. He slipped and fell in a slimy heap of cold meat fat, fruit rinds, coffee grounds – all of it stinking like hell.

'Fits the description,' panted the other officer as the two raced up to him, clubs ready. This time Carter was in no mood to fight. He lay there in the garbage, staring up at their coarse faces. The bigger officer leaned down and grinned:

'Say somethin', boy.'

'How – how'd you find me?'

'Why, Jim Olaf came to see the captain – Jim's got a lot of friends in town, y'understand. He described you and the rest was easy. We just started lookin' for a dark-haired well set-up Yankee tramp. Your accent just filled in the last bit of identification. You're a Yankee, all right.'

'An' he's right where a Yankee belongs,' said the other, grinning even wider than his companion. 'In the slops.'

He drew his booted foot back and kicked Carter's genitals. Carter screamed and clutched himself. After the fourth kick, he fainted.

The magistrate was an avuncular man with white side whiskers. He identified himself as another friend of Jim Olaf's. The crimp must have paid off half the damn town!

The charge was defrauding an innkeeper. Carter tried to speak in his own defence but was gavelled to silence. The magistrate sentenced him to thirty days in jail.

On the eleventh day of his jail term the fringe of a tropical storm brushed Galveston with heavy rains and howling winds, and Carter was glad to be indoors. The food wasn't bad in jail, either. Each meal included greasy grits, but at least the plate and tin cup were shoved into his cell three times daily.

Even so, he nearly went crazy in the confines of the six by ten foot cell with its plank sleeping platform, its bucket of tepid, bug-infested wash water, and its second, uncovered pail for his own wastes. The jailor was supposed to empty the waste pail once a day but he often forgot. Complaints were useless.

A small, high window in the cell overlooked a side street that Carter often watched for hours by standing on the plank platform. Late one afternoon, he saw Olaf drive by in an expensive buggy, two finely dressed girls riding with him under parasols, chatting and laughing. One was the little yellow-haired trollop. Carter clutched the bars and stared after her with a stricken look.

The month in the Galveston jail was an experience that scarred Carter, just as other brushes with violent death and deceitful people had scarred him. The cell was the most potent proof he'd yet encountered that if you didn't run others, they'd run you.

He thought about the yellow-haired girl, and of how foolishly he'd trusted her. Under the influence of beer and what surely must have been cigars impregnated with some kind of drug, he'd even got sentimental over her. And while the girl was no one he really cared about, her deception humiliated him.

He thought a lot about the Greek woman, too. In a way, he had also trusted Helen Stavros. He'd trusted her beauty, her warm eyes, her smile – and they had deceived him. She had meant for them to do that. Helen Stavros had made him suspicious of all women, and now the yellow-haired girl had confirmed and solidified that suspicion.

Women had their place, he supposed. A man needed them for physical satisfaction. But as for loving them – trusting them – he had been suspicious of that before he came to Galveston, and now he knew he was right.

As for trusting men – strangers such as Olaf who smiled and pretended to be decent, generous, helpful – well, the cell demonstrated where *that* got you. He concluded that the only people in the entire world it would be safe for him to trust were his mother, Will and Gideon – none of whom he'd ever see again, probably.

Therefore he was alone in a world of Olafs and Lu Anns – a world of potential enemies. He'd long suspected it. Now he knew it. So if he didn't behave accordingly, he was a damn fool—

Which was exactly what he'd been thus far in Galveston. Like the fearful lesson of the Red Cod, that was another he wouldn't soon forget.

On the day he was released, a policeman escorted him to the ferry and paid his passage across to the mainland. It was a grey November morning, unseasonably cold for Texas. A light drizzle was falling. The policeman turned up the collar of his old overcoat and said:

'On your way, now. Don't let us see you in Galveston again, boy.'

'You won't.'

'Where you headin'? North?'

Carter hadn't the slightest idea. He gazed out past the docked ferry and the rain-stippled Gulf to the coast; a vast, slate-coloured flatland embracing Galveston Bay. Earth, water, and dark grey sky seemed to fuse into one immense and hostile waste in which he had no home, countless enemies, little future, and less hope.

His spirits sank. What good were the lessons he'd learned? What good was cleverness, ambition – anything? He was alone and all that had happened to him in Galveston could well happen to him again, no matter how carefully he guarded against it.

Then the unquenchable Kent optimism came to his aid. He brought his chin up. Forced a smile that surprised the shivering policeman.

'Don't know where I'm going,' he answered. 'But you'll hear from me one of these days, you can bet. Galveston's going to feel bad about treating me the way it did.'

He said it with such conviction, the officer couldn't bring himself to laugh. Cocking his head, he asked:

'That a threat or just a promise?'

Carter held up both hands. 'Oh, a promise. Threats can get you killed.'

Smiling that dazzling smile, Carter stepped onto the ferry and tried to ignore the rain, the freezing wind, the great empty vista of water and forlorn sky in which he, of all human beings, had no place.

But surely, in a land so vast, there *should* be a place for him. He'd keep travelling in search of it, trusting no one.

And he wouldn't stop unless they buried him.

CHAPTER III

Jo

Will's collision with a fellow student on the steps of the medical school proved to be the start of a friendship.

Will soon discovered that Drew Hastings had a first-rate mind, an interest in medicine that was almost a passion, and a desire to succeed that matched or exceeded Will's own. Drew's ambition was due in large part to the dedication with which his mother and father had approached the task of educating him. His parents were storekeepers; people of modest means, to whom the annual tuition of two hundred dollars plus incidental fees was an enormous sum. They had scrimped for years to accumulate the money.

Drew was the sole recipient. He had a younger sister, Will learned, and he was devoted to her; but his devotion didn't extend to a belief that she should receive higher education. The family could afford just one standard bearer. Drew, older, and male, was the clear choice. He made no secret of liking it that way.

Each young man brought certain qualities to the friendship. Drew brought the steadiness and authority that went with being two years older. He liked having a friend to whom he could expound about medicine. He'd read extensively before coming to Boston, and he knew some startling things. On one occasion he astonished Will by telling him that Hippocrates, the famous Greek physician of the fifth century B.C., probably had little to do with the body of medical writing known as the Hippocratic Collection. Some scholars said he had no connection with the famous oath bearing his name.

Many skilled doctors had taught and written at the medical school on the island of Cos, Drew said. Hippocrates was among the most famous. He had also been born on the island. So it was undoubtedly inevitable that his name would be ascribed to aphorisms and bits of advice actually authored by others. Drew's favourite was, '*Not only must the physician be ready to do his duty, the patient, the attendants, and external circumstances must conduce the cure.*'

The first time Drew quoted the saying to Will, he went on, 'But tell that to someone living in a city slum. Those people don't have time to think about good health, let alone do something about it. All their energy goes into surviving. As to their circumstances – what could be more conducive to sickness than a tenement? The poor need doctors more than the rich do. Hippocrates knew that.'

Will didn't agree with Drew's conclusions, but he was fascinated by the breadth of his friend's knowledge. Hence one of his contributions to the friendship was the devotion of a pupil eager to learn. On the other hand, at certain times during the first term, he turned out to be the teacher.

The practice of medicine interested Drew, but not the preparation that was fundamental to it. He hated the scientific studies required of first-year students – general chemistry, physiology, materia medica. Only anatomy held any appeal.

Because of his attitude, he was soon flirting with dismissal. Even when studying physiology under an acknowledged master such as Henry Bowditch, he refused to attend most of the eight-man laboratory sessions. Instead, he relied on Will's notes, and Will's good memory. On the night before a test, Will would drill him for hours on the periodic table or Latin terms they were expected to know. Drew would absorb just enough information to squeak by.

There were two hundred and seventy-five students in the medical school, ninety-six of them in the first class. They lived in a closed universe consisting of the school building, its various annexes and laboratories, the City Hospital and Massachusetts General, where demonstrations took place and charity patients were observed, and the rooms in which they did their studying. Since Charles Eliot's inauguration as President of Harvard, the medical curriculum had undergone extensive revision and improvement. Courses were more complex and more difficult than they'd been just a few years earlier. Will and Drew had to keep up with daily and weekly work, but they also faced comprehensive examinations in the spring; examinations covering all the material studied during the year. Only by passing those examinations did a student earn the right to advance to the next class.

During his first term at the school, Will worked twelve, fourteen, sixteen hours a day – Sundays included. Sometimes the work load became so heavy, he existed for days in a state of near exhaustion. Once in a while he grew deeply discouraged. But when he did, he would recall standing in the rain outside the Vanderbilt mansion, or lunching with Vlandingham, or promising his stepbrother he'd amount to something. Any of those memories, but especially the last one, was enough to overcome his discouragement and keep him going without sleep and without complaint.

Occasionally there was a short respite from the routine. One came in mid-November. Drew announced that his father would be arriving on Saturday, to check on his son's progress. He'd be staying overnight. Will was invited to join them for supper.

To Will's surprise – and Drew's – another member of the family turned up, too. Drew's younger sister.

The three members of the Hastings family invited Will to eat at a Boston fish house not noted for low prices. Will had already heard that Mr Hastings had been forced to travel from Hartford in a borrowed farm wagon; he couldn't afford train fare. So Will insisted that he pay for supper, and made Drew's agreement a condition of his acceptance of the invitation.

Joab Hastings was a stout, soft-spoken man with rough skin and a red face. He was almost uncomfortably in awe of the two students, because they were venturing into intellectual realms wholly foreign to him. But his pride in his son was obvious.

Less impressed was Drew's fifteen-year-old sister, Joanna, whom everyone called Jo. Her father said she'd nagged him in such a cheerful but determined way, he'd been forced to bring her along. His smile said it wasn't an imposition, though. 'She clerks at the family store,' he explained to Will. 'She's a hard worker. She deserved a little holiday.'

Perhaps Joab Hastings was appeasing his guilt, Will concluded a few minutes later, when all of them were enjoying the first course – roasted oysters from a huge silver platter. Making conversation, he said:

'Did you enjoy the ride up here, Miss Hastings?'

'I enjoyed the scenery. But I couldn't help thinking how it all might have been different.'

'What do you mean?'

'If I were a boy, I could go to medical school. Since I'm a girl, I have to settle for a trip.'

Drew cracked a shell, then used his oyster knife to cut out the small, tender nugget inside. He forked the oyster into a dish of hot melted butter. 'You see, Will, five or six years ago, my little sister fell in love with the late Miss Nightingale. And with her profession.'

'Calling,' Jo said as Drew ate the buttered oyster. 'I've told you a million times, Drew – Miss Nightingale always referred to nursing as a calling. She said the word has more spirituality than profession does. Don't you agree, Mr Kent?'

She fixed her blue-green eyes on him with a directness for which he wasn't prepared.

'Oh, certainly, Miss Hastings,' he said with a straight face, reaching for another oyster. He found the girl's adolescent behaviour by turns funny and annoying.

She gave a vigorous nod. 'I knew you'd feel that way.'

Drew laughed. She shot a wrathful glare in his direction. Will lifted his napkin to his mouth to hide a smile.

He studied Jo covertly while they finished the oysters and awaited the chowder. Although she didn't share Drew's stoutness, she could easily be recognized as his sister. Will found her attractive, though not in a conventional way.

She was slim, and flat-chested. She had long, shining red-gold hair that gave off a pleasing smell of home-made soap. Her face was a well-proportioned oval, marred just a little by a nose many would have called too large. But the nose was counterbalanced by a nicely shaped mouth.

There was a light scattering of freckles on her cheeks.

Unlike so many girls, she didn't bother to powder them into invisibility. They gave her face a touch of the tomboy that Will found charming.

She was obviously bright, too. And quite conscious of the limits imposed on her by her sex. That was surely why most everything she said had an edge to it. Julia would have appreciated and encouraged her attitude, he supposed.

Gently, Joab Hastings put his hand over hers. He said to Will, 'Joanna would like to study at one of the Nightingale schools they're starting here in the States. I'm sure she'd make a fine nurse. But there isn't enough profit in selling corn meal and pins to pay for two educations.'

'So the world decrees it's the girl who stays home,' Jo said.

'The world and our circumstances,' Hastings agreed with a sad smile.

Jo wasn't willing to let the subject drop:

'One day brothers and sisters will have an equal chance. Do you understand what I'm saying, Mr Kent? I don't want Drew *not* to study medicine. I just want the same opportunity. What do you think?'

'I think I have no business meddling into a family's—'

'Oh, pooh!' she cut in. 'Answer the question.'

Her father frowned. 'You're being impertinent, Joanna.'

'I'll answer,' Will said lightly. 'I think your brother will need to support himself all through his life, while you'll undoubtedly have a husband to look after you. So in theory, Drew needs more education than you. That may not be right, or fair. But for the time being it's the way the world operates.'

'I don't care a fig for the way the world operates!' she exclaimed. 'Or for marriage, either. I have no intention of submitting myself to the whims of a man.

376

Or to the idiotic marital laws that prevail in this country.'

'Joanna,' her father said, a little more sharply.

She ignored him: 'I have no intention of doing any of that merely to pay the bills!'

Will said to Drew, 'Your sister should meet my step-mother. They'd certainly see eye to eye.' To Jo: 'My step-mother's a suffragist.'

'Young lady, I want you to settle down and mind your tongue,' Joab Hastings said, sounding severe for the first time. Jo glanced at her father, started to retort, then saw the set of his jaw. She looked at her lap.

During the rest of the meal, Will found himself avoiding the girl's eyes. They had taken on a strange intensity, and he seemed to be its object. For no reason that he could explain, the attention bothered him. His cheeks and neck were almost as pink as the lobsters they ate for the main course.

Jo made no further pronouncements, however. After dinner the two students escorted father and daughter back to the modest hotel where they'd engaged two rooms. Will and Drew said goodnight – Jo shook Will's hand for over ten seconds – then started walking down the dark, quiet street toward the river.

'I hope Jo's frankness didn't offend you,' Drew said. 'We're used to it around home. And to be fair, she really cares a lot about the family. Of course that doesn't mean she approves of everything that goes on. Such as Ma spending her entire life doing whatever Pa asks. Trouble is, Jo's protests hide all the kindness and love that are part of her, too. Strangers see the prickly exterior and think there's nothing else.'

My impression exactly, Will thought, though he wouldn't have said it.

'Pa and I hope that prickly attitude will disappear as she gets older,' Drew continued. 'Jo's – uh – somewhat late to develop. She'd deny it with her last breath, and kill me for saying so. But deep down, I think she craves a puffed-up figure.'

'You're probably right. Most girls these days want to look like Lillian Russell.'

'I certainly hope she gets her wish. Maybe she'll be less grumpy.'

Will laughed. 'Well, I wasn't offended by anything she said. She's a spirited young lady.'

'She's smitten with you, too.'

'What?'

'Didn't you see her start making sheep's eyes halfway through supper? That was when she realized she liked you.'

Will stopped under a street lamp, buttoning the collar of his overcoat against the night wind. With an awkward laugh, he fibbed, 'No, I didn't notice any special looks.'

'Then we'd best rush you to City Hospital. You've gone blind.'

They resumed walking. 'I've seen a similar expression on my sister's face once or twice before. She fell in love with her schoolmaster when she was nine or ten. At thirteen it was the man who directs our church choir. She always seems to pick the brainy ones. She certainly got fooled this time,' he finished with a chuckle.

Will ignored the joke. 'I can't believe she'd give two hoots about me.'

Drew's expression changed to one of puzzlement. Will's words struck him as strangely abrupt and serious for a conversation essentially light in tone. He tried to preserve the lightness:

'What's the matter? Don't you think you're good enough for my sister?'

Sometimes I don't think I'm good enough for anyone or anything. Again he kept the thought to himself.

Drew continued in a jocular way, 'Truth is, brother

Kent, I don't either. But we needn't worry about it. Adolescent girls have a crush a day, practically. They're in love with being in love. She'll grow out of it.'

Will believed him.

Both of them were wrong.

3

Two days before Christmas, Drew arrived at the Kent house with a cylindrical object wrapped in brown paper. Grinning, he handed the package to Will.

'It arrived this morning – along with a note asking me to give it to you with all due speed. I'm to wish you a Merry Christmas in the bargain.'

Will turned the package over and over. 'Who's it from?'

'My little sister.'

'Jo?'

'I have only one little sister, as I recollect. Seems she's still smitten. Unbelievable. Well, open it – open it!'

Will removed the paper and found an eighteen-inch-wide roll of fabric, which he carefully spread out on a table. He caught his breath.

On a dark blue background, in small, neat letters of white thread, Jo had reproduced a block of prose which began, *I will look upon him who shall have taught me this Art even as one of my parents*.

'My Lord,' Will said. 'The Hippocratic oath.'

'Every last word. Needlepoint, I think they call it. She made one for me, too. She must have done them at night. She works all day in the store.'

Will brushed his fingertips over the tiny letters. 'It must have taken her hours and hours. It's a beautiful present. I'll write her right away and thank her.'

Drew sat in a chair that creaked under him. 'Don't be too free with your compliments. She might turn up on your doorstep, pleading for a proposal.'

'I doubt that. She said she hates the idea of marriage.'

'And the idea of men dominating the world – and their wives. But those are merely *ideas*. You, on the other hand, are a living, breathing man. She can detest men in the abstract and dream about you and never see a smidgin of inconsistency.' A shrug. 'She's a young girl. That says it all.'

Will smiled. 'I guess so.' He was touched by the gift.

He thought of Jo's blue-green eyes, and the freckles she didn't bother to hide. He thought of how she longed for a woman's maturity, and that was funny, yet touching, too. She was a very engaging girl—

But one he mustn't think about with any seriousness. There was no room in his plans for a girl who lacked social connections. That might be regrettable, but it was also the way things had to be.

CHAPTER IV

The Students

Every few weeks throughout the winter and spring of 1887, Will received long letters from Drew's sister. Usually the letters contained comments on happenings in Hartford or events on the national scene; the comments were always made from the viewpoint of an avowed suffragist.

Usually Jo's ardour amused him. But there were unconsciously sad passages, too, as when she wrote about one wish that would remain forever unfulfilled; a wish that she could travel to London and study at St Thomas's Hospital. St Thomas's was the first Nightingale school endowed by subscription funds raised by Miss Nightingale herself.

Jo took pains to emphasize that she didn't want to become a nurse in order to flaunt herself as an educated woman. She wanted to serve others, as Will and Drew would after they graduated. Her humanitarian impulses were as strong as her brother's, Will soon realized.

No wonder she'd given him that particular Christmas gift. Will had framed the needlepoint and hung it on the wall of his room on Beacon Street. It quickly became as much a part of his life as the tea bottle or the Kentucky rifle downstairs.

He had no time to write letters as lengthy as hers. Now and then he sent her a short note, but these became even less frequent as he settled down to study for the year-end examinations. He also tutored Drew. When they passed, they got drunk in a North End tavern to celebrate. Drew went home to Hartford for the summer, and Will spent almost every day in the deserted medical school library, reading.

Fall arrived, and the programme this second year was more to Drew's liking. Even chemistry became tolerable against a background of courses in the clinical curriculum. Topographic and pathological anatomy. Clinical medicine. Clinical surgery.

Their surgical studies consisted of lectures, observation in the operating theatres at Massachusetts General, and demonstrations in the basics of bandaging. The bandaging section met six days a week at eight in the morning. It was there Will finally realized how innately suited for the profession his friend was.

Drew was the first pupil singled out by the faculty demonstrator, Assistant Professor Warren, to show that he'd mastered the lessons taught so far. The patient was a young male charity case at City Hospital. The day before, he'd had a small mole removed from his left shoulder blade by a student in the minor surgery class.

Drew took off the old, stained bandage and put on a new one. He worked extremely slowly. But when he was done, the bandage was perfect. Warren pointed that out.

'Hastings clearly possesses one of the most basic qualifications of the good practioner,' he said. 'Patience. You will all have to develop that patience, whether it is innate in your character or not. You see, gentlemen, modern medicine is structured so as to make the following an immutable law: if you are a practising physician, you will of necessity be a practising surgeon. The term surgeon is a very large umbrella. It covers many disciplines, and you must be expert in every one. Excellence, however, is far more than the sum of knowledge and a certain dexterity. But permit me to quote the head of our department, Dr Cheever. "To be an excellent surgeon, it is not enough merely to be a competent operator. One must be a painstaker." Mr Hastings is.'

And he had superb hands, Will discovered. Pudgy with fat, almost feminine in their gentleness and grace, they nevertheless possessed great strength. One night a drunken fourth classman teased Drew, pushing him and mincing back and forth in front of the door to his room in the dormitory. The upper classman kept calling Drew 'ladyfingers' until Drew had enough of the bullying and laid him out cold with three fast punches.

Will watched from the doorway; he and Drew had been going over the day's notes. Roosevelt all over again, Will thought. The comparison was accurate in other respects, too. They'd had some discussions about a doctor's responsibilities in which they'd disagreed sharply. And sometimes Drew sounded uncomfortably like a nagging conscience.

Drew dumped water on the upper classman, then helped him get up and limp away. Will's compliment about the way Drew had thrown punches led the older student into some half-joking remarks about his hands, and his weight:

'Know how I decided God must want me to be a doctor?

'First I realized I was fat as a tub. Next I found out I could do damn little about it. Still can't. Day after day, I eat nothing but melon and drink nothing but hot tea, and I never lose a pound. So these – ' He held out his hands. ' – these seem to be my only assets. It's always struck me as smart to work with what you have. I mean – what are the alternatives? There's really only one. You can refuse to make anything of what little you've been given, but if you do that, you're guaranteeing yourself a state of misery all your life. I'd rather try to be useful. Ergo – in God's grand if frequently murky plan, Hastings was meant to be a doctor. An obese one who will no doubt advise his patients to reduce their girth or face dire consequences.'

Will's amusement concealed a good deal of envy. He'd never be as skilful as Drew and he already knew it. But he could follow Drew's example and be a concerned, caring physician, a doctor who took to heart the words stitched into the dark blue fabric Jo had sent him.

That was a mark well worth aiming at, he decided.

2

The fall of '87 repeated the pattern of the preceding autumn. Will became more deeply immersed in his studies as the days went by, and less aware of events that stirred the collective mind and heart of the country.

Gideon, of course, remained fully aware of those events. One such – and a major one – took place on the eleventh of November. In Chicago, four of the accused Haymarket conspirators – Albert Parsons, August Spies, Adolph Fischer, and George Engel – were hanged.

A telegraphed account of the execution was delivered to Gideon's office at Kent and Son late that day. He put everything aside to read the dispatch from the *Union*'s mid-west correspondent. What he read filled him with dismay:

'Oh my God, Miss Vail – listen to this. Just before the trap dropped out from under him, Fischer cried, *"Hoch die Anarchie!"* Another of the four shouted in English, "Hurrah for anarchy!"' He flung the dispatch on his desk. 'What a sad, sorry business. The Haymarket set the cause of the working man back fifty years.'

Helene Vail was seated at a desk which faced Gideon's. From it, she could take his dictation or easily hand him a paper just pulled from her typewriting machine. The papers on her desk were neatly arranged, while those on his remained a jumble, despite her daily attention.

Miss Vail wasn't sympathetic to Gideon's views on the Haymarket issue:

'Which one of the traitors did that?'

'Engel. I remind you, Miss Vail – they were not proven guilty. That damn *Chicago Daily News* drove 'em to the gallows with its hue and cry for justice.'

He lit a match and touched it to a fresh cigar. Miss Vail continued to look at him with disapproval.

'Justice,' he repeated. 'What a joke. There was no conclusive evidence, and all the judicial niceties of a kangaroo court in a mining camp – Judge Lynch presiding. Yes, the views of those men were abhorrent to me – and counter to the views of a majority of people in this country. But by God, just because someone's views are unpopular – or even downright repulsive – doesn't mean they can be denied a fair trial. If anything, we have an obligation to be scrupulously fair with such people. Otherwise the right to dissent could be destroyed.'

'That's a subtlety I find hard to appreciate, Mr Kent.'

'You and a few million others. John Adams didn't fail to appreciate it. He served as the defence lawyer for the redcoats who caused the Boston Massacre in 1770. It nearly cost him his livelihood, but he understood that *someone* had to defend—'

The clanging of the telephone bell interrupted. Miss Vail rose to answer. Gideon puffed his cigar. He felt tired. Thanks to the *Union*'s position on the trial of the Haymarket defendants, he was constantly on the defensive these days.

White-faced, Miss Vail turned from the telephone.

'It's the telegraph office. There's a message from New York.'

'Who's it from?'

'Mr Jesperson, the copy editor at the *Union*.'

Gideon scowled. 'Why the hell didn't he put it on the direct wire?'

'Please don't keep cursing, Mr Kent. I don't know why. Perhaps he's upset and confused. He says that Mr Payne went for a noon walk along Park Row and on his way back, he was stricken with a heart seizure. He's dead.'

Theo Payne's sudden passing brought sorrow and consternation to the Kent household. Gideon was greatly upset by the loss of a close friend and invaluable associate.

Will travelled to New York with his father and stepmother to attend the funeral services. He returned to Boston alone; Gideon and Julia moved into the suite at the Fifth Avenue Hotel, planning to stay until Gideon could find a new editor – no easy job. Miss Vail packed up and joined them.

Saturday of the third week in November was a bitter, blustery day. Will spent it in a hired wagon heading for the New Hampshire border directly north of Lowell.

He and Drew had left Boston two hours before daylight. They didn't reach their rendezvous point until five in the afternoon. By then Will was nearly frozen despite his overcoat, two sweaters, muffler, and gloves.

Drew pulled the wagon into the shelter of some trees and scanned the autumn-withered landscape. A dirt road led into a large barren grove just beyond a stone marker at the state line. The sky had the look of dark grey paint.

'You still haven't told me who asked you to do this,' Will said.

Drew rubbed his mittened hands together. 'My answer's the same as it was an hour ago, and two hours before that. It's better you don't know.'

'You mean you can't tell your best friend where you got the money or directions to this godforsaken spot?'

'You can be assured it wasn't from the university corporation. They don't want to know where the medical school obtains – uh, demonstration material. We wouldn't be out here freezing our glutei if the damned state legislators could decide once and for all whether the release of bodies was mandatory or discretionary.'

Will knew that the current working of the state law, last revised in 1859, said unclaimed cadavers *'may be'* released to teaching institutions. It did not say *'shall be'*. At the moment, the Board of Health was not being cooperative. Hence expeditions such as this became necessary.

Suddenly the cold air came alive with the creak of wheels and the plodding of hooves. Drew manoeuvred their wagon out from behind the trees where they'd been concealed. A second wagon had emerged from the grove beyond the stone marker. Driven by a hunched-over man, the wagon was approaching along the road. Another man in a filthy coat and floppy hat rode a spavined horse out in front of it.

Presently the horseman reined in. He showed black, toothless gums in an insincere smile. An old musket lay across his thighs. From the seat of the wagon, the driver simpered at Drew and Will. He wasn't a normally proportioned man at all, but a poor, pitiable creature who looked barely competent to hold the reins. He had the body of an adult and a gigantic head with a strangely flattened and misshapen face. Slitted eyes were barely visible beneath a drooping hat brim.

'Brung you two of 'em,' the man on horseback said. 'But you ain't the one who usually picks 'em up.'

'He's sick,' Drew said quickly.

'That a fact.' A moment's thought. 'Mebbe I better tell you what I told him the first time he showed up here. If anybody ever comes to me and says I done this kind of business, I'll find you and kill you.' His grin was hideous. 'I know which school you're buyin' 'em for, y'see.'

Will shuddered. He didn't doubt for a minute that

387

the man would do exactly as he promised if he were betrayed.

The two students could not help staring at the pitiable thing on the wagon seat. Saliva trickled out one side of its mouth. It was male, but just barely recognizable as such, so distorted were the features.

'You understand me, boy?' the man on horseback said suddenly.

Drew started. 'Yes, of course. Completely.'

'Good. Let's get this over with. Price is fifty dollars apiece. You take 'em as is, wrapped up.'

'But surely I get to inspect—'

'Ain't got time for no damn inspection,' the man broke in. His horse whinnied and shied. He looked over his shoulder. 'They catch us at this, we'll be prison-bound for sure. Now get your fat ass over here and unload 'em, so I can hightail.'

'Come on, Will,' Drew whispered, heaving his awkward body into position so that he could step down off the spokes of the front wheel. While Will was climbing down, Drew paid the man in gold. The poor creature in the wagon was delighted by the glint of the gold pieces, and began to giggle and finger his drooling lips.

The two students hurried to the back of the wagon. They dragged the first canvas-wrapped body from under a concealing layer of straw. Will distinctly felt a lifeless arm and a head as he and Drew carried the corpse to their wagon. Then they loaded the second one, and covered both with burlap and scrap lumber they'd brought along.

The mounted man used his hat to slap the cheek of the witless man-child. After several false starts, the creature got the wagon turned and headed back toward the New Hampshire woods. The mounted man rode alongside with never a backward glance.

Will climbed to the wagon seat. He wasn't looking forward to the long ride back to Boston. They'd be

388

lucky to arrive by dawn the next day. But he understood why Drew had asked him to come along. A man like the one they'd just met might have robbed a solitary student, and abandoned the corpses somewhere – or, knowing he'd be safe from prosecution, never brought them at all.

Drew hawed to the horse. 'Someday doctors will understand what goes wrong in the human chemistry to cause a thing like that.'

'Do you suppose it was his son?'

A shrug. 'Son, brother, nephew – how could anyone tell? There must be a way to prevent such monstrosities. If I didn't think medicine could eventually find it, I sure as hell wouldn't be out here. Of course – ' Drew sounded disagreeable, perhaps because he was cold and tense, Will thought. ' – I'm sure I'm boring you by discussing what medicine may one day do for others. You care most about what it can do for you.'

Will scowled. 'Spare me the lecture, will you?'

'Why should I? Someone needs to wake you up! Someone needs to convince you that the purpose of medicine is to ferret out the causes of disease and heal the sick, not line the pockets of the practitioner.'

'Oh, for Christ's sake, Drew – enough! I know the rest by heart anyway. Practise in the city! Do good among the downtrodden! No thank you. I say every doctor should have the right to choose where he wants to practise, and how. You take the charity hospital, I'll take a drawing room. In ten years we'll compare notes and see who's happier.'

'All right, your life is none of my business,' Drew muttered. He didn't sound as if he believed it.

Both of them were silent for a while. The wagon lurched on along a road already rutted by the first hard freezes of the season. At the outskirts of Lowell they found a tavern. Will guarded the wagon while Drew went inside to buy two mugs of hot rum. When he came back, he uttered a quick raspy apology which concluded with the words:

'I sometimes forget you're my friend and think of you only as a damn good student—'

'So that's the new tack,' Will broke in, sarcastic. 'When bullying fails, try flattery?'

'No flattery. You didn't hear the rest. I meant to say a damn good student who's going in the wrong direction.'

With effort, Will held his temper. 'Not the wrong direction, Drew. Just a direction that isn't the same as yours.'

Drew managed a laugh. 'Amounts to the same thing, doesn't it? Anyway, I'm sorry. I won't lecture again.'

'Good!'

Will lifted the battered pewter mug; savoured the smell of the rum. He'd won a respite but he didn't really believe Drew's promise. He'd heard it too many times before.

4

Lecture on principles of asepsis & antisepsis. Dec. 4, 1887. Dr D. Cheever, Prof. Surg.
(1) Listerism presaged as early as 1843 in Dr O. W. Holmes' paper postulating contagion of puerperal fever & transmission of same by physician's hands.
(2) Semmelweis mistakenly given exclusive credit for this idea (Cheever claim!)—

The lecture notes blurred in front of Will's eyes. He laid the notes on his desk, stood, and turned away from the wall fixture with the shaded incandescent bulb. About three dozen of the fixtures were now installed throughout the house on Beacon Street. Will didn't like incandescent light. He found it harsh and unnatural.

He walked to the window, gazed down at the Common and the sleet slashing through the December darkness. For over two hours he'd vainly been trying to concentrate on his notes. It was well past midnight and he had a great deal of studying yet to do. Tomorrow he had examinations covering the anatomy course and the material from the surgery lectures.

But he was too upset to study. The morning mail had brought a letter from Carter, addressed to him. It was a short letter, mailed in Denver where his stepbrother was tending bar in a saloon:

Not exactly the fulfilment of my great ambitions, little brother! Over and over, I learn one lesson. You had better run others or they'll run you. Unfortunately, as my present low position testifies, I have yet to find a way to move from the latter state to the former. But by Heaven I will – count on it.

That was the only positive note in an otherwise cynical and despondent missive. Ever since reading it for the first time, Will had debated about showing it to his stepmother. Now he decided against it. He usually shared Carter's letters, profanity and all, but this one was too dark and defeated in tone. It would probably disturb Julia as much as it disturbed him.

Distantly, a downstairs clock rang the hour of one. Will rubbed his cheeks. Tomorrow's beard had already sprouted. He cast a disgruntled eye on the lecture notes and tried to forget Carter.

'All right, get to it,' he muttered, 'or you won't ever be called doctor.'

That, unfortunately, made him think of Drew. Even when Will earned a Harvard diploma, Drew probably wouldn't grant him the right to call himself doctor. Not unless he practised medicine exactly the way Drew thought it should be practised.

Damn his high-flown pronouncements! Will thought, savagely kicking his chair.

But he was wasting energy. He had examinations to pass tomorrow.

5

The two tests were harder than any he'd taken during his first year. This was in keeping with President Eliot's programme to make each year's curriculum more challenging than the one before, the over-all purpose being a general improvement in the reputation of the Harvard medical degree. For this reform, as well as others, Eliot had the backing of a substantial number of progressive faculty members. But he'd also encountered opposition from a group of medical school professors who were more conservative. That opposition was ferocious and unremitting.

Sometimes Will wondered how Eliot accomplished anything at all. The reactionary forces in the medical school were powerful and well entrenched. Even men of acknowledged intelligence resisted change.

Henry Bigelow, the former head of the surgical department and now emeritus professor, came to mind. Though Bigelow had a reputation as a fine teacher and an innovative practitioner, he had nevertheless steadfastly refused to accept Listerism for more than two decades; had even refused to grant the possibility of its value – and this in a decade in which doctors who didn't embrace all Lister's ideas were adopting some of them on a selective basis. Carbolic as the preferred antiseptic, for instance; surgical drainage with Chassiagnac's tube; use of silk or catgut ligatures that were short cut, carbolated, and buried.

Bigelow had closed his mind against every facet of Lister's techniques. Old hands at the school claimed he hadn't always been so reactionary. They said he'd been enthusiastic about ether anaesthesia when the Boston dentist, Morton, had first demonstrated it. But that was in 1846. Forty-two years ago—

At the moment, however, his primary feeling was relief. He'd passed the examinations. He could relax and enjoy the holiday season.

On Friday night at the end of examination week, some fellow students invited him to go out and celebrate. They were some of the more boisterous second- and third-class men. Drew wasn't among them.

Will needed a change in his routine. He accepted the invitation, thinking the others meant to go to a theatre, or to a beer hall for supper. Only after a hired hack picked him up on Beacon Street did he learn the actual destination:

'Nicest little whorehouse in Cambridge. High class. Most of the girls read novels and play the piano – and there's one *Deutscher* blonde with a contralto as big as her tits. She can treat you to some Wagner, if that's your persuasion.'

The speaker was a frivolous young New Yorker named Joe Marchant. 'You'll have a fine time,' he promised. 'You need to let down once in a while, Kent. You spend too much time philosophizing with Deacon Drew.'

Will laughed. 'Is that what you call him – Deacon?'

'Not to his face,' said another of the students crowded into the hack.

There was a tremor in Will's groin when he thought of their destination. In one way, he was more than ready to visit a bordello. But he was apprehensive, too. He must have showed it. Marchant said:

'The place we're going is perfectly safe. The crowd's respectable. Well, most of the time. Occasionally they let in regular Harvard undergraduates. Then everything deteriorates.'

Laughter.

'The girls are clean, too. One of us drives over every week to conduct an inspection. Madam Melba, the lady who runs the place, gives payment in trade. There are benefits to medicine you never imagined.'

'Amen to that,' Will agreed with a smile, hoping to forestall any questions that might reveal the prime cause of his nervousness. He had never been to bed with a woman.

He'd kept his inexperience a secret even from Drew. It made him feel inferior, especially among the older students, who bragged a lot. Even if half of their claimed conquests were fictitious, they still had impressive records. Though Will was nervous, he was glad Marchant and the others had invited him along.

The hack rattled on toward the Charles and the bridge at Cambridge Street. It was another foul night, and growing worse. In addition to a drizzle, fog had rolled in from the ocean. It blurred the gas lamps and occasional electric lights in passing houses. Will's mood became a blend of excitement and dread. He was afraid he'd inadvertently say or do something that would make his innocence apparent to the girls at the brothel.

His concerns were only for the events of the next few hours. There was no way for him to realize then that the trip to Cambridge, and all that would happen before the night was over, would have consequences affecting his life for years to come.

CHAPTER V

Trouble at Madam Melba's

'How old are you, dear?'

The simplest, most familiar tasks became hard all at once. Taking his left leg out of his trousers, for instance. He got impossibly tangled and almost fell over.

At the last minute, he braced his hand against the gaudily papered wall of the windowless cubicle. He answered the red-haired prostitute's question without looking at her:

'Twenty-one.'

'Come now, I don't believe that for a minute. You don't need to hide your real age. It has nothing to do with being able to give a lady a jolly time. Well, almost nothing – here, may I help?'

Damnably, his left leg was still caught. The woman glided up behind him. In the parlour she'd introduced herself as Aggie.

She was thirty or so. She had a long fall of red hair that reached to the midpoint of her back. Her nose was large and freckled under a thick layer of powder. Her lips were thin. The bodice of her nainsook camisole, all trimmed with lace and threaded with baby blue ribbon, accented the smallness of her breasts; a little bigger than ripe peaches. Yet her experienced eyes and her scent – warm skin mingled with perfume – gave her an air of sexuality that was dizzying.

'I do take back that remark about age,' she said as she reached from behind and grasped him through his linen drawers. He reacted with a quiver. She laughed:

'You see? The younger a fellow is, the larger and livelier. Now tell me your true age.'

'Eighteen, Miss—'

'Aggie.' Her fingers moved on him; caressing; teasing. 'Just Aggie. By the way – when it comes to getting your trousers off, it helps to take your shoes off first.'

He'd completely forgotten. Scarlet-faced, he lurched to the narrow bed. He sat on the edge and struggled to remove his shoes. One thumped to the floor, then the other. Aggie bore all his grimacing and heavy breathing with professional good humour. Before he knew it, they were both naked and she was drawing him down beside her on the bed. With a very slight note of urgency, she said:

'We mustn't be too slow, love. You only paid five dollars. Madam Melba doesn't like her employees to dawdle.'

There'd be no dawdling, she saw to that. She began to caress him and slide her mouth across his bare shoulder, his neck, his face. He was astonished that such a thin mouth could feel so warm and wet and passionate.

He slid into her with amazing ease. The amber bowls on the room's two small gas fixtures suffused their bodies with a rich, deep light that seemed to brighten and fade – brighten and fade – matching the accelerating tempo of their lovemaking. All too quickly, unstoppable forces were let loose.

'Oh my God,' he gasped, shutting his eyes.

A moment later, she said, 'That was very nice, dear.' The warm web of her hair touched his shoulder and spread over the small, heavily starched pillow. 'Your first time, wasn't it?'

She laid her palm against his perspiring cheek. He felt sublime, sinful, drained, grown up. Her smile had a touch of sadness:

'Wasn't it?'

'Yes.'

'Well, it was very nice indeed. Madam Melba doesn't require me to say that, you know. Here – ' She drew his head down on her bony shoulder. 'We still have a few minutes. Rest.'

Even though his eyes were closed, Will quickly came back to a sense of where he was. Madam Melba's was located on a sparsely settled dirt street between the river and the university. Only a couple of nearby cottages were visible in the fog. Weed-infested vacant lots adjoined the bordello on either side, and water filled deep ruts at the foot of the ramshackle steps out in front. The house itself was clapboard, with heavy curtains at every window to hide the business conducted inside.

Once through the front door, the depressing effect of the fog and the dark was banished, replaced by sounds and sights that soothed and pleased the senses. Polite laughter blended with dazzling piano arpeggios. All the gas fixtures made a soft glow through their glass bowls. The mingled scents of powder, perfume, and cigarette smoke gave the air a languorous quality.

Madam Melba was a proper, spinsterish woman in a high-necked gown. She had greeted the arriving students gravely and even pecked Joe Marchant's cheek as if she were his maiden aunt.

From the foyer they'd moved to the parlour, where the smoke and the perfume were much heavier. Girls lounged in their undergarments, nonchalant and overpoweringly sensual.

Will vividly remembered the first look that had passed between him and Aggie. He also remembered something that marred the otherwise pleasant picture. A huge, flat-faced man was posted beside a table just this side of the hallway leading to the rooms. The man took Will's money and gave him a surly look. In the hack, Marchant had issued a warning about the man:

'She has a big Hungarian working for her. Don't say anything smart to him. He hates the college crowd, and they say he's killed three or four men right here in Boston.'

Tonight the flat-faced man had a great many targets for his hostility. Harvard students made up most of Madam Melba's trade. Whether or not the fellow was indeed Hungarian didn't much matter. By looks and by occupation, he qualified for the name, which was widely if inaccurately used, especially by newspapers. Criminals whose origins couldn't be identified easily were always Hungarians. If not that, Slavs.

Watching Aggie walk ahead of him down the hall, Will realized he'd picked the only woman in the place with hair the colour of Dolores Wertman's—

Dolores. Her face floated in his mind as he drowsed on Aggie's shoulder. He could almost imagine it was Dolores who had responded so ardently to his lovemaking.

The thought of Dolores triggered an explosion of shame. Aggie felt the sudden tension in his body. She shifted her head far enough to get a view of his face. She touched his cheek again.

'What a guilty look you have! Didn't you enjoy—?'

'Very much,' he broke in. He didn't want her feeling bad.

'But you're as red as an apple. What's wrong?'

'Nothing.'

The lie was obvious. Trying to put him at ease, she snuggled closer. 'Please tell me what's wrong.'

He managed to gather his nerve and say with a shy smile, 'It was just – so easy to love you.'

'Did you think it would be hard, or complicated?'

'I didn't know.'

'Love should be easy. Pleasant. With no remorse afterward.'

His colour deepened. 'That isn't what I was brought up to believe.'

'Ah. That's it. Half the boys who come here have the same problem. Well – ' Another reassuring pat. 'You don't have to rush to the altar just because we made love. It may work like that elsewhere, but not in here.'

He was embarrassed that she'd guessed his secret thoughts. He had indeed been thinking that a respectable girl, compromised this way, would have sobbed and demanded that he marry her in return for what she had given him in a moment of weakness. And his own conscience would have insisted that he do what the girl, and society, said was only ri—

A crash brought his eyes open. From down the hall he heard an angry shout. Aggie sat up and pressed her palm against his chest:

'Lie still. I'll see what's wrong.'

Naked, her thinness pitifully evident, she ran to the door and peered out. Both of them heard loud voices – a man's and a woman's, the latter shrill and vindictive. Instantly, he had a sense of danger.

Aggie shut the door, leaned against it and scratched herself. 'Nothing serious. Just a small dispute down the hall.'

But it didn't sound small to him. The woman screamed an obscenity. The floor vibrated as someone or something fell. Boots pounded. Someone was in trouble. Maybe a fellow student. He remembered the Hungarian. If one student got in trouble, all of them might—

He pushed up from the bed. 'Let me take a look.'

Aggie protested but he ignored her. He pulled on his drawers, then his pants. With a nervous glance at his face, she moved away from the door.

Heart hammering, Will lifted the latch and stepped into the dim hall.

Two doors down, a wiry, curly-haired young man with a towel around his middle was confronting a naked blonde with shoulders and thighs as big as an ironworker's. She towered over her customer, but he wasn't intimidated.

'I *saw* you reach for my wallet.'

'Damn liar!' the blonde retorted. Marchant poked his head out of another door. Noticing Will, the blonde said to him, 'You should have heard what he asked me to do for him. Or *with* him, I'm not sure which. I said no, so now he's accusing me—'

'Of being a thief!' the curly-haired young man broke in.

Madam Melba hove into view at the end of the hall, followed by the lumbering thug with the flattened face. He unbuttoned his shabby jacket to show a billy club in his belt.

Madam Melba stepped between the quarrelling pair, shoving each of them roughly.

'I'll have no disorderly behaviour in this establishment, Mr Pennel. My unofficial truce with the college is a very delicate one. Now explain yourself.'

'I don't deny I was asking for – something special,' the student said. 'I'd have paid. What I wanted doesn't change what she did. She tried to steal my money.'

Will leaned against the wall, watching the flat-faced man, who was glowering at the angry customer. Pennel, Will thought. A familiar name. But he couldn't place it.

Madam Melba dismissed the accusation with one word. 'Nonsense.' She put her arm round the blonde's pudgy waist. 'Alice is the newest of our girls, but I screen every applicant most carefully. I run an honest house, and you and all the other young gentlemen from Harvard know I do, Mr Pennel.'

'Maybe I know it, but she doesn't,' Pennel shot back.

The flat-faced man was fingering the billy club. The corridor was growing crowded as whores and their customers popped out of the cubicles. The situation might have eased if Pennel hadn't made one last statement:

'I'm going to have the authorities look into this place.'

Madam Melba's gaze grew chill. 'Be careful about uttering threats like that, young man. We can't afford to treat them lightly.'

'You damn well better not! I'm getting out of here and going to the police.'

He spun and started back into his cubicle. Madam Melba pondered only a moment. She waved to summon her helper:

'You'd better do a little something to dissuade him, Rudy.'

A smile spread over the thug's face. He yanked the billy from his belt and sauntered toward the door of the cubicle, pleased to be the centre of attention.

Will was alarmed to see that none of the students moved to help Pennel. In a place like this, trouble for one of them meant trouble for all. Maybe a few conciliatory words would avert it. Impulsively, he stepped forward.

The thug stopped and glared. Will slid past him, blocking the doorway. Inside the cubicle, Pennel was scrambling into his clothes.

It took all the courage Will possessed to look past the flat-faced man and say to Madam Melba:

'Give him a chance to calm down. Maybe we can get him out of here and avoid a muss.'

Madam Melba was clearly anxious for a peaceful settlement. She rushed to Will's side:

401

'You mean no reports to the police?'

'I don't know Mr Pennel personally, so I can't promise. But I'll certainly talk to him. If there's fighting, someone else in the neighbourhood will call the police, and then we're all in dutch. I don't think anyone here wants to be involved in a scandal—'

Other students in the hall murmured anxious agreement. Headlines flashed into Will's mind. LAW INVADES SPORTING HOUSE. PUBLISHER'S SON ARRESTED. What did they do to you at the medical school for such an offence? Dismiss you, most likely.

'Please, Madam Melba, give me a chance to talk to him.'

The flat-faced man didn't like the interference. He grabbed Will's shoulder:

'I'll do the talking that needs to be done here.'

Will put a palm against the man's left arm, to hold him back. 'Let her answer me before you—'

'Don't shove me, you college fucker,' the man shouted. Before Madam Melba could step in, he slammed the billy against the side of Will's head.

CHAPTER VI

Marcus

Will crashed backwards into the wall. Flimsy panelling broke. He reached high over his head, snatching at a gas fixture to keep from falling. The blowsy blonde lunged at him, hands forming claws. 'Little bastard! Who asked you to interfere?' she shrieked.

The flat-faced man flung her aside and rammed the

end of the billy into Will's left hip. A little higher and it might have done some serious damage. But it glanced off bone and gave him time to grab the thug's wrist.

An unexpected twist of the wrist loosened the big man's grip. The stick fell. Will caught it. The thug fisted his hand and launched a punch that could have broken Will's neck if it had landed. Will ducked. The man's hand smashed a hole in the wall and disappeared up to the elbow.

Will hit the back of the man's head with the billy. The thug yelled, his arm tearing strips of wood from the wall as he staggered away. Will helped him along by ramming the billy into his groin. The man crashed against the opposite wall, screaming like a gored animal.

Madam Melba had abandoned all pretence of gentility. 'Carrie, fetch my horse pistol! I'll show these rich brats they can't tear up my house.'

The naked blonde kicked Will's shin and clawed his face. One nail nicked his left eye, momentarily blinding him. She tore the stick out of his hand, turned, and sought another target. Joe Marchant was hurrying to help Will at last. The blonde hit Marchant's head three times. The last blow broke the billy. The young medical student went down in a slow corkscrew, blood pouring from a gash in his scalp.

The blonde turned back to Will, charging like a jiggling white elephant. He didn't want to hurt a woman. On the other hand, he had no intention of letting her maim him. He put up both hands and shoved, managing to hurl her off balance. Cursing, she fell against Madam Melba, knocked her down and landed, buttocks first, on the madam's scrawny bosom.

Madam Melba flailed and shrieked. She might have been a longshoreman, so obscenely did she curse the students and so loudly did she scream for the horse pistol one of her girls was attempting to pass to her.

Alice was still floundering on top of her employer. 'Get your fat hams out of my face!' Madam Melba howled, pinching the blonde's backside. The blonde shot up like a cannonball. Will, meantime, took the only escape route left open to him – the door through which Pennel had retreated.

Pennel had his shoes and trousers on. The moment Will burst in, Pennel yelled and pointed:

'Watch out behind you!'

Will spun. The flat-faced man was lurching across the hall with one hand outstretched and the other still rubbing his groin. Desperate, Will hunted for a weapon. There was none.

A small, cheap armoire stood beside the door. He leaped to the end of the armoire, put his shoulder against it and pushed. The armoire moved easily; evidently there wasn't much inside.

He shoved the armoire diagonally into the doorway an instant before the thug appeared. The man's outstretched arm was pinned between the doorframe and the piece of furniture Will was pushing with all his strength. Bone in the man's arm cracked. He screamed.

Wild-eyed, he struggled to extricate his arm and kick the armoire aside. In the corridor, Harvard men were running to and fro while whores in various stages of undress punched and kicked and threw chamberpots at them. Panting, Will searched the cubicle. He and Pennel were trapped—

No! Next to the headboard hung a velvet drapery. Old; shabby – and rippling slowly.

Will leaped past Pennel, tore the drapery down and whooped. Unlike Aggie's cubicle, this one had a window. It was raised a couple of inches. Outside there was nothing but mist and dark.

'Out that way!' Will ordered. Pennel snatched up his shirt and coat, then tried to raise the window.

'Stuck!'

'Put your coat over you and go head first.'

In the corridor there was more punching and screaming and crashing, the pandemonium heightened by Madam Melba's torrent of oaths, and then by the boom of her pistol. Pennel swallowed, covered his head and dived at the glass, shattering it, and tearing his trousers as he plunged through. Will heard him as he hit the muddy ground.

Will scrambled through the sawtoothed opening and leaped, landing in watery ooze and sinking ankle deep. The footing was treacherous. He lost his balance and sprawled face first. But his only injury was a scratch on his left forearm.

Covered with mud and spitting, he scrambled to his feet. A spectral hand, equally filthy, shot toward him out of the fog. The other student was barely visible as he shook Will's hand and whispered:

'Marcus Pennel.'

'Will Kent.'

'Thanks for what you did.'

'Never mind that now. Got your wallet?'

'In my pocket. Let's get going!'

Madam Melba appeared at the broken window. 'I'll teach you to disrupt and vandalize a decent, orderly business establishment!' Beyond the other student's shoulder, Will saw her pistol glinting.

He dived against Pennel and knocked him into another puddle. There was a roar, a streak of fire in the dark. Before Madam Melba could fire again, they leaped up and ran. Neither paid any attention to the direction the other one took.

Will ran a block in the thick fog, too shaken to be amused by some of the brawl's comical aspects. All at once he slowed down. He looked to the left, to the right, and behind.

He was running alone.

He stopped; listened. In the murk, shouts reverberated, and loud crashings. At that precise moment a door in his memory sprang open.

'God above. Marcus *Pennel*.'

He'd come to the aid of a member of one of the very richest families in America; a family even wealthier than Will's, and so long entrenched in New York Society that by comparison, the Kents were upstart immigrants.

He started walking, moving rapidly but without a sense of fear. The thick fog would protect him from further danger. Rain began to fall again, dampening the mud that was drying on his arms and bare back. He was uncomfortable but he didn't mind.

'Pennel,' he said again. As he recalled, the first Pennel had been a rag dealer prowling the streets of Manhattan with a pushcart, sometime during the early years of the eighteenth century. Today the family had real estate holdings nearly as vast as those of the Vanderbilts. In the mid-nineteenth century, the Pennels had begun to accumulate a second fortune by constructing and leasing factory buildings on land they owned all along the East Coast. Their money was old money; polished into respectability by the passage of many generations.

For a moment Will fervently wished he hadn't become confused and lost Pennel in the fog. He'd have liked to get to know the young man he'd helped. It could have been a useful contact for the future.

But of course no member of the Pennel family would deign to speak to a Kent unless it became necessary during some commercial transaction. He'd never see Marcus Pennel again.

As it turned out, he saw him the following Wednesday night.

Marcus Pennel called at the house on Beacon Street. He wore a suit of expensive English tweed, complemented by a walking stick and pale grey gloves. He strolled around the Kent parlour with an air of authority quite at odds with the panic he'd displayed at the brothel.

'Didn't have a proper chance to thank you, Kent. Took a wrong turn and lost you somewhere. Trust you got back here in one piece?'

Pennel was at least two years older than Will. He had an amiable, boyish smile and gave the impression that he didn't take anything seriously, though Will knew better. He took the contents of his wallet very seriously. A family trait, no doubt.

In response to the question, Will smiled and nodded. 'I was damn near frozen. Luckily my parents had gone to bed by the time I got here. I didn't have to explain why I was half naked and covered with mud.'

'How's that other fellow? The one who got coshed?'

Embarrassed, Will said, 'I don't know what you mean by coshed.'

'Oh, of course. Little term I picked up in Britain last summer. Coshed means hit on the noggin.'

'Then you're talking about Marchant.'

'I s'pose. I don't know the chap's name. I was looking out the door just as he fell.'

'He's all right. Some of the others from the medical school sewed up the gash in his scalp after they all got away. I'm told Madam Melba handed out some bribe money to the proper authorities and is doing business as usual.'

Marcus sniffed. 'Last time I patronize the old slut. That Hungarian would have nailed my balls to the ceiling if I'd been forced to deal with him all by myself. I wasn't carrying enough cash to buy him off, and that's the only way I know to handle such scum. You came to my rescue—'

Will waved off the compliment. 'I'm just thankful we got out safely. Glad you got your wallet back, too.'

Marcus took a chair and crossed his legs, relaxed and elegant. He lit a cigarette. 'Oh, the girl didn't try to steal anything of mine. She just wouldn't perform the – ah – special service I requested. I got damned mad about it.'

Will felt victimized. But it was clear his visitor wasn't interested in his reaction; he didn't even glance in Will's direction. And Will decided his annoyance was worth it when Marcus said:

'The purpose of my call is to show you I'm genuinely grateful for what you did. If you've some free time over Christmas, I'd like you to join a house party we're having at our place down in Westchester County.'

Will was so overwhelmed, he couldn't speak for a moment. Marcus raised an eyebrow. 'That's outside New York City.'

'Yes, I know where it is. That's very kind of you, Pennel.'

'Call me Marcus. I think fate, or possibly our interest in women, ordained that we'd be friends. You'll like Pennel House over the holidays. Lots of bright young people around. Lots of charming females.' He scrutinized Will with mock seriousness. 'You might even take a fancy to my sister Laura. She's a year younger than I, but a pretty piece of fluff, if I do say so. The Harvard boys I bring home don't seem to interest her in the slightest. Perhaps a learned physician will break the pattern.'

Excited by the thought of what the invitation could mean to his career, Will nevertheless felt it prudent not to appear too eager:

'See here, Pennel—'

'It's Marcus, didn't I say?'

'Very well – Marcus. You needn't invite me just to give me some kind of – reward, as you put it. I was glad to help you.'

Even though I was scared as hell doing it.

'Of course I need to give you a reward! Buying, selling – balancing one favour against another – that's what the world is all about. That and nothing else.'

His smile was cordial, yet a little smug. He rose and held out his hand.

'My driver's waiting. I have other calls to make, but this was the most important. We'll expect you at Pennel House the day after Christmas.'

3

When Gideon heard the news, he never thought to probe Will's statement that he'd met Marcus Pennel through mutual friends at Harvard. He was too busy being exercised:

'Bunch of hypocritical robbers, the Pennels. Thurman Pennel, the boy's father, is a mossback of the worst kind.'

'You've met him?'

'Yes, unfortunately. I had a run-in with him at the last Republican nominating convention. He'd like to see us roll blissfully backward into the eighteenth century – or perhaps the Middle Ages. Then no one would presume to question his right to make money from human misery. Mr Pennel specializes in that. He puts up the most efficient factory buildings in New England. Companies stand in line to lease them. I shudder to think of the number of young girls and children who die because he designs those buildings to be free of distractions for the workers. I'm referring to distractions such as windows that admit sunlight and fresh air. I'm surprised you want to get involved with people like that.'

Irked, Will shot back, 'Papa, it's a social occasion. I'm not endorsing the way the Pennels live.'

Gideon cast a dour eye over his son. 'Don't be too sure.'

4

Drew was even more caustic about the invitation:

'By God, you are determined to be a Fifth Avenue doctor, aren't you? But ascending the social heights via the window of a whorehouse – that must be some kind of first.'

Will refused to be baited. His life was his to live as he chose, and he had no intention of missing a chance to visit the Pennels of Westchester County.

CHAPTER VII

The Pennels

Will first saw Pennel House through the slowly falling snow of a December afternoon. Even counting William K. Vanderbilt's place on Fifth Avenue, he'd never seen a more magnificent residence. Centrepiece of a two-hundred-acre estate forty minutes north of the city by train, Pennel House was not only stunning in its own right, but symbolic of, and appropriate to, the position of its owners. Their world contained everything that was worth having – or so Will had convinced himself while anticipating this visit.

The mansion had been designed in popular and eclectic style. It was a three-story, fifty-four-room castle with no two exterior elements matching. Shape pulled against shape, colour against colour, texture against texture. The ground floor was pale limestone trimmed with dark brick; the second story was shingled, the third half-timbered, gabled, and roofed with slates of several colours.

Balconies, porches, and dormers interrupted the facade at a dozen places. Two huge chimneys dominated one end of the house. At the other, an immense round tower jutted into the gloomy sky. The mansion's windows resembled painter's palettes; light of every conceivable colour was cast on the snow by intricate patterns of stained glass. Curiously, the jumble of elements and techniques was so overstated that it achieved a certain reverse elegance, its ostentation declaring to the world that a Midas lived here – for who but a Midas could afford such extravagant confusion?

The Pennel carriage, sent to meet Will at the railroad station, pulled up at the main entrance to the house. The postilion jumped down, eyebrows and hat brim snow-encrusted. He began unloading Will's three pieces of luggage. Marcus burst out the front door, a toddy mug in hand.

'Welcome, my friend! We've been expecting you for an hour.'

'The snow's getting heavy on the roads.' He shook Marcus' hand and moved gratefully from the cold air to the warmth of the immense baronial foyer.

Pennel House was as elaborate inside as out. Everywhere he looked he saw ornamentation, decorative scrollwork, heavy furniture, all in the Queen Anne style. Gas and lamp-light on polished panelling and a parquet floor created a warm atmosphere helping to offset the forbidding vastness of the foyer. Will quickly decided that despite the jumble of styles, motifs, and materials, the house had a definite appeal. It was just the sort of place in which he could be happy.

Servants took Will's coat, hat, stick, and gloves and whisked them out of sight. With a grin, Marcus said to him:

'I've built you up to Laura something fierce. Handsome, all-knowing physician to whom no crevice of a woman's body is a mystery – or sacred.'

Will turned red. 'Good God. Your sister will run the other way.'

'On the contrary. All we get here are chaps with pedigrees, never one with brains. Till you, I mean. She's mad to meet you.'

'I'm anxious to meet her too. Is she here?'

'No, not just now. She and the others went skating on the pond. But I'm glad the place isn't swarming with our friends. It gives me a chance to introduce you to Father.'

He grasped Will's arm and steered him toward massive, intricately carved doors of dark wood. A footman rushed forward, seized a heavy bronze ring and opened the right-hand door. Will said:

'I'm worried about the way you described me to your sister. She's in for a mighty disappointment.'

'Nonsense!' Marcus waved with his mug. Some of the toddy splattered the footman's coat. The man blinked but said nothing. Apparently Marcus didn't even notice. 'She'll be charmed. I keep telling you that you're like no guest we've ever had at Pennel House.'

That was probably true, Will thought, but not in the sense that Marcus meant it. He had done some investigation of the Pennels. In terms of social position, they were far above the Kents. For one thing, Thurman

Pennel no longer dirtied his hands with direct involvement in his business empire. He merely issued orders to underlings.

'Father has a guest but he said it's all right to break in. Follow me.'

2

Marcus led his visitor into a huge but surprisingly cheerful room which resembled pictures of English castles that Will had seen. The room – the living hall, Marcus called it – was crowded with furniture, potted plants, and bric-a-brac. A large open stairway dominated the inner wall. The outer one was pierced by narrow windows of leaded stained glass. In the wall directly ahead was a large, lofty recess.

Within the inglenook, two perspiring men sat on thickly padded bench seats which faced one another in front of an immense hearth. Fragrant logs blazed in the grate and set reflections to shimmering on polished floor tiles. Marcus and Will stopped at a respectful distance. The larger of the two men was saying in a slurred voice:

' – of course I intend to donate heavily to the war chest, Andrew. That damned Democrat is dangerous. He must be turned out before he engineers the ruin of the system under which we've both prospered.'

'I canna help but agree, Thurman. But he's the incumbent. We must start now if we mean to defeat him. That's why we're seeking your guarantee of support this far ahead of the election. We—'

The speaker stopped suddenly, warned by the nervous eyes of the heavier man. Marcus moved forward. Both men rose and stepped out of the inglenook.

Will knew that he and Marcus had interrupted a

413

conversation about President Cleveland. The Republicans had been infuriated by the President's annual address to Congress on December 6. The President had devoted the entire message to a carefully structured plea for reduced tariffs – a proposal which was anathema to the protectionists in the Republican party. Gideon had predicted that the tariff would be the major issue of next year's campaign. The conversation just overheard tended to confirm that.

'Father,' Marcus said, 'I'd like you and your guest to meet my friend Will Kent.'

He addressed the larger of the two men. Thurman Pennel stood well over six feet. He was paunchy and had lost most of his hair. Only a few dark, oiled wisps were left, combed across his hairless skull.

His visitor, fifty or a bit older, was noticeably shorter and leaner. White whiskers lent him a benign air, though his eyes were foxy, even hard. When Marcus spoke Will's last name, the visitor raked Will with an appraising glance. Meantime, Marcus' father said:

'How do you do, Kent? I'm Thurman Pennel. We're happy to have you here.'

He extended his hand and smiled, but there was no cordiality in his heavy-lidded eyes, just as there had been none in his welcome. Marcus didn't resemble his father, Will noticed. Perhaps he favoured his mother.

'I appreciate the invitation, sir,' Will said, determined to be polite. It was uncomfortably hot near the fire. Pine boughs hung up to decorate the living hall gave off an odour that was cloyingly sweet. There was another sweet smell in the air, but Will couldn't immediately identify it.

'This is Mr Carnegie,' Pennel said. 'Andrew – Mr Kent.'

The sinewy little man shook hands. His grip was strong. 'Related to the Boston Kents, by any chance?'

'Gideon Kent is my father.'

'I see.' Carnegie's lips twitched; it could never have been called a smile. 'Well, lad, we'll na hold that against you.'

Will kept his temper as best he could. He knew Carnegie's name and background, of course. Almost everyone in the nation did. An immigrant from Scotland, Carnegie had begun his working career as a bobbin boy. Today he controlled a steadily expanding complex of steel factories. Will had heard his father say Carnegie was pulling the American steel industry into a dominant position in the world market almost single-handedly. 'British steelmakers would like to see him dead,' was Gideon's summation. To judge from Carnegie's hale and leathery look, he would probably be around for many years.

Carnegie's smile remained as cold as the air Will had quitted a few moments ago. 'I'll na lie to you, young man. I cannot abide your father's views. They say he was once a Republican—' The little man clearly found that hard to believe.

Marcus looked unhappy about the trend of the conversation.

Thurman Pennel said, 'He showed his true colours when he deserted Blaine in the last national election. Your father and I had a discussion about Mr Blaine at the nominating convention. No, I guess discussion doesn't quite cover it—'

Pennel smiled just as his guest had done – to make it seem as if he were getting a little joke when he was actually indulging his malice:

'He started to knock me down. The same way he knocked down Ward McAllister—'

By God, I refuse to stand for this, Will thought. But politeness won out. Pennel was his host, and Gideon was the first to admit his opinions weren't popular among Republicans.

Still pretending to smile, Pennel added, 'Hot-tempered, these ex-Rebs, eh?'

Will's face was white. He kept his voice level:

'That's true, sir. They can be very hot-tempered when they believe something strongly. My father believed Mr Blaine was a crook.'

Pennel scowled. But Carnegie's expression changed from distaste to grudging admiration. Pennel noticed his guest's approval – and then his son's distressed look. He wasn't so tactless as to pursue the little quarrel further. He again resorted to that false joviality:

'In any case, Kent, you're the one invited for a visit, not your father—'

He stepped to Will's side and clapped him on the shoulder. Will smelled the sweet odour again, and recognized it. Gin. No wonder Pennel was so garrulous, so imprudent in what he said. *If I talked that way when I drank, I wouldn't drink.*

He continued to resent the criticism of his father. Then, on a more practical tack, he remembered some of the reasons he'd wanted to come to Pennel House. He decided he'd better do something to blunt that criticism:

'Perhaps I ought to explain something, Mr Pennel. My father's a publisher but I'm studying to be a doctor. Two different careers. Two different people. My father understands that. Politics has ruined many a friendship. I don't intend for it to ruin any of mine.'

'D'ya mean to say you stay neutral, lad?' Carnegie's disapproval of neutrality was quite evident.

Will stared him down and said, 'No, sir. I have my own views. But I don't debate them. Especially when I'm a guest in someone's house.'

Marcus smiled. Thurman Pennel was immediately more cordial:

'I expect you'll go far in your profession, Kent. A doctor doesn't develop a loyal clientele by stepping on the toes of patients with whom he disagrees. You seem to have learned that lesson early.'

Will squared his shoulders and met Pennel's lidded gaze. The man was opinionated and more than a little drunk; Will disliked him intensely. But he smiled, stifled a twinge of conscience and said:

'I've tried to learn it, Mr Pennel.'

Before he could say more, someone came rushing down the open staircase:

'We're back, Marcus. Is this your friend? You must present me at once!'

The men forgotten, Will turned toward the stairs. With considerable relief, Marcus said:

'Will, here's Laura.'

3

Will immediately lost interest in meeting the other members of the house party who followed Marcus' sister into the living room. The group consisted of four young gentlemen from Dartmouth and Yale, and three other young ladies, vapid and noisy, who attended private schools. All Will could see was their hostess.

Laura Pennel was a beautiful girl, a year older than Will, pale-skinned and immaculately groomed. She had slightly slanted grey eyes, and straw-coloured hair that fell in tight natural curls. Curly hair was a characteristic both she and her brother had evidently inherited from their mother; it certainly didn't come from the paternal side.

She was dressed fashionably, in a severely tailored suit. The mauve skirt and jacket contrasted with a snug white shirtwaist beneath. An ascot was neatly pinned at the centre of her full bosom.

Her face was sweet, though it was an animated

sweetness, quite unlike the insipid look of many beautiful girls. There was an innocence about her, too, an aura that told him she was a person incapable of wicked thought or deed, at least not an intentional one.

He tried to be pleasant and witty as he replied to a few inconsequential questions about his family and his trip from Boston. He felt he was making a fool of himself. Not that it seemed to matter. She was soon gone again, sweeping out of the living hall accompanied by her friends. He was so flustered, all he could remember of their entire conversation was one fact. She would see him at supper in half an hour.

Marcus showed him up to his bedroom in the tower wing. 'You and Laura seemed to hit it off instantly,' Marcus said when they were halfway up the stairs.

'She's a lovely young woman.'

'And you look like a gentleman who's been thoroughly smitten.'

'The instant I saw her,' Will said with a nod, his light tone concealing the strength of his feeling.

Still his conscience nagged at him:

Would you have been smitten if her name were something other than Pennel? Would you have been so quick to turn your back on your father and try to ingratiate yourself with hers?

'Here we are,' Marcus said, turning in at a bedroom door and temporarily relieving Will of the burden of listening to that accusing voice.

CHAPTER VIII

The Lioness

Will's luggage had been unpacked, the contents neatly put away in a bureau and an armoire. He set about changing his shirt. Marcus lingered. Something was on his mind. Presently he brought it into the open:

'You got a dreadful welcome from my father. You must forgive him, Will. He isn't too competent playing the role of gracious host. And when he's had too much to drink, he's far from tactful.'

'Oh, that's all right—' Will began.

'It certainly isn't.' Marcus blew his nose, then lit a cigarette. 'He insulted you. He'll never apologize, so I must.'

Will shrugged to suggest the apology was accepted, though not considered important or necessary. Marcus slouched in a chair and hooked a leg over the arm. He peered at the end of his cigarette.

'Might as well tell you something else. You'll notice it soon enough anyway. Mother and Father aren't exactly what you'd call loving spouses. Perhaps they were once. But these days things are strained. Father's got a shopgirl in town. He keeps her in one of those new French flats near Forty-fifth and Lexington. I don't believe Mother knows about it. But she certainly suspects. If she ever gets definite proof, I suppose she'll throw him out. The friction does nothing to improve the atmosphere in this house.'

Will was startled but tried to conceal it. Marcus expected him to take the revelations in his stride. A man was always free to enjoy a woman's favours so long as that woman had loose morals, and could by no

419

stretch of the imagination be considered a potential wife – although as the prostitute Aggie had sensed, Will had trouble being that cavalier about any girl.

He reached for a hair brush. In a calm voice he said, 'You surprise me, Marcus. You and your sister act as if there isn't a bit of trouble in the house.'

Now Marcus shrugged. 'We both try to stay out of range of the squabbling. I tend to take my father's side – I don't give a damn what he does. Laura sides with Mother.'

Was that a nasty note in his voice? As though he were the weaker of the two, and resented it? Will couldn't be sure, and Marcus concealed any ill feelings with another nonchalant lift of his shoulders.

'In any case, I don't want Father's behaviour to spoil your visit.'

Will thought of Laura's shapely figure and angelic face and said:

'Never.'

2

Mr Carnegie wasn't present for supper; Thurman Pennel said Carnegie had departed while the guests were refreshing themselves in their rooms. The main meal of the day had been eaten at noon, but supper was still a feast. It consisted of cuts of turkey and some other, more gamy fowl set out with a multitude of side dishes and a large selection of white wines and champagnes. The meal was served in a dining room so large and heavily hung with tapestries, Will again thought of some great baronial hall in England.

Before the meal began, Marcus presented him to Mrs Pennel. She was a small, curly-haired woman who seemed unusually shy. She murmured a word of welcome and then returned to her daughter's side, as if she had nothing further to say, and – being married to a man as important and dominating as Thurman Pennel – would have no right to utter it if she did. Will soon learned how mistaken he was in making that judgment.

Marcus had warned him that relationships in the family were strained. As the supper commenced, he saw signs of that; some were embarrassingly obvious.

Thurman Pennel lurched along the sideboard, filling his plate from the dishes set out in the light of silver candlesticks. Pennel spooned up candied yams but missed his plate, depositing a large, glistening mass of food on the floor. Several of the young house guests noticed and pretended they hadn't. Mrs Pennel's face grew stiff with disapproval.

Pennel started to stagger on toward his place at the head of the long table. He saw his wife watching him. With a scowl, he squatted and picked up the sweet potato with the serving spoon which he then handed to a serving girl who hurried forward. Only then did he move on, his neck red.

Will was watching Mrs Pennel. No smile broke her sedate face. But he thought he detected a gleam of triumph in her eyes – particularly when she exchanged looks with Laura.

To reach his assigned place between two of the house guests, Will had to circle Thurman Pennel's chair at the head of the table. As he did, he again smelled gin.

Pennel didn't try to sober up during supper. Instead, he drank a great deal of champagne. The moment his champagne glass was empty a servant refilled it and he started gulping again. Except for a certain slurring of his speech which had been evident earlier, he didn't act drunk. At least not until he called for everyone's attention and told an off-colour story that had no place in the conversation of mixed company.

The story angered Mrs Pennel. 'My dear – if you please,' was all she said when he finished, and that was said very softly. But Pennel had been tongue-lashed, and he and everyone else knew it.

Pennel started to retort, looked at his wife and then at Laura and said nothing. He snapped his fingers. The servant with the champagne bottle rushed forward. Pennel pointed to his empty glass.

While he drank, he again scrutinized his wife and daughter. Will was shocked to see the expression in the man's dull brown eyes. *Am I crazy, or does he hate both of them?*

The young men and women at the table were minimally polite to Will. But it was clear that they felt awkward – in a couple of cases, irked – to have an outsider in their midst. He was just as uncomfortable, unable to make much sense of their conversation about someone's yachting party last summer, or someone else's recent victory in a lawn tennis match. Laura always knew what was being discussed; her conversation was cheerful and animated.

Few remarks were addressed directly to Will. To those that were, he replied with a murmur, or a smile and a nod. He kept quiet for fear of making a fool of himself – then began to fear that his silence was creating precisely that impression.

After the meal, he was thunderstruck when Laura walked straight to his side. She'd barely spoken a word to him at the table. As Marcus led the group toward the music room, she took his arm:

'I suppose you found all that social chatter frightfully boring, Mr Kent. Your studies keep you occupied with matters ever so much more serious and important.'

Was she mocking him? He saw no sign. He wanted to jump up and click his heels; he hadn't come off as a clod after all. His shyness had been misinterpreted as intellectual boredom.

He didn't intend to alter the impression:

'I hate to admit it to a charming hostess, but you're

right. When you deal with life and death, it isn't easy to work yourself into a passion over lawn tennis.'

'Doctors in training must see sights that are positively shocking.'

A thoughtful pause; he wanted to drain every drop of advantage from the situation. 'On occasion. The real world isn't as sheltered and comfortable as Pennel House.' With difficulty, he framed a compliment. 'By the way – I've never seen anything quite so pretty as that outfit you're wearing.'

Marcus had kept the other guests moving. Will and Laura were momentarily isolated in a passageway designed to resemble an arched tunnel in a castle. Not too authentic a tunnel, though. Gas fixtures jutted from the walls; some illuminated large, conventional landscapes in heavy gilt frames.

'Ah, do you like it?' Laura spun into a pirouette in the centre of the passage. Will caught a flash of the toe of her shoe. Her skirt had no bustle, and fitted so snugly that he saw, or thought he saw, the suggestion of the cleft between her buttocks. Unbearably erotic, somehow—

She turned full circle, her cheeks flushed from wine. 'Papa doesn't like me to wear it. It's the very latest thing, but he thinks anything from France is immoral. Imagine, a judgment like that from someone like him! Mama's a modernist, though. She wants me to look up-to-date.'

Laura took his arm again. He felt the pressure of her breast against his sleeve. The contact was evidently unintentional. She drew away, turning still redder. A swift glance down the passage seemed to suggest she'd let her emotions carry her away.

But no one had seen them. Marcus and the other young people were trooping into the music room. Mrs Pennel and her husband had disappeared as soon as the group left the dining room.

'Mama probably struck you as a proper and dutiful wife, didn't she, Mr Kent?'

He wondered what kind of answer she wanted. Not knowing, he hedged:

'Very soft-spoken, certainly. I hardly heard her say a word except when your father told that story.'

'Wasn't that dreadful? The poor man simply can't control his tongue when he drinks. Sometimes he's just impossible.'

'Your mother acted with great restraint—'

'Don't mistake that for a lack of backbone, Mr Kent. Whatever you see in this house that pleases you – whatever you eat that you enjoy – be assured it's all Mama's doing. She even picks out Papa's clothes. The only area in which she defers to him is in the choice of some of the paintings.'

She nodded at one of the two canvases. 'Papa still considers Thomas Cole and the rest of the Hudson River painters to be very advanced. He's fifty years behind the times, but Mama humours him. I'm afraid you won't find a Matthew Kent at Pennel House. Not while Papa's alive, anyway.'

'Oh, you know my uncle's work?'

'I'm more familiar with – what do I dare call it? His social life—?'

Will grinned. 'Try escapades.'

She smiled too. 'That does fit, doesn't it? Your uncle's name pops up in the Saunterer's column every now and then.'

'The Saunterer,' Will repeated. 'You must read *Town Topics*.'

'Everyone in our set reads *Town Topics*. Don't you?'

He shook his head. 'My father won't allow it in the house. He says the Colonel is a blackmailer and a disgrace to journalism.'

Will was referring to Colonel William d'Alton Mann, a raffish adventurer who'd acquired the foundering weekly tabloid called *Town Topics* in 1885. Mann had instantly converted it to the most scandal-packed paper in the nation.

He piously claimed that his journalistic mission was to improve the behaviour of society by exposing immorality when and where he found it. Gideon had a different opinion. He said the ten- or twelve-page Saunterings column, which contained the week's juicy gossip and was written by Mann himself, was no instrument of moral reform but a blatant money-making device. Mann's biggest income came from items left out of his paper.

The Colonel kept a table at Delmonico's Restaurant for the convenience of wealthy men to whom he'd sent an advance galley proof of some scandalous item concerning them, their wives, children, or mistresses. Usually the victim was willing, not to say eager, to pay to have the item omitted from the next edition. Once a week the Colonel received the supplicants – and the bribes – at his table where he also managed to work in his favourite meal: six mutton chops, two heads of lettuce with a creamy dressing, a dozen biscuits, a huge portion of chocolate cake, two full bottles of champagne, and a cigar.

'Deserves to be shot,' was Gideon's opinion of the editor and publisher of *Town Topics* – which from time to time chronicled some of Matt Kent's rowdy exploits at Europe's fashionable resorts.

' – yes,' Laura concluded. 'I'd say the Kent name is a familiar one in this household.'

He laughed. 'Though not for the right reasons.' He indicated the paintings. 'If your mother's responsible for everything except the art in this house, she's to be complimented.'

'Thank you. In our set, a wife's expected to take charge. The husband only appears to run things. The power really belongs to what the newspapers call the lioness.'

'The what?'

'Lioness,' she repeated with a dazzling smile. 'I don't know who first applied the term to women like Mama, but I think it's rather appropriate. The male goes out to hunt for food while the female defends the home, tends the young, and disposes of whatever bounty the male dutifully brings back. The lioness runs everything. The limits of propriety are never exceeded because she sets those limits. You heard Mama speak to Papa when it became necessary—'

And saw him back down the moment she ordered it, he thought.

The rules in the Pennel household were clearly different from those under which Gideon and Julia operated. They treated their marriage as a partnership, not as a struggle for dominance between – God help him – carnivorous animals. Lioness struck Will as a ridiculous conceit. And yet Laura seemed taken with it. So taken, it made him uneasy.

A new thought troubled him. By describing the Pennels' relationship, was Laura also setting out the terms for any friendship she might develop with him?

His silence brought a frown to her face:

'Do you disapprove of Mama speaking to Papa as she did? Do you disapprove of a wife guiding her husband's life in his best interests?'

Three of the young people appeared at the door of the music room searching for them. One pointed:

'Oh, there they are.'

Will said, 'I don't think it's my position to approve or disapprove, Miss Pennel.'

Pink-faced over the stares they were receiving, she nevertheless stood her ground, whispering:

'I do wish you'd call me Laura.'

'Very well – Laura. I repeat, approval or disapproval

426

isn't mine to give. I don't move in the same circles as you do.'

The others started calling for them to hurry so the carolling could start. Inside the music room, near a great candle-decorated tree, Marcus was seated at a rosewood piano and was playing the opening notes of 'Good King Wenceslas.'

Laura turned so that the young people couldn't see her touch his arm for a second:

'You mustn't downgrade yourself. Politics aside, your family is eminently respectable—'

'Respectable is not the same thing as belonging to your set, as you call it,' he replied with a wry smile. 'Why, I've never even been invited to Mrs Astor's January ball.'

'But it could be arranged,' she said softly.

Suddenly something in him rebelled; he saw danger in the grey eyes and smiling demeanour of this sweet-faced girl. A lioness *devoured*. A lioness *killed*. He had no intention of being destroyed as Thurman Pennel had been. Laura's father had obviously been stripped of his authority and self-respect and driven to the arms of some shopgirl by the woman to whom he was married.

Stiffly, he said, 'I doubt it very much. The Kents don't receive invitations at that level. My father once struck Ward McAllister.'

'Yes, I know that. But—'

'I'd better say the rest, Miss Pennel.'

'I thought it was Laura.'

'We both know I'm a guest at Pennel House only because Marcus and I got acquainted through mutual friends in Cambridge.' It was the lie they'd agreed upon. 'I'm studying to be a doctor. That automatically puts my position in the world much lower than yours – as if it wasn't lower to begin with. The Kent money is new money. My father's a radical by trade and by temperament—'

'And you, Will? Are you a radical by trade and temperament?'

'That makes no difference.'

'It most certainly does. If the answer's no, people in our set will accept you – even given your notorious profession. Actually, your profession might even help. It's diverting to meet someone who uses his mind for more than the contemplation of a polo mallet or his own pedigree. People in my set respect intelligence so long as it isn't – what shall I say? Radical. Dangerous. You give every indication that yours is not. There should be no limit to how high you can rise – *if* you have the right guidance.' She averted her eyes. 'A wife with whom you share common goals—'

Marcus stopped playing and walked to the door. 'Laura, will you kindly come along and bring your friend? Or have you eloped?' he added with a smirk. One of the girls giggled:

'They're whispering back there as if they're planning on it.'

'Is that envy I detect, Charlotte dear?' Laura called out, her sweet tone not quite hiding her malice. Perhaps lioness wasn't such a farfetched term after all. Like her mother, Laura was proper; but she was also emotional, and quick to anger when she was threatened.

'We're coming,' she added, moving away from him. Over her shoulder she said, 'I suppose we have held things up. But they can just wait for us. Are you bored with carolling now that Christmas is over?' She gave him no chance to answer. 'I am, dreadfully. I'll see that Marcus cuts the singing short.'

She glided on toward the music room. A smile stole onto Will's face as he followed. She was a curious and complex girl. A girl of the very sort he'd dreamed about. A girl who could help him keep his promise about the future.

428

'I know you'll be staying with us for several days,' she went on, never glancing back to see whether he was there; she expected him to be. 'Marcus and I have planned a great many activities for the group. You and I may not find another convenient opportunity to continue this discussion. We must do so when we see each other at some later time.'

She added the last sentence as an afterthought, just before she made her entrance into the music room. She still didn't look back, but her meaning was unmistakable. She liked him. And if she continued to like him, she could and would take him where he could never go by himself.

A man didn't succeed in her world without *the right guidance*. Nor without a wife with whom he *shared common goals*. Let the lioness rule unopposed, and everything was possible—

And they would continue the discussion of the possibilities *when we see each other at some later time*.

Not if.

When.

He couldn't understand his good fortune. She could have a hundred eligible bachelors waiting on her. Why choose him? Was it for the reason she'd stated? Because he wasn't the sort of person she usually met in her crowd?

Whatever the explanation, he mustn't question his luck. She was beautiful – and she could help him realize all of his ambitions—

'Will?'

He glanced up. She was standing in the doorway of the music room. She'd spoken his name with an undertone of annoyance.

'Are you or are you not planning to join us?' she asked.

He smiled. 'Certainly.'

429

Her own smile, hard as glass, rebuffed him because he'd made her angry. She spun away:

'Then do hurry along, unless you don't enjoy our company.'

She disappeared into the music room. Worried, he called, 'I'm coming,' and rushed after her.

CHAPTER IX

A Doctor's Duty

The holiday at Pennel House sped by. It did so despite the activities Will was forced to join in merely to be near Laura.

The mornings weren't bad. Usually the group spent them ice-skating on the pond on the estate. But the afternoons and evenings were appalling. Following the main meal at midday, the group played inane parlour games such as wiggles and hunt-the-slipper. In the evenings, the young people sat with feigned expressions of interest while one of their number recited 'Thanatopsis' or some other poem Will found equally sleep-inducing.

When Will's turn came, he said with a straight face that all he could recite from memory were passages from the fifth edition of Dr Austin Flint's *Principles and Practice of Medicine*. If that didn't sound suitable, he might manage some of Professor Shattuck's observations on auscultation and percussion.

No one was amused, least of all Laura. Her smile grew stiff as she stung him with a reproving glance.

He didn't repeat the mistake. He also felt he'd learned a valuable lesson. The Pennels' set didn't appreciate humour, unless it was the bawdy variety heard when the gentlemen left the ladies and retired to another room with their cigars. Certainly Laura and her friends didn't like any kind of joke which implied disapproval of established customs or accepted ideas.

Because Charles Darwin defied accepted thinking, he was the favourite conversational whipping boy of the young people. Arguing about Darwin's theory of evolution was popular at Harvard, too; Gideon called such argumentation the greatest intellectual craze of the century.

The young people were quite opinionated on the subject, but Will wasn't particularly surprised to find that none of them had read Darwin, and only he and Laura had read the sensationally popular, fictionalized version of the 'ape or angel' debate, Stevenson's *Strange Case of Dr Jekyll and Mr Hyde*. It had been published the preceding year, and Gideon had negotiated to bring out an inexpensive reprint edition. Despite the demands of his course work, Will had read it twice.

One evening at Pennel House, there was a welcome respite from things literary. Laura persuaded Marcus to play the piano in the ballroom, so the young people could dance.

After a few minutes of intricate Virginia reels and Germans, Laura declared her boredom and the group paired off for more intimate waltzes and galops. Will was Laura's only partner. The others seemed to understand that already.

High above the ballroom floor, Marcus hunched over the piano in the musicians' gallery, smirking and puffing a cigarette as he played. He knew what his sister was up to, and was quite willing to cooperate.

Thus, for a few delicious moments, Will was able to hold the soft blonde girl in his arms. As they whirled and turned, he could feel the heavy steel stays of her corset against his palm. Occasionally the lace ruching of her high, boned collar tickled his chin – an erotic sensation, somehow.

He revelled in the nearness of her face. Her grey eyes were enhanced by the clarity and perfection of her pale skin. Being fashionable – and free of freckles that would need concealment – she didn't use cosmetics, save for a bit of rice powder and a touch of rouge so expertly applied, it might have been mistaken for the natural glow of her cheeks.

Altogether, she was the most desirable creature he'd ever met – and she knew he felt that way. He was overjoyed to realize there was a mutual attraction. She kept Marcus playing waltzes until he absolutely refused to run through another. When the last dance ended, she gave Will's hand a quick squeeze – the only real intimacy between them thus far. She might be wilful, but he knew beyond any doubt that she was morally upright. She was the kind of girl who would give herself only to the man she married.

Will had promised to be back in Boston to celebrate the New Year with Drew and some other classmates. His departure was set for early afternoon on the thirtieth. That morning, while servants packed his luggage, he planned to go on a sleigh ride with the others. He really didn't want to, but Laura was looking forward to it, so he didn't object.

After breakfast, he dressed for the outdoors and strolled to the foyer. He found Marcus and a young man named Taylor, a senior at Yale, discussing trends in men's clothes.

'They say the howling swells over in Mayfair and Belgravia are definitely going back to trouser creases front and back,' Taylor remarked. 'It's the British Army influence.'

Marcus sighed. 'What's next? Creases on the side? Cuffs?'

Taylor took him seriously. 'Very possibly, old man.

The Prince of Wales wore his trousers pressed four ways when he visited America in – oh, hello, Kent. All ready, I see.'

Will nodded. He searched for Laura in the group just entering the foyer. She was at the back, brushing something from her sable muff. She didn't look at him.

By now Will could recognize a deliberate delay. He was growing accustomed to Laura's need to dominate any situation. As long as that need didn't conflict with anything he considered important, he'd indulge her. Eagerly, in fact.

Finally she smiled at him. A manservant wearing a dark vest over his white shirt entered the foyer. He was carrying a large feather duster. Laura spoke sharply:

'Jackson, where are you going?'

The man stopped. 'The library, ma'am. Mrs Pennel wants all the books dusted. She gave me full instructions before going out this morning.'

'Be careful of the ladder when you do the top shelves. When it was delivered two weeks ago, I noticed it was none too sturdy. It came from a Scottish castle, you know. It can't be replaced.'

'I shall exercise care, ma'am.'

The man continued to the library, leaving the doors open behind him. Will frowned. He had trouble understanding a system of values which placed more importance on furniture than on the safety of a human being. There was a simple and cynical explanation, of course. Jackson wasn't a human being, merely a servant.

Laura joined Will as the group moved toward the front door. 'And how are you today, Mr Kent?' she said with mock formality, gazing up at him from beneath a little fur hat. He seemed to be drawn into those grey eyes as he answered:

'Very happy to see you. And sorry I have to leave this afternoon.'

'Well, we shall just have to make the most of the morning.'

She slipped her arm through his. He felt the contour of her breast again. The others, especially the girls, noticed her minor infraction of the rules of propriety but said nothing.

The young people trooped outside. The day was dark. The white lawns stretched away to woods that looked black under the heavy overcast. More snow was starting to fall. A pair of sleighs came gliding up the drive from the stables, the horses snorting and stepping smartly. The scene had a storybook quality; the look of one of the immensely popular Currier and Ives lithographs.

The girl accompanying Taylor made counting motions, then giggled:

'Ten people for eight places. We'll be packed tight as sardines.'

'Will and I are the only ones who'll be sardines,' Laura told her.

'What do you mean?'

'The first sleigh holds five passengers. I'll ride in the second one. I'll sit on Will's lap and risk being pilloried in *Town Topics*. That way there'll be ample room for all.'

The thought of that kind of intimate contact with Laura rekindled erotic feelings in Will. He had only a moment to anticipate the sleigh ride, though. From inside the house there suddenly came an anguished cry and a loud, prolonged crash.

2

The sleighs pulled up, bells on the horses jingled. Behind the hiss of runners and the clop of hooves, he heard a second outcry.

434

'Someone's hurt.'

He started away. She caught his arm:

'The servants will see to it.'

'Maybe it's something the servants can't handle. I should think you could wait five minutes without spoiling your ride.'

His sharpness brought a resentful glare. He turned away from it and strode into the foyer, melting snow glistening in his dark hair.

Servants were hurrying to the site of the accident. As Will followed them, he heard the front door open behind him. Then Laura exclaimed:

'Oh, its the library! I warned that oaf to be careful.'

The servant named Jackson lay in an awkward position on the library floor. Books and the broken pieces of the ladder were strewn on the carpet all around him. Midway between his left knee and ankle, something white and sharp stuck out through a bloody rip in his trousers.

'Stand back and let me examine him,' Will said as he hurried forward.

The servants quickly gave him room. He knelt, studying but not touching the leg from which the bone protruded.

Jackson was a man of about fifty. He gazed at Will with apprehensive eyes and tried to change position. The effort made him groan and squeeze his eyes shut. Tears trickled down his cheeks.

'Get me a scissors, please,' Will said.

A servant ran past Marcus and disappeared into the foyer. All the guests were trooping back into the library now. One of the girls complained about the delay. Jackson again tried to move; he clenched his teeth and uttered another groan.

'Try to relax and lie quietly,' Will said. 'I know it hurts.'

'Hurts – isn't the word for it,' Jackson gasped.

435

'I'll snip that pants leg off for a better look.'

The scissors arrived. He cut slowly and carefully, fearful of a mistake. Two fragments of bone, not just one, jutted through the bloody tear in the skin. 'An open tibial fracture—' he began as Laura walked up next to him:

'I'm sure Charlie Brassman can handle it. I've sent for him.'

'Who's Charlie Brassman?'

'One of our grooms.'

Disgusted, Will stood up. 'This man needs help from someone who treats people, not horses.'

'I tell you Charlie Brassman's perfectly competent!'

'I still prefer to take care of this myself.'

'Very well,' she said, her voice pitched low. 'But if you do you'll make me extremely unhappy.'

'Good God, Laura, that's unreasonable—'

'Please don't curse. There is no need for theatrics. Charlie Brassman—'

'Someone send for me?'

Heads turned. A small, shabbily dressed man bustled into the library. He touched a knuckle to his forehead, and Will noticed that he had hands like wrinkled hide.

'Miss Laura – Mister Marcus,' Brassman said, nodding a greeting. Then he looked down. 'What's this, what's this? Ain't you a sight, Jackie! What the devil did you do to yourself?'

He dropped to his knees beside the injured man. Jackson eyed him in fright and distrust. Laura tugged Will's arm:

'Everything's under control. Do come along.'

He didn't want to anger Laura. Didn't want to risk an abrupt end to a friendship so well begun; a friendship with so many auspicious possibilities for the future—

His hesitation annoyed her. Smiling, she slipped her arm in his and lashed him with her soft voice:

436

'I insist.'

Will turned away from Jackson's imploring gaze. His shoulders slumped. 'All right,' he said.

3

Taylor, the Yale man, pursed his lips. 'I'm thankful the ride won't be delayed any further.' He led the others back to the foyer. Will was moving toward the library door, Laura clinging to him, when the groom clucked his tongue and said:

'We'll have to set this, Jackie.'

In a terrified voice, Jackson breathed, 'Be careful, won't you? It hurts like sin. Go easy.'

'Sure, sure. Leave me to take a closer look.'

Will and Laura had just reached the foyer when Jackson screamed.

The scream rang through Will's mind, raising echoes of the cries of Chris Tompkins the night he died. Echoes of the little grey, Boston, bellowing and slamming his head on the ground in the glare of the lightning—

A few words about your duties.

Laura gasped as he took her hand and lifted it away from his arm.

Then he pivoted and walked back toward Charlie Brassman. He knew his decision would probably cost him dearly, but he couldn't silence his conscience any longer.

Brassman had both hands fastened on Jackson's bleeding leg. Livid, Will said, 'You're not treating a horse. Let go of him.'

Scowling, the groom obeyed. Jackson gasped with relief.

'I thought you were competent,' Will said to Brassman. 'Don't you know better than to maul him when you haven't given him anything for the pain?'

437

The groom was indignant. 'You're an expert, are you?'

'I'm a medical student.'

'Oh, yes, the Harvard boy. Someone did tell me you was visiting here. Well, *doctor*, I'm mighty sorry to inform you that we ain't got any spirits of ether sittin' around the house.'

'I assume you have brandy. Get some.'

The groom hesitated, his surly eyes communicating his instantaneous dislike of the younger man. The delay infuriated Will. He took a step toward the groom:

'*Go!*'

Brassman muttered something and stormed out. Trying to ignore the stony look on Laura's face, Will looked at the others. Only Marcus, who was leaning against the library door at the back of the crowd, looked sympathetic.

Behind him, Will heard Jackson's rough breathing as he said:

'The rest of you go enjoy the ride while I look after Mr Jackson. I'll send Brassman for anything I need.'

Laura fixed him with those imperious grey eyes. A smile slowly curved her mouth. An executioner's smile, he thought with sinking spirits. When she spoke, her voice was as cold as the winter day:

'Yes, let's go enjoy ourselves while Mr Kent does his humanitarian duty. Come along, now. Come along—'

She spread her arms and herded the others into the foyer without a single backward glance.

Will ran a hand through his hair, listening to the merry voices as the young people boarded the sleighs. The drivers whipped up the horses. The voices and the tinkling sleigh bells began to fade.

He looked down at Jackson, who said, 'Sorry – if I – ruined the outing for you, sir. Didn't – mean to fall. Damned ladder just – broke apart under me.'

Will waved. 'Never mind.'

438

His thoughts were less forgiving:
The outing isn't all you ruined, my friend.

CHAPTER X

Laura's Victory

When Brassman returned with a decanter of brandy, he met Will in the foyer. Will had been in the kitchen, scrubbing his hands with strong yellow soap. His coat was gone, his sleeves rolled up.

He gestured for the groom to precede him, then used the heel of his boot to close the library doors. Brassman poured some brandy down Jackson's throat. Will touched nothing in the room or on the patient until he started to work.

It took him forty minutes to reduce the fracture, close the wound and suture it with seven stitches, each put in place with straight needles Brassman found in the sewing room. Will kept the groom busy; he proved to be a competent if disgruntled helper.

All seven needles were first boiled in the kitchen, then soaked in brandy and brought to the library on a clean towel. At the prick of the first needle, Jackson's eyes rolled up in his head. He'd borne a good deal of pain, but he couldn't deal with the thought, sight, or feel of a steel sewing needle piercing his skin. He fainted.

One by one, Will aligned and inserted the seven needles through the edges of the wound, exactly as if he were sewing up a holiday goose filled with stuffing. To each needle he attached a strand of boiled cotton thread; the heaviest Brassman had been able to find.

When all the needles were in place, he went back to the first, pulled it through and tied the thread. Then he finished the second stitch in similar fashion, and so on until the wound was closed. Brassman soaked up the excess blood with wads of cotton.

During the entire procedure, Will fought off a pervading certainty that he wasn't doing things according to the instructions he'd received in class. The lack of confidence persisted until the last suture was tied off and he stepped back, gloomily wondering how he'd behave when confronted with his first major surgical procedure. Perhaps he'd never even start it for fear of botching it.

He passed a hand across Jackson's brow. The man's skin was clammy but cool. He was breathing satisfactorily. Will walked to a chair, sat down, and put his palms against his eyes, letting his tension drain away.

He had to wait another thirty minutes for Brassman to bring in the old-fashioned fracture box he had sawed and hammered together out of scrap lumber, following a crude sketch Will had provided.

'A good job,' Will said as he examined the hinged sides of the box. 'Doubly good considering the short time you had to make it. Where's the young lady who volunteered to take care of Mr Jackson?'

'Said she'd be right along.'

'Did you explain that the care entails extra work for seven, possibly eight weeks? It'll take at least that long for the fracture to mend. And Dr Barton's bran treatment has to be carried out faithfully, every day.'

'I explained,' Brassman told him, smirking. 'She don't mind the work. She's sweet on Jackie.'

Soon the subject of the discussion, a homely maid named Nell, appeared. She was carrying linen Will had requested because there was no gauze in the house. As Will dressed Jackson's leg, Nell watched carefully, making notes on a slate with a piece of chalk.

440

'A new dressing once a day,' Will said to her. 'Wet it here – here – and here with a five per cent carbolic acid solution. Have an apothecary prepare the solution so it isn't ten or fifteen per cent. When you apply it, do so sparingly. Lister himself isn't using the stuff as freely as he once did. He used to cover an entire operative field with carbolic mist sprayed continuously from a steam atomizer. Now there's speculation that too much carbolic may injure tissues. So be careful.'

The maid nodded, although Will suspected she had grasped little of what he'd just said.

'Now we'll position Jackson's leg in the fracture box. Watch how I do it. The foot must be tied to the end board exactly the way I'm going to show you.'

Nell asked no questions, so when he finished, he checked the slate to make sure she'd written down the essential information. She had. She promised to pack the box with fresh bran once a day.

'Good.' Will wiped his hands on a towel. 'The bran will absorb any discharge from the wound and help keep the dressing dry. Dr Barton's treatment is an old one, but it's very good and still very popular – oh, by the way. Replace the linen as soon as you can find gauze.'

'Yes, sir.'

Will rolled down his sleeves and took out his pocket watch. More time had passed than he'd realized. Soon he'd have to be on his way to the railway station.

Jackson was awake again. He'd listened to most of Will's instructions. Though obviously in pain and still intoxicated, he managed to mumble a garbled thank-you to the man who had helped him.

Will appreciated the thanks. He took satisfaction from having done his job with reasonable competence. Yet the satisfaction couldn't offset a larger disappoint-ment he was experiencing now that his mind was no longer focused on his patient.

As he put on his coat, he was conscious of the stillness of the house. Laura and her friends were still out in the sleighs, having a fine time. As he walked out of the library he realized the carriage would probably leave for the depot before Laura returned. He wouldn't see her – not today or ever again, thanks to what he'd done. That was bitter medicine.

'Will?'

Astonished by the voice, he looked toward the doors to the living hall.

'*Laura!*'

2

She hurried toward him. The silken dust ruffle inside the hem of her skirt showed briefly, a pale froth. Her stride, and her determined expression, kept Will from smiling to show his delight.

She'd taken off her fur hat and muff but still wore her fur-trimmed jacket, which was much too heavy for indoors. Perhaps that accounted for her flushed look. That, or anger.

'I thought you were with the others—' he began.

'At the last moment I decided not to go. I thought it was more important to stay and speak with you. Please come outside so we won't be overheard.'

'But it's snowing hard out—'

'*Please come outside.*'

This time he didn't argue. He was overjoyed at seeing her again, and anxious to know what had put such intensity in her voice.

He followed her out the front door, down the steps, and around toward the east side of the mansion. She seemed unconcerned about the snow, although it stuck in her hair, melted, and ruined her coiffure.

She stopped under a large window consisting of pieces of red, orange, and yellow stained glass arranged to represent a sunset. Gaslight inside cast a bloody glow on the white ground, and on Will and Laura as they faced one another.

'You quite spoiled my morning, Will Kent.'

Anger flared again. 'I'm sorry. A man needed help.'

'I decided to let you indulge your humanitarian instincts this once.'

'Christ, that's charitable of you!'

The force of that made her blink and step back. All at once, gazing at her through the curtain of the snow, he was again struck by her incredible beauty. His rage moderated. He even tried to excuse her behaviour by telling himself that no one was perfect: everyone's character – his own included – had objectionable aspects.

Laura, too, seemed in a gentler, more conciliatory mood all at once. Her grey eyes softened as she and Will stood gazing at one another in the falling snow. She moved closer again:

'I don't want to quarrel with you, Will. It's forward of me to say this – altogether improper, but I – ' She looked away. 'I've been taken with you since the moment Marcus first mentioned your name and what you did. You're ever so much more interesting and – well – substantial than the drones he usually brings home.'

Will's face lost its strained look. 'I don't want to

quarrel either.' A sheepish smile. 'And I owe you an apology for swearing again.'

'No you don't. In the library, I said what I did because I thought the others were listening. I disapproved of your profanity for the sake of appearances, that's all. You've no idea how important appearances can be in our circle. I'll have to impress that on you if we continue seeing one another.'

Not when. *If*. Was her turn of phrase intentional or accidental? He'd better find out:

'I thought that my decision to help Jackson made it certain that we wouldn't see each other.'

'Not quite. I like you, Will. I decided one indiscretion was forgivable – if we could strike a bargain. I admire your idealism, but it must be channelled, my dear. Kept within practical limits.'

He thought of their earlier conversation. Of the image of the lioness who allowed her mate to appear dominant but who in fact controlled everything he did.

She laid a hand on his arm. 'My proposition's a very straighforward one. If we permit our friendship to ripen – and I hope we can – this morning must be the first and last time you ever leave my side to do your horse doctoring.'

'*Horse* – ' Stunned, he couldn't go on. It took him a moment to recover and say, 'You still don't understand. That man Jackson—'

'Is the kind of patient who is not worthy of your attention. You squander your talent and your energy when you deal with people of his station. It's beneath you! What's worse, if you continue with that kind of work, you'll soon give everyone the idea that you want to do nothing else. That you're capable of nothing else.'

How icily calculating that sounded. She was concerned with subtleties of which he wasn't even aware. How was that possible when she was so young?

The face of her mother flashed into his mind. A modest, retiring woman. Deceptively so. '*My dear – if you please.*' She ruled her husband, and she'd evidently taught her daughter all her skills. Until this moment, he hadn't quite believed the word lioness was appropriate, but at last he did.

Laura was saying, 'If you'll realize that the impression you create is every bit as important as your actual ability, you can be a very successful doctor. Prosperous. Prominent, too.'

He smiled, surprised. 'I can't imagine that you'd be interested in the medical profession.'

She touched her upper lip to flick away a flake of melting snow. 'I am because you are. When Marcus first described you, Papa made disparaging remarks about doctors. He said they were undistinguished and poverty-stricken. That isn't true, is it?'

'Not for all of them. Some do exceptionally well – if they have a touch of luck, and a few friends in the right places.'

'Do you mean sponsors? Patron families who help them establish a practice?'

'Yes.'

Her grey eyes seemed to bore through him. 'Sponsors such as the Pennels, for example?'

He nodded, trying to soften the strange, almost uncomfortable intensity of the moment by smiling again. He had a curious feeling that she knew much more about his chosen profession than she admitted. Had she been asking questions? If so, why?

He could only find one explanation; but it was one which pleased him. She felt a physical attraction as strong as his. He saw it in the scarlet lights glowing in her eyes. She wanted him the way he wanted her—

Of course that could only come with marriage. But she seemed to be hinting that it surely would come if he obeyed the rules.

Her rules.

But would that be so hard to accept if she took him where he wanted to go? He decided the answer was no.

Again she startled him by doing the unexpected. After a swift glance over her shoulder, she put her hands on his upper arms and held him, tightly:

'I'm afraid I'm quite taken with you, Mr Kent. I don't know exactly how it happened, or whether it's wise. But they say the heart is seldom wise. Still – there *are* terms. If you can't agree to them, I'll feel terribly brokenhearted, but I imagine I'll survive. So tell me, my dear. Do you want to see me again?'

He was almost giddy with happiness. And yet, in a remote corner of his mind, some small voice protested that her performance was too perfect to be sincere. She couldn't possibly care for him as she said she did—

Or was that only his sense of inferiority trying to rob him of happiness by telling him he wasn't worthy of it?

She stood on tiptoe. No one would see; the storm was intensifying, and they had become the only living things in a vast white wilderness. The swirling snow blurred the limestone wall of the house just a few feet away, and bleached the red light falling through the window.

'Do you want to see me again?' she repeated, her mouth only an inch or two from his.

He thought of the Vanderbilt mansion.

Of Vlandingham ordering luncheon in French.

He thought of Carter.

Then he heard Roosevelt speaking from the sun-drenched platform in Dickinson. He fought to banish the memory. Emotion and ambition struggled with conscience and slowly, slowly overcame it—

'Very much,' he said.

'Then you must promise me that you've done your horse doctoring for the last time.'

He hesitated only a moment:

'For the last time. I promise.'

She flung her arm round his neck. She raised her face and body and kissed him, opening her mouth for a moment to let him savour the delicious promise of her tongue.

Then she withdrew, patting her hair and whispering, 'I shouldn't have done that. I've never done it with any other boy. I couldn't help myself. Don't think less of me.'

Tumid with excitement, he tried to speak calmly:

'No, I don't, I couldn't. Ever.'

Laura squeezed his hand. She looked much older than her nineteen years as she smiled and said, 'We'd better go back inside before we freeze.'

Without waiting for agreement, she swept past him, her shoes crunching in the deepening snow and her skirt leaving a trail. She kept her hand in his, leading him.

Since he was a step behind, it was impossible for him to see her face. Impossible for him to see her shut her eyes, as if immensely relieved about something; impossible for him to see the joy and satisfaction that flooded into those same eyes a moment later; impossible for him to see the smile that curled her mouth. It was a satisfied smile, as if a plan had been carried to a successful completion, and a victory won.

CHAPTER XI

Castle Garden

Every other weekend during the early months of 1888, Will took the train to New York City to visit Laura.

The Pennels' city residence was an opulent mansion located on the east side of Fifth Avenue above Fifty-second Street. They had formerly owned another place downtown, near Madison Square, but had sold it when the area began to decline. Will found it a good omen that their present home was within hailing distance of the William K. Vanderbilt chateau that held such significance for him.

Laura always had the weekends completely planned by the time he arrived. They watched Gilbert and Sullivan operettas from the Pennel box at the Standard Theatre; went sailing on Long Island Sound with friends of her and Marcus as soon as the weather grew warm enough; attended a number of subscription balls for which Will was forced to buy complete formal dress.

He didn't care much for the people he met at these weekend outings. Young or old, they seemed a self-centred, snobbish lot. But he learned to hide his feelings, reminding himself frequently that a doctor didn't have to like his patients in order to profit from their illnesses. Whenever he spoke to Thurman Pennel, he never discussed politics, or mentioned his father. It was soon evident that his restraint improved his standing with Mr Pennel. He assumed Mrs Pennel already approved of him; otherwise he wouldn't have been permitted to court her daughter.

His uneasiness about lacking social graces began to

disappear. Laura was free with advice on everything from proper manners to the proper attire for each hour of the day. Anxious to learn, he took the advice with good grace. Soon he found that he could wear his evening clothes with no sense of awkwardness, and could carry on trivial conversations with Laura's friends and not fret about whether his next word would be the correct one. Memories of his mother seldom bothered him.

Thurman Pennel had a stream of callers that spring. He was deeply involved in an effort to remove Grover Cleveland from the White House. One of the visitors was a portly but vigorous-looking Ohio congressman named McKinley. On the afternoon Will and Marcus were invited to meet him, he was still venting his fury over the President's tariff message the previous December: 'A body blow to every single native manufacturer! Let England take care of herself – and in God's name let Americans look after America!'

Laura's father was even less restrained when criticizing Cleveland. 'Marxist' was perhaps the kindest term he used. If there had been any doubt about the chief executive's radical leanings, Pennel declared, his signature on the Interstate Commerce Act the preceding year had removed it. Of course Cleveland quibbled and said he was 'suspicious' of the new legislation.

'But the blackguard signed it!' Pennel roared. 'It's nothing less than a shameless attack on the business community!'

The purpose of the new law was to regulate the railroad combinations, those lines which got together to fix rates among themselves. The practice resulted in rebates for volume customers of the cooperating railroads, and exorbitant rates for smaller shippers – especially the farmers of the midlands who moved their crops to market by rail. Under the new law, all discriminatory rates were forbidden, and the railroads

449

were required to file tariff schedules with the newly created Interstate Commerce Commission. Pennel deemed the whole thing an assault on American liberty, and predicted the decay of personal incentive and the collapse of the country unless the Republicans elected a man who was pro-business and pro-tariff. Senator Benjamin Harrison, grandson of the ninth president, was a name mentioned in Will's hearing.

In the late spring, Will and Drew prepared for year-end examinations. Drew was anxiously awaiting answers to letters he'd sent a month earlier. He was hoping to find a volunteer medical post for the summer, one in which he could gain some practical experience.

Two weeks before the examinations, Will again travelled to New York. He hated to take time from his studies but the Pennels – minus the head of the household – were about to sail for three months of sightseeing on the Continent.

The night before the departure, Will took Laura to Tony Pastor's variety theatre, then to supper at Delmonico's. On the way home in a hired carriage whose driver had been instructed to go slowly, she permitted Will to touch her breast while they kissed, and even put her own hand over his to increase the pressure. When they broke the embrace, she apologized for letting her emotions overwhelm her sense of propriety.

He laughed and told her he didn't mind a bit. Her ardour encouraged him to say what he'd been thinking all evening:

'I don't know how I'll survive the summer without you.'

'Nor I, my dear.'

Another moment of hesitation. Then:

'I love you, Laura.'

'Oh, my sweet boy—'

One arm curled round his neck. She pressed her

cheek against his, her eyes closing. Her voice was husky with emotion:

'I feel the same way. I know it's wrong, but when I'm with you, I want to do the most wonderful, shameful things—'

Then, as boldly as Aggie at Madam Melba's, she reached down and grasped him.

Her hand, working and working, almost drove him crazy. She moaned softly. It would have been so easy to hire a cheap hotel for an hour—

But he couldn't ask that of her. A man who respected a girl had a responsibility to help her maintain her honour. Old-fashioned as that might be, he still believed it. He moved just slightly. She understood the signal, and, with a small, disappointed sigh, let go.

'Will, I'm so terribly sorry. I got carried away all over again. It's never happened with anyone but you.'

'I'm glad.' After a pause he blurted, 'I want to marry you, Laura.'

He was terrified that she'd laugh. But all she did was hug him and whisper:

'When, my darling?'

'In two years. As soon as I've gotten my degree.'

'I don't know whether I can wait that long. But I'll try. In case you don't know it, Will Kent, I think you're a perfectly splendid catch. We're going to turn you into one of the finest, richest doctors in all of New York. In the whole country! It's about time the Pennels had a member of the family who can claim some intellectual accomplishment.'

Is that what I'm to be? A family trophy?

But what was wrong with that? he asked himself a moment later. The kind of plan she described would give him everything he wanted; absolutely everything. He'd have no worries for the rest of his life—

He gathered her into his arms and kissed her again.

451

The carriage creaked slowly on toward upper Fifth Avenue.

2

Will saw the Pennels off at the North German Lloyd's pier, then returned to Boston, where his father made some disparaging remarks about his fondness for his new-found friends. Will was too much in love to let the sarcasm bother him for long.

Besides, Gideon wasn't himself these days. In the wake of Theo Payne's death, four successive editors had been hired to take charge of the *Union*. Each had been found wanting. While the search continued, circulation fell steadily. Gideon was growing desperate.

'I have only one more possiblity,' he said to Julia. 'An editor on the night desk of the *World*. His name's Moultrie Calhoun. I've heard he's unhappy, so I'm going to write him a letter and ask him to have dinner. I don't like raiding a competitor – not even one like Joe Pulitzer – but if I must go raiding, I will. And I must say Joe's reputation gets worse by the week. I hardly ever agree with him anymore, and everyone on Park Row says his nervous disorders are making him almost too irascible to deal with. I'm not surprised Calhoun wants to leave.'

Will and Drew continued to cram for their examinations. Two days before the first test, Drew jubilantly reported that he'd got a job as an assistant at the medical inspection station at Castle Garden in New York. Castle Garden was the entry point for the hundreds of thousands of European immigrants swarming to the United States. The press regularly predicted that by the time the decade was over, the total number of arrivals for the ten-year period might reach five

452

million – much to the disgust of established families such as the Pennels.

Both young men passed their examinations, thus advancing to the third class. Drew left Boston and a few weeks later wrote from New York to invite Will to come for a visit.

The idea was appealing. Will was bored reading medical texts, and it would be some weeks before he began his studies in Dr Charles Green's special summer course in obstetrics. Until very recently, medical students hadn't been permitted to witness childbirth; that was the province of the midwife. Also, questions of the patient's modesty were involved. The only obstetrical training most doctors received came from lectures or study of anatomical models. Since 1883, however, Harvard had required that every third-year student attend at least two cases of labour before receiving a diploma. Dr Green's short course was intended as preparation.

In late July, Will boarded a train for New York.

3

Castle Garden, a huge building with a conical roof, was located at the upper west end of Battery Park.

The structure dated from 1807. It had been planned as a fort to defend lower Manhattan, but that use had been found impractical – as had its second function as a site for public entertainment. Although Jenny Lind had packed Castle Garden during her Barnum-sponsored concert tour in 1850, the building's shed-like design was simply all wrong for a music hall. Finally it had been leased to the Commissioners of Immigration.

Will reached sprawling Battery Park on a hot, humid morning. The hazy air all but hid the Jersey shore, and blurred the hull and superstructure of a rusty ocean-going vessel moving slowly up the river. As Will watched, the ship came to a dead stop. Tugs and a pilot boat steamed away while the vessel's anchor chain paid out noisily. At the ship's rail stood a couple of hundred men and women. Some held up infants, presumably hoping the babies would appreciate the heat-sodden skyline, or the huge copper-clad figure of Liberty out in the harbour. Bartholdi's gigantic statue with its flaring lamp upraised had finally been erected on its pedestal late in 1886. Small excursion boats took sightseers a mile and a half out to Bedloe's Island for a closer inspection. Will thought he should make that one of his stops before he returned to Boston.

He was fascinated by a group of about twenty men, most of them unsavoury looking, who lounged near the gates of Castle Garden. As the new arrivals emerged from the buildings, bundles of belongings slung over their shoulders and bewildered expressions on their faces, the waiting men took advantage of that bewilderment.

From the shadow of the park's bandstand, Will watched one of the men step up to an elderly couple, smile and tip his derby. The man spoke to the couple in a foreign tongue. Russian, perhaps; he couldn't be sure.

The old man and woman broke out in smiles at the sound of a familiar language. The man – a hard-faced sort with a large diamond ring on the little finger of his right hand – noticed Will watching and glared. Will moved on. The man stepped between the elderly couple and began talking in a confidential tone.

Another white-haired man came through the gates, a homemade crutch under his left arm. A laughing eight-year-old boy rode on his right shoulder. Next came the boy's parents – a big-shouldered man in ragged clothes, and a buxom, extremely ugly girl who was entranced by the sights around her. A man broke away from the loungers and sauntered toward the group:

'Good morning to you. Would you be interested in half-price railroad tickets to your destination?'

The grandfather said something in a foreign language to indicate that he didn't understand. He asked a question. The American grinned:

'Sure, I can talk bohunk. I was raised on it. My folks spoke nothing else.'

He proceeded to prove it, slipping his arms round the young couple as if he'd known them for years. The parents, the old man, and the child all looked at the stranger with expressions of trust and gratitude.

At the gates, Will sent in his name; he'd have to wait until Drew came for him. The guard, a florid Irishman, told him no one was allowed to leave without a permit – and no one was allowed to enter without being vouched for by an employee:

'Otherwise we'd have the damned rascals inside the buildings too.' He indicated the lounging men who were laughing and talking to one another. 'As it is, they pollute this place day and night. They pay off the police so they won't be run in for their dirty tricks. We try to warn the greenhorns. And there's a currency exchange inside where they can get an honest shake. But they've been packed in steerage for weeks, and most of 'em are tired and so nervous, they don't get around to doing business till they meet their new-found friends out here. Disgusting, that's what it is!'

Will pointed at the family he'd observed:

'I heard that man mention cut-rate railroad tickets to those four.'

'Oh, sure, he'll sell them a half-price ticket to Minnesota or Kansas or anyplace else they want to go. Only they won't be able to read it and see it's worthless. The sharps either speak a foreign language or learn enough of a few to get by. These are the very first Americans the greenhorns meet outside of Castle Garden. What a fine impression of our country it must give them!' The guard glowered at the men.

'Will!'

He turned at the sound of the familiar voice. There came Drew, a spotted linen smock flying around his legs. The heat plastered his red-gold curls to his pale forehead. In a moment, he was shepherding his friend through the gate.

'So you've seen our version of John, chapter two.'

'What?'

'The temple of the moneychangers that Jesus purged. I wish someone would purge Battery Park.'

'I was watching some of those men operate. They're very skilful.'

'Skilful crooks! They all have their specialities. Some only watch for prosperous immigrants. They buy them a meal, drug their drinks – and the newcomers wake up in some alley, prosperous no longer. Some of the men concentrate on befriending young girls travelling alone – you can imagine where *they* wind up. By the way – Jo sends you her regards.'

The thought of Drew's sister brought a look of embarrassment to Will's face. 'I haven't had time to answer her letters for months.' A wry smile. 'Do you suppose that's why she stopped writing?'

'That and the fact that she's seeing a boy.'

'Oh? Who?'

'The minister's son. He bores her to tears, but at least she has a suitor of whom Pa approves. She's filled out a lot. I've never seen anyone so grateful to be grown up.'

'You said you hoped she'd be less grumpy when that happened.'

'My hope has been fulfilled. Now she's only grumpy

456

when she looks in the mailbox and finds you haven't sent a letter. You're still her favourite.'

Will wished Jo Hastings would grow out of her adolescent devotion to him; he hoped Drew hadn't told her about Laura.

'Is Jo working at the store?' he asked.

'Six days a week.' Drew led his friend into the building and down a dark corridor ten degrees hotter than the outdoors.

'Is she happy?'

'I think she's miserable. She'll never get over the fact that she can't realize her ambition because we're poor and she's a girl. She sympathizes with Pa's predicament, but that doesn't make her like being the victim of it.'

He and Will entered a small office. Drew took Will's valise, then reached toward a wall peg. He handed his friend a heavy linen smock of the kind he was wearing:

'Put this on, if you don't mind. We have a patient.'

'We?'

'Yes, I need your help.'

'What about the regular doctors?'

'Too busy. I don't know whether I wrote you about the procedure here.'

'No.'

'Arriving ships anchor in the river—'

Will nodded. 'I watched a big one putting her anchor down.'

'They stay in the river while a Customs House launch takes the immigrants off in groups. We'll be receiving that ship's first load within the hour. A vessel that came in earlier this morning brought us two hundred and fifty, including our patient.'

'Who is he?'

'She,' Drew corrected. 'A Polish girl. She seems to be sans a husband, but she's very much pregnant. At full term, in fact. Some of the others on her boat spoke a little English. They say this is her first child. She's been in labour about twenty-six hours. Too long. Her pains have stayed steady and strong, but the baby's progress has stopped.'

'The fetus in the wrong position?'

'Yes. Almost a direct posterior position, as far as I can tell.'

'Wasn't there a doctor aboard her ship?'

'No.'

'Couldn't someone in the crew have helped her?'

'Medical care isn't included when you buy a steerage ticket, Will.'

'All right, but how'd she become your responsibility?'

'The captain ordered her off, and never mind her condition. An orderly's watching her in case there's an emergency, but I've delayed about as long as I can. I'm going to have to deliver her myself.'

Will frowned. 'Why? You told me only routine examinations were done at Castle Garden.'

'That's right. Serious cases are transferred to the hospital on Ward's Island. I don't believe I have time to ship this girl there.' He shoved the smock at Will.

'Drew, I've never seen a delivery! I haven't even had a course in—'

'Neither have I, for God's sake. But we've both read textbooks – and last summer in Hartford, I paid an old midwife to let me watch half a dozen accouchements. I had to pretend to be her son. Some women are insane on the subject of modesty. They'd rather perish than have a physician see their private parts. Anyway, for three of the deliveries, the woman had to use the forceps. Years ago she hired a blacksmith to make some to her specifications. She was masterful with them. I learned a lot watching her. Now come on – enough conversation. If we don't give this girl proper care, no one will.'

The old sense of inadequacy gripped Will then:

'I'm not sure I'm capable of being any real hel—'

'You can administer ether, can't you? I'll tell you how many spoonfuls to sprinkle into the inhaler.'

The contempt reddened Will's cheek. But he still didn't move.

Drew cast an anxious eye on a small desk clock. 'Now what's wrong? Do you object because the girl's poor and foreign? Do you only associate with rich patients now that you've taken up with the Pennels?'

'That's goddamn unfair, Drew!'

'Of course it is. But it got a reaction.'

'For your information, I don't need to be told how many spoonfuls of ether to sprinkle into the inhaler. I memorized a few things besides the tenth edition of Gray's!'

'That was my impression,' Drew said with a mocking lift of his eyebrows. 'Will you or won't you help?'

Will snatched the smock from Drew's hand, flung it on a chair and started to strip off his coat. Drew's quick smile couldn't quite hide his tension.

CHAPTER XII

Birth

In a small, badly lighted room bearing no resemblance to a modern surgical theatre, Drew examined a rectangular table with a large brown stain in the centre. Two blocks of rough wood had been nailed to the corners of the table nearest him. He touched each block, then spun to the loutish young orderly in the filthy white jacket:

'Couldn't you find wood without splinters, Clarence?'

The orderly acted as if the question insulted him. 'No, I couldn't.'

Drew pointed to the blocks. 'Then cover these with cloths soaked in the carbolic solution. Put a sheet soaked in carbolic over the whole table, and two dry ones on top. Where's the girl?'

'On my gurney, down the hall.'

'We'll bring her in after we fix the table. Get the linens.'

The orderly shuffled away. 'Fast, for Christ's sake!' Drew shouted. 'I'd like to deliver the child sometime before the leaves fall!'

The orderly moved a little faster. The door slammed. Drew sighed. 'Shouldn't have yelled at him. I'll need his help, too. Damn heat's getting me.'

The heat, and the problem confronting them, Will thought as he studied the room. For a moment the only sound was the faint bubbling of a kettle of water boiling on a ring above a gas burner. Drew noticed his friend's frown and said:

'We're splendidly set up, aren't we? No windows. No separate ventilated room for administering the anaesthetic. You'll have to do it right in here.' He cocked an eye at the gas fixture hanging above the table, its jets trimmed low. 'Be careful with the ether. Blowing the fetus into the world isn't the procedure I had in mind.'

'Where's your equipment?'

'Behind you – what little we have.'

Will moved to an old walnut cabinet. 'You sound nervous.'

'Why, no,' his friend replied as he pulled a book, then a forceps, from storage cubbies. 'I always keep a text handy when I work. It reassures the patient. If the doctor doesn't know what the hell to do next, perhaps the author does.'

Less sarcastically, he continued, 'I really am glad you're here. I wouldn't trust Clarence to give the anaesthetic. I didn't tell you all the complications. The fetus is extremely large. And the mother's pelvis is all wrong for child-bearing. It's the truncated kind – more like a man's than a woman's. Add my inexperience and you might logically conclude that the whole business is very chancy. Your conclusion would be right.'

2

Drew poured some of the boiling water into a smaller basin next to a second one containing carbolic solution. Will, meantime, began to lay out the anaesthesia equipment on a small table. He noted the title of the book Drew planned to keep handy. *A System of Midwifery*. It was a widely used text by Dr Leishman of the University of Glasgow.

Clarence returned with sheets and rags. Will and Drew took over preparation of the table. After it was draped, Drew tore strips of clean rag with which to tie the patient's ankles to the blocks once her heels were braced against them.

Next Drew washed his hands in the smaller basin of boiled water, relatively cool now. Once he'd rinsed off the soap he dipped his hands and lower arms into the adjacent pan of carbolic solution.

The room was intensely hot. Will asked about dispensing with the smocks. 'I prefer them, but I suppose we can.' Will got rid of his, rolled up his sleeves and drained the dirty water from the small basin. He rinsed and refilled it, then washed his hands and immersed them in the basin of antiseptic.

Drew, meantime, instructed Clarence to pick up the separate halves of the forceps. Each half of forged metal consisted of a long shank with a handgrip at one

461

end and, at the other, a blade somewhat resembling a large serving spoon from which most of the bottom had been cut out. Holding each shank at the mid-point, Clarence dipped the handles into the kettle of boiling water, then into the carbolic. Drew waited a few seconds to permit the handles to cool and took them in his own hands.

He studied the two halves of the forceps. They were meant to be united by an attachment mechanism near the mid-point of the shanks. When fitted together, the halves formed a single instrument with the concave surfaces of the blades facing inward for holding and judiciously pulling the head of the fetus. The design of the attachment mechanism allowed the two halves to slide forward or back; necessary for adjusting to irregularities in the shape of the fetus' head. In a posterior-position fetus, such irregularities were to be expected.

As Drew stared at the instrument, his expression suggested that he might be remembering horror stories he'd heard at Harvard; stories of infants marked or mangled before birth by doctors whose handling of the forceps was unskilful. Will started to feel an ache in the pit of his stomach, and a sense of concern and responsibility for the unknown mother that he didn't altogether welcome.

Drew immersed the unsterilized sections of the forceps in the boiling water, then the carbolic. At the same time, Will was sorting and arranging the apparatus for administering anaesthesia: a battered metal Allis inhaler; a Goodwillie mouth gag for holding the jaws apart; a tenaculum to draw out the tongue, and a large curved needle with attached silk thread for transfixing it, if that became necessary; a silver trachea tube; a basin for catching vomit.

Drew raised the forceps for a final inspection. The carbolic solution dripped from the blades. A professor on the Harvard faculty had once referred to the forceps as the great prime mover of obstetrics. No one knew who had invented the instrument. Its origins were lost in the past. But Avicenna, the great Persian physician who had lived in the tenth and eleventh centuries, had been familiar with the forceps. Watching the wet blades shine in the gaslight, Will had a strong sense of the worthy traditions of his profession.

In the hall, a woman moaned. 'Find the anaesthetic?' Drew asked as he laid the forceps on a square of linen that had come out of the carbolic basin a few minutes earlier.

Will nodded, holding up two corked cans of ether. It was Dr Squibb's, generally considered the best available.

The orderly opened the door. The moaning grew louder. As Clarence tried to manoeuvre his cart into the stifling room, Drew's eyes shifted past Will to the mother. Instantly, his anxious look disappeared, replaced by a confident smile. Will understood the abrupt change when he saw the young woman. She was awake, and terrified.

The girl was only eighteen or so. She had a pretty, high-cheekboned face, bright with sweat. Her hair was damp and stringy. Her abdomen pushed up beneath a soiled sheet. She tried to respond to Drew's smile with a shy and hopeful one of her own, but the fright in her hazel eyes was unmistakable.

How much greater that fear must be because she couldn't understand what was said by those around her, Will thought. Her expression had a sudden and unexpected effect on him. It made Vlandingham's greed seem contemptible.

They transferred the girl from the cart to the table. She said something to Drew in a foreign language. Even though her words made no sense to him, he responded with a nod and solicitous sounds.

'Don't worry,' he said, his round head bobbing. He

463

placed his left hand just above the mountainous belly. 'We'll take care of your baby. He'll be perfectly fine. 'We'll see to it, Doctor Kent and I.'

Somehow, she comprehended one word. 'Doctor? *Doctor?*'

'Yes, I'm Doctor Hastings.' He touched his chest, then pointed. 'That's Doctor Kent. We're both doctors. You're safe.'

He was stretching the truth by using the term doctor to refer to a couple of students; but it was what she wanted to hear. She nodded, her eyes fixing on Drew with unquestioning trust. She was in a foreign land, in pain, but the two young men were relievers of pain – deliverers of children. That much was clear, and it eased her anxiety.

Suddenly she clenched her teeth and her fists. Another contraction racked her body. Drew's eyes flicked to Will, a signal.

Will opened his pocket watch; laid it on a stool. His hand shook slightly as he picked up the Allis inhaler, a metal tube more oval than round. After a quick look at the gas flame hissing overhead, he began to sprinkle ether on the long gauze bandage threaded through the maze of wires within the inhaler. He hoped to God he didn't make a mistake.

No one spoke. Will pressed the inhaler's turned metal edge against the girl's mouth. He continued to sprinkle ether into the other end, glancing frequently at his watch. Its tick seemed thunderous.

Ten minutes passed.

Twelve.

The girl's face turned deep red, a sign of the first stage of ether narcosis. Will warned Clarence to be ready for the possible onset of violent struggling.

The young woman started to mutter. Soon she was babbling loudly, and tossing in a restive way: not quite sleeping yet.

Her hands spasmed toward her belly; she still felt the contractions. The pain should be lessening moment by moment—

The babbling stopped. The girl passed safely into the deep, completely relaxed second stage of anaesthesia. Will said:

'You're free to go ahead.'

3

Drew turned the gas jets up full. Then he lifted the sheet and bared the girl's lower body. The orderly started to snigger. Drew's murderous look silenced him.

Drew positioned the girl's feet and told Clarence to tie them. The loutish young man moved with surprising alacrity, tying both feet neatly. Drew complimented him. The orderly lost his sullen look.

The gaslight hissed; the pocket watch ticked. Will's clothing was soaked with sweat. He stood behind the girl's head, lightly holding the inhaler in place, his heart slamming fast and hard within his chest. He leaned down to check the girl's pulse. Drew looked at him.

'All right?'

'Yes, fine.'

With great care, Drew inserted his hand to examine the fetus trapped in the birth canal. The problem he faced was stark and simple. In the posterior position, the back of the fetus was toward the mother's back. This put the head in an attitude in which its largest dimension pushed against the walls of a uterine canal made too narrow by a pelvic bone structure Drew had characterized as inadequate. Had the girl been fortunate enough to be born with a normal pelvis – the luck of the draw, some doctors termed it – the fetus might have passed through the canal with no difficulty.

But that wasn't the case, and so a rotation was necessary. With the fetus in the correct position – its back toward the mother's belly – the head would be in a slightly different attitude, presenting a slightly narrower dimension to the canal opening. The difference was only a matter of one or two centimetres, but it was critical if the fetus was to be driven downward and outward to the air, and to life, by the mother's labour.

When Drew was sure the dilation of the os was complete, he took a deep breath. Then he moved his right hand forward again, slipping it up into the uterus, well out of sight. The hand was positioned between the side of the fetus's head and the uterine wall on the mother's left side. It would stay there as a guide and buffer for the potentially damaging blade of the forceps.

Drew's face shone under the gaslight. Will whispered an order. Clarence took a rag and mopped Drew's forehead and cheeks.

'Thank you, Clarence.'

Upper teeth biting down on his lower lip, Drew took the left forceps blade in his left hand. He slowly inserted the blade next to his right hand. The procedure seemed to take hours.

He pulled his right hand out. Jammed his sleeve against his forehead to swab sweat away. He glanced at Will again, his tension unmistakable. Once more Will checked the girl's pulse.

'Everything satisfactory.'

Drew reached for the right forceps blade. His palm must have been excessively slick. The metal handle slipped away from him.

Clarence caught the handle just before it hit the floor. He didn't touch the blade. Drew nodded his appreciation. Slowly and carefully, he inserted the blade into the opposite side of the uterus.

Deeper—

Deeper—

Drew swallowed hard; took another long breath. Then Will heard the faint click as the crossed blades locked.

With barely a pause, Drew began to rotate the forceps clockwise, like a man turning a key in a lock. Suddenly his face wrenched.

'*Damn.*'

'Hard?' Will whispered.

'Won't budge.'

With the fetus in a perfect posterior position, the practitioner had a choice of rotations – to the right or to the left. Either way, a turn of a hundred and eighty degrees was required. Sometimes a fetus was canted slightly in one direction or another, requiring a turn of only a hundred and thirty-five degrees or even less. Drew hadn't been that fortunate. And the direction he'd picked had been the wrong one.

Face twisted into a mask of concentration, he applied pressure in the other direction. It seemed to Will that his friend was barely breathing. He was undoubtedly conscious of the blades clasping the fetus's head, and of the potential for damage. One mistake and an entire lifetime could be blighted, even before the fetus was transformed into an infant by its first struggling intake of outside air.

'*Turning,*' Drew said abruptly. Under the flaring gas, he looked like a hunched cherub there at the end of the table. His whisper sounded remarkably like a prayer:

'Come on. Come on – a little more. *Come on—*'

Will's spine prickled. There was hope on Drew's face now; the fetus was rotating properly. And as Will continued to monitor the young woman's pulse and respiration, he knew he was witnessing a miracle. The kind of miracle of love and concern that made one human being minister to another not because there was money to be made, but because there was pain, and danger, and desperate need.

'*Done!*' Drew exclaimed, looking ready to faint. 'Done, by God!'

'And no advice needed from Dr Leishman,' Will said by way of compliment.

'Not so far, anyway. I swear, Will – this one's big as a lumberjack.'

Will grinned. 'Let's see.'

'Any minute now.'

With the fetus reversed in the birth canal, Drew removed the forceps and turned them over in preparation for delivering the baby. When the instrument was once again inserted, he formed a tight ring round the crossed shanks with his left thumb and index finger. Clarence reached over Drew's arm to place a sponge between the handles, both of which Drew held in his right hand. The sponge protected against accidental pressure on the head of the fetus as Drew grasped it with the blades and began the extraction.

He did it perfectly, simulating the contractions of the uterus in labour. He'd give a little tug, then let up. Another tug; another pause. Downward and then upward in the classic arc, he brought a small head through the canal and into the open. Amid the fuzz of black hair Will could clearly see the soft indentation of the posterior fontanelle.

He watched tiny red ears and the back of a neck come into sight above the mother's pubis. Then small shoulders, a backbone, and buttocks appeared.

Drew brought the newborn the rest of the way into the world, as proud and delighted as if he were the father:

'Damn if he won't make a lumberjack. Look at him! Ten pounds if he's an ounce.'

After one whack of his wrinkled red bottom, the baby howled. Will felt tears of joy in his eyes.

4

Drew's hands moved confidently as he cut and tied the cord. The newborn kicked and screamed while Drew lowered him to clean towels Clarence was holding. The orderly, too, had a soft, wondering look on his coarse face. Drew smiled in a weary but satisfied way. The baby boy was strong of lung, and apparently perfect.

Within a couple of hours, the mother had her first bleary look at her child. She was resting on a cot Drew had set up in his own office. While Will handed the young woman the warm, squirming bundle, Drew cooled her forehead with a cloth dipped in alcohol.

Although the mother understood none of what Drew and Will said as they murmured appreciations of her fine son, something in Drew's expression continued to communicate calmness, reassurance – a promise that the young woman had survived her ordeal in steerage, and her more recent one at Castle Garden to a good purpose. The purpose was wiggling and squalling in her arms.

'Very fine,' Drew said, lifting the blanket so the mother could clearly see the infant's sex. 'A very fine, strong boy.' He kept smiling and nodding as he said it. The exhausted girl understood. She burst into tears. The sight sent another shiver up Will's spine.

Then the young woman uttered a short sentence Will didn't understand. Her tone of pride was unmistakable, though. Drew seemed to grasp what she meant. As he tucked the starched sheet beneath her chin, he bobbed his head again:

'Yes, that's a very good thing. A good omen for his life.'

Softly, Will asked, 'What did she say?'

'She said *born in America*. She's glad her son came into the world on this side of the Atlantic.' He unfolded fresh swaddling clothes; the gurgling infant had wet the other ones. As he began to wrap the baby, he added, 'I'm glad I was here to help her.'

Will gazed down at the tired, pretty face of the young woman, so peaceful and happy now that her ordeal was over. He was deeply moved; as much as he'd been that first night he watched Lon Adam at work.

'So am I,' he said. Medicine wasn't a chateau on Fifth Avenue, an investment portofolio, an invitation to the Astor ball. This was what medicine was all about.

This.

CHAPTER XIII

'The Wretched Refuse of Your Teeming Shore'

The rest of Will's week in New York passed swiftly. He moved in with Drew at a run-down rooming house near Battery Park. Cost of an extra bed – thirty cents a night. He didn't mind staying in such a sleazy place; he and Drew were seldom there. They spent most of their time at Castle Garden.

Large as Castle Garden was, the facility was still taxed to capacity. Two or three shiploads of new Americans arrived almost every day. An atmosphere of confusion prevailed.

Nor was Castle Garden free of official corruption, Will discovered. Drew said he'd seen cheating and price-gouging at the currency exchange and general store inside the gates. One official who was supposed to give newcomers advice about honest boarding houses had recently been discharged for sending people to a filthy tenement owned by his wife.

Two middle-aged doctors supervised the Castle Garden inspection station. A few minor cases were treated on the premises, rather than at Ward's Island. Drew got most of these – not an easy assignment, because many of the patients were hard to handle. They feared the American doctors and were suspicious, even hostile, because they didn't know the language and customs of their new country.

Drew worked twelve to fourteen hours a day. Will accompanied him everywhere, and quickly discovered that his friend had a remarkable knack for putting the immigrants at ease and winning their trust. His air of competence and his innate kindness were instantly communicated to patients, no matter what language they spoke.

Will saw that when Drew bathed the feverish forehead of a young Bohemian boy, or palpated the flux-bloated belly of an old, surly Russian, he soon calmed them, won them, had them smiling, and swallowing whatever medicine he wanted them to take. He talked blithely about the medicine in English, as if he was confident they'd understand. Somehow, Will almost believed they did.

It struck him that in at least one respect, Drew was very much like Lon Adam. He did more than merely treat symptoms. He was a healer of the spirit. Will decided that the man whose style he wanted to emulate in his own practice was not Vlandingham, but Drew. It was a tall order. Although Drew wouldn't get his diploma for another year, he was already a skilled practitioner. Perhaps a better one than Will could ever hope to be.

The week soon came to an end. Castle Garden received no immigrants on Sunday, so the two friends decided to treat themselves to a good meal at August Luchow's restaurant up on Fourteenth Street. But first they'd visit the city's newest tourist attraction. They took a steam launch out to Bedloe's Island for a close look at the Bartholdi statue.

A midweek thunderstorm had cleared the air and brought a spell of cool, almost autumnal weather. Sunlight sparkled on the harbour and the rooftops of lower Manhattan. From Bedloe's Island the view of the city was impressive. And from the base of the granite and concrete pedestal designed by Richard Morris Hunt, the view straight up was breathtaking.

The colossal statue with its covering of more than three hundred copper sheets towered into the cloudless sky. The great torch upraised in Liberty's right hand was so far above them, Will could almost imagine that it was visible on the other side of the ocean.

They walked all the way round the pedestal, then entered a hallway which led to the stairs. On a plaque in the hall they found 'The New Colossus,' the sonnet by Emma Lazarus which the statue had inspired.

The friends stopped and silently read the poem. It had a special, personal significance for Will; his family had been founded by a young European boy *yearning to breathe free*, as the poetess had put it.

Still saying nothing, the friends walked outside again. The sea wind was raising white water on the Atlantic. Will took off his straw hat and let the wind cool his forehead. He squinted against the sun's glare and softly repeated the line he'd found most memorable:

'"The wretched refuse of your teeming shore – " I understand that now that I've seen Castle Garden. America takes them all.'

'We do, and we should be proud of it,' Drew said. 'It's hardly a pleasure to examine some of them after they've been cooped up between decks a week or so. But once you look into their faces, you forget the shabbiness and the stench. You understand what this country means to them. We take it for granted, but to them it's a haven like no other in the world.'

They strolled toward the jetty where the excursion launches docked. 'I'm glad I got a summer job here,' Drew went on, hands in his pockets and his eyes fixed on the ocean. 'It's clarified my thinking about what I want to do after I get my diploma.'

He pointed a plump finger at Castle Garden and the panorama of buildings beyond the Battery. 'That makes Harvard seem like the proverbial ivory tower. That's the real world, Will. There's so much squalor and pain in that one city, no single life's long enough to do all that needs to be done to relieve it.'

Will thought he knew the direction Drew wanted the conversation to take. The realization made him defensive, even a bit testy:

'If you're trying to say that only greenhorns and the poor get sick, you know you're distorting the truth. And I still believe every doctor ought to practise where he wants to practise.'

'I disagree. Doctors should practise where they're needed.'

'Meaning—?'

'Meaning that a doctor is seldom needed very urgently in the parlours along Fifth Avenue. There, the typical illness is some society girl's headache, which is usually imaginary.'

Will stepped in front of his friend, his dark eyes fierce and bright in the sunlight:

'Drew, why the hell are you constantly sitting in judgment of me?'

'Because we're friends.'

'Does that confer some special right to criticize?'

'I think so.'

'Well, whether it does or not, we won't be friends for long if you keep it up.'

Drew's cocksure smile turned a bit uneasy then. 'I've got to, Will. You have the makings of a fine doctor. But someone's got to set you straight before you waste your talent.'

Will couldn't help laughing. 'My God, I've never heard such gall. Is it a Yankee characteristic?'

'Can't say. I know it's a Hastings characteristic.'

Will's smile faded. 'Whatever it is, I damned well resent your constant hints that I'll turn out to be nothing but a medical hack.'

'Hints?' Drew's round head bobbed from side to side. 'No hints. I'm saying it straight out. Except for rare moments – helping me deliver that baby was one – you don't seem to care about anything but the financial and social rewards of being a doctor. I admit you can probably set up a very lucrative practice thanks to your liaison with Laura Pen—'

'*Leave my personal life out of this!*'

Drew sighed. 'Wish I could, but I can't.'

'Who the hell appointed you as my conscience?'

He didn't take offence: 'I'm self-appointed. You have talent, and I refuse to let you squander it. You're trying hard to do so.'

'Goddamn it, you're wrong!' Will slapped his hat against his leg. His loud voice attracted the attention of several sightseers just getting off a launch. Glaring at Will, a mother hurried two small girls out of the range of further profanity.

A part of Will's anger sprang from guilt. He couldn't deny that he'd been preoccupied with money and social position for the last year or so. But Castle Garden – and Drew – had done a great deal to remind him of medicine's true purpose.

474

'Wrong, am I?' Drew had a strange, almost sly smile on his round face. 'All right, prove it.'

'What's that?'

'I think I spoke clearly. I said prove that I'm wrong. If you're hell-bent on practising uptown, instead of taking your skills to people genuinely desperate for them—'

'And who might those people be?'

Drew turned and pointed to the doorway in the pedestal. He referred to the Lazarus sonnet, and those it described. The human garbage of Europe. The refugees from the slums, the ghettos, the failed farms and stagnating villages of a dozen ancient countries. The seekers of the second chance. The travellers who had risked all they had – savings, security, sometimes even sanity or life itself – to reach the American shore.

'Weekends, I've been poking around up in the Sixth Ward,' Drew continued, his tone more temperate all at once. 'The sixth contains the worst slum in the city. The Mulberry Street Bend. I've decided to practise there. And to open a free clinic.'

'Well,' said Will softly. 'That's a major decision.'

'The doctors at Castle Garden are already teasing me about it. They say I must have come of missionary parents since I plan to practise in Hell.'

'Sounds like you do. Why not go into the Roman priesthood and take the vows of poverty and chastity while you're at it?'

He was instantly ashamed of the sarcasm. A resigned, almost sad smile appeared on Drew's face:

'My decision takes care of the poverty part. Ensures it, I guess you could say. As for the chastity, I reckon I'll always have to pay for whatever feminine companionship I get. I see girls I like, but when I say hello, they won't even answer because I'm so fat.' He shrugged. 'By now I'm resigned to that. But look – here's what I was getting at when I said you could

475

prove you really care about helping people. I want you to go into that free clinic with me.'

Will thought of what was symbolized by the words free clinic. Failure. An admission to the world that a man couldn't practise medicine profitably. Incredibly, Drew wasn't forced into such a position. He was making his choice voluntarily!

'Out of the question,' Will said.

'Don't turn me down so fast. You've already said you plan to set up shop in New York too.'

'Yes, but—'

'Then give me a chance to show you what needs to be done in the Mulberry Bend. Stay over a few more days. We'll take a tour of—'

'No, I can't. You know I'm due back in Boston to study with Dr Green.'

'Next summer, then. Your social calendar isn't booked that far ahead, is it?'

'Don't be snide.'

'Well, is it?'

'Of course not.'

'Then come with me to the Bend next summer. I've met another doctor down there. An old fellow, ready to retire soon. It's his practice that I plan to buy – provided I can arrange a loan.'

A loan of ten dollars is probably all you'll need for a practice like that, Will thought, but he didn't say it. Growing more enthusiastic, Drew went on:

'Give me as much time as you can next year, but promise me at least a week. We'll help the old man a few hours every day, and you'll soon see there's plenty of work for two men.'

'How long have you been hatching this insane—?'

'Next summer. I want your word on it.'

He took hold of Will's arm. His deceptively soft hands constricted like bands of metal. 'Your word.'

Angered, Will shot back, 'All right! On one condition.'

'What is it?'

'I don't want to hear another syllable about my personal life.'

'Done,' Drew exclaimed. His pale grey eyes shone in the sunshine. 'Let's catch the launch and go to Luchow's to celebrate.'

'Celebrate?' Will snorted. 'Celebrate volunteering to spend a week in the midst of drunks and thieves and push-cart peddlers?'

'Americans,' Drew said, pointing back at the pedestal again. 'With just as much right to the name as the nabobs on Fifth Avenue. And ten times as desperate for your help.'

Will shook his head. 'What the hell have I gotten myself into?'

Drew laughed. 'The most important part of your life. Excepting your marriage, of course,' he added, but with a noticeable lack of enthusiasm or conviction.

2

The following night, an express on the New York & New Haven line rattled through a heavy rainstorm, carrying a thoroughly sick Will Kent toward home.

After dining at Luchow's – no, gorging was a better word – he and Drew had gone back to the rooming house and consumed a huge quantity of cheap bourbon. Now Will had almost every known symptom of subacute gastritis. Overpowering thirst and a coated tongue. Extreme tenderness over the epigastrium. Flatulence and eructation. Diarrhoea, slight pyrexia, and highly coloured urine. A hammering head, a weak pulse, and cold feet. Plus a general feeling of debility and depression. Dr Austin Flint's text-book commentary on the condition carried a faintly moralistic tone which made him feel no better: 'The affection sometimes follows a prolonged debauch. Patients who are spirit-drinkers should be told of the connection of the disease with their habits.'

A little late for that now! He couldn't eat, or even think about food, without coming close to throwing up. He'd tried a little of everything recommended as a treatment. Small pieces of ice. Carbonated water. Salts of morphia. Milk mixed with lime water and a bowl of farina, both of which had refused to remain at their intended destination. Nothing helped; he was a digestive wreck. He'd just have to wait until his system decided he'd been sufficiently punished for his foolishness.

But it wasn't even the sickness causing his sharpest concern – and confusion – tonight. It was what he'd promised his friend, and what the consequences of that promise might be.

In a way, Drew had tricked him. He'd provoked an argument in which Will's pledge had been drawn from him in a burst of anger. Drew understood very well that his friend had a conscience. And he knew just how hard to press Will in order to elicit the response he'd got.

Queasy, Will rested his forehead against the grimy window, his gaze lost in the dark of the Connecticut woodlands through which the train was speeding. He was in a trap. Squarely in a trap. Yesterday he'd made a promise which was in direct conflict with the one he'd given Laura – and with the monumentally important one to Carter.

He thought about his dilemma with as much clarity as possible, given his miserable condition. Certain facts, seemingly irreconcilable, had to be taken into account in any solution of the problem Drew had precipitated:

First, Will was in love with Laura Pennel. He worshipped her. But he also knew that Drew was right about the triviality of society practice. What he'd seen in the eyes of the young Polish girl after he and Drew had delivered her child had all but cancelled the impression left by Dr Vlandingham. Will wanted to be not merely a competent and successful doctor, but a useful one. That meant taking care of people who genuinely needed help. And as Vlandingham had suggested during their conversation at Sherry's, there was no shortage of doctors on Fifth Avenue. Just the opposite.

So perhaps, in order to reconcile that which seemed irreconcilable, something had to give way.

The promise to Laura?

The short term of service with Drew next summer hardly classified as horse doctoring in Will's mind. But it would be classified that way by Thurman Pennel's daughter. Every human being had failings, and one of hers was arrogance. Perhaps he could do something about that after they were married. He'd certainly try. But at present, it was an undeniable part of Laura's character. To her, the patients Drew examined at Castle Garden, and those he intended to treat in the city's slums would be – in Emma Lazarus' word – refuse. If he helped Drew treat such people next summer, Laura would object—

If she knew about it.

All right, then. She mustn't find out, ever.

To ensure that she didn't, he'd have to keep his promise to Drew – and his fulfilment of it – a secret known only to the two of them. He'd have to keep it from Laura, from Marcus, from the Harvard faculty and fellow medical students – from everyone.

It was unpleasant to think of deceiving the girl he

meant to marry. He knew of no other way out. He was torn, wanting the best of two worlds.

He'd try like hell to have both, without ever being forced to choose between them. He thought it would work but he couldn't be sure. There were many potential pitfalls. Many, he repeated to himself as he stared into the rainy night, the swaying lamps of the car reflecting his bleak face on the dark, wet glass.

CHAPTER XIV

The Only Hope

Gideon's letter to Moultrie Calhoun of the *World* brought about a cordial dinner between the two men, thus provoking a stormy outburst from Joseph Pulitzer. The publisher fired off a telegram from Chatwold, his mansion in Bar Harbor, Maine, where he was summering. He demanded a meeting with Gideon.

Gideon pondered strategy, then decided he could best blunt Pulitzer's attack by a show of politeness. He wrote a note inviting his rival to an overnight cruise aboard *Auvergne*. Julia told Gideon he was asking for trouble, but he insisted on sending the note:

'Dealing with Joe shouldn't be any worse than putting your head up next to the muzzle of a Yankee cannon. Besides, I doubt he'll take me up on it.'

To their surprise, they received an acceptance. So the yacht steamed up the coast, and the Kents welcomed their competitor and his entourage on board with appropriate ceremony.

Politeness forbade any immediate discussion of the successful outcome of Gideon's dinner meeting with

Calhoun. But the dinner had taken place three weeks earlier. Now Gideon was worrying that perhaps Pulitzer had presented a counter offer; one which was too attractive for Calhoun to resist. But if that were so, why had Pulitzer accepted the invitation? Merely to gloat? That wasn't like him. Answers would have to wait until evening.

Soon the yacht was headed south again, toward Mount Desert Rock. As dinner began, the Hungarian-born newspaperman was polite, but no more than that. His occasional smile was closer to a wince. Heavily bearded and wearing prim-looking eyeglasses, he resembled a professor of the classics more than he did a publisher with a taste for the sensational.

'I'm delighted we could meet here rather than in New York,' Gideon said after twenty minutes of trivial talk about Washington, world affairs, and various aspects of the newspaper business – not including the thorny one which had brought them together.

'I've never seen your yacht,' Pulitzer said. 'Very handsome.'

Gideon murmured thanks.

'Besides, even in the summer Chatwold's a mausoleum. You know I like company.' That was evident from the two male secretaries Pulitzer had brought along for the overnight trip. It was said he employed as many as eight of them. 'It's been some time since we've seen each other, Gideon.'

His host nodded. 'Eight or nine months.' And in that interval, Pulitzer's health had obviously taken a bad turn. Coming into the dining saloon, he had moved slowly, and squinted as if his eyesight were failing. Pulitzer was actually four years younger than Gideon, but a lung condition had forced him to relinquish day-to-day management of the *World* two years earlier, though he still exercised rigid control of the paper's policies.

Lightning glared on the glass of the portholes. A rain squall was moving across *Auvergne*'s bow. The subsequent drum of thunder made Pulitzer squirm and dab his eyes with a handkerchief.

A few seconds later, Julia accidentally dropped a teaspoon. It struck the silver sugar bowl; not a loud noise, but a sudden one. Within seconds, perspiration was pouring down Pulitzer's cheeks and gleaming in his beard.

He managed to say, 'I had another reason for accepting your invitation. It struck me as fitting to be on board your yacht when we discuss the subject of piracy.'

Gideon sat motionless. So did Julia. Both felt the emotional temperature drop.

'I made a bona fide offer, Joe. And I didn't ask Mr Calhoun to keep it secret.'

'Oh, believe me, he didn't. But I very much resent your manoeuvring behind my back.'

'Joe, come off it. With your circulation, you've been licking the *Union* and every other daily in New York. My editorial department's been in disarray ever since Theo Payne died. I have to do something about that. To continue your nautical metaphor – suppose I were the captain of a sinking vessel, and your ship were the only one in the area with a lifeboat large enough to hold my crew. Would you deny me the right to reach out and save their lives, and mine?'

Rain began to spatter the deck above the saloon. Pulitzer reacted as if rifles were exploding. He mopped his forehead, then struggled to collect himself. He looked hard at Gideon.

'Sophistry! Slick words that have nothing to do with the issue. You stole Moultrie Calhoun from my staff.'

'Stole – ? Past tense?' Gideon couldn't conceal his surprise.

'Yes. He submitted his resignation. I offered him

half again what he was making at the *World*, and he still refused to stay.'

Because he's unhappy with the working conditions and with your temperamental behaviour. But Gideon wouldn't have said that under any circumstances.

'He hasn't officially informed me—' Gideon began.

'*I'm* informing you! Calhoun's an able journalist. A valuable man. I want to keep him.' It had the sound of an edict.

Growing annoyed in spite of himself, Gideon shrugged:

'It appears you can't. I'd say our discussion of the issue is closed.'

'No it isn't. Withdraw the offer.'

'In my place, you wouldn't do that.'

'I *demand* that you withdraw it.'

Slowly, Gideon shook his head. 'Joe, I refuse.'

Pulitzer leaned forward, red-faced and wrathful. Before he could speak, another peal of thunder jolted him back against his chair. His eyes watered behind his schoolmaster's glasses. He thumped the table:

'All right! If the son of a bitch doesn't like the *World* any longer, you take him – I won't have him! But let me tell you one more thing – ' Again that wrenching grimace, intended as a smirk. ' – I don't forget things like this. One day I'll drive you to the wall.'

Gideon puffed his cigar and managed to smile. 'That comes as no surprise. You're already hard at it.'

The drumming of the rain intensified suddenly, forestalling another retort. Pulitzer pressed his palms to his ears, as if in extreme pain. He stumbled to his feet and accidentally lurched into Julia's chair. Before she could rise and help him, he whispered, 'Keep your seat, Mrs Kent. You'll have to excuse me.'

When Pulitzer was gone, Gideon called Anderson to refill his brandy snifter.

'Calhoun was right. Joe's getting more and more

peculiar. He can't tolerate noise, but he has those flunkeys who talk or read to him all night long because he can't sleep. I'm thankful the Almighty never made me a genius. You pay a high price for it.'

'Are you sorry you invited him?'

Gideon shook his head. 'At least everything's out in the open now. I can put Moultrie Calhoun to work with no qualms. If I can get the paper back on a sound footing, maybe I can concentrate on Kent and Son for a while.'

But it was neither the paper nor the publishing house that worried him most. Even the chest pains that still plagued him were inconsequential when compared to the mistake he'd made in judging his son. A year ago, he had decided that Will was finally on the right track. He had been wrong; blindly, devastatingly wrong.

He tossed down the remaining brandy as if it were water.

'My, you drank that rather fast.'

'I'd say that was my affair, wouldn't you?'

A moment later he jumped, circled the table and squeezed her shoulders by way of apology:

'I'm sorry. That was a churlish thing to say.'

'What's troubling you, dear?'

'The usual. Business problems.'

He leaned down to touch his lips to her forehead. She turned in her chair, reaching up to clasp him. He kissed her mouth. It was an awkward embrace, but for Gideon a comforting one.

As they were proceeding to their cabin, Nyquist, the deck hand, pointed out that the squall had already passed astern. Gideon thanked him and said goodnight. Alone in their quarters, he and Julia came into each other's arms – he needing the comfort of it, and she sensing the need. They made love during the yacht's last violent rolling. Afterward he felt better, and again apologized for his rudeness.

484

But he still couldn't tell her the cause of his deep-seated worry. He still couldn't repeat the things he'd been hearing from one of the *Union*'s most reliable reporters.

2

Mr Moultrie Calhoun was a portly widower of fifty-two. He disliked his former employer, but he favoured Pulitzer's brand of journalism. When he and Gideon concluded their negotiations and shook hands, Gideon told the Charleston-born editor that he could and should begin spicing the *Union*'s front pages with some crime and society news.

From his very first day at the paper, Calhoun took charge. In contrast to the vituperative Theo Payne, he was a quiet man who seldom raised his voice. But he had eyes of an arresting blue-grey. The colour of a pistol barrel, someone remarked to Gideon. Calhoun had been at his desk only two hours when he turned that gunmetal gaze on a reporter and asked him in polite and unprofane language to correct the factual errors and sloppy writing in a piece of copy. The reporter took one look at those eyes and jumped to it.

As soon as all the copy for the next day's paper was in the composing room, Calhoun convened a meeting of the staff. Gideon gave the new editor a short introduction, then sat down. It took Calhoun less than two minutes to state his expectations. He would dispense with the services of anyone who didn't obey orders promptly, or behave in a seemly way:

'You may drink yourselves to perdition, ladies and gentlemen. You may – I shall use frank language despite the presence of the gentler sex – debauch until you have guaranteed yourselves berths in the nether region. You may lie and cheat until the Devil himself

485

distrusts you. But you will keep all such activity separate from these premises, and never let it interfere with the performance of your duties. If my requirements are not to your liking, or your character is such that you cannot fulfil them no matter how good your intentions, I urge you to seek employment elsewhere. You will not last long working for me. We are responsible journalists upon whom the public depends for the truth. We shall behave accordingly – at least during working hours. Which, I must warn you, will not be short. Thank you for your attention. That is all.'

That night Calhoun kept the staff at their desks long past the normal quitting time. One by one he called the reporters and illustrators into his office, closed the door and interviewed them. By four the next morning, he had issued dismissal notices to three writers and one staff artist. Clutching their severance pay, they staggered into the dawn shaking their heads. Gideon woke on the cot where he'd been catching a nap. Calhoun looked fresh and full of energy:

'All personnel problems have been taken care of, Mr Kent. Shall we go out for breakfast?'

'Aren't you going to sleep?'

'I hadn't planned on it, sir. It'll soon be time to start working on the next edition.'

Yawning, Gideon sat up, folded the blanket and laid it on the end of the cot. 'Did you serve in the war, Mr Calhoun?'

'Please call me Moultrie, sir.'

'Very well, Moultrie. Did you serve—'

'I did.'

'Which side?'

'The same side as yours, sir.' He seemed anxious not to say that too loudly in a Northern newspaper office. 'I was a telegraph clerk.'

'Well, if we'd had a few more like you running things in Richmond, maybe we wouldn't have fared so badly. I'll join you for an omelette and some black coffee.

486

But you'll have to nudge me if I doze off. I'm only forty-five, but you put me to shame.'

From that first day, Gideon was completely satisfied with the work of his new editor. Calhoun's childless wife had been dead five years. He had no interests except his job. As the fall election campaign intensified – the *Union* endorsed Cleveland – Calhoun used the weekends to come to Boston to report on progress at the paper, and to listen to his employer's reaction. One of the meetings was held at Kent and Son. There, Calhoun met Helene Vail for the first time.

He kissed her hand, murmured some pleasantries, and managed to bring a pink glow to her cheeks. On Calhoun's next visit, Gideon asked his typewriter to be present to make notes on a number of important financial decisions. He was astonished when Miss Vail appeared with a new hairdo and a new dress. That night he said to Julia:

'I do believe our thorny rose may blossom. She was giddy as a young girl around Calhoun. Maybe she won't be listing herself as "disappointed in love" much longer.'

He was trying to act lighthearted, but strain was clearly written on his face. What secret anxiety was tormenting him? Julia wondered.

Grover Cleveland amassed nearly one hundred thousand more popular votes than Senator Harrison, but the Republican candidate had a larger total of electoral votes, and hence won the presidency. His party took control of both houses of Congress. The best that a disgruntled Gideon could say about the election was that his friend Roosevelt, who had remained loyal to the Republicans, might now find an outlet for his talent in Washington. He hoped so; the country would gain by it.

As winter approached, Gideon and Julia continued to entertain friends and well-known people at their dinner table. Samuel Clemens, the writer who called himself Mark Twain, paid them a return visit. On another evening, Professor William James, the anatomist, drove over from Cambridge. He said little about his developing interest in psychology but he couldn't say enough about his expatriate brother Henry, whose fiction was being hailed as the work of a genius. Regrettably, Gideon found that same work unbearably boring.

One week they entertained the evangelist Dwight Moody, who was saving souls up and down New England. The following week their guest was a man trying to rescue those same souls from folly – Bob Ingersoll, the successful Washington lawyer whom the press called The Great Agnostic. He was in town to deliver his famous lecture, 'Some Mistakes of Moses.'

An aging Edwin Booth spent an evening at the Kent house and spoke of the fine reputation Eleanor was building in the theatre; she and Leo were currently on tour with one of the troupes sent out by the famous producer-manager Augustin Daly. Booth seemed a hollow man, somehow; he was sombre and melancholy despite his international fame. Twice he made reference to 'poor Johnny.' He was obviously still haunted by what his actor brother had done that calamitous night at Ford's Theatre.

Two pillars of the women's movement – leaders of opposing factions within it – came to dinner on the same evening. Julia had gone to great lengths to arrange the reunion between the two, who had parted over a policy dispute years before.

One guest had often been at the house – Julia's mentor Lucy Stone, who headed the American Woman Suffrage Association which had its headquarters in Boston. She was small, seventy years old, and remarkably energetic.

The other was a newcomer to the Kent house. She was Mrs Elizabeth Cady Stanton, reputedly the first woman to refuse to include the word *obey* in her marriage ceremony. She and Susan B. Anthony directed the National Woman Suffrage Association in New York. The National was generally considered the more radical of the two wings.

Mrs Stanton had come to Boston for one of the lyceum lectures which kept her travelling a good part of each year. Like Lucy Stone, she was just a little over five feet tall. She had merry eyes and a tart manner. At seventy-three, she was as animated and good-humoured as her counterpart Mrs Stone.

There was tension when the two suffragists first greeted one another in the parlour, but soon the atmosphere was cordial and comfortable. Julia was clearly elated; a reconciliation between the two organizations was one of her highest hopes. She argued that the movement already had trouble enough. Influential politicians, preachers, and journalists regularly damned it and its leaders from every available platform. Why, then, should women further impair their own cause by quarrelling among themselves? They needed a united front, not a divided one.

To prepare the ground for this dinner party, she'd gone to Washington several months earlier, to the first International Council of Women, sponsored by the National Association. There she had stated her case to Mrs Stanton and Susan Anthony. Now there were signs that a resolution of differences, and a reunion of the two groups, might be forthcoming. At least Mrs Stanton and Mrs Stone were dining at the same table, and appearing to enjoy it.

Differences remained, of course; important ones. Lucy Stone still believed women should only work to gain the vote, and not damage that effort by involving themselves with issues such as divorce and child bearing, and debates about virginity and marital fidelity. Although a model of moral behaviour herself, Elizabeth Stanton had quite different views – especially on free love:

'Lucy, I don't care whether the sisters who march under our banner are spotless white or screaming scarlet. What counts is their conviction. We've had enough women sacrificed to this sentimental, hypocritical prattling about purity. It's one of man's most effective engines for dividing and subjugating us – nothing personal, Mr Kent,' she added with a crisp nod in his direction. 'I say we must put an end to that ignoble record and stand for one thing only – with no qualifications. Womanhood.'

A prolonged silence then. Julia looked crestfallen; surely the prospect of reconciliation was ruined.

But Lucy Stone spoke up with just the right blend of firmness and restraint:

'Friendship has many rare qualities, Elizabeth. One of the most precious is this. True friends can disagree about a few things and still work together. Whatever our differences on lesser questions, we have none on the greatest question of all. Freedom for women. I fear we may have forgotten that fact – and our friendship – far too long.'

Mrs Stanton's face softened. 'I fear we have. Perhaps it's time we remembered.'

She held out her hand. So did Lucy. They clasped hands for a moment, both of them smiling. There were no more disagreements that evening, and a spirit of good feeling prevailed. Julia was overjoyed.

But she noticed that Gideon had a preoccupied air, and a drawn look. *Why?*

In the days that followed, he began to grow snappish with her – behaviour not typical of him. For hours and even days at a time, he'd say little more than what was necessary. He seemed not only depressed but perpetually tired.

Julia urged him to see a doctor. He denied there was anything wrong with him physically. She felt he wasn't telling her the truth. Finally, on Christmas Eve, matters came to a head.

5

It promised to be a lonely Christmas. Perhaps the loneliest they'd spent together. None of the children was home. Will had boarded a train for New York at eleven o'clock that morning. At noon, the servants had been given their gifts and the rest of the day off. The house was still; heavy with shadows. Why turn on lights when no one was there?

Julia and Gideon had gone to the parlour after eating a simple supper she'd fixed. There was no illumination in the parlour except that from the candles on the small, fragrant fir tree. Hands locked behind his back, Gideon paced in front of the window overlooking the Common. Occasionally he stopped and peered out. He looked dejected; miserable. Finally Julia could stand it no longer:

'Gideon, come here and tell me what's wrong.'

Without looking at her, he said, 'What do you mean?'

'You know very well. You haven't been yourself for

months. You really must tell me what's troubling you. I can't help if I don't know.'

He turned from the window. It was a bitter, starless night. Behind him the Common was bleak and dark. There'd be no snow to soften the iron cold, everyone said.

His blue eye momentarily reflected candlelight. 'Has it showed that much?'

'I'm afraid so.' She moved to his side, her skirts rustling. 'Are you thinking about the children?'

He was silent a moment. Then he nodded. 'I miss them. They should be home on Christmas!'

'They're grown, darling. They have their own lives.'

'But what are they *doing* with their lives? Nothing worthwhile that I can see. Poor Eleanor's performing in some ten-cent town, spending Christmas in a hotel.'

'But she's with Leo, and she's happy.'

'God, I hope so. And what about Carter? He's hiding his life away in Colorado—'

'You mustn't take all the burdens of the family on yourself, dear. That's a Kent family failing, and frustrated idealism can become destructive guilt. You're not to blame for Carter's waywardness. I'm more responsible than anyone else. Besides, he isn't in Colorado any longer.'

'How do you know?'

'A letter came in the morning mail. We were so busy getting Will packed off to New York, I didn't have a chance to show it to you. Carter posted the letter in Denver but it says he's moving on.'

'Where?'

A sad laugh. 'That, he didn't say. I don't suppose he knew. Believe me, I fret over him as much as you do – ' She touched his shoulder. 'I suspect I know the real reason you're feeling so bad. You're angry because Will left to spend Christmas with the Pennels. That's it, isn't it?'

He didn't answer the question directly:

'Did you notice the way he kept talking about them all morning? As if he damn near worships 'em!'

'He's in love with Miss Pennel, Gideon. I suspect he hopes to marry her. It's perfectly natural for him to praise her parents.'

Gideon didn't seem to hear. 'All he wants to be is a Fifth Avenue doctor who dispenses headache remedies to anaemic girls. And now he's taken up with a pack of robbers.'

'He's almost an adult. Even if you feel that way, you mustn't say it.'

'Why not?' Gideon shot back. 'Must I leave his education – or should I say his seduction – to bandits like Thurman Pennel? Godamighty, Julia, the man makes millions from the misery of others! Factory owners fall all over themselves to buy the wretched buildings his architects slap together. And for years it's been rumoured that he owns whole square blocks of the worst tenements in New York City.'

'Rumoured, or proven?'

'What difference does it make?'

'A great deal. I want you to make objective judgments about Will and his friends.'

Gideon's jaw set. 'Then objectively speaking – he's gone the wrong way. I've allowed it to happen.'

Julia was equally firm. 'Regardless of your opinions, you can't choose the girl with whom he falls in love.'

'Even if she's the kind who'll ruin his life?'

'Oh, Gideon – that's terribly exaggerated. What you mean is that Miss Pennel may ruin his life according to your standards.'

'My God, whose side are you taking?'

'Please don't yell. You *cannot* dictate Will's choice of a wife.'

There was a lengthy silence. Finally Gideon let out his breath:

493

'I know. I suppose that's why I'm worried. Months ago, I – I began to hear some disturbing things about Miss Pennel.'

Instantly Julia's anger was gone. 'From whom?'

'One of the reporters on the *Union*. Her name's Hester Davis. She covers Mrs Astor's parties – that sort of thing. She's very reliable, and very familiar with New York Society families. When she heard Will was seeing Miss Pennel, she came to me and passed along certain facts. Out of consideration for us, she said.'

'Facts, Gideon? Or more rumours?'

'Well – rumours,' he admitted. 'But there must be something to them.'

'What's the nature of the rumours?'

'That the young lady Will is seeing isn't as pure as her doting mother likes to pretend. Far from it. I don't understand the why's and wherefore's, but Hester claimed that in the Pennels' circle, the girl's reputation is so suspect, she can't attract a single suitor who would think seriously of marrying her.'

'Oh, Gideon – those are vicious accusations. Probably completely unfounded. Spread by some spiteful person who has a grudge against the girl.'

His shrug admitted the possibility – but just barely.

'In any case, you mustn't repeat that sort of thing to Will. Unless you have irrefutable proof, you can't tell him that the girl he's fond of is – ' She gestured helplessly. ' – immoral.'

'But in many way's Will's an innocent. What if it's true?'

'What if it is? He's grown up. You have to let him learn the truth for himself.'

'Suppose he doesn't?'

'That's a risk you'll have to take. Unless you intend to destroy him by making all his decisions for the rest of his life.'

Gideon fumed. She patted his hand gently. 'The

Kent spirit's a worthy and admirable one. But you can't play the role of patriarch forever, controlling the lives of grown men and women—'

'And why not?'

'Because it's out of style! Times are changing, Gideon—'

'For the worse! Why shouldn't I step in if I think Will's headed for disaster? Someone has to guide this family—'

A glance at the shadowed room. A candle on the Christmas tree hissed and dripped wax down its side.

' – or what's left of it after I'm gone. I'll be forty-six years old next year. I must get things in order! I thought Will was the most likely candidate to take charge. That was a terrible mistake.'

He sounded hurt and angry. Julia's eyes softened as she saw his pain. He lit a match and touched it to a cigar. The flame put bright highlights and deep, contrasting shadows on a face no longer young.

He flipped the blown-out match into the sand bucket kept handy in case of fire. Then he slipped his arm round his wife:

'It has to be Eleanor. Now that Carter's wandering all over hell and Will's fallen in with a crowd of whited sepulchres, Eleanor's the only one left to lead this family when we're gone.'

He pulled Julia close to him. His face was stern in the candlelight – a Biblical patriarch's face – but she knew his sternness concealed a deep anxiety.

She was thankful he'd finally admitted the cause of his brusque behaviour of late. But she firmly believed in the rightness of every word she'd said to him. Even granting that the accusations about Laura Pennel might contain some truth, Gideon simply couldn't go to his son and repeat them. It was an unacceptable alternative.

Something else he had just said bothered her:

'You mustn't count too heavily on Eleanor. She's immersed in her profession, and in Leo.'

'Maybe something will change that.'

'What could possibly change it?'

Silence again; longer than the one before.

'I don't know,' he said, drawing her still closer against him. 'But she's our only hope now. Nothing must happen to ruin her life. She's our only hope.'

BOOK FOUR

The Waters Roar

CHAPTER I

The Troupers

In 1873, New York had been the first state to adopt the thirtieth of May as a holiday honouring the Civil War dead. Now the holiday was widely observed throughout the North. But Memorial Day offered no respite to a theatrical company on tour – and that was the case on this last Thursday of May 1889. While most citizens relaxed and enjoyed a day of leisure, twenty-seven-year-old Eleanor Goldman, her husband, and the members of their troupe were rattling eastward through the Allegheny mountain valleys in a dingy Pennsylvania Railroad coach. According to Regis Pemberton, the company manager, they were about a half hour from the town in which they were scheduled to give a show that evening.

The company had been sent on tour by Augustin Daly, one of the half dozen most successful producing managers in the United States. Daly's Theatre was one of New York City's best playhouses, and Daly's productions were almost always hits because he mounted them lavishly, neglected no details, and insisted on absolute personal control of every phase of a show. The newspaper writers called him 'the autocrat of the stage' with good reason.

Daly was also a prolific playwright. Every season he turned out several scripts, both original ones and adaptations. Eleanor and her husband were touring in a very successful comedy called *A Night Off* which Daly had adapted from the German of Franz von Schönthan six years before.

Tonight's performance would be professional, but

499

certainly no pleasure, Eleanor thought. She felt tired and depressed this afternoon. She sat by the grimy window, her chin in her palm and her dark eyes fixed on the misty dark green peaks passing slowly above her. An unread letter lay in her lap. She was hungry. She'd overslept and had had no time for breakfast before boarding the train. And when she'd awakened, her first sight had been an upsetting one – Leo, standing by the window of their hotel room and gazing out at the streets of Pittsburgh. On his face was a forlorn and faintly bitter expression which was becoming all too familiar.

What tricks life can play, she thought then, before he realized she was awake. An outside observer would study the visible evidence and conclude that everything was going splendidly for the Goldmans. The truth was quite different.

Leo sat beside Eleanor, dozing and swaying with the motion of the train as it switchbacked along a track above a racing creek. A few raindrops spattered the window. From two seats behind, one of the actresses sighed, 'More rain. That'll keep the audience at home.'

'Maybe not, Minna,' Pemberton said. 'This place is supposed to be one of the best theatre towns in Pennsylvania. I've never played here myself, but Daly told me the houses are usually excellent. And the town's accustomed to springtime floods. People are used to going out in bad weather.'

'Seems like it's been raining all month,' someone else complained. 'Won't we ever see the sun?'

Pemberton again: 'Don't count on it soon. The Pittsburgh paper said the Signal Service is predicting another big storm today or tomorrow.'

His voice blended with that of the company stage manager across the aisle. The stage manager doubled in brass as Prowl, a minor character in the play. He was saying to his assistant:

'We've been guaranteed possession of the Opera House by three-thirty. I told them that if we couldn't start shifting our scenery by four, there'd be no performance. The house manager promised to make sure the patriotic programme ended on time. Of course the start of the programme really depends on when the parade finishes.'

'I hope to hell it doesn't pour before we arrive,' the assistant grumbled. 'If it does, we won't be able to find any pick-up labourers.'

The voices droned on, punctuated by the sudden loud laugh of an actress reading a copy of the humour magazine, *Life*. Eleanor wished she could find something to laugh about. Leo's mood made that almost impossible these days. Why couldn't she soothe or humour him out of his despondency? Why, when so many things were going just right for them?

Professionally, their position was enviable. They were well established in the organization of a fine manager. Daly was temperamental, but he tolerated no temperament in his actors and actresses. He also despised the star system, and refused to permit it in his shows! As a director, his chief goal was to achieve an excellent performance by the ensemble. He never permitted one actor to shine at the expense of others.

That held true even in New York, where four of the most accomplished performers on the American stage formed the core of Daly's stock company. The so-called Big Four – leading man John Drew, the son of Mrs Louisa Drew of the Arch Street Theatre, the two comedians Jim Lewis and Mrs John Gilbert; and the ingenue Ada Rehan – all knew better than to try to upstage one another, or anyone else in the company.

Membership in the Daly organization was also desirable because Daly believed in modern acting methods. Like any art, acting was not static; during the century it had gone through a steady evolution.

The first great American star, Edwin Forrest, had summed up the evolution within his own career. He'd started as a disciple of the stately declamatory school of acting popular in Britain. Then he'd fallen under the influence of the stormy emotional style of Kean. By the time Forrest had done his last season in 1871–72, that style, too, was passé, and Forrest was dismissed by the avant-garde as a 'bovine bellower.'

Now a more natural and realistic technique was developing. Men such as James Murdoch and Edwin Booth exemplified it best. Of course there was still an important place for performers who could shift to the style known as extreme emotionalism. Women who could cry copiously on cue were in great demand for the many melodramas staged every year.

Once categorized as emotionalistic, however, an actor had few chances to try other kinds of roles. Eleanor had struggled to avoid that kind of pigeonholing by producers. She deliberately sought varied roles. She'd started her professional career as Eva in a travelling Tom show. She'd played Juliet, Ophelia and, in different productions of *The Taming of the Shrew*, Bianca and Kate. She'd understudied the title role in *Camille*; ranted and sobbed in three Daly melodramas; been menaced by revolvers while defending her virtue in frontier dramas – even done knockabout comedy in a revival of Harrigan and Hart's huge hit of ten years before, *The Mulligan Guard Ball*.

Unlike some of Daly's performers, she enjoyed all sorts of plays, from ancient to modern. A lot of actors were traditionalists, despising modern playwrights such as Ibsen or Mackaye. Daly's ingenue Ada Rehan, for example, loathed the work of both men and would appear in nothing that was not light, innocuous, and – to use her words – morally uplifting.

Eleanor didn't quarrel with Ada for holding those views, but she felt sorry for her. Just as there was a new kind of acting emerging, so there was a new, more realistic and powerful dramaturgy. In America its foremost exponent was Steele Mackaye. His play *Hazel Kirke*, first produced in 1880, was still widely toured. *Hazel Kirke* took place in a mill and featured working-class characters – a shock for audiences accustomed to the convention that serious plays were only set in ancient palaces or upper-class drawing rooms. The new dramatists thrilled and excited Eleanor. The theatre was a banquet, and she had no intention of settling for a one-course meal.

Despite Eleanor's efforts to keep from being categorized, it was happening. Like it or not, she was beginning to be thought of as an actresss of the personality school. Such actresses developed a personal following; their audiences paid to see them regardless of the vehicle.

Some personality actresses tended to be more than a bit bizarre; the famed Madame Bernhardt kept a lion cub as a pet and slept in a satin-padded coffin in her Paris apartment. Eleanor abhorred that kind of exhibitionism. Yet it was flattering to be thought of as one who someday might have roles tailored to fit her talents because she, not the play, was the reason the audiences came to the theatre.

Since she and Leo worked regularly, they were able to put money away in the hope of one day realizing a personal and professional dream. They'd started talking about the idea almost ten years before. They wanted to own and manage their own playhouse in New York. During seasons with Daly and with Mrs Drew at Arch Street, they'd learned the business side of theatrical management. Lately Eleanor had begun to think they were almost ready to stop working for others and start working for themselves.

Why, then, with everything going so splendidly, was Leo constantly unhappy?

She knew, of course. The fault was hers.

She turned to look at her husband. Her classically-featured, dark-eyed face that men found so beautiful revealed nothing of her worry and unhappiness. She was a good actress. She never permitted herself to show emotion of the kind surging through her now. And no matter how miserable she became, she never cried. Never.

Leo was still dozing. Sleep had smoothed away some of the strain on his face. One area of their marriage hadn't worked out and never would, because of what had happened that night in 1877 when men had broken into the Kent mansion and driven Margaret Kent to her death, and cornered Eleanor and—

She clenched her hands in her lap. Fought to blank out the memory of the pain, the humiliation, the incredibly soiled feeling as, one by one, those men—

No. She would *not* dwell on it. She closed her eyes and breathed deeply, failing to notice the letter slip out of her lap as she changed position.

The moment of strain passed, the details of that harrowing night successfully pushed out of· her mind. She opened her eyes, noticed the letter on the floor and quickly recovered it.

The letter was from Papa's brother, Uncle Matt; the man who had first encouraged Eleanor to try a professional stage career. Matt Kent had served as a genial and expert guide when she and Leo had honeymooned in Paris. Among the theatres they'd visited was the Comédie-Française, where Eleanor's great-great-great-great-grandmother, Marie Charboneau, had performed.

For a few moments she immersed herself in the letter. Its only real news concerned Tom, the son Uncle

Matt had never seen. Before the boy's birth, Matt's estranged wife Dolly – of whom he still wrote and spoke in the most affectionate terms – had gone out to the North-West Frontier of India as a schoolteacher for officers' children. Now, Matt said, Tom was hoping for a career as an officer in the Indian Army – an organization not to be confused with the British Army in India, he pointed out. Down to the very last soldier of the line, those in the British Army in India were Englishmen. The Indian Army included many native-born noncommissioned officers and enlisted men.

India was a colourful, if dangerous place to soldier, Uncle Matt concluded. He wanted to visit it and sketch its sights one day. Eleanor suspected that what he really wanted was to get his first look at young Tom.

She folded the letter and put in her reticule. The train was rumbling past shanties and wooden tenements standing on mud flats beside a river which looked unusually swift and turbulent. Across the river, large brick homes perched on a steep hillside, their fronts supported on pilings. The train passed a factory complex. Eleanor recalled Pemberton saying the town's main industry was steel.

But trivial things couldn't keep her mind off Leo for very long. They had been married almost four and a half years. In all that time, despite mutual tenderness and consideration for the feelings of the other, they had been unable to solve the problem which was Eleanor's legacy from that dreadful night in '77. Her father had sensed the existence of the problem. Of course she couldn't discuss it with him.

But the problem was so serious that discussions with Leo were inevitable. Time and again she told him the difficulty didn't matter. He agreed – or pretended to agree – then contradicted that attitude a day or so later by another desperate attempt to prove that the problem didn't exist. He always failed.

505

She repeatedly told him the fault was hers. But she couldn't bring herself to do the one thing that might have convinced him. She couldn't open the imaginary door and, by sharing the secret with her husband, destroy its power over her. She simply could not do it. And so Leo's despondency and bitterness grew steadily worse.

Now the train was rolling across a huge stone bridge at least fifty feet wide. The bridge carried four sets of tracks. 'Looks like we're coming in,' Pemberton said. 'Our hotel's the Hulbert House. It's supposed to be the newest in town. Before we left New York, they wired that they were heavily booked. But I think we managed to squeeze everyone in.'

'Leo?' Eleanor tapped his arm. His eyes opened. 'We're here,' she said, leaning over to kiss his closely shaved cheek.

In *A Night Off*, Leo played Marcus Brutus Snap, an eccentric and flamboyant theatrical manager – a role far removed from the sombre silence with which he regarded her now. Others in the company stood up, gathering hand luggage from overhead racks. On either side of the train spread a panorama of tenements and business buildings made indistinct by the rain and the dark sky.

'Feeling a little more rested?' she asked.

Leo shrugged. 'I slept. I don't think I got much rest.'

She held back a retort. Melancholy was becoming a way of life for him. She hated that. She knew he had many more reasons than one for becoming embittered. Yet that understanding didn't make it any easier to live with him.

He tugged the brim of his derby down over his forehead, slouched on the seat and stared out the window. What he saw quickly soured his expression:

'God. Someone in Pittsburgh told me they manufacture a lot of barbed wire here. A fitting product for such a depressing place.'

506

'Regis said it's an excellent theatre town—'

'Oh, certainly. In this weather I'm sure we'll play to all of a dozen people.'

It hurt her to hear his sarcasm. These days he was so unlike the merry, confident, and outgoing Leo Goldman she'd first met at an amateur theatrical club in New York. He was still handsome. But the frustration caused by their failure to achieve a satisfying physical relationship seemed to be eroding his good looks as well as his good spirits.

One indicator of his unhappiness was the frequency with which he reminisced about the past. Although he'd spent his boyhood in poverty in New York's Lower East Side, he already regarded that boyhood with great nostalgia. Often after a performance, he would lie on the bed in their hotel room, lock his hands under his head and deliver a long, rambling monologue about the days when there had been a mezuzah on the doorpost and pushcarts selling oilcloth, garlic, fish, and a hundred other items in the street. 'After a skimpy meal, those carts could provide dessert if you were clever and fast. Apples went down your shirt front, bananas up your sleeve.'

He'd worked hard running newspapers from Park Row, but there had been moments of relaxation, too; wonderful moments. There were breathtaking vistas of the city to be seen from tenement rooftops; bright immies to be won in a marble shoot; a rubber ball to be solidly whacked in the Hester Street equivalent of a baseball game—

'Good times.'

That was his summation. He'd been among his own people. Not constantly jostling against bigots who turned on him because of his name or his dark, Semitic face. He'd been full of hope and ambition. She blamed herself for most of his dreams going bad.

Pemberton bustled along the aisle of the lamp-lit

507

coach. He was a runty, red-faced man of sixty, inclined to be brusque. Now, though, he sounded like a mother issuing instructions to a brood of children:

'Take hacks if they're available, a trolley if they aren't. It's the Hulbert House, remember—'

A conductor shouted the name of the town, but a screech of the wheels muffled it. There were twenty in the company travelling in the coach: five men and five women who took the principal roles in the play, plus musicians, scenery and property people, the stage manager, his assistant, and Pemberton. One of the musicians had evidently played the town before:

' – that's the Little Conemaugh out that way, and the Stonycreek there. The two rivers meet just above that stone bridge we crossed. What I don't like about the place is the dam. It's fourteen or fifteen miles up the south branch of the Little Conemaugh, and four hundred feet higher than the town.'

'What's wrong with that?' someone wanted to know.

'It's an earth dam. Largest in the world, and the reservoir behind it is the biggest artificial lake in the country. The dam holds back four and a half billion gallons of water. That's twenty million tons. I guess the dam was safe once, but now it's leaky as a sieve.'

'My heavens, Waldo, why doesn't someone fix it?' a young woman asked.

'*Laissez-faire*, my dear Ellen. *Laissez-faire*. The dam was built forty or fifty years ago, as part of a rail and canal system connecting Philadelphia and Pittsburgh. When the system became obsolete, the land near the dam was put up for sale. Now the reservoir's called Lake Conemaugh, and on the shore there's a private fishing and hunting club for the Pittsburgh swells. The Mellons, Carnegie, Frick – that crowd. No one's going to tell them how to run their businesses or maintain their property. They refuse to repair the dam. I'm glad we're not staying here any longer than one—'

Pemberton interrupted with a hard tap on the shoulder:

'That's enough, Waldo. The weather's doing a fine job of depressing everybody. Don't help out with scare stories.'

'It's no story, Regis. That dam's been in wretched shape for—'

'Waldo!'

'All right,' the musician said, turning away with a sullen shrug.

Eleanor knew Pemberton's edict was not just a whim. A company's mood had a significant effect on a performance; subtle influences could result in a superlative show, or a drab one. And audiences were quick to sense when a company wasn't up to the mark.

She saw no enthusiasm in the company this afternoon. The gloomy weather and the drab town had destroyed it little by little; Waldo's comments hadn't helped, either. Voices grew subdued as the train slowed for the depot. The women readied parasols that wouldn't be of much use against the rain beginning to fall heavily outside. The sky had grown so dark, it might have been dusk instead of mid-afternoon. Lamps had already been lit in the station.

As she and Leo prepared to leave the coach, she heard a second, somewhat louder noise above the drum of the rain.

'What on earth is that roaring?'

Waldo answered. 'The rivers.' Something in his tone made her shiver and recall his remark about the dam:

Now it's leaky as a sieve.

The Goldmans stepped down on the wet platform. Leo pointed. 'Look at that.'

Beyond the depot, a red, white, and black three-sheet billboard was visible in the falling rain. The three-sheet advertised the evening's performance at

509

the Opera House with a mammoth capital-letter heading which Leo read aloud:

'"Intensely funny." Surely they can't mean us.'

No one smiled. Pemberton scowled. It didn't promise to be a successful engagement, and it was certainly a wretched way to spend Memorial Day. What Eleanor saw of the town only depressed her further. The main business district was situated on a triangle of land bounded by the two noisy streams. From the steep, dark hillsides, homes of the well-to-do looked down on the commercial buildings, and on shanties and tenements along the rivers, which were already close to overflowing their banks. The rain was falling harder than ever.

Eleanor shivered. 'What's the name of this gloomy place?'

Leo pointed to the dripping depot sign.

JOHNSTOWN

CHAPTER II

The Other Cheek

Pemberton sent the stage manager to the Opera House to check on the progress of the Memorial Day program. Hacks proved to be nonexistent around the depot. So did trolleys. Pemberton left two men at the station to arrange for transportation of the scenery, then he and the others trudged through the downtown carrying their own luggage. By the time they reached the four-story Hulbert House at Clinton and Main Streets, nearly a mile of walking had left them soaked and in a bad temper.

Leo carried both his valise and Eleanor's. He sneezed loudly several times. Finally she asked if he felt all right.

'Marvellous. I do this for my health all the time.'

She tried to cover him with a parasol that offered little protection. He pushed it away.

The hotel was sturdy, elegant, and obviously new. Leo didn't like to stand in line, so he and Eleanor sat down in the lobby until all the others had signed the ledger and claimed their keys. Then they approached the desk. Pemberton was at the front door, conferring with the man he'd sent to the Opera House. The holiday programme wouldn't end till about four-fifteen. Pemberton's curse could be heard all the way across the lobby.

'Goldman, Mr and Mrs,' Leo said at the marble counter. They travelled under their married name but at the theatre Eleanor was always billed under her maiden name. It was as Eleanor Kent that she received bouquets and written invitations from men in the audience who didn't realize she was married. Displeasing her with his morbidity, Leo sometimes joked that if he died, her suitors would attend his funeral.

'Goldman, Goldman—' the buck-toothed clerk studied some card or paper beneath the counter. Eleanor stepped up next to her husband, a wary look in her eyes. This had the smell of something familiar and infuriating.

The clerk turned round to examine the pigeonholes containing room keys. After a moment he pivoted back to face them.

'I'm afraid I just rented the last room, Mr Goldman. We have nothing left.'

Leo exploded:

'Our manager made reservations for the entire company weeks ago!'

'Be that as it may – ' The clerk's eyelids drooped as he shrugged. 'We have nothing.'

Leo gripped the edge of the counter, his fingers white. 'Would the situation be different if our last name was Smith?'

'I beg your pardon?'

'You heard me, you lying fraud.'

The clerk stepped back. 'I'm not required to listen to that sort of—'

'Some trouble here?' Pemberton said, bustling up to them.

Eleanor spun to face him. 'The hotel doesn't have enough rooms. At least not enough for us.'

'Regrettably, we are one short,' the clerk told Pemberton. His face showed a pious regret. But his narrow brown eyes were far from pious as they slid from Leo's face to the swelling curve of Eleanor's breast.

'This is disgraceful,' Pemberton said. 'Artists aren't accustomed to being treated in this fashion. We were assured by telegraph that your establishment could accommodate my entire troupe.'

'Well, someone made a mistake. And I don't have to stand here and be insulted by this Je – this gentleman. If you want to take your troupe somewhere else, feel free to do so. We won't suffer bankruptcy, I assure you.'

He turned sharply and disappeared into his cubicle.

Pemberton whacked his soft hat against his plaid trouser leg. Dismayed, he eyed the lobby. All the others had disappeared, anxious to reach their rooms and change to dry clothes. One fat guest sat with a newspaper in his lap and a smouldering cigar in his mouth. The man's head was exceptionally large; too large even for his obese body. Protruding eyes added a final touch of ugliness.

The man had been amused by the incident at the counter. He chewed the end of his cigar as he studied Eleanor's face. A moment later he heaved himself up from his chair and waddled around a pillar where he fell into conversation with someone the pillar concealed.

'We'll all go somewhere else—' Pemberton began.

'And turn everyone out into the rain again?' Eleanor shook her head. 'That isn't necessary.'

'But if we stay, we're condoning—'

'Never mind, Regis,' Leo interrupted. 'Eleanor's right. It would be all right to protest if it weren't raining, but the others are worn out. Let them stay. We're used to this kind of reception.'

And in truth so was the company manager. He was only one of many who'd urged Leo to Anglicize his last name. Even Gideon had made the suggestion to Eleanor. But the one time she'd mentioned it to Leo, he had lost his temper. Ever since the attack on his father in Philadelphia, he refused to put up with slights or insults caused by his being Jewish. With bleak humour, he often said it was easier for Christians to turn the other cheek because the first one didn't get pummelled and spat on like the cheek of a Jew.

Eleanor slipped her arm in his, picking up her valise

with her other hand. 'Don't worry about us, Regis. We'll find another hotel.'

Leo nodded. 'There must be one in town that isn't run by bigots.'

He said it loudly, so that the clerk in his cubicle was sure to hear. A clearing of a throat said he had. Leo smiled in a humourless way, then snatched up the other valise with a suddenness that betrayed his suppressed rage.

They walked toward the street entrance. Eleanor's travelling cape and skirt were sodden and she was bone-cold. Leo sneezed again, then a third time. Pemberton called after them:

'Don't walk in this weather. Find a hack. Offer the driver double or triple – whatever it takes. I'll reimburse you from company funds.'

'Thank you, Regis,' Eleanor called back. It was a kind offer but a futile one. They all knew no hacks were operating in the downpour.

As they passed the pillar, they came upon the fat fellow and the man to whom he'd been talking – a thin, white-haired porter in rank overalls. Three steps more, and the Goldmans had nearly reached the street door. Suddenly Eleanor heard the fat man snicker and reply to a question. A few words of his heavily accented English carried clearly:

' – sure he's a kike, can't you tell? *Gröss gott*! It's almost as shameful as a white woman giving herself to a nigger.'

Leo dropped his valise and whirled.

'Leo, don't, he isn't worth it!' Eleanor exclaimed. But her husband was already stalking toward the fat German, who had turned grey as oatmeal.

Leo poured out invective in Yiddish. The porter scuttled away. But the fat man, momentarily puffed up by anger, brandished his cigar and shouted:

'Don't swear at me in your heathen tongue, you black sheeny!'

Leo's cheeks turned plum coloured. He kept walking. In a panic, the fat man jabbed his lighted cigar at Leo's left eye.

Eleanor clapped a hand to her mouth. But Leo was quick. The cigar's glowing end only came within a couple of inches of his face. He seized the fat man's forearm with both hands and pushed. The man could move the cigar no closer.

Leo squeezed the German's arm. The man's hand opened. The cigar fell out, hit the carpet and rolled. Leo kept applying pressure to the arm.

The fat man gasped curses in German. Tears began to run from the corners of his eyes. He dropped to his knees, moaning and pleading for mercy in his native tongue. Leo didn't release him.

The fat man kept pleading. His bladder let go, staining his crotch. The clerk peeked out from his cubicle. A twist of strong-smelling smoke was rising beside Leo's muddy left shoe. He pointed to the burning circle in the carpet and called to the clerk:

'Your rug's on fire. Maybe this gentleman will help put it out.'

He seized the back of the fat man's collar and hurled him down. The man's chest crushed the hot cigar. He floundered, squirmed, squealed like a girl—

Leo grabbed Eleanor's arm, practically jerking her to the door. 'Maybe it'll rain forty days and forty nights and wash this benighted place off the map.'

'Don't say that, Leo. Not even as a joke. That man doesn't represent the whole town.'

'I'd like to think not. But I wonder.'

Luggage in hand, they lowered their heads and went through the door into the downpour. Although it was only late afternoon, the sky was almost completely black. Behind them, the fat man began yelling:

515

'Sheeny Jew bastard! If I see you again, you're in for it. You better not stay in Johnstown or they'll ship you out in little pieces!'

Hard rain battered Eleanor's face as they headed up the street. Sometimes she felt a flash of pride when Leo stood up to the kind of witless bigot they'd just encountered. Yet what did you really gain when you offered resistance? Only trouble and more trouble – and you changed nothing.

But she could never persuade Leo of that now. She'd lost that battle after Papa Goldman had visited Philadelphia.

The fat man had lumbered to the lobby window. He pounded the window frame and continued to shout. Were the threats merely bluster, or something to worry about? She didn't know, but she didn't care to learn.

CHAPTER III

A Dream in the Rain

They found a room at the Penn Hotel, four blocks from the Hulbert House. The room was cramped and shabbily furnished. A few sticks of kindling in the grate provided the only heat, a single dim gas jet the only light. One small window overlooked an alley that resembled a river in flood. The storm showed no signs of stopping.

An hour after they checked in, Leo was down the hall in the bathroom used by all guests on their floor. Eleanor was finishing a note to their friend and some-time employer, Louise Drew. She had loosened her hair. It hung over her shoulders and down her back, long and dark and glossy. As she wrote, she snuggled deeper into the garment she always took along when she travelled – an old, faded cotton flannel robe of Leo's, much too large but exceptionally comfortable and warm.

She'd decided years ago that she would never make a society woman for a variety of reasons. One was her almost complete lack of interest in clothes. A large, expensive wardrobe simply wasn't important to her. She'd often been told that she looked stunning in the lavish gowns provided for some of her stage roles. But her very favourite garments were old, familiar ones like the disreputable robe, which she wore with nothing underneath.

Leo walked in, drying the back of his neck with a worn towel. His robe was much like hers, but somewhat newer. Suddenly he sneezed loudly.

'Oh, Leo, you're catching something.'

'The Johnstown grippe. In this kind of weather who could avoid it?'

He stretched on the bed in the familiar position, hands laced under his head. He closed his eyes. Another melancholy monologue about to begin? Eleanor kept her head bent over her writing to conceal her disappointment.

All at once Leo coughed and opened his eyes; something was on his mind.

She signed the note, folded it, and smiled at him. He smiled too, but in a wan sort of way. He jumped up and stalked to the window.

Eleanor turned in her chair, watching him. As she changed position, the robe's lapels fell away from her deep cleavage. She clasped the lapels together, not for modesty's sake but for warmth. The kindling in the fireplace had nearly burned away. A roach went scurrying along the skirtingboard beside the bed. She took notice without being unduly upset; she and Leo had stayed in far worse places.

Leo eyed the streaming window. 'The theatre's liable to float away by eight o'clock. But in case it doesn't, I should go over those lines I had so much trouble with last night.'

So that was it; he was fretting about his performance again. Well, that was better than longing for a past that would never return.

'Which lines do you mean?'

'Third act. Where Snap's describing how the professor's play failed.'

She looked dubious. 'I'd hardly say you had trouble. I noticed a moment's hesitation, that's all.'

'It was more than that,' he shot back. 'I paraphrased half a dozen words. It threw my timing completely off.'

Eleanor said nothing. Leo's insistence on perfection made him a highly dependable actor; one whom other actors trusted and enjoyed being with on stage. But that same perfectionism played its part in many of his personal disappointments. He expected too much of himself, of others, and the world. He always expected relationships to be flawless, and his career, and Eleanor's, to be free of major difficulties. Was there such a thing as being too idealistic? she wondered.

He walked to the bureau, there rummaging among personal articles they'd unpacked and put away. She reached under the note lying in her lap:

'I have the *bikhl*, if that's what you're searching for.'

She held up the frayed playscript. She'd picked up his habit of referring to it by the Yiddish word for small book. Leo had prepared the script by hand. It contained the dialogue for the entire play; normally, actors were issued only their own scenes. He laboriously wrote out a similar playbook for every show in which they appeared.

'I was using it to write on,' she added. 'Let me find the page—'

One of the plot lines of *A Night Off* dealt with Marcus Brutus Snap's attempt to make a killing by producing a classical tragedy written by a college professor named Babbit, who taught in a town where Snap's troupe was playing. The production was a catastrophe, and in the scene Leo wanted to rehearse, Snap was bemoaning the result of some scenic improvisation: a borrowed parrot in a tubbed orange tree had been part of the stage decoration for a scene in ancient Rome – for no very clear reason.

'Here it is,' Eleanor said. There were several characters on stage with Snap in the scene. She lowered her voice to read the line of the first to speak, a doctor: 'How is it going?'

Leo sat on the edge of the bed, immediately in character as the manager whose production had just met with catastrophe:

'"It's all over. It's all over!"'

She changed her inflection, playing the professor: '"I knew it!"'

Leo clutched his heart. '"When I think of this happening to me in my old age—!"'

She struggled to keep from smiling as she read the next line:

'"Tell us all about it."'

'"I've been a manager twenty-five years, but I never had such a failure as that!"'

Again she was the disappointed playwright. '"How did it end?"'

'"How did it *end*? It ended in a riot, that's how it ended!"'

'"A – a riot?"'

'"We had to ring down in the middle of the second act! I never heard such a hissing and whistling on a railroad train!"'

Leo jumped up, waving his arms; his personation of the flamboyant, excitable manager made her laugh aloud.

'"The audience jumped up and down like madmen – but the tragedy was not all to blame. Half the calamity was your fault, doctor. It was your parrot in the tubbed orange tree that capped the climax. Picture the pine grove in the second act – Cassius had just come on, and the audience was quiet. I was standing in the centre – "'

He took a long step toward the window. '" – as King Titus Tatius, with my arms folded just so – "' He folded them with great exaggeration. '" – glaring at the Roman soldiers. My wife had just finished Virgia's great speech, defying the haughty Romulus—"'

Leo pitched his voice much higher, raising one finger as he declaimed:

'"What would'st thou, king? Thy stubborn silence break – what would'st thou, tyrant? Answer. Speak!"'

He looked at Eleanor. '"Then your confounded parrot squeaked at the top of his voice – "' He flung his arms wide and went falsetto:

'"Kiss me, darling!"'

Eleanor burst out laughing again. 'Oh, Leo, you're wonderful. Absolutely wonderful!'

He dropped out of character. 'That did go a little better.'

'A little better? Letter perfect!'

He walked to her side; put his hands on her shoulders and leaned down. 'Undoubtedly that's because I have such a fine dialogue coach this afternoon. Thank you, Madam Goldman – ' He planted a chaste kiss on her forehead. ' – but we both know where the genuine talent lies in this family.'

'Now, Leo, please don't start that.' She raised the playbook. 'Do you want to go over it again?'

He ignored the book. 'It's true, though. I realized it

years ago. I'm a competent actor – sometimes even a good one – but there are thousands and thousands of those. You have talent and something else. You have that rare quality of holding every eye the moment you enter a room or walk onto a stage. It can't be learned and it can't be bought and only a very few possess it. The truth is, my dear, it's a precious gift, and you should capitalize on it—'

His right hand strayed to her face; his knuckles moved gently back and forth along her cheek. That and the expression in his eyes told her that he was falling into one of his despondent moods.

He continued to stroke her cheek slowly. 'You should use that gift to attract a more suitable husband. Some *goyische* nabob with a lot of money and a talent for getting more.'

She slapped his wrist lightly with the script. 'Leo Goldman, I don't want to hear you talk that way.'

'Why not?' His face bleak, he turned towards the window. 'I've given you damn little, Eleanor. When I was a boy – long before I ever met you – I ran into your father one winter night on Printing House Square.'

'Yes, he's often told me the story.'

If he heard, he gave no indication; he seemed to be staring straight through her:

'We talked for a few minutes, and I said I meant to make my fortune in America. I predicted that very blithely at the time. You notice I hardly ever predict it these days. I haven't made a fortune and I never will.'

'No one who goes into the theatre expects to get rich. Not unless you move from acting into managing and producing, and even then it's chancy. We've always known that.'

'But you really could do much better when it comes to a husband. You could easily find one who isn't turned away from good hotels. One who doesn't drag you down to mediocrity with—'

'*Leo, don't!*'

He inhaled sharply, shrugged and leaned on the window sill, staring at the rain. He no longer looked handsome, only tired and defeated.

Eleanor's eyes shone with anger. How she loathed these dark, self-pitying moods. They filled her with a special frustration because she was incapable of talking him out of them.

She supposed a certain amount ot disappointment was natural for him; he really had expected to grow rich in America. It was the eternal dream of the immigrant. Reality and the passage of time had slowly chipped it away. But that happened to everyone's dreams. Living with the disappointment was part of growing up.

Don't evade, she thought. *Of course being poor hurts him. But you're the one who gives him his deepest wounds. You strike at his manhood. If only you didn't make him feel a failure that way, he might be able to stand everything else.*

With a shuffling step, he returned to the bed. He didn't look at her. She stood up and thrust her suddenly chilly hands into the pockets of the old robe. Then she took his place at the window, gazing at the rain-blurred rooftops and the steep hillsides beyond.

Somewhere on the same floor of the hotel, a man laughed. She wondered whether Leo would ever again find anything to laugh about.

2

She heard Leo throw himself down on the bed with a melodramatic sigh. It did no good to remind herself that all actors over-dramatized their own emotions. He was hurting. He needed her help.

She knew of only one subject that might draw him

out of his melancholy. She straightened her shoulders, composed her face and walked to the bedside. She sat down with her right hip touching his and began to stoke his forehead.

'Darling, we mustn't let this terrible weather, or what happened at the other hotel, get the better of us. I don't want any husband except you. No – ' She covered his lips with her fingers. ' – don't say anything. We're both adults. We know some of the dreams we had when we were younger won't come true. But we needn't be rich to be happy. We must keep our eye on the goal we've set for ourselves. Owning that theatre in New York. Running it. Hiring actors and actresses we respect, and producing the kind of plays we want to produce.'

She leaned down and kissed his mouth, adding a whispered word:

'Together.'

At that he showed a little more animation. 'Maybe we've toured long enough, Eleanor.'

'I was thinking the same thing.'

'Daly's a good employer, but I'd rather work for myself—'

'So would I.'

'I don't know whether we have enough money to make the move, though.' Over the past few years they'd put every spare penny into a special account at the Rothman Bank in Boston. Under the bank's management, the principal had appreciated.

'We have at least nine thousand dollars,' she said. 'Not a fortune, but we shouldn't let that hold us back. New York real estate prices keep rising. We should start looking for a theatre immediately, and when we find one, we should try to buy it. If we don't have enough for the down payment, I'm quite willing to ask Papa—'

'No gifts, Eleanor! I'll accept no gifts from anyone.'

'I know that, darling. It would be a loan, that's all. A loan we'd repay, with interest, just as if we'd gotten it from a bank.'

He considered it a moment. 'Well, that would be all right—' He wasn't wholly impractical. They had often discussed the negative feelings of most banks when considering actors as credit risks.

'I do think this might be the time to launch out on our own, Leo. While we're young enough to do all the work that will have to be done to launch a new company in a new theatre. We could stay with Mr Daly until this tour's over, then start searching for a property—'

At at once, Leo raised himself on his right elbow. His old, charming smile appeared suddenly; the smile that had quite won her heart long before she'd married him. She was thankful her effort had been successful. His self-pity was gone, and he was more cheerful than he'd been in weeks:

'I think you're exactly right. If we wait for every circumstance to be perfect, we'll still be waiting when we're seventy.' He swept his left hand in an arc above her head, as if imagining a poster. "Eleanor Kent and Leo Goldman present Bronson Howard! Sardou! William Shakespeare—'

'Don't forget Ibsen.'

He laughed and hugged her. 'By God, Eleanor, that's as fine a dream as getting rich.'

'And it's one that can come true. We must definitely leave Daly when this tour's over. We can go to New York and work there until we find the right theatre. It might not take too long. Regis has a nephew who's scene designer for the Knickerbocker. Regis heard that the principal stockholder is in poor health. The rest of the stock's owned by the man's family, and none of them is experienced in operating a theatre. We might make an offer—'

Leo's face lit with enthusiasm. 'The Knickerbocker's a splendid little house. Good location right off the Rialto. The right size – four hundred and eighty-five seats—'

She smiled. 'Four hundred and ninety.'

Up went his eyebrows. 'You've been doing homework.'

'Quizzing Regis,' she nodded. 'I'm tired of the road. We've served our apprenticeship – my heavens, it's been twelve years since we first went with Bascom's Tom show. Let's take the step while we can. Commit ourselves to it! I know we'll make it work.'

A troubled look dulled the glow in his eyes. He raised a cautioning finger. 'Provided—'

'Provided what?'

'Provided you're still sure you want to be married to a Jew.'

She took his cheeks between her palms.

'Listen to me, Leo Goldman. I am saying this for the very last time. No, I do not want to be married to a Jew, or to a Christian, a Berber, a Pole, or any other conveniently categorized type—'

She leaned down again, her hair falling soft and dark on both sides of her face. She loved him, but there was always a certain fear when she demonstrated it. She knew where such demonstrations could and frequently did lead.

Yet there was no equivalent way to tell him she considered him the most important person in the world. With only a moment's hesitation, she whispered:

'I want *you*, Mr Goldman. As for your religion, and your faults—'

She tried to put a teasing note in her voice to overcome the tension already starting to build within her.

'—not so numerous as mine, of course, but still considerable in number – all those things, dear sir—'

She kissed him, wondering how she could be so eager for such a normal human contact and at the same time dread it.

' – those things are incidental. I love you.'

Just as she'd feared, he put one arm gently behind her neck and pulled her mouth down again. His other hand slipped beneath her robe. Gentle fingers closed on her breast. She wanted to pull away. There was a wild, hysterical feeling within her; an irrational urge to run—

But she was an actress. And she did love him. She kissed him with feigned ardour, pressing her breast against his hand even though she knew what the outcome would be.

No, by heaven, she said to herself. Only moments ago they'd agreed to give their lives a different direction. It was time for their marriage to have the same kind of new start. She would make it all end differently for once. She swore that as Leo began fumbling with the cord of the old robe.

He pushed the robe down her back, baring her full, dark-nippled breasts. She *would* succeed this time. No fear was so great that courage could not overcome it—

Leo knew Eleanor well, and was a considerate husband:

'Darling, are you sure you're up to this?'

'Yes, Leo, yes, please – I love you. I do love you so!'

Her suddenly husky voice gave no hint of her terror.

3

From the first, Eleanor had wanted to be a good wife. The rape had made that impossible.

She and Leo had always got along well as colleagues and companions. It was as lovers that they failed. Their

526

wedding night – and most of the European honeymoon – had been a disaster of awkwardness and deep hurt. Only Leo's innate kindness and understanding had seen her through that terrible time, which should have been so joyous.

Once back in the States, this part of their relationship improved very little. Whenever she and Leo started to make love, Eleanor was instantly in an agony of fear. She knew the physical contact would inevitably result in discomfort; even severe pain. The knowledge fuelled her fear, and generated tension he could feel in her naked body long before they were united. The tension was like some virulent disease, quickly infecting him too, and growing worse in both of them as they came closer and closer to union. The result was disappointment and constantly reinforced failure for him, and unremitting guilt for her. The guilt was enhanced because she was incapable of doing the one thing which might have resolved the situation. She couldn't tell him *why* she felt pain when they made love.

How ironic that was, she often thought. She and Leo were members of a liberal, free-thinking profession. And although she did discuss certain sexual matters with him, she positively could not bring herself to confess that she'd been raped.

She'd come close to telling Leo many times. Once, on New Year's Eve, she'd drunk a whole bottle of wine in secret, hoping it would wash away her hesitation and permit the truth to spill out. It had almost worked. She'd blurted one sentence and part of another. The exact words were forgotten now. But she vividly recalled how he'd stared at her, puzzled, while her heart pounded and her stomach ached and the confession ended abruptly.

When he pressed her for an explanation of her strange behaviour, she lied and said it was too much wine. The sad truth was, she hadn't had enough. Was there enough in the whole world? She doubted it.

She hated herself for that. She knew silence didn't represent strength, but weakness. She truly believed Leo might be relieved of some of his worst feelings of inadequacy if he knew she was damaged goods when she married him.

Damaged goods. Deep down, that was the root of all the difficulty. Not only had she concealed the foul thing that had happened to her, she'd entered into marriage dishonestly.

She knew Leo would be outwardly forgiving if she told him. He was that sort of man. But what would he be thinking? *The woman I married is a slut. A woman other men dirtied before I took her, foolishly imagining her to be a virgin*.

How cleansing just a little frank talk would be. And yet doubt and fear continued to keep the secret sealed away, even when she saw the consequences of silence.

Of course, she realized that in the view of some, she was a sinner damned to hell simply because of her wish to break the silence. Conventional wisdom in Victorian America said that a wife did not sully her mind with undue attention to the physical side of marriage. A wife was supposed to submit to her husband without complaint, no matter how uncomfortable or distasteful she found that submission. The purpose of the act was procreation, not pleasure, and thus contemplation of it for any purpose other than marital duty was immoral. So was candid discussion of the act, even between spouses—

Well, the devil with the dictates of convention. Their problem demanded thought, and a resolution. Just once she wanted to make Leo happy by successfully hiding the pain a sexual union produced. She dreamed of being free of that pain herself, and – most unrealistic dream of all – of actually finding joy in the moment when, with utmost care and tenderness, he came into her.

This time, she thought as she lay in his arms. Let it be different this one time.

But it was not.

4

She shuddered and winced uncontrollably. The dry, abrasive contact stiffened her body. He felt that, and the tension transmitted itself to him:

'I hurt you again.'

'No, Leo. No, darling, please – go on. I'm fine.' Her voice was hoarse; barely audible above the beat of the rain.

'Goddamn it!' he said softly, pulling away. 'I can never do it right.'

She started to speak but somehow couldn't. She covered her eyes to hide tears of self-loathing. Capable actress that she was, she still couldn't control the workings of her own body. The dream of finally lifting some of Leo's guilt died stillborn once again.

He swung his legs over the side of the bed and sat up, his broad back toward her. He reached for his shirt. She turned on her side and sat up, too. She put her cheek against his back and huddled there, both of them silent and cold in the dark, mean room.

CHAPTER IV

Attack

Shortly before six, Eleanor suggested they make a dash to the Hulbert House, despite the rain, so they could join the rest of the company for supper. Sharply, Leo said he didn't care to give the Hulbert House one penny of his money.

She knew there was another reason he snapped at her. As he turned up the gaslight in an effort to brighten the room, she walked to his side:

'Darling, don't fret over what happened a few minutes ago.' It was the first time since they'd got dressed that she was able to speak of it. And it was instantly clear that she shouldn't have. He whirled to face her:

'Fret? Why, no. By now I'm accustomed to hurting my wife every time I touch her.'

'But it isn't your fault! I've said it over and over, but you never believe me.'

Nor did he now. He turned away, and she went on:

'You mustn't continually scourge yourself for something I'm responsible for—'

'Eleanor, we've been married four and a half years. That's a long time. Enough time, surely, for me to learn how to make love so that you at least find it bearable. God knows I'm unable to make it enjoyable.'

'Don't keep saying things like that! There's something wrong with me. Something I—'

She drew in a quick breath. She ached to tell him, and perhaps he sensed that. For a few seconds, expectancy smoothed the bitterness from his face. But then the silence lengthened, and the old shame and fear took control again. The door must stay closed. *Forever*—

'Something I've always been at a loss to explain,' she blurted finally.

'Well, a better man would be able to do something about it.' He turned back to the window, eyes gloomy as he watched the rain.

A feeling of futility swept over her. How dare she scorn him for weakness when she could not tell him the truth? More practically, what could she now do to break the mood of tension? She thought of one reminder that might help:

'At least we won't have to put up with places like this much longer. We'll soon be off the road, and new owners of the Knickerbocker. I feel sure of it.' She slipped her arms around his waist from behind; hugged him. 'That's something to look forward to, isn't it?'

'Yes,' he replied in a low voice, 'that's something—'

The last word trailed off, as if to suggest he couldn't see much else in their marriage that was worth anticipating.

2

They ate supper in the dining room of the Penn Hotel. Both of them ordered pot roast which turned out to be stringy and dry. Before Leo had finished half of his, he tugged out his pocket watch and began to drum his fingers on the tablecloth. Old, familiar signs, Eleanor thought, smiling at long last.

Leo hated to be late for a performance. So did she, but with him, punctuality was a passion, if not an outright mania. He was proud that he'd never missed an opening curtain, or an entrance, in his entire professional career – except once. In Chicago, a stage-hand had moved a saw horse in the dark wings during a performance. Coming back after a change of costume, Leo had tumbled headfirst over it, delaying his entrance a full fifteen seconds.

Consequently, Eleanor understood his sudden response to an internal clock, and his sudden impatience. Without finishing his meal, he left the table. He returned in fifteen minutes to say that he and the hotel's elderly porter had finally located a hack.

The rain showed no signs of letting up. If anything, it was heavier than it had been an hour ago. The cabman drove with one hand and used the other to hold an umbrella over his broad-brimmed hat.

The horse splashed through wide streams of water running in the streets. The electric lights of Johnstown looked pale and shimmery in the downpour. The cabman delivered them to the stage door of the Opera House, took the fare and Leo's generous tip and said:

'You folks leavin' town tomorrow?'

'That's right,' Leo answered.

'Well, you better git ready to swim to the depot.'

'What do you mean?' Leo said, while Eleanor hurried toward the building.

'When it starts rainin' this hard, most of the streets flood out.'

Eleanor reached the porch by the stage door. It was kept almost completely dry by a projecting roof. She shook water off her parasol. Suddenly, down at the corner of the building, she thought she saw a man standing motionless, watching.

No sooner had she seen him than the man stepped back out of sight. Almost immediately half a dozen people appeared at the same corner, complaining about the storm. Early arrivals at the theatre. Surely the man she'd glimpsed had been part of that group—

Or had he? She remembered the fat man at the Hulbert House. Remembered his threats. Had he come hunting them—?

No, that was too far-fetched, especially on such a bad night.

The storm certainly wasn't inhibiting the cabman's desire to talk. Hunched under his umbrella, he called down to Leo, 'Happens dang near every spring. Most businesses have to close up for a few days. Looks like they may be doin' it again. Lot of folks with two-story houses are already carryin' their rugs and good furniture upstairs. Friend of mine told me the first shift at Cambria Iron might not work tomorrow. But if you're headin' out early, I expect you'll miss the worst of the flooding. What's your next stop?'

'Altoona,' Leo told him. She heard the impatience in her husband's voice. Rain dripped from the brim of his rakish crush hat.

'Well, good luck to you. Give a good show an' don't think too poorly of Johnstown. It's a mighty nice place when it's dry – which is what I hope to be in half an hour. I'm callin' it a night.'

He raised his umbrella in a kind of salute and drove away. Leo ran to the porch and sneezed again. Eleanor said, 'Why on earth did you stand there chattering with that man?'

'I certainly didn't want to. But he brought us here when he could have gone home. The decent people of this world ought to be encouraged. God knows there are enough of the other kind, and they don't seem to need one damn bit of encouragement for what they do.'

His smile was vivid white in the gloom. He took off his hat and shook water from it. In just a few seconds, the rain intensified so that it was hard to see more than a yard or so. Protected by the overhang, they watched the downpour. Suddenly Leo said:

'"God is our refuge and strength, a very present help in trouble." The people of Johnstown may want Him to make a practical demonstration of that. If I lived here, I'd pray for a rowboat. Especially since I can't swim.'

Eleanor laughed. 'I'm glad you're feeling better. What in the world made you think of a Bible verse?'

'Do you suppose I'm just another one of those pagan actors, Mrs Goldman? I know several Bible verses. In two languages! I didn't skip all the sessions of Hebrew school when I was growing up. That verse is from a psalm that talks about bad weather. "Therefore will not we fear, though the earth be removed – though the waters thereof roar and be troubled—'

'That's certainly appropriate. But we should go in. You're sneezing so much, you'll probably have influenza by the second act.'

Leo didn't move. There was still plenty of time for them to don makeup, and he seemed fascinated by the water cascading from the edge of the roof:

'I don't think I've ever seen a worse storm. While I was hunting for the hack, the hotel porter told me the spring flooding could be moderated if the river channels were widened. But the Cambria Iron Company wants them narrow for a technical reason I completely fail to understand. In any case, the porter said that what Cambria Iron wants in this country, Cambria Iron gets.'

'You mean they deliberately ignore the town's welfare? That's despicable.'

'I agree. But as you've often remarked in other circumstances – it isn't our fight. All we have to do is give a performance and stay afloat another ten or twelve hours. Then Johnstown will be just an unpleasant memory.' He started to sneeze, jerked out a handkerchief, and held it to his nose. He sneezed anyway.

'We'd better go in before I blow my own head off.'

Leo offered his arm. She was happy about the noticeable improvement in his mood; he always grew more cheerful and energetic as curtain time approached.

They turned toward the door. The man Eleanor had seen lurking was forgotten. But he wasn't gone. He stepped from behind the corner of the building and watched the Goldmans disappear through the stage door. Then, taking a step backwards, he settled down to wait. Not happily; but at least he was getting paid for the night's work. It would be two or three hours before it was over.

3

Inside the Opera House, Leo immediately seemed to be his old self. He took a long, deep breath, inhaling the odours that were so familiar to all actors. Smells of lumber and backstage dust; the stale tang of old gas fixtures and the quite different smell of the new, hot electric lights that were revolutionizing the theatre. He stretched, tossed his hat in the air, and caught it:

'I think it's going to be a damn good show tonight. Everyone will want to please those few hardy souls brave enough to come – and those who show up will want to demonstrate to one another that it was worth the effort.'

He was right. Both Goldmans had a strong intuitive grasp of what lay behind an audience's reaction. A fine performance was not solely due to the actors; the audience also played a part, and that was especially true in comedy. Good response early in the play spurred the cast to a greater effort. Tonight, as if in defiance of the storm savaging the city, players and audience were quickly joined in perfect interaction.

A Night Off consisted of four acts. Before the first act was even half through, Eleanor had the exciting feeling that she was witnessing and helping to create a performance as nearly flawless as any in which she and Leo had ever appeared. Contrary to their expectations, the nine-hundred-seat Opera House was filled almost to capacity. And the men, women, and children out front recognized the extra effort the actors were putting into their roles, and the perfection with which even the smallest part was being played.

The audience rewarded the cast with loud and frequent laughter. Lines or bits of business which never even drew a chuckle on a bad night produced a roar of mirth, and even applause. The clapping after each curtain was increasingly longer and louder. Eleanor had never known the first three acts to fly by so fast.

She played Nisbe, one of Professor Babbit's daughters; it was a choice role. By the middle of the last act, Nisbe was about ready to succumb – with all due propriety – to Jack Mulberry, the young British actor with whom the convoluted plot had romantically involved her. Mulberry was a favourite of producer Snap, because he was the only leading man Snap had ever employed who owned eight suits of clothes – thus making it possible for Snap to stage 'society plays.'

Snap's career was in ruins by this point in the comedy. But thanks to a convenient coincidence, he found a new post as manager of a London theatre which just happened to be owned by Mulberry's long-lost father – with whom he was of course reunited before the final curtain.

It was a complicated and nonsensical play, but well written, and the audience loved it. Snap's dialogue in the fourth act gave Leo a chance for a bravura performance. Tonight he took maximum advantage of that, drawing spontaneous applause when he made a flamboyant exit just minutes before the end of the show.

He caught an admiring glance from Eleanor as he swept off stage. The stage manager squeezed his arm. 'Grand, Leo. Just grand.'

'Thanks very much,' he whispered. On the other side of the flats representing Babbit's study, dialogue produced another explosion of laughter. Leo pulled out his handkerchief and carefully dabbed his warm forehead; he didn't want to wipe off greasepaint.

Rather than wait in the wings for his final entrance, he decided to catch a breath of air on the protected porch. He tiptoed away in the dark, ignoring the stage manager's anxious glance. Leo knew he had plenty of time. About five pages of dialogue had to be played before he came on stage for the last time.

He stepped outside and immediately regretted it. Wind drove the rain into his face with unexpected force. He turned, reaching for the doorknob. Just as he did so, there was a sudden movement in the shadows a few feet beyond the porch.

'Someone there?'

Almost as he said it, he saw the man. He wore a slicker and a slouch hat and came striding out of the dark along the side of the building. Leo was surprised but not alarmed; not until the man jumped to the porch.

Leo backed away quickly, trying to see the man's face beneath the hat brim. In a rough voice the man said:

'Didn't expect you to come out so soon, sheeny. You stayed in Johnstown one night too many.'

Astounded, Leo could only think. *The fat man hired someone. He actually* hired *someone—*

Then there was no more time for thought. The other man yanked something from under his slicker.

'Let's see how the audiences like your looks after this, Jew-boy.'

The man's right hand streaked toward Leo's face, fingers clasped around the broken neck of a bottle.

Leo didn't jerk his head back fast enough. The jagged glass missed his eye but raked the skin below. He grabbed his assailant's wrist, smelling tobacco and liquor. The man lunged one way, then the other, shaking him off. Leo's left shoe slipped on the slick porch. He almost fell. He twisted on his left heel as he righted himself. Pain shot from his ankle all the way up to mid-calf. He held back a groan and rammed his right knee into the attacker's midsection.

The man bent over, gasping in pain. He dropped the neck of the bottle. Leo caught it and slashed upward. The man howled and clutched the underside of his chin. He stumbled off the porch and fell on hands and knees.

The stage door opened suddenly. The doorkeeper stuck his head out.

'Who the devil's makin' all the racket?'

The man in the slicker was floundering in the mud. Leo started for him. But his injured left leg betrayed him. He would have pitched off the porch if he hadn't grabbed one of the roof posts.

The attacker regained his feet. Blood ran between his fingers as he held his chin and staggered toward the corner of the building where he'd first appeared. He vanished there, leaving Leo clinging to the post and taking out his frustration with loud profanity.

He wanted to run after the man but he knew he couldn't. He'd need all his strength just to finish the play.

The stage manager appeared, pushing the door-keeper out of the way. 'Leo, where the devil have you got to? Your entrance is coming up – God above.' He gulped at the sight of blood leaking from the cut below Leo's eye. 'Are you all right?'

'Splendid!' Leo snarled, trying to favour his left leg as he pressed his handkerchief against the gash. He hobbled back inside and in half a minute stepped on stage dizzy with pain and sweating under the greasepaint that was now streaked and smeared.

CHAPTER V

Stranded

Leo came on stage with the kerchief pressed to his bleeding cheek. His limp was clearly apparent to the audience. But his entrance and the final curtain were separated by just fifteen short speeches, and he kept the play's momentum going by sheer will. He ignored glances of consternation from Eleanor while he announced that the disastrous premiere of Professor Babbit's tragedy had been saved at the last moment by quick thinking on the part of Mrs Snap, a character never seen in the comedy:

'When she saw that your piece was irretrievably damned—'

He paused for a beat; just long enough to allow the professor and all the others on stage to register astonishment. Earlier in the act, Babbit had been misled into believing his play had turned out well after all.

'In the second act, she—' Again Leo paused deliberately.

'Well?' exclaimed the actor playing Babbit. '*Well?*'

'She dropped your tragedy altogether and substituted in its place—'

'What?'

Leo summoned all his energy for the curtain line:

'*A Night Off!*'

A cannon-burst of laughter greeted the unexpected twist. The curtain came down to the beginning of applause. Leo heard voices all around him – Eleanor's most clearly:

'What in God's name happened to—?'

'Places, take your places!' the stage manager yelled from the wings. 'Here we go with the call.'

Up went the curtain. Leo fixed a smile on his face, joining the others in a line stretching across the stage. In unison, they bowed slowly into the blaze of the incandescent footlights.

When he leaned over, he was afraid he'd fall. He clenched his teeth and came upright again. Pain was scorching the wrenched muscles of his left leg. But he managed five more calls before Regis Pemberton personally grabbed the ropes and lowered the curtain for the last time.

Pemberton had been told about Leo's injury while he was counting box office receipts in the office. Now he rushed to Leo's side, joined by Eleanor and the others. They all wanted to know how he'd got hurt.

'I made the mistake of going out for some air,' he said, his voice weak all at once. 'One of the local Jew-baiters was waiting with a piece of broken bottle.'

'I thought I saw someone when we came in!' Eleanor said. 'Here, darling, lean on me. You look dreadful.'

'Perfectly – all right. Perfectly – capable of standing.' It wasn't true. His head was clanging like a fire bell, his left leg was threatening to collapse again, and all at once he was sure he was hallucinating. The walls of Professor Babbit's study were rippling and swaying—

He realized it was only the scene shifters. They were already starting to strike the set.

'I'll get a doctor,' Pemberton said to Leo. 'I'll see

540

that he comes right to your hotel. I'll also get the police on the case. These small-town simpletons can't mistreat a member of a Daly troupe and get away with it. Do you know the identity of the man who attacked you, Leo? Was it that fat German Eleanor told me about?'

'Didn't see the man's face.' Leo limped upstage toward an upholstered chair. 'I'll bet it was someone the German hired. The man wasn't expecting me outside until the play was over. I took him by surprise. Otherwise he might have done a better job.'

He sank into the chair and took deep breaths. Pemberton growled another promise of swift action by the police. Leo shook his head, a glazed look in his eyes:

'No use, Regis. The police won't – find either of them. Not on – a night like this.'

'Well, it's a *wretched* piece of business, just *wretched*,' said the rather prissy young actor who played Jack Mulberry. 'But you were splendid, Leo. A trump to the very last.'

Eleanor knelt beside her husband. He was growing groggy. His right hand slipped off the chair arm. The crumpled handkerchief touched Eleanor's white sleeve and stained it red. Unconcerned, she took the handkerchief and gently wiped blood from his cheek.

No longer fully aware of what he was saying, Leo muttered to the young actor who'd complimented him:

'Thanks, Tom. This audience – deserved—'

Before he could finish, his head lolled over and he fainted.

2

The custom of performing an afterpiece was nearly gone in the American theatre. So when *A Night Off* rang down its final curtain at ten thirty-one – five

541

minutes later than usual because of all the laughter – the show was over. It took half an hour for a police wagon to arrive. Leo was placed on a stretcher and moved to the Penn Hotel in the wagon. Eleanor rode with him.

Pemberton conferred with a detective from the Johnstown force. As Leo had predicted, the effort was wasted. An hour's investigation by the police revealed that the fat man had paid the Hulbert House the day rate and left with his sample cases shortly after six that evening. The hotel management knew little about him. The register said his name was Kleinerman, and that his home was Baltimore. He had told a dining room waiter that he was a traveller specializing in ladies' and gents' stockings.

But there was nothing to prove he'd hired some local thug, the detective said to Pemberton when the two met again in the lobby of the Penn. Leo hadn't got a clear look at the attacker, so that closed the matter. Pemberton was disgusted but could do nothing.

The manager sat down to wait for Eleanor. The hotel's elderly porter and the night clerk were rolling up the lobby carpet when she finally came downstairs a few minutes after midnight, followed by the doctor. He gave Eleanor a few last words of instruction, fastened his cape overcoat at the collar, picked up his satchel and vanished into the storm.

Pemberton stood waiting. A damp, wrinkled Pennsylvania Railroad timetable stuck out of his pocket. Eleanor walked toward him in a dispirited way. She was exhausted.

'How is he?' Pemberton asked.

'Asleep again. He woke up when we put him in bed. The doctor gave him a draught that should help him rest till morning.'

She sank down in an old chair. The lobby had an eerie air. The two men working silently to remove the

542

carpet seemed like spectres under the old-fashioned gas chandeliers.

Eleanor's dark eyes drifted to the front entrance. She frowned. An inch-wide stream of brown water was trickling between the door and the sill. The water carried bits of mud and refuse. It was already a foot into the lobby.

'My God, Regis, look at that.'

Pemberton turned, as did the young night clerk. As they watched, the stream widened and lengthened. Gaslight reflecting on its surface made it resemble some primitive form of life that kept changing shape, its growth out of control.

The night clerk didn't take the sight as seriously as his guest:

'Don't worry, ma'am. We get water in here most every springtime.'

She wasn't reassured. She could only think of remarks she'd heard earlier in the day: *That's four and a half billion gallons . . . Four hundred feet higher than the town . . . It's an earth dam. Leaky as a sieve—*

By now the sound of the rain had become nerve-wracking. She felt herself losing control and dug her nails into her palms until a measure of calm returned. The clerk added:

'No matter how hard it rains, you'll be snug and dry in any of the rooms upstairs.'

The old porter tried to do his part to soothe her: 'And don't get all scairt if you hear some fool yelling that the South Fork dam's busted. That's an old joke around this town.'

'How comforting!' she said.

The porter and the clerk exchanged eloquent looks and walked away. Pemberton studied his hands. How infantile to snarl at two men who were only trying to help, she thought. She turned to apologize but both men were already back at work. She covered her eyes a moment, then said to the manager:

'Regis, I've got to make a decision. The doctor said that if Leo wants to perform tomorrow evening, he should stay flat on his back with his leg elevated for at least twelve hours. Otherwise the injury may take much longer to heal. When are we scheduled to leave?'

Pemberton pulled the limp timetable from his pocket. He peeled the pages apart until he located the one he wanted. 'Here it is – ' He showed her. 'The Chicago–New York Limited. Departs at seven-fifteen in the morning.'

'I was afraid of something like that.' She pondered. 'We'll be on board if I have to carry him to the station.'

'But I thought the doctor said—'

'He did. Leo's supposed to stay in bed. I want to get out of here. If Leo can't go on tomorrow night, his understudy can do the role.'

Pemberton chewed his lower lip. 'Whatever you say. Tomorrow night's Altoona. A very big house. We're completely sold out. I'd rather have Leo on stage than sitting in the wings. And you know how he hates to miss a performance—'

Eleanor couldn't deny that. But the manager's tone produced a flare of anger:

'I refuse to say in this wretched town one moment longer than necessary.'

He shrugged. 'As you said – it's entirely your choice.'

'You act as if I made the wrong one!'

'No, Eleanor. He's your husband. But maybe there's a way to resolve the problem. Here, look.'

Again he showed her the timetable. 'This eastbound train leaves at eight minutes past three in the afternoon. It arrives in Altoona in plenty of time for you and Leo to reach the theatre and do your makeup. Taking the later train would give Leo the rest he needs, and he could still get there in time to perform tomorrow night.'

Eleanor uttered a tired laugh. 'Stranded in Johnstown. Sometimes I can't get over the thrills of a life in the theatre.'

'Stranded? No one's stranded!' Pemberton exclaimed, bending to clasp her chilly hand. 'It's just a delay of a few hours. I'll stay too, if you like.'

'Oh, come, Regis – you're embarrassing me.' She sat up straight, wiping her cheeks with her palms. 'I'm behaving like a child. I'm tired and upset, I guess. I apologize. You go in the morning and we'll catch the later train. Then Leo can do the show and everyone will be happy. Unless, of course, the rain doesn't stop, and the bridges wash out, and the three-oh-eight fails to arrive in Johnstown.'

The night clerk had obviously been listening as he wrapped twine around the roller carpet. 'She'll be here, all right,' he called. 'Nothing can hurt the old bridge your train comes in on. It's seven arches of solid stone. We'll get you and the mister to the depot even if we have to paddle a canoe.'

The clerk ambled toward them, so anxious to be helpful, Eleanor couldn't possibly take offence at his eavesdropping. The young man went on:

'The storm'll probably pass by morning. Even if it doesn't Johnstown's been through a downpour like this nearly every year that I can recollect, and I was born right here in Cambria County.'

The clerk smiled again, shy, yet eager to persuade the visiting actress to think better of his hometown. She couldn't be unkind to him. She put on a smile she didn't feel and said:

'Well, if we can't trust a local resident, there's no one we can trust. What's your name, young man?'

'Hack, ma'am. Homer Hack.'

'Well, Homer, I'm very sorry I spoke sharply to you

545

and the other gentleman a while ago. I'm Mrs Leo Goldman, by the way.'

'Yes, ma'am. I signed you in, remember?'

'That's right, you did. Lord, that seems eighty years ago.'

The young man blushed at her mention of the Deity. She tried to forget how weary she was as she rose from her chair. 'All right, Homer, it's a bargain. You and I will both paddle the canoe if necessary.' She turned to the manager. 'Leo and I will be on the three-oh-eight to Altoona.'

'I'll have a cab waiting at the depot. Shall I look in on you a few minutes before we board the Limited in the morning?'

'Not necessary. Thank you for worrying about us.'

'It's my job, Eleanor. I've been a bachelor all my life but I always wanted a flock of children. When I started managing road companies, I got my wish.'

She laughed. 'You're terrible.'

'No, I just understand actors. Along with liking them, of course.'

She laughed again, and kissed his cheek. The familiarity brought another amazed look to young Hack's face. He nearly dropped the end of the rolled carpet he and the old porter were carrying toward the stairs.

Pemberton waved as he turned to leave. 'Good night, then. See you in Altoona.' His boots splattered and spread the muddy water that had widened until it measured eight or ten inches across. The forward point had reached the centre of the lobby.

Pemberton opened the front door. The wind tore it from his hands. Homer Hack had to drop his end of the carpet, run, and force the door shut with his shoulder. But the wind had sprung it, and ripped the screws in the lowest hinge halfway out of the wood.

Instantly, Eleanor felt she'd made a dreadful mistake solely out of loyalty to the company. She thought about running after Pemberton to tell him she'd changed her mind. Somehow she couldn't.

She trudged upstairs. In the room she wrapped a blanket round her legs and tried to sleep sitting in the chair beside Leo's bed. But the constant sound of the rain began to grate on her nerves again. The sound seemed to develop a terrifying resonance, like the roar of a waterfall. Pictures filled her mind. Frightening pictures of an earth dam high in the mountain darkness. It began to spout water from a few holes; then from a dozen—

She shook her head, rubbed her eyes. She was an adult. She mustn't give in to childish fright. She and Leo would be perfectly safe overnight in Johnstown, and would take the afternoon train for an uneventful trip to Altoona—

But if all that was true, why did the sound of the rain and of her husband's drugged breathing continue to depress her spirits? Why did those sounds make her feel – to use the word she'd used with Pemberton – stranded in a lonesome, even dangerous place?

'*The dam's busted.*' *That's an old joke around this town.* Suddenly she thought of the Psalm Leo had quoted:

God is our refuge and strength, a very present help in trouble.

Though the earth be removed—

Though the waters thereof roar and be troubled—

She wasn't on familiar terms with the Almighty. She believed in God, but she didn't practise religion in the formal sense. She'd always considered her religion to be the way she lived her life; especially the way she treated others. Tonight that philosophy seemed trivial and of little use. She wanted a strength greater than her own to touch her and relieve the unreasonable fear mounting within her.

She wanted that relief and couldn't find it. She

huddled deeper into the blanket, exhausted yet sleepless. Outside, the rain continued to fall.

CHAPTER VI

Adrift

That same night, far across the continent from rainsoaked Johnstown, a footsore Carter Kent limped into the Southern Pacific ferry terminal in Oakland.

Mellow California sunshine had bathed the dirt road he'd followed into town, but now the sun was down. Cold fog was billowing in from the Pacific. It was seven o'clock on a spring evening but it might have been midnight. And he might have been seventy. He felt that old.

He paid the fare at a booth, then went on board. Just beyond the gate at the stern of the ferryboat, he stopped to count his money. Less than three dollars left. He trudged to the large midships cabin, pushed through a swinging door, and sank down on one of the lacquered benches. Across the bay, the lighted hillsides of San Francisco had disappeared in the fog.

He shivered and clenched his teeth to keep them from chattering. His old corduroy trousers, cracked boots, and cast-off gentleman's jacket provided little warmth. The jacket's plaid was faded by weather and hidden by dirt. The stiff bill of his large cap was broken in the middle.

Carter was heading for San Francisco at long last, though he didn't know precisely why. Maybe it was because the city had been his original destination, and some inner sense told him nothing would go right for him until he finally got there.

He knew Willie Hearst was in San Francisco, managing his father's newspaper. Willie had taken over the *Examiner* two years earlier, when the California legislature had at last been persuaded that it should send George Hearst to the US Senate. That made his son Willie a publisher at twenty-six. Willie could be proud of that. Carter had no intention of looking up his friend right away, however. He couldn't stand to have Willie see how low he'd fallen.

He couldn't stand to have his mother or stepbrother know, either. In the past six months he'd written only two letters to Julia. Both of them, extremely short, had consisted entirely of lies.

2

When Carter had stepped off the train in North Platte five years earlier, he'd been convinced he was taking his future back into his own hands. He was further convinced that it would be a fine future since he personally controlled it. Both judgments had been wrong. When he added up those five years, the sum of them was exactly nothing.

He'd travelled from the Nebraska prairie to the parched plains of Texas, then further south to Galveston, where he'd learned how foolhardy it was to give anyone your trust until they proved worthy of it. From Galveston he'd drifted to Colorado and, eventually, on to the Pacific Northwest.

In all that territory, he'd never been able to find a town or a job in which his glibness and his infectious smile could be put to good use – or were even wanted. When he took a job, it was almost always some backbreaking menial task an African ape could have done nearly as well. Carter still hated to obey orders. It was a supreme irony of his life that since leaving the train in North Platte, he'd done virtually nothing else.

He'd learned some harsh lessons in five years. Life was much more hazardous if you were poor and far from friends and family. Earlier this spring, he'd lain ill under a pier on the Seattle waterfront for two days, only rats and mongrel dogs paying him notice. One old yellow hound had pissed all over his pants. Wouldn't that be a fine story to tell his stepbrother, to whom he'd given so much advice?

He hoped Will hadn't taken the advice too seriously. Some of it could damn well ruin him, and one squandered life was enough for the current generation of Kents.

It was after his illness that he'd finally started south down the timbered coast to California, making the long, slow journey by foot and by boxcar. Several times he'd run into some rough-looking tramps. When it wasn't possible to avoid them completely, he always assumed they were planning to rob or kill him. He credited that wariness as the reason he hadn't been molested once.

Now the journey was over, at least for a while. The ferry whistle shrilled. Men closed and latched the wicker gates at the stern. Lines were uncleated, tossed aboard, and secured. The engines chugged as the vessel nosed into the fog, its bow wake faintly phosphorescent.

In the distance a bell buoy clanged. By the time the ferry reached open water, the fog was even thicker. The whistle sounded a signal every fifteen seconds. Carter, feeling queasy, weaved to his feet and headed up the aisle toward the doors leading out to the bow.

There were only four other passengers in the cabin. One, an elderly Chinaman, sat on a bench which faced the aisle. The Chinaman was dressed all in black. A derby covered the root of his long pigtail. Carter smiled feebly and touched two fingers to the broken bill of his cap.

The gesture of friendliness terrified the Chinaman, somehow. He huddled down on the bench with his hands in his lap, trying to look inconspicuous. A ferryman appeared outside, glaring at Carter through a window. By greeting the Oriental, Carter had evidently done something wrong.

Carter pushed through the swinging door. The ferryman's truculent stare infuriated him. He hooked a thumb over his shoulder to indicate the Chinaman:

'Just saying hello to an old friend. He used to cook for my mother at our ranch in the valley.'

Then, almost jauntily, he walked on across the wet deck. The ferryman scowled. The sallow young man in the cap didn't look as if his family could afford a servant, let alone a ranch. The ferryman walked off shaking his head.

At the bow Carter turned and leaned back, his elbows resting on the rail as he tried to control a growing dizziness. His teeth started to chatter. He asked himself why he was standing out here as casually as some dandy on a Sunday excursion trip. The fresh air wasn't doing him a bit of good.

The thick fog closed around him. He felt rootless; lost; adrift in a world in which he had no place. The feeling had become very familiar. Practically thirty years old, he had mishandled his past and left himself without a future.

But the defeated feeling passed. He willed it to pass. He was a man, and he was a Kent, and the Kents were survivors. Part of his inheritance from the family was the streak of optimism no amount of failure could destroy. He was *not* lost. The city of San Francisco was out there somewhere. It was just temporarily hidden, that was all. Hidden like the success he knew could be

551

his if he only had a touch of luck. Besides, he'd learned too many painful lessons not to put them to use somehow. He'd do that in San Francisco. He'd make a new beginning. That was what America was all about, wasn't it? New beginnings. Hell, over the past few years he'd made dozens.

But this one, now. This one would be different. This one would count. This one would put him on the right road at last—

A moment after he made the vow, he saw faint lights flickering ahead. The whistle blasted three times.

The wind felt stronger suddenly. It blew against his face and tore the fog away. He gripped the wet rail and watched the lights loom up on the hillsides of San Francisco. More and more lights appeared every second, and all of them grew steadily brighter. He had a destination after all.

He stayed on deck in the wind and damp as the ferry lumbered on to the terminal at the foot of Market Street. And although there was no reason for it except the hope or brass or whatever it was that kept him going, he had a smile on his face.

CHAPTER VII

Danger on a Dark Street

Carter left the ferry with the few other passengers who had made the crossing. In the terminal he spied a newspaper in a trash barrel. He fished it out. Luck was with him; it was the morning *Examiner*.

He paused under a lantern just inside glass doors leading to Market Street. He peered out at the fog, which was thick again. He must have looked lost, because one of the other passengers walked up to him:

'Need directions, mister?'

He turned to see a sturdy boy of twelve or thirteen with curly brown hair, large blue eyes, and a soft, almost delicate mouth. There was nothing delicate about the boy's hands. They were red and calloused. In each of them the boy held several books.

Carter nodded. 'Matter of fact, I do.'

The boy eyed Carter's shabby clothing. 'Need a job too, I'll bet.'

Carter was amused. The boy was as poorly clothed as he was.

'Eventually,' Carter told him.

'Well, you've come to a good place. There's plenty of work to be had all around the Bay. I know. I've had four jobs since I turned eleven.'

'Why'd you change so often?'

The boy looked insulted. 'Four at one time! I carry papers in the morning and evening, on Saturday I apprentice at an ice house, and Sunday I set pins at a bowling alley.'

'But it looks like you have time for reading.'

The boy's blue eyes grew hard. 'I find time. I make time. The first day I walked into the Oakland Public Library, it was like discovering a palace full of treasure.' He held up the books in both hands. 'These can help you be something besides a drudge all your life. I learned that from Miss Coolbrith.'

The special emphasis on the name failed to draw a response from Carter.

'Ina Coolbrith,' the boy said.

Again nothing. Condescendingly he explained:

'I thought they'd heard of Miss Coolbrith everyplace. She'd the head of the whole free library system. I'm returning these to her right now. They're books from her own collection. She runs what she calls a literary

553

salon at her flat on Russian Hill. Mark Twain's been there, and Bret Harte – all the big writers. If you want to see famous people, you're in the right place. You can see just about everything else, too. Out in the estuary, there are ships from all over the world. Pacific whalers. Chinese junks. South Sea schooners—'

Carter broke in, 'Right now I'd like to see the offices of the *Examiner*.'

The boy pointed to Market Street and gave directions. 'You can't miss it, mister—'

'Kent.'

'Sounds familiar – wait a minute. I've read books from a publisher named Kent.'

Carter's eyes grew remote. 'A relative of mine. But not a close one.'

'I see. Well, you'll like the Bay. Take it from a native son. One you're going to hear about, too. They say it's too late to be a gold or silver millionaire so I'm going to get rich being a writer, or maybe the prince of the oyster pirates.' He waved and started out of the terminal. 'Good luck, Mr Kent.'

'Thanks,' Carter called after him. 'But how will I recognize you when you're famous? What's your name?'

'First name's John, but I go by Jack.' A trolley bell on Market Street muffled the rest of what he said. He waved a second time and disappeared in the fog.

Tough little beggar, Carter thought. Likeable in spite of a certain arrogance. Like so many millions of Americans – like Carter himself a few years ago – the boy believed that his own sweat and diligence, plus the unparalleled opportunity the country afforded, would automatically combine to make him wealthy. But only a few realized that dream. Very likely the boy wouldn't.

Still, you never could tell. Some were born with a

gift for sucessfully capitalizing on what they were given, be it a little or a lot. Willie had that gift.

Carter studied the newspaper. Doing so was almost like meeting his old friend. The *Examiner* even sounded like Willie, from the masthead which proclaimed him 'editor and proprietor' to the box on the front page which promised:

> *The most elaborate local news, the freshest social news, the latest and most original sensations, and the relentless exposure of every scheme to rob the common man of hard-earned money or dearly-won rights. This is our pledge no matter how loftily positioned the perpetrators of such schemes may be.*

' – oughtn't to let passengers bring that damn rag on our boats. Hearst's always attacking the line.'

Carter glanced up. Two ferrymen with lunch pails were passing, evidently on their way home. In reply to the first man, the second grumbled, 'Oughtn't to let Chinks ride in the same cabin with white men, either.'

Carter recognized the ferryman who'd disapproved of his friendliness, and was in turn recognized with a contemptuous glare as the men went out the door. The hostility surprised Carter. San Francisco was supposed to be a tolerant, cosmopolitan town. It had enjoyed that reputation ever since the great discovery at Captain Sutter's mill brought Europeans, Orientals, and South Americans flocking to California to join the Americans in the search for gold.

The *Examiner*'s front page revealed the reason the Southern Pacific ferrymen disliked the paper so much. Next to a short, lurid account of the knifing of an Italian sailor in a 'foul Chinatown crib,' there was a longer piece about a Southern Pacific derailment in the Livermore Valley. It was a minor accident; two passengers were slightly injured. But the reporter, a Mr

Bierce, made the derailment sound like a wreck of huge proportions, and used it to justify an attack on the line:

This is but one more harbinger of an even greater disaster yet to come. For accidents will inevitably happen when timetables become forlorn jests, and profit is the only god the railroad serves. How can there be anything but catastrophe after stupefying catastrophe on the Southern Pacific when schedules are never adhered to, and trains are invariably so late that the passenger is exposed to senility?

But Southern Pacific management does not care about such matters. Let its wretched road-beds be littered with the mangled bodies of trusting women and innocent babes in arms! – no one in the board room will deign to notice. The road to wealth is the only road which concerns humanitarians such as Mr Leland Stanford.

One of the railroad's owners, if Carter remembered correctly. He was amused to see that Willie's wrath extended even into typography. The paper had set the name as £eland $tanford. Carter knew his old friend well enough to suspect that some of Willie's crusading spirit sprang from his knowledge that controversy improved circulation.

God, what he wouldn't give to see his friend again. Perhaps the boy named Jack was right. Perhaps he could make money in California, just as his grandmother had. Then, when he once again encountered Willie, he'd be able to look him in the eye with no shame.

Of course he had less than three dollars for a stake, and absolutely no notion of how he'd survive in San Francisco. But he still had his wits. He'd put them to use to solve the problem—

Provided he didn't perish of pneumonia or starvation before the night was over.

He tossed the paper back in the barrel. With his hands in his pockets, he stepped out into the fog. He immediately began shivering. He knew why he'd stayed in the terminal so long. Not merely because it was warm, but because passing through those doors plunged him into the city.

And into the possibility of failing again.

2

He wanted to buy something to eat. But Julia's peace of mind was more important. He found the nearest Western Union office and spent all but fifty cents of his money to send her a telegram. He told his mother that he was in San Francisco, and in good health. The clerk who took the blank darted a look at Carter's pallid, sweat-drenched face, but said nothing.

His stomach was hurting because it was so empty. He had no idea where he'd sleep tonight. Some alley, probably. Out on Market Street again, he observed a couple of sinister men drifting along in the fog, eyeing the few pedestrians who were abroad. He heard raucous laughter and rough language from several grog shops.

He found the *Examiner* as easily as the boy said he would. He smiled as he gazed up at the impressive gold-leaf signboard, well lit, which proclaimed the paper the MONARCH OF THE DAILIES. Typical Willie.

Reporters were hurrying in and out since there was a new edition to be readied for tomorrow morning. A crowd of people stood reading news bulletins block-printed on long sheets of paper which were hung side by side on the front of the building. A man in a waterproof came out to put up a new one. It dealt with torrential storms and damaging floods in the East.

Carter blew on his stiff hands, shoved them back in his pockets and turned north along a street with a moderate slope. It soon brought him to a public square surrounded by solid buildings, including several brightly illuminated, obviously first-class hotels. One of them on the east side of the square bore the words *Hope House* above its canopied entrance.

He stopped out in front, impressed by the finery of the guests coming and going through the main doors. It was his grandmother's friend, the mulatto for whom Gideon had wanted him to work, who owned this establishment. He approached the doorman, a burly fellow in a kind of bastardized hussar's outfit.

'Excuse me, sir. Is Mr Israel Hope still alive?'

'Why the devil do you want to know about Mr Hope?' The doorman shoved him. 'Get up to the Coast with the other riffraff! If I see you loitering here again, I'll call the foot patrol.'

Carter swore. The doorman started towards him, huge hands raised. Carter dodged across the street and was soon safe from the man's wrath.

He moved on up the hillside and quickly found himself in a neighbourhood of quite a different character. The shops were narrow, the lighting within them dim. The shopkeepers wore embroidered robes and queer caps. Young Chinese toughs in American clothing lounged in doorways, watching the passing crowds as closely as did their robed elders.

Carter turned into an even narrower street teeming with people. Paper banners decorated with Oriental characters and fire-breathing dragons hung down from clotheslines strung above the thoroughfare. Beyond an open door he glimpsed men lying in tiered bunks in a sweet-smelling haze. Before the door closed, he saw a huge woman in a silk robe pass a pipe into one of the bunks.

In the next block, the merchandise offered for sale was female, and most of the potential customers were sailors – German and French, Italian and American. Loudly, often obscenely, they commented on the women available, some of whom posed inside their windows. Most of the women were well past youth, and ugly, but a few were pretty. One of the latter, frail and no more than fifteen years old, caught Carter's attention. She was seated on a stool. She pulled up her blue silk gown, spread her legs, and smiled.

The callousness of the display shocked him, but no more than what was revealed by the girl's smile. Only one tooth remained in the rotted black interior of her mouth. He waved to show he wasn't interested. The prostitute spewed a string of filthy English words and slammed a shutter in his face.

He hurried on, ignoring hands that plucked at him and whispering voices that offered a cup of plum wine; a pipe of opium to promote lovely dreams; a bag of ginseng to make his ladylove want to copulate all night.

After another block or two, the neighbourhood began to change again. He was in a congested area of secondhand clothing stores, pawn shops, cribs containing white girls, and elaborate saloons with names such as the Fierce Grizzly, the So Different, The Nymphia, the Bella Union. There were plenty of whores on the sidewalks, searching for customers, and scores of men drifting among them; many of the men were reeling drunk.

Carter was thankful he was sober. Bright and cheerful as the district seemed at first, he soon noticed watchers in cul-de-sacs or the dim doorways near the grog palaces. Watchers hunting for a man just a little too drunk to defend himself—

A reed organ in a saloon called the Thalia pealed

'Oh, Susanna!' into the foggy night. Carter presumed he'd arrived on the Barbary Coast, named years before in memory of the equally infamous pirate coast of Africa. Here, too, there were pirates – as well as at least one man trying to put a stop to the ubiquitous sin. The man marched through the crowd shaking a tambourine and calling, 'A free meal and a helping hand always available at the Salvation Army. Eight-oh-nine Montgomery Street, where Major Wells receives those in need!'

Carter saw rolls of bills clenched in fists, and heard coins clink. Visitors to the Coast who displayed their money were clearly fools. They'd soon be penniless if the platoons of sauntering pimps, whores, and thieves had anything to do with it. He decided he'd better find some other part of town in which to spend the night. Some of the people around him looked vicious enough to kill a sleeping man for his bootlaces.

He was feeling feverish again. He'd lost track of directions, but he thought Market Street lay behind him. He turned round and started back down the sloping street.

Almost without his noticing it, dance halls and gaudy bars were replaced by stores and offices shuttered and chained up for the night. The only other men he saw in this all but lightless section were two husky specimens wearing white blouses and tams with red pompons. They were going uphill on the other side of the street. Foreign sailors in port for the night and bound for the Coast, he surmised.

The sailors' laughter faded away. Carter reached an intersection. He was about to cross when he heard a soft tapping, and two voices midway down the next block on his side of the street.

He stepped to the corner of the building and leaned there, studying the block ahead. The two men were going in his direction. He studied them to be sure he wasn't coming up on a couple of roughnecks.

No, they looked respectable enough. The one on the outside, tall and frail, had his left arm crooked so the other could hold on. The man on the inside, older, had a cautious, shuffling gait. He poked his stick out ahead of him, tapping the walk. A blind man.

The fog hung heavily here. The men almost disappeared as they reached the next intersection. More visible were the other two men who startled Carter by stealing out of an alley half a block behind the first two men. The two began to slip along the sidewalk, creeping up on the blind man and his escort.

Light from up the hill speared through the fog, creating an eerie effect and affording just enough illumination for Carter to see that there was no one else on the sloping street. He was about to be the sole witness to a robbery.

Or worse.

3

Whatever the crime, it was no affair of his. He'd be smart to slip away.

Yet a new idea held him motionless on the corner. He had only fifty cents to his name. The hour was late, he felt feverish, and the thought of going hungry and sleeping in the open had become unbearable. He might have stumbled on a way to improve that situation.

From a distance, the intended victims looked prosperous. Suppose he warned them of the impending danger – he could practically do it from here. If he did, there was an excellent chance that he'd earn a reward.

After Ortega's death, he'd vowed that he'd never again voluntarily involve himself in anything that might lead to violence. But the danger here seemed exceedingly small. Surely a shout would scare the thieves away—

Mercenary considerations aside, there was another reason he lingered on the corner. Although he wouldn't have admitted it aloud, his conscience demanded that he step in. One man outwitting another – even robbing him, if they were evenly matched – that was the way of the world. But picking on a blind man? That was too much.

He took a deep breath, jumped down from the walk and ran across the street to the corner of the next block. He kept his attention fixed on the two men gliding along the plank walk behind their prey. The blind man and his friend would certainly have heard a telltale creak if they hadn't been talking so boisterously and having such a good time; the blind man's rich, mellow laughter carried all the way back to the corner where Carter crouched.

He cupped his hands round his mouth, yelling as loudly as he could:

'Watch out behind you!'

The frail man pivoted first, then his companion. Carter could discern a moustache on the blind man's face but nothing else. The thieves whirled to see who had sounded the alarm. Carter could only tell that they were young, and dressed in dark clothing.

He expected the thieves to bolt. When they didn't his stomach started to hurt.

The larger of the two thieves yanked something from his coat pocket. Light penetrating the fog flashed on a pistol barrel. The man waved the gun and shouted at the second robber:

'You take care of that meddling son of a bitch. I'll handle the other two. I want the boss's bundle.'

What that meant, Carter didn't know. But he did know he'd miscalculated badly. These weren't common thieves who fled when discovered and outnumbered. These were crazy men. And one of them was running back along the sidewalk toward him. The diffuse light flashed on a long knife in the man's right hand.

Ortega, Carter thought.

Over the head of the running man he glimpsed the other thief closing on the victims. Panic dried his mouth. He'd sworn to start over and squandered the chance in a single moment of greed and misguided altruism.

The thief was coming fast. Even as Carter stepped back, the man shot out his right hand, driving the long blade straight at Carter's midsection.

CHAPTER VIII

The Weapon

He'd forgotten how close he was to the edge of the sidewalk. When he stepped backward, there was only air under his right foot.

Off balance, he tumbled into the street, and landed hard. But that misstep and fall kept him from being disembowelled by the slashing knife.

The thief had trouble checking his momentum. He skidded to a stop, recovered, and made a lithe turn toward Carter. Distant light from the Coast showed dark eyes and curly hair that glistened as if the man dressed it with Macassar oil.

Panting, Carter scrambled to his feet. He took three long steps backward. The man on the walk spoke to him in a British accent:

'Too late to run, mate. I can catch ye if ye try.

Shouldn't've shoved yer bleedin' nose where it don't belong. Now I'm obliged to cut it off—'

He leaped into the street and ran at Carter, who darted to one side just as the man again shot his knife hand forward. The thief cursed and tried to shift the direction of his charge. He couldn't. Carter brought his right knee up. The tip of the knife tore through his trousers at the thigh, narrowly missing flesh. Then Carter's knee jolted the thief between the legs.

The man grunted, stumbling to one side. *Too close*, Carter thought as he swiped the back of his hand across his eyes. He smelled the stench of fish. A second knife seemed to overlap the one in the thief's hand. Then Carter saw Ortega at the Red Cod. Flickering and flashing, the past hid the present for a heartbeat of time—

He heard cursing and came to his senses. He wasn't out of danger. Fortunately the angry thief was still groggy. Carter ran at him and rammed his knee into the man's groin a second time. The thief yelled, clutching himself. The knife clacked on the wood blocks with which the street was paved.

Carter had an impulse to duck down and grab the knife, but he was afraid of losing his momentary advantage. He laced his fingers together and pounded the back of the thief's neck. Once. Twice. Three times—

The man gave an exhausted sigh and fell over, barely breathing.

Carter eyed the knife. Taking huge, gulping breaths, he crouched and closed his fingers around the rough hilt. The fish stench nearly made him gag. *It's only in your mind*. He had difficulty convincing himself of that.

Down the block, the frail man was grappling with the other thief for possession of the thief's pistol. To Carter's surprise, the frail man looked anything but helpless now. He had a bung starter in his left hand,

and brass knuckles on his right. Ordinary citizens didn't walk around carrying such weapons. The man was either a thug, the blind man's bodyguard – or both.

Clutching the knife, Carter raced toward the struggling men. The blind man stood near them, his back against the building and his lacquered walking stick raised in front of his chest. A few steps more, and Carter could make out some of the man's features. He looked to be in his forties. His ruddy cheeks and forehead suggested he might be English or Irish. His eyes had a curiously commanding quality – perhaps because they were so large, dominating his face.

An elegant wide-brimmed hat lay at the blind man's feet, and the earlier impression of prosperity was confirmed by what he wore: an expensive tweed sporting suit cut in the popular Norfolk pattern, but with long trousers, not the usual knee breeches.

'Shove him over here where I can shillelagh him!' the blind man shouted as Carter sped down the last half of the block. But the blind man's companion needed no help. He beat the thief's wrist with the bung starter. The thief let go of his pistol. The frail man tossed the bung starter away and snatched up the gun.

The thief weaved on his feet, clutching his wrist and moaning. Suddenly the frail man looked past the thief and saw Carter running with the knife in his hand. Confused by the darkness and the sight of the knife, the frail man yelled:

'The other one's coming back, boss!'

'Wait, I'm not—'

Before Carter could finish, the frail man aimed and fired.

Carter dived for the sidewalk, hitting hard and skinning his jaw. The bullet thumped wood somewhere above him. To hell with humanitarianism. It had nearly got him killed twice in only a couple of minutes. He began to crawl toward the edge of the walk, where he intended to drop into the street and keep crawling until he was safe.

Even that plan went wrong. The frail man let out a hurt cry. Carter raised his head and saw the man stagger, struck on the skull by the bung starter the thief had managed to pick up.

The blind man knew something had happened to his companion. He kept poking the air with his stick:

'Alex? Alex, where are you?'

The man named Alex didn't answer. Dazed, he couldn't defend himself when the thief hit him a second time. His eyes rolled up in his head. He slumped to his knees and toppled sideways off the walk, dropping the pistol.

The thief seized the gun, then darted in beneath the blind man's jabbing stick. Astonishingly, the blind man seemed to have no concern for his own safety. He sounded irked:

'Alex? Answer me, can't you?'

Out of the thief's throat came a curious sound; a chuckle distorted by nervousness. The thief whispered, 'Boss?'

The blind man drew his stick back by his shoulder, ready to jab. He looked alarmed for the first time:

'Who's that?'

Watching the stick, the thief kicked the blind man's right leg, then his left one. The blind man fell, sprawling on his back. The thief tore the stick from his hands and hurled it away. *He's going to kill him*, Carter thought, still on his belly and creeping toward the edge of the sidewalk.

The thief paid no attention to him. Evidently he thought Carter had been hit by the bodyguard's bullet and was no threat. *Let him go on believing that till I get out of here*. To appease his conscience Carter told himself he'd done all he could.

He was about ten feet from where the thief stood

over the blind man. Slowly, cautiously, he worked his way toward the edge of the walk. He heard the thief say:

'Can't you tell who it is, boss?'

'Now – ' The blind man was short of breath. 'Now I can. You sound very pleased with yourself, Charlie Schmidt.'

A hard laugh. 'Want to shake hands to make sure it's me?'

'I only shake hands to identify a friend, never an enemy. Never a poltroon to whom I gave an honest job with the push, only to have him reward me by stealing from my cash box.'

'I took only a little.'

'Don't whine, Charlie. You always did strike me as a whiner. You took a hell of a lot.'

'And you fired me for it! That should have made us even.'

'Not in my book.'

'No, that's right. Firing me wasn't enough. You had to make a stink all over town.' He put his right foot on the man's shoulder, pointing the pistol down at his eyes. 'I can't get work because of you.'

'What did you expect when you robbed me, a proclamation honouring your honesty? You got what you deserved. Now let me up, you damned rogue, or—'

'Or nothing!' Schmidt broke in. He stepped down on the blind man's shoulder; the man let out a short, pained cry. 'I'm going to blow your fucking head all over this walk, boss. Then I'm going to help myself to that bundle of bank notes you always carry. After that I'm going to catch a coasting ship for Los Angeles.'

Only about six inches separated Carter from the edge of the sidewalk. The faint music of a melodeon drifted down the hill from the Barbary Coast. Holding his breath, he braced his left elbow on the walk, then his left knee. In a moment he'd be down in the street; less visible.

He started to move—

A loose board creaked.

The thief spun round; saw him:

'I thought you were done for. Well, I can take care of that. A little payment for putting my partner away. Stand up.'

Carter remained awkwardly propped on one elbow and one knee. A part of his mind urged him to leap up and lunge with the knife he was still holding. He might be able to surprise the man. Force him into a wild shot, then reach him before he could shoot again. But memories kept flickering in his head. Ortega; his knife, his ripped throat—

Get up and go at him!

He refused to listen to the voice. He remembered the Red Cod, and what the weapon in his hand had almost cost him tonight. And besides, he was too far from the thief. A wild charge stood no chance of succeeding. There had to be another way out of this. Another weapon with which to disarm and overcome the man.

He knew of one. Would it work? Did he dare gamble?

'You son of a bitch, I said stand up.'

'All right. But I have your friend's knife. Don't shoot when I throw it away.'

The blind man reacted to what he'd heard with surprise and disgust:

'Whoever you are, boyo, you must be daft. If you have a knife, don't toss it away or he's sure to kill you, too.'

Carter paid no attention. Sweat ran into his eyes. He slowly raised his right hand. Flicked it outward—

The knife sailed into the street; thumped on a paving block. The sickening fish stench receded.

In a strained voice, he said, 'It's gone. Can you see?'

'I see. On your feet.'

Carter clambered up.

'Hands in the air!'

Carter obeyed. He heard a groan; a faint stirring out in the foggy street. The thief glanced that way, apparently saw nothing alarming, and returned his attention to Carter.

The thief was about Carter's age. A colourless man with a moon face and stooped shoulders. Carter eyed the pistol pointed at him. He guessed he had only a few seconds to prevent the blind man's murder – and his own.

2

With all the urgency and conviction he could muster, Carter said:

'You'd better run for it, Schmidt.'

It took the thief a moment to realize what he'd heard; his first reaction was a laugh of disbelief:

'You're giving me orders when I've got this?'

He waggled the gun. Carter broke out in a sweat again. Trying to ignore the small, round muzzle, he struggled to maintain a blustering tone:

'Listen to me, you damned idiot.' The man was stunned to be addressed that way. 'Why do you think I took a chance and interfered with your little adventure? I'm being paid to patrol this district along with four other detectives.'

The thief laughed, but less confidently. 'Bullshit. No San Francisco coppers patrol this part of town after dark. If they did, they sure wouldn't be as sorry looking as you.'

'Think we're going to carry signboards? Our job's to

blend in and watch for tinhorns like you.' The lies came more easily all at once:

'We've been working these streets since a week ago Monday night. The saloon owners on the Coast and the merchants along here whose places keep getting broken into took up a special collection. They pay us for the extra duty.' He turned toward the blind man. 'Isn't that the God's truth, boss?'

Whoever the man was, he had brains. He picked up the intent of the ruse instantly:

'The gospel, officer. You'd better heed him, Charlie Schmidt.'

Schmidt blinked, clearly confused. Carter's hands were still raised. He hoped their trembling didn't show. The longer he kept Schmidt from firing, the greater his chances. But he couldn't afford to pause too long and give the man time to think:

'How long has it been since that pistol went off? Two minutes? Three? I guarantee at least one of the others in the special patrol heard the shot. One or more of them will be coming along soon to check on—'

'Shut your mouth!' the thief yelled, his voice so ragged Carter knew he'd successfully planted a seed of fear. The man might never swallow the farfetched story but he was wondering about it. If he wondered long enough, he might lose his nerve – and his will to do murder.

When he spoke again, he sounded as if he were trying to convince himself: 'I don't believe a damn word of what you're telling me, mister.'

Carter shrugged. 'Your privilege.' He was positive he heard a footfall in the street. But he didn't dare look. 'You'll find out soon enough whether I'm lying. You'll find out when we string a noose around your neck.'

The thief looked shaken; even in the near-darkness,

Carter could see that. The man was an amateur. Carter's hopes soared. He bore in hard:

'Every man on the special patrol is empowered to act under what's known as a municipal writ. That's a writ signed by a municipal judge and kept in a vault at police headquarters. Those of us on the patrol don't carry any papers, but that writ gives us the right to raise a *posse comitatus* – a posse of citizens which can legally pass sentence and carry it out right in the street. Under the supervision of any man in the patrol, the posse can hang an offender caught committing a crime.'

'I – ' The man swallowed. ' – I worked for the boss six months. I never heard of anything called a municipal writ.'

'Am I responsible for that? You'd better cut and run. Do that and we'll give you a sporting chance. You've hurt people but you haven't killed anybody. But if I'm found dead, all that money you stole won't do you a damn bit of good. Four other San Francisco detectives will catch you and hang you. And they'll do it before the sun comes up.'

'*You're lying*,' Schmidt whispered. 'There's no way a man can be lynched without a trial and—'

He stopped, hearing the same sound Carter and the blind man heard; the wonderful, unmistakable sound Carter had been hoping and praying for. Men coming down the hill from the Barbary Coast.

How many had banded together to investigate the gun shot, he couldn't tell. It sounded like at least a half dozen. The thief began to breathe in short, hard gasps.

'They're coming for you, Schmidt. I told you they would. Go while you still have time. *Go!*'

The command, almost shouted, made the thief back up as if he'd been punched. He blinked again, lowered the pistol and swung around to peer at the moving silhouettes visible against the lights further up the hill. The men were coming rapidly. Carter was euphoric.

He'd staved off a killing by using only his ability to think quickly, speak quickly, sow doubt and thereby—

The blind man's companion came lunging up from the street so fast Carter barely saw what took place. In his hand was the knife Carter had discarded. He rammed it into the thief's back halfway between shoulder blades and buttocks. Then he seized the thief's arm and flung him to one side.

The thief screamed. His trigger finger jerked, but the bullet he fired thunked harmlessly into the sidewalk.

The thief fell, dead before he rolled into the street. Raging, Carter turned on his killer:

'You murdered him. Why? He was ready to run. *I had him ready to run!*'

3

Boots hammered on paving blocks as the men came closer, shouting questions. The blind man's companion sounded surly as he said:

'We're grateful. Not nobody turns on the boss that way. Nobody.'

He picked up the thief's gun and shoved it into his belt. Then he extended his hand to the blind man, who was sitting up now:

'Let me help you, boss.'

Carter stared at the knife jutting from the dead thief's back. He'd thrown the knife away and bet everything on his own ability to spin out words that would make the man hesitate. He'd been successful, and then this damnfool bodyguard had ruined everything!

Elongated shadows of eight or ten men appeared on the wall of a warehouse on the other side of the street. The fog had thinned somewhat during the last few minutes. The huge shadow of a pointing hand was clear on the wall as someone yelled:

'That must be one of them. Catch him!'

Down at the corner, the Britisher darted away into the cross street. Two men raced in pursuit. The others came on, their shadows looming. The bodyguard helped the blind man to his feet.

'You all right, boss?'

Carter didn't catch the answer. What did it matter? All the effort had been for nothing. Despairing and angry, he leaned against the front of a store, his forehead resting on his forearm. He heard the new arrivals clamouring around the blind man. They seemed to know him well.

A new thought struck him. On top of everything else, he was an accomplice to murder. He clenched his fist and hit the siding on the front of the store. From somewhere – the night streets or the recesses of his own imagination – there came again the terrible odour of rotting fish.

CHAPTER IX

The Blind Boss

In the crowd surrounding the blind man, Carter suddenly spied two new arrivals, both in uniform. A badge threw off a flash of reflected light.

He swore softly. Why had he waited to run? Why had he involved himself at all? His reasons – the hope of a reward, and the prodding of a conscience he hated to acknowledge – now seemed completely absurd. There was a corpse in the street.

A curious thought struck him then. He seemed the only person worried about the corpse in the street. The man responsible for it certainly wasn't. He'd seated himself on the edge of the sidewalk, lanky knees drawn up in front of his chest, and was carefully fingering his temples and forehead.

The blind man didn't act worried either. Smiling, he thanked those who handed him his broad-brimmed hat and stick. He grew positively ebullient when someone said policemen were on the scene:

'Splendid. Who's on duty tonight? Don't speak, officer. Shake hands with me first.'

The older policeman did so. The blind man nodded: 'Sean Phelan.'

The grey-haired patrolman grinned. 'Right, boss.' The crowd murmured; a couple of men clapped. The blind man asked:

'How does your sister like that teaching job, Phelan?'

'She likes it just fine. Thanks to you, she's able to salt a little into the Bank of California every payday. My Lord, it's uncanny, the way you recognize people by a handshake.'

'Only my friends, Phelan, only my friends – as I told poor Charlie Schmidt. I understand he's no longer among the living.'

The second policeman, quite a bit younger, rose from a quick examination of the corpse. 'That's right, boss. Somebody planted a knife in his back.'

Carter swallowed the sour fluid burning his throat. He backed up half a step, hoping to slip out of the crowd, turn and walk away unnoticed. It might be possible. The blind man was the centre of attention as he explained:

'There were two of them, Charlie and some Limey. I suppose they planned to split the loot. I hired Charlie as a candidate for my push, you see. But I soon found him untrustworthy and discharged him. Robbing and killing me would have been his way of getting even.'

Phelan's expression was sympathetic. 'Can you tell exactly what happened?'

'Certainly. My companion and bodyguard, Mr Alex Gram—'

The blind man raised his cane and, without an instant's hesitation, pointed it straight at the frail man. Someone let out a soft whistle of astonishment.

'—accompanied me to the Coast, where I took care of a small errand. We were on our way back down to Bush Street when Charlie and his accomplice ambushed us. Then another fellow came along – where is he, by the way?'

Heads turned. Eyes fixed on Carter's face as he swore again. An aisle opened. He'd backed almost the whole way out of the crowd, but now he was caught. And when he saw the stern look on the face of the other policeman, he thought:

The blind man's someone important. He'll probably pin it on me to save his pal. And the coppers will play along.

The young policeman moved in beside Phelan. One hand rested on iron handcuffs hanging from his belt. 'Step up here!' he ordered. When he motioned, the cuffs rattled.

A last impulse to run seized Carter. But it quickly faded. With so many people available to help the police, he had no chance. No chance at all.

The two policemen were scowling at him. The crowd stared. Run, stay – what difference did it make? They had him either way.

'Didn't you hear my partner?' Phelan said. 'Up here, if you please.'

Carter shuffled forward, completely exhausted. The fever was raging through him again. His face was sticky with sweat and his ears rang. He wasn't sure how long he could stay on his feet.

The older officer pointed the billy at Carter's chest. 'What's your name?'

Should he lie? Invent something?

Glowering, Phelan raised the club. 'Lad, I'll ask you but once more. What's your name?'

'Kent. Carter Kent.'

The blind man took charge then:

'Well, Mr Kent, my friend Mr Gram told me you did a game job of coming to our assistance. That will not be forgotten. No, indeed – not forgotten for one moment.'

He reached for Carter's right hand and found it with only a little fumbling. He held it a moment, as if memorizing its contours. Then he shook it, as if he was working a pump handle. At last he let go. His sightless eyes had been fixed on Carter's face the whole time. Carter was too surprised to say a word.

The blind man again addressed the older officer:

'Mr Kent's hand feels feverish. I want to offer him the hospitality of my saloon—'

The suggestion sounded wounderful to Carter, though he knew he should be careful; far away, on the coast of Texas, another man had once offered him shelter, and a job – and he'd nearly lost his life.

'—so let's conclude this business.'

'Yes, sir,' Phelan said, so meekly he could barely be heard. Carter held his breath, fearing that at any second the reprieve would be withdrawn. But it wasn't. With a sweeping gesture of his stick, the blind man went on:

'And get rid of the body. We've enough of them on the streets of this town as it is.'

'Be happy to take care of it, boss. But – ' Phelan licked his lips; unconsciously began twisting a button on his jacket. ' – I do need to clear up one or two details.'

'Be quick about it. I told you Mr Kent's feeling poorly. And night air tends to give me catarrh. Mrs Buckley is always nagging me to stay indoors after dark.'

Nervous, the older officer asked, 'Can you just give me a concise account of what happened?'

Though clearly irritated, the blind man did so, starting with Carter's shout of warning:

'I expect ordinary footpads would have run for it. But an outcry wasn't enough to drive Charlie off. As I told you, he bore a grudge. He also knew, as do all my associates and employees, that I always carry a sizable roll of cash. He didn't intend to leave until I was dead and the cash was in his pocket. Despite Mr Gram's best efforts, he might have carried out his plan had it not been for this young man's intervention.'

'Jumped Schmidt and fought him off, did he?'

The blind man chuckled. 'No, Phelan. He talked him out of it.'

The officer's brows shot up. 'What did you say, sir?'

'I said Mr Kent talked Charlie Schmidt out of his violent reprisal. He did so with the finest flow of blarney I've ever heard. Mr Kent gave Charlie no time to think, and bombarded him with some very impressive threats about being a detective in plain clothes. A detective patrolling these streets under the authority of something called a municipal writ. Mr Kent said this fictitious writ gave him power to summon a posse and hang Charlie on the spot. No smart fellow would have

believed it for an instant. But of course when someone's smack in the middle of robbery and murder, he's
heated up and not thinking clearly. To that you must
add Charlie's inherent stupidity. Mr Kent bamboozled
him just long enough for us to get out of the scrape.'

Carter was stunned to hear the blind man speak with
such obvious relish. Buckley had acted as if he were
telling a humorous story, not describing a crime.

Phelan was insistent on one point, though:

'I'm afraid you still haven't told me who killed
Schmidt.'

Carter tensed. Again Buckley waved his stick:

'Oh, Mr Gram did. By then he had recovered from
blows which took him out of action temporarily.'

The acknowledgment of guilt obviously didn't worry
the frail man. He didn't even turn round, just continued to rub and poke his head. The grey-haired policeman twisted the jacket button so hard the thread broke.
He was afraid to speak, but finally did so:

'Boss, you know that because of what you've just
told me, I'm required to put Mr Gram in the lock-up
overnight. I don't want to do it, but the law
explicitly—'

'Come by the saloon in an hour or so,' Buckley
interrupted. 'I have a supply of orders of discharge. I
keep them for emergencies like this. I'll sign Judge
Toohy's name and then Mr Gram won't be
inconvenienced.'

Phelan let out a huge sigh. 'A fine solution. That
way, I needn't even take him in.'

Forge the name of a judge to a legal document?
Carter couldn't believe a man would publicly announce
his plan to do such a thing. The laws of logic didn't
seem to apply in San Francisco though. Buckley's
statements caused no comment among the crowd left
at the scene.

Several men had already departed, their curiosity

satisfied. One burly fellow prodded the corpse with his boot, and then made a joke about it as he and a companion strolled back up the hill toward the Coast. Carter didn't consider himself overly scrupulous, yet he was appalled. As Buckley had suggested, death was evidently a common occurrence in the city, right along with circumvention of the law.

Suddenly Phelan seized his arm. 'I'll also need some information about you, Kent. Place of residence, in case we have further need to contact you—'

The man's peremptory tone angered Carter:

'I don't have a place of residence. I just arrived today.'

Phelan whipped his club up over his shoulder. 'Damn you, don't speak smartly to me, or—'

There was a swish and a loud clack. The blind man's cane had blocked the policeman's stick in mid-air. Buckley was furious:

'Phelan, you're taking advantage of your authority and harassing a stranger. Evidently I didn't make my wishes sufficiently clear. This young man assisted Mr Gram and me, and we're in his debt. If you need to reach him, follow the instructions I already gave you. Come to the saloon! I also suggest you permit us to go on our way at once. Unless, of course, you're bucking for a new job with some hick department down the peninsula—'

The blind man's eyes seemed to fasten on Phelan's and hold there:

'If that's your wish, Phelan, it can be arranged.'

The policeman wilted. 'Boss, I'm sorry. I didn't think you—'

'That's quite correct,' the other broke in. 'You didn't think. Which is why you're fifty and still a foot police-man. Mr Kent – Alex – come along. I don't want the damned catarrh.'

And, displaying all the wrath of a king insulted by a

commoner, he moved majestically down the sidewalk, his stick extended six inches in front of him to tap and test the way.

3

Carter fell in step beside Alex Gram. Phelan caught up with them, clutching the bodyguard's arm:

'Gram, I can't afford to lose my job. I've a big family to feed. Try to fix it, for God's sake. Put in a good word—'

'I'll do what I can, but you angered him. He doesn't get angry very often. Bring some cash around. That might placate him.'

'How much should I bring?'

'As much as you can get together. Even then I can't promise he'll relent. You'll just have to take your chances.' Gram put his hand on the policeman's shoulder and rudely pushed him aside.

The policeman didn't protest, just redirected his wrath at those people still loitering by the corpse. He ordered them to move along or face arrest. One man laughed and Phelan struck him twice with his billy. A friend dragged the man away before Phelan could do more damage.

Gram kept an eye on Buckley as they walked. Presently he said to Carter, 'It isn't far to the saloon. You look like you could use a drink and a meal.'

'Both,' Carter nodded. 'But more than that, I need a place to sleep. Mr Buckley was right. I'm not feeling very good.'

'There's a stable near the saloon. The owner owes the boss a favour—' Gram stopped, waiting for Buckley to negotiate the drop-off at the next corner.

'Will there be any more trouble because that man got killed?' Carter asked.

Once Buckley was across the intersection, Gram moved on and finally answered:

'Not a whit.'

Carter shook his head. 'Seems incredible.'

A chuckle. 'You *are* new in town. You don't know who he is, do you?'

'Obviously someone with influence—'

This time Gram laughed aloud. 'Yes, you might say. You might say that a man who runs his party's central committee, decides which way the primaries will come out, and tells a majority of the city supervisors how to vote has influence. Let me give you a fast introduction to local politics, Kent. My employer's a pal of Senator Hearst and every other important office holder in California. No, I'll put that a better way. They're pals of his – because they never stop needing what the boss can deliver on demand. Extra ballots. Our price is five dollars a vote or ten dollars for a straight ticket. That includes a little cream on the top for us.'

'You mean your boss can always find as many votes as someone needs?'

'Usually,' Gram nodded. 'But he isn't just my boss. He's *the* boss. Remember that.'

'I will. Where do you get the extra votes?'

'Wherever we can find extra voters. Flop houses. The drunk tank. Sometimes we use our own stalwarts to vote names from the cemeteries or the obit columns. Hell – ' An amused shrug. ' – in an election a couple of years ago, the boss came up short. But there was a French warship in port. We rounded up half the crew and voted *them*. Believe me, Kent, nothing important happens around here without the boss okaying it first. If your sister wants to teach in the San Francisco schools, the fee for the job is two hundred dollars. Every municipal job has its price. That isn't to say the boss doesn't have a conscience. He does. His father came here from Ireland, and he knows what it means

581

to be poor. He hates the damn gougers who run the railroads. He wants the streets to be safe for everybody. And he's a prince to work for. If you're loyal to him, he'll always be loyal to you. Altogether, I'd say he's the most powerful man in the city – probably the state. They don't call him the Caesar of the Democracy for nothing.'

Carter was impressed. Sick and worn out though he was, he felt a stir of hope. His luck might have taken a favourable turn at last.

CHAPTER X

Steam Beer

Christopher Buckley's saloon on Bush Street was a gas-lit place full of cigar smoke, beer fumes, and noisy, cheerful men. The moment Buckley walked in, he was besieged by a well-dressed man and four others in much shabbier clothing. All obviously sought favours.

Buckley waved his stick to acknowledge greetings from several customers. Then he took the five suppliants into an office at the rear. The door closed.

In about two minutes, one of the poorly dressed men emerged. He was grinning. The others came out at short intervals. All looked satisfied except the prosperous-looking gentleman, who was the last to appear. Buckley shouted at him from the office door:

' – and tell your cronies at the Southern Pacific never to approach me again with that kind of filthy scheme. Otherwise the push may visit their fancy Snob Hill palaces some night!'

Pale, the man fled. Carter was leaning on the beautiful turned rim of the mahogany bar. Gram stood next to him. Buckley walked to the bar and stepped behind it. 'What was that about?' Gram asked.

'Ah, one of their high-toned officials messed with a conductor's twelve-year-old daughter. The girl's mother was pimping for the child in the hope of furthering her husband's career. The father found out, immediately quit the SP and pressed charges. Now the railroad wants me to spring its man from the clink. I said I'd be damned if I would. Men like that should rot in jail and burn in hell. When I expressed that view, the rogue who was just here grew a trifle testy. I told him to shove his five thousand dollars up his rosy ass.'

Buckley had hung his coat on a rack and rolled up his sleeves. Now he tied a white apron around his waist. 'The fellow threatened me then. It was at that point that I threw him out. He won't be back. They know better than to tread on Boss Buckley. Mr Kent—?'

'Right here, sir.'

'Feeling any better?'

'Since we came inside, much.' But he still didn't feel good.

'Are you hungry? Thirsty?'

An embarrassed laugh. 'I confess to both.'

'Well, we usually have some dabs on the stove in back.'

'Dabs, sir?'

Buckley spaced his index fingers a few inches apart. 'Small Pacific coast flat fish. Very succulent when properly broiled.'

Carter swallowed. 'If it's all the same to you, Mr Buckley, fish isn't a favourite of mine.'

'Boiled beef, then. And something to drink – and perhaps a chance to put a little money in your pocket?'

Carter's excitement overcame his caution. 'That would be very welcome, too.'

'Where are you from, my boy?'

'Boston.'

'Ah! A good Irishman's town. Nearly as fine as New York, where I grew up. By the way, what may I pour you? The hard spirits sold in this establishment are safe to drink.'

'You mean they aren't elsewhere?'

Gram laughed cynically. 'This place is an exception in town. A rare exception.' He snapped his fingers at another bartender. It was obvious to Carter that the man didn't like being ordered about that way. With a sullen stare, he passed Gram a quart of whiskey and a glass. Meantime, Buckley continued:

'Depending on whether a saloon owner wants you dead in order to rob you, or alive in order to ship you out to some heathen port, you're liable to find your drink laced with opium or laudanum or chloral. That kind of thing gives San Francisco a foul name, but we can't seem to eliminate the practice, much as we try. There are a few places you can safely enjoy yourself. I run one of them.' He gestured to the gleaming bottles ranked behind the bar. 'Name your poison – no, wait.'

A smile spread on his pink face. Without hesitation, he extended his hand and plucked a schooner from among a dozen arranged on the back bar. Taking two steps to the left, he pulled the handle of a keg tap. Beer spouted into the schooner.

'Since you're new to the area, you must sample this,' he said.

Carter drank. 'That's delicious.' He wiped his upper lip and set the schooner on the bar. 'I've never tasted any beer half as good.'

Buckley nodded. 'I venture to say you haven't. That's a special brew unique to the city. San Francisco steam beer.'

584

He went on to explain that ice, required for conventional brewing, hadn't been available when San Francisco boomed at the time of the Gold Rush. What little ice there was had to be brought all the way from the mountains. So a canny brewer had formulated a beer which could be manufactured without refrigeration.

Carter barely caught half of Buckley's remarks. He was feeling increasingly feverish, and the walls seemed to ripple like windblown cloth. The beer didn't help matters.

'Barley,' the blind man went on. 'And malt and hops only – no rice or corn.' Then came something about, 'Steam mash bubbled up by what they call krausening, a natural carbonation process.' The rest of the explanation was lost on him.

His next sip was a tiny one; he was again afraid that he might pass out. He rubbed his eyes and stared at a fat bronze cupid holding up the milky globe of a gaslight behind the bar. Slowly the cupid's navel came into focus. By the time it was sharp, he felt a little better.

Gram noticed his drawn look. 'I think the lad needs food more than he needs steam beer, boss.'

'Coming up!' Buckley sent another bartender hurrying to the kitchen. It was the same man who'd brought Gram his whiskey. He didn't act resentful when Buckley gave the orders.

'Let's sit down at that corner table,' Buckley said. 'You needn't worry about a place to sleep. I believe I can persuade Hanratty's Livery to accommodate you for a night or so.'

The blind man emerged from behind the bar, obviously familiar with the dimensions and placement of all the fixtures and furniture; he never bumped into a chair or a guest as he led the way to the secluded table. As he sat down, he chuckled:

'A municipal writ. Glorious! If there isn't such a

585

document, there should be. I'll have to speak to the supervisors about it. There are twelve of those gentlemen. Seven of them can usually be counted on to vote as I ask. Sometimes I can even swing nine if it's necessary to override the mayor's veto.'

He laid smooth pink hands on the table top. A waiter arrived with a plate of steaming beef surrounded by thick slices of brown bread. Carter tore a slab of bread in half and stuffed the pieces into his mouth. Buckley continued to smile, but a hard tone came into his voice:

'As you may have gathered, Mr Kent, a great many matters affecting the municipality are discussed in these somewhat unlikely quarters. So are some things pertaining to the state and the nation, for that matter. My enemies call this place Buckley's City Hall. I consider that an honorific, not an insult. Because I'm a busy man, I can always use helpers who don't allow scruples to interfere with their duties or diminish their party loyalty.'

Carter cut and ate the tender beef as fast as he could. With his mouth full, he asked, 'You're talking about the Democratic party, aren't you?'

'Yes, but to anyone on the inside of San Francisco politics, that's incidental. I'll explain what I mean in a moment. From your voice I'd guess you to be in your twenties. Am I right?'

'Yes, sir.'

'That was the decade in my life when I discovered my passion for politics. My first job in San Francisco was conductor on a North Beach horse car. From that I rose to the eminence of tending bar at Snugg's, a very cosmopolitan saloon on the lower level of Maguire's Opera House on Washington Street. At Snugg's, murder was not infrequent. But a great many fascinating and influential men congregated there. I was soon on a first name basis with gamblers, actors, and politicians of both parties. Of the lot, the politicians seemed the most worthy of emulation – at least to my impressionable eyes.'

He realized what he'd just said and laughed – this time it had a melancholy sound. 'In those days, you understand, I could still see.'

Gram poured another stiff shot of whiskey. He'd obviously heard the story before. He looked bored. Carter wasn't. The blind man fascinated him. Behind the deceptively congenial face, Carter sensed the presence of a man to whom weakness was loathsome and defeat a mortal sin.

'Soon I was busy involving myself in local politics. My training ground was the Fifth Ward. I learned how to drag votes out of boarding houses as well as less savoury places. I developed a knack and a liking for all the rough work that accompanies a primary which comes out the way someone wants it to come out. Within a couple of years I'd built a reputation as a handy fellow to have around. Of course I had a splendid group of tutors. Republicans, every one of them.'

'You mean you didn't start out a Democrat?'

'Indeed not. My best mentor in the Fifth Ward was a young Republican who attended Harvard. Bill Higgins is his name. He still runs the party here in San Francisco. In any case, there came a time – oh, twenty years ago now – when I decided that if I wanted to continue to move ahead in politics, I'd need to work for myself. So I could apportion my time as I saw fit. I left town and went up to Vallejo to establish myself as an independent businessman. I opened a saloon. It wasn't an entirely wise decision. It was consumption of spirits which later caused me to lose my sight.'

Cigar smoke drifted slowly in the air. All around them, men talked and laughed. But it was suddenly quiet at the table where the three sat. Buckley's eyes appeared to be fixed on his hands. For a moment Carter had the strange feeling that he could see them.

'I did well in Vallejo,' the blind man resumed. 'I worked my way in as secretary of the Solano County Republican Committee. But by '72, I had a yen to come back to this side of the Bay – where there wasn't any way to climb higher on the Republican ladder. All the rungs were filled. It took me about ten minutes to decide what to do. I walked out of Vallejo a Republican and into San Francisco a member of the Democracy. I've remained a Democrat, although Bill Higgins and I still close the door occasionally and strike a bargain if it suits our mutual purpose. A few minutes ago I said belonging to the Democracy was incidental. Now I hope you understand what I meant. Politics is the grandest game a man can play, but it isn't the party organizations that make it so. It's the power.'

The quiet declaration send a prickle along Carter's spine. The ruddy man with the sightless eyes could teach him what Willie Hearst had talked about such a long time ago. How to hold the reins. How to run others, rather than letting them run you. The thought of taking orders didn't appeal to him, but the advantages of the situation far outweighed that.

Eagerly, he said, 'I'd like to work for you, Mr Buckley. I got to know Willie Hearst. Willie once suggested that I think about being a politician.'

For some reason the atmosphere at the table had chilled in just a few seconds. 'Willie,' Gram repeated. 'You call him Willie?'

Baffled, Carter nodded. 'Everyone did.'

'They don't do it any more. Around the paper it's Mr Hearst or nothing. He's a stuck-up young snob.'

So that was it. Carter came to his friend's defence:

'A lot of people think he's snobbish, but it's really shyness—'

He stopped. The explanation changed nothing. In fact, Buckley had a scowl on his face:

'Mr Hearst and I try to cooperate because of his father's position in the party. On some things, we fully agree. He hates the Southern Pacific as much as I do. But newspaper publishers are a queer breed. Most of them are a menace to an established political organization. Young Hearst falls into that camp, I fear. He's a crusader. Dangerously unpredictable. If you were to work for me, I'd want to be sure of where your loyalties lie.'

Carter's hands tightened on the empty schooner. This was the test. He didn't dare fail it.

'You'd be sure, sir. They'd lie with you.'

'What if I asked you not to renew your friendship with Hearst?'

Carter let out his breath slowly. 'I'd refuse.'

'Hell,' Gram snorted. 'Why the hell are we arguing this? Hearst's so snotty these days, he probably wouldn't let someone as ordinary as Kent clean his privy.'

'Let him finish, Alex.'

'I don't have much more to say, Mr Buckley. If I work for you, I'll give you my loyalty, and my word that you have it. But if Willie Hearst can't trust me not to abandon him, how can you? Until he tells me otherwise, Willie's my friend.'

A silence. Ten seconds passed. Twenty. Suddenly the tension left Buckley's face:

'Good. That tells me all I need to know about you. We don't have to make an issue of Hearst. I've had no significant trouble with him so far.'

Carter relaxed a little. But if he landed a job, it was obvious that he'd be wise to play down his friendship. That much he was willing to do. What Gram said might also turn out to be true. Willie might not want to associate with him any longer. He didn't intend to

589

explore that question for some time; not until he could afford a decent suit of clothes, at least.

There was another moment of silence. Gram poured his fifth drink. Buckley's hands began to move in slow circles on the table top. He seemed to think out loud:

'I had in mind that you might join the push—'

'I've heard that word several times, sir. What's it mean?'

'The push is a gang of rockrollers, mostly. Roughnecks from south of Market Street.'

'What do they do?'

'Exactly what the name says. They supply a push when a push is necessary. They push some to the polling place, and they push others away. The push is important to me. I pay every member handsomely.'

The blind man paused, and though Carter knew he might be bringing a quick end to a relationship not even fully begun, he had no choice but to say:

'I don't want that kind of work, Mr Buckley. I don't want roughneck work.'

That didn't set well with Gram. He pulled his hand down from the bruise he was fingering. 'What's the matter? Not respectable enough for a Harvard boy? Or is it that Harvard boys don't have the belly for it?'

Buckley spoke softly but firmly:

'In view of the help Mr Kent gave us, Alex, those remarks are not only rude, they're stupid.'

Gram turned red. Carter looked him in the eye.

'Mr Gram, I don't mean to insult your position as Mr Buckley's bodyguard. But it's no use covering up how I feel. Violence only comes back to hurt the man who deals it out in the first place.'

'Oh?' Gram was sneering. 'You don't think it's ever necessary? It was necessary tonight.'

'No, it wasn't.'

'That son of a bitch Schmidt would have killed us all!'

Carter shook his head. It was hard to do, considering all he stood to lose.

'No,' he said. 'I had him ready to run. If you hadn't knifed him, you'd never have seen him again.'

Gram uttered a curt laugh. 'Sure of that, are you?'

'Pretty sure, yes.'

This time Buckley defended his employee:

'You may be right in this case, Mr Kent. But you aren't completely right. Violence is sometimes the only means to reach a desired end. There are times when everything else fails and you're left with no other choice.'

At that point Carter felt he'd lost the battle. But he still tried a tactical manoeuvre:

'Then if it's necessary, I don't want to be the one to do it. I'd hire it done, if need be, but I'd never involve myself. When I'm your age, Mr Buckley, I want to be walking around enjoying the rewards I've earned.'

Buckley raked a fingernail lightly along his lower lip. 'Hire it done, eh?'

'Yes.'

'For that answer and the ones about Hearst, I'll hire you, Mr Kent. Five dollars a month and all you can take from my free lunch counter.'

Gram swung sideways in his chair, disgusted. Buckley laid a hand on his sleeve.

'Alex, I can hear you fairly seething. Don't. Each of us has his own calling in this life. You needn't approve of Mr Kent's, or he of yours, so long as we all work together.'

Gram replied with a shrug which only pretended agreement, as did his muttered, 'Sure, boss. You're right.' Carter knew he'd alienated the bodyguard for good. He didn't care. Buckley was smiling.

'Boss,' Carter said, 'do you mind if I order another schooner of this steam beer?'

In a few minutes, Gram went off to his rooming house. Buckley called a bartender over and dictated a note to the night man at Hanratty's Livery. He gave the note to Carter.

'Come see me when you've had a good night's rest,' he said as he ushered Carter to the door on Bush Street. 'And don't worry about Alex. He's a fine fellow, but he has his limits. And you're right, he's in a bad trade. I expect both of us will outlive him. You needn't fear he'll cause you any trouble. He wants to keep on earning his high salary.'

The blind man gave Carter's arm an almost fatherly squeeze, but when he spoke it was without sentiment. 'I'm getting older, Mr Kent. I've been looking for a pupil in whom I could finally place some confidence. Perhaps I've found him. You'll get your hands dirty working for me. But if you're willing to do that within the limits we discussed – and if you're willing to take my guidance – you ought to go far. I'm impressed not only with your talent for blarney, but with your attitude in general. I think you have the makings of a remarkably successful politician.'

The cynicism grew heavier:

'Beg pardon. Public servant.'

He waved Carter into the fog like a doting parent.

3

Blissfully soft, the straw in the loft of the livery stable sank beneath Carter Kent. There was no heat in the building, and it stank of horse manure and all the garbage and human slops dumped in the alley running along one side. But those smells were transformed into perfume by his sudden good fortune. Even the stinking horse blanket given him by the grumpy night man smelled wonderful next to his nose.

He began to shiver again, alternately roasting and freezing. But he knew he'd get well, and work hard for Boss Buckley, and prosper. What if he did dirty his hands, as Buckley put it? Wealth could buy you a carload of soap. And then one day his hands would be holding the reins.

Carter was sure of that now. He was exhilarated; happy for the first time in months and months. San Francisco had been Amanda Kent's lucky town and it was going to be his. He was going to like its politics as much as he already liked its steam beer. And to think he'd jumped off that train in North Platte and wasted five whole years getting here!

With that thought he turned over and fell asleep.

CHAPTER XI

Puncher Martin

In Johnstown at eight o'clock next morning, the rain still showed no sign of slackening. Leo was awake and feeling fairly comfortable. Eleanor tucked the covers round him and went to the lobby to look for some rolls and coffee.

From the bottom of the stairs, she saw young Homer Hack cranking the handle of the lobby telephone. Seven hotel guests – all men, and all commercial travellers, she suspected – were sitting or standing near the clerk, anxious looks on their faces.

593

Hack spoke into the mouthpiece. Eleanor picked up her skirts to cross the lobby. The entire floor was submerged beneath a quarter inch of yellow-brown water.

As she approached, one of the men was saying, 'He's calling the central telephone office for a late report.'

On what? she wondered. The words *late report* had an ominous sound. Beyond the window, a wagon rumbled by, filled with a swaying pyramid of household goods. The street was covered with water; up to about ankle height, she judged by watching the wagon wheels.

'Thanks very much, Imogene,' young Hack said, ringing off. He turned back to the others. 'Most of the early shifts at Cambria's divisions were sent home. Too much water on the floors. Morning, Mrs Goldman.' He struggled to smile. 'Bet your friends wish they were back here.'

Politeness kept her from laughing at such a ridiculous statement. 'Why is that?' she said, her attention drawn to the hardware store across the street. A man who looked like the proprietor was frantically motioning at the door. One after another, four adolescent boys appeared, arms laden with merchandise which they carried away down the street. Then the owner went in, presumably for another load.

Hack's remark turned out to be far from ridiculous:

'Your friends went out on the New York Limited, didn't they?'

'That's right.'

'She's stalled up at the mountain summit. According to the telegraph report, there's some kind of obstruction on the tracks. Imogene at the telephone office just told me about it.'

'Better to be sitting up there than down here,' one of the guests complained. 'I walked over to the Little Conemaugh a while ago. Saw two dead heifers float

594

by. And more tree trunks than I could shake a stick at. If it doesn't stop raining, the mountain will slide right down on top of us.'

'I do think we should all move to the third floor,' Hack said. 'Can your husband do that, Mrs Goldman?'

'He isn't supposed to move for another five or six hours. In an emergency he'll do whatever's necessary.'

She started for the dining room, then saw that the gas fixtures hadn't been lit; the room was dark and empty.

'Isn't there any food this morning, Homer?'

Chagrined, he shook his head. 'The cook didn't show up.'

'Or the owner of this damned rat trap, either!' another of the men exclaimed. 'He's probably moving his family to high ground.'

'I expect that's pretty close to the truth,' Hack admitted. 'But we'll be fine on the top floor. I've unlocked all the rooms. Take any one you like.'

Panic began to gnaw at Eleanor then; panic fed by her weariness – she hadn't slept – and by the incessant rain. The young clerk started away, but she caught his arm:

'Is the dam all right?'

'Far as I know. At least there haven't been any reports of trouble.'

'Would you get a report like that?'

'Most likely. I've been calling the telephone company every few minutes. The central office is located in the same building as Western Union. Mrs Ogle who runs the Western Union office keeps the telephone girls advised of any dispatches from up near the dam. That's how Imogene knew about the Limited.'

'That makes me feel better. Thank you, Homer.'

'Surely, ma'am.'

The clerk gave her a smile meant to bolster her confidence, then splashed toward the lobby counter in rubber fishing boots Eleanor noticed for the first time. He stepped behind the counter and found an old coat and cap. Then he splashed back to the main door, stopping there to say:

'I'll trot over to Konig's Bakery and try to find a couple of loaves of bread. Meantime I'd appreciate it if all of you would go on upstairs.'

Eleanor returned to the room. Leo asked about the situation. She tried to sound more cheerful than she felt:

'There seems to be no danger from the dam. That nice young man who handles the desk is just suggesting we move to the top floor. I hate to make you do it, but I suppose we'd better be safe.'

'Absolutely.'

He swung sideways in bed and carefully lowered his left foot to the floor. 'This may sound stupid, but all at once I wish I knew how to swim.'

'Well, sir – ' Again she forced a smile. ' – if a rescue becomes necessary, you can count on me.' She bent and kissed the tip of his nose. 'Provided you're nice to me, never start your line before I finish mine, and never upstage me for as long as we both shall live.'

He laughed. 'Bargain.'

'Let me help you stand up—'

She took his arm. The sound of the rain on the window grew louder. She frowned as she went on:

'Lean on me and don't put weight on that leg – good, very good. A little effort and we'll be upstairs and perfectly safe until this blasted rain's over.'

But statements like that, from her own lips or from others, were beginning to have a decidedly false sound.

From the room they chose on the top floor, they were able to see more of the downtown area. Quite substantial-looking, Eleanor decided. Its many brick and stone buildings looked sturdy enough to withstand a severe storm as well as high floodwater.

Here and there she noticed abandoned trolley cars. Two young men on horseback went cantering through the streets, the hooves of their mounts shooting up geysers of water. Not a bad way to see the flooded downtown, she thought.

Now and again the rain let up a little. When it did, she could glimpse the towering stacks of the Cambria Iron Company's blast furnaces, and the cupolas of its Bessemer plant in the borough of Millville across the foaming water of the Little Conemaugh.

She kept the door of their room open. Some of the other guests drifted in from time to time, the storm having cemented everyone in the three-story building into enforced camaraderie. One of the salesmen staying at the Penn had been raised in Ferndale, just a short way down the Stonycreek. The man knew a lot about the area. The population of Johnstown was around twelve thousand, he told Eleanor in response to her question. She soon wished she hadn't asked it, because it brought a torrent of information she didn't really want, including the population of the nine surrounding boroughs and a capsule history of the development of Cambria Iron into an industrial complex producing everything from steel ingots and heavy track bolts to railroad car axles, ploughshares, and of course the world-famous Cambria Link barbed-wire.

She and Leo nodded politely at each new fact or statistic. That encouraged the man to describe the large

Pennsylvania Railroad marshalling yards up at East Conemaugh, between Johnstown and the dam. All at once Homer Hack appeared carrying three loaves of bread and a big blue enamel pot of lukewarm coffee; happily, the food ended the description of Johnstown.

As the morning dragged on, she found the room increasingly confining. She began to pace. Leo suggested she go off by herself for a bit – downstairs, if the lobby wasn't under water, or outside if the rain wasn't too fierce and Homer Hack would lend her the boots he was wearing.

'I don't need boots,' she said, eager to get away.

'The devil you don't. Your feet'll get soaked.'

She tied her cape around her shoulders and picked up her parasol. 'I don't care. These are old shoes, and I'd love some air. It doesn't seem to be raining so hard. I'll walk around the block.' She kissed his cheek and hurried downstairs, holding her skirts high as she crossed the lobby. Young Hack came out of the lightless dining room, shaking his head when he saw her leave.

The rain had indeed let up a little. Her parasol offered some protection and rain or not, she was glad to be outside. She put her head back, shut her eyes, and inhaled the damp air. How much better it smelled than the hotel, which already reeked of mould.

She tilted the parasol outward from her left shoulder and started walking, staying close to the buildings on her right. The overflow of the rivers swirled and gurgled through the street, completely covering the raised wooden sidewalk with a half inch of yellow water.

She reached the corner and started to turn right. Just then she saw men watching from the large window of a saloon on the corner diagonally opposite. Like targets in a shooting gallery, their heads were visible above gilt scrollwork on the lower half of the window. Weak lights shone inside. Evidently the owner had decided to remain open to serve those who had nothing to do but drink until the storm passed.

One man raised a stein, pointing her out to a companion. What caught and held her attention was another face at the opposite end of the window.

She stopped abruptly and stared. The man holding the stein assumed the attention was meant for him. He waggled the stein and grinned. The true object of her interest quickly stepped back out of sight. But the huge head, protruding eyes, and venomous scowl had been unmistakable.

Would it be possible to find a policeman this morning? She doubted it. For a moment she entertained the idea of charging into the saloon and accusing Kleinerman herself. But that wouldn't get her anywhere either. Suspicion wasn't evidence. There was no way to prove that the fat man had paid for the attack on Leo, even though they both believed it to be a certainty.

She couldn't forget the bulging, hate-filled eyes behind the saloon window. Shivering, she turned and resumed her walk. She fervently hoped she and Leo had seen the last of the man.

3

She planned to make a complete circuit of the block. At the next corner, three boys of twelve or thirteen were romping in the street. They slapped up handfuls of muddy water, shouting as they doused each other. As Eleanor went by one of them pointed:

'Hey, look. There's a lady who needs a bath.'

A second boy laughed. 'That she does. She ain't wet enough by half—' He whipped his right hand toward

599

the water. One slashing scoop and Eleanor was drenched.

Sputtering, she wiped her face. She was about to charge into the street and whack the young oafs with her parasol when she saw their attention shift to someone behind her; someone coming along the submerged sidewalk with swift, noisy strides.

'Get the hell away from her or I'll toss you all in the Little Conemaugh!'

The boys replied with some obscenities and a couple of feeble threats. One started to scoop up more water, but another grabbed his arm to stop him. The surly trio splashed away down the street while Eleanor turned to see her benefactor.

Her first glance explained why the boys had fled. The man was exceptionally tall; two or three inches over six feet, with wide shoulders and the roughened, ruddy complexion of someone who spent a lot of time outdoors. She noticed a paper sack tucked in the crook of the man's left arm. From the sack came the fragrant smell of coffee.

She judged the man to be thirty or a little older. His face was neither handsome nor ugly, yet it was instantly memorable and eminently likable.

His teeth were a bit irregular, and he showed a lot of them when he smiled. The ingenuous charm of that smile didn't quite jibe with the worldly look in his pale grey eyes. His brows were dark and thick, his hair the same. It curled out beneath an old fisherman's cap. He wore dark clothes; shabby but not dirty. Their drabness was relieved by a bright red railroad kerchief knotted around his neck.

He touched his cap. 'Sorry I swore, ma'am. Seemed the best way to get rid of those louts. Here – better step closer to the building.'

Flustered, she did so. She knew how silly she must look, strolling in the rain and soaked to boot.

600

She took the man's advice, moving to his side beneath a roof at the front of a tobacco shop. There, virtually no rain reached her. The shop was dark. A carved and painted Indian chief on the sidewalk was fastened to the wall by a chain around his throat.

After she caught her breath, she said, 'I appreciate your help – cusswords and all.'

The man grinned again, taking in her figure with one swift glance. The inspection was more admiring than lustful. Yet it made her uncomfortable, and not a little sad. She'd seen other men look at her the same way. She could never be flattered and let it go at that. Such looks always touched off feelings of insufficiency, and bitter speculation about what the men would think if they knew she was an incomplete woman. Acting a role in everyday life just the way she enacted roles for Daly—

The silence stretched out longer than she intended. Embarrassed, she touched her soaked sleeve:

'Those boys were boorish, but more water wouldn't have hurt me very much.'

He eyed the sky. 'If the object is staying dry, I'd say we both chose the wrong week to visit Johnstown.'

She wondered about his choice of a verb. How did he know she wasn't a resident?

The man was impeccably polite, and yet he continued to fluster her. All those irregular teeth somehow added up to a smile of great warmth. His grey eyes, capable of the anger she'd seen when he drove the boys off, were cordial now.

'I take it this isn't your home—' she began.

'Yes and no.' He leaned against the wooden Indian and gestured to the west. 'I was born up in the hills behind Sang Hollow.'

She wondered why in heaven's name she was interested. Perhaps it was because she'd run into so much hostility in Johnstown. It was good to talk to someone friendly. She found herself listening closely as he continued:

'I left town years ago, but I still have relatives here. My brother-in-law works for Cambria Iron. My sister's the one who sent me out for this.' He shook the sack of coffee. 'She and her husband have eight children. The whole caboodle's crowded into one of those tenements down by the river, the ones Cambria built – at a pretty fair profit, I might add. I have a brother with the company too. But he isn't married. He lives in a nice brick barracks the company maintains for bachelors. Cambria likes to watch over the morals of single employees.'

'It's obvious the company pretty well controls the town.'

Cynicism ruined the man's smile a moment. 'You might say that. Still, King Cambria can be a benevolent despot.'

Those words told her more about him. Obviously he hadn't come from a well-off family, but he'd educated himself. How and where? she wondered.

The man folded his arms and gazed past her, seeing something other than shuttered shops along a flooded street:

'Cambria really does take care of anyone who goes to work there. The company store over on Washington sells you everything from chewing tobacco to goose-down comforters. The Cambria Benefit Association pays you when you're laid up, and the Cambria Hospital takes you in when it's time for you to die. If you've been sufficiently loyal and had a spot of luck, there might even be some fellow members of the Cambria Club at your funeral. You have to rise pretty high in the company to get into the club, though. I suppose working for Cambria's fine for those who want that kind of existence. It takes most of the fear and insecurity out of living. But it takes away all the surprise and

602

joy, too. I couldn't tolerate it. That's nothing against my brother and sister, you understand.'

'No, of course not. What do you do, Mr—?'

'Martin. Cornelius Raphael Martin. My mother hung two fancy Christian names on me and I hate both of them. I use Rafe instead.

'When I was growing up here, I worked in the barbed-wire plant. But only long enough to save money for college out in Oberlin, Ohio. Oh, I don't mean the regular college – the fancy one. I went to Oberlin Business and Telegraph College. I'm a puncher. That's—'

'I know what it is,' she broke in. 'My father publishes a newspaper. You're a telegrapher.'

'Good for you. But I don't work for anyone on a regular basis. I'm a boomer. I travel a lot. I suppose a more honest word would be wander.'

'A gypsy of the key.' She smiled. 'I've heard my father use that expression, too.'

'Fits,' Martin nodded. 'Some of us can't hold jobs; and some don't want to. I like to think I'm in the second category but maybe I'm really in the first. I go wherever I can find work. Fill in when someone's sick, or when there's a lot of extra wordage to be sent. After a big fire, or a flood—'

'Let's hope you have no call for your services here.'

His smile faded. 'No, let's hope I don't. Those nabobs up at the Lake Conemaugh club have refused to repair the dam for too many years. Well – enough chatter. I expect you want to change into dry clothes. And if I don't deliver this coffee, my sister'll think I've drowned.'

She extended her hand, man-fashion. 'Thank you again for your help, Mr Martin.'

He held her hand longer than necessary:

'Pleasure, ma'am.'

'I can understand why you wouldn't want to consign

603

yourself to one company for life. I'm something of a boomer myself.'

He surprised her when he nodded and said, 'I know.'

'You do? How is that?'

She'd overlooked the obvious: 'I saw you at the Opera House last night. From the gallery. Best I could afford – but you were fine. Just fine. Your performance was a bonus I didn't expect when I came home for a visit, Miss Kent.'

'Thank you indeed. But Kent's only my stage name. My maiden name. My husband Leo Goldman is also in the company.'

'Goldman, Goldman – the fellow who played Snap!'

'You have a good memory.'

'I have a liking for good performances. Just like good women, there aren't enough of them in the world.' He paused before adding, 'Your husband did a splendid job, too.'

It struck her as something he felt obliged to say, but she didn't let on:

'I'll tell him, Mr Martin. He'll be pleased to hear it.'

'I knew you were married,' he said. 'I saw your rings when I chased the boys off. Well – goodbye again.'

One more touch of his cap, and he turned up his collar and started across the street, moving through the foot-deep water with long, strong strides.

Eleanor watched him go, wondering why she'd found the past few minutes so enjoyable. She was wet, she was cold – and despite a twinge of conscience, she was wishing she could have kept Martin talking longer. Why?

Shortly after he vanished round a corner, she found a possible explanation. It had nothing to do with a lack of love for her husband. She'd enjoyed herself with Martin because the encounter had been an inconsequential one; an agreeable conversation completely

604

free of the kind of pain and guilt that accompanied her relationship with Leo.

Then, staring into the rain, she saw Martin in her mind's eye and felt an emotion sharply at variance with her conclusion of a moment ago. She didn't want to acknowledge that emotion. It was disloyal; shamefully so—

She banished the feeling; turned back the way she'd come and soon reentered the room at the Penn.

'You were right, I shouldn't have gone out,' she said as she closed the door and pulled off her wet cape. 'It's raining hard again.'

From the bed, Leo said, 'I thought you'd bumped into old man Noah and decided to buy a ticket for the ark.'

She averted her face. Unexpectedly, Rafe Martin's smile had flashed into her thoughts.

She concentrated on getting into dry clothes. She was thankful she was enough of an actress to keep her guilt hidden. After everything else Leo had endured because of her, he didn't deserve so much as one moment of infidelity.

But she was giving him more than that; much more. She kept thinking of the stranger. She felt an undeniable attraction that was all the more pathetic because she was a sexual cripple.

The attraction, and her own shameful response, mystified and angered her, adding more tension to a day already too heavy with it.

CHAPTER XII

The Deluge

By noon the downtown area was completely flooded. Some streets could only be traversed by rowboat or improvised raft. Yesterday's farfetched jokes about swimming to the theatre and canoeing to the depot had become today's reality.

Black clouds pressed down overhead. The rain poured without letup. The two narrow rivers continued to spill over their banks upstream of their junction near the stone railroad bridge. One of the men who'd taken refuge on the top floor of the Penn worried about the possibility of water reaching the boilers and hearths of the Cambria mills. If that happened, he said, there could be catastrophic explosions.

From her window Eleanor watched people splashing along the submerged sidewalks and poling rafts down the centre of the street in an effort to reach higher ground. Others were still carrying merchandise out of stores. Here and there children romped in the water, laughing and beating at it with sticks. Why a parent would send a child out to play on such a day, Eleanor couldn't understand.

At a few minutes past one, Homer Hack looked in. He confirmed something Eleanor had suspected for a couple of hours:

'No more trains are running. I can't raise the central telephone office, either.'

From the bed where he was sprawled with a bedraggled copy of the previous day's *Johnstown Tribune*, Leo asked, 'How deep is the water in the lobby?'

'About three feet.'

'Good God.'

Suddenly, down the hall, a man began to weep:

'We're going to drown. We're going to drown and die in this goddamn place.'

Young Hack looked upset, and uncertain about what to do. Eleanor strode to the door and gently pushed him aside. Her hand white as she gripped the door-frame, she spoke to the sobbing man in a low, ferocious voice:

'Don't do that. It doesn't help you and it doesn't help the rest of us.'

The man – the same one who had described Johnstown at such length – was leaning against the wall to Eleanor's right. He looked at her with eyes reddened by tears:

'Then what will, lady?'

'Patience,' she said, suddenly aware of how tired and hungry she was. 'Just patience.'

Disbelieving, the man shook his head and turned away. Leo said, 'Patience and maybe a prayer – just in case the foundations of this fine hostelry aren't as strong as we assume they are.'

He sounded nonchalant. But his face was nearly as pale and strained as Eleanor's.

2

At four o'clock, a faint, shrill sound roused Eleanor from the chair where she'd been dozing. Men were running past the open door, but it was difficult to see much else because the hall was so dark; Homer Hack had shut down the main gas valve hours ago.

Leo had been resting too. Now his eyes flew open. Someone shouted, 'What's that crazy sound?'

Another voice: 'Train whistle.'

Like a faraway scream, the sound continued. 'The

whistle's tied down,' a third man exclaimed. 'Homer, get up on the roof and see what the devil's happening. Maybe there's been an accident in the Pennsy yards.'

Eleanor rushed to the door, waiting there until the young clerk clattered back down the stairs connecting the third floor hall with the roof. Just as he appeared, the whistle stopped.

Men crowded around the clerk, shouting questions. He shook his head:

'I couldn't see far enough. The rain's too heavy. And there's a lot of white smoke over in Woodvale. But I heard an explosion. Could be the wire works.'

'Bet you saw steam, not smoke,' said the man who'd been crying earlier. 'The boilers must have exploded. All that wreckage will be coming down the river into town – we have to get out of here. *We have to get out!*'

He shrieked the last, slumping against the wall with his arms clasped over his stomach. Childlike, he bent his head and sobbed.

'Maybe the worst is over – ' young Hack began. Jeers and humourless laughter greeted that, but he went on in a dogged way. 'No, no, I mean it. The rain's still coming down pretty hard, but the sky isn't so black. Go look for yourselves.'

It was the first hopeful word they'd heard all day. Men hurried past Eleanor and rushed up the stairs to the roof. Hack went with them.

She turned to the window of the little room. In the northwest, boiling black clouds were yielding to grey. Jubilant, she clapped her hands.

'Leo, I think Homer's right. The sky's definitely lighter.'

He pushed himself up from the bed. 'Let's go upstairs for a better view.' She started to protest but he cut in, 'Look, I've been flat on my back for the prescribed length of time. And we'll never reach

Altoona tonight, so it hardly matters whether I walk, limp, or crawl the rest of the day.'

Once on his feet, he slipped his left arm over her shoulder and she put her right arm round his waist. They made their way slowly along the corridor redolent of dust, leaking gas, and wet wool carpet.

In a moment, Eleanor felt almost lightheaded with relief. Above her, the oblong of the doorway at the head of the stairs changed from dark grey to pearl.

She helped Leo up the steps. All at once she heard sounds like claps of thunder. Then came another distant howling, deeper than the first. A factory whistle, perhaps. Just as she and Leo reached the top of the stairs, a man began to yell:

'Oh, my God. Look up there. She gave way. *The dam gave way!*'

Eleanor and her husband staggered into the rain and looked northeast along the steep-sided valley. Dimly at first, then with increasing clarity, she saw a sight so incredible, so numbing to the mind, that it made her bite down on her lip until blood ran.

Filling the valley from wall to wall, its noise like that of a runaway locomotive, a foaming rampart of water forty feet high was rushing down on Johnstown.

3

For a moment everyone on the roof stood motionless, numbed by the sight. From the streets below rose shrieks and shouts. One of the travelling men tugged out his gold turnip watch, as if compelled to fix the exact moment of the catastrophe:

'Nine minutes past four. No, make that ten.'

The man snapped the lid shut and put the watch back in his pocket. He had a curiously peaceful expression on his face. What could be done now? It seemed to say. Everyone shared his silent resignation for a few more seconds.

Then the calm shattered. The man who'd cried downstairs turned his back on the moving wall of water and ran, screaming and waving his arms. He failed to see the low roof coping. Still screaming, he stumbled, pitched into space and fell. But even such a calamity could only briefly draw Eleanor's and Leo's attention, so huge and horrifying was the wall of water travelling toward them at incredible speed.

4

A few short blasts of factory and train whistles were Johnstown's only warnings that up in the mountains, the earth dam had collapsed beneath the weight of the water behind it. The resulting floodtide, pouring down through nearly fourteen miles of river channel, had wiped out farms, homes, factories, and the Pennsylvania marshalling yards. Eleanor had no knowledge of all that. Yet, she was able to understand the enormity of the disaster by looking at the rolling mountain of water – and at what it contained.

Appearing and disappearing within it she saw broken timbers that once might have supported bridges or buildings; she saw a big steel boiler with a great hole blown in its side; lengths of iron cable unreeling from tumbling drums and lashing back and forth like fifty-foot whips; the front half of a locomotive thrusting up like a great whale's head, then sinking down again; the shingled roof of a house with two tiny human figures clinging to it; a log jam of uprooted telegraph poles; wheels from farm machinery; bricks, chunks of mortar, pieces of siding and – worst of all – once-animate things. She saw the bloated bodies of calves, dogs, and human beings. The bodies were borne along like limp dolls, sucked under by the current one moment, flung to the surface the next. There were scores of corpses in that incredible wall of water that shot off smoke and vapour as it inundated everything in its path.

The scene might have been conceived by a demented designer of theatrical effects. The water-wall lifted a young woman into view; she'd been impaled through her breastbone by an iron rail and hung dead halfway between the ends. Mercifully, rail and corpse soon sank from sight.

When the flood wall encountered the somewhat greater resistance of the larger buildings downtown, the water appeared to split. One branch rushed along the Little Conemaugh toward the stone railroad bridge; the other surged into the business district. Eleanor was stupefied with terror. The water was now only a few blocks from the hotel. All over downtown Johnstown, on rooftops and in the upper windows of buildings such as the Hulbert House, people stared at the flood wall and knew, as she did, that escape was impossible.

The earth seemed to rumble and shake as the water shattered building after building and swallowed the remains. The flood wall was so high, nothing was visible behind it but a few hilltops and the sky.

One of the travelling men cried, 'Run – run, all of you!' She was tempted to break into hysterical laughter. Run where? And to what purpose, with the churning, foaming apocalypse sweeping down, indiscriminately tossing on its forward crest half a barn, three Pullman cars, a dozen bodies; crushing houses and substantial buildings and grinding them together into wreckage as it roared on—

Homer Hack had grown befuddled. He was staggering toward the edge of the roof where the other man had plunged off. The sight of the dazed clerk walking to his death jolted Eleanor back to her senses.

But it was Leo who moved first. Despite his injured

leg, he lunged and pulled the clerk back from the coping just a step away:

'This way, Homer! You can't stay up here—'

Hack turned his rain-drenched face toward Leo. 'What? What's that?' The young man's eyes were vacant, his mind no longer functioning coherently. Leo grimaced at Eleanor and half-dragged, half-carried the clerk toward the head of the stairs.

By the time Leo got there, Eleanor was already shoving frightened men down the steps into the darkness: 'Hurry, you've got to hurry—'

She could barely be heard. She looked back, and the water seemed to tower to the top of the sky. One calm question flashed into her mind:

I wonder if dying hurts very much.

'Get in there!' Leo shouted, pushing her. She stumbled down the stairs, her husband and Hack right behind her.

All at once Leo lost his footing. He came crashing into her from above as the flood noise peaked, loud as a thousand trains at full throttle. The water struck the hotel and tore it whole from its foundations.

CHAPTER XIII

Flood Tide

An instant after Leo tumbled against her, Eleanor heard the incredible sound of the flood crest striking the hotel. The building immediately began to tilt, pushed from its foundations by the enormous force of the water. Simultaneously, a great yellow wave came crashing down the stairway from the roof to the light-less hall.

'Hang onto me, Leo!'

He wrapped his arms around her waist as the wave thundered over them, hurled them against a wall, and receded for a few seconds. The building kept tilting.

The water was knee high, then breast high a moment later. Men screamed, waved their arms, sank from sight. Eleanor saw a flood-borne length of steel cable flick out and touch young Homer Hack's neck, instantly decapitating him.

The moment was forever seared into her mind: the boy's head sailing past, mouth and eyes agape. Blood from the severed neck pattered on her hair, her cheeks—

'Don't let go, Leo,' she screamed as the ceiling collapsed and the walls burst apart, driven outward and shattered by the water that engulfed the hotel and everyone inside.

2

It took ten minutes for the wall of water to rage through Johnstown, smashing a three-block-wide path to the point of land where the rivers met. The flood demolished building after building, tearing them apart and mingling the debris with that from further up the valley.

In those ten minutes, courage and resourcefulness had little to do with determining who lived and who died. Some of the bravest perished; some of the most cowardly lived. Most of those who did survive the initial disaster weren't even aware of what happened to them immediately after the flood crest struck.

That was the case with the Goldmans. When Eleanor came to her senses, she and Leo were clinging to the top of a four-drawer bureau which bobbed in fast-moving water. Rain and Homer Hack's blood were trickling down her cheeks. The bodice and skirt of her dress were in shreds. Her shoulders ached from clutching the bureau, which had a familiar look.

Hotel furniture, that's what it was. The flood had evidently swept the Goldmans into their room or one like it. They must have grabbed hold of the first solid object they could find. She didn't remember.

She looked over her shoulder. The hotel was gone, and – God above – half the downtown as well. In the water she saw cupolas of houses, roofs of Pullman cars, the horns of cows, and pieces of lumber to which men, women and children clung. Some of the survivors were calm but a great many of them were screaming.

Hanging onto the other side of the bureau, Leo gasped:

'Are you all right?'

'I – ' She struggled for breath. 'I'm alive. That's more than I expected when the water hit.'

He gulped air and bobbed his head in agreement, trying hard to conceal his terror of the water.

3

The current spun the bureau round and round. But the momentum seemed to be slowing. Eleanor heard a cry of alarm from nearby. Leo pointed past her left shoulder. She twisted her head till her neck ached and saw a man riding a door as if it were a raft. He cradled an infant in his arms. The man had called for help because the capricious current was rushing the door straight toward the brick wall of a half-submerged building.

Eleanor kicked and paddled, clinging to the bureau and trying to reach the man at the same time. It was no use. The man's face drained of colour as the brick wall loomed.

Without warning, the gable of a sunken house rose from the yellow water like a ship's prow. The steeply pitched roof pressed upward from beneath the door, tipped it vertically, and hurled the man and the child against the brick wall. The gable pressed in from behind, crushing them.

When the current shifted the section of the roof away from the wall, Eleanor saw a red paste mingled with scraps of clothing on the bricks. She vomited in the water.

'Look,' Leo exclaimed a moment later, pointing past the site of horror she'd just witnessed. 'Everything's piling up at the stone bridge. Creating a dam—'

She turned again, nearly losing her hold on the bureau. She saw sections of buildings being driven against the arches of the railroad bridge by the water whose height she judged to be fifteen or twenty feet above the Johnstown streets. More timbers, portions of houses, and chunks of wreckage impossible to identify were accumulating behind the bridge like a great log jam. Here and there the Goldmans spied people clinging to the debris, and calling frantically to others on the hillsides; the lucky ones who'd reached high ground. But far worse than the cries of the survivors in the water were the moans and shrieks of people imprisoned within partially sunken buildings.

'Leo – ' Eleanor kicked as hard as she could, trying to guide the bureau. Her effort was rewarded. The bureau turned a hundred and eighty degrees, then came to rest in a patch of relatively quiet water. ' – we've got to do something. If we're carried down to that jam, this bureau will break up like matchwood.'

'Where do you propose that we go? We can't reach the shore, the current's too strong.'

As he gasped the words, he kept blinking. Heavy

spray blew across the surface of the water. Or perhaps it wasn't spray but rain mingled with smoke; there was no way to be sure. But it added a murky distortion to an already unbelievable scene.

And over it all, unforgettable as the sight of Homer Hack's decapitated head, there were the cries:

'*Help us. Help us down here!*'

'*My grandfather's dying and we can't get out—*'

'*We're trapped in the attic with the red shingles. Can anyone see it? IS ANYONE OUT THERE?*'

Before Eleanor could answer Leo's question, her hand slipped off the bureau a second time. Terrified, she caught the top, raking her palm on one of the metal drawer pulls as she did so. Threads of blood trailed from her wrist into the water. It was of no importance; the current had caught the bureau and was moving it swiftly again – straight towards the pileup of wreckage at the bridge.

Between the bureau and the bridge, she suddenly saw something that offered hope. A half-sunken Pullman car formed a rampart straight ahead of them. The upper halves of its windows were visible above the water. Most of the glass was gone, but not all. Sharp fragments remained in almost every frame—

'We must get on the roof of that car,' she shouted. But Leo saw the same danger she did. A powerful undercurrent was tugging at them. It might drag them down and hurl them through one of the shattered windows. They could be torn apart on the jagged glass—

Still, the car was their only hope. Leo saw that:

'All right. Let's try.'

4

Vision was difficult because of the spuming water and the gloom of the day. It couldn't have been much past four, but the sky was dark and growing darker. Once more the bureau revolved in a full circle. As it turned, Eleanor saw some people struggling across floating rooftops and jumping yard-wide gaps between them, thus working their way toward buildings left standing near solid ground at one side of the main flood channel. Those people were no more than half a block from the Goldmans, but because of the current, Eleanor and Leo had no chance of reaching safety in the same way.

A glance at her husband's face told her how frightened he was. This was turbulent, dangerous water. Deep water. Since Leo couldn't swim it was up to her to make certain he reached the roof of the Pullman car.

They were only about fifteen feet from the car now. A whimsical current sped them toward it more quickly. For the moment, Eleanor's side of the bureau was closest to it.

She could feel the current dragging at her skirt and undergarments as the bureau hurtled on. She gauged the narrowing distance carefully. At the critical moment, she used all her strength to lift herself to the top of the bureau. She clung there precariously, praying the bureau wouldn't revolve again. If it did, Leo would be trapped between the side and the car.

They were lucky. Her side thumped the edge of the roof. The impact was followed by a prolonged cracking sound. 'It's breaking apart!' Leo cried.

Eleanor was already clambering from the bureau to the more substantial, if slippery, top of the Pullman car. She dropped onto her stomach, heedless of the way the impact hurt her breasts. She clung to the edge of the roof with one hand and shot her other one out over the water. The bureau disintegrated.

'*Leo!*'

He was already sinking. She leaned out. His wet fingers touched hers, then slipped away.

He kicked frantically, not knowing how to propel himself toward her. Three inches separated their outstretched hands.

Then four.

Five—

'Paddle, Leo! Cup your hands and pull them down to your sides!'

He understood; tried it; made enough headway to reach her wrist, seize it and pull himself to the car. Once he'd taken hold of the roof, he was able to kick against the wall below and throw one knee up and over. She slid backward to give him room.

Panting, he clambered to safety. Her arm hurt ferociously because he'd pulled so hard. That didn't matter, though. Nothing mattered except the miracle of their survival.

The car seemed buoyant. Or perhaps it was supported from below by other wreckage. Half a dozen boards went floating by, borne toward the debris at the bridge. The rain continued to fall in the near-darkness. But at least they had a respite; a few moments in which to draw air into burning lungs, then crawl toward one another and take comfort in each other's arms. She buried her cheek against his torn and sodden shirt.

'My God, Leo, it's beyond belief. It's like hell without the fires.'

But those were soon to come.

They rested five minutes. The screams and entreaties continued. The rain fell and the remaining light faded.

The Pullman car had already become part of the jam of debris building behind the upstream side of the bridge. Other wreckage was collecting there: gutted locomotives, twisted rails, uprooted trees. Some of the debris was literally bound together by steel cable and barbed wire freakishly tightened by the flood.

Some open water remained at one end of the car. The entire upper story of a house floated into the space. Just as the house bumped gently against the car, the Goldmans looked at one another:

'Voices?'

'I heard them too,' Leo said, scrambling to his feet and helping her up. In the panic of the last hour he had not given a thought to his injured leg.

As they rushed toward the house the voices grew quite distinct. A man's, a woman's, and those of several children – all pleading for help.

A gable with horizontal siding was jammed against the end of the car. Leo leaned close to it and called, 'We hear you. We'll get you out of there. Just hold on.'

He began to tear at the siding, but the nails had been well driven. Eleanor added her effort to his. Painful though it was, they managed to squeeze their fingertips beneath one length of siding. Just then something beneath the house collapsed. The gable tilted away from the car, and just as abruptly stopped. If it tilted a few more feet, those inside would find it impossible to jump to safety.

Leo's face dripped with sweat and rain. She saw blood on his fingers where they were wedged beneath the tight-fitting siding. 'Pull, Eleanor!' Together they heaved backwards. Then again. And a third time.

On the fourth try, nails wrenched with a metallic screech. The end of the board stood out from the wall about two inches.

Face close to the gable, Leo shouted, 'Listen to me. Can you see any light?'

The man's voice:

'I can see some between the studding. Not much.'

'Well, push against the plank where you see it. All of you push. Hurry. Your house may go down any minute.'

The man inside issued rapid orders. Soon a series of blows drove the length of siding outward another four inches. With Leo and Eleanor pulling at the same time, the plank abruptly cracked in the middle.

The sudden breaking of the wood sent Eleanor skidding wildly backwards. In a panic, Leo saw that if she didn't regain her balance, she'd tumble into the water. He knew she could swim but that would do her little good. Behind her, at the spot where she would fall, floating strands of barbed wire waited to slash and entangle her.

CHAPTER XIV

Fire in the Water

The strength and control required for stage movement served Leo well. He lunged forward as if he were Mercutio duelling in front of the footlights, catching Eleanor an instant before she pitched into the water.

She rested against him for a moment. He could feel

her heartbeat through his soaked shirt. 'Don't worry,' she gasped, 'I'm all right – ' Her eyes widened as she saw something beyond his shoulder. *'The house is going!'*

The Goldmans rushed back to the end of the car. The people inside had battered another board halfway off. Leo wrenched it loose and flung it into the water. With frantic pushes and pulls, two more were removed – enough to create an opening between two studs; an opening in which the members of the family could brace themselves before jumping to the Pullman car.

In the gloom, Eleanor and Leo made out five people – husband, wife, two small boys, and a girl. The girl might have been twelve, the youngest boy seven or eight.

One by one they leaped to safety. Just as the last one, the smallest boy, prepared to jump, the house gave another precipitous lurch. The man shouted for his son to hurry.

The boy jumped, barely clearing the strip of water that widened suddenly as the house fell away from the car. The entire upper story quickly sank from sight.

The boy snuggled in his father's arms, frightened but trying to smile. 'Fine catch, Papa.'

The father was a stout man with a pasty complexion. Though short of breath, he managed to say to Leo, 'Rasmussen's the name, Daniel Rasmussen. You saved our lives. There are no windows in that attic. How can I possibly express—'

He was interrupted by a heavy clanging sound. It reverberated across the wreckage and the great expanse of dammed flood water stretching from hillside to hillside. Rasmussen's wife, a small, plain-faced woman, looked upward with a stricken expression. When the mournful bell rang a second time, she burst into tears.

'That's our church. The Lutheran church. It's still

standing. Why couldn't the church have gone and Mama's house been spared! Why, Daniel!'

'Loretta, you don't know that your mother's house is gone.'

'She's dead. I know she's dead. I should have insisted she move in with us but I didn't and now she's dead, that's why the bell's ringing—'

Clang! Echoes of the third note rolled across the valley of the Conemaugh. There was something jarring about a church bell striking the hour in the midst of such carnage. It rang five o'clock quite as if life in Johnstown was proceeding normally. The bell should have been tolling for the dead. How many so far? Eleanor wondered. Hundreds? Thousands, more likely.

She noticed Leo watching her, and understood his look of concern. Rasmussen's wife was close to hysteria, and Leo wanted Eleanor to help if she could. She moved toward the small woman:

'I know how you must feel, Mrs Rasmussen. But perhaps your mother is all right, and—'

The woman flung off the arm placed around her shoulders. 'Don't touch me. Mama's dead.'

'Even if that's true, it isn't your fault. It's no one's faul—'

'Yes, it is! It's Daniel's. I pleaded with him to find a job with another railroad, so we could leave Johnstown and take Mama with us. I begged him. He wouldn't do it. He was wedded to the Pennsylvania, and to this town. For years people have been saying the dam was weak. Now Mama's dead and it's his fault.'

Loose hair hanging in her eyes, she glared at her husband. Eleanor was eerily reminded of Margaret Kent. Bewildered and frightened, the Rasmussen children watched their mother lurch to the other end of the car where she stood with her back to them, crying.

Eleanor knew she'd better leave the woman for a little while. She was walking back to Leo, when her expression suddenly brightened.

'Look over toward the bank, Leo. That way.' She pointed in a direction she thought was east. 'The debris is almost solid from here to the shore. There are some people crossing it right now.'

His eyes followed her outstretched hand as it pointed upstream about a quarter of a mile. There, two men and a woman were gingerly stepping from one piece of floating wreckage to the next. Sometimes a plank or a part of a building sank six or eight inches beneath them. They were forced to proceed with great caution. But while the Goldmans watched, the three people travelled another hundred feet and one by one jumped to solid ground. Outstretched hands helped them up the hillside in the dusk.

Leo turned to Rasmussen. 'See how they did that? I think we should try it.'

Rasmussen's nod was emphatic. 'I agree. I don't want to stay out here when it's dark. Not if we can possibly reach the bank –' For a moment he'd managed a touch of enthusiasm. It vanished as his gaze returned to his wife. She was still standing motionless, head down, at the other end of the car. 'I'm not sure Lorette can make it, though.'

Leo nodded. 'We'll wait a little. Perhaps she'll calm down.'

'I'll see what I can do,' Rasmussen said. He put his young son down next to Eleanor and walked towards his wife.

The level of the water dammed by the wreckage was

falling, Eleanor noticed. Falling very slowly, but definitely falling. Upstream, another building toppled with a grinding crash. The noise was becoming familiar; every few minutes, something collapsed. The human cries and groans remained almost constant.

Rasmussen's younger son watched his mother and father, tears shining in his eyes. Eleanor stepped in front of the boy to hide the sight of his parents. Then she slipped her arm round the boy's shoulder and drew him to her side. The child huddled against her, grateful for the gentle fingers patting him to soothe away the horror of this day.

As if that could be done. As if those who had survived could ever forget the experience. Again her mind showed her the moment in which Homer Hack's severed head went sailing past, spouting blood—

Tears came to her eyes. She rubbed them away. Drove the memory from her mind. She mustn't break down. Mustn't feel sorry for herself. She and Leo had survived. Just as important, they were in the open. Scores of others were still trapped in sunken houses and buildings, crying for help that might never come.

Though cold and frightened, she struggled to keep a positive frame of mind. If they could reach shore, there'd be plenty of work to be done. She must be part of it. Only work, movement, activity – the effort to help others – would stave off the hysteria lurking at the edge of her mind. She felt no contempt for Loretta Rasmussen. She understood exactly how she felt.

Mrs Rasmussen's overwrought state proved a formidable obstacle to their plan to set out across the dam of wreckage. Her husband spent almost half an hour trying to calm her with words and clumsy caresses. Each time he touched her, she recoiled and demanded that he leave her alone. Over and over, she accused him:

624

'We should have moved, Daniel. We should have moved years ago. My mother died because of you.'

Defeated, the man finally trudged back to Leo, who was sitting on the roof, resting.

'No use,' Rasmussen said. 'She won't listen, and she won't go.'

'Then we'd better force her.'

'Force—?'

Leo's mouth had a hard look as he nodded. 'What other choice do we have? It's almost dark. Before long we won't be able to see our way to—'

There was a sudden boom. A geyser of flame shot from the water a hundred yards west of the car. The Rasmussen boy burrowed against Eleanor as the pillar of fire rose skywards, then spread laterally. The flame reached a floating tank car, ate through the wooden exterior, heated the steel inner shell – and the car exploded like a hundred cannons fired together.

All of them were spattered by drops of scalding water thrown by the explosion; they felt the fire's intense heat, too. Eleanor's mind could hardly accept this latest shock:

'It isn't possible for fire to ignite in *water*—'

'I'm afraid it is, under certain circumstances,' Rasmussen said. 'The Pennsylvania carried a good many shipments of lime, and lime's combustible when it's slaked with water. That must have been the first explosion. I think the tank car contained crude oil.'

Flames shimmered in Leo's dark eyes. 'Well, I don't give a damn about the cause. I don't propose to stay here and be roasted. Get your wife.'

'Let me get her,' Eleanor said, hurrying down the length of the car. Behind her, she heard the fire roaring as it spread to floating debris. She glanced back and saw the upper floor of a house being consumed. Within the cherry-coloured flames, black stick figures ran to and fro, screaming as they were incinerated.

625

Eleanor took Mrs Rasmussen's arm. 'We're leaving. You must come with us.'

'*No!*' The sobbing woman clawed Eleanor's wrist and jerked away. The violent motion nearly toppled her into the water. But Eleanor caught her. She slapped the woman's face twice, as hard as she could.

'Your husband won't leave without you – and we're not going to allow three children to die because of you. You're alive. Be grateful and come along!'

She gave the woman a sharp tug. Together with the slaps, that seemed to jolt her into a semblance of self-control. She didn't resist when Eleanor pushed her toward the others.

Leo was showing Rasmussen a possible route to shore. It took them away from the spreading fire, and with luck would bring them to the hillside after they worked their way between two housetops and across a sizable area of lumber and steel cable. By ones and twos, people were carefully crossing that mass of floating material.

'I'll go first to test the footing,' Leo said. 'Each of you take charge of one of the children. Whatever happens, don't let go of them.'

Eleanor wanted to fling her arms around her husband's neck and kiss him. Fearful as he surely was about the water they were about to traverse, and despite the injury to his leg, he was yet willing to take the lead. And because he was a superb actor, none of the Rasmussens knew how he felt. In fact he seemed to exude confidence – a deliberate attempt to bolster theirs, she was sure.

Leo pushed hair out of his eyes and threw her a swift look. The others saw the affection in it; she saw the anxiety. She closed her eyes a moment to tell him she loved him and understood his fear.

He visually measured the distance to the next roof. About three and a half feet. In one easy jump he cleared the flame-reddened water. The roof sank a few inches but bobbed up immediately.

Leo turned, widened his stance to brace himself, held out his arms and smiled a dazzling smile:

'Send that first youngster over. This'll be a picnic. We'll be on dry land in ten minutes.'

In that moment, she loved him more than she ever had. Daniel Rasmussen caught Leo's spirit and did his best to convey confidence as he swung his daughter across the water into Leo's strong hands.

3

The way was treacherous but they made progress in spite of it. Leo's prediction wasn't far off the mark. In ten minutes, all that remained between the little band and the hillside was about a hundred feet of lumber and debris entangled with wire, the whole none too firm, Leo warned as he stepped back from testing it. On the far side, four other people were scrambling to shore while a crowd of watchers called encouragement. To the right, a man was working his way across the jam on a path that would intersect theirs.

'Ready?' Leo motioned the others forward.

They'd crossed twenty feet of wreckage when Eleanor caught her breath. The man she'd noticed was just a few feet from them now. Instantly, she recognized his huge head. So did Leo.

The recognition was mutual:

'Well, well, look at this. The sheeny.'

The fat man didn't seem the least intimidated by the people accompanying the Goldmans. Scowling, he took a step toward Leo. His right foot slid off a wet, tilting plank but he recovered and planted himself directly in front of Eleanor's husband. The left side of the man's face was cut open; he'd bled all over the front of his suit. He looked less than rational, but that was no wonder, given his temperament and the events of the last few hours.

Leo spoke as if he were dealing with a vexing child:

'I'd like to settle with you, Kleinerman, if that's your name. These people are more important. Move aside and let us pass.'

Something ugly glittered in the protruding eyes. The man spread his feet, steadying himself on the plank. 'Not just yet, sheeny. Not until I'm good and ready.'

Leo went rigid. But he was too sensible to involve himself in a fight. With a disgusted shake of his head, he stepped sideways to another board:

'Then we'll go around, you damn fool.'

'Not unless I say so!' Kleinerman fisted his right hand and shot a weak punch at Leo's stomach. The fat man's sudden change of position threw him off balance. He toppled forward, knocking Leo into the water with a great splash.

Panicked, Eleanor started forward. The Rasmussens didn't mean to impede her, but they all seemed to be in her way. And it was impossible to move quickly on the mud-slimed mass of wood and wire.

She heard Leo kicking and sputtering. Saw his head bobbing above the red-lit water. If she could reach him, she could easily pull him out. But her foot missed a board and slid down into a knot of steel cable, just as Kleinerman picked up a length of dripping two-by-four and swung it hard against Leo's skull.

She cried his name but the cry was lost as another building roared down into ruin. Leo sank from sight.

'Oh my God, help him, help the poor man!' Rasmussen shouted. Eleanor twisted back and forth, trying to free her leg. The cable's rough surface ripped her underskirt and raked her calf. Blood ran into her shoes as she extricated herself and struggled to the spot where Leo had gone down.

People on shore were shouting loudly; pointing and waving. Two had even leaped into the wreckage. Kleinerman turned and attempted to run. He slipped and pitched head first into the water, flailing his arms and wailing like a child:

'Jesus Christ, help me! I can't swim—'

Eleanor's eyes shone with hate. *'Neither can he!'*

She flung herself to her knees on a big piece of siding that sank four inches under her weight. A huge bloodstain showed on her petticoat now. She thrust her hands into the water up to the wrists, then to the elbows, crying Leo's name again and again. Tears began to spill down her face.

It gave her no satisfaction to see Kleinerman's plight. The harder he kicked, the faster he sank. His eyes bulged as he choked and went down a second time.

Eleanor didn't care whether the man lived or drowned; she only cared about her husband. Even half conscious from Kleinerman's blow, he should have floated to the surface by now. Had he got trapped down there? Had he become too frightened and somehow entangled himself in the debris? The water gleaming with firelight returned no answers.

Against her back she felt the heat of the spreading flames. But her hands were cold as she groped below the surface. Suddenly she touched something. Human hair, she thought.

Hope lighting her face, she called her husband's name again.

She closed her hands—

Nothing there.

Kleinerman disappeared, the water bubbling for a moment after it closed over his head. The last bubbles burst. Someone seized her shoulders from behind. It was Rasmussen:

'It's too late.'

'No.'

'Yes, it is, he's gone.'

'*No.*'

'I tell you he's gone. You must be careful or you'll drown too.'

She writhed in Rasmussen's grip, screaming at the water:

'Leo. *Leo!*'

Patterns of reflected firelight shone and shifted at her feet. Suddenly strength drained out of her. Limp, she leaned against Rasmussen. She'd reached a point at which it was impossible to feel more shock or grief, because the load had already become unbearable. The universe no longer contained any rationality; the flood denied all rationality, and so did Leo's death.

He had died because he was hated.

Was hated because he was a Jew.

Was a Jew by accident of birth—

And he'd died in a country in which accident of birth supposedly made no difference. Her country's self-proclaimed idealism was a cruel shame, it was a—

It was a—

Her overburdened mind went blank, as swiftly as if a sponge had suddenly been swept across a slate. She didn't remember being lifted gently; supported; guided toward shore by Rasmussen and his younger son. On shore, people were still yelling encouragement.

She seemed calm as she stepped on solid ground. At

Rasmussen's behest, half a dozen men filed out onto the wreckage to take up the all but hopeless search for the bodies of the drowned men. Eleanor didn't notice.

Her wet hair gleamed with red highlights, as did her cheeks. The dampness there could have been the rain, not tears. Her face was composed; eerily so.

But memory was coming back.

She stood motionless. Inside, she was in turmoil. Over and over, she heard accusations. Not accusations about responsibility for Leo's death. Her mind chose something else to hurl at her in silent condemnation:

You never told him why you hurt every time he loved you.

You never had the courage.

He died thinking it was his fault, you bitch, you worthless bitch.

CHAPTER XV

Confession

A temporary aid station had been set up in a large brick house two hundred yards up the hill from the place where Eleanor and the Rasmussens had clambered to shore. Candles burned in all the first floor rooms. The owner's small supply of blankets had been laid out for shivering survivors of the flood.

The Rasmussens didn't linger at the house. Mrs Rasmussen was still not herself; her husband wanted to take her to a friend's cottage higher in the hills. He said he felt bad about leaving, especially in view of Leo's death, but Eleanor urged him to go, saying it wasn't necessary for anyone to keep her company.

'Besides, many people need help far more than I do, Mr Rasmussen. I want to keep busy here.'

Because if I don't, I'll break down.

She didn't admit that to Rasmussen. After a few more words of condolence, sincerely meant but awkwardly delivered, he shepherded his wife and children into the darkness.

Eleanor went straight to the kitchen. There she helped an elderly black woman prepare and cook a watery vegetable soup. When the soup was done, Eleanor filled crockery bowls, pewter mugs, anything she could find, and served those huddling in blankets throughout the candle-lit house.

The survivors were all citizens of Johnstown – young and elderly; individuals and entire families. A good many of them cried unconsolably; now and then one wailed a loved one's name. The crying helped Eleanor keep her own emotions under control. Although Leo was dead, and rage and guilt and sorrow were battering her mind, she vowed she wouldn't weep. When she mourned, it would be in private. Meantime, there was work to be done.

The rain fell steadily. Every half hour or so, Eleanor stepped out on the wide front porch for a breath of air. Her face was filthy. She wore an old blouse the grey-haired woman of the house had given her. The blouse was threadbare, but at least it covered her arms and breasts. Her skirt showed three great rips, and bedraggled lace beneath.

Well back from the dripping eaves, an oil lamp had been set on a wooden bench. The lamp cast long, distorted shadows of the tired men who continued to bring the living and the dead to the house. The living were taken inside, the dead put on the wet lawn beyond the end of the porch. Fifteen or twenty corpses were already laid in rows out there. Eleanor heard one man say bodies kept surfacing down at the water's edge. Perhaps she'd find Leo before the night was over.

From the porch she could look down on the panorama of the Conemaugh Valley. The waters hadn't receded very far. A vast, debris-filled lake remained behind the stone bridge. Throughout that debris fires burned. She still found it difficult to accept the reality of all she saw.

A few courageous men had located and launched some rowboats. She could see the boats moving near half-submerged rooftops as the search for survivors continued. Many people saved themselves, working their way ashore as she and the Rasmussens had done.

The firelight revealed a few buildings still intact downtown. One was a substantial structure with three stories visible above the water. She asked about the building. A man told her it was called Alma Hall, and was located on Main Street. From the building's dark interior, mournful cries drifted through the downpour.

Gradually, those arriving with the injured added small pieces of information to create a crude mosaic of the disaster. Johnstown was cut off from the outside world. The telegraph lines were down. Railroad tracks had been swept away, though for how great a distance in either direction, no one could say.

Of more than thirty doctors who practised in the city, five to ten couldn't be located; the exact number depended on who was talking. But it was a certainty that most of the medical supplies and blankets in the boroughs along the river had been swept away.

The police force had ceased to exist. The gas and electric plants were in ruins, leaving Johnstown dark except for candlelight or the light from the burning debris. One man claimed two or three thousand survivors had gathered on another hill nearby. But it seemed clear that as many, or more, had been trapped in the city and drowned. The valley at which Eleanor gazed was quite literally a valley of the dead and those who grieved for the dead. The rain continued to fall. The fires kept burning. The screaming never stopped.

2

About three in the morning, she steeled herself to go down to the side lawn. The rain had let up a little. By the light of the lamp on the porch, she examined the bodies covered by pieces of sodden bedding. She knew the search was almost certainly futile. Yet she lifted the sheets or comforters one by one, hunting for Leo.

She didn't find him.

As she turned back toward the house, she felt something wet and warm on her left leg. She paid little attention. The sight of so many white, lifeless faces had unnerved her. Hysteria was threatening her again.

She fought it; pushed it away as though it were an enemy with a tangible form. She climbed to the porch. Another half dozen men arrived. Three carried children in their arms. The rest supported exhausted adults. Eleanor thought she recognized one of the men but he had gone into the house before she could be sure.

She leaned against a porch pillar. Behind her, through an open window of the music room, candlelight showed a toothless old man praying on his knees. Further back in the house, a woman began to sing 'Rock of Ages' in a weak soprano voice.

The grief and guilt and anger lapped at her mind like rising water. She rested her forehead against the pillar; clenched her fist; whispered:

'Leo. *Leo*—'

She reminded herself that they needed her inside. She mustn't break down. She *would* not—

She turned sharply, aware that someone had spoken

634

to her. But her attention was concentrated on the way her leg felt under layers of damp clothing. Her leg was wet and all at once she understood why. Tonight, on top of everything else, her own body had betrayed her.

'Dear God – not that too,' she said half-aloud, pressing her palms against her skirt as if to hide any telltale sign. There was none. No one would have taken much notice if there were. But to Eleanor it was the final cruelty of whatever malignant power had arranged the events of the last twenty-four hours; a cruelty her battered mind could barely accept.

A shadow bent across her line of sight. The man who'd spoken. A tall man with mud on his cheeks. Rain shone in his curly hair. There was concern in his pale eyes as he said:

'Mrs Goldman? It is you, isn't it? I thought I recognized you when I brought that youngster into the house.'

The man pulled up the red bandana; wiped his chin and his mouth. The neckerchief triggered her lagging memory:

'Mr Martin—'

'Are you all right?'

'Yes.'

'And your husband—?'

'No.' She turned toward the red-lit smoke billowing in the valley. 'I lost him down there.'

'My God. How?'

'Drowned. We were crossing to shore and we met a man we'd had trouble with the night before. He knocked Leo into the water.'

'Why?'

'Because Leo was a Jew.'

'A—?'

'Jew, Mr Martin. The word is Jew.'

'I can't believe one man would kill another just because he was Jewish.'

'Especially not in this wonderful country – is that what you're trying to say? This country's a mire for pigs.'

Seldom in his life had Rafe Martin heard a voice so poisoned by bitterness. It hurt him. That and his tiredness made his shoulders slump.

'I'm truly sorry, Mrs Goldman.' With hardly a conscious thought, he took hold of her forearm gently. 'If there's anything at all that I can do—'

The touch of his hand – a *man*'s hand – was enough to set memories exploding like long-buried mines, to shatter her already-weakened defences:

'*Leave me alone!*'

She turned and dashed to the end of the porch. She stepped off without realizing there was a two-foot drop to the ground. She landed hard on a sheet-covered mound, unhurt but momentarily stunned.

Her cry had brought people running from the house. Martin ignored them, just as he ignored her plea to be left alone. He jumped off the porch to help her. She was floundering atop the covered body. Somehow her hand tangled in the wet sheet, pulling it away.

Six inches from her eyes lay the head of a blonde child; a girl of six or seven whose cheeks had been horribly cut before she died. For a moment Eleanor stared at the deep, crusted wounds. Then she leaped to her feet and ran up the hill, screaming.

3

Afterward, Eleanor had only fragmentary memories of the next few minutes:

The coldness of the rain; harder suddenly and beating against her face. The feel of the secret flow soiling her; draining what little of her strength remained. The brick house, seen from higher on the hill and silhouetted against the fires of Johnstown—

And the terrifying sight of an unknown man loping after her. 'Mrs Goldman,' he called. 'Come back inside!'

No longer rational, she turned to confront him. She dropped into a crouch, her hands held in front of her. She clenched those hands, as if rage could somehow change what she railed against:

'Why did Leo have to die before I told him? I never told him—'

The words were shrill; punctuated by her gasps for breath. Martin stopped and stayed motionless while trying to decide how to deal with her.

Softly, he said, 'What do you mean, Mrs Goldman? Never told him what?'

She beat the air with her fists to emphasize each spat-out word:

'That it – wasn't his fault – I couldn't – love him – the right way – I was – raped in my own house – in New York – the men – *took turns with me*—'

A flicker of sanity lit the chaos of her thoughts. Her eyes registered horror as she realized that the dark door, kept closed at such great cost for so long, was open.

'Oh – my God—'

The words began to dissolve into sobbing. 'My God, what a – foul mess – I've made of – everything—'

She fell against him, crying uncontrollably and trying not to think of what she'd confessed to a stranger.

Martin put his arms round her, supporting her as best he could. One of his calloused hands came up behind her head. He knew it would afford her no real protection from the rain. But he wanted to keep it there because she was so hurt, and because of the way he felt about her.

In a moment, the abrupt limpness of her body told him she'd fainted.

He picked her up so that she lay horizontally across his arms. Her hair trailed down behind her head; her cheek pressed against his worn jacket. He could hardly believe what he'd heard her say. And yet it must have been the truth, because it had come pouring out with such unmistakable pain.

Martin moved down the hill with steady steps. Eleanor was no burden at all. But he experienced guilt because of the emotions churning inside him. There was sweet enjoyment in holding her so close.

What a damned, shameful way to feel with her husband no more than a few hours dead! Yet he couldn't help himself. He was an incurable romantic, though he usually tried to hide it because the world scoffed at romantics, and often punished them. Nevertheless he'd conceived an instantaneous passion for Eleanor Goldman when he'd seen her perform at the Opera House. Now, despite his conscience, he was glad that chance and the events of the night had thrown them together.

But could he ever look her in the eye after what she'd told him? He wondered.

A grey-haired woman with a massive bosom barred the front door of the brick house:

'Another one? We've no more room.'

'This is the lady who's been helping you.'

The woman bent for a closer look. 'Lord yes – so it is. Put her down here on the porch. I'll bring some flour sacks to cover her. What happened?'

'She collapsed. Probably from exhaustion.'

'I heard her cry out, then someone said she'd run off.'

'Can't say I blame her,' Martin replied. 'Her husband's missing.'

A moment later, he carefully laid Eleanor close to

the house, well out of the rain. When the older woman returned, he covered Eleanor with three coarse pieces of burlap she'd brought.

He knelt beside Eleanor; studied her dirt-streaked face. Unconsciousness smoothed away its agony. God, how beautiful she was.

Of course it was ridiculous, not to say sinful, for him to entertain such a thought at such a time. Yet he was powerless to deny his feelings; they were too strong.

He rested the fingers of his right hand against her cheek. What were the exact words she'd used? *I was raped in my own house. The men took turns with me.*

His lips barely moved as he whispered, 'Poor thing. Poor thing.'

He jerked his hand back, noticing the grey-haired woman watching from the front doorway. He stood up; walked to the steps leading down from the porch. He told the woman, 'I'll come back early tomorrow to see how she is.'

But he never did.

4

When Eleanor woke, the rain had stopped. A balmy wind blew against her face. The sun shone above the dark summits of the hills to the east.

She sat up, drowsy and almost smiling despite the soreness of her body and the soiled feel of her skin and clothing. Then, in an instant, memories returned. Memories of Leo vanishing in the water. Memories of the man responsible for his death. Memories of what she'd admitted to that stranger, Martin.

She could recall few of the circumstances of that revelation, and none of the words. Yet she knew she'd opened the secret door and let its horrors spew forth.

Martin knew something known to no other human being.

For a moment she experienced a sudden, overwhelming sense of relief. Then a curious longing began to sweep over her. A longing for Martin to come back; speak to her; simply be with her. Except for the Rasmussens, he was the only person she knew in what was left of Johnstown. She felt guilty craving his company, yet the craving persisted.

But as she stood on the porch, shielding her eyes and gazing down at the sunlit smoke and floating wreckage, shame returned, and the longing was banished. Martin was a kind and decent man. But how could she even speak to him again? He *knew*.

But no one else would. Ever.

The scene below soon disappeared, replaced by an image on which she concentrated with an almost crazed intensity. A new door. Stronger than the old one, thicker, too. She imagined elaborate bolts, chains, extra padlocks. It was an impregnable door; one whose integrity she would guard and defend with her whole being.

As for Martin – she hoped she never set eyes on the man again.

5

Now it was Saturday, and the sun shone. In the valley of the Conemaugh, a flotilla of small boats continued to search the smoke-covered water for survivors. Many of the fires were finally out. The waters began to recede slowly. Large numbers of people were visible on the heights. Life was returning.

The first word of the disaster had gone out late Friday, transmitted in a telegraph message from Sang Hollow to Pittsburgh. After that, details reaching the outside world were few, though it was soon known from coast to coast that a great flood had devastated Johnstown. By the end of that sunny Saturday, many people in other parts of the state and nation were making plans to descend on the town as soon as rail service was restored. The people included the Pennsylvania militia, journalists and photographers, and relief workers from numerous organizations. Hundreds of ordinary citizens were preparing to travel to Johnstown, too. Some would bring food and medicines, some just their morbid curiosity and greed.

Rafe Martin spent the day doing rescue work. It was an exhausting job, using a hammer and crowbar to open jammed doors in order to liberate those trapped in houses that had been spared. The work had its infuriating aspects, too. Four times, in four different attics, Rafe and his fellow workers came across women who initially refused help because their torn clothing revealed too much of their bodies.

Rafe quickly developed a technique for dealing with such women. He'd walk away from the door through which he'd been speaking to them, making certain they heard his voice fade:

'All right, ladies – whatever you say. The moment we locate an all-female rescue group, we'll send it along. May take a few days, though.'

In every case, false modesty was immediately replaced by pleas that the men break the door down.

The corpses revealed after the waters fell weren't pretty. The warm sunshine created a fearful stench from the mud, the smoke, and the putrefying flesh. Among the men with whom Rafe worked, there was anxious talk of the possibility of disease, especially typhoid.

Hour after hour, he thought of returning to the brick house to check on Eleanor. But every available man was needed down in the city, so he delayed. Around noon he was approached about going to work professionally.

A Colonel William Connolly of Pittsburgh sought him out. Connolly identified himself as the agent for the Association Press in Western Pennsylvania. He wanted Rafe to help with telegraphy once three new wires were strung to connect the valley with the outside world. He said one wire would be used by the Pennsylvania militia who would soon be policing the area. Another would link Johnstown with the capital of Harrisburg. He'd secured the third wire for exclusive use by the AP.

Connolly didn't bother to explain how he'd pulled that off. But the wages he offered Rafe were handsome. Rafe told him making money had to wait until his present work was finished. The AP agent urged Rafe to look him up as soon as it was.

At twilight Rafe was tramping alone through the mud of Napoleon Street, near the downtown. He had a crowbar tilted over his shoulder. He could hear some of his fellow workers a block or two behind.

He approached a small house; one of the few private homes left intact near the main flood path. All at once he stopped, swallowing down revulsion. Above the thick mud covering the front yard, a flag still drooped at half staff; a flag raised but never taken down on Memorial Day. Close to the base of the pole, a single human hand jutted from the mud like some grotesque piece of statuary.

A man's hand, he judged. A drowning hand reaching for help it had never found—

Shaking his head, Rafe crossed the yard. *This will be the last one*, he said to himself as he moved into the heavily silted entrance hall. *Then by heaven I'm going back to see her.*

He heard a peculiar grunting in the darkness at the rear of the house. A rat came scurrying toward him from behind a half-buried umbrella stand. Sensing his presence, the rat stopped, then ran the other way.

Rafe moved farther down the hall, glanced into a parlour, and nearly dropped the crowbar. Silt covered the parlour floor. Just above it, brown eyes looked at him. The lifeless eyes of a boy of ten or eleven.

How had he died? There was no way to tell. Maybe he'd been trapped in the cellar just before the water rushed in, and had managed to chop a hole in the floor of the room above, only to drown while he tried to climb to safety. Just the upper half of the boy's head showed above the mud. His nose rested in it.

'Jesus,' Rafe whispered. He heard the grunting again, and a faint voice:

'Come on, you old bastard. *Give.*'

The intruder was in the kitchen, he thought. Who was he? No one should be in the house except someone trapped there, or rescue workers. The gruff voice didn't fit either circumstance.

Rafe walked forward quickly, making no effort to conceal his approach; the thick, wet silt made that virtually impossible anyway. He stepped into the kitchen and saw an unkempt man struggling to open a back door jammed shut by the mud.

Footprints clearly showed the intruder's path of entry. He'd climbed through an open window Rafe could see in an adjoining pantry. On the kitchen floor, partially buried in mud, a second man lay on his back.

Near the man's shoulder lay a discarded knife, the blade smeared reddish-brown. Overlapping footprints and deep furrows in the mud showed the body had been moved. A stick held the dead man's jaws apart. Judging from the slashed and bloodied gums Rafe glimpsed, the intruder had been trying to cut gold teeth from the mouth of the corpse.

'You fucking ghoul,' Rafe said, taking one long step.

He smashed the crowbar down on the intruder's left shoulder, breaking it.

The man yelled and staggered. He yanked a small pistol from his coat. He shoved the pistol against Rafe's side and fired.

Before the echo of the shot died, the thief was gone the way he'd come. Members of Rafe's search party, two carrying lanterns, soon rushed up the front walk:

'Who fired? Where are you, Martin?'

Rafe hurt too much to answer. He was on his knees, arms crossed over his belly. He tried to keep from keeling over. He couldn't. As lantern light filled the mouldy-smelling kitchen, he fell forward into the mud.

His last thought was of Eleanor.

CHAPTER XVI

'Not Known to Be Found'

That same Saturday night, Gideon, Moultrie Calhoun, two reporters, a photographer, a sketch artist, and a pair of telegraphers were riding a special one-car train chartered by the *Union* for the trip to Johnstown. Gideon had been at the Fifth Avenue Hotel when he got word of the disaster. His first act had been to root frantically through the litter on his desk and locate Eleanor's itinerary. He let out a long, loud sigh when he saw she and Leo had been playing Altoona on Friday.

The one-car special was frequently side-tracked due to heavy traffic on the Pennsylvania's main line. At several of these enforced stops, relief workers came aboard and begged Gideon to permit extra cars of food and medical supplies to be coupled on. Much as he hated the delay, he couldn't bring himself to refuse. Fortunately the paper was being supplied with copy by the Associated Press, whose representatives had been the first newsmen to reach the scene.

Soon the special train consisted of eleven cars. At the unscheduled stops in various small towns, Gideon always stepped off to smoke a cigar and ask for whatever new details had come in on the local telegraph. All he heard were conflicting stories, and wildly varying estimates of the death toll. One man said six thousand were dead; another said it was eight. When Moultrie Calhoun wrote a dispatch datelined *Rolling toward Johnstown aboard the Union Special*, he used the figure twelve thousand in his opening paragraph. Gideon read it and slashed it out with a pen.

'We're supposed to report the truth, not merely sell papers, Moultrie. I appreciate that we're dealing with the biggest story since Appomattox. But New York already has a full quota of irresponsible reporting.'

He picked up two special flood extras published on Saturday, and flourished one:

'The prestigious *Times* has Johnstown being wiped out by a waterspout. And this other rag – have you seen what's on the front page?' He read from the second paper:

'Johnstown's foreign population, particularly a group of whiskey-maddened Slavs and Hungarians, is running amok dynamiting bank safes, looting private homes, and relieving pitiable corpses of jewelry and other valuables. These crazed Europeans do not understand our way of life, let alone the simplest rules of human decency. They have no right to enjoy the privileges of citizenship. They should be promptly deported, if they are not first lynched by outraged Americans.'

He flung the paper across the car. 'Neither news-paper as yet has a single representative in Johnstown, for God's sake! And as far as I know, the AP isn't transmitting any dispatches about crazed Slavs and Hungarians.'

'You're correct, sir. They are not.'

'Then the paper simply invented the story. Make sure we don't pick up any items like that and rewrite 'em just to fill space.'

'I will, Mr Kent.'

'And watch that business about the body count. If you can't print facts, don't print rumours unless you clearly identify them as such.'

Calhoun shrugged. 'Very well. I was only trying to do what every other newsman will be doing. The more bodies reported, the more papers sold. I thought you'd want—'

'You thought incorrectly,' Gideon interrupted. 'You don't know me very well yet, Moultrie.'

'I'm learning, sir. I'll be happy to omit the figures. I too dislike compromising editorial standards for the sake of extra circulation – whether the advertising department approves or not.'

He leaned forward to peer out the window. 'What now? We're slowing again.'

'Good God. What town is it this time?' Gideon spied a depot in the spring sunshine. 'Altoona!' He reached for the signal cord.

Two sharp tugs brought the train to a standstill. Gideon easily located the Daly troupe. They'd announced a special Monday night performance to benefit the flood victims, and everyone in town knew where they were staying. But Gideon's hope of finding Eleanor and Leo was shattered when he spoke with Regis Pemberton at the troupe's downtown hotel.

Pemberton explained why the Goldmans hadn't taken the same eastbound train as the rest of the company, who had only straggled into Altoona aboard a work train after the passenger express had been delayed for hours up in the mountains.

Gideon bolted out of the hotel and ran all the way back to the depot despite chest pain and shortness of breath that began before he'd gone a third of the distance.

2

The train chugged on. Gideon sat brooding. Pemberton's news had left him shaken and fearful. This was just another example of the way fate surprised a man at the very moment things seemed to be going well. Only Friday, a telegraph message had informed the Kents that Carter was safe and well on the Pacific Coast. Julia had enjoyed her first night of sound sleep in many months.

As a consequence, so had he. But peace never seemed to last long any more. His had lasted less than forty-eight hours.

The train neared Johnstown late Sunday afternoon. East of the city, the Pennsylvania rails had been swept away for a distance of almost twenty miles. The special was forced to come to a halt behind six other trains lined up at the end of the track. Gideon's men fanned out to search the countryside. One found a farmer who would take the *Union* contingent the rest of the way in his wagon. The farmer's price was outrageous but Gideon paid it without so much as a question.

The wagon jolted up and down precipitous mountain roads. By the time the *Union* men reached the devastated city, the sun had been down half an hour. Gideon left the affairs of the paper in Calhoun's hands and immediately set out to look for his daughter and son-in-law.

He tramped through the ruins for three hours, searching everywhere: some kitchens; the aisles of an improvised tent hospital; marshalling stations at which homeless survivors were being assembled for transportation to emergency shelters in nearby villages. He even spent half an hour in a temporary morgue.

He didn't find the Goldmans anywhere.

He asked questions again and again. It was impossible to get consistent answers. Almost every version of the disaster was different. But one central fact was clear. Hundreds and hundreds of people had simply disappeared in the flood crest and its aftermath. He was increasingly fearful that Eleanor and her husband were among them.

3

He finally gave up the search and trudged wearily back to the temporary headquarters members of the press had established in a half-destroyed firebrick plant. Inside a large kiln which had somehow been spared, reporters and artists worked by lantern light, writing and sketching on top of whatever they could improvise for desks – everything from planks to the backs of shovels and the lids of coffins. There were reporters from most of the New York, Philidelphia, and Pittsburgh papers on the scene now, and correspondents on the way from more distant cities as well as from abroad. A new telegraph station was already clicking out copy from a hillside above the stone bridge.

Gideon sank down on a keg and watched Calhoun pencil a headline:

HORRENDOUS TOLL STILL UNKNOWN
IN DEATH'S VALLEY.
*Casualties of the Fearsome Flood
Said to be Ten Thousand or More.*

'Said to be,' Gideon read, smiling without humour. 'At least you're being honest about your dishonesty.'

Calhoun remained imperturbable. 'Do we have a reliable figure yet, sir?'

'We do not. The best guess seems to be somewhere between twenty-two and twenty-three hundred, but I've no proof that's correct. I've just heard it more often than some other estimates.'

Calhoun's pencil remained motionless above the sheet of foolscap. 'Shall I change the headline?'

An indifferent wave. 'Don't bother.'

Calhoun frowned. Gideon's answer told a good deal about his mental state. Softly, the editor asked:

'Did you find them, sir?'

'No. The damn town's a madhouse. Militiamen everywhere. Relief workers stumbling over one another. Some of the townspeople are starting to set up relic booths.'

Calhoun's jaw dropped. '*Relic* booths, Mr Kent?'

'That's right. Any unbroken plate, tarnished spoon, glass eye, or hank of hair has suddenly been transformed into a fabulous souvenir of the flood. The natives seem to perceive a sizable market, and they're pricing the items accordingly.' He grimaced. 'They're probably smarter than we'd like to think. When people from the outside arrive in large numbers, I expect the souvenir trade will boom.'

The editor nodded sad agreement. 'I never cease to be astonished by the human appetite for the tasteless and the macabre.'

He stood up; reached for his overcoat. The night air was growing chilly.

'The other men are off hunting up material, Mr Kent. I'll go up and stand in line with this copy. It will undoubtedly take at least an hour to get it on the wire.'

Shortly after Calhoun left the kiln, a handsome

young man appeared at the entrance. Gideon recognized him at once. The other reporters were dressed conventionally at best and poorly at worst, but the new arrival wore an English lounge suit, a yellow ulster with green stripes, and swung a cane from one kid-gloved hand. It was a standing joke in the profession that Mr Richard Harding Davis of the Philadelphia *Press* never removed those gloves to write his copy. Though only in his mid-twenties, David had already acquired a reputation as the most elegant newsman on the Eastern seaboard; perhaps in the whole country.

'They'll be putting up the first casualty lists in thirty minutes, boys,' Davis called to the others.

'Where?' shouted a man from the *World*.

'By the main tent. See you there.' With a jaunty wave, he left.

Impatiently, Gideon waited for the half hour to pass. When it was nearly up, he hurried to the tent where long strips of crudely inked paper were being nailed to a board made of pine planks. A noisy crowd pushed and shoved in order to get a first look at the columns of names. Gideon was about to start working his way toward the front when he spied a grimy face he thought he recognized.

He thrust a reporter out of the way; ignored the man's scowl; looked again—

'Eleanor!'

4

Struggling and shoving, he fought toward her. He called her name a second time. She turned.

What he saw on her face chilled him. There was a lack-lustre quality in her eyes; a dead look. Her cheeks were red, as if she'd been crying.

'Eleanor – child—' Gideon felt tears in his own eye

as he folded her against him. 'Thank God you're alive. I talked to Pemberton in Altoona. He told me you and Leo had stayed behind. I've been searching for you ever since I arrived four hours ago. Is Leo all right?'

'No, Papa. Leo's gone. I came to make sure they posted his name up there. I told them to be sure to include it. I told a military officer, I think. I don't remember that part clearly.'

Gideon was numbed by what she said, and by the remote way she said it. He'd never seen his daughter so bedraggled, or acting so strangely. With the utmost gentleness, he asked:

'What happened to Leo?'

A bitter smile. 'He met a man who never read your Independence Day editorials.'

'I don't understand.'

She came to life then. Anger stiffened her shoulders as she said:

'You know, Papa – one of your editorials saying how splendid it is to be an American. It isn't splendid if you have an accent or go to the wrong church. It isn't splendid if you're a darky or a Jew. You love to write about the opportunity in this country. I finally understand what you mean. The opportunity to be hated. The opportunity to be killed solely because of who you are.'

'Eleanor, you still haven't told me about—'

'Leo *drowned*, Papa. A man pushed him in the water, and you know he couldn't swim. The man didn't like Jews, and – and—'

She couldn't sustain the anger. Her eyes grew dull again. Her shoulders sagged.

'What does it matter? Leo's gone. I've been searching for him all day. I searched yesterday, too. There's no trace of him. Finally I told someone to put his name up there. Do you see what it says?'

In the light of a windblown torch held aloft so the

reporters and relatives could scan the list, Gideon read the heading scrawled above the columns of names:

NOT KNOWN TO BE FOUND

She laughed. 'Isn't that a fine turn of phrase? "Not known to be found." It's like the pretty talcum the undertaker dusted on Mama's cheeks after she died. Why don't they say what they mean? Lost. *Lost.*'

Then, weeping like a child, she slumped in his arms.

He continued to hold her as a photographer set off flash-light powder with a whoosh of smoke and a dazzle of light. The man smiled, pleased at having recorded the scene for posterity.

Spots danced in Gideon's good eye. Finally his vision cleared. Staring over his daughter's head, he hunted among the names beginning with G. At last he found *Goldman, Leo.* Put there by Eleanor herself – an act that made him fear for her well-being.

He held her close and let her sob. He'd always worried about Eleanor and her husband encountering all-too-prevalent bigotry. But he'd never imagined bigotry could cost Leo his life. That it had only made his daughter's future the more uncertain. For a moment, Gideon actually feared for her sanity.

More torches were streaming around him. Nearby, a young man wept; had he lost a wife? A child cried in his mother's arms; had he lost a father? The dead were not the only ones lost, Gideon thought, just as another charge of flashlight powder exploded. The photographer had set up his camera within three feet of the grief-stricken young man, taking his picture while he wept.

When Gideon saw that, he left Eleanor, moved quickly through the crowd, picked up the photographer's camera by the tripod and hurled it to the ground. He was too angry to wonder why the photographer didn't attempt to stop him.

He stamped on the wooden body of the camera and on the tripod, breaking all the legs. He twisted the lens ring, loosened the multiple discs of glass, and broke them under his heel. Finally, he made sure the plate was ruined. He flung it at the photographer's feet:

'For Christ's sake let these people mourn in privacy!'

'Mr Kent – ' Nervously twisting a corner of his black camera drape, the incredulous man stammered out the words. ' – don't – don't you recognize me? I work for you.'

Gideon saw it was true. 'Not any more,' he said. 'Collect your wages from Calhoun.'

5

He walked back toward his daughter. Eleanor simply stood waiting, hands at her sides, dirt and blood all over her skirt, a blank look in her eyes. A profound despair filled Gideon as he put his arm round her shoulder.

'We'll start for home in the morning,' he said.

It took great effort for her to rouse from whatever reverie had claimed her. Comprehension returned to her eyes only slowly. At last she said:

'We must tell Leo's father. I'm sure there's some – ritual of their faith that ought to be carried out.'

'I don't know. But we'll stop in New York before travelling on to Boston. I'll personally find Efrem Goldman and tell him what happened. I know words are no good at a time like this, but I want you to hear this much, Eleanor. You must let Julia and me care for you in Boston during this terrible period. That way, perhaps it won't be so long before the grief passes.'

'It won't pass, Papa.'

'I know you feel that way now, but—'

'It won't,' she cut in, with a savagery that raised echoes of the past. 'I never told him—'

'Told him what?'

After a long moment, she answered, 'That I loved him.'

Her voice was remote, and the words weren't the ones she had intended to say, of that he was sure. A mask had dropped into place. She turned to stare at the columns of names.

A half minute went by. Very softly, he said:

'Eleanor?'

She didn't answer, or even give any indication that she'd heard.

6

Flood relief committees were organized in almost every American city of any size. Gideon served on the Boston committee and, because of his business interests, on that in New York as well.

On the New York committee he worked with men such as August Belmont, the financier, Daniel Frohman the theatrical producer, New York Central president Chauncey Depew, rival newspaperman Charles Dana, and former president Cleveland. Together the men directed the raising of funds and the purchase and shipment of supplies for the stricken town.

There was also an old friend on the New York committee:

'I got this at the meeting. Theodore brought it.'

Disgust on his face, Gideon laid the souvenir spoon on a small rosewood table at Julia's side. It was a sultry afternoon in late June. Sunlight cast bright patches on the carpet of the Fifth Avenue Hotel parlour, but sections of the large room lay in shadow.

The spoon glowed in a sunbeam. Julia leaned over

the left arm of her chair to study it. 'How on earth did he get hold of such a thing?'

'An acquaintance mailed it from Johnstown – along with a letter of protest. Theodore didn't unwrap the package until our committee was in session. The minute he saw this charming item, he went off like a mortar. He demanded that the jeweller who designed and sold it be arrested and sent to jail. On what grounds, he didn't quite make clear. He shouted that he'd take the case to Washington if we refused to become involved.'

'Did the committee become involved?'

'No. We persuaded him that there's no way on God's earth to legislate greed out of existence. In his calmer moments, Theodore knows that.'

Julia picked up the spoon. 'By the way, you never told me whether Theodore made a decision about Washington. Is he going to take the post with the Harrison administration?'

Gideon nodded. 'The salary's a munificent thirty-five hundred dollars a year. But he really feels he can do something worthwhile as a civil service commissioner. I hope he's right. God knows the government needs a comprehensive merit system. Right now, a congressman can get his favourite nephew a good job even if the boy's the village idiot.'

He noticed Julia moving her thumb back and forth over the raised designs on the spoon. He frowned:

'Logic aside, I agree with Theodore about that thing. The man who's peddling them should be flogged.'

'I'm not sure I recognize everything depicted on it. Do you?'

She handed the spoon to him. He held it up; pointed to the handle:

'That's the dam that gave way.'

His finger slid down the shaft. 'This is supposed to be the Conemaugh River coming down in full flood upon—' He touched the bottom of the bowl of the spoon. 'The stone bridge.' Colour in his cheeks, he flung the spoon back on the table. It made a loud clacking, and stirred motes in a sunbeam. The two Kents started at an unexpected voice:

'Please get that thing out of here.'

Gideon turned to see Eleanor standing at the bedroom door. She wore widow's weeds, unadorned by even a trace of white. That and the deep shadow surrounding her made it seem as if her pale hands and face floated in darkness.

With a tone of apology, Gideon began, 'I had no idea you'd returned from your shopping—'

She didn't let him finish: 'I shouldn't have gone. The crowds were frightful. I don't think I'll try again. I was resting with the door open when I heard you and Julia talking. There are enough reminders of Leo's death as it is, Papa. Get rid of that filthy thing!'

Her skirt rustled as she glided out of sight.

With a stricken look, he slipped the spoon in his pocket. 'I really thought she was still out. Otherwise I'd never have shown you the infernal thing.'

'I know, darling.' Julia gave his forearm a gentle pat. 'I know that. It's a small mistake. You mustn't feel so guilty.'

Gideon's blue eye fixed on the patch of darkness where his daughter had disappeared. He stood up suddenly; struck a match and held it to his cigar. Wreathed in blue smoke, he started to pace.

'She's a very strong girl, Julia. But this unfeeling manner she's adopted since she came home upsets me. The only time she displays an iota of emotion is when she tells me how vile this country is. She's developed an unreasonable hatred of America—'

'Not so unreasonable,' Julia countered. 'Think of the way immigrants are treated. Think of what the Negroes' lot has been for years. Eleanor's feelings are completely understandable when you recall what she went through as Leo's wife. Large and small humiliations. An attack on his father. And finally his death. You must see her side of it.'

'I do! But we aren't talking about some sort of — intellectual posture. We're talking about her response to the death of her *husband*. She ought to show some sorrow. Weep! She did the night I found her in Johnstown, but she's held back ever since.'

'Well, she's always been a very private sort of person. She's never told us what happened to her in '77, for instance, and we've agreed that she probably never will. Perhaps Leo's death was the same kind of shock. Perhaps it hurts too much for her to mourn him in a conventional way.'

'She should let it hurt, so she'll recover. Bottling everything inside is just no good.'

'I'm sure she's acting.'

'*What?*'

'Acting,' Julia repeated with a small shrug. 'Playing a role. It may be that she's been offended by all the howling and breast-beating that sometimes accompanies the death of a loved one. I suspect she's picked another role. A more restrained one. Your daughter's very accomplished at playing any role she chooses for herself—'

Role. That was it. Julia had said it without understanding it. Days ago, he should have realized what Eleanor was doing. It had nothing to do with a dislike of the hysteria that often followed funerals. It was something she'd done before — something so frightening in its implications that his mind must have evaded an acknowledgment of it.

'Darling, what's wrong?' Julia said, noting his stricken look.

'I know why she hides her feelings.'

'What's that?'

'I say I know why she hides her feelings! It just came to me. You used the word role a moment ago. Don't you see what role Eleanor's playing? No, I suppose I shouldn't expect that. You never knew her.'

Confused, Julia shook her head:

'Knew Eleanor—?'

'*Margaret.* Eleanor's acting like her mother.'

'Oh, dear God, Gideon – what are you saying?'

His expression was anguished. 'I've caught glimpses of it before. In the last few years before Margaret died, she was rigid, secretive, obsessed with herself. Eleanor's playing the part to perfection, whether she realizes it or not. It's to be expected that she'd somewhat resemble her mother. I suppose most daughters do. But Leo's death—' He could barely utter the rest. 'Somehow, it's pushing her beyond the bounds of a normal family remembrance. Eleanor's responding to her loss just the way Margaret responded to her problems. By shutting out the world as completely as she could. To a certain extent, Eleanor did that when Leo was alive. Now that he's gone, she's still doing it – but now it's her entire existence.'

Silence. Julie pondered, looking as upset as her husband. Finally she said:

'What a terrifying thought. I fear you may be right. It explains so many things. She's never impolite when I speak to her. But neither is she remotely interested in what I have to say – or in sharing her thoughts with me.'

'Nor with me – except when she reviles the whole damn country for what one man did.' He reached out to squeeze his wife's hand. 'You mustn't take her behaviour as any kind of personal insult—'

'Oh, I don't. But I'm desperately worried about her.'

'With good reason.' He pointed to a six-inch stack of letters and telegrams on a side table. 'No wonder she hasn't replied to any of those messages of sympathy from her colleagues – or to the offers of work. She's read a few, but she hasn't answered a single one. I asked her.'

As if trying to disprove Gideon's frightening thesis, Julia countered, 'Well – conventionally speaking, she's supposed to mourn for a year.'

'Julia! When have actresses – or the Kents – ever worried about convention? She ought to go back to work the moment she's able. It would help her survive the grief. But she's no longer interested in the theatre. She isn't interested in anything.'

And neither was her mother after she began her descent to madness.

Husband and wife were silent then. Another punishing thought struck Gideon:

Lost is truly the word for this whole family now.

The word had come to mind that night six years ago when he'd wandered down to the Boston piers, speculating about the family's future. Much had changed since then. But nothing had improved. If anything, the situation was far worse.

Carter was off at the other end of the continent and might never amount to anything. Will was pursuing his ambition to be a Society doctor, and was completely dominated by a girl of questionable reputation. Eleanor hated and scoffed at everything the Kents stood for – and not long ago he'd regarded her as the family's only potential leader.

What a misguided fool he'd been. Not only was she lost to the family – she might be lost to life itself. He recalled another fact about Margaret's descent to madness. Once begun, it had been unstoppable.

He and Julia stared hopelessly at one another in the blue-tinted sunshine. Soon she rose, murmuring:

'I want to see if she's all right.'

She walked to Eleanor's door, tapped softly,

659

received no answer and reached for the knob. Even before she spoke, Gideon knew what she would say:

'It's locked.'

With a sad shake of her head, she disappeared into her own room. While the disturbed cigar smoke slowly came to rest again, Gideon at last relaxed his face and let his discomfort show.

He fought for breath as a spike of pain in the centre of his chest held him in his chair. It was the worst pain he'd ever experienced. He knew with certainty that his days were fast running out.

BOOK FIVE

The Marble Cottage

CHAPTER I

Summer of '89

For Will, it was a tense and troubled summer.

He was twenty that year. A difficult age, Julia teasingly remarked to him once. Too young to be fully launched in life, and too old to be at home under the scrutiny of a strong-willed father.

Will's response was a vigorous nod. Relations between Gideon and his son were polite, but that was all. Each felt angry with the other, and suppressed it. As the days passed, it became more and more likely that some insignificant event would shatter the artificial calm and let that anger erupt with disastrous consequences. Some days Will dreaded it; at other times, he couldn't wait for it to happen. Often he didn't know how the hell he felt.

He had volunteered as a ward orderly at the Massachusetts General Hospital. He preferred working and learning to idling around Beacon Street while he waited for the end of July. At that time he planned to spend eight or ten days with the Pennels at their new summer home in Newport. Gideon knew about the trip, of course. It was one of the reasons he was testy with his son.

Will was eager to visit Newport, but much less enthusiastic about the trip he was to take immediately afterward. From Rhode Island he planned to go straight to New York, to fulfil the promise made that morning at the Statue of Liberty.

Drew was part of the reason Will felt so unsettled. For three years, the two friends had studied, worried, argued, and joked together. Now Drew had finished his course and graduated. Doctor of Medicine, 1889. He was already at work in Manhattan's notorious Sixth Ward, caring for some of the patients of the doctor whose practice he shared. His brief letters reminded Will in cheerful but pointed fashion that he was counting on his friend's visit.

Will loathed the idea of going into the slums, but he'd made a promise, and he'd honour it. He told no one, though. Not his parents, and certainly not Laura.

Laura. He thought of her often. At night he lay in the humid darkness and imagined how she would look stripped of all those layers of silk and cotton and steel boning that produced the Lillian Russell figure – tiny waist, swelling bosom – that young ladies wanted so badly. The waking dreams were painful for Will. He was strong and in good health, and he hadn't been with a woman since his first and only visit to Madam Melba's.

One thing did please him, though. Carter was happy for a change. He was in San Francisco, working for a politician named Buckley.

'My God, I've read about that rascal,' Gideon had exclaimed when he first read the news in a letter. 'They say he makes Boss Croker and the rest of the Tammany thieves look like heavenly cherubs by comparison. Where the hell is this family going?'

Carter seemed to have found his niche. He ran errands and drafted letters for Buckley, who exercised phenomenal power in the Bay Area. He said he was enjoying the life, learning a lot, and making important connections that would favourably influence his future.

Will hoped all of that was true. Whether it was or not, he was glad to read cheerful letters from Carter at long last.

Will was working hard to fulfil his promise to his step-brother. In another year, he'd be ready to establish a practice like that of the very successful Dr Vlandingham – whether his father liked it or not. By doing that, it was also conceivable that he could carry the family one rung higher on a ladder Gideon and Julia would be forever unable to climb. In fact he might be able to lift the Kents to the very highest level of American Society – a goal not entirely unworthy of a family which prided itself on achievement, he frequently reminded himself.

And yet, thoughts of Drew's situation sometimes soured the taste of Will's ambition, generated doubt, and drove the promise to Carter from his mind.

Gideon frequently made unflattering comments about the Pennels. And, in a household in which daily events were the grist for the family business, there was seldom a meal without some talk of politics. Those discussions provided additional opportunities for Will and his father to quarrel.

A storm of social protest was rising in the West and South that year. Farmers in both regions felt they were being exploited by the railroads, whose owners still formed secret combinations to fix freight rates, and by bankers who did the same for interest rates. High interest made it almost impossible for farmers to borrow for expansion, let alone survive one or more seasons of drought.

Even the government had become the farmer's enemy. Most politicians were in the pockets of the capitalist manufacturers – or so the farmers said. There was certainly some evidence to support the claim. A high tariff imposed by Congress reduced the flow of imported goods. Thus farm families could only buy domestically made products – but the prices had been set so high, the farmers couldn't afford them.

Finally, the farmers wanted an increase in the money supply. They proposed to bring this about by removing the US from an exclusive gold standard and supplementing paper money that was backed by gold with unlimited coinage of silver.

Organizations were formed to fight for farmers' rights and redress their grievances. Successors to the Grange of a decade earlier, the new organizations – the Southern and Northwestern Alliance – were considerably more militant. Gideon called them evangelists of an agrarian revolt, and did so with the enthusiasm of a man anticipating a championship prize fight.

Will often found himself speaking against the Alliances, since that was the position taken by Laura's father. Thurman Pennel damned the members of the two Alliances as illiterate immigrants and Southern traitors who had banded together to promote anarchy. Will repeated that assertion. But he had no evidence to support it. Gideon easily demolished his arguments with facts and sarcasm.

The farmers were allied with the powerful Knights of Labor, and loomed as a formidable political force in the decade ahead. Will parroted Pennel's view that the Republican Party had nothing to worry about. Its control of all branches of the federal government created a barricade no wild-eyed reformer could ever breach. Gideon countered with the argument that the party was essentially powerless, because its majority in the House of Representatives was so slim. The Democrats had the votes to block almost any legislation. The result would not be a pro-Democratic Congress, of course, but one which did nothing.

And yet that summer, the powerful Republican Speaker of the House, rotund Tom Reed of Maine – Czar Reed, some called him – was already predicting that the Fifty-first Congress scheduled to convene in December would be the first in history to spend a billion dollars. Only fitting, Reed declared. America's wealth had reached a phenomenal level. A billion-dollar country deserved a billion-dollar Congress.

Meantime, huge sums had been raised for relief in

Johnstown. The city was setting up its rebuilding programme and trying to erase the horror of the flood from collective memory. That horror lingered like a ghost in the house on Beacon Street; Will felt its eerie presence whenever he spent time with his sister.

Eleanor kept to herself a good deal, and continued to wear black to honour Leo's memory. Occasionally she denounced the country in fiery, almost incoherent language – performances Gideon endured in red-faced silence – but those outbursts were her only displays of emotion. She seldom mentioned her husband's name.

Yet in Eleanor's dark eyes, Will thought he glimpsed a pain, a memory – an unmentionable *something* – she was constantly fighting to suppress. He asked her about it one Sunday afternoon when he took her for a walk on the Common.

She assured him there was nothing specific troubling her, only the general exhaustion and shock that were the legacies of Johnstown. Her replies were uncharacteristically sharp, and Will wasn't satisfied she was telling the truth. But there was no way to prove otherwise, and he let the matter rest.

One thing that was emerging plainly was that Eleanor had no interest in returning to the theatre. That became certain soon after the day a large package arrived for her. When Julia asked about the package at dinner, Eleanor said it contained a script sent by a producer, Daniel Frohman's younger brother, Charles. He wanted her to read it. She said no more.

After dinner, Will went to her room in the hope of getting her to talk about the script. He knocked but Eleanor didn't open the door. She asked him to come back another time because she was sleepy.

She sounded wide awake.

The next day Will found the script on the floor beside a wicker chair in the solarium. Gideon had built the solarium a few years earlier, at the third story front. It provided a magnificent view of the State House dome, the rooftops of Boston, and the leafy Common just across Beacon Street.

Will sat down and opened the cover of the script; he found a note tucked inside. With only a slight feeling of guilt he unfolded the note. Charles Frohman apologized for intruding on Eleanor's grief, but did so because he considered the accompanying script superior in every respect. He hoped she would read it, and think about taking a role when he produced the play in September. He was sure it would be a huge success.

He browsed through the first couple of acts of the hand-copied manuscript. The play was entitled *Shenandoah*. Its author, Bronson Crocker Howard, had turned to the Civil War for his theme and setting. It seemed a dramatic and well-written play; Will regretted his sister's lack of interest.

He left the script where he found it. Gideon picked it up in the same place a day later. That night he brought it into the dinner conversation:

'When I saw your script, Eleanor—'

'Not mine,' she interrupted. 'Frohman's.'

He drew a deep breath and went on, ' – I realized the war was truly over. Playwrights and novelists only return to a war for subject matter when the older veterans start dying off, and it's no longer so painful for the public to recall the conflict. It certainly took long enough in this case – twenty-four years. The funny thing is, sometimes it doesn't seem long at all. Sometimes it seems like only a moment ago that Jeb Stuart was leading a troop of the First Virginia up to the Yankee lines so we could get accustomed to the sound of cannon. Only a moment—'

A melancholy expression had erased his earlier pique. He went on matter-of-factly:

'You aren't interesting in auditioning for the gentleman, then?'

'For a play about this country?' Eleanor laughed, and Gideon's cheeks darkened again. 'No, I certainly am not. Besides, Charles Frohman's never had a success in New York.'

'I see,' Julia murmured. Scarlet, Gideon concentrated on his food. He kept silent with great effort.

That evening, for the first time, Will stopped looking at Gideon as a parent and considered him as a man exhibiting symptoms. The result was unexpectedly alarming. From now on he must keep his eyes open.

As for Eleanor, Will didn't believe it was only Leo's death which had caused her cold rejection of the outside world. Something terrible had happened in Johnstown. He was positive of it when he came home late one night from an outing with friends from the hospital. He passed his sister's door; heard her tossing and ranting in a nightmare.

He paused in the silent hallway, listening. A few words were clear:

' – No, you didn't hear me say that. I never said such a thing. *Never!*'

The rest was muffled. But the fright and anger in her voice spoke eloquently. He shivered. What had she denied saying? And to whom?

He might never know. Whatever the nature of her secret, he feared it was destroying her.

2

Underneath his resentment, Will harboured a deep love for his father. So, as the summer wore on, he began to pay more attention to Gideon's physical condition. What he saw upset him.

Early in June he developed a tentative diagnosis.

Then one boiling afternoon he came into the down-stairs office and discovered Gideon sitting absolutely still in a chair under old Philip's portrait. It was hard to tell that he was breathing.

Although Gideon was only forty-six, his beard was rapidly turning white to match the hair at his temples. Permanent wrinkles already creased his face. He would admit to his family that he suffered from rheumatism, but nothing more; nothing to explain his pale, sweat-stippled skin, or his peculiar pose of breathless rigidity.

But Will understood that pose perfectly. It fitted his diagnosis. It was the classic self-immobility of the person trying to calm the anguishing pains of angina.

Will was determined to try to validate that diagnosis, which at this stage was little more than an informed guess. Gideon winced and stood up. Will clasped his father's hand in greeting – something he seldom did. The action so startled the older man, Will was able to feel for Gideon's pulse without detection.

He only managed to catch two beats. But they seemed unusually far apart. A slow, laboured pulse was another symptom of the inappropriately named angina, which had nothing to do with strangulation, even though its Latin root, *angere*, suggested otherwise.

That night after dinner, Will commented on the hot weather, then casually asked Gideon whether the heat was causing him any discomfort. Any problems with sleeping or breathing. Any chest pains—

'No!'

Gideon's answer was quick, sharp, and presumably final. Still, the vehemence of it only served to convince Will that his father had meant exactly the opposite, and was deliberately hiding the truth from the family.

To add to the emotional strain in the household, Gideon's stepmother, Molly Kent, was stricken with heat prostration down at Long Branch. Molly was sixty-six. She hadn't been well for the past eight or nine years.

The news came on the twenty-second of July; two days before Will's departure for Newport. Julia was in Scranton, lecturing. Gideon sent her a telegram. As soon as she received it, she immediately dispatched two of her own. One was to the headquarters of her association, cancelling the remaining week and a half of her tour of Pennsylvania and Ohio. The other was a reply to Gideon, telling him that she knew he was busy, and assuring him that she could handle the emergency by herself. She'd send for him only if it became necessary. She boarded the next express for Philadelphia, and changed there for Long Branch.

Just in case he received a sudden summons from Julia, Gideon that day visited the Boston shipyard where *Auvergne* was careened for repairs to her hull. The yard superintendent told him the yacht couldn't be ready for at least four days. That enraged Gideon, even though he was the one who had ordered the scraping and painting. When he returned home, he grumbled and complained – he was becoming an irascible old man, Will thought sadly. Perhaps a very sick one, too.

At breakfast the next day, Gideon confessed he'd slept hardly at all. Will knew he'd better tread lightly. His father seemed determined not to permit it:

'Still leaving for Newport tomorrow?'

'Yes, sir.'

'Nothing worthwhile on that damned island except Mahan and the college.'

The installation to which he referred, the Naval War College, was barely four years old. There the Navy trained officers for future command responsibilities. Captain Alfred Mahan, one of the professors, had recently made a name for himself with a series of lectures on the influence of sea power on world history during the years 1600 to 1783. The lectures were soon to be published as a book. Kent and Son had already purchased the right to reprint it in a cheap edition.

Mahan was what Gideon called an expansionist: a man who felt it was the United States' destiny to extend its influence around the globe, via warships, just as it had extended itself from the Atlantic to the Pacific, buying or swallowing up the territory of others until it became an ocean-to-ocean country.

Gideon didn't approve of all Mahan's ideas, but he considered them to have a certain inevitability. Political thinkers such as Mr Roosevelt were fascinated by Mahan's theories – and that strongly suggested the course America might follow in the next couple of decades.

At the moment, however, Gideon's reference to Newport had a much more personal motivation. Will resisted an urge to retort, saying instead:

'I'd be happy to offer my services to Molly. I can easily delay my trip and go to Long Branch instead.'

'No, thank you,' Gideon shot back. 'I prefer to have my stepmother attended by a doctor who takes medicine seriously.'

'And I don't?'

'In my opinion, you're training to treat the nerves and vapours of debutantes.'

Livid, Will rose and flung down his napkin. Before Gideon could say anything, he walked out of the dining room.

He only kept his anger in check by reminding himself that his father was in poor health and undoubtedly worn out from a night of worrying about Jephtha Kent's widow. Besides, he'd be on his way to Newport in a little more than twenty-four hours. No point in causing a scene before he left. All the ingredients were certainly present for one. Will knew he'd better continue to tread lightly.

Events of July 23 conspired to rob Will of sleep, too. That night he again met a group of friends from the hospital. They had dinner at a tavern near the office of the Boston *Globe*. Every few minutes the *Globe* received telegraphic dispatches from a secret site in Mississippi where Jake Kilrain was meeting John L. Sullivan for the world's boxing championship. The men were fighting bare-knuckle style. That was already illegal in thirty-eight states, hence the secret location.

The telegraphic reports, summarized on chalk boards in front of the newspaper, were slow to come in. It was late when the outcome was posted for a small but noisy crowd which included Will and his friends. The Boston Strong Boy had won the $20,000 purse by knocking out the half-dead Kilrain in the seventy-fifth round.

A cheer went up. Will and his friends decided it wasn't too late for one more round to celebrate Sullivan's victory. One round became several. It was four-thirty in the morning when Will staggered up Beacon Street, lascivious thoughts of Laura chasing through his head and a bedraggled cat miaowing at his heels.

Will's ears seemed to be buzzing as he lurched up the front steps. He stumbled; fell against the projecting metal key which sounded an inside bell when twisted. He thought he heard the bell ring. Flung a finger to his lips:

'Sssh!'

He'd better not go in until he could walk a little more steadily. He sat down on the steps under the paling stars and again thought of Laura. She'd never been carried away to the point of losing control and letting him do anything he wished. But he suspected that under the proper circumstances, she might—

Laura Pennel was a shining and wondrous creature; desirable; altogether perfect. She was also his entreé to a world from which his father would be forever barred.

The wind blew gently, sweet with the smell of the ocean. The sky began to lighten. At last Will tottered to his feet and turned to the front door. A drunken determination surged through him. He knew Gideon wasn't a healthy man, but compassion had its limits. If his father refused to accept Laura as a prospective daughter-in-law, he could go to hell. Will was old enough to marry whomever he wanted. And he was ready to say exactly that – or anything else that became necessary – should Gideon force the issue.

Later that same day, he did.

CHAPTER II

Quarrel

Will folded shirts and piled them in his valise. It was two in the afternoon. His head still ached from the previous night's binge; every noise was an irritation, whether it was the buzz of a fly near the ceiling or the happy shout of a youngster careening down Beacon on a bicycle. Bicycling had recently become very popular with children and even with some adventurous adults.

Will had his mind on pleasure of a different kind. A letter from Laura had arrived in the morning mail. She said she couldn't wait to see him.

To protect the next item he packed, he surrounded

it with several pairs of socks. The object thus protected was a brand-new, box-like affair with a pebbled black finish; one of George Eastman's amazing Number One Kodak Cameras, put on the market just the preceding year.

Eastman was revolutionizing photography; transforming it from a tool of portrait makers and journalists to a pastime anyone could enjoy. Eastman's factory packed and shipped the camera with roll film already inside. After Will had snapped all his shots, he'd mail the camera back to Rochester where the film would be taken out and processed and the pictures printed and returned together with the re-loaded camera.

He folded a pair of white flannels into the valise, then pulled out his watch. Soon it would be time to go. He had a ticket on a four p.m. train to the little town of Wickford, Rhode Island. He'd stop overnight at an inn there, and in the morning board a side-wheel steamer which made daily runs between Wickford and the flourishing summer colony at the south end of Aquidneck Island.

The passenger and freight steamer *Eolus* was one of the two favourite means of transportation of Newport's many warm-weather tourists, the other being the Fall River boats out of New York. Of course the rich didn't sully themselves by taking public transportation to the island – not even a steamer as opulent as one of those on the Fall River Line. The elite arrived in private rail cars, or on personal yachts far larger and grander than *Auvergne*. It struck Will that his father would probably hull and sink his own yacht rather than see it docked at Newport among the boats of the people he loathed.

He heard footsteps ascending the hall stairs, out of sight beyond the open door of the bedroom. Without listening closely he assumed the steps to be Gideon's. On hot afternoons the owner of Kent and Son often came home early.

The last thing he wanted right now was an encounter with this father. To keep calm, he concentrated on closing and locking his valise.

The footsteps grew louder. He strode to the window and looked down at the Common.

'Will? Are you in there?'

He swung toward the door, hearing a second sound his anxiety had made him miss; the sound of rustling petticoats.

He pulled out a handkerchief and mopped his face.

'Yes, Eleanor. Come in.'

2

His sister was still shockingly pale, and a good twenty pounds thinner than she'd been when Gideon brought her home from Pennsylvania. Will assumed she'd just returned from Watertown. Once a week she drove there with flowers for Leo's empty grave. She had wanted Leo's monument placed in the Kent family burying ground despite his father's wish that it be located in a Jewish cemetery in Manhattan. Finally Efrem Goldman had relented.

'I see you're ready to go.'

'Almost.'

'I just wanted to wish you a happy journey.' She picked up her black bombazine skirt, rearranging it as she sat on the bed with that natural grace which drew and held every eye when she was on stage.

'Thank you. Did you see the mail I put outside your door?'

Her nod was listless.

'There was one from Philadelphia. The Arch Street Theatre—'

'Louisa Drew,' she said. 'She heard what happened,

and she wants me for a full season. Leo and I had a wonderful year with Louisa.'

'I remember. Don't you think you'd like going back to work?'

'I couldn't stand it. I couldn't face people. The questions, the continual talk about Johnstown, and Leo—'

'Well, I see your point. Perhaps if you wait a little longer, you could go back to Daly's.'

She shook her head. 'Mr Daly's been very kind. But he had to find two replacements immediately. Otherwise the touring company couldn't have fulfilled its bookings. I can never go back with him. The memories would be too immediate. God knows they're bad enough here, where I'm by myself—'

Despite the indications that her temper was short, his conscience forced him to press his views:

'That's precisely the point, Eleanor. Working might take your mind off all that's happened.'

'I don't *want* to work again, can't you understand that?' His heart almost broke as she stared at him – and through him – to some terrible moment in the past. Her voice lost strength: 'All I want to do is keep from losing my mind.'

She jolted and frightened him with the last statement, and with the strange look she gave him for a moment. A supplicant's look; the look of a terrified child pleading for help. He decided to push ahead:

'Eleanor, if there's anything you'd like to discuss – you know, on a confidential basis – I have some understanding of problems of the nerves. I'd be glad to listen to—'

'There is no problem except forgetting Johnstown – which can't be done. There is nothing to discuss!' It was as abrupt as a fire curtain thudding down.

He glanced away and shrugged. 'Whatever you say.'

Suddenly he heard a noise at the door. He'd been so

preoccupied with the conversation, he'd missed the approach of other footsteps—

And now, unprepared, he faced the person he least wanted to see.

3

Gideon had a smouldering cigar in one hand, a telegraph message in the other. Eleanor gathered her skirts and stood. Gideon waved the cigar, leaving a heavy blue tracery in the humid air:

'You needn't leave, Eleanor. You should both hear this piece of news. Happy news for a change – though I'm damned if we need extra commotion just now.'

Gideon's sleeves were rolled above his elbows and a palm leaf fan was stuck in his back pocket. His rumpled appearance coupled with his tone of voice told Will that he needed to be extremely careful not to antagonize him.

Eleanor pointed to the telegram. 'Does that concern Molly?'

'No.' He handed her the paper. She read it, then gave it to Will and said:

'Mr Calhoun and Miss Vail plan to be married.'

'It comes as no surprise to me,' Gideon said. Chewing on his cigar, he stalked to the window.

'I just wish to hell they'd wait a while,' he added. 'As you can see from Calhoun's message, they'd like to have the wedding in the suite at the Fifth Avenue Hotel. That's no problem. But Julia will undoubtedly want to supervise the reception, and we'll have to attend as a family. With Molly ill, I'm not certain we'll be able—'

He stopped, noticing Will's frown. 'You have a comment?'

Will tapped the telegram. 'The wedding's to be the first Saturday in August?'

'That's what it says.'

'And you want us all to attend?'

'Yes, I expect you to be present.'

That weekend Will would be helping Drew in New York – secretly. He certainly didn't want to show up at the Fifth Avenue Hotel and be forced to explain in the presence of guests, hotel help, and a clergyman why he was in the city. Laura said the publisher of *Town Topics* had spies everywhere. And since Will's name had been associated with hers almost constantly during the past months, if Colonel Mann found out about his little vacation in the Mulberry Street slums, he would surely print something about it. The Pennels wouldn't like that kind of notoriety. More important, he'd promised Laura that he'd do no more horse doctoring, as she called it.

All in all, the situation was extremely tricky; for that reason he finally said:

'I'm not sure it'll be possible for me to be there, Papa.'

Gideon jerked the cigar out of his mouth. 'Too busy with that crowd of socialites?'

'Something like that,' Will replied in a cold voice. 'I surely wish you'd tell me one thing, sir. Why the hell are you so antagonistic toward the Pennels?'

'It's no trick to explain that. In fact I thought I'd already done so. I despise the way the Pennels live, and I despise what they represent. I particularly despise what they represent.'

'Oh? Since when has this family begun scorning money?'

'Don't be snide, young man. It isn't money I object to, it's something else entirely. President Jefferson identified it best. He said—'

Will raised his hands. 'Spare me the history lesson.'

'No, by God. You need it. Jefferson said men are naturally divided by temperament into two classes. Those who fear and distrust ordinary people, and want to concentrate power in the hands of a small, select elite – and those who trust and cherish ordinary people, and think of them as the safest, if not always the wisest repositories of power.'

'Papa, I really haven't time to listen to a lecture on theories of government.'

'But a lecture is what you need! The Kents have always belonged in the second group. Your newfound friends are entrenched members of the first. They seem to have enticed you into it as well.'

Will flushed. Eleanor stepped between the two men:

'Papa, you have no right to say such things to Will. And that quotation is perfectly ridiculous! It's the dear, wonderful, *ordinary* people who killed my husband!'

Gideon spun on her, sweaty and red-faced in the heat:

'I'm sick of hearing that. I respect your grief but I cannot respect the errors in your thinking.'

'Don't take it out on her because I'm going to Newport,' Will exclaimed as Eleanor picked up her skirts and rushed out. In the hall, her high-topped shoes drummed on the carpet. The sound quickly faded.

'Yes, you are going there, aren't you?' Gideon retorted. 'I wouldn't brag about associating with a pack of self-anointed aristocrats.'

Will's temper was almost at the breaking point. '*Why* do you hate them so?'

'Because they're the antithesis of everything this family stands for! They're a disgrace to the country.'

'Christ. They're as American as you!'

Gideon shook his head angrily. 'They're Americans in name only. They may lack hereditary titles, but

680

they're of a piece with the rotten nobility old Philip despised and fought.'

'Oh, bullshit! You hate them for one reason. They don't want any part of an ill-mannered Southern brawler who—'

'God*damn* you!' Gideon shouted, his right hand fisting above his head.

Before Gideon could strike him, Will grabbed his father's wrist; held it high while Gideon pushed down – strength against strength. For a moment there was a stalemate. Then, with a loud exhalation, Gideon relaxed the pressure, unable to best his son.

Will let go of Gideon's wrist. Disgusted, he stepped back. 'Be decent enough to answer one question.'

'What is it?'

'Did your father choose the people you associated with?'

Gideon's good eye shone like a blue flame. 'No. Jeff Davis did.'

With an embittered laugh, Will reached for his summer blazer hanging on the bedpost:

'Oh, that's right. You were off to war when you were my age. The great cavalry hero – how could I possibly forget? You never permit us to forget. You even grew a beard like all the GAR veterans, just to be sure we wouldn't—'

Gideon's face shaded from red to plum, and Will was afraid he'd goaded his father into a seizure. He held very still.

Ten seconds passed. Ten more.

The unnatural colour drained from Gideon's face. His breathing grew less stertorous. He began rubbing his right wrist with his left hand, as if to eradicate the memory of being defeated by a younger, stronger man. When he spoke again, his voice was surprisingly moderate:

'We've gotten far from the subject. I ask you to

think of Moultrie Calhoun's wedding as a family obligation.'

Will shook his head. 'I'm sorry, Papa. You're deliberately making it an issue. You're giving the wedding an importance it doesn't deserve.' Gideon's startled look showed he knew he was guilty of the accusation.

'And if you count on me being there,' Will added, 'You'll be disappointed.'

A pause. Then Gideon whispered, 'Those Pennels will ruin you.'

Will snatched up his valise. 'I doubt it.'

'If you were aware of the questionable business practices of that girl's father—'

'I'll appreciate it if you make no more remarks about Laura's family.'

'I must. Before you entangle yourself further, it's important that you realize some of the things they—'

'Papa, that's enough!'

Silence. Longer, this time; interrupted eventually by the drone of a fly coming in the window. Down on Beacon Street, the bell of an ice wagon clanged.

Looking old and tired, Gideon sank onto the bed and stared at his son. Softly, he said, 'What the devil is going to become of you, Will?'

For a moment Will actually hated his father. Gideon's face accused him – as did other faces that abruptly came to mind. Drew's face. Roosevelt's—

A few words about your duties.

'Why do you do that?' he cried. 'Why do you all act as if you have to supply me with a conscience?'

'Because yours is missing.'

'I don't want or need your kind of conscience!' Will slammed his straw hat on his head. He stalked toward the door, valise in one hand, blazer trailing from the other. He heard his father say:

'No, not among the Pennels. And especially since you've abdicated your place among the Kents.'

You arrogant son of a bitch! Will shouted – but not aloud. He stormed down the stairs. Ignored the anxious face of a footman peering from the dining room. Heard Eleanor call his name from somewhere but didn't pause. He was going to Newport tomorrow – to the girl he wanted – and Gideon Kent's opinions be damned!

As soon as he had discharged his obligation to Drew, he'd have no more claims on him. He'd be free to do whatever he wanted with his life. Free of pious voices forever crying platitudes about duty, democracy, and God knew what else. He was beginning to think some of Eleanor's diatribes were justified.

He stopped at the first corner he reached, struck by another pang of guilt. During the past few minutes he had violated a fundamental precept of medicine: the physician must use every means at hand to protect and preserve the health of others. He had done the opposite; by his own anger, he might well have provoked his father into a fatal paroxysm. He vowed never to repeat the mistake.

How would it all work out? He didn't konw. But he saw a sad pattern reappearing. Once, Gideon's eldest child had fled his house. Of course Eleanor had left thinking her father guilty of deeds for which poor, demented Margaret had actually been responsible. Will's case wasn't quite the same.

But the result could be the same, he thought as he walked on in the scorching sunlight. If Gideon's stiff-necked antagonism continued, Will too would walk out. And although it was sad to contemplate, he knew that if he ever decided to do that, the parting would be permanent.

CHAPTER III

Newport

Flykyns – So she loved not wisely?
Sylykyns – Yes, it's a case of sin and bear it.

Will shook his head and turned the page.

Winkle – You're the last man I'd expect to marry
outside the fashionable set.
Binkle – Oh, I fancied I'd like to have a wife
of my own, don't you know?

He shut the paper, frowning. The jokes in *Town Topics* didn't strike him as funny. The one he'd just read was especially disagreeable. Laura was a member of the so-called fashionable set.

He sat on the open deck of *Eolus*, his dark hair tossed by the wind. The steamer was chugging slowly round the southern tip of Goat Island, on its way to one of the Newport piers.

The pier extended from a waterfront street which resembled that of any small New England maritime town. Will had bought a little guidebook in Boston. He knew that at one time slave ships had sailed out of Newport bound for West Africa. Now the vessels in the harbour were mostly small sailboats running before the breeze, or dumpy lobstermen putting out to the offshore banks. In the main channel of Narragansett Bay, two dozen crewmen were aloft spreading canvas on a three-masted yacht. She was a splendid, stately sight as she glided toward the Atlantic in the summer sunshine.

Will had never seen so many sailboats moored in one

place. Colonel Mann must have been thinking of Newport when he wrote a comment Will had just read in the *Saunterings* column. *The man that does not own a yacht is a poor, despicable creature indeed.*

That kind of condescension pervaded Mann's so-called *Journal of Society*, a tabloid containing articles, short fiction, and those wretched jokes. But the heart of it was *Saunterings* – ten pages of short paragraphs which started on page one. He guessed that *Saunterings* attracted two groups of readers – ordinary people who wanted to peep through a journalistic keyhole at the rich, and the rich themselves, anxious to see whether their names or escapades were included in the column.

An item on page one was typical. It began, *There is a little comedy, or tragedy, if you like, going on just now.* Then two paragraphs piously deplored the various affairs of an unfaithful wife.

The wife was never named. But the street in New York on which she lived was mentioned twice. Will supposed that was how Mann made sure his victims were identified. Obviously the woman or her cuckolded husband hadn't paid the amount necessary to keep the item out of print.

Will had lived in a newsman's house long enough to recognize Mann's moralizing for what it was – a screen behind which otherwise objectionable material could be published. Altogether, he found the paper as distasteful as his father said it was. He tossed it into a waste can.

At the rail he squeezed between two heavy-set gentlemen, obviously tourists. A gust of wind almost lifted his bright-banded straw hat from his head. He raised his hand to hold it in place and, with mounting excitement, scanned the shore.

Behind the busy piers and the straggle of houses and shops along the main street – Thames Street, if he recalled the guidebook – small, neat saltbox houses perched on the side of a moderately steep hill. Aquidneck was a hilly island, with outcrops of rock and patches of scrub growth breaking up its expanses of farmland.

Fifty years earlier, Newport had been a popular summer retreat of wealthy Southern planters. The Civil War had driven them home to stay. Then, a few years ago, the ladies at the top of Northern Society had rediscovered the place. It had happened about the time that the prestige of the New Jersey resorts – Deal Beach, Elburon, Long Branch – had begun to decline. Thurman Pennel identified the cause of that decline as an 'Infestation of New York Jews.'

Two local land speculators named Joseph Bailey and Alfred Smith had responded to the interest in New York by developing a parcel of a hundred and forty acres on the island's southeast side. They offered land as a kind of private preserve of the rich. Now more and more of New York's leading families were buying property and building vacation homes. Earlier in the year, Mrs Astor had officially sanctioned Newport as the nation's premier summer colony when she let it be known that she would be in residence during July and August.

The Bailey and Smith land had been subdivided into large lots. The choicest ones were located on the east side of Bellevue Avenue, overlooking the public Cliff Walk and the Atlantic. The Pennels had purchased one of these lots almost three years earlier. At that time, Laura's mother had somehow become attuned to the resort's imminent popularity. She'd persuaded her husband to commission Richard Morris Hunt to design and supervise construction of the Pennels' summer residence.

The choice of Hunt turned out to be a remarkable stroke of foresight. Now that Mrs Astor had given her imprimatur, everyone wanted a cottage at Newport – no matter how large, the homes were always called cottages – and everyone wanted Hunt for the architect. The rush had only started, and the Pennels were already settling into place at Maison du Soleil. All Newport cottages were required to have special names, it seemed. The Wetmore cottage was Château-sur-Mer, that which the Cornelius Vanderbilts had bought from the Pierre Lorillards, The Breakers, Mrs Astor's cottage was Beechwood.

The Pennel cottage had been finished and furnished during the spring. Maison du Soleil had forty-two rooms, and was constructed chiefly of Siena marble. Laura said it was a copy of a Northern Italian villa, though she called the style American Renaissance.

To Will it seemed a gross waste to build such huge places and move forty or fifty servants all the way from New York for a season only eight weeks long. Of course, in the Pennels' circle, cost was usually the factor of least importance in any decision. Laura boasted that marble imported for the cottage had cost four million dollars just by itself. Will was almost as anxious to see Maison du Soleil as he was eager to see Laura.

The pier at which *Eolus* docked was crowded with people, including a good many men with the robust look of fishermen. Their faces were cheerfully contemptuous as they eyed the pale vacationers on board the steamer. The tourists jostled for a position near the gangway while the vessel was warped in the last few feet.

There were ordinary townsfolk on the pier, too. Even a few aristocratic servants who kept themselves noticeably apart from the rabble. Perhaps the servants had come to await a freight shipment.

Will searched the crowd for Laura. Slowly his smile faded. She wasn't there. She'd promised he would be met, and he'd assumed she would be the one to meet him.

What had happened?

3

Suddenly, up on Thames Street, people scattered. There were shouts; curses, fists shaken. A lacquered victoria came careening into sight from behind some waterfront houses.

The top-hatted driver whipped the four matched sorrels, heedless of pedestrians. He didn't slow down until he had to turn at the head of the pier. There, too, people were forced to run. As the victoria came bouncing down the pier, Will recognized the driver. Marcus Pennel.

With four sets of reins in his hands and a gleaming black boot on the brake, Marcus brought the victoria to a swaying stop. When he jumped down he was caustically rebuked by a woman who'd snatched a toddler out of the path of the coach. Marcus strolled right by, not even glancing at her to acknowledge her existence.

By then the steamer was snugged to the pier with hawsers. The gangway thumped down. Passengers started to elbow and shove one another. Marcus swaggered to the edge of the pier and put one shining patent leather boot up on a bollard. He took off his black silk hat and wiped his forehead with a handkerchief plucked from his cuff.

His curly hair glistened in the sunshine. He was wearing an emerald green coaching jacket with gilt buttons, a yellow waistcoat, spotless white breeches, and gloves. In his lapel he sported a yellow flower that matched the four bouquets decorating the throatlatches of his horses.

'Marcus! Hello!' Will waved.

'Hello, there!' Laura's brother raised his top hat, then tilted it in an exaggerated way. A passing sailor looked at him and spat. The spittle landed near the toe of Marcus's right boot. The young man pretended not to see. The sailor snickered and walked on.

Will struggled down the gangway with his valise. He was uncomfortably hot in his blazer; Marcus looked dry and cool despite the obvious heaviness of his driving clothes.

'Nearly thought I wouldn't get here,' Marcus said, laughing. 'I came through the tail end of the noon coaching parade. Damn near ran over four or five townies.'

His laugh bothered Will, but not as much as Laura's absence. Perhaps it wasn't proper for a girl in her position to meet a beau at a public pier. All the same, he was disappointed.

'Seems like a year since I last saw you,' Marcus went on. He relieved Will of his valise and carried it through the crowd toward the victoria, which was upholstered in rich maroon.

'Well, it has been six months,' he replied. 'How've you been?'

'I manage to survive. Real estate's a boring business, but then I'm afraid I'd find any business boring. I'd much rather be driving or sailing.' Since graduating from Harvard, Marcus had been managing some of the Pennel properties from the family offices in New York's financial district.

Marcus flung Will's valise into the open carriage.

'Laura's at the beach with some of her girl friends. She should be back by the time we reach the cottage. Maybe you'll even have a glimpse of her bathing costume.'

He winked, and a moment later Will felt himself go rigid. The words bathing costume had done it. Contemporary beach fashions showed very little flesh, but they were still considered quite daring by most people, and flagrantly immoral by a few. Hiding his embarrassing reaction as best he could, he climbed up on the coachman's seat next to his host.

Marcus pulled the whip from its socket. 'The girls are required to clear the beach by noon. After that it's reserved for nude bathing by gentlemen—' He noticed an older man and woman who appeared to be having a reunion with a younger girl directly in front of the horses. The girl had been on the steamer.

Marcus waved the whip at the man. 'Clear the way, Edmonds!'

Edmonds, a plain-looking sort, turned toward the elegant man as if ready to object. Before he could, Marcus again brandished the whip:

'I said clear the way, you clod.'

The starch went out of the man suddenly. He took the two women by the arm and guided them to the other side of the pier. Amused, Marcus said to Will, 'He'd better move when I tell him. His son's one of our gardeners. Edmonds himself needs the cold water cure. Failing that, he needs his son's wages so he can buy whiskey.'

Now that the man and his family had got out of the way, Marcus was in no hurry to drive on. Edmonds noticed that, and glowered.

Marcus ignored him. 'How was the trip from Wickford?'

'Smooth. I spent most of it reading *Town Topics*.'

'God almighty. What'd you do with it?'

'I threw it away.'

'Good. That rag isn't allowed in our house any longer.'

'Why not? Your family used to read it. Laura said so.'

'We still read it, old boy. We just aren't permitted to let it lie about the cottage as if we approve of it. Father skims *Saunterings* once a week at a men's club I'll show you on the way home. He skims it nervously, I might add. A year ago I got involved with a Chinese girl down in the city. Never told you about that, did I?'

Will shook his head.

'Somehow Mann discovered I was buggering the wench. He presented Father with a galley of an item on the subject. No names, of course. But the piece was written so everyone would know I was the fellow trying to erase the natural colour barriers between the American and Asian races, as Mann so delicately put it—'

Marcus shuddered, his smile gone. 'It was horrible. Naturally, Father paid Mann to suppress the story. But the language of their discussion got pretty heated. The very next week, to retaliate, Mann condensed the story to half its original length and published it anyway. I couldn't show my face for weeks.'

Will was aghast. 'How could Mann pull a trick like that?'

'How could he? Because he's a damned crook. Of course he kept the letter of his bargain. He'd been paid to kill the copy he showed Father, and he did. Nothing was said about other versions. He joked about it afterward. I tell you, Will, everybody on the island is terrified of the son of a bitch.

'There isn't a first-rank household that isn't fearful of harbouring at least one of the Colonel's informants on its staff. We think we have two or three. Trouble is, we don't know who they are and we can't find out. Mann pays them too well.'

'You mean servants actually spy on their employers?'

The naïveté of the question made Marcus snicker. 'How else do you suppose the Colonel digs up all that dirt? Someone else on the island acts as a clearing house for the information and a conduit for the money. We can't find out who it is, either. Another of our footstools, I suspect.'

'Footstools?'

'Those of us who come up for the summer call the townies our footstools. I'm told the term originated with King Louis the Fourteenth. I like it.'

Will said nothing. He was appalled by the remark, and by all he'd heard in the past few minutes. He'd seen little of Marcus Pennel during the past year, and he realized something had changed. Perhaps it was his own viewpoint. How had he ever been able to consider this callous young man his friend?

The truth was, he hadn't. As he looked back, he realized Marcus had impressed him because of his family name, nothing else. And after he'd met Laura, he had tended to overlook Marcus's faults because he was her brother.

The presence of the victoria in the centre of the pier was an inconvenience to pedestrians and cart traffic. Marcus sensed that the appropriate moment for departure had come. He picked up the reins and quickly separated them.

'Here we go.'

He whipped up the horses and started them into a wide hundred-and-eighty-degree turn. He whipped them a second time as the carriage rumbled toward the head of the wharf, picking up speed. He was grinning again. He clearly assumed that any sailors, fishermen, or townspeople would remove themselves from his path before he ran them down.

Remarkably, they did.

CHAPTER IV

The Shacker

The high-stepping sorrels drew the victoria north along Thames Street. Occasionally Marcus flicked one of the leaders with the whip. He was an expert driver, Will observed as Marcus guided the carriage round a corner and up a sloping brick street.

'How long are you going to be here, Will?'

'A week or a little more. Till Laura gets bored with my presence.'

'Oh, my dear sister has many a devious method of combating boredom,' Marcus replied with a sly smile. Will found himself disliking that smile, though he couldn't say why.

Marcus realized he'd annoyed his friend. With a straight face, he added, 'She's awfully anxious to see you again. I think you two would make a capital match.'

Redness showed in Will's cheeks. 'How does she feel about that?'

'I haven't quizzed her, but I have a feeling she agrees. I was expressing the opinion of some of the rest of us—'

He pointed the whip at a small, grey-painted colonial building on their left. 'That's the Touro Synagogue. Oldest Jew church in America. Established a good ten years before the Revolution.'

Will held onto his straw hat and turned to look at the building. Marcus guided the horses down the middle of the street. A delivery wagon coming from the other direction was forced to give way.

Sparks shot from the hooves of the sorrels as they

pulled hard toward the summit of the hill. Over the noise of iron shoes and wheel rims, Will shouted, 'What do you do for entertainment here?'

'I'll show you when you can tear yourself away from Laura. The family dinghy's berthed at the local yacht club. I like sailing even more than driving, I think. Pierpont Morgan said you can do business with anyone, but you can only go sailing with a gentleman. Managing Father's estate, I meet a lot of low-class people. You can't imagine what illiterate grafters I'm forced to deal with. Some of them come right out of the foulest sl – well, never mind that,' he amended, keeping his eye on the horses.

He turned into another tree-shaded street. This one headed roughly southeast along the crest of the hill. 'We were discussing recreation. You have your choice of the yacht, polo ponies, this and several other carriages – you enjoy coaching, as I recall—'

Will nodded.

'Then you'll be right at home in Newport. You can also play tennis, swim, or visit Blanche's and get royal treatment for your cock.'

'What's Blanche's, a whorehouse?'

'A very fine and discreet one. The girls would object to the use of such a crude term. All our crowd goes there. Keep it in mind if Laura's busy.' He chuckled and watched the road a moment. 'Seriously, old fellow, she's working very hard on your behalf these days.'

'What do you mean?'

'Ward McAllister summers here, up at Bayside Farm. He puts on picnics that are all the rage. Earlier this month Laura attended one. She flattered and wheedled McAllister until he was in a good mood and she could bring you into the conversation. I'm afraid Wardie hasn't forgotten what your father did. But Laura reminded him your name is Will Kent, not Gideon. He admitted that was true. Before she was finished with him, he'd virtually promised to get you an invitation to Mrs Astor's ball next January.'

It was incredibly good news. Why, then, did Will have trouble summoning any excitement?

He tried. 'That's wonderful, Marcus.'

'A little more enthusiasm, if you please. Once you attend Mrs Astor's winter ball, your membership in Society is forever certified. You're recognized as *crème de la crème*, as Wardie likes to put it—'

Promise me you'll be somebody.

And promise me you'll make sure everybody knows it.

'I appreciate Laura's effort,' he said with greater animation. 'I didn't mean to act as if I don't. Something else had crossed my mind—'

'What?'

'That servant whose leg I set the first time I visited Pennel House.'

The victoria turned down another broad street. Through dust raised by the horses, Will saw a marker identifying the street as Bellevue Avenue. Marcus looked blank for a moment, then said:

'Jameson – wasn't that the fellow's name?'

'Jackson. Is he still with you?'

'No. I think he married one of our house girls and went west. Why do you ask?'

'I'd like to know whether the leg healed properly.'

'Afraid I can't say. To tell you the truth, I never inquired. Does it matter?'

'No. It was just my first fling at – well, call it horse doctoring.'

The carriage continued up the street toward a frame building with a shaded front porch. On the porch sat several old gentlemen with sizeable paunches. One of them nodded – the only greeting Marcus received. The rest regarded the victoria and its driver with disapproval. Will had the feeling the old gentlemen would have regarded any source of noise or motion with disapproval.

'Those are some of the august members of The Reading Room,' Marcus told him. 'That private club I mentioned.'

'Private?'

'Very. But the membership roster includes damn few readers. Mostly it's a bunch of old rips who drink and reminisce about chorus girls they've fucked in private booths in some New York lobster palace. The club used to be Commodore Bennett's hangout.'

'Gordon Bennett, Junior? The publisher of the *Herald*?'

'The same. I always admired his style, but he was too much for some. A few years ago, he had a British officer up here as his guest. Chap named Captain Candy. Bennett challenged Candy to ride a pony across the Reading Room porch and straight on inside. Damned if the limey didn't do it. The stunt didn't set well with some of the old farts in the club. They slapped the Commodore's wrist. Sent him an official reprimand. Made him so mad, he dropped his membership and built the place just ahead. The Commodore's long gone but that's his memorial – the Newport Casino.'

Marcus pointed his whip at the sprawling structure on the east side of Bellevue Avenue. The victoria jolted over shiny tracks in the centre of Bath Road. Down the hill on Bath, Will saw a trolley climbing from the waterfront. He noticed overhead wires:

'You really have electric trolleys here? It's a pretty small island for that—'

'The trolley line's new this year. Some like it. I don't. Isn't good for anything but hauling tourists from the ferry to the beaches – here, I'll stop so you can get a better look at the Casino. Stanford White designed it.'

He pulled to the right side of the road, at the edge of a field in which more than twenty vehicles were parked; everything from a Demi-Daumont to a dog cart. The drivers and postilions were tending to the horses or lounging in the shade of nearby trees.

The Casino across the street was a low, rambling building painted green and heavily decorated with the wooden scrollwork so popular these days. From where he sat, Will could look straight through the entrance arch. On a grass court, two men and two women wearing white were languidly batting at a tennis ball. Fashionably dressed couples watched from parasol-shaded seats at the sidelines.

'The Casino's damned popular,' Marcus told him. 'It's always packed at eleven o'clock every morning. That's when Conrad's Orchestra gives its daily concert. And unless your family owns permanent seats in the grandstand, you positively can't get through the turn-stile during Tennis Week in Aug—'

'Pennel. Hey – Pennel!'

A stocky, dark-haired young man stepped out from the shadows of the Casino's entrance arch. In one hand he held a smouldering cigarette.

He stared at Will and Marcus with a derisive expression. He was about Marcus's age and wore patched trousers, a sweat-marked red jersey, and a dirty cap with a broken visor. The shabby clothes did nothing to detract from his swarthy good looks. Behind him, two

697

other boys leaned on a railing beside a turnstile, watching. Both were dressed like their companion.

Marcus whipped up the horses. But not so quickly that Will missed what the swarthy young man yelled next:

'Tell your sister that when she gets another itch, we're all ready to take her on again.'

3

'*Bastards.*'

Marcus brought the whip down so hard on the left leader, the animal whinnied.

The victoria veered toward the centre of the avenue, the lead horses on a collision course with those of a second victoria coming from the opposite direction. The other driver shouted and swore. His passenger, a man of about sixty with a Vandyke and a Napoleon III moustache, recognized Marcus and glared.

By expert driving Marcus narrowly avoided a crash. When he'd got his victoria back on the right side of the street, he groaned, 'This isn't my day. That was Wardie.'

'McAllister?'

'Right. Jesus! As for that loudmouth – I hope you didn't pay any attention to what he said.'

'I didn't take it seriously, if that's what you mean. Turn the carriage around.'

'Why?'

Will's dust-covered face had a hard look. 'I'll give him a chance to take back his remark and apologize. If he won't, I'll call him out.'

'Bare knuckle?'

'Anything he chooses!'

Marcus kept driving. He was unenthusiastic about a fight:

'Listen, that shacker was just spouting hot air. You don't want to get mixed up with his kind.'

'Why'd you call him a shacker? What's that mean?'

'It's the name for ball boys at the Casino. Townies, every one of them. They delight in harassing the summer crowd. Every so often the complaints get too numerous, and the Casino managers fire one or two. But two more are hired to replace them, so it's a losing battle.'

Marcus turned to look earnestly at his companion through the dust blowing up behind the horses. Here Bellevue Avenue ran in virtually open country, treeless except for obvious new plantings which screened a few large houses on either side of the road. To the left, a break in shrubbery afforded glimpses of a turreted mansion against a glinting expanse of the Atlantic.

'Shackers will say the worst possible things about anyone,' Marcus went on. 'Tell the crudest and most outrageous lies. They delight in it. In a brawl they stick together. Always win. And Muldoon – ' Marcus caught himself. 'The one you just saw is the worst of the lot. That's why I wouldn't go back and start anything if I were you.'

Marcus's cowardice sickened Will. How much easier and safer it was for Laura's brother to demonstrate his bravery by threatening a miserable, middle-aged drunk like that Edmonds. And obviously he didn't want Will to know the shacker's name, in case Will went back looking for the boy.

What ingratitude, he thought a moment later. Marcus Pennel was his host and one day might be his brother-in-law. He should be on Marcus's side, not that of a bunch of illiterate oafs who didn't know how to behave toward their betters.

'Laura's never spoken a friendly word to any of those wretches,' Marcus assured him. 'Never. Count on it.'

'I do. I recognize dirty talk for what it is.'

Marcus looked relieved. 'I'm glad. Ah – here we are.'

4

He swung the leaders into a left-hand turn. The victoria passed through an immense wrought iron gate onto a long, broad driveway of crushed marble. The drive was flanked by closely planted, neatly trimmed hydrangeas.

Ahead, a magnificent house rose. Will hardly noticed. Marcus had been upset about the shaker's remark, yet unwilling to do anything about it. To Will it was puzzling behaviour. No, more than that; upsetting. Marcus should be interested in defending his own sister's reputation. Why wasn't he?

Will began to think his earlier explanation was wrong. He wasn't absolutely convinced Marcus was a coward. But if not, what kept him from fighting? Again Will had no idea.

He didn't dignify the shacker's taunt by wondering whether it might be true. He knew it wasn't. Laura might lose her self-control with someone she loved, but she'd never sully herself by being promiscuous. Yet the incident continued to trouble him. He decided the problem was Marcus. Reluctantly, he realized he didn't like Laura's brother very much.

A bad way to begin a visit, he thought as the victoria rolled up in front of the awesome three-storey mansion looming against a backdrop of cliff, ocean, and summer sky. But Laura would help. By her mere presence, she'd settle his doubts and put everything right again. He was sure of that much, at least.

CHAPTER V

Maison du Soleil

Servants met the victoria outside the huge front doors of carved oak. One man whisked Will's valise away, a second relieved Marcus of his top hat, two more held the horses while grooms came running from the stable. At a touch of Marcus's index finger, one of the tall, perfectly counterbalanced doors swung open without a sound.

Delighting in Will's amazed expression, Marcus led him into the marble-floored entrance hall. 'Come along, now. There's more to see than a doorway that cost a mere fifty thousand.'

So there was – and Mrs Pennel, small and polite yet exuding that aura of steely strength, was determined that Will see it immediately. Laura was still at the beach. 'And Thurman is in New York attending to business.' It had the sound of an afterthought.

Maison du Soleil had been built by a combination of local and imported European labour, she said as they began the tour. The plan of the house devoted the first floor to rooms for entertaining, the second to nine family and guest bedrooms, and the third to much smaller rooms for the servants. The mansion's focal point was a central hall whose walls rose two floors to a fresco so realistically painted, Will had to look closely to be sure he wasn't staring at the summer sky.

On the east side of the hall, directly opposite the front entrance, six glass doors with ornate bronze fittings opened on a wide loggia. This overlooked a well-tended lawn and provided a breathtaking view of the sea. As Will faced the loggia, a sweeping staircase was on his left. On his right he saw four closed doors behind a splashing fountain recessed into the floor. Like the walls, the floor was marble quarried in Europe.

Mrs Pennel next led him to the morning room, but he could no longer absorb or appreciate most of what she said. His mind was already numbed by the size and extravagance of the so-called cottage. Still, in room after room he was forced to murmur compliments about wall facings of Campan marble, inlays of green Spanish leather stamped in gold, panels of Circassian walnut, mosaics painstakingly created in Rome. He spent ten minutes studying a hooded fireplace. It took that long just to discover all the tiny, exceedingly realistic human figures in medieval costume which ornamented the stone chimneypiece.

His hostess was relentless. She showed him gilt furniture, intricate metalwork, Flemish tapestries, porphyry vases, grisaille. She said Richard Hunt had personally supervised every detail, right down to selection of the furnishings. 'And we still don't know the total cost of the house. It will be somewhere above ten millions.'

Will felt like a guest at a banquet; sick from too many courses. He could only smile in a bleary way and murmur, 'It's very beautiful, Mrs Pennel.' Laura's mother nodded happily to acknowledge the remark – as if it was exactly what she'd expected to hear.

To his relief, the hostess's tour didn't extend beyond the first floor. Marcus accompanied him upstairs. The second floor, in contrast, was comfortable, and much less ostentatious. Obviously the largest amount of money had been spent where the results would show. Now that Will's astonishment was passing, he decided he didn't like the house much. It had all the warmth of a museum.

Marcus seemed quite at home, however. He threw himself down on the bed in Will's quarters – a bedroom with adjoining tiled bathroom. A servant was already waiting when they walked in. The man stood motion-less in a corner.

Marcus pointed through the bathroom door to a gigantic, claw-footed marble tub with four faucets of fluted silver:

'Two are plain water collected from the cisterns. The others give you salt water, hot or cold, in case you'd like a romp in the ocean without leaving your room.'

Will couldn't help laughing. 'Good Lord – what other wonders do you have in store?'

'Well, in case you haven't noticed, I'm the main decoration in here – ' He indicated a marble statue on a free-standing Ionic column. The statue, two feet high, represented a small boy. He had a lot of curly hair, wore a classic toga, and was pensively gazing at a bunch of grapes in his hand.

'They had that done for my fifth birthday,' Marcus added.

'That's you?'

'Of course.' He rose and put a hand on his friend's shoulder, his smile faintly condescending. 'If you mean to be part of the Pennel family, old chap, you must get used to this sort of thing. Take it in stride without letting your jaw drop. One favour, though—'

He changed position so that his back was toward the waiting servant. The man's gaze was fixed on the ceiling frescoes, which featured plump female personifications of the four seasons.

'Don't say anything about – ' He mouthed the rest. ' – the shacker. Eh?' Another brotherly squeeze, and he started out. 'This gentleman standing so still is named Ridgely. He will gladly draw a bath or lay out new linen. Just tell him what you want. We'll expect you downstairs in a little while.'

After Marcus strolled out, Will studied the bedroom more closely. It had no closets, but there was a large and elaborate armoire. He said to the servant:

'Unpack my things and put them in there, if you please.'

Instantly, he was ashamed of the arrogance that had crept into his voice. The man called Ridgely didn't seem to mind. He evidently expected the owners of the marble cottage as well as their guests to behave as if they were superior to everyone else on earth.

2

Twenty minutes later, Will went downstairs carrying his camera. Another servant informed him that luncheon would be served at two. Meantime, a light appetizer was available. Local whitefish; lobster in wine; freshly roasted corn. He politely turned it down and joined Marcus outside in the formal garden.

The garden was sunken, laid out in parterre on the south side of the mansion. Will counted nine gardeners at work on the Pennel property. Some were planting new pin oaks out near the avenue, some were trimming the Japanese maples and Chinese ginkgoes and African blue cedars closer to the house. Two were weeding around a row of copper beeches which partially hid the lot to the south. There, about a hundred bare-chested workmen sweated with picks and shovels, digging the foundation of another cottage. A dozen horse-drawn tip carts carried off the excavated dirt. Dust billowed, and almost continuous swearing counterpointed the crash of the waves below the cliff walk.

Will concentrated on composing a snapshot. 'A little to the left, Marcus. By that bench. I want to get a picture of you while the light is—'

Feminine laughter mingled with the sound of hooves and iron wheel rims in the driveway. Will turned, drawing a quick breath as Laura jumped down from a carriage crowded with six other girls. Laura was the only one who hadn't changed her bathing costume before coming home.

The carriage turned around and rattled back toward the gate. Laura barely waved at her departing friends; she was looking at him.

Her hair streamed out above her shoulders as she ran barefoot into the garden. She carried sandals and an embroidered bag. True to his expectations, the sight of her bathing costume was almost unbearably erotic; demure as it was, it revealed far more of her figure than did her everyday clothes.

It was serge; dark blue, and trimmed with white pique. It consisted of a snug-fitting, high-necked dress whose hem reached to mid-thigh, and matching drawers gathered below the knee. Of course the bathing costume wasn't damp. Proper young ladies didn't go to the beach to swim or get a sunburn. They went to meet their friends and gossip – and always under a sunshade.

Even taking that into consideration, Laura's skin was abnormally white. Her lack of colour disturbed him. Was she ill?

She rushed straight to him, her breasts bouncing in the serge bodice. 'Oh, Will. How delicious to see you!'

She flung her arm round his neck; pressed her cheek against his. Will's hand strayed to her waist, plump and uncorsetted. She let him hold her a moment, then stepped back, depositing her sandals and bag on the bench.

She sat down, her hair blown in the wind that made a hissing sound in nearby clumps of junipers. 'I've been anticipating this moment for days and days. I couldn't sleep last night just thinking of it.'

'It's grand to be here, Laura. This place is breathtaking.'

She jumped up again, taking his arm and leaning in close enough for him to feel her breast against his forearm. For a moment her grey eyes seemed to convey

705

frank sexual desire. The reaction of his body was instantaneous. He didn't dare glance down to see whether it was noticeable.

'I'm so happy you like it, my dear.' She led him toward the arches of the small south porch. Marcus followed. 'You must learn every nook and cranny of the cottage. All of us hope you'll spend your summers her for a long, long time.'

Behind them, Marcus laughed. 'Damned if that doesn't sound like a proposal.'

Her voice was airy. 'Does it?' She concentrated on a cloud. 'Interpret it any way you wish, gentlemen.'

Elated, Will said, 'I'm supposed to do any proposing that's necessary.'

She squeezed his arm. 'Ah, but you're such a shy one, I'm forced to be bold.'

'It really must be love,' Marcus said with good-humoured sarcasm. 'Look here, you two.'

They turned. He was holding Will's camera in his left hand, Laura's bag and sandals in the other. 'Have you forgotten your own names, too?'

Will laughed. 'Nearly.' His father certainly thought so. They strolled into the house, talking about the beautiful weather, his trip, her outing at Easton's Beach. Marcus continued to amble along behind the young couple, eyeing Will in a thoughtful way. A satisfied, almost smug expression settled on his face, exactly as if some prearranged plan was working to perfection.

3

What Mrs Pennel termed 'a simple midday meal' consisted of six courses including poached salmon, rack of lamb, and *filets de boeuf aux truffes et champignons*—'Mr McAllister's recipe.' There were numerous side dishes as well, the whole served by half a dozen footmen in Pennel livery.

The dining room was another of those caverns whose size and opulence elevated an ordinary human function to something of a rite. Its ceiling, too, was two stories high, decorated with murals of dawn and dusk. From the ceiling hung a pair of mammoth crystal chandeliers equipped for gas and also wired for the less dependable electricity. Columns of red Numidian marble with gilt capitals were ranged all around the walls. An intricately carved fireplace trimmed in silver leaf dominated one end of the room. At the other was a large window overlooking the Atlantic.

Storm clouds were darkening the horizon out there, Will noticed. He was hot and a little dizzy from all the red and white wines served with the various courses. Still the dutiful guest, he'd taken a glass of each.

The dining table was a square of carved mahogany with inlays of satinwood. There were five chairs with red damask upholstery at each side. The table could be expanded to seat forty, Mrs Pennel had informed him. But even in its normal configuration it dwarfed the four diners. Marcus was opposite his mother, Will across from Laura.

She had changed to a fluffy summer organdy and tied her hair with a lavender ribbon. Despite her odd pallor, she looked beautiful. But he began to notice that she occasionally darted worried or questioning glances at her mother. She was clearly under some strain. Could it have anything to do with that shaker's remark about—?

No. He wouldn't even entertain such a thought.

During the meal conversation ranged over a variety of innocuous topics. Mrs Pennel asked about Will's studies, but her attention to his answers struck him as perfunctory at best. She preferred speaking to listening. Will concluded that she was chiefly interested in herself and the impression she made as mistress of Maison du Soleil.

For that reason, anything pertaining to Society claimed her full attention. This was brought home while the dessert ices were being served. Laura abruptly clapped her hands and said:

'Will – did Marcus remember to tell you about Mrs Astor's ball?'

'That I might get an invitation? Yes, indeed.'

Mrs Pennel beamed. 'That's wonderful news, don't you think?'

He did his best to show enthusiasm:

'Wonderful.'

Mrs Pennel leaned forward, her eyes bright. 'Perhaps Mrs Astor will even invite the two of you to her divan for a chat. Every year she favours a few of her ball guests that way. Should you and Laura be chosen for that honour, your position would be secure for life.'

How seriously she made the statement. As if such a thing truly mattered—

Then he wondered what was wrong with his own attitude. Here he was, on the threshold of gaining everything he wanted in the way of prestige and position, and he found himself being cynical about the whole business.

A cigar in his mouth, Marcus leaned back in his chair and waited for one of the footmen to rush forward with a match. When he had the cigar going, he blew out a puff of smoke and asked in a slurred voice:

'What are you children planning to do the rest of the day?'

Mrs Pennel coughed and waved her hand in front of her face. 'The afternoon is occupied, Marcus. You know that.'

He grimaced. 'I thought that in view of Will's arrival, we would skip the dreary business of exchanging visiting cards.' To Will: 'You drive up and down the

708

Avenue. The footmen carry the cards inside. No one else ever leaves the carriage. Believe me, it's two hours of absolute torture.'

'Nevertheless,' said Mrs Pennel, 'it is one of the Newport proprieties, and we observe it.'

Will didn't intend to argue. But Marcus had put away a large amount of wine, and he didn't hesitate:

'Good God, Mama – I'm sure Will would rather take Laura driving. He's a first-class whip, you know.'

Uninterested in the accomplishments of her guest, Mrs Pennel gave her son a withering look. Will tried to keep the conversation going on a note of modesty:

'Well, I do enjoy coaching—'

'Have you always liked horses?' Laura asked.

'Yes, as long as I can remember. I got some fine experience with wild mustangs when I was out west on Mr Roosevelt's ranch.'

Mrs Pennel reacted as if he'd uttered a filthy word. 'I believe you mentioned something about that once before. You're speaking of Mr Theodore Roosevelt, are you not?'

'That's correct.'

'He's become quite a champion of the unwashed. Most of us who summer here consider him a traitor to his class. There is no more serious crime.' She pressed heavily beringed hands on the polished wood. 'Are you still friendly with Roosevelt?'

At first he evaded: 'I haven't seen him in a year or so. He's in Washington, you know.'

Out on the Atlantic, thunder boomed in the depths of massing clouds. Will was disgusted with himself. Politeness was one thing, cowardice quite another. His love for Laura was threatening to turn him into a gutless sycophant.

Mrs Pennel responded to his last statement with a chilling smile:

'No, I don't know. I never keep track of people who prove themselves unworthy of the trust of their peers.'

It was said quietly, but it was scathing. She'd gone too far.

'I happen to admire Mr Roosevelt, Mrs Pennel.'

Marcus again leaned back in his chair, enjoying the confrontation. Laura looked upset. Her mother's smile never wavered. But her hostility was evident. Will was sure she'd never forgive his remark.

Somehow, he didn't care. He disliked the small, stiffnecked woman even more than he disliked her house. With amazement, he recalled how shy she'd seemed the first time they met. But Laura had warned him that her manner was deceptive, and he'd seen evidence the night she humiliated her husband because he'd told a dirty story. She continued to stare. Now Mrs Pennel stared at Will as if she expected him to cave in too. He didn't, which made her seethe.

'Young man, I've always believed one should be charitable, and overlook a few faults in others. Provided those faults are not too obnoxious.' Her eyes flashed. 'I regret to say I find your defence of Roosevelt very obnoxious indeed.'

'Mama, that's rude!' Laura burst out.

'Is it? I'm so sorry.'

But she wasn't. The dining room had grown dark. Storm clouds were racing in from the Atlantic. Outside, shrubs and trees began to bend, lashed by wind out of the north-east. Mrs Pennel continued:

'I was only trying to be candid. If Will wishes an opportunity to become a part of this family, he should know what the family expects of him.' Abruptly, she fixed her gaze on him. 'Unacceptable opinions or behaviour will not be tolerated.'

Thunder boomed. The large window whined under the buffeting of the wind. Caps of white water had appeared on the ocean.

Having spoken her mind, Mrs Pennel now changed the subject:

'It will rain soon. I fear the afternoon drive is ruined.'

There was venom in Laura's eyes as she said, 'Along with other things!' She jumped up, overturning her chair. It fell with a crash before a servant could catch it. She ran from the room.

'Come back here!' Mrs Pennel called. The hollow sound of footsteps on marble was all the answer she received.

Marcus scowled at the ash of his cigar. Will sat motionless. There were strange emotional currents swirling around him. Something was very wrong in the Pennel house.

CHAPTER VI

Whispers

The rain came pouring down then. For the next two hours Marcus and Will shot billiards.

Even a room devoted solely to amusement had been planned and furnished with spendthrift magnificence. The billiard room had walls of grey-green Cippolino marble. Six-foot bronze candelabra stood in the four corners. The table was a Baumgarten, of Central American mahogany.

Marcus's only reference to the tempers on display in the dining room was a nonchalant one:

'You'll have to excuse Mother and Laura. Both of them have been extremely upset lately.'

'Is it impolite to ask why?'

'Not at all. But I don't think I should answer. It's a family matter. I believe it's your shot, old boy.'

Presently a servant brought word that both Mrs Pennel and Laura were still indisposed. Will received the news in disappointed silence.

Marcus excused himself, pleading another engagement. Will roamed the first floor, hoping Laura would suddenly appear on the staircase. The rain continued to fall. Night came on and the gas fixtures were lit. Still no sign of her.

Will wandered to the gloomy, dark-panelled library. Servants looked in from time to time to see to his needs, but he wanted nothing to eat or drink. By eight-thirty it was already pitch dark because of the storm. He gave up and went to his room.

Passing a closed door, he heard female voices raised. Though he knew he shouldn't, he stopped to listen.

' – can handle the matter. But not if you're rude to him!' That was Laura.

'I'm sorry. I lost my temper. You know how I feel about turncoats like Roosevelt.' Laura's mother. Her next words were muffled. Then Will heard, ' – has let me down. So many problems at the same time—'

'Well, you mustn't allow nerves to ruin the solution we devised for mine. This is one case in which you can't simply dictate the outcome, Mama. It must be carefully—'

A thunderclap shook the cottage. Beyond a massive marble railing to Will's left, a grotesque shadow grew on the wall of the landing below. A servant must be coming upstairs.

He hurried on to his room, puzzling about the curious conversation he'd overheard. He had no idea what Laura and Mrs Pennel were talking about, although an urgent, almost conspiratorial note had come through quite clearly. Mother and daughter had obviously patched up their quarrel.

He supposed that was good. But the whole business bothered him, for reasons he couldn't adequately explain.

2

The morning dawned rainless but grey. Heavy air carried the promise of new storms.

Will was cheered when Laura came down to breakfast in the morning room. Despite lingering signs of fatigue, she seemed in much better spirits.

They agreed to go driving in an hour. She whispered to one of the servants and sent him out of the room. When Will asked what she was up to, she hugged him and said it was a surprise.

When they'd finished eating, she asked him to come with her to the loggia. Once outside, they walked on across the damp lawn to the bluff overlooking the serpentine Cliff Walk. Only then did she tell him what was on her mind.

'I'm dreadfully sorry yesterday was such a botch.'

'And I'm sorry I made your mother so angry.'

'She isn't any longer. I finally saw her before breakfast.'

Before breakfast? You saw her last night. But all he said was, 'You're sure?'

'Positive.'

'That's good news.'

'The problem isn't you, it's Papa. For the past few months he's been – call it inattentive.'

He thought a moment. 'I noticed he wasn't around much this spring.'

'It's gotten worse. He invents excuses for spending all his time in the city. Most Newport men are absentee husbands. They've grown indifferent to their wives. But in Papa's case, there's talk—'

She glanced toward the mansion, as if she feared eavesdroppers. Remembering *Town Topics*, Will understood why she'd brought him outside. She went on:

'Talk that he consorts with other women. I mean women of the very lowest kind. I wouldn't be surprised. Things have become so strained, he seizes every opportunity to spite Mother. I shouldn't tell you this, I suppose. But we're friends, and you *are* training to be a doctor. I presume you're familiar with the – the symptoms women experience in mid-life?'

'Yes, of course.'

'Mama experienced them in a very acute way. And although she's too decent to discuss the particulars, I gather the change only aggravated her lifelong dislike of – the physical side of marriage. That's why Papa's never here – and why I believe the rumours we've heard.'

'That's certainly unfortunate.' *But eminently understandable.* An image of Mrs Pennel's autocratic face had flickered in Will's mind. 'I saw that your father was gone a lot. But I'm embarrassed to say I wasn't aware of other changes in his relationship with the family.'

'Don't be embarrassed. It all happened very gradually.'

'Marcus did hint at some difficulties, after you left the dining room yesterday—'

'Our friends in the city are starting to do more than hint. They tell us Papa's drinking a lot – for him, even a little is too much. One or two champagne cocktails and all control disappears. He hardly knows what he's saying—'

Will remembered. 'I'm very sorry to hear all this, Laura. It makes me doubly unhappy that I upset your mother yesterday. I hope the problems between your parents won't lead to – ' How to phrase it politely? ' – something more serious.'

714

'You mean divorce? Absolutely not. I expect Mama would like to be free of Papa, but the price is too high. In our set, both parties to a divorce are ostracized. Mama *is* under great strain, though. For the first time in memory, Papa's defied her openly. She has difficulty accepting that. And of course she dreads a scandal.'

But had Laura been referring to Thurman Pennel when she spoke of 'her' problem behind a closed door last night? He probed for an answer:

'Is that why you're looking so exhausted?' He touched her chin gently. 'It's the doctor's considered opinion that someone as fine and beautiful as you shouldn't be worrying every waking moment.'

She tried to lighten her tone: 'Perhaps if I had a husband to share the burdens, I wouldn't.'

A nod of exaggerated gravity. 'Professionally, I agree.'

A whisper: 'And personally?'

'Yes, there too. Are you searching for a husband, may I ask?'

She linked her arm in his. 'Yes, doctor, I am. Quite diligently, in fact.'

'And has your search been rewarded?'

'No.' A slow, almost smouldering flicker of her eyes. 'But I'm hopeful it may be soon.'

He faced her. The wind blew her straw-coloured hair against his cheek. It had the feel of a disembodied hand caressing him. Nervousness made him hoarse:

'Teasing aside, you know how I feel about you. The search can end any time you say.'

'How sweet you are. How very sweet—'

With another swift look toward the house, she raised herself on tiptoe and brushed her lips against his face, the swell of her soft breasts pushing against his jacket. He reached for her. She eluded him; started toward the loggia:

'But you mustn't press me, Will. I haven't made up

my mind. Not yet. I like you very much. But the trouble between Mother and Papa reminds me how cautious we must be. Marriage is such an important step—'

Suddenly she pirouetted to face him, her grey eyes wide with emotion. 'It's a lifetime promise. I'm just not completely sure, even though – ' Her voice dropped lower, the very sound of the whisper exciting him. ' – even though I want you more than I dare admit. I admire my mother. But I'm not like her in every way. I won't be – cold to my husband.'

Stunned by her candour, he held out his hand. 'Laura—'

'We'd better get ready to go driving.'

She whirled away and hurried toward the house. He followed her, his emotions in turmoil because of what she'd confessed.

I won't be cold to my husband.

I want you more than I dare admit.

He was sceptical of her statements about being unsure of her own feelings. Laura's character was complex, but that complexity didn't include being indecisive. She always knew what she wanted; in that way she was exactly like her mother.

He felt traitorous for questioning something she'd said, but he couldn't help it. He also couldn't understand why she'd put him off, unless it was a feminine tactic designed to make him want her all the more.

If that was her aim, she'd succeeded. The thought of her eyes, her mouth, the light touch of her hand and her body filled him with aching expectation as he raced to catch up with her beneath the ominous sky.

716

The Pennel carriages were housed in an enormous twenty-stall stable on Coggeshall Avenue, which ran parallel to Bellevue and one block west. In the stable, Will and Laura found the sorrels already hitched to a splendid landau with a two-section folding top that permitted it to be converted to a half-head barouche or a fully open carriage, or to be kept completely closed as it was this morning.

Will felt nervous about driving unfamiliar horses, just as he felt self-conscious about his outfit – a duplicate of the one Marcus had worn to meet him. It was the suprise Laura had mentioned. She'd ordered it from a fashionable gentlemen's shop, just for his visit.

The four sets of reins were exactly where they were supposed to be – hitched behind the tug strap supporting the trace buckle and pad of the off-side wheel horse. Will took the reins in his left hand and carefully let out the proper amount of slack on the two sets belonging to the off-side horses.

He put the reins in his right hand and mounted the wheel to the coachman's seat. Then he transferred the reins back to his driving hand so that they were in the right order: the near-leader's rein between thumb and forefinger; those of the off-leader and near-wheeler between the next two; and the off-wheeler's rein lowest of all, between the middle and third fingers. The feel of the reins had become part of him long ago. Without conscious thought, he could tell whether the four sets were correctly arranged. That was essential. On the road there was no time for conscious selection and manipulation. You had to know where each rein was, how to get hold of it without looking at it, and how to handle it without disturbing the other three. Will knew of several careless beginners who'd been killed because they mistook one rein for another.

He grasped the whip in his right hand, then shortened rein until he could feel just a slight tension of the bits against the mouths of the two leaders. Laura sat close to him on the next seat; one of the grooms had helped her climb up on the other side. Will grinned at her:

'Ready?' She nodded. 'Here we go.'

They set out southward along Coggeshall, turning right where it intersected a muddy, deserted road Laura identified as Ocean Avenue. She clung to his right arm as the landau lurched in and out of several ruts.

Ocean Avenue switchbacked along the shore. He had trouble keeping the horses under perfect control on the sharp turns. But Laura complimented and encouraged him, and once he'd discarded his top hat and stopped worrying about mud splashing up from the road, his driving improved. He accustomed himself to the size and weight of the landau and began to feel the mouths of the sorrels a little more positively. The horses were well schooled, responsive animals, and soon he had them clipping along briskly.

'Marcus was right, you're a first-class whip,' Laura exclaimed as the landau bounced and swayed round a curve. Will was showing off a bit; turning so that the right wheels lifted away from the road for a moment or so.

She gasped delightedly as they came down again. To the left, fans of white spray rose above boulders lining the shore. Ocean Avenue was low and close to the water at this point. The waves were noisy; Laura had to shout to be heard:

'What does it take to be a good driver?'

'Two of the same qualities it takes to be a good

doctor. Patience and practice. Plus the money to maintain a fine outfit like this.'

'And what else?'

'Strong wrists. Strong forearms. Above all, you need what they call good hands. That's a kind of instinctive feel for the reins. Expert drivers develop it, poor ones never do.'

They were rolling along a straight, fairly smooth stretch of road parallel to the rock-strewn shore. He shook the whip in his right hand. 'You also have to be able to touch the whip to any one of those four horses and miss the other three. If you can't do that and do it perfectly every time, you're not a true four-in-hand man.'

A quarter of a mile further on, the racing horses rounded another bend. Will pulled them frantically to the right to keep from running down two men and a shabbily dressed girl who'd emerged from the damp underbrush on the left side of the road. Laura lost her last trace of colour:

'It's those creatures from the Casino—'

Will recognized the shacker who had accosted Marcus. The shacker recognized him in turn, just as the lead horses flashed by the trio. The slatternly girl's clothing was disarrayed, leaving little doubt as to what she and the boys had being doing this warm, windy morning.

Behind him, Will heard the boy shout. He was about to ask Laura about the shacker when something sharp struck the back of his neck with enough force to draw blood.

He twisted round, scowling. The shacker flung another rock. This one hit the near wheel horse on the left flank.

The impact frightened the animal. It whinnied and lunged forward, throwing the other three off stride. In a moment the smoothly running quartet became four frightened runaways. Will sawed and hauled on the reins in a desperate effort to stop from overturning in a ninety-degree turn just ahead.

CHAPTER VII

Love and Honour

'Hang on!' Will shouted.

Laura ducked her head. He leaned back, tugged frantically. The lead horses plunged into the turn.

On the far side of the road, the shoulder dropped steeply to a natural ditch. The lead horses raced straight toward it for a moment more. Finally they responded to the reins and made the turn. So did the wheels.

But the four runaways exerted a tremendous whip-lashing force on the carriage, skidding it sideways toward the ditch. Will feared one or both axles might snap.

There was a terrifying instant in which he felt the right wheels slide onto the shoulder and slip downward. If the landau tipped and crashed into the standing water, Laura could be injured or killed—

The near wheels rose from the road. '*Will, it's going over!*'

Without conscious thought, he fed slack into all four sets of reins, keeping only minimal pressure on the bits as he stroked the off-leader with the whip – Hah!' – then the near-leader – *Hah!* – The response was a sudden forward surge of the horses down a short straightaway – enough to arrest the landau's sideways skid and settle its near wheels on the road with a jolt.

Will's gut hurt. His mouth felt dry as he pulled on the reins again, tightening up on the bits. Badly frightened, the horses didn't respond. He shortened rein again, trying not to dwell on the fact that by now the bits would be tearing at the mouths of the sorrels.

In a moment the horses began to slow down. By the time the landau bumped into the next turn they were down to a walk, snorting and bobbing their heads in response to the pain of the bits. Will hated hurting them; he'd had no choice.

He slacked off on the reins and pushed his boot against the brake lever. The landau came to a stop.

His shoulders slumped from the sudden release of tension. After two deep breaths, he turned to Laura expecting to see a bleached look of fear. To his astonishment, she was flushed with exhilaration.

Her grey eyes fastened on his, communicating a message he could hardly believe. She ran the tip of her tongue over her lower lip and brushed at the hair blowing past her cheek. She gripped his forearm with her left hand, kneading his flesh through the green coat. Her voice was husky as she said:

'That was splendidly done. You were very brave.'

He shook his head. 'No bravery involved. I just drove and hoped we didn't upset. If we had, it could have been serious.'

'You were brave, Will. Don't deny it.'

Breathing almost as loudly as he was, she leaned toward him, opening her lips. *My God*, he thought, aroused. *The danger* excited *her*.

'So brave,' she murmured as her mouth came against his, all moist and soft. He tasted her tongue; felt her hand glide across his leg. He thought of the shackers and the girl; what had become of them? Was anyone else driving on Ocean Avenue today? This *was* a public road—

Southward above the Atlantic, the sky was solid

grey. On a nearby hillside, a collie ran back and forth
along the skyline, barking at a farmer carrying a milk
can. Laura's breathing was rapid now; as if she were
no longer in control of herself. She kissed him more
ardently, and moaned. Her hand tightened. The pressure between his legs was almost more than he could
bear.

One by one he forgot the things that had been
worrying him. There was no sign of the two boys from
the Casino. The road remained empty. The man with
the milk can was gone; the collie silent; the heavens
dark as evening.

A fissure of white lightning split the sky in the south.
Laura's other hand moved in his hair. She teased his
tongue with hers; whispered:

'Let's go down to the shore. Please, Will.'

'What if someone comes along and finds the
carriage?'

'They won't find us. Tie the horses! I can't help
myself. I can't wait any longer. I've waited and wanted
you too long as it is—'

'All right, just a minute.'

Awkwardly, he disentangled himself and climbed to
the ground. The only tree close by was a low, stunted
evergreen at the roadside. By reaching under – scratch-
ing his face in the bargain – he was able to tie the
sweating horses securely. They seemed content to
stand, spent from their run.

As he stood again, he used his cuff to wipe dirt from
his cheek, then rubbed at the blood on the back of his
neck. He extended his other hand to Laura. She
clasped it and led him into the wet underbrush separating the road and the shore.

Their passage raised miniature rain showers when
they disturbed branches still wet from last night's
storm. 'Laura, you're getting soaked. Your clothes will
be ruined.'

722

'I don't care. It's warm and we can lie on your coat. Please, Will – hurry. Unless you don't want—?

He squeezed her hand. 'You know I do.'

2

They found a patch of sand in the shelter of some seaside rocks. The sand was damp but level and smooth. The tide was running out, leaving bits of driftwood and small, jelly-like creatures behind.

Will kicked a piece of wood from the spot he'd chosen. Standing, he looked back toward the road. He could just see the roof of the landau over the top of the largest rock. Lying down, they should be invisible to anyone up there. Unless, of course, someone grew curious about the abandoned carriage and came searching—'

'Will, your coat!'

Her voice was so urgent, it made him apprehensive about his ability to please her. The surf thundered as he flung the green garment on the sand. Lightning gashed the dark sky. Side by side, they dropped down on the coat, their arms going round one another.

He put a hand on her breast. She cried out in delight. Her fingers strayed to his neck and came away faintly red. That seemed to excite her even more.

He got his breeches off, then everything else. She bared her body without embarrassment, pleading for him with almost shocking intensity. He brought himself over her and her entreaties became a roar in his ears. His mouth savoured her damp hair, her sandy cheeks – all of it sweeter than anything he'd ever experienced. The hasty, almost frantic coupling climaxed when they rolled off the green coat onto the sand, he below, she above, arms and legs locking them into a heaving convulsion—

Seconds later, the rhythmic noise of the sea began to lessen. Or so he thought. Gentle lassitude filled him. Despite the forbidding day – darker by the moment – he was content.

The wind intensified; it smelled of salt and of vast reaches of open water stretching into the distance. They savoured their intimacy and their nakedness a moment longer. Then, cooling, they separated. They put on their wrinkled and sandy clothes, all the while murmuring endearments.

He manoeuvred her toward a rock, so that she sat with her back partially against it, partially against his side. His arm was behind her, cradling her. She rested her forehead against his cheek. Eyes closed, she murmured:

'You were too much for me, darling.'

'What do you mean?'

'I lost control. I couldn't stop.'

'Neither could I.

'It was bliss—'

He touched her nose. 'Because of you.'

'I knew it would be,' she finished.

He was proud and happy. How lucky he was to have such a girl, so fine and soft and white. He remembered the feel of her waist naked under his hands and shivered with pleasure.

Abruptly, a little stick-legged shore bird rushed from behind a rock and stopped to peck at the damp sand. The bird sensed intruders; turned to regard them with a bright eye as distant lightning flashed again.

Undisturbed by their presence, the bird marched on, pecking at the sand; pecking—

The omens for the future were fine, he thought.

They clung to one another in silence, both of them with relaxed, almost dreamy smiles on their faces. After about ten minutes had passed, conscience compelled him to say:

'We should start back.'

'Soon.' She snuggled closer. 'Do you know you're the first lover I've ever had?'

Reassured, he said, 'I'm glad.'

'I'll confess something else. When I met you, I set out to trap you. Now I've succeeded. Once a girl's done what I just did, honour demands that her suitor marry her.'

She spoke in a teasing way, yet he thought he detected a serious undertone. It was heady to realize what her words promised. He laughed softly.

'Yes, I've been told that's the way things work. But don't say you set a trap. Traps are for the unwary. I've wanted to marry you since the day Marcus introduced us. So if your parents will have me—'

She kissed his cheek. 'They'll have you. If I say I want you, it's settled.' Another quick peck. 'Now I admit a physician in the family may not be quite as grand as a European duke. But dukes are becoming common. All the girls in my set want a title along with a wedding ring.'

'And what do you want?'

Her hand dropped down, caressing:

'Need you ask?'

Then she looked at him, her gaze steady; almost without emotion. The bantering tone was gone:

'I'll tell you the truth, Will. Until this morning I *thought* I wanted to marry you, but I wasn't sure. Now I am.'

'Then I'm delighted that roughneck from the Casino threw the rock. He seemed to know you—'

She pulled away sharply, crossing her forearms over her breasts, and rubbing her upper arms. She avoided his eyes, staring instead at the mountainous waves.

'At the start of the season, Marcus and I went to the Casino nearly every day. We went to hear the concerts, or to watch Dickie Sears play tennis. But the shackers soon changed all that. They make it a point to push themselves on nearly every female visitor under fifty. Some of the more jaded members find that amusing, but I don't. Once, just as I was leaving, the boy with the scar accosted me. Marcus threatened to thrash him, then other people stepped in to prevent the fight. But before I left I gave that boy a piece of my mind. We tried to get him discharged, but we failed. He's some-one's relative. That's the whole story.'

Will nodded. 'I figured it was something like that.'

Her story certainly explained the shacker's behaviour. The boy was getting back at her. Just one thing in the account troubled Will; Marcus's purported eagerness to fight. That didn't jibe with his reaction when Will suggested the same thing. What had been different the first time? Had there been a crowd present? People Marcus felt he must impress? Undoubtedly that was it.

'Island filth, that's all those shackers are,' Laura said. 'Because of them, I can't go back to the Casino. I haven't been there since the day I had the trouble.'

That's one more score I must settle. I knew the bastard was spreading lies about her.

'Oh, but we shouldn't waste time talking about some dirty Irish ball boy. Do you plan to speak to Father about an engagement?'

'Yes. The moment I can get an appointment with him in New York.'

She sighed. 'I wish we could be married tomorrow. I dread the rigmarole if Mama insists on a huge church wedding. Wouldn't it be grand if we could just slip away and surprise everyone afterward?'

'You mean elope? Could we?'

She grew thoughtful. 'It's a very exciting idea. We can certainly think about it.'

The sky erupted at last, spilling fat raindrops on the sand with loud plopping sounds. Will scrambled up.

726

'Right now we'd better think about running for the carriage. This looks like a cloudburst.'

So it proved. By the time they reached the landau they were drenched. Neither minded very much. And while most girls would have wanted to ride inside, Laura insisted on sitting beside him. Will took that as another fine omen.

They laughed and talked all the way back to Coggeshall Avenue. He drove the carriage into the fragrant stable, imaginary scenes of an elopement vivid in his mind.

Quite suddenly, the swarthy face of his stepbrother was there too, equally vivid. Will laughed loudly.

Laura brushed at her wet hair, ignoring the grooms waiting to help her down. 'What's funny?'

He fibbed:

'I was thinking of how ridiculous we must look.'

He told the lie because he was fearful she'd misunderstand the truth. He wasn't sure he could clearly explain one of the reasons he was so happy. She might misinterpret his words if he said, *What happened this past hour will help me keep a promise.*

3

That night, Will had trouble sleeping. One minute he was consumed with excitement at the prospect of marrying Laura; the next, his mind churned with thoughts of repaying the shacker. He planned to do that tomorrow.

Will had never been prone to settle anything by fighting. But this case was an exception. He knew what Roosevelt would have done in similar circumstances, and that helped him make up his mind. He didn't intend to tell Laura of his plans, though.

If Laura wanted to elope, he'd have to contact Drew

right away; tell him that he couldn't come to New York just now. So much to think about—

Despite his wakeful night, he was in a fine mood when he went down to breakfast. His euphoria soon disappeared. He found Laura looking paler than ever. She was cross with the servants, and with him.

After they finished their coffee, they walked out on the loggia. With a smile, he asked whether she'd had any further thoughts about an elopement. She reacted as if she'd been stung:

'I know we discussed that. But I hope you didn't take me seriously.'

He stiffened. 'I beg your pardon. Am I talking to the same young lady with whom I spend the morning yesterday? Or have I met some disagreeable twin sister she never mentioned?'

Her irritable look faded. She sighed and offered a lame smile:

'I know it must seem that way. I apologize. Today all of a sudden, I just feel – oh – blue. It happens to women periodically, you know.'

She gave him a significant look before she turned away. *So that's her trouble*, he thought. At least she wouldn't become pregnant as a result of their hour on the beach.

Laura leaned on the balustrade, gazing out to sea. The grey clouds were beginning to fragment along the horizon, revealing swatches of blue beyond. It might turn out to be a splendid day.

At length she said, 'I'm sorry you took my remarks about eloping too literally.'

'Yes, I did. I honestly thought you disliked the idea of a church wedding.'

'I dislike the idea of being disinherited even more.'

'All right,' he said equably. 'We've settled the misunderstanding. I'll speak to your father soon.'

'There's no hurry.'

It took him a moment to recover from the shock of hearing that.

'Laura – if you didn't mean any of what you said yesterday—'

'I meant it, darling. I love you. I want to marry you. You'll make a fine, distinguished husband. But we – we needn't rush things. A long engagement is ever so much more fun than a short one. There'll be lots more parties for us to enjoy – you'll see.'

Baffled by her abrupt reversal, he was still anxious to please her:

'We'll do it any way you wish. The marriage – our life together – that's what counts.'

A footman opened one of the great glass doors from the central hall just as Laura patted his hand:

'I knew you'd be understanding.'

'Miss Penel?' the servant said. 'Your mother wishes to remind you that her guest will be arriving at one.'

Laura dismissed the man with a brusque nod. 'What guest?' Will asked.

'Mamie Fish. Stuyvesant Fish's wife.'

'I've heard of him. Wasn't his father Grant's secretary of state?'

'That's right. He's president of Illinois Central. His wife's a perfectly dreadful person. Barely able to spell or read a newspaper. But socially, she's nearly as important as Mrs Astor. I forgot to tell you she'd be dining with us this afternoon. She and Mama are planning a ball at the Casino.'

The word reminded him of his obligation.

'I hope you and your mother will excuse me if I don't join you. I have an errand.'

'Can't it wait?'

'It could, but I'd prefer that it didn't.'

'At least have the courtesy to tell me where you're going.'

He grinned. 'I gave in to you on horse doctoring. You'll have to give in to me on this. I'll tell you afterward.'

He walked toward her, intending to give her a kiss. She stepped quickly to one side and stalked into the mansion.

4

Will began to pace the loggia, hands in the pockets of his jacket. She was confusing him mightily – and angering him into the bargain.

It was possible to understand her quarrelsome mood, but not her abrupt reversals on important matters. Could her behaviour be ascribed solely to the fact that she was suffering a familiar feminine complaint? He knew some women went through torment every month, year after year; Laura might be one of those. The explanation didn't satisfy him, but he could find no other.

Ah, well. He'd always been told women were difficult to understand, and that romance never proceeded smoothly. If Laura was to be the mercurial half of the family, he supposed it would behoove him to be the calm, steady, forgiving half. Most of the time his disposition inclined him in that direction anyway. He could play the role if it would help him get what he wanted.

Or what you've convinced yourself that you want.

'Damn!' Elbows on the balustrade and a scowl on his face, he stared at the whitecapped Atlantic. Where did these traitorous thoughts keep coming from? He didn't know – any more than he knew why he was unable to get rid of them.

CHAPTER VIII

Accusation

Mrs Stuyvesant Fish had brilliant black eyes, an ugly face, and a surprising lack of pretension. Laura and her mother were nervous and almost sickeningly obsequious in her presence, Will observed when he made his brief courtesy call on the ladies.

The Pennel women and their guest were seated in the morning room. Mrs Pennel performed the introductions. Mrs Fish knew Gideon by reputation, and immediately told Will how much her husband disliked the *Union*'s editorial positions.

He silently shrugged off the familiar criticism, determined to be polite. He asked Mrs Fish where her summer cottage was located. Just down Bellevue Avenue, she replied. He asked how large it was. Instantly, she said:

'Why, my sweet lamb, I can't tell you. It swells at night.'

She tossed her head back and uttered a loud, raucous laugh; she sounded very much like a cackling parrot.

Will laughed too. He found her remark funny – probably because it was so outlandish, and she'd said it with a perfectly straight face. The Pennel ladies were not amused, however. Mrs Pennel tried to smile, but the best she could manage was an insincere moue. Laura stared at her lap to hide her disapproval.

When Will offered an apology for leaving so soon, Laura didn't hesitate to show her annoyance. In spite of it, Will bowed and walked out. She'd get over her pique. And he wouldn't feel comfortable until he'd done something about the shaker.

Marcus caught him as he was crossing the main hall:

'Not staying to keep the old bat company?'

'Mrs Fish isn't so old. I like her sense of humour. But the answer's no.'

'That explains why the dear girls are acting miffed. I'm afraid they've dragooned me to take your place. Being a house guest, you can get away with doing whatever you please. Once or twice, anyway,' he added. 'Going any place interesting? Blanche's maybe?'

'I have an errand at the Casino,' Will said as he left.

'The *Casino*—?'

When Marcus recovered from his shock, he dashed to the front door and peeked out. He thought about chasing Will, who was already halfway down the drive. He didn't for two reasons. First, his mother expected him to help entertain her guest. Second, and more important, the ladies were in charge of this little affair involving Will; he had no intention of making decisions on their behalf. He'd just keep quiet and hope Will learned nothing.

That conclusion reached, he turned round and proceeded toward the morning room with a worried look on his face.

2

Early that same afternoon, in the house on Beacon Street, Gideon lost his temper with his daughter.

A visitor provoked the outburst. A visitor, and the tension he'd felt ever since he grew aware of the emerging pattern in Eleanor's behaviour.

To be sure, Eleanor still showed flashes of her former personality. But the changes were unmistakable. Consider the matter of her refusal to work. In Philadelphia, she'd have been among friends, and busy. But she had said no to Louisa Drew's offer.

So despite the chaos in the household – Molly's illness, the trouble with his son – Gideon knew something had to be done, and soon. The question then became – was he the one to do it? Did he have the ability to arrest the transformation taking place within his daughter? He didn't know. The mind was a far, dark country only just now beginning to surrender its secrets to the first explorations by doctors specializing in mental disorders.

Gideon had used the resources of the *Union* to turn up the name of the best alienist on the Eastern seaboard – but he had not yet raised the subject of medical help with Eleanor. He continued to feel that her problem was first and foremost a family problem. *His* problem. And when he was in one of his confident moods, he believed he had a real chance to help her – if only he had the courage to try. What held him back was fear of a mistake, and of doing even more damage.

Today, Eleanor's behaviour had cancelled all those nice concerns, and plunged him into a rage. Harsh words spilled out almost without being aware of it:

'You insulted him! You insulted him so badly, he didn't even finish his meal. While Julia's down in Long Branch looking after Molly, you're supposed to make my guests welcome, not drive them away!'

The first floor office was hot and still. Eleanor struggled to open the window as she said, 'But that man's a buffoon. A hypocritical fraud.'

'In your opinion! Levi Morton is also vice president of the United States. He agreed to come here and share the president's thinking on a voting rights bill that will come up in the next Congress. Morton's only in town for two days, and when he's willing to give up part of that time to come here, it's my duty to treat him courteously.'

'You feel you must treat him courteously when he spouts homilies?'

'Politicians are *allowed* a certain amount of rhetoric.'

'Well, kindly don't subject me to it.'

'Then why the hell did you agree to help me entertain?'

She covered her eyes. 'I don't know. I shouldn't have.'

'That's quite right. You shouldn't have!'

Abruptly, a melancholy feeling replaced the anger that reddened his face and made breathing difficult. Eleanor sensed the momentary lessening of tension; she spoke more calmly:

'I apologize, Papa. I just couldn't tolerate Morton's pious cant about—' She lowered her voice, imitating the visitor. ' – *our – great – country.*'

'So you ridiculed it. In effect, you ridiculed him.'

'I—'

'Eleanor, I want to say something you'll no doubt receive with as little enthusiasm as your brother receives my warnings about the Pennels.'

'Papa, I'm tired.' She rubbed her palms on her black skirt. 'Another time—'

'*Now!*' His fist struck the mantel so hard, the tea bottle jumped. 'I don't want to add to your unhappiness, but what I'm going to say is long overdue.'

'Papa, I beg you – no platitudes. I hate—'

'I know you hate this country,' he broke in. 'You say it constantly. Theodore Roosevelt has a name for people who talk the way you do. Fireside moralists.'

His bitterness astonished her; even frightened her a little. On Beacon Street, two ladies carrying sunshades clucked at the unseemly noises issuing from the open window of the office.

Gideon knew he was on treacherous ground, but his patience was exhausted. 'Fireside moralists,' he repeated. 'I regret to say you've become an accomplished member of that group.'

Her voice was small suddenly. 'I don't understand.'

'Oh, I believe you do. We argued about the same thing before you and Leo got married. I'm sure I can't convince you any better now than I could then. But by God, your attitude compels me to try.'

She sank into a chair, chin resting on her palm. He tried to lower his voice but found it difficult:

'I am not arguing that this country is peopled by saints, Eleanor. Any sane man knows better. But neither is it populated exclusively by devils, as you so blithely imply. The one thing you fail to comprehend about America is that it's malleable. It is nothing more or less than what we make of it by our action or inaction. Most of the Kents have understood that, and acted accordingly. You, however, bemoan a lack of national virtue while refusing to lift a finger to promote that virtue. You prefer to sit by the fire, utter your condemnations, and let others improve things – if they're so inclined. I realize you have good reason to be bitter. A vicious man killed your husband. But you're blaming too many of the wrong people.'

'Oh? Just whom should I blame?'

'You might try blaming yourself.'

A whisper – deliberate; theatrical; stinging:

'Do me the courtesy of explaining what you mean!'

How much like Margaret she sounded then, he thought. He blunted the attack with a curt laugh:

'I expected you to be insulted. But it's true – you do bear responsibility for what happened to Leo. You did nothing to prevent the spread of the hatred that was Kleinerman's stock in trade. Whenever you encountered it, you attempted to convince yourself it didn't exist. And by ignoring it, you permitted it to grow. Stop blaming this country for Leo's death. The fact is, America's given you far more than you've ever given to it. Stop blaming the kind of bigots you encouraged by your silence. Start placing some of the blame where it belongs. At your own feet. The Kents have been a lot of things, good and bad, but I can't think of one of them who's been a fireside moralist. I'm sorry for you, but I'm sick of hearing your self-righteous proclamations. From now on kindly keep them to yourself!'

Tears appeared in her eyes. Furious tears or hurt ones, he couldn't decide which. Some reaction was better than none, he told himself. His anger cooled; the forgiving parent replaced the stern one. His expression softened. She failed to notice.

He realized he'd reached a critical point; a point at which he could and perhaps should pull back, leaving the truth only half uttered. Speaking the truth, he'd learned long ago, was a difficult and dangerous business. People did not welcome it.

Gently, he took her hands in his. 'Eleanor—'

She jerked away. Discouraging; but to be expected. He would press on. The two of them had effected a reconciliation, and become reasonably close again, after she had come to understand Margaret's warped thinking. And Eleanor was still a rational human being. It was on those two facts that he was basing his gamble:

'There is one other thing I must say to you. The most hurtful thing of all, perhaps. I don't know whether you realize it – I doubt it – but I think there is a reason why you're behaving as you are. Scorning the whole world. Turning away from involvement with it—'

He drew a breath. 'You're hiding from more hurt in a way you learned long ago. Your mother did the same thing, remember? You're starting to act just like her.'

There. It was said. The fearful words – the most terrible accusation he could possible have made – *said*. He felt drained.

He expected a torrent of abuse in return. Instead,

she gazed at him as if he were a simpleton. She began to laugh:

'That – Papa, that's – preposterous.'

'I don't think so.'

'It is the most ludicrous, insane—'

'*Look at yourself!* he shouted. The wild smile left her face, replaced by a sick, stunned expression. 'Your mother closed herself off from the world, and that's exactly what you're doing. She wanted nothing to do with her home, her family – you want nothing further to do with your profession. Or with us, if we ask for anything more than polite conversation. She locked all her pitiable secrets behind the door of her room – a habit I notice you are beginning to imitate—'

At that, Eleanor's eyes flew wide. Her expression was so shocked, he wondered why the mention of the locked door had such special significance. Obviously it did.

Then her face changed again, showing outrage. Something seemed to break within her. Without warning, she ran at him, fists flying:

'You cruel *bastard – IT ISN'T TRUE!*'

He seized her wrists and shouted, 'It is!' He shook her hard. 'Don't hide from the truth. You *know* what she did to herself!' He felt the tension leave her body suddenly. Her forearms relaxed; she stopped struggling. His breathing slowed. There was remorse – even grief – in his voice:

'I don't want the same thing to happen to you. Sometimes lately, you even sound like her.'

'Oh, my God,' she wept, turning away; burying her face in her hands.

Cruel bastard doesn't begin to say it. You should be horsewhipped for speaking to her that way.

And yet he'd said what needed saying. He might have chosen the wrong time, but the words were right.

The trouble was, he couldn't tell whether the words

737

had helped, or only made things worse. From the savagery of her sobs, he suspected the latter.

He shook his head, worn out. He stepped to her side; cautiously put his arm round her. He was afraid she'd pull away. She didn't, but neither did she look at him. He pitched his voice low:

'I'm sorry I shouted at you. I know you don't believe a syllable of what I said – especially the part about your mother. But I think about it constantly. I don't want you destroyed the same way she was. So you think about it too, Eleanor – please. I beg you. I'd do anything if you would just think about it. I'd cut off my arm – lay down my life – if you would—'

Slowly, he turned her; lifted her chin; looked into her red, stunned eyes.

'I'm your father. I want you to live, not die a slow death in a darkened room for the next thirty years. You have too much to give the world—'

A sharp knock turned him toward the doors. 'Yes? What is it?'

A servant entered. Eleanor chose that moment to rush out of the room, skirts held high. As she vanished and a feeling of defeat overpowered him, the servant held out a piece of yellow paper:

'Telegraph message, Mr Kent. I'm afraid it's bad news.'

CHAPTER IX

Summons

The clouds blew away and sunshine flooded Bellevue Avenue by the time Will reached his destination. He was breathing hard from the fast walk. But he barely broke stride as he turned in beneath the entrance arch, walked halfway down the dim tunnel leading into the Casino, and stopped at the turnstile.

One of the four men on the tennis court directly ahead scored with a powerful backhand return. There was loud applause. A guard seated on a stool near the turnstile held up his hand as Will started through.

'I'm sorry, sir. Members only.'

Will frowned. Should he attempt to force his way? No, that would only create a worse scene. The one he was planning would probably be bad enough.

'I'm a guest of a member. Marcus Pennel. I just want to speak to one of your employees. He's a ball boy. Muldoon, I think his name is.'

The guard was less hostile now that the Pennel name had been invoked. 'That would be Donny Muldoon.'

'I guess so. He nearly caused a serious accident on Ocean Avenue yesterday. I'd appreciate it if you'd get him out here right away.'

Will's obvious impatience prodded the guard off the stool. 'Very well, Mr—?'

'Kent.'

'Just a moment.'

The man shuffled away and disappeared to the left of the inside arch.

Will leaned against the green-painted wall near the turnstile, thinking of what he was about to do. A good

739

many people would consider him a brawler and no gentleman, merely for contemplating it. Others, anxious to look out for themselves, would call him an idiot for fighting over a girl's honour. None of that mattered very much.

The turnstile guard reappeared, the shacker a step behind. Will stepped away from the wall, his pulse quickening. His eyes widened when he saw two other ball boys slouch into sight. They stopped by the inside arch, but it was clear they'd come along in case their friend needed help.

Muldoon strolled up to the turnstile, smiling in a smarmy way. His heavy, closely-razored beard had a sweaty glint. Black stains showed at the armpits of his jersey.

He took hold of the turnstile and whirled it. One of the other shackers put his hand into the pocket of his grimy knickerbockers. Reaching for a weapon?

More applause from the grandstand. The four players acknowledged it and left the court. Muldoon leaned on the rail separating him from Will and fiddled with the broken visor of his cap. The guard finally realized what was about to happen. He raised frail hands:

'There'll be no fighting on these premises. If that's your intention, step across to the field.'

'Me fight? Shit, Harry—' Muldoon shrugged. ' – you know I'm a peacable fellow. Can't speak for this howlin' swell, though.' He walked through the turnstile, his dark eyes fixed on Will. 'Let's see what he has in mind.'

One of his friends called, 'Want a hand, Donny?'

Contemptuous, Muldoon gauged Will's size and strength. 'Nah, he's nothin' but a college boy.'

Will fumed. Muldoon went on, 'Truth is, I didn't expect to see you again.'

'You very nearly didn't. When you threw those rocks, we damn near overturned.'

An expression of feigned innocence: 'That a fact! Sorry to hear it, college. We were just havin' a lark. Didn't mean any harm.'

'I don't believe that for a minute. But that isn't the issue. Miss Pennel could have been maimed or killed because of what you did.'

'Miss Pennel, is it.' The shacker strolled past Will, chuckling. When he reached the sidewalk and the sunshine, he turned. Will was only a step behind. 'My, my – sounds like she's got you bamboozled. Got you believin' she's a proper lady, that *Miss Pennel*.' He exaggerated her name, snatching off his cap and touching the ground with it as he bowed. 'I'll tell you what she really is, college – a swell actress. And I'll tell you what she really fancies. It isn't the likes of you. Me an' my friends know. We've all taken turns with her.'

Will grabbed the shacker's jersey with both hands. 'What pleasure do you get from telling lies about her?'

'Lies?' Muldoon laughed. 'You ask *Miss Pennel* whether I'm lyin'.' He reconsidered. 'No, I s'pose she wouldn't tell you the truth. Now, college—'

Slowly, he reached up and across with his left hand. He tapped Will's right arm. Smiling, he said softly:

'Take your hands off me or I'll rip your balls out and stuff 'em into your asshole.'

'*You foul-mouthed son of a bitch*—'

The shacker reacted by driving his fist toward Will's stomach. Will dodged and threw a punch, clumsy but with plenty of force behind it. It struck the point of Muldoon's chin and slammed his mouth shut. Muldoon's upper teeth tore into his lower lip.

Blood spewed. Muldoon grabbed his red chin, sputtering. Will punched the shacker's stomach. Muldoon staggered.

Will knew his advantage wouldn't last. He made the most of it, knocking off the shacker's cap and grabbing his oiled hair as he started to sag. He held Muldoon's hair with one hand and with the other battered his face three times, taking only one ineffectual punch in return.

But Muldoon's two friends were coming. They dodged round the guard and jammed through the turnstile as Muldoon shuffled from side to side, groping for Will who had backed off. The shacker looked ghastly. One of Will's blows had opened a cut above his right eyebrow. Blood leaked down through his brow, streaking his cheek and mingling with mucus and blood from a battered nose and chewed lip.

'Fucker,' he said, blowing out spit and blood between his teeth. 'College fucker!'

He charged. Will jumped sideways, avoiding a flailing fist. The other shackers were close now. One did indeed have a weapon; sharp knuckle dusters glinted on his right hand.

Will lunged to one side, then the other. Muldoon's clenched hand missed him only narrowly each time. He was barely aware of all the coachmen running from the field to see the fight, or of a carriage pulling up at the kerb behind him. Someone called his name.

He paid no attention, breathing hard and watching Muldoon. The shacker swung wildly again. Will dodged, then ducked under the outstretched arm and pushed with all his strength. Muldoon yelled and went tumbling into his friends.

They flung him aside, harder than they intended. He crashed into the wall and the impact finished him. As he slid down, his bloody face left a broad wet stripe on the green paint.

The boy with the knuckle dusters rammed them toward Will's face. From behind Will's left shoulder, a whip popped. Something blurred past the corner of his eye.

The shacker with the knuckle dusters pulled his punch and shrieked. Blood spurted form a cut under his right eye or from the eye itself – Will couldn't tell which. At the sight of the damage done by the whip, the third shacker lost interest in the quarrel.

A hand seized Will's shoulder; whirled him round—

'Marcus!'

'Get in the carriage, you damn fool.'

Spectators from the tennis match were pouring out of the Casino. Marcus shoved Will around a small crowd of coachmen to the victoria, to which a pair of lean grays were hitched in tandem. 'God,' he fumed as he pushed Will into one of the passenger seats. 'Mother'll have apoplexy when she hears about this.'

Will was still breathing hard. The complaint infuriated him:

'That's too bad! The shacker was spreading lies about Laura. He had it coming. Why'd you follow me?'

Marcus yanked a crumpled paper from his pocket as he settled himself on the driver's seat. He reached back to give Will the paper – it was a telegram – then whipped up the horses and set them into a wide turn. 'That was delivered ten minutes after you left,' he shouted.

The carriage sped south along Bellevue Avenue. Will tried to unfold the telegram. Suddenly the wind snatched it from his fingers. He swore.

Marcus twisted his head and saw Will watching the paper tumble in the dust behind the carriage. Will cupped his hands round his mouth:

'I didn't get a chance to read it. Who's it from?'

'Your father. He wants you in Boston right away.'

'I'll be damned if I'll leave till I'm good and ready!'

'You'll have to go,' Marcus called back, 'if only to spare us further trouble with Muldoon's bunch. Besides, it's an emergency. Your father's stepmother has died down in New Jersey.'

Marcus took him into the cottage by a servant's entrance, and showed him a secondary stairway to the upper floor. Will was able to reach his room without encountering anyone.

He cleaned himself up so there'd be no sign that he'd been fighting. The others would find out soon enough anyway, Marcus had gloomily predicted. 'They don't yet know where you went. I said I thought you'd gone out shopping for a house gift. I'll have to tell them it was sheer luck that I found you so quickly.'

Will packed in ten minutes. Downstairs, he said his formal goodbye to the family. Mrs Pennel expressed sympathy but the words were perfunctory. Marcus took her arm and the two of them disappeared into the music room.

Will and Laura stepped into an alcove under the main staircase for a moment of privacy. He told her that as soon as the funeral was over, he'd be spending a week in New York; an obligation, he said.

She wanted to know the nature of the obligation.

'It's too complicated to explain, Laura. It's just a piece of business I have to get out of the way. The moment I do, I'll be back. We must make plans—'

She kissed him and smiled, but he felt she wasn't entirely teasing when she said:

'Indeed we must. I'm counting on you to make an honest woman of me.'

The second-class day coach which took him south on the mainland was airless and sooty. It made little difference to Will; he was uninterested in his surroundings or in the other passengers. He could only think of what had happened with Laura.

He wanted to be pleased about the consequences of that hour on the shore. But something was wrong. He finally realized the cause of the feeling. Her remark just before he left.

She had meant it.

Like it or not, a new element of coercion had entered their romance. Before his visit to Maison du Soleil he'd had a choice. Now he had none.

It wasn't even a matter of pregnancy. That worry had been removed just one day after they'd been together. It was a matter of honour. He'd made love to her, therefore he had to marry her. His mother had always been insistent about that. Never mind that Carter called the idea ludicrous. This was one instance in which his stepbrother was wrong. Carter had never associated with girls like Laura Pennel. He had no understanding of the rules that governed behaviour among her class of people.

If Will did the honourable thing, as he knew he must, he'd achieve his highest ambition. An alliance with the Pennels would bring him absolutely everything he wanted. So why the hell wasn't he as happy as he'd been yesterday?

He knew. The answer lay in the imperative way Laura had spoken to him. As if he weren't her lover but her—

Her property.

He spent the rest of the trip trying to forget that one remark. He couldn't.

CHAPTER X

Parting

'Then said Martha unto Jesus, Lord, if thou hadst been here, my brother had not died.'

While the vicar read the Bible, mourners fidgeted. Summer heat made an oven of Christ Church in the North End of Boston.

The Kents were seated together in the high-sided box pew that had belonged to the family for almost a hundred years. The pew was situated directly across the aisle from that belonging to the Revere family.

Will sat nearest the aisle, sweating in his black alpaca suit. He hadn't worshipped in the church for a long time. Gideon belonged to the congregation, but his participation consisted of writing a very large cheque once a year.

Directly ahead of Will hung a painting of Christ at the Last Supper. The picture was flanked by panels on which the Ten Commandments, the Lord's Prayer, and the Apostles' Creed had been lettered in gilt. From above the central painting, summer light flooded through a clear window. Stained glass had been avoided in order to make hymnals and prayer books easy to read.

Eleanor sat at Will's left, then Julia, and finally his father. Gideon looked more exhausted and irritable than ever. He and Eleanor were barely speaking – for reasons no one would explain to Will. As yet, Will hadn't told Gideon that he planned to marry Laura Pennel. Because of his father's mood, he was now thinking of waiting until he got back from his week in New York. He'd telegraphed Drew to expect him in a couple of days.

'Jesus saith unto her, thy brother shall rise again—'

Not counting the family, only about a dozen people sat in the tiny sanctuary. They included Moultrie Calhoun and his new wife; one of the sons of the former *Union* editor, Theo Payne; and a representative of the Rothman Bank. Molly's body was already in the hearse outside. The coffin had been surrounded by blocks of ice because of the heat.

It was Friday. The funeral had been delayed two days to allow for the arrival of the three mourners seated immediately behind the Kents. Michael Boyle had been especially close to Molly's husband Jephtha. The Irishman had come all the way from Cheyenne together with his wife, Hannah, and their son.

Nineteen-year-old Lincoln Boyle was a tall, red-faced young man with a deceptively mild manner and his father's pale, gold eyes. Just a few minutes' conversation told Will that the Boyles' son was bright and, for his age, extremely well read.

There was an immediate kinship between Will and Linc, as everyone called him. The reason had become clear the night before, during the Boyles' first meal at the Kent table. Michael had been critical of some books his son had brought along on the trip. 'Radical rot,' was the way he characterized them. Linc had defied his father by offering a cheerful correction to Will:

'The truth is, they're just books I borrowed from one of the free libraries run by the Farmers' Alliance. Universal literacy only gets lip service in the Boyle house. Hand a man a book and the next thing you know, he's smart enough to realize he's being victimized.'

Michael reddened but held his tongue. After the meal, Will discovered Linc in the first floor office. Books were piled on a table at his elbow. Will asked him what Michael found so objectionable about them.

The sunburned young man leaned back, a homespun sort of figure in his corduroy travelling suit, faded blue shirt and scuffed knee boots – a wardrobe ideal for the cool nights of summer on the high plains, he'd said earlier, but unbearable in sweltering Boston.

'They're all keystones of the agrarian movement.' Link tapped book spines one by one. 'Bellamy's *Looking Backward. Caesar's Column* by Ignatius Donnelly. William Harvey's *Coin's Financial School.* Henry George's book on the tariff. The Alliance makes these titles and a lot more available to farm families who can't afford books. Of course—'

He drew out a tobacco pouch; filled a long-stemmed clay pipe. 'Pa would just a lief burn every one. As far as he's concerned, anything which doesn't champion the tariff, the trusts, and the gold standard is unpatriotic and dangerous.'

Voices drifted through the open doors of the office. Across the hall in the parlour, Gideon and Michael sat with their chairs close together. Though they'd been hostile to one another in the past, tonight they were acting like old cronies. Michael handed his host a small wooden box with brass corners. Gideon accepted it with a strange, almost reverent expression.

'So you and your father are at odds?' Will asked.

'Very much so, I'm afraid.' Linc exhaled pipe smoke. 'I've been courting the daughter of a man who makes his living raising hay and alfalfa. It's through my girl's family that I got interested in the farmers' movement. Pa hates the movement because that's the attitude required of all good Republicans. Pa's an admirable

748

man in many ways. He accomplished a lot in his time. Fought for the Union. Helped build the Union Pacific. Made a few millions in general merchandise and cattle. But he's sixty now. You know what a bad combination age and a little money can be. Not only does he think like a plutocrat, he despises anyone who doesn't. It's a hell of a situation,' he finished, melancholy for a moment.

Linc's candour made it easy for Will to speak:

'I'm in the same spot, only in my case the political poles are reversed. My father can't stand the parents of the girl I'm seeing. They're somewhat like your father. Rich and conservative. It causes a lot of trouble.'

He walked to the marble hearth; stared into the cold fireplace. Only half joking, he added, 'Since we both seem to be up against the same problem, maybe between us we can figure out an answer.'

'How about trading fathers?'

Will laughed. 'Not a bad idea. Think it'd work?'

'I wish it would. I'll tell you the conclusion I reached a couple of years ago, when Pa and I started having really ferocious battles. I decided that my only course was to go right ahead – do what I believe is right – and at the same time try to keep differences from splitting the family for good.'

'Does it work?'

'Certainly – provided I'm willing to sit like a stump and never express an opinion,' Linc said glumly.

'You aren't, are you?'

'Of course not. The truth is, my solution doesn't work. Not often, anyway. Trouble is, I can't find another that's any better. Things would smooth out if I backed down. But there I take a lesson from Pa. He never backed down. So, hard as it is, I just go right ahead and keep hoping for the best.'

'What if the worst happens?'

'You mean what if Pa disowns me? Something like that?'

'Yes.'

Linc laid a hard brown hand on the top book of the stack. 'That's a risk I'm willing to bear. I love Pa. And I owe him a certain respect because he's my father. But I won't change what I believe just to please him. Slavery in the house of a benevolent master is still slavery.' He gestured to Philip's portrait. 'The old fellow who started this family knew that, I'm told. But fathers have an infuriating way of forgetting.'

'You're right,' Will said. Across the hall, he saw an astonishing sight. Gideon embracing the Irishman like a lost brother.

' – absolutely right.'

And there's no point in delaying the discussion of marriage. 'Go right ahead,' Linc said. It's the only way. I'll tell my father about the engagement before I leave.'

He'd do it as kindly and tactfully as he could. But he wouldn't let Gideon's opinions change a thing.

' – *Jesus said unto her, I am the resurrection, and the life. He that believeth in me, though he were dead, yet shall he live.'*

Will came out of his reverie. The vicar's voice rose in ringing affirmation:

'*And whosoever liveth and believeth in me shall never die.'*

He closed the lectern Bible. 'Let us pray. Unto God's gracious mercy and protection we commit you. The Lord bless you and keep you. The Lord make his face to shine upon you, and be gracious unto you. The Lord lift up his countenance upon you, and give you peace, both now and evermore. Amen.'

His hand slowly traced the cross in the air.

Will had the feeling someone was watching him. He turned slightly to the left; saw Gideon leaning forward and looking at him, as if he's sensed Will's defiant thoughts.

Will looked away and bowed his head.

2

There was grief in the Kent family that day, but it was acceptable grief. Molly had lived a good, full life.

Gideon held back tears as the coffin was lowered into the dry ground at Watertown. He and Julia had agreed that they wanted no long faces in the house that night. The kitchen was already at work preparing a big meal which would be served with plenty of wine.

Before supper, the Boyles went upstairs to pack. They were scheduled to leave in the morning. Gideon knocked at the door of his son's room and asked him to come to the office:

'I have something splendid to show you.'

Apprehensive, Will followed his father downstairs. Gideon seemed in good spirits; especially good considering what had taken place today. It might be a propitious moment to mention Laura.

Looking pleased, Gideon swung round beside the mantel in the office; pointed to the small brass-cornered box:

'See what Michael brought us?'

'I'm afraid I don't know what it is.'

'It's his most treasured possession.' Gideon lifted the box from its place beside the partially filled green bottle. He opened the lid. Inside, Will saw a small mound of ordinary dirt. Gideon's face fairly glowed:

'Michael collected this just before he left the Union Pacific. It's earth from the roadbed he worked on. He *is* a Kent by adoption. He wants the box kept with the other mementoes, so people will know someone in the family had a hand in that incredible achievement—'

Gideon closed and replaced the box. 'Michael and I didn't always see things the same way. Frankly, I was the one at fault. For a long time I considered him a fortune hunter. I was wrong. We still disagree on most political questions, but on the importance of traditions of this family, we are in perfect agreement.'

He paused, then walked past his son. He shut the double doors and turned round before resuming:

'But I've been anxious to ask about your trip to Newport.'

Although the office windows were open, the room was oppressively hot all at once. The curtains hung motionless in the heavy humidity. Outside, a damp grey dusk blurred the trees and footpaths of the Common. A strolling couple moved slowly, like sleepwalkers.

'I'd like to know what happened up there,' Gideon went on. 'I'd also like to know the current state of your feelings towards Miss Pennel.'

Will didn't want to anger his father. Not today. But Gideon was making restraint difficult; he leaned against the double doors as if he intended to guard them until he got answers. *He's acting as if this is Jeb Stuart's cavalry, and I'm some enlisted man to be ordered about any way Major Kent pleases!*

He thought of Linc Boyle's simple, if risky advice. '*Go right ahead.*' If his father wanted to force the issue on the day Molly Kent had been buried, so be it.

Will took a chair, crossed his legs, and said, 'My feelings toward Laura aren't hard to explain. I'm going to marry her.'

After a moment, Gideon shook his head.

'Surely you're joking.'

'No, sir. I know you don't care for the Pennels or their politics. But I see no reason why that should affect—'

'I had no notion it had gone this far,' Gideon broke in. 'Julia kept warning me, but I didn't believe her. It's more important than ever that you listen to me. Thurman Pennel is a jackal. A profiteer without conscience or scruple!'

Will covered his eyes a moment; tried to suppress mounting anger:

'Why the hell must we go over and over the same ground? We argued before I went to Newport, and I see no point in repeating that scene. First of all, I'm marrying Laura Pennel, not her father. Furthermore, I'm old enough to marry whom I please. If you can't accept that, it's pointless to talk, and pointless for me to stay here. I'll pack my bag and go.'

Gideon leaped on that:

'Go? Where?'

'I'm taking another trip. I thought I'd mentioned it.'

'You most certainly did not.'

A resigned shrug. 'Well, perhaps not.' *Or perhaps it slipped your mind. They say it happens to old men.* 'Things have been confused lately. It's natural that one of us might forget—'

'I forgot *nothing*. You failed to inform me you would be leaving again. Kindly do me the courtesy of telling me where you're going.'

He's tired, Will thought. *Think of what he's been through today.* But his father's arrogance overrode charitable impulses. Gideon made things worse by prodding:

'I said you will do me the courtesy of telling me where—'

'The hell I will.'

'What?'

'I believe you heard me.'

Gideon's face began to redden. Will cautioned himself not to repeat the mistake he had made last time. He mustn't push his father to the brink of a seizure.

In a tight voice, Gideon said, 'What I hear is your defiance. Your absolute contempt for all the values which have sustained and enriched this family. Even Michael Boyle, who isn't a Kent by birth, understands them better than you.'

'Oh God, Papa. Don't start with that kind of—'

Gideon ignored him:

'I don't need your answer. I know where you're going. Back to that crowd of thieves and poseurs. Back to Newport! That's it, isn't it?'

If you think so little of me, what's the point in telling you the truth?

'That's it, isn't it, Will?'

Silence. Will stared at his father with fury in his eyes. Gideon pivoted away:

'I thought so.'

Gideon lifted one of the curtains and stared into the humid dusk. He was breathing loudly. His right hand moved out of sight in front of his chest, as if he'd experienced a sharp pain.

'Tell him where you're going!'

But if he did that, it would lead to a full explanation. And when Gideon learned he had no intention of joining Drew in his practice in the slums, he'd think even less of him.

'Papa—' he began. Gideon spun, the very movement

754

intimidating. *Bungler*, said a remote, superior voice Will hadn't heard in some time.

He knew why he heard it now; he was making a botch of every response. Instead of speaking his mind with patience and reason, he was acting like his father; losing his temper. He forced a calm tone:

'You obviously have little respect for me, or what I'm doing—'

Gideon yelled: 'I don't respect anyone whose chief ambition is to curry the favour of people like the Pennels! They represent everything that's wrong with this country!'

'You're so quick to sit in judgment. You might be a little more understanding of—'

'Nonsense! The evidence against the Pennels became conclusive long ago! They are dangerous people. Amoral exploiters of the poor. And you seem as obedient to their wishes as a tame puppy.'

Livid, Will said, 'If you feel that way, perhaps I shouldn't merely take a trip. Perhaps I should move out.'

'Perhaps you should! First, however, I have one more thing to say. You evidently are unaware of certain – statements widely made about the young lady you say you plan to marry.'

Will came up from his chair as if a branding iron had touched him.

'*Statements?* What kind of statements?'

'Concerning Miss Pennel's character. It's been charged—'

His voice ominously low, Will interrupted:

'Be quiet, Papa. I've listened to the rest of your fulminations, but I refuse to hear one word about Laura. If anyone's to criticize her, it'll be me.'

'I only mention it in an effort to protect—'

'Goddamn it, I'm not *interested* in your protection! I

am a grown man. I am capable of doing my own thinking and making my own decisions!'

For a moment, rage robbed Will's thoughts of coherence. Then a measure of reason returned. *Don't prolong this. No matter what he's done, don't be the one to bring on his attack. You owe him that much as a doctor, if not as a son—*

Will fought back tears that unexpectedly sprang into his eyes. He walked past his father and said one word – 'Goodbye' – before he slammed the door behind him.

4

Twenty minutes later, he slipped down the rear stairs and out the back way. Not once during the twenty minutes had he heard the office door open. Gideon didn't attempt to stop him; didn't care enough to try.

Very well, he thought as he walked into the summer darkness. He'd never step inside the Beacon Street house again.

5

To stave off the moment when he'd be alone with his thoughts, Gideon pulled a book from one of the office bookcases. He sat down and opened the book with trembling hands.

It was a political tract called *The Chains of Slavery*, originally published in England in 1774. The author was Jean-Paul Marat, the Frenchman who ultimately led the most extreme faction of the Revolution, and who was stabbed to death in his bathtub by Charlotte Corday. Years before the Revolution, Marat had offered a pessimistic view of its outcome:

Liberty shares the fate of all human affairs; it yields to time, which destroys all; to ignorance, which confuses all; to vice, which corrupts all; and to force, which crushes all . . .

Try as he would, Gideon couldn't get beyond those words. He didn't have to stretch them far to find them applying to contemporary America – or the family's own situation.

Time had destroyed whatever principles Carter might once have believed in. Ignorance had confused Will, and made him prey to the subtle but ultimately cancerous vice of ambition. Force had crushed whatever idealism Eleanor had possessed before Leo's death, as well as whatever chance for happiness she once might have had. Since their fiery scene, she'd said little to him, and his one attempt to suggest that she see an alienist had met with an instantaneous rebuff. He knew he'd failed.

And because of all that, there was no one left to shepherd the family through its next generation, no one who gave a damn about the cornerstone of the family's strength – the liberty for which old Philip had first borne arms; the liberty of which Marat wrote with such disillusionment. Gideon shared that disillusionment now.

Suddenly, though, he saw what he was doing. The same thing Eleanor had done. He was placing the blame everywhere but upon the shoulders of the one person to whom it rightly belonged. Gideon Kent.

Time passed while he pondered his alternatives. Carter was beyond help, Eleanor almost so. But Will, now. That was another matter entirely.

He threw Marat's treatise on the floor and hurried out of the office. He would apologize to his son. Try to smother his own frustrations and make amends. Try to substitute fatherly affection and reason for the anger of an exhausted, spent man—

It was too late. Will's closet had been emptied. He was nowhere to be found.

6

At two in the morning, there was a brief shower. Then the sky cleared. The moon shone. Gideon stared out the window of his bedroom, ostensibly speaking to Julia in the darkness behind him, but in truth speaking mostly to himself:

'What's happened to him? Ridiculous question. He's caught the fever of the age. The fever for wealth. The fever for position—'

Despairing, he leaned on the sill and shook his head. Then he turned to face the darkened room, a bent silhouette against the moon.

'What's wrong with the people in this country, Julia? Are we nothing but a nation of self-indulgent snobs whose only concerns are the size of a house and the cost of the furnishings? Have we gotten so greedy and indolent, we're satisfied to stand for nothing except a bank balance while we're alive – amount to nothing but an estate when we're dead? Did old Philip go to the Concord bridge solely to secure the right to have a family pedigree approved by some simpering eunuch? By God I don't think so. But I see precious little evidence to support my point of view. In fact, my views have alienated my daughter, and now they've driven my son away.'

'Gideon—' she began from the shadows where she lay.

'He's gone, Julia. Gone to that worthless crowd.'

For the first time that day, he cried.

After a moment, she whispered, 'Gideon, come to bed.'

She held him in her arms for a quarter of an hour, listening to him score himself for Eleanor's disaffection and Will's sudden departure. He no longer held them responsible for the disintegration of the family. And though he didn't retract a word of what he'd said about the country or the Pennels, he couldn't hold others responsible either. The blame, he said, was his alone.

Finally he was silent; motionless. She kept him close, his chest crushing the thin nightdress against her right breast, her right arm curved round him so that she could stroke his temple gently. In a flat voice, he asked:

'Do you suppose we'll ever see him again?'

'He's a man. We've been guilty of forgetting that.'

'I know. He said so. But do you think—?'

'That's what I'm trying to say, dearest. He's a grown man. It's entirely up to him.'

'Then the answer's no. He's gone for good.'

Her silence was devastating agreement.

BOOK SIX

The Education of Will Kent

CHAPTER I

The Bend

'Che cosa? Non ho sentito ciò che hai detto.'

The speaker was an old Italian with a black clay pipe and the wheezy voice of someone suffering a lung disorder. He was the fourth person Will had asked for directions. The old man didn't understand Will any better than the others had. He made that clear by raising his hands, his shoulders, and his eyebrows in a gesture of bewilderment.

The din on Mulberry Street this Saturday afternoon was incredible. Men, women, and youngsters packed the sidewalks, bargaining or socializing. Other people leaned out the windows of the four-and five-story tenements lining both sides of the street. Will had stopped on the west side of Mulberry, at the point where it made a slight change of direction – the bend for which the neighbourhood was named.

Two ragged boys scrambled after pennies they'd been pitching on the sidewalk. One penny had landed near the valise Will had put down. In the act of retrieving the coin, one of the boys made a grab for the valise. Will kicked it six inches to the right, just out of the boy's reach. The urchins ran off, laughing. The old man laughed too.

Will didn't find much to laugh about. He was soaked with sweat and worn out from the all-night train trip. The pitiless August sunlight was giving him a headache. He felt terrible about the circumstances of his departure from Beacon Street.

A permanent separation from his family had been inevitable; a long time coming, but inevitable. That

763

was the conclusion he'd reached during his sleepless night on the local from Boston. The last hope of a good relationship had been destroyed when Gideon resorted to innuendoes about Laura's character in order to discourage his interest.

Still, the parting hurt.

Now, on top of everything, this old man couldn't or wouldn't help him.

Will had his coat slung over his shoulder and his vest open, but even so, he was obviously dressed too well for the neighbourhood. The quality and newness of his clothing would have branded him an outsider even if his language hadn't.

The old man started to turn away. 'Wait,' Will said. 'Surely somebody around here has heard of Bayard Court.'

He showed the old man the note Drew had sent several weeks ago. Unfortunately Will's friend had provided no directions, merely an address. 'Bayard Court,' he repeated, emphasizing each word. 'Number four and a half. Bayard – Court.'

'*Oh, è quello ciò che vuoi?*' the man said with dawning comprehension. Then Will heard an accented version of something familiar: 'Bay – ard Court—?'

'Yes. That's it.' Will nodded several times.

Slowly, the old man pivoted until he was facing north. Then Will was again forced to wait while the man acknowledged a friend; a younger man pushing a two-wheeled cart along the sidewalk. On the cart sat one of the barrels which could be seen on the kerbstones at half-block intervals, overflowing with ashes and cinders. The barrel on the cart was empty, and a pert little girl in a ragged dress was balanced precariously on the front rim. She was obviously enjoying the ride.

The old man beamed. '*Buona giornata a te, Pasqual. E buona giornata alla tua bellissima bambina.*'

'*Buona giornata, Chiro.*' The younger man indicated Will. '*Chi è il tuo amico pallido?*'

That too was incomprehensible, but not the suspicion with which it was said. In answer to the question, the old man shrugged in an expressive way. The young father gave Will another suspicious stare, then went on.

'Bay – ard Court?' the old man repeated at last.

'Yes, that's what I want. Where do I find it?'

The old man pointed north to the next intersection; rattled off directions which he supplemented with gestures. Will gathered that he was supposed to proceed to the corner, turn left, then right again. Precisely how far he went before he made the right turn, it was impossible to say. But at least he had a start.

He thanked the old man, who simply stared until he picked up his valise and moved on. Other people watched him too. Only a few smiled. He felt more and more uncomfortable with every step he took.

2

The Mulberry Street Bend was just a few blocks from the New York *Union* and the solid, relatively uncluttered commercial area surrounding City Hall Park. The Bend, by contrast, was a colourful neighbourhood, but a crowded and abysmally poor one. A slum.

Drew had written that the neighbourhood population was chiefly Italian with some Irish sprinkled in. Most of the Italians were recent arrivals. They eked out a subsistence by picking rags, or by working at the municipal dumps where garbage was loaded onto scows for disposal at sea.

Years ago, Italian newcomers had begun to gravitate toward the dumps for reasons no one could adequately explain. It wasn't an elegant way to earn a living, but a few of the more unscrupulous had discovered ways to make it pay, and pay handsomely. Today, those men were powerful. They were addressed by the respectful title padrone. They controlled the dumps. With one hand they bribed municipal officials in order to maintain their exclusive rights to do all the work and all the hiring. With the other they held out jobs to their fellow Italians.

The padrones employed the immigrants but paid them a pittance, and in addition deducted a weekly percentage – only fair, they said, since they had generously extended themselves and taken a chance on inexperienced workers. To the trusting newcomer, the padrones were benefactors. To those less naïve they were merely businessmen doing business in the American way. It was a sad introduction to the new homeland, Drew said.

The whole of Mulberry Street for several blocks had turned into an outdoor market this sultry Saturday afternoon. On the kerbstone to Will's right sat women ranging in age from thirteen to ninety. Their heads were wrapped in red or yellow bandanas. Their tongues were busy with the day's gossip. Beyond them, in the street, was a row of pushcarts. A similar row ran along the far kerb, which was equally crowded with women.

The two lines of carts in the street were supplemented by two more on the sidewalks near the buildings. Displayed on the carts Will saw sticks of stove kindling; cabbages and carrots blackened by mould; long loaves of bread already stale and crumbly; big fish with phosphorescent scales; thick, bloody-looking sausages; small mountains of snails.

Behind the sidewalk pushcarts were grubby shops which advertised themselves in Italian and English as banks, steamship agencies, or employment bureaus. Each shop and cart had its gilded religious plaque or its painted plaster image of a benevolent-looking saint.

Most of the saints cast their eyes up to heaven, no doubt because their earthly surroundings were so grim.

Will passed a pushcart from which a toothless old woman was offering what appeared to be secondhand stockings and undergarments. Beyond the pushcart, a couple of dark-eyed, rough-looking men sat talking on a crumbling cement stoop. They noticed Will. Their interest increased when they saw the obviously expensive gold watch chain hanging between the pockets of his open vest.

The interest of the two men didn't strike Will as precisely innocent. One squinted at him through the blue smoke of a cheroot; he was younger than his companion, and wearing a derby. He grinned at Will and pointed to the gold chain:

'*Ehi amico. Porti una bella catena d'oro. Hai un bell' orologio appeso alla fine?*'

Will kept walking. When he'd gone about six steps beyond the stoop, the two men exchanged sly looks, stood up and fell in step behind him.

3

His neck prickled. He didn't turn but he knew they were following him. He worked his way through the crowd, the pounding in his head growing worse.

He wasn't overly surprised at the unwelcome attention he was receiving. Drew had written that a certain few in every one of New York's many racial and ethnic groups were totally unwilling to better themselves by honest means. Hence every slum had its gangs. There were Irish gangs on the West Side; Chinese gangs on Mott Street; Negro gangs in enclaves along Seventh and Eighth Avenues; Greek gangs, Polish gangs, Bohemian gangs – even a gang in the small Arabian community down near the Battery. The gangs preyed on outsiders who ventured in, and when there were no outsiders, on their own neighbours. The slums guaranteed every man the opportunity to become embittered and desperate, Drew had said in one particularly caustic letter.

Will passed a saloon. From its open doorway came lusty singing and laughter. Two elderly men stood still as statues in the entrance, smoking those ubiquitous clay pipes. The men's eyes slid from Will's face to a spot somewhere behind him. Then the men glanced at one another. Those small signs told Will the two roughnecks were still stalking him.

Ahead, the sidewalk was drenched with spray from an open hydrant. A crowd of small boys frolicked and splashed. Will walked right through the spray, not minding the soaking he got. The water felt cool on his aching head.

A genial, moustached man in a fine, thigh-length coat of black alpaca leaned against the front of a shop identified as a bank. The man was peeling notes from a thick bundle. He handed the money to an eager customer who babbled thanks in Italian. Both banker and customer noticed the men following Will. The banker reacted with cynical amusement; the customer's look was one of pity.

On both sides of Mulberry Street, tilted telephone and telegraph poles angled toward the hot August sky. The lower sections of the poles bore marks of frequent battering by wheeled vehicles. Wagons stood hub to hub between the pushcarts. Just across the street, a hearse had its rear doors open to receive two children's coffins of unpainted wood, each carried by men in dark suits.

Will tried to listen for footsteps behind him. The noise made it difficult. Preoccupied, he stumbled against the outstretched arm of a butcher skinning a kid. The dead animal hung from a metal hook on a kind of gallows attached to the butcher's cart.

The butcher's hairy forearm was wet with blood. The blood spattered Will's vest when the two collided. Will apologized in English, the butcher in Italian. Then the butcher looked over Will's shoulder, blinked and bobbed his head – a clear warning of pursuit. Will nodded his thanks, then walked on to the corner – the intersection of Mulberry and Bayard Streets, according to a sign.

To his left along Bayard Street, tenements faced one another across a thoroughfare even more crowded and noisy than Mulberry. Portions of the cross street lay in heavy shadow. If he went on, he'd have to pass through those dark sections. He decided that would be foolish with the two men still on his trail. He had a better chance of dealing with them here in the sunlight.

Heart beating fast, he rounded the corner, stopped and dropped his valise. With his foot he pushed it into the shade near the building. His head was pounding as he turned to confront the pursuers.

CHAPTER II

Unexpected Help

The two men were taken by surprise when they rounded the corner and discovered Will standing there. But they recovered quickly enough, swaggering up to him while passersby hurried round without a second look. One stout man did perceive that something was wrong, but his thin-lipped wife refused to let him stop.

The two roughnecks closed in on Will from either

side. The one on his right, the older of the two, reached for Will's vest and started to finger the material. Will jerked his fist up and batted the hand aside.

The younger man instantly reached under his soiled shirt and produced a clasp knife. He opened the knife one-handed, without so much as a downward glance.

'Hey, my friend – ' The young Italian's English was heavily accented but clear. Beneath the brim of his derby, his eyes glittered. ' – that's no way to treat my pal. You come wandering into the Bend in your fancy suit, you have to pay visitor's tax.'

The other man guffawed. 'That's good, 'Sep. Visitor's tax. That's rich.'

'Get the hell away from me,' Will said. The men weren't impressed. 'Sure, sure,' said the older one. 'Soon as we collect that visitor's tax – huh, 'Sep?'

The young man in the derby grinned, nodded, and put the point of his knife against Will's vest:

'We'll take the tax or we'll take your gizzard. In your case the tax is this good-looking chain – ' He flicked the knife upward, touching the gold links. ' – and whatever's on the end. Hand it over and you can go along.'

Will didn't move. The knife moved lazily away from the gold chain and rose to a spot just below his collar. The point was perhaps half an inch from this throat.

'Did you hear what I said, friend? We want the tax and we want it *now*.'

The young man's other hand shot toward the chain. Will jerked backwards, ramming his fist at the young man's face.

The young man was quick and agile. He easily side-stepped the punch. His companion swore and grabbed for Will, but he too missed as Will ducked away from the slashing knife. It whispered past his left side. The point raked the brick wall and left a trail of sparks.

Will slammed his left fist against the young man's

770

outstretched arm, driving it against the wall. He yelled and dropped the knife. Will bashed the older man's throat with his elbow. He was desperate – and enraged at being robbed in broad daylight. On the corner, a small crowd had gathered to watch. No one moved to help him.

'*Ti sistemerò io, bastardo!*' the young man snarled as he crouched to retrieve his knife. Will kicked it out of his reach, at the same time using both hands to hold off the other thief.

The young man groped for the knife. Over his bent back Will saw the crowd stir. Suddenly a woman bellowed, 'You mean to say you'll stand by and let those two loafers attack a visitor to our neighbourhood? *Feccia indolente!*'

The crowd parted as she shoved through, a stout dark-haired woman with a baby bouncing on her sizable bosom. The baby rode in a kind of sling hanging from her neck.

The woman ran up behind Will's assailants. Folding both arms to shield her howling infant, she lifted her right knee. 'Get out of here, low-life!' She rammed her knee into the buttocks of the young man groping for the knife.

The man's derby fell off. He crashed head first into the brick wall.

'*Preziosissimo sangue di Gesù il Salvatore!*' The young man clutched his scalp. His fingers came away red. 'You've killed me, woman.'

'No,' she said with a shake of her head. Her English was only slightly better than his. 'But I will if you don't take yourself out of my sight. I know who you are, Giuseppe Corso. I know your mother, your poor abused wife, and half your kin from Naples. I see them all at Sunday mass. But I never see you because you're busy swilling wine and congratulating yourself on your manhood after robbing some helpless stranger.'

771

Protecting the yelling baby with her left arm, she used her other hand to shove the young man's shoulder. 'But you never commit a crime alone, do you? You prefer two or three against one. By yourself it would be too chancy.'

Her brown eyes flashing, she swung to the older man. Will had released him, but he was too thunderstruck to move.

'I recognize you also, Rocco Amato. Your wife hangs her laundry in the court behind Baxter Street.'

The man blushed and grabbed his companion's arm, pleading with him in Italian. The younger man fingered his bloody head. Then he fixed Will with a vengeful stare; raised his right hand; bit the tip of his thumb. He spilled out a stream of furious Italian:

'*Ti rivedrò, bastardo! Ci puoi contare!*'

Still shouting, he let the older man pull him round the corner out of sight.

Will shivered. 'What the devil was he saying?'

Unsmiling, the woman looked at him.

'It's better you don't know.'

2

A moment later, she began to croon, 'Now, now, baby. Hush, little one.' She began rocking her child to soothe it.

Soon the baby stopped crying and gurgled. Then the gurgling stopped too. The child was falling asleep again. The woman turned her attention to Will who had dusted himself off and was picking up his valise.

His benefactor was a powerfully built woman, heavy, and quite short. Her eyes were on a level with his upper arm. She had the blackest hair he'd ever seen, wound into a big bun. There was some grey in it, although she couldn't have been more than thirty-five.

He studied her more closely. Wrinkles, weight, and a downy black moustache increased the impression of age. But they did nothing to diminish an impression of strength tempered by a good disposition.

'If you're ready, young man, I'll conduct you wherever it is you're going.'

'Thanks very much,' Will said. 'I'm grateful for the help you gave me with those two. But I'm a little embarrassed too.'

'Why?' she shot back. 'You'd better not say it's because I'm a woman. You needed help and you wouldn't have gotten any from those gutless loafers.' She gave a withering look to the small crowd of spectators just breaking up. 'I don't recognize any of them. That means they don't live in this neighbourhood. You mustn't judge Mulberry Street by their behaviour – or by that of men like 'Sep and Rocco either. 'Sep – the young one with the knife – he's totally worthless. But Rocco Amato is just weak. He's a working man. He supports a wife, a father, a mother-in-law, and four wee ones. When a man earns only seven dollars a month trimming the scows and must spend five to rent one filthy room with no air except that which comes up the shaft and no water except the foul stuff from the community sink – well, it's easy for a man like that to grow bitter and disregard his conscience. That doesn't excuse what Rocco did. But perhaps it explains it, eh?'

The woman's brusque pronouncements made Will smile. He began to relax a little. 'Yes, it does.' He draped his coat over his arm. 'I'm looking for Bayard Court.'

'You are? Fancy that! Grimaldi's there right this minute.'

'Who's Grimaldi?'

'The father of this little beauty – ' As they began walking, she patted the infant's head. Will could see the anterior fontanelle beneath a fuzz of dark hair; a newborn, then. 'Little Miranda. Plus eight more. I don't doubt he'll want to plant another one the moment I permit him close to me again. Grimaldi's a regular bull. I'm not complaining, you understand. Many of my friends are envious. But sometimes I do crave a night's rest. Ah well – that's life, hah?'

Again he smiled. 'You're Mrs Grimaldi, then—'

Her plump cheeks grew pink and her moustache quivered. 'Who else would I be? Do I look like some slut who'd bear nine children out of wedlock? Is that what you think?'

'No, no, I didn't mean to imply that.'

'Good.'

'I apologize.'

'I accept.' She studied his obviously expensive summer suit. 'What are you doing in the Bend, Signor—?'

'Kent. Will Kent.'

'I'm happy to know your name, but that isn't the information I requested.'

He chuckled. 'I'm looking for a friend. A doctor who practises at number four and a half Bayard Court.'

'Imagine! That's exactly where Grimaldi is – number four and a half.'

'Is that a fact?'

Again the thunderous brow: 'Of course it's a fact. Why else would I say it? Do I strike you as a frivolous woman who makes idle jokes? Is that what you mean to say?'

He quickly raised his free hand. 'No. Absolutely not.'

'Good. I don't want to think I made a mistake about you.'

'Is your husband seeing one of the doctors?'

'Yes. He's having a cough looked after.'

'What a coincidence. Our meeting, I mean.'

'Coincidence? It's proof of God's guiding hand in

774

human affairs. Tell me, Signor Kent. Do you know the doctors?'

'I know one of them. He's a good friend of mine.'

'They are both good men. One is newer to the neighbourhood than the other, but they are both Christians. They know that those of us who live here have little or no money, but they also know we have a need, so they never demand that we pay. And they never force us to sign anything, as the bankers do. Good men,' she repeated with a nod that said she'd brook no other opinion. 'Which doctor is your friend? The old one or the round one?'

'The round – ? Yes, that one.'

'Come on, then. Let's move a little faster. You wouldn't have found Bayard Court by yourself. Mind your step and hold your nose and we'll be there before you know it.'

3

Mrs Grimaldi was right. He couldn't have located Bayard Court alone. When she turned into a narrow passage between two tenements, he was sure he would have missed the passage completely.

They walked in semi-darkness, between windowless walls. Over her shoulder she said, 'I've lived in the Bend five years and I still don't know all the alleys and courtyards. Of course the property owners and rental agents keep adding onto the buildings and putting up new ones to further confuse matters – be careful! Don't fall over the garbage.'

There was more than garbage littering the lightless passage. Will's shoes stank of offal. Mrs Grimaldi marched right through it with her skirt hiked up in both hands. The stench didn't bother little Miranda, who was still sleeping in the sling.

Just short of the spot where the passage opened into a gloomy courtyard, Mrs Grimaldi stopped, gazed down, and said softly:

'*Madonna Santissima*. Look at that. Another one left to die.'

Will moved up beside her. On the ground he saw the feebly moving hands of a dirt-crusted baby no more than four or five weeks old. The child was swaddled in greasy rags. A fat fly walked on its face.

Will couldn't hide his astonishment. 'You mean people just – discard their children?'

The question saddened her. 'You honestly don't know what it's like to live in a district like this, do you?'

He thought of Maison du Soleil; of the comfortable house in Boston that he'd never see again. He said softly:

'No. I don't.'

'When people cannot feed the extra mouth God has seen fit to give them, they grow desperate. Several children are abandoned in this section every week. Some are found dead of exposure but some have been suffocated before being abandoned. I suppose their misguided parents believe that to be an act of mercy.'

She bent with a grace surprising in a person so heavy. With great care she picked up the filthy bundle. The small, squashed face looked lifeless. The tiny hands made only the feeblest of waving motions.

'This one's almost gone. I'll see whether I can give the poor thing a fighting chance. Grimaldi won't like me bringing it home, but he'll have to humour me if he wants his marital privileges. Come along, Signor Kent. We're only a few steps from the splendours of Bayard Court.'

The court was bounded on the Bayard Street side by the two buildings which the passage separated and on

the other three sides by the backs of five-story tenements. Each building had at least one fire escape. The
fire escapes were crowded with wash tubs, broken
chairs, sofas with ripped cushions and other pieces of
useless furniture.

Shabbily dressed men and women relaxed on the old
furniture. The people filled every bit of usable space
on the fire escapes – the verandas of the poor, Will
thought with dismay. Mrs Grimaldi greeted some of
the residents with a wave and a few words in Italian,
all the while carrying Miranda on her breast and
cradling the abandoned baby in her left arm. The mud
of the courtyard was strewn with bales of rags, as well
as more garbage and dung, human and animal. The
stink was overpowering.

Directly overhead, a maze of pulley-lines criss-
crossed the open space. The lines were strung from
every floor. Each was laden with laundry, some of it
no better than rags. Thick smoke twisted between the
hanging clothes. The source was a cooking brazier on a
third floor fire escape.

The combination of the tall buildings, the smoke,
and the hanging laundry kept the courtyard dark. In
fact, the only scrap of summer sky visible to Will was
so beclouded by smoke, it looked stormy. He could
hardly believe the sun was shining up there.

Mrs Grimaldi noticed him gazing upward; she
clucked her tongue. 'That, I believe, is what the priests
call *cielo*. Heaven. It's no wonder that even in a good
Catholic neighbourhood, the churches are half
empty—'

Suddenly she grew more animated:

'Grimaldi! Here I am!'

She marched toward the dark door of the tenement
directly opposite the passageway by which they'd
entered. Will took a final look at the faces on the fire
escapes, vaguely ashamed of where he'd come from

and very much ashamed of what he wanted from life. What did the residents of the Bend want? He suspected the answer was a simple and fundamental one. They wanted to survive – not easy to do down here where there was so much dirt and poverty and violence.

'Grimaldi, get a move on!' the stout woman called to a man with curly grey hair and a pie of a face. His leather vest couldn't hide his huge paunch. He'd just come out of the tenement clutching a small bottle of reddish-brown liquid. Behind, in the hall, a woman was saying:

' – a spoonful of that elixir whenever the cough bothers you, Signor Grimaldi. And don't forget to come back next Saturday and let the doctor see whether you've improved.'

Curious, Will thought. *That voice sounds familiar*.

'Thank you, thank you very much, signorina,' Grimaldi said. His wife thumped his ear with her index finger:

'Don't flirt with the nurse. Turn around and see what I have for you. A little surprise.'

But Will was the one who was most surprised when the nurse emerged into the dim light. He recognized her red-gold hair, and full mouth. As for the rest – it was new; a product of her passage into young womanhood.

Gone were the skinny limbs and the sharp angles of adolescence. Instead, he saw a hint of a rounded hip under her plain skirt; breasts beneath a vertically striped shirtwaist and white surgeon's apron.

'Miss Hastings? Is that you?'

'Certainly, Mr Kent. We've been expecting you since noon,' Jo Hastings said.

CHAPTER III

'One Notch Above Hell'

Will was astonished at the difference three years made. When Drew's younger sister had visited Boston, she'd been a child; now she was a young woman, and a handsome one. That was true despite the freckles, still visible on her cheeks, and the nose that remained a fraction too large.

Mrs Grimaldi called a goodbye as she left the court. Her husband followed a pace behind. Will waved, then said to Jo:

'What in the world are you doing here?'

She used the hem of her apron to wipe her hands. With a nod toward the fire escapes, she said, 'This was my birthday present to myself.'

His scepticism kindled wrath in her blue-green eyes. 'A chance to help Drew for a few weeks! A chance to learn nursing by being a nurse. I had no money for a Nightingale school.'

'Yes, I remember. I didn't mean to make fun of you. I apologize.'

She smiled. 'You're forgiven. This is what I've wanted to do all my life. Last winter I took a second job in addition to the one at the family store. Every week I put forty cents of that extra money into a jar. When I had enough, I gave it to my father so he could pay a boy to take my place at the store for the summer.' Defiance glinted in those eyes he found oddly fascinating all at once. 'But to be perfectly truthful, Mr Kent, I'm not sure I can ever go back to Hartford or that store.'

'Please – ' He extended his hand. 'I'd like you to call me Will.'

With a grave expression she shook his hand. Her palm was cool and firm. He imagined her fingers would be surpassingly gentle with a patient.

'Very well. It's Will from now on. And you must call me Jo. When I was a little girl, I hoped we'd be on a first name basis someday.'

The directness of her gaze made him nervous. Was he crazy, or was her expression more than merely cordial? Surely her adolescent crush was a thing of the past—

She surprised him by asking, 'Do you know the meaning of the name Jo?' He shook his head. 'It's a Scots word. Very old.' Teasing him with her eyes, she added, 'Look it up some time.'

'I surely will. Meantime, may I ask you a question?'

'Of course. What is it?'

'Do you think an environment like this is good for someone like you?'

Her eyes blazed. 'What do you mean – someone like me?'

He dodged an empty tomato can that came whizzing down from a rooftop. Several boys were leaning over a crumbling cornice. One dropped a second can. It hit a mongrel defecating in the middle of the courtyard. Yelping, the dog ran off.

Will couldn't decide whether he liked or disliked Jo's forthright, challenging manner; a little of both, probably. He tried to explain himself tactfully:

'The Bend isn't exactly a resort—'

'Drew mentioned your familiarity with resorts,' she said with a tart smile. That told him she knew about the Pennels, and undoubtedly about Laura, too. 'Are you trying to say I shouldn't be here because I'm a girl?'

'Well—' His hesitation was an admission.

'That's utter nonsense. The idea that women are too delicate for some kinds of work is a fiction perpetuated by men. The same kind of men who claim that all female diseases have one cause – women deviating from their ordained function. If a girl tries to educate herself instead of letting her womb function, she'll get sick!'

'Jo, that's widely accepted medical theory.'

'I'm not surprised, considering the sex of most doctors. Men are determined to keep women in their place.'

As he started to object, she gave him a radiant smile. 'Oh, those aren't my words. I heard them used by a suffragist who lectured in Hartford. I spent twenty-five cents of my savings for a gallery seat and I'm glad I did. She was a fine, inspiring speaker. Her name was Julia Kent.'

He turned red. 'Oh good God.'

Jo's smile was sweet. 'I beg your pardon? What did you say?'

He knew he was beaten. 'Nothing,' he muttered. 'Not a thing.'

2

Inside the tenement, a pump handle began to squeak rhythmically. Contentious voices were raised in the lightless hall. Jo went on:

'If Miss Nightingale could go to the Crimea by herself and Dorothea Dix could venture into madhouses, I can certainly help my own brother here. You have no idea how desperately these people need us.'

'I'm beginning to,' he told her with an eye on the filthy courtyard.

'How long do you plan to stay? Drew hasn't said.'

He wanted to tell her that the Bend so depressed

him, he'd have left immediately if his conscience would have allowed it. Instead, he said:

'I'll be here about a week.'

'Oh, no longer than that?'

The faint tone of disapproval irked him. Before he could say anything else, there was an interruption:

He recognized Drew's voice. The familiar round face appeared in the tenement door. 'Will! You're finally here!'

Will hurried toward the doorway, both to greet his friend and to escape the curiously unsettling gaze of Drew's sister. Why the devil did he have to justify his opinions and his behaviour to an adolescent girl? The question nagged at him as he clapped Drew in a bear hug and exclaimed without thinking:

'It's wonderful to see you, Deacon.'

3

Drew laughed. 'Deacon, eh?'

Will's face reddened again. He started to offer an apology. Drew held up a hand:

'Don't look so stricken. I've heard that name before, though I assume most of my classmates thought otherwise. I just never heard it from you. I guess it fits. You've met our nurse, I see—'

'I have indeed.'

Drew bobbed his head at the grey and greasy-looking bricks of the tenement. 'What do you think of our little medical missionary station?'

'Want me to be honest? It's appalling.'

'I agree.'

'I never imagined that you'd practise in a tenement,' Will said as he walked back to pick up his valise.

'Neither did I. Dr Clem says Bayard Court is just one notch above hell, and sometimes I think that's

782

stretching it. But we've found it's the best place for us. Come on, I want you to meet my partner.'

He led Will into a dark, dismal hallway. A few old floor tiles remained, but most had been torn up, leaving a spongy sub-floor that reeked of urine. Huge holes had been punched in walls whose paint had long ago been overlaid with dirt and deposits of airborne grease. The steady *squeak-squee* of the pump handle came from an old sink at the rear of the hall. Despite hard pumping, only a trickle issued from the spout. Half a dozen women and youngsters were lined up waiting their turn with cans and bottles.

'That's the building's source of water,' Drew told him.

'Not the only one, surely.'

'Yes. This isn't Newport. Every morning Dr Clem and I pump a couple of gallons and boil it.'

'Even more reason for not having your office in a place like this.'

Drew stopped at an open door. 'Dr Clem used to have a store-front office on Mulberry. He practised there until he discovered that a lot of neighbourhood people thought the office was too fancy. It scared 'em off. I didn't believe that the first time I heard it, but it's true. Our patients are afraid of all American doctors, but they're less afraid of ones who practise in the kind of building the patients live in themselves.'

'Do you live here too?'

'No, I'm afraid we aren't that idealistic. I've got fairly decent lodgings a few blocks east of Bayard Street. In the section people call Jewtown. Jo's staying there, and I've rented a room for you. Our landlord's an energetic Russian Jew named Nevsky. He's a sweater.'

'A what?'

'He operates a sweat shop in his flat. He's doing well. Last month he took over the entire top floor of the tenement. Some of the older children in this neighbourhood work for him.'

'If he's doing so well, why does he have to rent out rooms?'

'It's a way of life in his neighborhood. He told me a lodger fulfils the same function for a Jewish family that a cow does for an Irishman. It puts a few extra pennies in the cookie jar.'

Drew conversed while leaning against the frame of the open door in a relaxed way. Jo had stepped down the hall and was examining a cut on the cheek of a boy in a line near the sink. She was talking to the boy in what sounded like a pidgin Italian. It was hard to say who looked more nervous, the boy or his mother. A couple of the women watched Jo as if she were a sorceress.

Will looked in the door and inspected the reception room – a windowless chamber about ten feet by six, lit by keresone lamps that added noticeably to the heat. On a collection of old chairs and boxes, five patients sat waiting: two elderly men, a handsome black-haired youth, a nondescript middle-aged woman, a mother with twin babies in her arms. There was a burlap rug on the floor and an uneven coat of whitewash on the walls. Yet in spite of the imperfections, the room had an air of cleanliness and order completely at odds with the filthy hall just a step away.

Will spent a moment studying the expressions of the people waiting. Frightened expressions, every one of them. Drew noticed his interest and said:

'Like a lot of immigrants, the Italians want to live among their own kind.' Will was surprised that his friend would speak within earshot of his patients. 'This country's so new and strange, they need the reassurance of familiar customs – a familiar language. Trouble is, by hanging onto the old ways, they're slow to adopt new ones. Many of them never even learn English.

784

That plays right into the hands of the padrones who pose as their friends.'

Now Will understood Drew's candor. 'But there must be exceptions. Walking over here, I met a woman named Mrs Grimaldi. Her husband's a patient of yours. She knew English.'

Drew laughed. 'Signora Grimaldi's got a spine like a ramrod and a will as strong as my dear sister's. Now that she's in America, she's determined to become an American. But a lot of these people are just too timid or too ground down by poverty. It's the same in every slum. A few strong ones fight their way out. There are thousands more who can't – but I'm chattering too much. Trying to tell you everything in ten minutes. My partner'll be wondering what happened to me.'

'I know his name's Clem. But your letters never said whether that's his first name or his last.'

'It's his nickname. His real name's Vlandingham.'

Will blinked. '*Vlandingham?*'

'That's right. Clement Chase Vlandingham. Do you know him?'

Will's thoughts turned back to the interview at Sherry's Restaurant. The fat society doctor had mentioned an older brother whose altruism – and whose slum practice – he regarded with contempt. Surely this must be the same man—

'No, I don't know him. But I'm anxious to meet him.'

Drew led him toward a closed door on the far side of the reception room. 'Then come on.'

CHAPTER IV

Warning

The whitewashed surgery was three times the size of the waiting room. On four home-made shelves on the wall to Will's left stood twelve kerosene lamps. To provide light for surgical procedures, he supposed. At the moment only two of the lamps were lit.

The current patient was a middle-aged man, stooped and sallow. He stood beside an old examination table, fastening the buttons of his trousers. He turned red and whirled away as Jo entered the room a step behind the two young men.

On a stool beside the examination table sat Drew's partner, a stringy fellow with a stern air. He was in his mid-sixties at the very least. His cold grey eyes briefly examined Will before returning to the embarrassed patient:

'Signor Abruzzo, you come back and see me Tuesday, all right?'

Another nervous glance at Jo. Then the old man nodded. '*Martedì. Sì, dottore.*'

'Meantime – ' The white-haired doctor picked up a small cardboard box which he handed to Signor Abruzzo. ' – use one of these whenever you have bad pain. I've explained what you're supposed to do with them. You understand, don't you?'

'I understand, *dottore*.' Eyeing the box apprehensively, the old man shuffled out.

When the door clicked, the white-haired man said to Drew, 'He'll throw them out. I don't know how I'm going to persuade him to go up to Bellevue for surgery. His wife practically had to put a knife to his throat just to get him here. Actually, I think it's too late for an operation to do much good.'

Drew grimaced. 'Is it what you thought? Rectal cancer?'

The white-haired man nodded: 'Goddamn it.'

Jo looked close to tears as she walked toward the wall on Will's right. There, curtains of cheap red gingham hung between a pair of ancient equipment cabinets. The curtains decorated what at first appeared to be a regular window opening onto an airshaft. A second look showed the window to be merely a ragged hole knocked through plaster, lath and brick. Between the curtains a pot of crimson geraniums was visible. The pot rested on a sill improvised from a piece of rough lumber.

Drew's partner rubbed his eyes a moment, then stood up. He looked at Will again. His apology for his profanity was a terse, 'Sorry.' He extended his hand, firm and brown. 'Clem Vlandingham.' His voice was that of a born New Englander.

'Will Kent, sir.'

Vlandingham's next remark caught him off guard:

'I know something about your background, but I don't know why you're here.'

It was Drew who answered:

'I invited him, Dr Clem. Will graduates from Harvard next year. I thought he might be interested in seeing the need for doctors in this part of New York. Maybe he'll be interested in joining our practice.'

Will was irritated with his friend for presenting him under false colours. 'Drew—' he began, but Vlandingham cut in:

'Well, we certainly have a lot to offer, Kent. We treat two entirely different and distinct populations here. The first is the permanent one. People who live in these fire-traps, renting rooms for seven to ten dollars a month – twice what it costs for decent quarters

787

in a good neighbourhood. Then there's our transient population. That consists chiefly of tramps who live in the streets and alleys. They survive by stealing. Neither group can afford to pay us a red cent, though a few people try. And they suffer all the maladies ever conceived by God and perpetuated by man. On top of that, we work amid the constant presence of typhoid and smallpox, and the constant fear of cholera. We make house calls in rooms where a thermometer registers a hundred and fifteen degrees this time of year.'

He gestured to the furnishings. 'Most of our equipment was donated and, as you can see, it's old. We save what little we earn in fees and use it for supplies. Lately, income's been lean. We have to buy drugs soon. That will take all the money that's left. In every respect, we offer a splendid opportunity—'

Once more the grey eyes raked him. Vlandingham's contempt angered Will, as did his next remark:

'I'd say you're the type who wouldn't be interested. Maybe I should send you to my younger brother who practises uptown.'

In a level voice, Will said, 'That's where I intend to practise.'

'Then what the devil are you doing in the Bend?'

'Honouring a promise I made to Drew.'

'What kind of promise? A promise to come down here and sneer at our primitive methods?'

With a sympathetic glance at Will, Jo tried to intervene:

'Dr Clem, people are still waiting—'

'Let them wait,' Will said. 'Why are you so angry with me, Doctor? I wasn't aware that I'd sneered at anyone or anything. I certainly don't know what the hell I've done to offend you. But I'll be damned if I have to stand here and be insulted.'

Will's words produced a look of grudging respect from Vlandingham. He put his palms on the cracked leather top of the examination table and leaned forward, obviously tired.

'You've done nothing, Kent. I apologize for my bad manners. I'm taking my anger out on you because I'm powerless to save the life of that poor old man who was just here – and yet I have to keep trying. We'll be glad to have you spend a week with us. We'll happily accept whatever help you can offer.'

That was all the time he gave to making amends. He turned to Jo:

'Let's have the next one. It's Saturday, after all, and it might be nice to get out of here by six or seven o'clock.'

'I'll walk Will over to his room, then come right back,' Drew said. Vlandingham's answer was no more than a mutter. Passing Will on her way to the reception room, Jo accidentally brushed against him. The curve of her breast touched his forearm, reminding him again of how much she'd grown and changed.

But there was no excitement in the brief contact. He was still too upset with his friend.

2

'Deacon Drew!' he finally exploded when they were by themselves. 'Reforming the world and everyone in it! What gave you the right even to suggest I might want to practise down here?'

They were moving east on Bayard Street, a block past the Bowery. Signs in Hebrew hung on the telegraph poles and Hebrew characters were painted in gilt on the windows of shops closed for the Jewish Sabbath.

Hands in the pockets of his white duck trousers, Drew kept his eyes on the ground as he replied, 'I don't think the idea's so ridiculous. I don't believe you really want to spend the rest of your life prescribing headache powders up and down Fifth Avenue.'

'You seem to know a hell of a lot about me!'

His friend gave him a penetrating stare. 'More than you know about yourself, maybe. Look – ' He faced Will on a corner. Two bearded men in long black twill coats and broad-brimmed hats passed them, speaking an unfamiliar language. ' – I realize I haven't much chance of weaning you away from the future you've planned so meticulously. But Clem Vlandingham's sixty-four. Thinking of retiring. You can't blame me if I'd like to have my best friend come in as my partner. You can't blame me if I try to persuade you.'

Less angry, Will said, 'No, I guess I can't.' He even managed a smile. 'Given your missionary temperament.'

'I'll ignore that. I'm not the only one pleased that you're here. Jo is, too. She's still quite enamoured of you, or didn't you notice?'

He evaded by shaking his head and saying, 'I was too busy noticing that she's grown up.'

'Grown up and still rebellious. I'm afraid she won't stay at the store in Hartford forever. She means to have a career as a nurse. By the way – I've told her all about the Pennels. She knows you're taken.'

Will didn't smile. Presently Drew asked, 'How is Laura these days?'

'Fine. We hope to be married by this time next summer.'

'I see. Are congratulations officially in order?'

'Not until I've spoken to her father.' An image of Jo's eyes drifted into his thoughts. For no very clear reason, he added, 'I wish you wouldn't mention an engagement just yet.'

'Whatever you say. We should clear up one thing, though. As Dr Clem said, we'll be grateful for your help at the office. But it's voluntary. You don't have to earn your keep. You're here as a guest.'

'And possible convert.'

'Don't sound so cynical. You could do worse.'

Will didn't voice his doubt of that. Drew went on:

'In any case, I want to show you around the neighbourhood. By day and at night too. I'll introduce you to a couple of interesting acquaintances I've made. One is a police sergeant named Banks. He's an expert on the Bend, and so is his friend Jake Riis. Riis does police reporting for the *Evening Sun*. He's going to have a book published soon, about the tenement districts. He prowls around after dark taking flashlight pictures of them.'

'Sounds like it could be dangerous.'

A wry laugh. 'On occasion – though the danger isn't always the sort you'd expect. Once Jake arranged a picture in a room occupied by some blind beggars. The quarters were just too crowded. Jake almost set himself and the whole tenement on fire with his flash powder.'

Will looked dubious. 'I don't know whether I need any slum tours, Drew. I've already met my quota of unsavoury types.'

'What do you mean? Have you had some trouble?'

'Yes, on the way to your sumptuous office. That's how I met Mrs Grimaldi.'

'What happened?'

'A couple of the local unemployed tried to relieve me of this.' He touched his watch chain. 'Mrs Grimaldi came along and helped me get rid of them. She knew them both.'

'Did you hear their names?' Drew said, stopping at the foot of a cement stoop so well scrubbed and swept, if fairly shone.

Will was struck by the note of concern in his friend's voice. 'Why? Is it important?'

'Might be. There are some bad actors in the Bend.'

Will thought a moment. 'One of the men was named Amato.'

'Rocco Amato?'

'Yes, that's it.'

'He's harmless.'

'The other was Giuseppe Corso.'

'He isn't. He holds grudges. Last week we treated his wife for cuts and contusions. She said he beat her because she didn't buy a bottle of Fiano for him to drink with supper. Of course he hadn't brought any money home. But *she* got the beating. Tells you what sort he is, eh? Might be better if you didn't walk around the Bend by yourself too much.'

'You're exaggerating.'

'No. I've worked here a month and a half. You start hearing things in a fraction of that time. The Bend may be grim, but it's still a neighbourhood, and a small neighbourhood at that. The people seem pretty much like people everywhere. Some of them scoundrels, most of them decent – and a few, like Mrs Grimaldi, nothing short of wonderful. And everyone's acquainted with everyone else. That's how I know Corso's no good. I've heard he does roughneck work for a couple of the padrones who control the trimming of the garbage scows – not to mention a fair amount of crime in the area. While you're here, you'd be wise to keep your eyes open and your wits about you,' was Drew's final, unsettling opinion on the matter.

CHAPTER V

The Policeman

The Bayard Court medical office was open seven days a week, from eight in the morning until six at night; later if the case load made it necessary. Unless there was an emergency, the hour from noon till one was set aside for the main meal of the day.

On the Sunday following Will's arrival, Drew, Jo, and Will took that meal in a small restaurant near the corner of Bayard and the Bowery. They paid thirteen cents apiece for beef soup, beef stew, fresh bread, peach pie, and a big bowl of pickles. The price also included a small schooner of beer. The two men drained theirs and split Jo's.

The restaurant was crowded with cheerful, gregarious Jews. The neighbourhood had come back to life after the Jewish Sabbath. Pushcarts lined both sides of Bayard Street, and peddlers shouted their wares. Outdoors or in, most of the men wore black silk skull caps.

Many of those eating in the restaurant had brought their work with them. They carried bundles of unfinished pieces that would be stitched together in a tenement sweatshop. A few had stacks of finished garments – mainly boys' jackets, gentlemen's cloaks, and knickerbockers – or knee pants, as Drew said they were called.

Fascinated, Will watched the men laughing and gossiping in Yiddish, their hands moving frequently to the pickle bowls or the bread baskets. 'Did you notice all the bakeries close by?' Drew asked. 'The Jews have a passion for fresh bread. It's good for you, and it's cheap – ' He drank some beer, flicked foam from his upper lip and smiled. 'You look like you don't quite believe all this is real.'

'I don't,' Will admitted. 'I've been to New York dozens of times, but I've never seen this part of the city. It might as well be a thousand miles from the Fifth Avenue Hotel.'

Jo's blue-green eyes fixed on him. 'Or Newport?'

Drew frowned, making sure his sister saw. Will didn't notice; he was recalling the studied ostentation of the cottages along Bellevue Avenue; the museum-like formality so different from the noisy, hectic yet somehow vital spirit of the lower East Side.

'You're right,' he said to her presently. 'It's hard to believe Newport and this neighbourhood are both part of America.'

'But which part's yours?' she asked.

Drew drained his beer. He was only half joking when he said, 'I've tried to discover that for years.' He thumped his schooner on the tablecloth. 'It's time we got back.'

That ended the conversation – for which Will was grateful.

2

They strolled back to Bayard Court in the hot summer sunshine. When they'd gone half a block, they came upon two boys of fifteen or sixteen punching one another while a small crowd looked on. Will stopped to watch, but Drew motioned him away:

'Those two belong to the same neighbourhood gang. They aren't mad. They stage a fight like that every few days.'

'Stage a fight? Why?'

Drew pointed, and Will saw what he hadn't noticed before – other boys, about the same age as the fighters,

794

standing behind the adults in the crowd. One of the boys slipped his hand under the coattails of a well-dressed man in front of him. The man was obviously not a resident of the area. A moment later, Will saw the boy hide a fat wallet under his shirt.

'You mean it's just a diversion so the others in the gang can pick pockets?' he asked.

Drew nodded. 'That's what it is.' Will laughed, shook his head, and the three walked on.

Soon they crossed Mulberry Street. Will felt a prickle on the back of his neck. He glanced to the right; saw nothing suspicious. He looked the other way, and stiffened—

A few doors down, a man on a brownstone stoop was watching him.

The man stood motionless among cronies with whom he'd been talking. Even though the brim of a derby kept his face shadowed, Will recognized him. It was Giuseppe Corso.

A shiver chased down Will's back. Fortunately Drew was talking to his sister; neither noticed.

Once across Mulberry Street, Will didn't look back. But he felt Corso's eyes following him until the three of them were out of sight on Bayard Street. Drew began to explain some things about the practice:

'We've worked the schedule out so that Dr Clem always takes Sunday off to relax and attend to personal business. He also takes every other Saturday. I take Tuesdays. We plan to add a third person, though that isn't absolutely definite yet.'

'He means me,' Jo said. 'If I can't pay for nursing school, I can at least learn by apprenticing myself to a couple of exceptional doctors. I've decided to tell Father I won't stay in Hartford past the end of this year.'

That confirmed a prediction Drew had made only yesterday. 'How will your father take it?' Will asked.

Drew laughed in a humourless way. 'He'll squeal like a gored bull.'

'But my mind's made up,' Jo added.

'Ultimately, Pa will give in,' Drew went on. 'He won't like the decision, but he'll understand it.'

She sighed. 'I hope you're right, Still – ' She glanced at the tenements simmering in the sunshine. 'I'd come work here even if he didn't. Life's very short. I refuse to squander mine standing behind a counter when there are so many people who need what little help I can give.'

By God, they're still trying to convert me! Will thought. But he didn't utter a protest. Jo's dedication, like Drew's, had a strong appeal to a certain part of his nature. So all he did was smile and say:

'Spoken like a true disciple of Julia Kent.'

Jo laughed. 'Right you are, sir.' Without embarrassment, she linked her arm with his. Drew looked a bit unhappy about his sister's forward behaviour, but Jo ignored him. She and Will strolled arm in arm for half a block. A most enjoyable half block, Will thought as they separated to walk single file through the passage leading to Bayard Court.

'I'm confused about one thing, Drew,' he said.

'What's that?'

'The place we're going. Which is it, your office or the free clinic?'

Drew laughed again. 'All depends. If a patient can pay us a few cents, it's the office. If he can't, it's the clinic. You don't imagine we earn enough to cover two rents, do you? Now I'll ask you something. Supposing we get busy this afternoon. May I put you to work?'

'I wish you would.'

He didn't expect the office would receive many patients the rest of the day. There had been none during the morning, as the Bend had come slowly to life while church bells rang the summons to mass at regular intervals. But two young men were already waiting outside the tenement. Both looked groggy; both were covered with blood that attracted a great many big black flies.

The men were brothers, explained the one who knew a little English. After church, he went on, they had retired to their fire escape and started drinking and playing cards. There'd been an argument; knives were drawn. Each brother suffered a wound—

An embarrassed shrug ended the story. With no warning the brother who'd been speaking fell forward against Will, his eyes rolling up into his head.

'Get 'em inside,' Drew ordered. After a brief examination of the unconscious man, Will dragged him through the waiting room to the surgery, covering himself with blood in the process. That was the start of work that didn't let up until after five.

Will soon came to appreciate why Drew derived such satisfaction from his work. The people who came to the office didn't come with trivial complaints. It took pain, and attendant fear, to overcome their natural unwillingness to visit a doctor. The language barrier compounded their difficulties. When they walked into the surgery, they were in need, and terrified.

Will's first patient was a weeping mother with a four-year-old girl in her arms. Three rat bites marked the child's legs. In broken English, the mother explained the youngster had been playing in the alley when she was bitten. The explanation brought on more sobbing.

Will managed to calm the woman, who was far more upset than her child. The little girl bore the experience stoically, as if rats were an accepted part of life in the Bend. He cleaned the wounds and told the woman to bring the girl back if fever or other symptoms developed.

Next Jo brought him a burly young man who was weak and in severe pain. Will diagnosed acute enteritis, administered opium, then turned the patient over to Jo for fomentation.

The young man stretched out on the examination table, blushing as she applied the warm water poultices to his belly. When he left, he took along a little vial of opium tincture. Will hoped the patient had understood the directions Drew had given in slow, halting Italian. The young man probably couldn't do what would be most beneficial for his condition – stick to a bland diet. People in the Bend didn't have the luxury of choosing the foods they ate. Most of their energy was consumed in an effort to find any food at all. He felt helpless when he realized that; helpless and not a little angry.

He experienced the same sense of helplessness with a seventy-year-old woman suffering from subacute rheumatism made even more painful by the humidity. How could he tell her of the remedies enumerated in his textbooks? How could he urge her to eat better food? Get more rest? Move to a milder, drier climate? The thought was ludicrous. All he could do was spoon out some tincture of guaiacum mixed with sarsaparilla and ask Jo to prepare a tepid alkaline bath behind a folding screen.

After much balking, the woman was persuaded to step behind the screen where Jo helped her bathe. All this went on while Drew examined a portly, well-dressed padrone with a rasping cough. The padrone accepted a bottle of medicine and paid nothing.

After her bath, the rheumatic woman smiled and

acted a bit more spry. She shook Jo's hand, pressed a dime into Will's, and impulsively kissed his cheek.

Will thought a moment, then handed the dime back. Drew didn't object.

The final patient Will saw that afternoon raised a ghost that had troubled him only once in recent months – the night of his last quarrel with his father. He'd begun to think he was finally free of the past. With a jolt, he discovered how dangerously wrong that assumption was.

The patient was a middle-aged man suffering acute pleurisy. It was obvious that fluid had to be drained from the left side of the chest cavity. Will prepared the trocar. For the first time all day, he started to perspire.

Soon his hand was trembling. Drew noticed. Will fought the trembling; brought it under control. But by that time the patient had noticed too.

Will's reassuring smile did nothing to ease the man's anxiety. He stood up, obviously ready to leave. Drew stepped to Will's side and held out his hand for the trocar. Reluctantly Will surrendered it. Drew got the patient seated again, then performed the procedure with no difficulty.

Jo took charge of the cannula and the basin to catch the discharge. Will pulled Drew out to the reception room – empty at last – and attempted to apologize:

'I'm sorry you felt you had to take over. I've never done an aspiration before.'

'That was evident. Trouble is – ' A nod toward the surgery. ' – you let the patient see it too.'

'Damn it, Drew, the Harvard faculty doesn't offer a course in confidence!'

Instantly, Will regretted the outburst. It brought a scowl to his friend's face. 'No,' he said, almost curt. 'You have to learn that on your own.'

He went back into the surgery. Will leaned against

the whitewashed wall, one fist clenched. He saw his mother vividly.

Laughing at him.

4

Just as they were closing the office, a florid man in a white suit and wide-brimmed straw hat walked in.

The man had a curling moustache waxed at the points. A silver toothpick jutted from between his lips. There was a lot of silver in his mouth, too; all his front teeth had been partially replaced, Will noticed as he scrubbed his hands with carbolic solution.

'Sergeant Banks!' Jo exclaimed, smiling.

'How do you do, Miss Hastings? Dr Hastings—'

The visitor touched his hat. He had a low, husky voice. A second chin hid half of his cravat. Despite his girth, the man seemed to radiate strength and controlled tension. He was around forty, but something in his brown eyes said he'd been examining the world – and finding it wanting – for much longer.

The man was obviously among friends. Yet the wary brown eyes examined every cranny of the surgery. He looked behind the folding screen, then lifted the curtains and peered out the improvised window. Only when he was satisfied did he inspect Will, then say to Drew:

'This the friend you were telling me about?'

'That's right. Sergeant Eustace Banks – Will Kent. Doctor Will Kent in another year. I mean it'll be official then. He's already a pretty good practitioner.'

Drew's remark made Will appreciate the meaning of friendship. By what Drew said and didn't say, he made it clear that Will's problem of a few minutes ago – part inexperience, part fear of failure – would never be mentioned in front of strangers.

'Glad to hear it,' Banks replied. 'Didn't stop by purely to be social, Doc.'

'You seldom do.' To Will: 'The sergeant operates out of the Sixth Precinct station house over on Elizabeth Street. You're out of uniform, Eustace.'

The policeman sat down on a stool. He pulled his hat off and fanned himself. His pink forehead glistened. His hair was parted in the centre, and had been shaped at the temples into a pair of perfect spit-curls. A bit of a dandy, Will decided. But not a man to be dismissed for that reason.

'Of course I'm out of uniform,' Banks retorted. 'It's my day off.'

'You never take a day off.'

The policeman laughed; it was more a snort than anything else. 'You learn fast, Doc.' While speaking, he somehow managed to work the silver toothpick to the other side of his mouth without touching it. 'I came to ask whether you've heard anything about a new stale beer dive. It's supposed to be operating in Robber's Row.'

Drew shook his head. 'Haven't heard a word.'

Banks sniffed. 'Must be newer than I thought. Maybe we can padlock it before anyone perishes of poisoning.' He stood up suddenly, resetting his hat on his head without disturbing the curls. Will noticed his hands. They were calloused. The wrists were thick and powerful.

'Thanks for your time,' he said in a voice lacking any emotion. 'Good day, Mr Kent. Miss Hastings—'

As he turned to leave, Drew caught his arm:

'Are you going to check on this new dive before you close it?'

'Sure. I figure on giving it the once-over tomorrow night. Jake's going with me.'

'I'm anxious to show Will the conditions we're fighting down here. Truth is, I've never seen a stale

801

beer dive myself. Would you and Riis mind if we came along?'

Again the wary eyes examined Will. 'Sure he's got the stomach for it?'

'I'd say so,' Will replied with a smile, 'seeing that I don't know what it is.'

The attempt at humour failed. Banks stared:

'Be thankful. Even the wops who live in these chicken coops won't patronize a two-cent restaurant. That's the fancy name for a stale beer dive. A few of 'em actually serve mouldy rolls and some black swill they call coffee. But the staple is beer from the bottoms of kegs that decent saloons put out on the curb. The kegs are supposed to go back to the brewery for refilling, but the stale beer boys get to 'em first, and drain the dregs.'

'You mean the dives *serve* that kind of stuff?'

'Yes sir, that's exactly what I mean.'

'Who'd be crazy enough to drink it?'

'People who can't afford better. Tramps, mostly. They know they're taking their lives in their hands. They don't care. Why, we can't stay ahead of the stale beer trade in this part of town! And the politicians don't help, either. We'll close this new place and ship the patrons out for a six-month vacation on Blackwell's Island. But it's likely none of them will serve a full sentence. Some alderman will get a friendly judge to spring 'em as soon as their votes are needed, and they'll go right back to killing themselves in some other dive.' He sighed and let some of his anger drain away before he said, 'It's a losing game. I'll show you this new place if you've the belly for it, Mr Kent.'

He sounded as if he were doubtful. Will said, 'Absolutely.'

'I'd like to see it, too,' Jo said. 'But I know better than to ask.'

Banks's gaze flickered to her. 'Let's hope so. If my

wife ever asked to visit a stale beer joint, I'd break her head.'

Jo bristled but kept quiet. The policeman turned back to Will and Drew. He took the silver toothpick out of his mouth and said:

'Tomorrow night. Dress like you don't have a cent. Smear a lot of dirt on your faces and hands. Be ready at nine sharp.'

It wasn't a suggestion; it was an order.

CHAPTER VI

Stale Beer

On Monday, Drew found jackets and some ragged pants for them to wear that night – not a difficult search in this neighbourhood. The landlord, Nevsky, helped locate the clothing. Drew asked Nevsky's wife to boil the old clothes and hang them out to dry. She was quite willing; her own husband was the one who had urged the precaution. Nevsky had spoken of infants lying or playing in stacks of garments in their parents' sweat shops. The children were later found to be ill with smallpox. The garments had transmitted the disease to employees of the companies which had contracted for the sweat work. In one documented case, the disease had been carried into a fine Broadway store displaying the finished clothing.

As the summer evening darkened, the two young men escorted Jo from the office to the tenement. There they changed clothes, smeared dirt on their faces and hands, and started back to Bayard Court.

The streets were dim; electrification hadn't yet

reached the Bend. Shops and tenement rooms were for the most part lit by lamps and, in a few instances, by gas. There were plenty of dark areas to conceal crime.

As Will and Drew walked down the passage to Bayard Court, a church bell struck nine. From up on the fire escapes, Will heard tired, quarrelsome voices. Sergeant Banks and another man were waiting near the tenement entrance.

The clock rang for the ninth and last time. In the silence that followed, Banks said, 'You're late.'

Without waiting for an explanation, he stalked past the two friends. Will heard a clicking sound. He couldn't be sure, but he thought Banks was examining the mechanism of a revolver.

In a hushed voice, Drew introduced Will to the reporter Jacob Riis. All three hurried after the stocky policeman, who had already entered the passage leading to Bayard Street.

Once on the street, Banks turned right. The others kept pace. The darkness made it impossible for Will to tell just what Jacob Riis looked like other than that he was husky, with a frame much like Roosevelt's. The reporter's voice was deeper than Roosevelt's, yet there too Will discovered a resemblance. Riis spoke with a seriousness and an intensity that immediately brought the other man to mind.

Riis was much more willing to answer questions than the policeman who led them round the corner into Baxter Street, then on through a succession of black passages that seemed to go nowhere – at least not until Banks travelled unerringly to some unseen doorway in a decaying brick wall, or lifted some loose plank in a solid-looking fence.

In just a short time, Will got a good deal of information out of the reporter, starting with some facts about his book. It was called *How the Other Half Lives*. Riis hoped it would shock the complacent public into doing something about the poverty and disease endemic in the New York slums.

Riis explained how the city's tenements had developed. Seventy or eighty years earlier, many residential lots in lower Manhattan had had two houses on them. The smaller, rear-of-the-lot house was usually leased to a tenant. Soon someone got the idea of subdividing such houses to produce even more income. As fashions in neighbourhoods changed, better-class families abandoned the older sections and moved uptown. The tenant houses were expanded outward and upward, thus creating tenements. Now the blight was everywhere – block after block of it.

'I've done research on the subject of slums, Mr Kent. The Americans have succeeded in developing overcrowding to a high art. Even in the worst stews of old London, people were never packed more densely than at the rate of about a hundred and seventy-five thousand per square mile. In parts of New York, the density's twice that. One result is that areas like this one become a breeding ground of disease. Has your friend Hastings mentioned the infant mortality rate for the Bend?'

'No.'

'It's four or five times that of the rest of the city.'

'Good God.'

'The pestilence of the slums spills over into other sections and kills rich and poor alike. But that isn't the end of it. The slums are the nurseries of the paupers and criminals who fill our jails and police courts to overflowing. They throw off a scum of forty thousand human wrecks every year. Forty thousand who wind up in the asylums and work houses! The slums create half a million beggars who by their very numbers doom our charities to failure. Above all, the slums touch family life, the very keystone of society, with death and deadly moral contagion.'

'Doesn't anyone try to solve the problem?'

'Oh, yes – people try. But you might as well try to dam Niagara with a quart bottle.'

Crossly, Banks ordered them to lower their voices. Riis did so as he went on:

'For more than ten years I've fought the landlords and the rental agents and their chief allies and protectors, the aldermen they pay off. Do you know what I've managed to accomplish in all that time? Two years ago, the small Parks Act was passed. The worst block of tenements on Mulberry Street – the block on the west side, where the street bends – will be razed and the land converted to a park. But heaven knows when it will happen. I tell you this, Mr Kent. One park won't obliterate the Bend. It's bigger than a single block. The Bend is a state of mind composed of equal parts of ignorance, fear, greed and un-Christian disregard for fellow human beings. The Bend isn't so much a geographical spot as it is a cancer whose growth is out of control.'

'And no one does anything?'

'Oh, efforts are made. The Board of Health and the sanitary police and the society for Improvement of the Condition of the Poor do their best, but it isn't enough. In '67, the Tenement House Act cut forty-six thousand new windows in buildings that had never known daylight. But that still amounts to very little when compared to the size of the problem and the moral indifference of those responsible for it. Influential people don't want changes, Mr Kent. For one thing, the slums have been absorbed into the political system. The greater the density in a tenement, the greater the number of votes that can be easily located and controlled. Tenement votes can be bought very cheaply. But the tenements are much more than a source of extra votes. They're a source of immense profits. That's why so much money is paid to bribe city officials and inspectors to ignore the prevailing conditions.'

'The owners pay the bribes?'

'The owners, and those who operate the buildings.'

'Aren't they the same people?'

'No, generally not. Most often, each building has a rental agent. A middle man whose main responsibilities are to collect the rents and to keep erecting partitions to create more rooms – without spending money on fripperies such as toilets or running water that's safe to drink. The agent makes a handsome profit off the rents, and returns an equally handsome percentage to the owners.'

'How much?'

'It varies from fifteen to thirty per cent. Twenty-five is usual. As one honest builder put it, why should a man take seven per cent and save his soul when he can lose it and make three or four times as much?'

'Goddamn it, pipe down!' Banks hissed at them. 'We're getting close.'

This time Riis obeyed the order. One at a time, the four men stole through an opening in another plank fence, then moved down a narrow passageway. A cat miaowed. Will stepped in something with a rank smell and a slippery feel. From the darkness overhead, a voice called, '*Chi è là?*'

No one spoke. Will's heart was beating fast. He kept his eyes fixed straight ahead. He feared they'd gotten lost.

All at once he heard singing. Saw a few faint horizontal slits of light. 'Look sharp!' Banks warned.

Will realized there were no longer walls on either side of him. They were in another courtyard. Several stories above, he glimpsed faint stars behind a haze of stove smoke.

'School's in – mind the step,' Banks said. The singing

807

was louder; a filthy song, Will realized when he listened to some of the lyrics.

The light came from behind slatted shutters whose tops were level with the ground. The shutters covered windows in a sunken entrance way; the bottom was reached by a flight of stone steps. Banks was already down there. Drew's soles scraped softly as he went down next, followed by Will and Riis.

Will discerned a door between the shuttered windows. Banks opened the door. His big shoulders and broad-brimmed slouch hat leaped out in silhouette against the feeble light of kerosene lamps trimmed low. A moment later, the four men were inside the stale beer dive.

Will followed the others to a pair of dilapidated benches that served in lieu of tables and chairs. Somehow he moved across the room without showing his shock and revulsion. If the tenement where Drew and Dr Clem practised was a notch above hell, then the subterranean lair to which Eustace Banks had brought them was hell itself.

2

The room measured roughly fourteen feet on a side. It had been dug from the ground beneath the tenement, perhaps to serve as a storage cellar. A few pieces of studding had been nailed over the scraped earth which formed the walls. The floor was hard-packed mud, the ceiling low; Will and the policeman had to stoop to avoid exposed joists.

Will took a seat next to Drew on a bench. Riis and Banks walked to an open space in the centre of the room. Will kept his dirt-smeared face averted from the eight patrons who were still awake. Several others appeared to be sleeping.

All at once his eyes focused on the wall. Bile rose in his throat. Dozens of brown slugs crawled on the dirt, and in the two darkest corners, larger lozenge-shaped bugs darted back and forth.

He felt something crawling over the top of his shoe. He glanced down and shook his foot. An enormous roach fell out of his pants legs, then another.

He turned his head so the proprietor and his customers wouldn't see him gag. Drew looked green. He'd seen the roaches too.

Will forced himself to examine the room more carefully. In the back, four patrons lay unconscious behind some packing crates. In the centre, two broken chairs supported a beer keg. Beside the keg stood an immense, long-jawed man with slitted eyes and a bulging forehead. The man rattled coins in his pants pocket as Banks held up four fingers.

The proprietor slowly counted the fingers with his eyes. Then, with a witless grin he picked up two battered tomato cans and filled them at the keg tap.

He handed the cans to Riis. The reporter turned and started toward Will and Drew. Banks waited for the other two cans, counting out four pennies to pay for the order. What made Will nervous was the utter stillness of the place. The other customers – five men, three ragged and incredibly filthy women of indeterminate age – said nothing. They stared at the newcomers from seats near the keg.

All the customers wore clothes whose original colors were unrecognizable; dirt and grease had turned them black. Two of the men were afflicted with advanced cases of venereal disease; their faces and hands showed a great many weeping lesions. These, then, were part of the pitiable tramp population he'd heard about—

Suddenly one of the customers lurched to his feet. A sore-speckled hand shot out and closed on Banks's left arm.

The policeman's eyes registered anger. The other man, a hatless fellow whose greasy hair hung over his ears, peered at Banks and said in a drink-blurred voice:

'Ain't I seen you before? Sure I have. I know where it was! Elizabeth Street!'

Hearing that, the hulking proprietor reached for something hidden behind the keg. Will held his breath. Banks stared down his accuser:

'That's the fucking truth, brother. We have met before. When the coppers closed that fine spot Salvatore Passaglia was running, I got shoved into a holding cell next to yours.'

'At Elizabeth Street?'

'That's right, brother.'

'Oh.' Slowly, the man drew his hand back. He wiped his nose. 'Oh, tha's it—'

'That's it,' Banks said with a nod. Under the hat brim, his eyes shone with an intensity that made Will shiver. Banks wanted to hurt the man who'd accosted him. The man was too drunk to see that, or to hear it when Banks asked:

'All right with you if I get on with serving my mates?'

The man tried to answer with a mock bow. In the middle of it he sagged suddenly, passing out on his feet. He might have struck the keg and knocked it off its supports if the proprietor hadn't given him a push. The man slipped sideways and sprawled, his mouth open and his upper teeth partially embedded in the mud.

The proprietor relaxed. After an exchange of nervous glances, so did Will and Drew.

Riis and Banks distributed the tomato cans. The four men huddled together, facing one another on the benches. The other patrons had lost interest in them.

Will raised his can and glanced inside. The so-called beer was the colour of weak lemonade. Only a few bubbles showed on top. He swirled the contents of the can, a move Banks misinterpreted.

'For Christ's sake don't drink it!' he whispered. 'That stuff's brewed to kill at long range. They doctor it with drugs to bring back a head.'

So the foursome sat, merely pretending to drink until the proprietor was called on to dispense refills for two other customers. While the proprietor was thus distracted, Banks lowered his hand and emptied his can into the dirt. One by one, the others did the same.

A few minutes later Banks rose and stretched. With studied nonchalance he called goodnight to the tramps. One responded with a wave and a grunt but the rest were oblivious. A second man had collapsed beside the one who'd gone down a while ago. By the back wall, another customer had climbed on top of one of the scrofulous women. The man's bare buttocks jerked up and down. The woman kept time by waving a tomato can above his shoulder. The proprietor's tongue moved back and forth over his lips as he watched. No one else paid any attention.

The four men filed outside. 'Jesus, Drew,' Will whispered when the door had thudded shut behind them. 'That's unbelievable.'

'But not unusual, I'm told.'

'You're right,' Banks said as he marched up the steps. Will drew a deep breath. The heat-laden air smelled sweet compared to that in the cellar. He was queasy all at once.

As they moved along, Banks spoke to Riis in a low voice:

'I recognize that cretin running the joint. A Cherry Street roughneck named Dave McCauley. We'll give Dave and his crowd one more night of revelry and take 'em out on Wednesday – ' A little louder: 'What the hell's all that racket back there?'

Although Will was responsible for the noise, he

couldn't answer. He was leaning against a brick wall, violently sick.

3

Banks got them out of the vicinity of the stale beer dive without incident. Feeling somewhat better, Will caught up with the policeman and asked him a question he supposed was naïve. Yet what he'd seen had so shocked and sickened him he had to have an answer:

'Who's responsible for a place like that, Sergeant?'

Banks didn't laugh at him. 'Jake here would say every one of us. We really don't care whether such dives exist because we don't give a damn about the poor – neither the old poor who have been here for years, or the new poor arriving at Castle Garden every day. So we let 'em live in places we wouldn't keep a dog, and we hope to God that disease and their own self-destructive behaviour will keep 'em from our sight. Above all, we don't give them any help. I know that's how it works because my poor mother was Dublin Irish. She came here with just a few coins tied in a scarf and her soul brimming with hope. She went to work for a young swell as a household girl – about the only kind of job an Irish lass could find. I learned long afterward that the swell and two of his best friends were members of the Know-Nothing party. Despisers of the foreign born. One night the three forced my mother to drink a lot of wine. Her employer told her that if she didn't, she'd lose her job and he'd see she never got another. She got sick from the wine but that made no difference to the swells. Each one of them carnally abused her. One of the three swells was my pa, but of course I don't know precisely which—'

There was a vicious sound to those last words. His voice was barely audible:

812

'She bore me and five years later died of shame because of her mortal sin. I reckon I'd like to kick those swells to death if I could find 'em. I never learned their names. I was too little. Trouble is, if I killed them I'd be sent to the Island. Maybe that's why I do my kicking around here instead. When I'm in uniform, it's legal.'

They'd reached the end of a passage. Banks took hold of the bricks at the corner and turned, a commanding, even frightening figure. 'All here, are we?'

There were murmurs of assent. Will saw lighted windows along a street he recognized as Mulberry.

They moved on in a more relaxed way. Banks said to Will, 'Want to come along and watch the sport Wednesday night?'

'Very much.'

'Nine o'clock. Elizabeth Street station. Be prompt. This time we won't wait.'

'I'll be there.'

'Then so will I,' Drew put in, though without enthusiasm.

Will said, 'You didn't really answer my question, Sergeant. Who's responsible for that place?'

'I expect it's owned by one of the padrones. My guess would be a big boss named Don Andreas Belsario.'

'Know him?' Will asked Drew.

'I've never met him, but I hear a lot about him,' Drew replied.

'Well, this I guarantee,' Banks went on. 'Everything about him's shady, including the title he hung on himself. He's no don. He's a Neapolitan thug who happens to look like your favourite grandfather. Good protective colouring, that. He takes advantage of it. He started a string of stale beer dives two years ago. A couple of tramps died from drinking his brew. One turned out to be the brother of a member of the Board of Health. Overnight, Don Andreas got out of the business and covered his tracks. We couldn't charge him with a thing. Now I hear he's back in the same trade, but we'll never get him. Soon as we close one of his spots, he'll open two more.'

'And you're sure he's behind the place?'

'Pretty sure. I don't think Dave McCauley is working for the building's rental agent. The agent's dirty work is confined to bullying tenants who are late with the rent. For that, he hires a rockroller named Giuseppe Corso. Neighbourhood boy. Good family connections,' he added with sarcasm. 'It's a cinch the building agent knows what's going on in his cellar, though. Don Andreas wouldn't open up without making an arrangement. Maybe the agent takes a cut and doesn't tell the owners. Or maybe he passes a percentage along to them. Either way, it wouldn't amount to more than pennies. Dives like that are worthless as a source of income. But as a source of votes – that's another story.'

'But what about the owners?' Will persisted. 'The men who actually hold title to the land and the building? Do they know about the stale beer dive?'

'Probably not. But they have to know in a general way that most everything happening in the tenement – and especially the overcrowding – is against the law. They couldn't be ignorant when they're drawing thirty per cent, which I've been told is the rate of return for that particular tenement.'

'What kind of bastard would permit such conditions in a building that belongs to him?'

'A bastard who wants to get rich and stay rich and isn't too finicky about his methods. We have a lot of bastards like that in America, Kent – where've you been? The whole tenement system is nothing but American enterprise at work.'

'You mean respectable people own such places?'

Banks guffawed. Then, with the faintly weary tone of a teacher instructing a hopeless pupil, he said:

'Yes, Kent, very respectable people. I've studied the tax books on every tenement in the Sixth Ward, and I can testify to it. The building we just visited – that's owned by a real estate corporation which is in turn owned by a holding company. The holding company has a splendid, impressive name. Pen-York Property Trust. It's known but not legally provable that all the shares of Pen-York are held by a single family. A fine upstanding city family named Pennel. Ever heard of them?'

CHAPTER VII

The Tenement

Will's room on the top floor proved too hot for sleeping. Finally he picked up the clean, threadbare, and wholly superfluous comforter Nevsky had given him, and carried it into the hall.

He passed Drew's door, then the landlord's. Nevsky's flat contained not only living quarters but eleven Singer machines – four owned, seven leased. Light showed under the door. Nevsky was complaining to his wife in Yiddish; perhaps it was the same complaint Will had heard before – Nevsky was unable to amass a decent dowry for each of his four daughters. All were of marriageable age, but still single due to the lack of a dowry.

Nevsky claimed that he detested sweating. It was, after all, a system of labour designed to circumvent the new laws regulating hours and working conditions in factories. But the landlord was devoted to his daughters, and he was determined to capitalize on the opportunity in America, and give the girls a better start than he and his wife had had in Russia.

Beyond Nevsky's flat there was light under Jo's door as well. Will almost knocked, but held back at the last moment. As he climbed the stair at the end of the hall, he found himself picturing her eyes and the contours of her mouth.

On the roof it seemed slightly cooler, even though the air was oppressively damp. He almost stumbled across three youngsters sleeping on a ragged sheet. He apologized in English; they murmured sleepily in their own language. Soon he became aware of more than a dozen people occupying improvised pallets on the roof. He found a place against the stone cornice and spread the comforter.

He yawned. He was worn out. But sleep still wouldn't come. Troubling questions chased through his mind. He got up and gazed out across the rooftops of the Bend. Lamps glimmered in some of the buildings. Eastward, the colossal span of the bridge to Brooklyn hung across the night sky. But all he saw was the stale beer dive.

Do the Pennels really own that filthy place?

He didn't want to believe it, but he knew it was possible.

And if Laura's family owned one tenement, wasn't it likely that they owned others? The basis of the Pennel fortune was New York city real estate. Was Maison du Soleil built on the money Thurman Pennel collected from slum rental agents? If so, how much did Marcus know about the business? And Laura?

The questions led on and on, like conjuror's boxes that opened one after another to reveal one more box each time. The result was continuing wakefulness, and a decision about what he must do.

816

The next day, Tuesday, was Drew's day off. At breakfast he announced his intention of going across town to a pharmaceutical supply house. There he planned to purchase a long list of drugs the partners needed for compounding medicine.

He and Will and Jo walked to the office. Soon Dr Clem arrived from his bachelor rooms in the Bowery. He unlocked a cheap tin box kept on a shelf, and removed all the bills but one. Drew took the money and left.

The older doctor easily took care of the morning's few patients. Will read a text from the small collection in the surgery. He found it hard to concentrate. Around a quarter to eleven, he gave up and asked whether he could be excused for an hour or so. Dr Clem replied with a nod, concentrating on the mortar in which he was preparing a purgative for a patient waiting outside.

Jo was folding sheets for the examination table. She'd boiled the sheets first thing that morning and hung them up in the passage outside the improvised window. When Will asked to leave, she gave him a quizzical look, then followed him out to the courtyard. There she asked:

'Is anything wrong?'

He mopped his forehead with his handkerchief. The sun was hidden by dirty grey clouds, but the temperature still felt like ninety or better. There was no wind to disperse the odours of cabbage and fish and offal.

He shook his head. 'I'm going over to the police station.'

'Whatever for?' She took hold of his hand. 'You haven't had more trouble with Corso, have you—?'

Spots of colour brightened her cheeks as she realized she'd been forward. She pulled her hand away quickly.

'No,' he said. 'I just want to go back to that tenement we visited last night. I want to see the upper floors by daylight.'

The harshness of his voice made her frown. 'Drew said reaching the place was like travelling through a maze. Do you know how to find it?'

'I know someone who does. Banks. I'll see you in an hour or so.' He started away.

'Will—'

Her tone of concern brought him back. Grey eyes held his a moment before she said:

'Do be careful.'

He smiled. 'I will.' He took pleasure in knowing she worried about him.

3

He found Eustace Banks at the precinct house on Elizabeth Street. The sergeant questioned the advisability of a return visit to the tenement:

'You don't exactly look like one of the renters. I don't want Dave McCauley smelling a rat before we come down on him.'

'I can pretend to be looking for one of Vlandingham's patients. If anyone questions me, I'll tell 'em I got lost and wound up in the wrong building.'

'Are you sure you have to see that particular tenement? Wouldn't another one do just as well?'

'Absolutely not.'

'All right,' Banks grumbled. He reached for a sheet of paper and a steel-nib pen. 'I'll put down the directions. Just stay away from the cellar.'

With the directions in hand, Will started back into the Bend. He'd gone no more than a block when he encountered Mrs Grimaldi. On her arm was a hamper containing a cauliflower, two carrots more brown than orange, and a large, fragrant onion. Perspiration shone in her dark moustache. She greeted him with a smile that didn't quite reach her eyes.

'Are you enjoying your visit to the Bend, Signor Kent?'

'There's certainly a lot to see.'

'Maybe you'll want to leave sooner than you planned. 'Sep Corso's doing a lot of talking.'

'About what?'

'About you. I wouldn't go too many places as you are – ' Her eyes flicked past his shoulder. 'Alone.'

Will's stomach began to hurt. Drew's warning hadn't been an idle one, then.

'Thanks for telling me. I'll keep my eyes open. How's that baby you found?'

Matter-of-factly, she said, 'The poor little thing died. It happened last night around midnight. We did the best we could. Grimaldi and the children and I. But the little girl lacked strength. I've already paid for a mass for her soul.'

Suddenly, instead of the uncomplaining stoicism he'd come to associate with her, there was bitterness:

'You should be thankful you are only visiting the Bend. You can escape its miseries whenever you wish. The rest of us – we aren't so lucky. Good day to you, signor,' she said, marching round him with the dull grey daylight shining in her tear-filled eyes.

She clearly didn't like the weakness the tears represented. Before she'd taken three steps, her knuckle was in her eye and her shoulders were squared again, ready to receive whatever burdens the Bend would put on them.

In the daylight, and guided by the written directions, Will had no difficulty finding the tenement. He climbed its dark, crowded stairs. The familiar squeak of a pump handle followed him upward – as did the eyes of the old men and women and children he passed. Those eyes were suspicious; even hostile. He was well dressed. The tenement dwellers couldn't be sure he wasn't some official from the city.

But no one bothered him. He paced the halls. With every step, he grew sicker and angrier.

Insects crawled in cracks in the floor. Roaches ran along broken skirting boards. The air was hot, still, and foul. Doors stood open in the hope of catching a puff of breeze, but there was none. Through those doorways he saw quarters hardly fit for animals, let alone human beings. None of the rooms measured more than ten feet on its longest side. Only one in every seven or eight had a tiny window. Although it was the middle of the day, oil lamps were needed for light. They added to the heat and spread a faint, smoky haze.

In one room he counted nine straw pallets. In another, two infants lay fretting in wooden boxes, and a four-year-old boy swung in a large shawl hung in a corner to supplement the mattresses on the floor.

There was almost continuous conversation, plus a good deal of shouting – all in Italian. Infants cried. Dogs barked. He even heard a goat bleating in one apartment. The narrow corridors and confined spaces amplified the sounds to a din. Finally, unable to take any more, he ran down to the ground floor and outside.

He approached an old man seated on a crate near the steps leading down to the stale beer dive; its door had a heavy padlock this morning.

'Do you speak English?'

A frown of suspicion wrinkled the old man's face. He took a black clay pipe out of his mouth. '*Si* – a little.'

'How many people live in each room in this building?'

'The sanitary police – they ask the same question.'

'I'm not a policeman. I'm a doctor. *Dottore. Medico.*'

'Ah.' Some of the wrinkles disappeared.

'Can you tell me how many?'

The old man thought about it. 'The least I know of is six, the most twenty.'

'In one room?'

'*Si.*'

'How much is the rent?'

'It depends on the size of the room. Seven, eight, nine dollars a month.'

Red-faced, Will said, 'Jesus Christ.'

He turned away, trembling so hard, he barely knew where he was going. He still had to marry Laura, of course. But in exchange for the performance of that duty, Marcus or her father had to give him some assurance that they weren't responsible for the misery and squalor he'd just seen.

Abruptly, he realized he hadn't thanked his informant. He turned round. The crate was gone and so was the old man.

5

The sights and sounds of the tenement had so unsettled Will, he could hardly keep his mind on the patients who came to the office that afternoon. To make things worse, a couple of ragged boys kept racing up and down the passage outside the window of the surgery.

They peeked through the curtains several times, startling Jo and the two men, and embarrassing the patients.

The last time the boys did it, Jo was busy removing some hardened wax from a woman's ear. One of the boys yelled. Jo started, and the tip of the syringe scraped the ear canal. The woman cried out. Vlandingham ran to the window, flung the curtains back, and cursed the fleeing boys. Then he stormed over to Jo and criticized her carelessness with a ferocity all out of proportion to the offence.

For the rest of the afternoon, the older doctor was in a bad mood. When the waiting room was empty and they were closing up, he apologized to Jo and explained why he was upset. The man with cancer hadn't returned. Vlandingham looked defeated as he shut the door and bid Jo and Will goodnight.

An hour earlier, a rumbling thunderstorm had dispersed most of the clouds. But it hadn't relieved the heat. If anything, the rain had made things more uncomfortable. Steam rose from the sidewalks. Will felt as if he'd bathed in machine oil. Jo kept dabbing her cheeks with a bit of lace-edged linen.

They walked slowly across the Bowery and into the Jewish section. Behind them, above the tenements to the west, a huge, dark orange sun dominated the sky. The storm's passing had brought the pushcarts out again. Women were haggling over the price of tin cups, neckerchiefs, peaches, eyeglasses, even eggs with broken shells. Over the squawking of several not-quite-dead chickens hung on the metal hooks of a cart, Jo said:

'What did you see in the tenement?'

'Nothing I care to remember.' That wasn't quite true. When next he spoke to Marcus, he'd remember well enough.

In response to a customer's gesture the chicken peddler seized one of his birds by the neck and pulled if off the hook. He flung the chicken on a bloody chopping board and decapitated it with one stroke of a cleaver. Then he began to section the bird.

'As I recall, Mr Riis took a photograph of a hallway in that building,' Jo told him. 'I hope his pictures will help convince people such places do exist.'

'By God, I hope so too.'

The slow-sinking sun only seemed to intensify the heat and humidity. Will suggested dinner. Jo said she wasn't hungry. She seemed edgy, which was exactly how he felt. His head was aching again – another by-product of the insufferable weather.

They walked the last block to the tenement. Conversation lagged. They climbed the stairs and parted with only an exchange of good evenings. He found his room broiling. He slammed the door and peeled off all his clothes. He lay down, fell into a doze, and was soon dreaming.

In the nightmare he saw infants squalling and suffocating in shawls strung in corners. He saw cockroaches crawling over mounds of dirt. He gagged on the smells of waste and yesterday's cooking. He heard the weeping and cursing of people penned in a tenement whose rooftop carried a huge sign blazoned with the name Pennel.

And then he saw Roosevelt's scornful face silently condemning him for doing nothing about any of it.

CHAPTER VIII

Jo's Confession

He woke abruptly, struggling for breath. The room was pitch black and hot as a furnace.

He lit a lamp; consulted his watch. Only a quarter after ten.

He pulled on a singlet and his oldest pair of trousers, then went into the hall. There was a light under Drew's door. He knocked. No answer.

He looked in. The room was empty. But the coat Drew had worn that morning lay on the cot. He shut the door and moved on.

Jo's door was dark. He took the stairs to the roof. The red sun had gone, replaced by blurred stars. He walked around the small, shed-like structure which enclosed the head of the stairs. His foot collided with something soft.

'Oh, I'm sorry.'

'Will?'

'Jo?'

He crouched down. 'I didn't see you sitting there. I must have tramped all over you. I apologize.'

'I should have brought a light. But even a tiny flame seems to raise the temperature ten degrees.'

As she spoke, he heard rustling sounds. He balanced beside her on the balls of his feet. At last he realized the significance of the rustling; she was slipping into a blouse she'd discarded.

Soon his eyes grew accustomed to the darkness. He could see her push her hair back over her shoulders. She fastened the lower buttons of the blouse but left the upper ones undone.

He sat down next to her, his back against the wall of the stairwell and his eyes on the lamp-lit tenement windows in the distance. His shoulder was only an inch from hers. That proximity and the evening heat conspired to produce a physical reaction. He was surprised but not altogether displeased.

'I've been up here for an hour,' she said. 'Did Drew get back yet?'

'Yes, but he isn't in his room. He must be out to supper.'

'Did you eat?'

'No. I still don't feel hungry.'

'Neither do I.'

'Sorry I wasn't very talkative on the way home. I was just damned depressed by that tenement. What's the name of Jake Riis's book—?'

'*How the Other Half Lives*.'

'Yes. I never knew. I never imagined. I'll say one thing – ' He tried to see her face in the starry darkness, but it was little more than a pale oval. ' – now I understand why your brother decided to practise in this part of New York. I only began to understand it at Castle Garden, when I helped him deliver a baby. Did he ever tell you about that?'

'Yes.'

'Well, that was when I first admitted that he really knew what medicine was all about. But I tried to deny that he was right.'

'You don't now?'

He shook his head. 'And that's something new. Up at Harvard, I thought he was crazy. The more he scoffed at my ambitions, the more I resented and laughed at his. I don't think our disagreement was all my fault, though. Drew's my friend, and a wonderful doctor. But sometimes he can be pretty self-righteous.'

'How well I know. I'm guilty of the same thing. It

must run in the family. Will you accept an apology for both of us?'

'It isn't necessary.'

'I think it is. Because I'm going to ask you a blunt question about your feelings. When Drew talks about his work, do you feel guilty?'

'Of course. That's the reaction he's looking for, isn't it?'

'Perhaps it was at Harvard.'

'What do you mean?' Nothing's changed. He still dwells on the importance of his work—'

'Not to shame you. There's a different reason, I think.'

The conversation was beginning to make him edgy; perhaps because he couldn't prevent guilt feelings. His annoyance showed when he said:

'Oh? What is it?'

He sensed rather than saw her shift her shoulders against the wall then draw her legs up closer. She sounded melancholy when she answered:

'Drew's been working with Dr Clem since graduation. Do you know how much the two of them have earned in fees in that time? Two dollars and eighty cents.'

'I thought Drew didn't care about profit.'

A bitter laugh. 'I'm not talking about profit. I'm talking about survival.'

'Maybe the Kents could donate some money to the practice.'

'That's nasty. Charity is the last thing anyone wants from you.'

His annoyance drained away. 'I'm sorry. I guess the heat's getting me down. You were starting to explain why Drew talks the way he does.'

'I can't be certain, of course. But I have a theory. At best, a slum practice is depressing. You make so little progress. And there are so many barriers. You've seen

826

some of them. Language. Ignorance. Fear. And you saw what happened today. Rather, what didn't happen. A man who desperately needs medical help refused to come back.'

'Do you mean Drew is starting to ask himself whether he made the right decision?'

'He doesn't say so, but I'm afraid he's doing just that.'

'And when he tells me how noble the work is – how important – he's really trying to convince himself?'

A sigh. 'Yes.'

Far away, a gun fired. Someone screamed. A dog began to bark, the sound quickly muffled by a hubbub of voices. Then those too melted away, and the hot night was quiet again.

There had been a note of vulnerability in Jo's voice a moment ago. Touched by it, he spoke gently:

'And how do you feel? Is working here less satisfying than you let on?'

'Oh, I'm learning things I couldn't learn otherwise. I could be content to spend my life in this kind of neighbourhood. Very content in – in the proper circumstances.'

'What might those be?'

She didn't answer. Instead, she countered his question with another:

'When do you plan to be married, Will?'

He jerked his wrists tighter against his legs. 'No date's been set.'

'But you *are* engaged to that young woman Drew told me about?'

'The engagement isn't official. There's one matter to be settled first.'

'But you love her, don't you?'

'Would I think of marriage if I didn't?'

Then he thought, *Yes. Marrying her has become my*

responsibility. That had changed everything, somehow; that and all he'd seen and heard since Saturday.

He started when her hand stole across to his forearm. 'That isn't an answer, Will.'

A brusque laugh. 'You're pretty forthright, Miss Hastings. And, might I say, pretty damn nosy, too.'

'For a purpose. When Drew says the practice is important, he's telling the truth. The people in the Bend need good doctors. Dr Clem will retire soon. You could take his place. Together, you and Drew could make a go of it.'

'Misery loves company, eh?'

His attempt to relieve the tension failed. There was urgency in her voice as she leaned close to him in the dark:

'What better way do you have of spending your life? Do you really care about that girl?'

'Jo – forgive me, but – why—'

He couldn't bring himself to say it. She said it for him:

'Why is it any of my business?' Amazed, he felt her fingers against his cheek, softly touching. 'Because, Mr Will Kent, at the risk of again being considered much too forthright—'

She brushed her lips against his.

'—I lost my heart to you the first time Father brought me to Cambridge. I'd never try to take you away from someone you love. But you don't speak of that girl with much conviction. If you don't love her – well—'

Another light kiss. Her breath was sweet on his face as she whispered:

'I'll fight for you.'

All he could say was, 'My God.'

Now, at last, she was able to tease again:

'Don't chatter so much. You know what we've both wanted for the last ten or fifteen minutes.'

This time her mouth came against his with passionate force.

The next few minutes passed at dizzying speed. They lost themselves in emotion, kissing and holding one another tightly. Against his chest he could feel Jo's body, firm yet soft beneath her half-open blouse. Just as his hand moved to her breast, a door opened at the head of the stairs.

'Jo? Are you up here?'

She pulled back. His left hand caressed her cheek and came away damp. Tears?

'I know I'm too forward,' she whispered. 'But who decreed that it must always be the man who speaks first?'

'Jo?' Drew's voice faded slightly as he walked to the far side of the roof.

She swiftly kissed him again. 'Now that I've confessed and made a complete fool of myself, there's nothing left to say – ' She clambered up, her skirts falling into place. Her hands flew to her blouse to straighten it. ' – except this. I'll be here if you ever decide what you really want. I don't believe you know yet. When you're with that rich girl, think of me a little, too. Think of the name my parents gave me.'

'*Dammit, Jo, are you up here or not?*'

'Coming! Will and I were just sitting over here, talking—'

Talking and throwing my whole life off the rails, he thought, overcome with emotion. She started past him. He caught her arm:

'What do you mean about your name?'

She pressed her open mouth against his cheek for a second, giving him a last tender kiss before she said,

'Didn't I tell you that Jo is an old Scots word? It means sweetheart. I love you, Will. Don't ever forget that.'

Hair streaming behind her, she ran round the corner and out of sight.

CHAPTER IX

The Raid

Will slept poorly again that night. Memories of Jo bedevilled him; memories of her warm, ardent kisses. In the morning he awoke from a restless sleep and began an inevitable comparison between Jo and Laura.

Laura got the worst of it. Her passion had a furtive, guilty quality. Jo was far more honest and direct. He imagined that she'd be a stimulating wife – and not just in bed. She wouldn't be the typical docile spouse who never permitted herself an original thought or opinion. If anything, she'd err in the other direction. He found that appealing – and a definite contrast to Laura's studied ignorance of the world and its problems.

But what good were comparisons? Events in Newport had dictated that he marry Laura. A year ago – even a month ago – he'd have been overjoyed about that. He recalled an old maxim he'd heard somewhere. A warning to be careful when you chose the things you wanted from life, since you would undoubtedly get them.

On Wednesday morning it rained hard again. The hour-long downpour created muddy rivers in Bayard Court, and cooled the air only a little. In the surgery, Will and Jo went about their work with a self-conscious politeness that was almost a parody of good manners. Drew soon noticed, but he said nothing.

Around noon, he and Will left to get something to eat. Jo pleaded a lack of appetite. Dr Clem's midday meal was always the same – two pears bought fresh that morning from one of the Bend's numerous fruit peddlers.

On the street, Drew said, 'You and Jo are certainly tiptoeing around each other. Did you have an argument last night?'

'No.' Will said, too quickly. How could he admit the truth – especially to her brother?

Drew accepted his answer without comment. They crossed the Bowery, their destination a new restaurant in the neighbourhood. The place was trying to attract customers by offering not only a complete meal for thirteen cents, but two schooners of beer instead of one, and a complimentary cigar.

'Haven't changed your mind about going tonight?' Drew asked.

'No.'

'I grant you Banks will have a squad of men with him – maybe more. All the same, it could be dangerous. I didn't peg you as the adventurous sort.'

'I'm not.'

'Then why are we taking chances? You certainly don't have a personal stake in seeing that dive cleaned out.'

Will thought of Thurman Pennel. And Marcus; charming, sociable Marcus. Always impeccably dressed. Always carefree. Will's most important question for Marcus and his father was a simple one. How could they draw income from real estate and not know its location or its condition? The answer seemed clear. They couldn't.

'You're wrong, Drew. It is a personal matter.'

Drew looked dubious. 'I can't see how – unless Jake Riis has suddenly turned you into a reformer.'

Will managed to smile. 'If that's what I'm becoming, the person responsible is someone I've known a lot longer than I've known Riis.'

Drew sighed. 'You mean if one of us gets shot or bashed in the head tonight, I've only myself to blame?'

'That's right, Deacon.'

2

Banks brought two full squads.

The policemen wore dark blue trousers and frock coats with brass buttons and wide belts. Tall, conical grey hats completed their uniforms. They marched two abreast, swinging their long locust-wood billies.

Garbed in old clothes, Will and Drew brought up the rear. They speculated quietly about the wisdom of this formal parade from Elizabeth Street. Loungers along the route made derisive remarks. But nothing was thrown, and there was no trouble. The marching men finally halted in a dark courtyard Will thought he recognized.

A man in a tattered shirt and cap broke away from the wall near the cellar entrance. The man started to confer with Banks. Will moved closer to hear what the man was saying.

' – not much business for the last hour. I don't believe they've been tipped. I've been right here the whole time.'

Banks clapped him on the shoulder. 'Good work. You had risky duty tonight. It'll be noted on your record. Now fall in. I brought an extra stick. Wouldn't want you to miss the fun.'

Will was disturbed by the barely suppressed excitement in the sergeant's voice. Banks handed the stick to the ragged man.

'Thanks kindly, sir.' The man touched his cap with the billy, then stepped into the ranks.

In a hoarse whisper, Banks issued orders. The first squad would invade the stale beer dive. The second was divided into teams responsible for guarding the various exits from the courtyard, in case any customers slipped past.

Will cast a nervous eye at the cellar steps. Lamps gleamed behind the slitted shutters, just as they had Monday night. A couple of voices made raw by drink were raised in a chorus of a minstrel tune. Will started when Banks loomed at his left, prodding him with his stick:

'You and your friend be careful. Most of the customers of a place like this are revolvers – in and out of a cell regular as the seasons. But that doesn't mean they're harmless. The drugs in the beer can do queer things to a man's brain. So watch your step. I don't want to be writing reports to explain an accidental death.'

He waggled the locust stick and added, 'If anyone dies by chance, it'll be McCauley or one of his patrons.'

Will shivered. Cheerfully, Banks said to his men, 'Heads up, lads. Here we go.'

3

The sergeant led the way down the steps. He'd just reached the bottom one when the door was jerked open by a tipsy tramp. The tramp saw Banks and started to shout a warning. Before he could, Banks laid his stick against the man's temple.

The blow didn't seem particularly hard. But the tramp shrieked, and Will heard bone crack. The man fell. Banks jumped over him and plunged through the door with an enthusiastic yell.

The police who stormed after him didn't bother to step over the fallen man. Hobnails came down on an exposed cheek; an outstretched hand. From the top of the stairs, Will gazed at the tramp, horrified. The man's open mouth, glazed eyes, and sudden fetid smell said Banks had killed him.

There were shouts; oaths; sounds of wood splintering. Will ran down the stairs. Drew followed, breathing loudly. From the doorway, Will saw that the police had already pulled the tap from the beer keg, broken the keg open, and shattered most of the rickety benches on which eight or ten patrons had been relaxing.

The customers received no quarter. The patrolmen swung their locust sticks at the nearest dirty face, male or female. One middle-aged crone had all her front teeth knocked out. Then a pair of officers beat her to the ground.

The only resistance came from McCauley, the man with the bulging forehead and slitted eyes. He broke away from one policeman, gut-punched another, and bolted toward the doorway where Will and Drew were standing.

He battered a path for himself by means of his sheer size. He kept one arm crooked over his head, protection against the clubs hammering at him. His other hand groped for something inside his greasy vest.

To Will's right, Banks finished clubbing another victim. He flung the man aside, hunted for McCauley, spotted him and charged. But there were several struggling policemen and patrons between the sergeant and his quarry.

McCauley pulled a brightly plated derringer. The policeman nearest him saw the multiple barrels aimed at his face. He yelled in fright. McCauley fired. The policeman's hat fell off and his forehead disintegrated. He tumbled back over a packing case, crushing it.

'You murdering son of a bitch,' Banks howled,

struggling toward him. A policeman inadvertently stepped into his path. Banks yanked the policeman's arm so hard, the man fell. Banks stepped on his leg and kept going.

McCauley's misshapen mouth jerked in a grotesque smile. Again he took aim. From the side, another policeman grabbed McCauley's trousers, fastening on a bulging pocket. McCauley wrenched sideways. The fabric tore. Out of the ripped pocket spilled copper pennies – the pitiful profits he'd tried to carry away.

The derringer exploded, its small sound made thunderous by the confines of the room. Banks dodged, losing his hat. His cheeks were red but not a hair of his moustache had been disturbed. McCauley's bullet knocked a shower of insects off the wall behind the police sergeant.

McCauley turned. A couple of yards remained between him and the doorway, where Drew stood at Will's right.

What happened next took place very quickly. McCauley pointed his gun to clear the door. Will ducked, and somehow his foot slipped. He stumbled against Drew, pushing him to the right. Drew grabbed the doorframe with his right hand. McCauley fired and missed.

Will straightened up and launched himself at McCauley's legs, bringing him down with a flying tackle. He sprawled on top of the big man, who promptly flung him off and regained his feet.

The fall left Will winded and dizzy. But he grabbed McCauley again and hung on. Banks was only a few steps away, his path clear at last. McCauley cursed and shoved the derringer against the top of Will's head.

On his knees, Will jerked backwards. The derringer roared, the slug scorching past his left shoulder. McCauley jammed a knee in Will's face, toppling him.

Banks smashed his billy into the back of McCauley's neck.

The big man staggered. But he didn't go down. He lurched on toward the door, blinking rapidly. Banks darted around Will; flung his right arm back, readying another blow—

More pennies poured out of McCauley's torn pocket. He slid past Drew and out of the door, reaching the foot of the steps just as Banks swung the stick in a savage arc. Will called a warning but the words were covered by the sickening crunch of the stick.

Drew cried out. He'd been holding the doorframe with his right hand and hadn't been able to let go in time. It was that right hand which Banks had accidentally hit.

'Goddamn it, stop him!' Banks shouted as McCauley looked back. The slitted eyes fixed on Will for an instant. Then, like a sprinter, he was up the stone stairs and into the dark.

Drew leaned in the doorway, gasping and massaging his hand. Banks didn't seem to notice. He pulled Drew out of the way and plunged through the door, bellowing curses.

He was gone ten minutes. He came back without McCauley.

4

Soon afterward, in the courtyard, the police lined up the four prisoners who could still walk. A black maria would be sent to collect the rest, one of the officers said as he lit a fat green cigar.

Three or four more matches were struck and passed from hand to hand. A thick cloud of smoke began to collect. Will said to one of the policemen, 'Is that the way you celebrate a successful raid?'

'Hell no. The smoke masks the stink of the prisoners. I expect the boys back at the station house are smoking too – 'specially the ones who tend the cells.'

'Where's Banks?' Drew said in a harsh, high voice that signalled displeasure. His right arm hung motionless at his side.

A moustached face loomed out of the dark. 'I warned you two to watch yourselves. Jake Riis has been on a dozen raids and never gotten hurt.' He whacked his stick against his right leg. 'If you'd been quicker on your feet, I wouldn't have lost McCauley.'

'Well, I'm damn sorry.'

'Believe me, so am I. Don Andreas is probably pouring wine for that son of a bitch right now. Congratulating him on getting away! He got a look at you, I noticed,' the sergeant added to Will. 'If I were you, I'd shorten my stay in the Bend.'

He brushed a frayed serge cuff across his sweaty face, disturbing one of the points of his moustache. Only then did he indicate Drew's dangling hand.

'Didn't break it, did I?'

Calmer but still disgusted, Drew said, 'Not quite. But I'll need liniment and bandages for at least a week.'

'Better stay home next time.'

Banks spun and moved to the four prisoners. He recognized one white-haired, emaciated fellow, and prodded him with his billy.

'Look who's here. Roscoe the Revolver. Back to Blackwell's for another vacation, eh, Roscoe?'

The old man, stooped and benign-looking, unleashed some of the foulest profanity Will had ever heard. Drew coughed from all the cigar smoke as the old man said, 'You didn't have to hit Mag Stephens that way, Banks. You could have kilt her, you dog fucker.'

With his left hand Banks seized the old man at the scruff of his neck. With his right he jammed the stick

837

horizontally against the prisoner's windpipe. The man's tongue popped out. His eyes rounded and started to water. Leaning down, Banks whispered:

'I'll do the same for you unless you swallow that tongue and keep it swallowed.'

He pushed on the stick again. The old man made gagging noises. Banks released him and began issuing orders for his squads to reassemble. He posted two men to guard the dive until the wagon showed up.

Mocking voices called down from the fire escapes. Will thought he heard Banks's name shouted once or twice, and not in a complimentary way. A few empty cans were thrown. But the police marched out without incident.

'Banks doesn't exactly generate respect, does he?' Will said as he and Drew followed the marchers. Drew had put his right hand into the pocket of his old jacket, letting it rest there. He shrugged wearily:

'One way or another, the Bend gets to everybody. Eustace is no worse than most on the force, and he's better than a lot of them. I'd take his advice about leaving. Along with Corso, now you've got McCauley against you. Maybe the padrone, too.'

'I haven't heard from Corso and I probably won't hear from the others. I'm staying till Sunday – just the way I planned.'

Drew laughed for the first time all evening. 'You sound as tough as Banks.'

'You said the Bend gets to everybody.'

'But I wouldn't want to be responsible for anything happening to—'

'It's my decision, Drew. My father once told me that every sensible man in the First Virginia Cavalry was scared to death of Yankee shot and shell. All the same, they didn't run away from it.

Still trying to lighten the situation, Drew said, 'That's the way it is with Virginians and Kents, eh?'

838

Fearful as he was of again encountering Giuseppe Corso or Dave McCauley, Will found a measure of courage in the words he'd just spoken. He'd made a decision, and although the fear stayed with him, he slept better that night than he had for several weeks.

5

That same night, Eleanor paced her room in Boston. Outside, thunder boomed. Occasional storms had drenched the city all week, but had done nothing to relieve the stultifying heat. Hand pressed to her lips and head bowed in thought, she barely heard the rain begin, so thick were the muffling draperies which hid the locked windows.

A single shaded light burned above her writing desk. On the desk lay a second letter from Louisa Drew in Philadelphia. An urgent plea this time. It forced Eleanor to think.

Her father's words that well-remembered afternoon in his office had shaken her almost as much as Leo's death. Gideon had called her a fireside moralist, had charged that before Leo's death she had convinced herself that hatred would never touch her if she pretended it didn't exist. And that since his death she had only gone on hiding.

Just like her mother.

For several days afterward Eleanor had denied the accusations vehemently in her own mind, especially the idea that she was imitating Margaret. But then doubt had begun to creep in. Doubt and a slow, shameful realization that her father was right. At a time of tragedy, after the horror of the flood and her inadvertent revelation to Martin, reality had been too much for her. She had begun locking real doors, just as she'd locked an imaginary one for years. And had turned her back on the one solid chance she had to resume her life, by going back on the stage.

It was frightening to realize that her flirtation with madness had gone so far. Yet now, aware of it at last, she felt a sense of redemption; rescue. She had her father to thank for that, and this evening, she had been gathering her nerve to go downstairs and tell him.

But first there was another decision. *If* she was strong enough to make it.

She stopped in the centre of the room, turned toward the desk and gazed at Louisa's letter. Showing that determination which had made her so successful as a manager, Louisa had refused to accept Eleanor's initial, negative answer to the offer of a place in her company. This latest letter renewed the offer of employment for the entire season. But, Louisa had noted, a prompt reply was necessary.

Finally, after perhaps a minute, Eleanor's expression grew more determined. She picked up her skirts.

But before she moved toward the desk, her eye fell on the closed door of the bedroom. She stared at it, frowning. If she were going to take the step she contemplated – take it because it was essential for her survival – then it was time to stop the outward imitations of her mother as well.

She walked to the door, twisted the key, and flung the door open, pushing it all the way back against the papered wall. A stir of air from the corridor touched her cheek.

She turned round and crossed the room. The bedroom had three windows. One by one she flung back the draperies concealing them, raised them, and pushed the shutters outward.

Rain splashed her face; the storm was heavy now. But the air felt deliciously cool, and the rain had a sweet taste when she ran her tongue over her lip. At the final window, she stood for a moment, head back and eyes closed, savouring the freshness of the swirling air and the dampness it bore.

Then, swiftly, she returned to the desk, inked a pen, and began to write:

My dearest Louisa,
Thank you for yrs. of the most recent date. I hasten to answer immediately, in order to tell you that I have reconsidered my original decision—

In the dark beyond the windows, the storm intensified over the Common. The gusts rattled the writing paper until she had to hold it down with her left hand as she wrote.

A small smile on her face, she bent over the letter, feeling a joyous freedom as she wrote in the wind that rushed through the room, cleansing it of its staleness and its ghosts.

CHAPTER X

Ultimatum

A stream of patients kept the Bayard Court office busy on Thursday morning. To judge from the number of coughs, sneezes, and runny noses the doctors saw, an epidemic of summer influenza was sweeping the neighbourhood.

Will had been up before dawn; thinking of Jo, and Laura, and the Bend. All that he'd heard in the past day or so – from Drew, Jake Riis, even the brutal Banks – had started him moving in a different direction. He wasn't sure where he'd wind up. But the next step was clear. He must speak to Marcus, and perhaps Thurman Pennel, as soon as possible.

He yawned as he brought Vlandingham a bottle of cough mixture from one of the cabinets. The doctor gave him a stern stare:

'You should go to bed at night, instead of chasing Banks and his flying squad.'

Drew turned from the patient whose throat he was about to examine. At the moment there were two middle-aged Italians in the surgery. Drew was taking care of one, Vlandingham the other. Neither patient could speak English; both had made their symptoms known by sign language.

'You know about the raid?' Drew asked his partner. Neither he nor Will had mentioned it; Jo had only been told that it had been successful.

Vlandingham snorted. 'Don't act so blasted surprised. Everyone in the neighbourhood knows. While I was walking over here this morning, four people informed me that you two had gone with the police to close that dive.'

Jo looked at Will, as if for confirmation. An abrupt silence had descended over the surgery. Will saw the expression of Vlandingham's patient change from anxiety to outright terror. The man was staring past the doctor to the doorway.

Drew glanced in that direction and frowned. His patient, too, had a fearful look. Will turned and discovered the cause. A man had entered unannounced, evidently opening the door so as to make no noise.

The man was about sixty-five, slender, and slightly stoop-shouldered. He had merry brown eyes, a Van Dyke which had been neatly trimmed and combed, and magnificent white hair that covered the tops of his ears and brushed his collar.

Jo was the first to react. 'You can't come in here!'

Vlandingham's grey eyes remained on the visitor. 'The gentleman is accustomed to doing whatever he pleases.' He glanced past the stranger to the outer room. Five minutes earlier, eight or nine people had been waiting. Now the room was empty.

The stranger's clothing was neat, though heavy for summer, and considerably out of date as well. The black trousers and matching sack coat were tailored in a style popular in the 1850s. His shawl was a reminder of a masculine fashion that had disappeared soon after Lincoln's death. A black silk cravat, grey gloves, and a cane with a silver knob completed his outfit. Every item contributed to his air of quaint gentility. But despite his age and his attire, he appeared alert and vigorous. He continued to smile in an avuncular way as Vlandingham walked toward him:

'I see you've frightened away all our patients,' Vlandingham growled.

'Have I, Doctor? It wasn't intentional.'

The stranger spoke English with a heavy accent. Still smiling, he glanced at the man Vlandingham had been examining. '*Per piacere andatevene.*' His eyes darted to Drew's patient. '*Anche tu. Immediatamente.*'

The second man knocked his stool over in his haste to beat the first to the door. The visitor stepped aside to permit them to flee. Drew righted the stool, a scowl on his face.

'Who is this man?' Jo demanded.

Drew shook his head. 'Never saw him before. But I suspect—'

'You know him by name,' Vlandingham cut in. 'I know him personally. We were introduced several years ago at a *ristorante* just around the corner on Mulberry.'

'An occasion I recall with immense pleasure,' said the visitor.

'You may, but I don't.' Vlandingham turned to

843

Drew. 'The gentleman no longer lives in the Bend, he merely continues to exploit it.' Will's stomach flip-flopped. He knew the stranger's identity now.

'That was one of your operations they raided last night, wasn't it?' Vlandingham asked.

'Alas, yes.' the visitor's smile lost some of its warmth. He gave Will a swift glance that was frightening because of its total lack of emotion. The man treated Drew to the same quick scrutiny, then said:

'Permit me to introduce myself to the young *signori*. I am Don Andreas Belsario.'

2

'I don't give a damn if you're the sainted ghost of Billy Tweed,' Vlandingham exclaimed. 'Get out of my surgery.'

Don Andreas' manner grew soothing:

'Please – there is no need for voices to be raised. What I have to say can be said politely. And you needn't become involved, Dr Vlandingham. Neither you nor the young lady bear any responsibility in this matter. I have come to speak with the two young *signori*. Dr Hastings and his new acquaintance—'

Will quickly supplied his name. He was damned if he'd let some elderly grafter buffalo him.

The padrone fixed him with another chilling stare. 'Are you by chance related to the New York family which publishes the *Union*?'

Will felt as if he'd been struck. For the padrone to make that connection by guesswork alone was too improbable to be believed. The man knew who he was because he'd made it his business to know.

He returned the padrone's stare. 'That's right.'

'A fine newspaper,' Don Andreas said. 'We read it regularly in my household.'

844

Vlandingham grabbed the padrone's arm. 'What the hell do you want?'

Quickly, the man stepped back. Vlandingham let go. Don Andreas glanced down at the wrinkles left on his sleeve by Vlandingham's fingers. Using his right glove, he flicked away invisible dirt, then murmured:

'I told you, Doctor. It is for the ears of the two young—'

'Say it and get out,' Vlandingham broke in. 'I'll have to disinfect the whole place to get rid of your stink.'

The sally infuriated the padrone. But he maintained his control. Even smiled again:

'Very well. As you said, Doctor – it *was* one of my two-penny restaurants which the police invaded and padlocked last night. There were those in the raiding party not officially attached to Elizabeth Street—'

Again the brown eyes slid to Drew, then Will. 'My employee, *il signor* McCauley, knew the two of you were not policemen. But he knew nothing else. Not your names, or where you might be found. Early today we circulated your descriptions in the neighbourhood. My apologies, Dr Hastings, but the mention of your girth led to a quick identification. I have come here to protest your interference in my affairs.'

Drew's face reddened. His voice took on that high, rasping sound:

'You've got it mixed up. I didn't close your place. The police did. Not to say I wouldn't shut all such establishments if I had the chance. They're pest-holes. Even tramps don't deserve to be poisoned.'

'Your moralizing is extremely tedious,' Don Andreas said with a smile. 'Of course I know you didn't instigate the raid. But by your interference, you and your friend almost deprived me of an able lieutenant. *Il signor* McCauley isn't the brightest man in my employ, but he is one of the most useful. I will not brook a similar interference again.'

845

He glanced at Drew's bandaged hand. 'I notice you earned a small reward for your meddling. How sad it would be if some mishap crippled you permanently. Never again able to perform surgery – you would hardly deserve the title doctor then.'

Jo was white. Drew shook with anger:

'Your effrontery is unbelievable—'

'No, Doctor. Yours!' the padrone shouted. 'You, all of you, are permitted to practise here by my sufferance alone. Sergeant Banks has harassed me before. My patience with him has worn thin. Last night he again closed a valuable commercial enterprise—'

'How can you call a dive like that valuable?' Will demanded.

Don Andreas controlled his anger; shrugged and lowered his voice as he said:

'Oh, I am not speaking of monetary value. The profits of a two-cent restaurant are of course insignificant. But the friendships made through operation of such places – the votes that can be harvested one or two at a time, then brokered – those are extremely significant. Those votes enhance my authority in this district, and my worth at City Hall. When you rob me of even one restaurant, as the two of you helped Banks do last night, the loss is not inconsiderable. When you compound the injury by nearly sending a valuable man to Blackwell's Island for six months or more – that is not easily borne, *signori*.'

His brief burst of temper might never have occurred; he sounded almost genial again:

'Put yourselves in my position. Imagine what would happen if I allowed this affront to go unpunished. I would quickly become a laughingstock. A toothless old grandfather devoid of power and prestige. Regrettably, I am unable to have Banks removed or held in check by his superiors. So I must find other means to demonstrate my displeasure. You—'

He pointed a gloved finger at Drew. Like a gun barrel, the finger swung toward Will.

'—and you. Both of you will leave the district by noon Saturday. If you are seen in the Bend after that, the consequences will be unpleasant. You, doctor Vlandingham – you may stay. Also the young lady who assists you. The voters must be kept in good health! But if either of you is found abetting the police, your dispensation will likewise be withdrawn.'

No one moved or spoke. Will and the others were stunned. Like an accomplished actor holding the stage, Don Andreas was in control and knew it:

'You may, of course, think of scurrying to Banks or some other police functionary to report what I have just said. No action will be possible against me, however. Several reliable witnesses will be prepared to swear in court that I was never anywhere near these rooms today – that I was, in fact, entertaining some of my seventeen grandchildren in Central Park. I bid you all good day.'

With a little nod, he strolled out, gently pulling the door shut behind him.

3

Drew sank down on a stool. Almost unconsciously, he brought his bandaged right hand into the palm of his left and cradled it there as he shook his head.

'My God. I can't believe it. People don't say such things in the civilized world.'

Vlandingham tried to smile. It was only a jerk of the corners of his mouth. 'I'm afraid that's your error, Drew. Thinking you're still in the civilized world.'

'He's an ignorant man!' Jo exclaimed, as if trying to shake off the spell of the visitor. 'Only stupid people threaten violence.'

'Stupid people or very confident ones,' Vlandingham said. 'Don Andreas has tremendous influence in the district. I suppose he feels he must demonstrate that occasionally. We had the misfortune to provide him with a convenient opportunity.'

'Not we,' Will said. 'Just Drew and I.'

Jo's anxious eyes sought his. 'What happened during the raid? With that man he talked about, I mean?'

Drew told her, concluding, 'Will tried to stop him, but he got away.'

Musing aloud, Vlandingham said, 'Wonder what he's got up his sleeve for Banks? In the past he's tried bribing him, but Banks can't be bought.'

Carefully closing his left hand around the bandaged one, Drew looked monumentally annoyed. 'I still don't know how the devil a doctor gets involved in this kind of mess.'

'By deciding to practise in this kind of neighbourhood!' Vlandingham snapped. He strode to one of the equipment cabinets and pulled a small key from his vest pocket. He bent to insert the key in the keyhole of a bottom drawer as Drew went on:

'Well, I can't let some crook run me off. But you didn't bargain for this, Will. There's no reason for you to stay and run the risk of getting hurt.'

'You know I wasn't planning to leave until Sunday,' Will said. 'I see no reason to change my plans. Tomorrow I have to do an errand on Wall Street, but I'll be back by evening.'

Slowly, his gaze travelled from Drew's face to Jo's. What he thought he saw there – admiration mixed with anxiety – warmed him and somehow made his decision seem less foolhardy. *How did old Philip feel, staring into the muzzles of British guns at Concord bridge a hundred and fourteen years ago? As frightened as I feel right now?*

'Ever fired something like this, Drew?'

848

Vlandingham's voice made them turn. From the cabinet drawer he'd taken an old maroon cloth and unfolded it to reveal the oiled metal of a revolver with a long barrel.

'No,' Drew said. 'But I had a squirrel gun when I was younger.'

'Then you should be able to get the hang of this without much trouble. It certainly isn't the sort of instrument I planned to give my partner any time during our association—'

He polished the already spotless barrel with the sleeve of his smock, then started to hand the gun to Drew. He blinked.

'Good God. You can't fire it. You couldn't fire it if your life depended on it.'

An unfortunate turn of phrase, Will thought gloomily. Drew laughed and held up his bandaged hand.

'No, not very well. I wondered when you'd realize that.'

'I can fire it,' Will said. 'I know how to handle a revolver. That looks like a fine one.'

'It is. Forty-four calibre Adams. Five shot, double action. The Union Army bought five hundred of them during the war. This one came from a Reb prisoner – one of D. H. Hill's men who was killed running away from the Bloody Lane at Antietam. I think one of his own must have shot him in the back. He was dead by the time he was brought to our hospital tent. And since he'd obviously stolen the revolver off a Federal, I – ' He cleared his throat. ' – I thought it all right to take it from him. It shoots well. I did some target practice with it over on the Weehawken Heights a year after the armistice. I have some ammunition I bought at the time. I've kept it dry, perhaps it's still good—'

Fiercely, Jo shook her head. 'Must we go through this? Do you really think that awful man will do what he said?

849

'It all depends on how badly he feels his prestige has been injured,' Vlandingham told her. 'I'd hate to gamble that he was bluffing. I think it's safer to assume he isn't.'

She walked to the door. The reception room was still empty. She turned back suddenly. 'Why couldn't Banks provide a police guard?'

'On what grounds?' Vlandingham replied. 'A threat? If the police gave special protection to every person in the Bend who was threatened by someone, they'd need a thousand patrolmen just for this precinct.'

Will licked his lips; they were dry all at once. 'If the padrone's threat was serious, we'll know by Saturday night or Sunday. Till then all we can do is look out for ourselves.'

Drew nodded. Jo's silence signalled reluctant agreement.

'May I see the gun, Doctor?'

Every eye shifted to the bright weapon as Vlandingham laid it carefully in Will's open hand.

4

No patients appeared the rest of the day. Don Andreas had marked the doctors, and communicated the stigma to the neighbourhood. The silent reception room was proof of the padrone's influence.

Late in the afternoon, Will walked out to the courtyard. The Adams .44 was thrust into the waistband of his trousers. Above him, only a scrap of sky was visible between the laundry on the pulley lines. Tenants of the buildings stared at him from fire escapes. Their faces were sober, as if they knew he was under some kind of sentence.

Jo came outside. 'Will?'

He turned. How lovely she was—

'What is it?'

'I've been wanting to apologize for being so forward the other night. I hope you'll forgive me. Forget what I said.'

'Nothing to forgive. But as to forgetting – I can't.'

'I wish things had worked out differently all around.'

'Yes,' he said. 'All at once I do too.'

Their eyes held a moment. Then she turned and hurried back inside. But not before he caught a glimmer of tears on her cheeks.

CHAPTER XI

Questions

At the end of the day, Will, Drew, and Vlandingham returned Jo to the protection of Nevsky and his wife, then walked on to the East River. There Will fired half a dozen practice rounds at the wake of a passing scow. Two crewmen shook their fists and shouted, presuming the scow to have been his intended target.

Will handed the revolver back to the older doctor, then rubbed his right forearm. He said he hadn't expected the gun to buck quite so hard. 'But I imagine I can hit a man at close range if it's necessary.'

Feeding bullets into the Adams, Vlandingham smiled coldly. 'I expect so too. There's a lot a man can do when he must.'

The two friends saw Vlandingham back to his rooms in the Bowery, then called for Jo. The three of them went to their favourite thirteen-cent restaurant. They chose a table from which they could watch both the front door and the family entrance at the side. Will felt ridiculous with the revolver hidden under his coat. But to banish that feeling, he only had to recall what Don Andreas had said.

Conversation faltered during the meal, and all of them turned in early that night. Will lay awake for hours, or so it seemed. He wondered what the next few days would bring. Or even if he'd survive them.

In the morning, he put on his straw hat and a good jacket. He gave the revolver to Vlandingham and promised to be back as soon as possible.

'Don't hurry, we don't need you,' Drew said with a gesture at the reception room. It was empty again this morning. 'There are usually one or two patients here when we open up. The people in the neighbourhood are more afraid of the padrone than I imagined.'

The city baked in the August heat. Will was sweltering by the time he reached the offices of the Pennel Company, a luxurious second floor suite of rooms on Nassau Street just round the corner from Wall. Three typewriting machines clicked in a large, dark-panelled anteroom. A tiny, mummy-like man wearing a cardboard eyeshade and sleeve garters approached the mahogany railing where Will stood waiting.

'Mr Pennel, please.'

'Mr Thurman Pennel is not here this morning,' the old man said regally. 'Mr Marcus Pennel is handling matters in his absence.'

'Please tell Marcus that Will Kent wants to see him.'

'He's extremely busy reviewing the books. If he's willing to see you, I'm sure it won't be for an hour or more.'

'All right,' Will said, his voice harder. 'But you tell him right now that I'm here.'

The clerk hesitated, scanned Will's face, and marched out of sight. He was back in less than a minute, looking amazed:

'He'll see you immediately.'

He unlatched the gate in the railing and opened it so Will could step through.

2

'Lord above! What a surprise.'

Marcus circled a paper-strewn desk placed in front of the windows overlooking Nassau Street. The room could have accommodated a dinner table seating thirty people. It was decorated with expensive walnut wainscoting and furnished with dark, heavy pieces with claw feet. In one corner, two stock market tickers on marble pedestals clattered softly, spewing paper tapes into collection baskets on the floor.

Marcus' damp shirt was open at the collar and his sleeves were rolled up. He pumped Will's hand. 'I'm forced to stay in the city all this month, but I didn't think anyone came here by choice. Are you in town on business?'

Will twisted the brim of his hat in his hands. On the wall to his left, he noticed a multi-coloured map. The map was framed in half-inch mahogany moulding and measured about twelve feet by six. It depicted the southern end of Manhattan Island, with north at the right hand margin. The lower East Side was studded with numerous pins with bright red or blue heads.

'Not business in the conventional sense,' he said. 'I'm helping a colleague from the medical school. He practises down in the Mulberry Bend.'

'Good God. That's a frightful area. Is this something you're required to do to earn your diploma?'

'It's something I'm doing because I want to.'

'I see.' Marcus cleared his throat; the edge in Will's voice was unmistakable. 'You never mentioned it in Newport, that I recall.'

'I didn't think anyone in Newport would be interested.'

The blunt reply made Marcus frown, though he still tried to be cordial:

'Well, I'm happy to see you, whatever the reason. Sit down, sit down.'

With a gesture at one of the chairs, he returned to his own, which was high-backed, throne-like, and finished in leather. Just as Marcus was about to sit, Will said:

'I'd prefer to stand. I have only one or two questions to ask you.'

'Questions?' Marcus was starting to sweat heavily. He plucked a cigarette from an ivory box half buried amid ledgers and memoranda. His hand looked less than steady as he put the cigarette in his mouth. His eyes kept moving between Will's face and the map Will was studying.

Marcus fumbled with a match. It burned out before he got the cigarette lit. Finally he was successful. He flipped the burnt match into a cuspidor, and said:

'What kind of questions? About the protocol of engagements? I'm the last one to ask about such things.'

'I haven't come to discuss a wedding.'

'Didn't you and Laura reach an understanding before that telegram took you away?' Marcus squinted at him through curling smoke, wary now. 'Of course, I know neither of you said anything about it, but after you left, she was absolutely buoyant.' A cynical smile returned. 'No one ever leaped to the defence of her honour the way you did, old boy.'

Will's cheeks grew warm. 'I suppose everyone in Newport's laughing about that.'

'No, no! I didn't mean—'

'Never mind. It isn't important – I'm not here to discuss Laura, either.'

'But there *is* to be an engagement, isn't there? An engagement and a wedding?'

'I don't know. It may depend on the answers I get from you.'

What a pathetic lie, he thought. No matter what corruption he found in this eminently respectable office, the discovery wouldn't cancel his obligation to Laura.

Then why was he doing this? He knew, of course. For the past year or so, he'd lived comfortably with distortions. The opulence of Pennel House and Maison du Soleil were the norm; poverty had been abnormal – even nonexistent – in the world as he saw it. He'd deluded himself because he wanted Laura and all she stood for. Or so he thought.

Now the Bend was removing the distortions; restoring perspective and a clear, true vision of things. He was learning what Laura and her family actually represented. Wealth and position built on human suffering, if those coloured pins meant what he guessed they meant. He was still obliged to marry Thurman Pennel's daughter. But if he did, by God he'd understand the full meaning of the bargain.

Marcus flung his half-smoked cigarette into the cuspidor. 'You haven't exactly been cordial since you came in here, old chap. I'm growing rather tired of your truculence. Perhaps you'd better be explicit about what you want.'

'Does the Pennel family control a company called the Pen-York Property Trust?'

Marcus turned pale. But he hesitated only a second:

'Of course. There's no secret there. See here – what's gotten you onto such a tedious subject as—?'

'And does the Pen-York Trust own a five-story tenement down in the Bend, in a cul-de-sac that goes by the name Robber's Row?'

Hostile now, Marcus sneered: 'Do we have another do-gooder on our hands? Another Jacob Riis?'

'I should imagine his work does bother your conscience,' Will said with a nod.

Marcus laughed curtly. 'Nothing bothers my conscience, old boy, except failure to earn a maximum return on every dollar the Pennel family controls.'

'What do you consider a maximum return, Marcus? Twenty per cent? Thirty? I know one section of town where you can make at least that.'

'What the hell are you ranting about?'

Will stalked toward the map.

'About the kind of return you get when you put a building in the hands of a rental agent who subdivides it into tiny, filthy cubicles that rent for twice what it costs for a decent flat in a good section. I'm talking about the return from slum tenements.'

He struck the map with his fist. Marcus had bolted from behind the desk. He rushed to within a yard of Will before stopping abruptly, unsure of what to do.

Will's angry eyes raked across the clusters of pins inserted in the wards of the lower East Side. He located the intersection of Mulberry and Bayard. For several blocks around it, pins crowded one another. He pointed:

'I guess you can't tell me whether you own that particular tenement. It appears you've got a dozen in the area. You must have trouble keeping them all straight. The profits from each, I mean. You don't seem to worry about all the misery and death you may be causing.' He snatched four or five of the pins and flung them on the carpet.

Baffled and angry, Marcus stared at him a moment. 'That was cheap and showy.'

'I know. But it made me feel damn good.'

'What's happened to you, old fellow?'

'I swallowed a dose of reality. It got all the delusions

out of my system. For years, I admired the kind of life your family leads. Because I thought I wanted the same kind of life. I never asked myself whether it had a price. Now I've started asking.'

'Who the devil's been filling your head with this socialist nonsense?' A weary smile showed on Marcus' face. 'How do you suppose great fortunes are made in this country? Out of thin air and Christian piety? Of course the Pennels have some dirt on their hands. I expect the Kents do, too. You'll have to accept that if you intend to be part of the fam—'

'Shut up, Marcus,' Will broke in. 'All I want is the answer to one question. Do the Pennels own a tenement on Robber's Row?'

'Jesus,' Marcus breathed, pivoting away and retreating behind his desk. He braced his hands on some ledgers, leaning toward his visitor. 'You've turned into a regular roughneck. What comes next? Do you throw me out of a window the way your father knocked down McAllister?'

'Don't tempt me. Answer my—'

'*No!*' Marcus' voice broke as he said it. Recovering, he went on, 'That answer will have to come from my father. I won't take the responsibility.'

Will stepped forward, then checked himself. Marcus was pale and sweating hard; his forced nonchalance had completely crumbled. Suddenly Will felt he'd been bullying a child.

'All right,' he said. 'Where can I find your father?'

'You might try his club. The Apollo. Uptown, at—'

'I know where it is.'

He jammed his hat on his head as he stalked toward the door. Marcus groped for another cigarette and called:

'Hurry and you may catch him while he's still sober.'

The door slammed.

Marcus sank into his chair, his sullen face shiny with sweat. He struck a match and burned himself before he got the cigarette going. He took several puffs. His breathing slowed.

Then suddenly he jumped up and hurried to a door so artfully designed, it was all but invisible in the wainscoting. He jerked the door open, stepped into a dark cubicle and began cranking a wall telephone.

When the operator made the connection and the call was answered at the other end, he said:

'This is Marcus Pennel speaking. I must talk with my father. Get him to the telephone as fast as you can. Tell him it's an emergency.'

CHAPTER XII

What Pennel Said

A massive grandfather clock rang ten-thirty. Thurman Pennel said, 'Robber's Row? I'm not familiar with the name. But I probably own the building. Been buying tenements all over the lower East Side for years. Splendid investments. Splendid. That tell you what you wanted to know?'

He covered his lips with a wrinkled hand, and belched. Then he reached toward a filigreed silver tray bearing five champagne glasses. Two were empty. He picked up a full one and sipped.

Standing in front of the older man, Will was momentarily at a loss for a response. He'd expected hostility from Laura's father, not an immediate, if bleary, admission of the truth. Of course Laura had said that her father was drinking heavily these days. And when he drank, he lost all caution.

Once Thurman Pennel had impressed Will with his commanding presence. Now the bald and paunchy man looked sadly ordinary. His shirt and summer suit were stained and wrinkled. He smelled as if he hadn't bathed for days. He slumped in a velvet chair in front of tall windows hung with lace curtains so heavy, only a glimmer of morning light penetrated. The curtains muffled noise and effectively hid the squalor of the world outside. Except for the two of them, the book-lined clubroom was empty.

In a vague voice, the older man went on. 'Impossible to be positive about one building. The family's holdings are pretty extensive. I'd bet we own it, though.' He sipped again. 'Otherwise Marcus wouldn't have been so agitated when he told me you were asking questions.'

Will was startled. 'When did you speak to Marcus?'

'Right before you got here. He called me on the club's telephone. He was damn near hysterical. I'm afraid my son will never make a businessman. He's short on nerve. He isn't a bad administrator if he's told exactly what to do. But he can't deal with emergencies, and he has no mind for the creative posh – possibilities of real estate. Fact is – to be absolutely candid – ' He drank. ' – you have it all over Marcus. Even if you do come from a family of damn radicals.'

He consumed the rest of the glass at a gulp, heedless of the way some of the liquid ran down his chin to his shirt. Another belch, and he went on:

'Hate to admit it, but my son's no good with anything

except polo ponies or a tennis racket. An ineffectual Harvard-educated fart, is what it comes down to—'

Pennel replaced the glass on the tray and reached for another. Then, peering at the young man begrimed from his trolley ride, he said:

'Oh. Not minding my manners, am I? Care for a champagne cocktail? I can ring for more. I probably will before the day's much older.'

Softly, Will said, 'No, thank you.' There was no point in badgering a drunkard. The sooner he left, the better.

'Mustn't have any secrets from you, my boy.' Once more Pennel took a sip. 'You're to be a member of the family soon. Snaring you has been their design, Laura's and my wife's, ever since Marcus fetched you home that Christmastime.'

'Snaring? That's a pretty hard word, Mr Pennel.'

A sloppy shrug. 'Fits, though.'

'But I'm the one who's been doing the courting.'

The older man gave him a pitying look. 'You only think so. They played you like a violin, my boy. Fact is –' Another large drink. 'Even though I abom – abomin – hate your father's newspaper, I have felt increasingly sorry for you. You may think marrying Laura is an attractive proposition. You'd get a fine dowry to add to your own inheritance, plus the social standing your father can never hope to acquire—'

The words disturbed Will, and not merely because they were true. Something poisonous was gathering within the drunken man, and slowly working its way out of a deep, concealed place.

'But I'll tell you this, Kent. You needn't ask my permission to marry Laura. She and her mother decided the question months ago. I have nothing to say about it.'

He reached out to put his empty glass on the tray, but he wasn't watching. As he put the glass down, he bumped another. It fell, striking the raised edge of the tray. A half moon of crystal broke from the rim of the overturned glass.

'Glad it wasn't a full one,' Pennel said with a snuffling laugh. The library was utterly still save for the heavy *tock-tock* of the clock pendulum. Pennel's face grew twisted and sour; the poison was near the surface.

'Another thing,' Pennel resumed after he drank. 'Those two harpies need you more than you need the Pennels. Don't ever make the mistake of thinking otherwise. My sweet daughter can't get a regular suitor from her own social group.'

'Oh, sir, I can't believe—'

Pennel didn't seem to hear: 'There's no shortage of ordinary suitors, y'understand. Penniless attorneys. Merchants mortgaged to the hilt. But the ladies don't want someone like that. They want a man with money and some sort of pedigree. That rules out most of those European dukes and earls. They've got the titles but nothing else. So it comes down to an American. Trouble is, mothers in the best families won't let their sons near my daughter. They've heard too many stories. It's been that way ever since Laura – matured.' He shook his head. 'My fault, I reckon. But I don't know how it happened—'

His voice strengthened. 'I do know I had to move out. I couldn't stand those damn women one day longer. Seems to be the familiar complaint of Newport husbands,' he added. He drained the glass, rose, and lurched across the room to jerk a satin bell pull.

Will was in such turmoil, he didn't know what to say. Pennel came lurching back, stumbled against his chair and almost fell. He seized the back of the chair and held himself up. He smiled at Will again, half in contempt, half in pity:

'Guess you're surprised to hear me speak of my wife and daughter the way I do. I'll tell you the reason. I hate both of 'em. My wife's a pretentious, domineering

861

bitch. All she cares about are *things* – oh, and maybe the approval of a bunch of dry-titted, half-crazy old hags she fancies to be her betters. You've no idea how frantic she is to keep from being ostracized because of Laura. You've no idea how many backsides she must kiss so it won't happen. That social stuff is shit, my boy. Pure shit. I like feeling important as well as the next man, but by God I know I came from nothing and will go right back there when I'm all through. My daughter – she's caught the taint in that house. It's ruined her. She's worse than her mother. At least my wife isn't a whore.'

A seventy-year-old man wearing club livery entered with another tray bearing five more champagne cocktails. He set it down, then removed the first tray without so much as a lifted eyebrow – as if finishing five drinks before a quarter of eleven in the morning wasn't at all unusual.

When the waiter had gone, Pennel helped himself. He stood sipping his fresh cocktail with an owlish look. At last Will spoke:

'That's a terrible thing to say about your own daughter.'

'Terrible? I s'pose. Trouble is, I don't know a better word than whore. I tell you again, my boy – you don't need my permission to marry Laura. You've no competition. No one in her own set will have her. Here—'

In the process of placing his cocktail on a book shelf, he nearly fell again. He rummaged for something in his pockets; finally pulled out a wrinkled piece of newsprint about seven inches wide. One edge was ragged, as if the paper had been torn from a longer galley.

'Here's her latest escapade. I was one of Colonel Mann's supplicants at Delmonico's earlier this week. He arranges to let you know when he's written an item for *Saunterings* that he thinks you should see – the

862

fucking robber. I paid eight thousand dollars to keep this out of the next issue of *Town Topics*.'

Pennel shoved the typeset paper at Will, who was already numb from all he'd heard. His feeling of horror worsened as he read the torn galley:

A hurricane of scandal is about to disturb the tranquil waters of Newport's summer scene. This particular storm promises to make its landfall near a cottage where the sun was thought to shine perpetually.

Will looked up. 'The sun? Is that his way of saying Maison du Soleil?'

Pennel nodded with grudging admiration. 'The bastard always finds a way to reveal identities without naming names. Read on. Read all about your dear, sweet intended!'

Not so, the Saunterer discovered a fortnight ago. Next spring will bring more than the traditional blooming flowers to the young mistress of the aforesaid cottage, we are informed. The unfortunate maiden in question may one day discover that her presumably unwanted offspring has inherited a penchant for tennis – though for fetching the spheroids, not lobbing them.

'Godamighty,' Will whispered. For a moment he wanted to believe Mann had invented the story, but that was too farfetched; how could the publisher hope to collect hush money for a fabrication? But Will didn't see how Laura could be pregnant if what she'd told him the day after their lovemaking was true—

Wait. The story said *a fortnight ago*. She might have thought she was pregnant then, only to find before he left Newport that she was not.

It explained some things, but not all. Who was the

father? Did the reference to fetching tennis balls mean it was Muldoon? If it did, Laura had lied to him.

And the shacker had told the truth.

Pennel saw his confusion and chuckled in a gloomy way. Sipping his champagne cocktail, he gazed out through the ecru curtains with eyes that almost failed to focus. Will forced himself to read the rest:

> *If true, the story is a sorry ending to the season for one of the colony's premier families. Alas, it is not an unexpected ending, however. The erring maiden is said to have erred many times before, thus ensuring an absence of quality suitors upon her doorstep. Ah, la folie d'été! Ah, la folie de la jeunesse!*

Will crumpled the galley. 'Where do they get material like this?'

'Mann depends on spies. Didn't anyone ever tell you that?'

He nodded, remembering; Marcus had said exactly that.

'There's no telling how many informants may be scurrying around our own household, each one hoping to overhear something saleable. That must be what happened in this case.'

'You're acting as if this could be true, Mr Pennel.'

'Am I, now?'

'You're pretty damn calm about it. He's written filth about your own daughter! Is it true?'

'Kindly keep your voice down, Kent. You'll have the club stewards on my neck.'

'*Is it true, goddamn it?*'

'Why, my boy, I don't know. It very well might be.'

Will felt as if a knife had been rammed into his stomach. Pennel went on, 'I'd say learning whether it's the truth is your responsibility, not mine. You're the one foolish enough to think of marrying her. My only

864

concern was to keep Mann from printing the item. If he did, I'd look like a jackass in the business community. Couldn't allow that—'

He stumbled to Will; squeezed his shoulder with clumsy cordiality:

'Brace up, Kent. Brace up and have a cocktail. If you still want to acquire social standing overnight, my possibly pregnant daughter can give you that much.'

He stared into Will's dazed eyes. There was genuine sympathy in his voice as he continued:

'Don't feel bad that they gulled you. They gulled me for years. I don't know you well, but you strike me as honest and decent. That's why you mustn't feel bad. Being honest and decent immediately puts you at a disadvantage with my wife and my daughter, since they –' He drank. ' – they are not.'

The tall clock ticked. Fifteen seconds passed.

Thirty.

The confused look cleared from Will's eyes. His head came up.

'Thank you for your time, Mr Pennel. The only person who can answer the rest of my questions is Laura.'

He held out the galley. Pennel didn't move to take it. Will dropped it between them and walked out.

2

Despite the intense heat, he walked all the way back to the Bend from midtown. It took him about an hour, and failed to produce the result he'd hoped for – a lessening of the anger and humiliation consuming him. *'Being honest and decent immediately puts you at a disadvantage with my wife and my daughter.'* What a fool he'd been!

Red-faced and perspiring, he stormed across Bayard

Court and into the reception room. It was still empty. But someone from the neighbourhood was inside – Mrs Grimaldi.

She and the others turned toward the door as he entered. He took note of their faces. 'What's wrong?'

Mrs Grimaldi sighed. 'Word has passed in the Bend that anyone visiting these rooms will incur the displeasure of a certain padrone. Nevertheless, conscience compelled me to bring news which otherwise you might not have heard for hours. Grimaldi agreed that I must come.'

Jo watched Will with anxious eyes. Vlandingham wiped his palms on his trousers; the revolver bulged under his surgical apron. He said, 'A fisherman found Eustace Banks just after sunrise.'

'Found him where?'

Drew said, 'Propped against one of the piers of the Brooklyn bridge. With his throat cut.'

Will felt lightheaded for a moment. Mrs Grimaldi said:

'That is not the worst of it. I did not have a chance to tell the others before you came in—'

'Tell us what?' Jo asked.

The older woman hesitated briefly. 'It is being said in the streets that the death of Banks is not the end. It is being said that—'

A doleful glance at Will and Drew.

'That the two young doctors will be next.'

CHAPTER XIII

Carnage

The rest of Friday dragged, dark with the threat of rain.

They had one patient; a woman of about thirty with a lined face and exhausted eyes. Her forearm was badly burned. Vlandingham dressed and bandaged it in about fifteen minutes. Even that seemed too long for the woman, who nervously explained that she'd fallen against her stove and wouldn't have troubled the doctors except that her arm was the one she used for twenty hours of ironing which she did every week for a Bayard Street sweater.

'What she meant,' Mrs Grimaldi said after the woman left, 'is that if there were any neighbourhood doctors *not* in disfavour with Don Andreas, she would have gone to them. But at least she came. That showed more courage than most have exhibited.'

Drew looked sceptical.

'Maybe the people in the Bend are showing common sense. Maybe we should, too.'

From the cabinet where she was rearranging bottles, Jo looked at her brother. 'Are you saying we should lock up and leave?'

'I'm suggesting we might think about it. Does it really make sense to stay here when we've been threatened, and Banks has been murdered?'

Vlandingham's swivel chair squeaked as he swung round; he'd been reading one of the texts from the shelf above his desk. But he hadn't turned a page in almost twenty minutes. In reply to Drew's question, he said:

'No, it doesn't make a whit of sense – not if your sole concern is self-preservation. I can tell you this much. If we leave before noon tomorrow, we might as well not come back. The confidence I've worked years to build will be gone like that.'

He snapped his fingers. Then, chair squeaking again, he returned to his study of the same page.

2

Around six that evening, they extinguished the lamps in the office, locked up and walked slowly toward the Bowery. Heavy thunderclouds rumbled in from the northwest. Wind billowed grit and rubbish through the streets. Neighbourhood people ran for cover, some of them casting pitying looks at the three men and the girl.

On the corner of Mulberry, peddlers were hurriedly covering their carts with tarpaulins. Will checked the street for oncoming vehicles and got a shock. Four doors down on the far side of Mulberry, Giuseppe Corso was just turning into a saloon.

Corso recognized the foursome at the intersection. He took a cheroot from his mouth and, his eyes on Will, dropped the cigar to the pavement and stepped on it. Then, laughing, he ducked inside.

Will looked to see who else had noticed. Drew and Dr Vlandingham were engaged in conversation about the comparative merits of catgut and silk ligatures. But Jo had seen Corso; her expression made that clear.

Bayard Street grew almost pitch dark under the heavy clouds. After the four of them had crossed Mulberry, Jo dropped back and took Will's arm. Her touch was comforting and familiar, somehow. Her hand seemed to belong right where it was.

'You've been very quiet ever since you got back from Wall Street.'

He shrugged, as if to indicate he had nothing to say on that subject. She went on:

'I do agree with what Drew said yesterday. This really isn't your fight. I wouldn't think less of you if you left. Drew wouldn't think less of you.'

He remembered the contemptuous way Corso had reached for his watch chain with the knife. Remembered some of the people he'd seen in the surgery; people desperate for the care the doctors offered. Now they'd been frightened away—

'But I'd think less of myself,' he said. 'And it is my fight. I'll stay until Sunday.'

He reached across with his other hand, closing it on hers. They gazed at one another and let their eyes speak eloquently of their feelings. They might have been alone on the dark, windy street.

Several steps ahead, Vlandingham grabbed his derby as a gust lifted it from his head. 'Hurry up, you two!'

They ran to catch up. But each knew something had changed, and changed profoundly, in that moment in which they'd looked at each other.

The grit-laden wind blew harder than ever. A butcher shop sign over the sidewalk creaked on its iron rod. Creaked and screeched and threatened to tear loose, just as old confusions and uncertainties were tearing loose within Will Kent. Tearing loose and blowing away – gone for good—

'I wish you'd go,' Jo whispered suddenly. 'I don't want anything to happen to you.'

'I feel the same way about you.' The feeling had been struggling for release for days, he realized. Even in the midst of their predicament, he experienced a moment of almost unbelievable happiness. 'That's one reason I have to stay.'

'You're more stubborn than I gave you credit for at first.'

He smiled. 'Being stubborn is one of the chief pastimes of the Kents.'

'Tell me why you've been so quiet all afternoon.'

He frowned. 'Oh – thinking.'

'About Don Andreas?'

'Not entirely'.

Memories cascaded through his mind; memories of Thurman Pennel and the torn galley from *Town Topics*; of Muldoon's taunts; and of Laura's puzzling behaviour – suggesting a quick marriage one day, only to reject the idea the next. He'd thought Laura was just a proper young woman carried away by her feelings. Her feelings for him and no one else—

Damn fool, he said to himself as he and Jo walked arm in arm. *Muldoon as much as told you what she was. You thought he was only saying it to settle a grudge.*

In the last few days he'd made a lot of discoveries about Laura Pennel. But he'd made even more important ones about himself. He'd discovered how badly false ambition could distort perception and judgment: he had believed what he wanted to believe about Laura, never what the facts suggested. He'd discovered how wrong he was to want all that the Pennels represented. Most important of all, he'd discovered Jo.

The clouds burst with a blaze of lightning, a clap of thunder. He rushed Jo toward a covered passage between buildings. It was just half a dozen steps away but they got soaked.

He heard Drew calling from shelter farther down the block. He shouted a reply but the storm muffled it. In the darkness of the passage, with thunder shaking the pavements and rain cascading from black clouds, he took Jo's waist in both hands:

'I don't know any way to tell you except straight out.

I've fallen in love with you. You're the only one I want.'

She put her hands on his shoulders. For a moment her face shone. But a sudden memory erased the radiant look:

'What about the girl in Newport?'

'I'll see her once more. To say goodbye. Maybe one of these days I can explain how she misled me. How I let myself be misled. But it's pointless right now.'

'You mean because of Don Andreas?'

He nodded and kissed her. They held one another without speaking, their tightly clasped arms communicating their love, and their fear that they'd found each other too late.

3

The most severe weather passed in less than an hour. But it rained all night and on into the next day. Drew, Will, and Jo reached the office shortly after eight-thirty Saturday morning. Dr Clem was already there. This Saturday would regularly have been his day off. But he'd changed his schedule, he said. They all knew the reason.

They kept the waiting room door closed, to provide more warning if anyone tried to come in that way. The Adams revolver lay on the examination table. In the hallway of the tenement, the pump handle squeaked with its familiar rhythm.

By ten Jo had cleaned the entire surgery. Will had read a chapter on delivery of a child by surgical section. Drew and Dr Clem had used the time to go over the account book for the practice – a study good for producing a lot of dismayed laughter from both of them.

About ten-fifteen, Mrs Grimaldi appeared with a

strapping, black-haired young man she introduced as her son, Tomaso. He would be staying with her in the surgery until twelve o'clock had come and gone, she said.

No amount of argument from Drew and the others did any good. She had made up her mind about staying. If Don Andreas sent roughnecks at noon, at least those roughnecks would have to deal with more people than they'd bargained for.

Eleven came.

Eleven-thirty.

Twelve.

Two lamps illuminated the gloomy surgery. Rain dripped steadily in the passage beyond the curtains – which bore constant watching since there was no way to close or shutter the window.

From twelve until half-past there was scarcely a word of conversation. The temperature dropped. A dank chill began to pervade the room. Soon Jo was shivering and chafing her arms.

At one o'clock Mrs Grimaldi rose from a stool where she'd been sitting for over an hour. 'Come, Tomaso. I think it is safe for us to leave. If the padrone meant to make good his threat, he would have done so by now. Something changed his mind. I always suspected he was a cowardly windba—'

'Mrs Grimaldi,' Jo whispered, pointing at the home-made curtains. 'I thought I heard someone—'

There was a loud explosion in the passageway. One of the curtains whipped wildly. Jo screamed as something struck Vlandingham's shelf of books and sent one spinning to the floor.

Tomaso Grimaldi leaped at his mother and flung her to the floor. Someone outside yanked the curtains apart. In the window, looking like a goblin, Corso crouched, his derby tilted down over his eyes and a small silvery gun in his right hand.

High up in the tenement, people began to shout and scream. Corso hunted a target. Will lunged for the revolver on the examination table. Behind him he heard the crash of the reception room door flying open, then heavy footsteps and Drew's warning:

'*Look out, it's McCauley—*'

A thunderous explosion. Jo cried, 'Dr Clem!' Something thudded to the floor.

It was McCauley's shot that killed the older doctor. Almost immediately, Corso fired at Jo. She was hit as she ran to the fallen physician. She rose on tiptoe, an astonished expression on her face. Her hands groped toward a small black hole in the lower right side of her apron.

She staggered against Vlandingham's desk, breathing hard and blinking rapidly. Will had the Adams in his right hand now. Corso tore down one of the curtains with his free hand, flinging it behind him and laughing as he pointed the muzzle of his gun at Will through the swirling smoke—

Will fired.

Corso's derby flipped up in the air and over the back of his head. A red cavity had been scooped from the centre of his forehead.

'*Ahhh!*' He seemed to be struggling for breath. Parallel streams of blood ran down the sides of his nose and dripped into his open mouth as he toppled backwards into the passage.

Behind Will, Drew was panting and struggling with someone. Will spun, saw Drew break free of McCauley's grip and lurch toward one of the equipment cabinets. Mrs Grimaldi and Tomaso were getting to their feet. Jo was bending forward, her arms crossed over her stomach as if to contain her pain.

Drew managed to open the cabinet with his unbandaged left hand. Instruments came clattering out. Slitted eyes shining with enjoyment, Dave McCauley grabbed Drew from behind. With his other hand he brought a huge old horse pistol up to the back of Drew's head.

'Let him go!' Will yelled.

McCauley pivoted, squinting. Will squeezed the Adams' trigger. He felt sudden stiffness in the mechanism; applied more pressure—

Nothing happened. Something had jammed or broken.

McCauley held Drew's collar with his left hand while levelling his gun at Will. The round black muzzle aligned with Will's forehead. Will dodged to one side. McCauley followed him unerringly.

Drew wrenched away from McCauley. Will dived for the floor and landed next to the examination table, expecting to feel the impact of a bullet any second.

McCauley let out a choked cry just as his gun boomed. His explosion of breath escalated into a moan, then to a shrill cry of pain.

The bullet from McCauley's gun missed Will by a foot or so. Groggy, he climbed to his feet. Jo was walking in a small circle, moving rapidly and shaking her head as she talked to herself:

'I didn't get hurt. Somehow I didn't get hurt, it was like a bee sting, can you imagine—?'

He recognized the delirium and wild excitement produced by a gunshot wound. She was in shock. The wound might be far more serious than she realized.

He turned to find Drew, who was reaching to yank the horse pistol out of McCauley's hand. The big man was mewling like a child. Finally Will saw why. Drew had snatched a scalpel from the cabinet. Its handle jutted from a rip in McCauley's left sleeve. The blade was imbedded in the big triceps muscle.

'Jesus Christ, don't let me die. Don't let me die like a dog,' McCauley babbled, slipping sideways to the wall and then dropping to his knees. Tears of terror trickled down his face. It was a wound easily survived, but McCauley didn't know that. Drew seized the advantage:

'No one will help you unless you tell us who sent you here.'

Weaving back and forth on his knees and crying, McCauley managed to say, 'Don Andreas. Who else do you think it would be?'

Over the sound of Jo's agitated voice, Mrs Grimaldi spoke to her son:

'*La polizia, Tomaso! In fretta!*'

The husky young man cast one more awed glance at the carnage in the surgery, then bolted out through the reception room. In the outer hall, Will glimpsed pale faces; tenement dwellers wanting to see what had happened, yet too frightened to step over the threshold.

Drew grabbed McCauley's jaw with his left hand. 'Confessing to me isn't good enough. You'll have to speak your piece at Elizabeth Street. And in a courtroom.'

'I will if you don't let me die, I swear to God I will. Just help me. *Help me.*'

Wrathful, Drew reached across with his left hand, grasped the scalpel and tore it out. McCauley shrieked and fell sideways, fainting. Drew looked at him with disgust. Then he dropped the bloody scalpel on McCauley's shirt.

875

He turned to his sister. She was still following that small circular path and holding her stomach. Fear on his face, he hurried to her with Will only a step behind.

5

A sergeant and two patrolmen from Elizabeth Street arrived shortly. Ten minutes later attendants from a horse-drawn ambulance carried McCauley out on a litter. Will had applied a Spanish windlass tourniquet to arrest the bleeding of the man's arm.

The attendants returned and wrapped Vlandingham's body, then Corso's. They took both from the tenement.

Will struggled against the shock beginning to build up within him. He'd shot and killed a man. He told himself he'd had no choice – or even any time for rational decision. Still, the fact was inescapable. He'd killed a man. A worthless thug, maybe. But a human being.

One thing helped stave off the full impact: the sight of Jo lying under a sheet on the examination table where Drew had carefully placed her. She was white as milk. And awake, although her eyes didn't quite focus. From time to time she spoke softly, laughed, or sang snatches of a song. All of it was incoherent.

Mrs Grimaldi watched Jo anxiously. Will walked to the cabinet for a decanter of medicinal whiskey. He tugged at the stopper but seemed to lack strength. His fingers had a queer, lifeless feel.

Killed a man.

The police sergeant said to Drew, 'Should we dump the two bodies in the courtyard and let your sister have a place in the ambulance?'

Drew's voice took on that high, nasal quality. 'We can't risk the ride to the hospital.'

876

'Hurt that bad, is she? Sure don't look it. There ain't much blood—'

Drew exploded: 'How long have you been on the force? That's a classic gunshot wound. Very probably clotted already. There may be bad internal haemorrhaging.'

Will's hands froze on the decanter. He had just realized what had to be done.

' – I won't risk dislodging a clot during a rough ride. We'll remove the bullet here, and determine the extent of the injuries.'

Drew folded the sheet back and studied the hole in Jo's apron. It was a small black crater into whose centre scraps of cloth had been driven by the bullet's passage. There was some blood showing, but not much.

Talking more to himself than to the others, Drew continued, 'Maybe the bullet spent itself in the abdominal wall. But it's more likely that the cavity was penetrated. From the position and angle of the wound, I'd suspect a perforated small intestine. That generally means several holes rather than one – ' Suddenly his eyes focused on Will. 'For God's sake put that whiskey away.'

'Why?'

'Because—'

Drew brought his bandaged right hand up from behind the examination table. 'You're the only one who can open her up and see how badly she's hurt.'

6

The accumulated shock and horror of the past hour overwhelmed Will then. His hands started to shake.

He pushed the glass stopper back into the decanter and held it tightly.

'Look, Drew, I know she needs help. But I don't think I can—'

'Jesus, let's not repeat Castle Garden. You've had surgical training. Heard all the lectures. Watched the demonstrations—'

'But I've never done a procedure like this.'

'Are you afraid to try?'

'I—'

Bungler.

Drew mistook his frightened silence for consent:

'We'll go slowly. Step by step. I'll give you advice if you need it, though I don't think you do. Mrs Grimaldi will help too.'

The stout woman raised her eyebrows, then frowned. 'I'll do anything you ask, *dottore*. As best I can.'

Will fought to overcome a sense of certain failure.

'Drew, I don't have the skill!'

His friend stared at him.

'You'd better. Unless you want her to die.'

7

Will fixed his attention on Jo's white face. Her eyes were nearly closed but her lips were still moving, uttering airy, cheerful words he couldn't understand. Suffering from shock, she was in some other, happier place.

He struggled to collect himself. As Drew had said, Jo's was almost a textbook wound. Gunshot victims frequently reported little pain. Most said the wound felt as if a small stone had hit them, or a light blow of a cane.

He recalled a Harvard lecture on the tragic lessons of 1881. On June 30 of that year, President Garfield had been shot. He had languished and ultimately died in September because exploratory surgery was still suspect; no attending physician had been willing to probe for the assassin's bullet and remove it. The two young men didn't want to make the same mistake.

Drew's gaze fixed on his friend's face. So did Mrs Grimaldi's and that of the police sergeant. Will stared at the freckles which Jo's pallor emphasized so dramatically. He thought of all she'd come to mean to him – and what she meant to his future.

She meant everything.

His head cleared a little more. He rubbed his eyes with his palms—

'All right. I'll do it.'

A moment later, he said to the sergeant, 'Please keep people away from that window, and out of the waiting room.' The sergeant pivoted and left.

'Mrs Grimaldi, light those lamps. Every one of them. What kind of surgical books do you have, Drew?'

'Let's see. We have an Ashhurst, and a Wyeth. A *Smith's Operative Surgery*, too.'

The last was a Harvard text. 'Get all of them.'

Drew nodded. For a moment, intense emotion misted his eyes. He knew, as did Will, that physicians with close personal ties to a patient should never operate on that patient. But circumstances had forced the abandonment of the rule. Drew's glance said he'd be forever grateful to his friend.

Trying to keep his mind from the frightening possibility of failure, Will went on, 'Anaesthetic, now. Do you have ether?'

'Yes, plenty.'

'An inhaler—?'

'That too. We have everything necessary.'

'We'll need the carbolic – ' Again he rubbed his eyes. Mrs Grimaldi put the chimney back on one lamp and removed another. 'With all that's happened, I can't seem to remember where you keep it.'

879

Drew laughed in a ragged way. 'You know something? Neither can I. But we'll find it.'

Together they started the search as lamp after lamp spread blazing light in the room.

CHAPTER XIV

Under the Knife

Under Drew's supervision, Mrs Grimaldi uncorked a can of ether, poured the proper amount onto the gauze inside the inhaler, then lowered the inhaler over Jo's face. Drew watched for signs that the ether was irritating his sister's respiratory passages. The first few minutes would be the most critical.

Will, meantime, cut away Jo's clothing, struggling to maintain a dispassionate professional attitude as he did so. It was impossible to be completely free of emotion. He was pink-faced when he pulled the last of her undergarments from beneath the sheet with which he'd draped her.

He folded the sheet down, laying it so the turned edge covered her to just above her pubis. He was struck by the fragile whiteness of her body. A deep sense of love swept through him, followed by an overwhelming fear of losing her through chance or, worse, lack of skill—

No. He wouldn't let that happen. He *would not*.

If he wanted to be with Jo for the rest of his life, his mind had to function clearly, and without error. His hand had to be steady. He concentrated on achieving that steadiness as he temporarily covered the wound with a layer of gauze soaked with carbolic, then added a second layer, and a third.

Jo's sputtering cough brought Will's head up sharply. Drew whispered urgents instructions to Mrs Grimaldi. She grasped Jo's forearms while he took hold of her shoulders as best he could. Will got ready to step in, should the ether produce the violent resistance that it sometimes did.

But Jo only coughed once more, lightly; she was resisting less than the average, uninjured patient. In this case her state of shock had been of benefit.

When Drew told Mrs Grimaldi that she could let go, Will went back to work. He hurriedly dipped surgical instruments, including a Nélaton probe, in a tray of antiseptic solution. One by one he laid the instruments within easy reach on a small, towel-draped table.

Next he soaked a number of elephant-ear sponges that would be used to remove blood an secretions from the wound and the peritoneal cavity. Just a couple of days before, Drew had spoken of the new gauze sponges being adopted in many hospitals; as yet no one at the little clinic had had time to cut and sew any of them, so it was necessary to stick with the marine sponges that had been in wide use for years.

Drew was at the head of the operating table, Mrs Grimaldi next to him at Jo's right shoulder. Will could feel his friend's eyes on him as he scrutinized the wound – a small, relatively bloodless hole two and three quarter inches to the right of the umbilicus, and half an inch below.

He drew another deep breath. Reached out to dip both hands through the carbolic solution one last time. Then, with the utmost care, he inserted his right index finger into the wound.

Blood oozed. 'Not large enough,' he muttered, and quickly expanded the wound with scissors. The added quarter of an inch afforded him the room he needed. But he couldn't locate the bullet.

Next he tried Nélaton's probe, an instrument capped with unglazed porcelain. When the probe came in contact with a bullet, the bullet would mark the porcelain with a metallic streak. This time there was no mark. Grim, Will withdrew the probe and looked at his friend.

'I can't find it. And the peritoneum's torn. The bullet's gone into the abdominal cavity.'

It was what they'd feared – the possibility of visceral damage. Drew quirked the corners of his mouth, as if the thought of the next step was almost too painful. But he recovered quickly, giving a little nod:

'Go ahead and open her, then. The quicker the better.'

Once more Will studied the wound. 'The direction of the entry is anterior to posterior and the angle seems to tend toward the centre – a median incision would be indicated. Do the texts go along with that?'

Drew glanced down at the books open on the floor between the head of the table and the place where Will stood with his back to the lamps. Drew kicked one of the texts and said with that nasal tone:

'You don't need the books. You know what to do. Get busy and do it, for God's sake.'

2

Will reached for the scalpel. Adjusted it for proper fit in his hand. Stepped a half pace to the left in the hope of obtaining better light. As best he could, he obliterated Jo's identify from his mind. Then he touched the scalpel to the skin at the chosen site.

He applied downward pressure. Watched the indentation appear in her skin, then a thin redness as he started the section.

He lengthened the incision to an inch.

Two inches.

Three.

He heard whispering: Drew giving instructions. Mrs Grimaldi stepped to Will's side:

'Stop a moment. I'll wipe your face.'

Gratefully, he held the scalpel steady while she reached round with a towel to pat his forehead and eyebrows dry. He blinked to express his thanks, somehow incapable of uttering so much as an extraneous word now. Every bit of his concentration was fixed on what had become his universe – the operative field, and the incision which he now completed to its initial length of six inches.

He'd made his incision directly in the midline through the linea alba, without disturbing the muscles on either side. Fortunately, as he'd hoped, there was minimal bleeding. Mrs Grimaldi responded speedily when he summoned her and deftly sopped up the blood with one of the marine sponges.

He reached for the forceps. Transferred them to his left hand and carefully picked up a little fold of the peritoneum, into which he cut with the scalpel. The incision was small. He left it that way as he caught each side of the wound with a haemostat, then temporarily closed the belly while he stepped away from the table and again ran his hands through the antiseptic solution. Several trays of it had been set up on the desk beforehand.

With scissors, Will enlarged the peritoneal incision until he was sure he could introduce his disinfected right hand. Then, softly:

'Drew, can you manage the anaesthesia from now on?'

'Yes.'

'Mrs Grimaldi, give him the inhaler. Then clean your hands and come here beside me.'

As soon as she was in position, he said, 'I hope your stomach's strong.'

Almost annoyed, she shot back, 'Worry about the poor child, not me.'

'Very well. Here's what I'm going to do.'

He described the procedure. Despite her protest a moment ago, she swallowed and blinked rapidly when he concluded, 'Each section must be supported under some of that towelling stacked on the stool. And you mustn't let the gut slip or fall back into the cavity – understand?'

White-faced, she nodded. He closed his teeth on his lower lip and, after a last glance at Drew's tense face, slipped his hand into Jo's body.

3

He began with the loops of small intestine which presented at the incision. When he'd slowly withdrawn about nine inches of gut, he found the punctures; five of them.

Where was the bullet? That would have to wait. For the moment, his work was with the ragged multiple perforation in the gut wall.

Mrs Grimaldi's eyes were huge. Despite obvious fear and her unfamiliarity with the glistening internal organs of a human body, she was doing an expert job of cushioning the portions of intestine brought out through the incision and placed on towels soaked in Thiersch solution.

There'd been no time to properly empty Jo's gut, so before attempting to close the wounds, Will had to gently express the contents upward beyond the last puncture, then prevent their return by applying a clamp across the intestine. He expressed some remaining material downward and applied a second clamp. He was sweating heavily again, but he could no longer call on Mrs Grimaldi for relief.

He reminded himself that he'd have to cleanse the cavity of material which had escaped from the small intestine. He'd nearly forgotten that. With a human life in his hands – literally in his hands, as it was now – nothing could be forgotten. *Bungl*—

No.

The past was reaching out to snare him; drag him to failure. He wouldn't permit it. He meant to save Jo's life so they'd have time together—

Drew was staring at him with a strange, questioning expression. Will's jaw set.

'I'm all right,' he said. 'How does she look to you?'

'Her breathing is satisfactory. So is her heart rate. I'd say so far, so good.'

'All right. Just a little while longer, Mrs Grimaldi.'

'I'm fine, just fine,' she said in a hoarse voice, her eyes fixed on the strands of exposed gut. Will turned the intestine so the first section to be repaired was directly in front of him. The first puncture began to ooze a little more material that hadn't been expressed away. Quickly he positioned a sponge so the material wouldn't drain back into the cavity.

His right leg started to ache and throb. From tension, he was sure. It was worrisome. A severe spasm could throw his hand awry at a critical moment. He bent the leg slightly, alleviating the strain, and gently picked up the torn gut to decide how best to suture it.

The first and second punctures had to be treated as one, he decided. They were quite close together because the bullet had passed through both gut walls while they were folded against one another. Visually, he measured the distance between the two punctures. Only a fraction of an inch of tissue separated them when the gut was extended.

He cut out the tissue between the punctures, thus

forming a single elliptical opening more easily sutured. Carefully he trimmed away the opening's ragged edge, leaving a new and smooth one.

Next he took a narrow section of each of the two long edges and tucked them inward, so that the gut's outer sheathing on one side of the opening touched similar sheathing on the other. Drew passed him a curved needle with a long, twisted strand of carbolated black silk attached. Mrs Grimaldi had prepared the needles after Drew had chosen them from the collection in the office, to be sure they weren't too sharp.

He intended to use the Lembert suture, standard in intestinal procedures. He'd seen it demonstrated in the operating theatre, but had only tried it on inert laboratory material, never on a living patient. When correctly placed the suture passed through the two outer layers of intestinal tissure – the very thin, membranous serosa, and the muscularis – to the next layer, the submucosa, which carried the blood vessels. The Lembert suture was an inverting stitch, pulling all outside tissue to the inside without penetrating the mucosa, the intestine's inmost layer. If penetration accidentally occurred, the contents of the intestine could touch the suture, perhaps cause infection, and even disrupt the entire suture line.

Drew was clearly nervous over the procedure Will was about to attempt:

'You mustn't go too deep – but if you don't go deep enough, the sutures will tear out.'

'I'm worried about hitting the blood vessels in the submucosa.'

'Go under them. Miss them. You're a doctor – you're supposed to be able to do that.'

Slowly, Will pushed the needle into the tucked-together edges of the opening, kept pushing it with no difficulty, then felt a slightly increased resistance which told him he was into the third layer of tissue. He turned the needle to point it outward again. Following Drew's instructions proved a hellishly difficult and time-consuming process. But once the sutures were set, they were firm, and he was positive they'd hold.

Three other punctures, one hardly more than a nick, had to be closed before he could consider that phase of the work complete. Finally he stepped away from the table, his right leg hurting so fiercely he wished he could anaesthetize it.

Drew watched him in silence. An hour had passed, or a little more. At least another hour remained – even assuming he could locate the spent bullet.

Mrs Grimaldi looked exhausted, her face so pale, her moustache stood out with great prominence. She stared at Will, then at the strands of intestine draped over the blood-smeared towels like so much sausage. To buoy her, Will said:

'You've done wonderfully, Mrs Grimaldi. Better than many professional assistants.'

Her voice was strained. 'Don't talk. Just get done with it.'

Once more he introduced his hand, probing through the viscera with great care while trying to remember the Gray's memorized so laboriously as part of his first-class studies. Suddenly he touched something foreign and hard against the posterior mesentery near the lumbo-sacral area.

He lost it just as suddenly. But now he knew the bullet was free. It hadn't struck major blood vessels, the aorta nor the iliacs, and it hadn't lodged in the bones of the spine. If he could just find it again—!

His mouth opened in a kind of ghastly parody of a smile. Barely breathing, he shifted his hand downward, searching.

Stiff with tension, his right leg began to shake. The trembling became a violent spasm. God, not now!

The rod loomed in his mind, whipping toward his shoulders—

Bungler.

BUNGLER.

Drew stared, fear on his face; Will had a remote, lost look in his eyes.

Drew started to move toward his friend, as if prepared to take over using only his left hand. Will clenched his teeth, struggling with the inner enemy:

No.

Not this time.

NOT EVER AGAIN.

'Will—?' Drew asked in an anxious voice, moving to his side.

Will thumped his right heel on the floor, hard. He did it again. A moment later the peculiar glint faded from his eyes. They seemed to refocus on his surroundings. His reddened hand came slowly back up into sight. In his palm lay a mashed bit of lead.

With a sudden sag of his shoulders he said, 'That's all of it.' He flung the bullet behind him. It struck the floor. He closed his eyes and smiled a brief, tired smile.

4

Drew wiped the back of his bandaged hand across his upper lip, his relief evident.

'Congratulations.'

'Not time for that yet,' Will countered. 'We're a long way from finished.'

But he knew they'd make it. *He* would make it and, more important, so would Jo. Sometime during those last moments of intense concentration, as he'd located and withdrawn the spent lead, he had found comfort in a sudden image, and a very faint sound within the confines of his mind.

A single sharp crack: a rod of punishment breaking.
No, *being* broken. By his own hand.
Forever.

5

An hour and fifty-eight minutes after he'd first probed
the wound, Will finished the final suture and stepped
back.

He'd carefully cleansed the abdominal cavity with
sponges attached to long holders, then repaired the
incisions one by one. Now the girl on the table was
changed again; she was no longer a patient he was
required to think about in a narrow professional way,
but a woman with a name, a unique appearance, and a
set of traits that had become dear to him.

He put his freshly scrubbed left hand against Jo's
cool cheek. Despite his good intentions, his control
broke. He burst out laughing.

Drew and Mrs Grimaldi were thunderstruck. He
couldn't stop. He laughed so hard, tears streaked his
cheeks. He laughed because the strain of the operation
was behind him; and because he was happy; and
because he'd won a victory.

When the laughter diminished, he thought about
that victory. And about his mother.

*I don't know why you thought so little of me. Maybe
you couldn't help it, I don't know. I only know that to
save her, I had to prove you were wrong.*

6

'Will?'

He was leaning against the wall near the window

where the curtains had been torn down. He wiped his cheeks with his palms as Drew spoke again:

'You did a splendid job. Just splendid.'

He shrugged, as if to minimize the compliment. He looked past Drew to the girl sleeping peacefully beneath fresh sheets. Mrs Grimaldi sat beside her, keeping watch.

Then he took note of the admiration and affection on his friend's face, and he knew he needn't be afraid to believe Drew's compliment.

To realize that – to grant that to himself – opened him to a new emotion he hadn't expressed for years. Pride. He had done the job he had been trained to do. He had done it well.

Most important, he'd saved the life of the one person he loved above all others.

I'm sorry, Carter, he thought as he gazed at Jo's calm, lovely face. *The promise you asked me to give you was the wrong promise, for the wrong purpose. As long as I have work that matters, and a woman I love, I don't need anything else. I certainly don't need a mansion in Newport or a ball invitation from some arrogant old woman. I don't have to show anything, prove anything, to anyone except myself. It's taken me all this to learn that.*

He didn't know whether he could ever explain his change of heart to his stepbrother. He'd certainly have to try. He owed Carter that much, even if the result was a painful confrontation. Of course it might be years before he saw Carter again; his stepbrother might never come home from San Francisco now that he'd found some success there.

Well, that confrontation could wait. The confrontation with Laura could not.

CHAPTER XV

Laura's Confession

On Sunday, while bells rang the call to church, Tomaso Grimaldi brought a wagon to the mouth of the passage leading to Bayard Court. Mrs Grimaldi had padded the back of the wagon with clean blankets. Drew and Will carried Jo out to the street and lifted her into the wagon with great care.

Will took over the reins. Drew sat beside him. Tomaso rode in back with the half-conscious girl. The wagon completed a turn in the street and headed east along Bayard.

Will and Drew had stayed awake all night watching Jo. One or the other of them had administered an opiate when she needed it, and both of them had spent a lot of time answering questions from several police inspectors.

The two young men had also discussed the question of Jo's care. They'd decided the best place for her was Nevsky's tenement. Some member of the Nevsky family was usually on the premises and could see to her needs. She would also have a room to herself, as opposed to a bed in a ward at a public hospital. The constant presence of a doctor wasn't necessary; she'd come through the operation splendidly, and all she needed now was rest.

'Out of the way, out of the way!' Nevsky shouted as the wagon drove up. He had cleared a section of kerb in front of his building. He elbowed a peddler with many pairs of suspenders draped over his shoulders, and motioned the wagon to the kerb. Soon Jo was settled upstairs.

Will packed his valise. When he was done; he returned to her room. He pulled a small wooden box up next to her cot and sat down.

He gazed at her silently for a minute or so. Her red-gold hair was neatly tied behind her head; Nevsky's wife had got her into a nightgown and used a comb and brush on her hair while Drew held her up, loudly disapproving of the whole business. Jo's eyes were closed now, and she was still abnormally pale. But Will didn't think he had ever seen a woman half so beautiful.

Presently he took her right hand in his. 'Jo? Can you hear me at all?'

Her eyelids moved slightly. Her tongue brushed across her lower lip. She almost smiled. She heard him.

'I have to leave for a few days.' The words brought a tightness to his face. 'But I'll be back.'

She murmured something; a small, pleased sound. Drew had walked in a moment earlier. He reacted to what he'd just heard:

'Great day in the morning! That's wonderful news.'

Will chuckled as he stood up. 'Don't sound so surprised. Do you think I saved your sister solely for humanitarian reasons? I wanted to keep her around so we could see each other. Myabe even discuss plans for the future—'

Drew's smile faded a little. 'Maybe? You mean you're not sure?'

'I am. I don't know about Jo.'

'I don't know why you say that. She's had her cap set for you ever since that night we dined at the oyster house.'

'Then she and I will have a lot to talk about. As soon as I get my diploma – ' He didn't hesitate; he knew what he wanted, and where he belonged. ' – I'd like to take Dr Clem's place if you'll have me.'

'*If?*' With a roar of delight, Drew clapped his friend

into a clumsy embrace and waltzed him into the corridor, where Nevsky was fuming over a broken sewing machine belt. 'Nevsky, meet my new partner – Doctor Kent.'

Nevsky wasn't impressed; he waved the belt.

'Can he repair this? Of course he can't. What good is he?'

Doctor Kent. It had a very good sound.

As the two young men walked down to the street, Will thought of Drew's partner. Vlandingham's body had been removed to a local undertaker's. 'Is there going to be a service for Dr Clem?' he asked.

Drew shrugged. 'I suppose so. I doubt we'll be invited.'

'Why not?'

'Oh, just a feeling. Last night I sent a boy uptown to find Dr Clem's brother Cyrus. The undertaker said he showed up with an expensive hearse and took the body away as fast as he could. I don't suppose he'll be anxious to see any of Dr Clem's downtown acquaintances at the funeral.'

Will shook his head. Once, he'd admired the younger Vlandingham. And he'd come close to being the same sort of doctor. Drew and Jo had saved him from it. Laura too had played a role, though an unintentional one. In a way, he owed her thanks for that. But he knew he'd never utter them. When he saw her again – tomorrow, if he were lucky – he'd have all he could do just to keep his temper.

2

They emerged from the tenement. The weather had changed dramatically during the night. The sky was bright blue and cloudless. A refreshing breeze carried a cool foretaste of autumn.

The two young men discovered Mrs Grimaldi waiting on the stoop. She was dressed in her Sunday finery. She said she'd prayed for Jo in church, and she wanted to know whether those prayers and all the others said during the long night had been answered. Gravely, Drew told her they had.

The three walked to Mulberry Street, whose kerbs and sidewalks were beginning to overflow with the usual Sunday crowds. He recognized one – Rocco Amato, the man who had joined Corso in the attempt to rob him.

Will's hand tightened on the handle of his valise. He anticipated trouble. And indeed, Amato stared fixedly at the trio as they approached. Mrs Grimaldi glared right back.

Amato smiled nervously, then raised his hand to his forehead and pulled it away in a kind of salute. To Will he called, 'Eh – *Dottore Pistol*.'

Will frowned; said to Mrs Grimaldi, 'What the devil does that mean?'

'It's a nickname. Doctor Pistol. Ever since you dispatched Corso, I've been hearing it all over the neighbourhood.' She beamed at him. 'It's a compliment.'

'A compliment for killing a man?'

'Life down here is not so refined as it is where you come from,' she told him cheerfully as they walked on. The loafers went back to talking and joking. 'People in the Bend didn't like 'Sep Corso. Even his own relatives feared and detested him. You have earned widespread respect whether you want it or not.'

Will was about to say something when Drew exclaimed, 'Police!' They watched a horse-drawn wagon clatter round the corner, race past them and stop in front of an establishment whose gaudy signboard said *Ristorante Napoli*. A plain clothes detective opened barred doors at the back of the wagon and jumped out. Three uniformed men with locust sticks and handcuffs leaped out after him. The men ran inside the restaurant. The policeman driving the wagon watched the entrance warily.

A crowd gathered, murmuring questions. Sounds of commotion issued from the café: a table overturning; crockery breaking. A familiar voice cursed in fluent Italian.

The man was shouted down by others who spoke English; the police, presumably. People gasped and pointed as the policemen emerged into the sunlight with an elderly man in tow.

Don Andreas Belsario's face was dark red. He held his handcuffed wrists close to his vest, as if hoping to hide the most evident sign of his downfall. The moment people recognized him, they stopped talking. The fear the padrone generated was all too evident.

Don Andreas saw Mrs Grimaldi and her companions at the back of the crowd. He stopped and addressed Will and Drew:

'Ah – what a surprise. The young gentlemen responsible for my predicament. Did you come here to enjoy my humiliation?'

One of the policemen pushed him. 'Shut up and move along. The magistrate's waiting.'

Don Andreas wrenched away. His defiance was carried off with such arrogance, the officers were more amused than angered.

The padrone's white hair blew fitfully in the cool breeze. Again he fixed his eyes on Drew, then on Will. The venom in that gaze made Will catch his breath. When the padrone spoke, his voice was pitched low. But it carried clearly through the hushed crowd:

'These *ufficiales* have informed me that someone named McCauley – ' He mispronounced the name; intentionally, Will suspected. ' – a person of whom I have never heard – is accusing me of misdemeanours I have not committed. As soon as I have cleared up the misunderstanding—'

'In about twenty years,' said the plain clothes detective standing behind him.

'—you will see me again. This is my district.'

He meant it as a warning. His eyes were on Drew. But it was Will who replied:

'It's ours, too. When you get back, we'll be here.'

Mrs Grimaldi laughed. It broke the tension. People began talking softly. A few even smiled and pointed at the prisoner. Faces gradually lost their look of strain, as if there was a realization that the padrone was, perhaps, not omnipotent after all.

Don Andreas tried to glare the onlookers to silence but it was too late. The policemen lost patience; jabbed him with their sticks. The detective sprang forward and jerked the wagon doors open.

When the padrone saw the bars on the doors, he began to curse loudly again. A policeman yanked his arm. He resisted. The officer pulled harder. In a moment Don Andreas was howling, and struggling so violently he had to be subdued by blows of the locust sticks.

He was half carried, half thrown into the wagon. Finally, with the detective standing on the rear step and clinging to a hand rail, the wagon rattled away.

For a few more seconds, the prisoner's cursing and raving could be heard in the unnatural silence. Then the wagon turned a corner and Mulberry Street grew noisy again.

3

Will travelled all the way to Newport even though he wondered if Laura would refuse to see him. She didn't. But she sent word that they would have to speak in the formal garden – out of earshot of the servants.

She arrived twenty-five minutes after he was sent to

the garden to wait. Her curly hair, so reminiscent of her brother's, straggled over the collar of her dress and down the back. She had a haggard air, as if from sleeplessness or worry.

Unsmiling, she remained some distance from the marble bench where Will had been sitting. Out on the Atlantic, a long white yacht steamed south under a Wedgwood-blue sky crowded with small, fluffy clouds. The garden lay in sunlight one moment, shadow the next.

'I didn't expect you to come here again,' she said. 'Marcus sent a telegraph message from the city. He said you spoke to Father, but not about us. He said you asked questions about the family business. Matters that are really none of your affair.'

'I did see your father,' Will said, nodding. 'But we didn't talk much about real estate. He was more interested in discussing an item he paid to keep out of *Town Topics*.'

'Oh, dear God.' Laura covered her mouth with both hands. She looked vulnerable all at once; Will was almost sorry for her. But sympathy vanished when he recalled how she'd tricked him.

'This isn't pleasant for me, Laura. But it's necessary. I've tried to establish the sequence of things. I figure it must have gone like this. Some days before we – before the morning we went to the shore – someone supplying items to Colonel Mann overheard you say you feared you were carrying a child.'

She pivoted away, a reaction he took to mean that his guess was correct.

'On the morning I spoke of, you still thought you were pregnant. So a quick wedding – even an elope-ment – was an idea that had some attraction for you. And you also went out of your way to remind me that because of being – with you, I was obliged to marry you. Then, the very next day, you completely reversed everything you'd said the day before. I wondered why, and you gave me the answer, only I wasn't bright enough to see it just then. You told me you were cross because of a – feminine complaint. In other words, sometime during the night you'd discovered you weren't pregnant after all. You were still willing to marry me – your father explained the reason for that – but there was no longer any need for haste. No longer any need to cover a mistake – though of course, once we were married, I'd always be available to legitimize any others you might make.'

Despite his best intentions, he was beginning to speak angrily. She heard that. Fear crept into her eyes. He took a step in her direction.

'That's all I was good for, wasn't it? Legitimizing any bastards you might conceive by accident?' His hands clenched at his sides. 'What a damn fool I was. I was so dazzled by you, by – ' He lifted a hand toward the house. ' – this—'

He couldn't go on.

She made a steeple of the tips of her fingers; concealed her mouth with it. From behind her hands, she murmured, 'God, you sound so bitter.'

'Do you blame me? You told me you cared for me. I believed you. I trusted you. I thought you'd never made love to anyone else – or that if you had, it hadn't happened more than once or twice, and only then because your emotions carried you away. But that isn't the way it was at all.'

Again he moved toward her. She backed away, but not quickly enough. He seized her arm:

'When you thought we should get married right away, who had you been with, Laura? If there'd been a baby, who would have been its real father?'

'Damn you, let go! You have no right—'

'After the way you gulled me, I have every right.'

'I said let—'

He shook her; hard:

'*Who, Laura?*'

She looked closely at his threatening face. Said:

'One – one of the shackers.'

Even though he expected that, it shocked him. He lost colour.

'Which one? Muldoon?'

His anger had been drained away by sorrow and disgust; she sensed a chance to strike back. She tore free of his hand. Pushed wind-blown hair from her eyes and smiled sweetly.

'I really can't tell you, my dear. It could have been any one of six or seven.'

CHAPTER XVI

Reunion

Silence.

From the loggia on the east side of the mansion, he heard the rhythmic click of garden shears. He wanted to hit her but pity held him back. He groped for the straw hat he'd dropped on the bench when he arrived.

'I guess that says it all. Goodbye, Laura.'

Her anger faded as quickly as his. With an almost imploring note in her voice, she asked, 'Where are you going? Back to Boston?'

'Yes, then back to New York.'

He jammed the hat on his head; the movement had a swift, threatening quality. She retreated a couple of steps. Something had changed her mood and left her uncertain, even sad.

She clasped her hands at her waist; held them tightly

together as she whispered, 'What will you be doing in New York?'

'I intend to practise there. But not in the section of town we talked about. Not on Fifth Avenue. Downtown – in an area called the Bend. It's a slum. Full of Italians and Irish. I know you aren't interested in the world at large, but you must be familiar with this particular section. The Pennels own a lot of property in the area. Tenements. Filthy buildings, but very productive as investments. Surely you've heard the Bend discussed at the dinner table. It provides some of the income that enables you to enjoy all this splendour—'

Her response was a blank stare. He'd been wrong; she didn't know a damn thing about the nature of the family's real estate holdings. If she'd ever heard the Bend mentioned, she'd probably paid no attention.

'In any case,' he went on, 'as soon as I finish my studies, I'm going to practise in the Bend. You might pass this along to your brother. When I'm permanently settled, I'll do everything in my power to help the authorities punish the people who run tenements. I don't mean just the rental agents. I mean the owners.'

'My, you're getting very sanctimonious—'

'Call it whatever you like.'

'You're turning into a radical like that father of yours.'

He looked at her for several moments before he said:

'If that's true, I'm pleased.'

'You're *disgusting*! You and that whole family of yours. You're canaille, that's all you are. *Canaille!*'

'By your standards, and McAllister's, I suppose we are. I don't mind a bit.'

He'd stayed too long. He had a bad taste in his mouth. He turned and started walking. He was halfway across the garden when he heard her coming, screaming at him:

'You're an idiot, Will Kent. You're not going to use your training to help your own kind, you're going to squander your life among a lot of foreigners – ' She was growing hysterical; her shrill voice was cracking. ' – a – lot of – dirty foreigners, they – aren't – even – Americans—'

He faced her. 'Yes they are. Better ones than you.'

He said it quietly, without rancour. She stopped three feet from him, hair blowing wildly round her head, fists balled at her sides, grey eyes filled with tears of fury.

She stared at him; saw the determination on his face. All at once she began to weep like a girl much younger:

'Oh, Will – don't walk out on me. No one else – who's decent – will ever marry me if – you walk out—'

Once more he said, 'Goodbye, Laura,' and quickly left the garden. Moments later he was striding down Bellevue Avenue. Free.

2

It was ten minutes past midnight when Will climbed the front steps of the Kent house. The wind gusted along Beacon Street, sharp and cool out of the northwest. A light still burned behind the curtains in his father's office. He was tired but strangely exhilarated as he rang and waited for someone to answer.

The door opened. Instead of a servant, Eleanor stood there, clad in nightgown and robe.

'Will!'

'Hello, Eleanor.' He stepped in. 'I didn't expect you to answer the bell.'

'I was just on my way to the kitchen. I was closest. Are you all right?'

'Fine – just fine.'

With a delighted smile, she hugged him. Then she began, 'Everyone thought—'

She stopped. He finished for her:

'That I'd gone for good. That was my intention when I left. I made a mistake. Where are Father and Julia?'

'Julia's still at the Association office, working on the next issue of the newspaper. She just telephoned and asked Papa to send the carriage in half an hour. He's in the office. Mr Calhoun left about twenty minutes ago. He and Papa have been conferring for hours.'

Will covered the distance quickly. Eleanor followed. He knocked, then pushed the door inward.

A dishevelled figure in shirtsleeves, Gideon looked up from his desk. A cigar jutted from his mouth. His face had a dark, mottled look, but Will was too overcome to notice.

Gideon's frown changed to an expression of surprise, then to delight that was quickly masked by caution:

'You're the last person I expected to see tonight.'

'I came home to tell you I made a mistake. One that nearly became permanent. I'm finished with Laura Pennel. There's another girl. I'll tell you about her if you'll forgive all the rotten things I said to you. Forgive them and let me stay a day or so—'

Gideon, too, was overcome. He could only say, 'By *God!*'

He rose from the desk, flung his cigar into the fireplace, and walked toward his son. 'I'm the one to apologize. I tried to say the right things but I used the wrong words.' He rubbed his good eye with the knuckles of his right hand. 'We'll have time to talk of that. Plenty of time. Oh, I'm glad you're home again—'

His voice broke on the final words. Father and son put their arms round one another with unashamed affection.

'Yes, she's awake,' Drew said. 'She's been sitting up most of the day. She began to make a noticeable improvement when we got your telegram announcing the date you'd be back.'

He opened the door. Jo was in the midst of conversation with Mrs Grimaldi, who was seated at the bedside. The tenement room was steaming; a late summer heat wave had set in. The bedlam of Bayard Street drifted up to the open window.

Will found himself overwhelmed with emotion at the sight of the girl propped against pillows at the head of the cot. 'This is no place for me,' Mrs Grimaldi said. 'No place for you, either, *dottore*.' She took hold of Drew's arm, pulled him into the hall, and shut the door.

Will moved to the box on which Mrs Grimaldi had been seated, bringing it closer to the bed. Jo fussed with her hair:

'I must look frightful.'

He shook her hand. 'You look grand, Jo.'

'How fine you make that name sound.'

'It's because I finally discovered what it means.' He leaned forward and kissed her, tasting the sweet warmth of her breath. 'And how much it means to me.'

Her cheeks turned pink. Bewildered, he drew back: 'What did I do?'

'Nothing. It's just that – all at once I remembered who took out the bullet. I'm not exactly a prude. But I'm embarrassed by the fact that I no longer have any secrets.'

'You're wrong, Miss Hastings. There's one.'

'What?'

'The answer to a question.'

'What is it?'

'Before I tell you, I want you to know I'll be coming back to the Bend next summer. I want to take Dr Clem's place.'

Her eyes shone. 'That's what Drew said.'

'Did he? Well, then, I think you know the question. Will you marry me?' Nervous all of a sudden, he didn't give her time to answer: 'If you're wondering about the girl in Newport, that's finished.'

She flung her arms round his neck and hugged him.

He slipped his arms round her waist and held her tightly. When she gasped, he knew he'd squeezed too hard. Red-faced, he muttered an apology, then said:

'I hope I didn't put too much pressure on the sutures.' He reached for the sheet covering her. 'Better let me have a look.'

She slapped his hand lightly. 'Drew can take care of it. It doesn't seem right for a girl to have her intended poking and peering at her. That should wait until after the wedding, at least,' she finished with a teasing look.

'You mean you will marry me?'

'Oh, Will – don't you know the answer? I decided a long time ago that you and I would be married. It was just a matter of making it all work out. Didn't Drew tell you?'

'Were you always sure it would?'

'Not always. But I am now. I'll help you with your work, and we'll raise fine children named Kent and have a wonderful life together.'

They whispered and kissed and soon fell to discussing the details of a marriage. Jo's eyes softened, focusing on some remote but pleasing vista in the future. 'Where shall we go on a wedding trip?'

The question jolted him into remembering his step-brother. They had a lot to talk about, and some of it wouldn't be easy.

'What about San Francisco?'

'Oh, yes! I've always wanted to visit the West.' But a moment later she wondered if it was a good idea; at the mention of San Francisco, Will's face had grown troubled. She deliberately changed the subject:

'Were you in Boston these past few days?'

He nodded, his mind elsewhere.

'And how is your family?'

She had his attention again. 'I'm worried about my father. He isn't in good health. He refuses to admit it, though. When I was home, I tried to ask some very general questions about the way he's been feeling. He practically bit my head off while assuring me he was feeling splendid. I don't believe it, but I don't know what to do. He won't let me examine him, and my stepmother can't get him to a doctor. I will say he's been in somewhat better spirits since we patched up our differences. But he's still fretting about my sister. So am I. Eleanor's not as bitter as she was right after Johnstown, and she's decided to go back to work, but there's still something wrong. I know her. Even though she's a good actress, I can recognize the signs—'

He shook his head, and spoke his deepest concern:

'I sometimes wonder if she'll ever be happy again.'

CHAPTER XVII

Someone Waiting

After the curtain came down, Eleanor took off her makeup, put on her street clothes, and returned to the stage to wait another thirty minutes. Every night at the same time, a carriage called for her at the actors' entrance on Sixth Street. The carriage returned her to the theatrical boarding house where she'd rented rooms for the season. She could have left with the rest of the company, of course. For the first couple of weeks, she had. But certain experiences outside the stage door had caused her to resort to this later departure, which by now had become a comfortable ritual.

She didn't mind the wait. In fact she enjoyed spending a few minutes alone on the stage when it was empty and lit only by two dim incandescent work lights.

She liked to pause and touch the stacked flats which only a little earlier had been standing behind the footlights in gaudy representation of a railroad passenger car. The play being presented from the twenty-fifth to the thirtieth of November was *The Tourists in a Pullman Car*. It was a bit of comedic fluff, but audiences liked it. Eleanor played a major role, but her mind was really on the play which the company would open on the second of December – Sheridan's *The Rivals*. Joe Jefferson was producing as well as starring in it. The cast included bright and pretty Viola Allen, whom Eleanor had known at Daly's, and of course the owner-impresario of Arch Street, Louisa Drew.

Of Mrs Drew's many famous stage personations, Mrs Malaprop in the Sheridan comedy was perhaps the greatest. At seventy, Louisa was as energetic and funny in the part as she'd ever been. Together, she and Jefferson had made *The Rivals* an institution in the American theatre. Whenever the two of them revived the play, sold out houses were a certainty. Eleanor was looking forward to playing Julia Melville in the new production.

Pacing the stage slowly, she gazed past the footlights to the parquet, with the parquet circle above it, then the regular balcony and, highest of all, the family circle. White and gold trim throughout the theatre complemented the bright red plush of its seats. A magnificent domed ceiling decorated with floral paintings arched over the whole; in the centre hung a great crystal chandelier, barely visible in the darkness. The Drews had completely remodelled the play-house in the early 1850s, and audiences liked the result. The seating was comfortable and the sight lines superb.

Eleanor was very glad she'd chosen to make her return to work here. Almost without exception, a new show was mounted every seven days. The demanding production schedule forced her to concentrate on the external world, and helped keep her mind off the past.

The return had been hard in many respects, but she'd known it would be. Most difficult, now that she was no longer a married woman, was the presence of men in her life – including those she sought to avoid by her delayed departure from the theatre.

Well, she supposed she couldn't ask for all her problems to be solved. Life didn't work that way. On balance, the year in Philadelphia promised to be a fine one. She loved the companionship of her fellow actors, and especially that of Louisa Drew. Yesterday, for example, Eleanor would have been alone on Thanksgiving Day, had not Louisa invited her to dinner.

The Drew residence had been noisy and festive. The oldest of Louisa's four children, Georgianna – a superb player of comedy, just like her mother and late father – had been in town for twenty-four hours. With her was her husband, the handsome and flamboyant Maurice Barrymore, and their three charming, extroverted children. Lionel was eleven or twelve, Ethel ten, and already a beauty. John, the one who most strongly resembled his handsome father, was seven or eight.

Georgie and Maurice were currently members of the stock company of Countess Helena Modjeska. The Polish-born beauty, a former star of Warsaw's Imperial Theatre, was enjoying one of her most successful seasons. Consequently the Barrymores were too.

That success had been quite apparent all day long. Maurice had been merry and flirtatious – although he did drink a little too heavily. As the mince pie was being passed, he'd tipsily informed Eleanor that the name with which he'd started life in India was Herbert Blythe – and since he was already married under the name Barrymore, would she slip away and become Mrs Blythe?

He kissed her hand as he said it, and his own wife laughed. Blythe or Barrymore, he was devilishly handsome, Eleanor thought. So handsome that she certainly would have looked twice at him if he'd been single, and she had been interested in men.

But of course that part of her life was over. One failure as a woman was enough. The moment his lips touched her hand, she froze inside. In the limbo of her mind, huge and forbidding, was the door. It was the one phantom she could not banish.

2

A little of the sorrow about Leo was passing. She could reflect more objectively upon the past. In the hours she spent alone at the boarding house, she occasionally turned from studying her next role to thoughts of other aspects of her life. During those hours she had come to a decision. She had decided that of necessity, her only interest for the rest of her life would be her career. Such a future might not be a very satisfying one. But it was sensible in light of the secret she carried, and the misery it had brought. She would never love another man, only to hurt him as she had hurt Leo.

That was the safest way. And yet, a part of her – shamefully disloyal to Leo's memory – occasionally longed to discover someone else with whose help she *could* open the door, share her secret, and thereby begin to overcome its crippling power.

She wasn't totally unresponsive to men. During Thanksgiving dinner, for example, she'd found herself quite taken with Maurice Barrymore's handsome face, flirtatious banter, and occasional warm glances – until that moment when he'd kissed her hand. So she knew that her wish was an impossible one. To pretend otherwise was cruel self-deception—

Her reverie was interrupted by the distant rattle of a cleaning pail. Through a curtained doorway in the lowest tier of boxes, she saw the glow of a cleaning woman's lamp. Had a half hour passed yet? She didn't think so. But she could walk to the stage entrance and ask Charlie, the elderly doorkeeper, what time it—

'Eleanor?'

The voice made her start. It came from behind some flats stacked at stage right. Hand to her breast, she turned as the speaker appeared. It was Louisa Drew.

'Louisa,' she said, letting out a breath. 'I didn't hear you coming—'

Mrs Drew walked into the dim light at centre stage. Smiling, she said, 'I hope you were busy thinking of Mr Sheridan's dialogue.'

Eleanor laughed. 'I'm sorry to say I wasn't. But I promise to study that new business for Julia's curtain speech before I go to bed tonight. I marked it all down during rehearsal. Half an hour in front of a mirror will smooth out any rough spots.'

'Good,' Louisa said. 'Joe and I have toured in that play so long, we tend to forget that last year's staging can always be improved.'

Louisa Drew was a small, queenly woman with a sizable bosom, a prominent nose, and large blue eyes. When viewed from certain angles, those eyes showed a decided bulge. Louisa's son, young John – one of Daly's stars, though Daly disliked the term – laughingly

909

maintained that without 'the Drew pop-eyes,' the family would never have produced so many performers who were successful at comedy.

Eleanor's employer had been born of theatrical parents in Britain in 1820. As far as Louisa knew, her actress mother had first put her on the stage when she was around a year old. As a young woman, she'd married the Irish comedian, John Drew, and together they had managed the Arch Street Theatre until 1862, when John died. Immediately, those in the profession had predicted either a speedy sale or a speedy failure of the playhouse. Instead, Louisa set to work to build a strong company, and had turned the theatre into one of the most profitable in America. By herself, she was far more successful than she'd been while dividing responsibility with her husband. Even such formidable theatrical figures as Daly and the Wallacks acknowledged her to be the country's foremost producing manager.

Louisa cleared her throat. 'I did have one observation I wanted to make before you left. You were a few seconds late with your third entrance this evening.' The criticism was delivered in a straightforward way, without rancour. Mrs Drew wanted every aspect of her productions to be perfect. No one was above criticism; not Jefferson, and certainly not she herself.

'You're quite right,' Eleanor admitted. 'My timing was off, and it had a strong effect on the whole scene. We got much less laughter than we usually do. I'm sorry about the whole thing.'

'I know there are extenuating circumstances. The callboy said you slipped and almost turned your ankle just before making the entrance.'

'I did. But that isn't an excuse.'

Louisa patted her arm. 'When I saw Dan Prince at the Wallack benefit last year, he told me he'd once predicted a fine future for you. I told him I agreed with his prediction. Besides being extremely talented, you're thoroughly professional.'

Eleanor smiled. But hearing the name Dan Prince tinged her thoughts with sadness. Prince had been the featured player in the first company with which she'd toured, the Tom show she and Leo had joined together. Prince was a superb actor. But because of his drinking he was no longer able to get any roles except walk-ons.

How different everything had been just a little more than ten years ago! She and Leo had been eager young actors, and Prince had stil been able to give a creditable performance. Now Prince's career was in ruins, and Leo—

Leo—

She bowed her head. Again Louisa touched her arm. 'What's wrong, my dear?'

'Oh – the usual. Memories. Leo would have loved working here this season. We had such a wonderful time when we were here before. He had such a grand future—'

'Leo was a fine man,' Louisa agreed. 'And a generous one. He always said that of the two Goldmans, you were the one with the first-rank talent.'

'Oh, no, Louisa—'

'It's true, my dear. He told me that time and again. One of the qualities that made Leo such a thorough professional was a grasp of his own limitations. He used to watch you rehearsing and whisper to me – in delight – that you had no limitations at all. You could play any role. Go as far in this queer business as you wished. Climb up to the pineapple of success, as Mrs Malaprop would say.'

And that's all I have left – the prospect of reaching the pineapple of success, she thought. *I wish it was enough.*

But it wasn't. In spite of her decision, there was one role she could never play, and it was the role she sometimes longed to play most of all. The role of a woman who felt and responded as other women did—

Softly, Louisa said, 'I believe I heard the hack arrive.'

'Did you?' Eleanor shook her head. 'I was wool-gathering again. It's getting to be a bad habit.'

'But understandable,' the older woman replied in a sympathetic tone.

The two women walked toward the stage door. When they'd gone half a dozen steps, Louisa asked:

'You leave at this time every evening, don't you?'

She answered carefully: 'I prefer to let the crowds clear away. I dislike fighting my way through a lot of stagestruck people. I know they pay my salary, but I'm just not up to being courteous to them when I'm tired.'

They had reached the exit. Louisa was silhouetted against the shaded incadescent lamp on the door-keeper's desk six feet away. Eleanor couldn't see her face, but her voice was kind:

'I understand. Quite a few of the men in those crowds are waiting for you – as I think you know. Given your good looks and the striking impression you create on stage, that's to be understood. It's one reason I've ordered Charlie – ' A nod toward the elderly man behind the desk. ' – never to admit strangers to your dressing room. I appreciate that you aren't prepared for attention from gentlemen, and may not be prepared for months or possibly years.'

I'll never be prepared, she thought. But all she said was:

'That's very considerate, Louisa. I must get my wrap. Are you leaving now?'

'No, I have to stay and total the receipts for this production. I'll be done in an hour. Charlie will keep me company.'

'All right. Good night.'

'Good night, Eleanor,' Louisa Drew murmured.

Only when Eleanor turned away did the older woman premit herself a sorrowful shake of her head.

Eleanor walked to her dressing room for her hat, coat, and gloves, then returned to the stage entrance. She said goodnight to Charlie and stepped out into the frosty November darkness.

The same hack driver called for her every night. She was getting used to his silhouette on the driver's seat, his generally grumpy mood, and the ripe smell of his swaybacked mare. The horse stood motionless now, head down and steam pluming from her nostrils.

A chilly kind of light fell from the street lamps along Sixth Street. There was no one waiting near the stage door. Eleanor had found that men would seldom linger for more than ten or fifteen minutes after the rest of the cast had left.

Some of the men who waited for her were wealthy; some were socially prominent. Many were both. Often one of them would send his card in, or hand Charlie a bouquet for delivery to her dressing room. Many young actresses loved the ritual of stage door courtship, knowing where it could lead if a girl was sufficiently careful about the man she chose to favour. Not a few highly profitable marriages had been made on the doorsteps of theatres. It was a fact of life in the profession, but one of which she wanted no part—

'Mrs Goldman?'

For the second time tonight, a voice from darkness startled her. The voice came from her left. Vaguely alarmed, she wondered about the stranger's identity. She was billed at Arch Street under her maiden name.

'I didn't mean to frighten you, Mrs Goldman.'

Now she recognized the voice. She didn't believe her ears.

The man had been leaning against the wall, hidden by shadows. He stepped forward into the light. He was bundled in a fur-collared overcoat; and hatless, so she was able to confirm her identification. She saw the curly hair; the thick, dark brows; the irregular teeth revealed by that smile she'd found so infectious—

'Oh my God,' she said in wonderment and dismay. 'It is you, Mr Martin.'

CHAPTER XVIII

The Secret

'Forgive me for startling you – ' Rafe Martin began. Still astonished, she interrupted:

'Where did you come from?'

'Altoona. I've been working there ever since I got out of the hospital.'

'*Hospital?*'

'That's right. After we saw each other last, I went back to work searching for flood survivors. It was my bad luck to go into one house while a looter was at work. I started to collar him and he took a shot at me. Luckily the wound wasn't a fatal one. But it took me a good ten weeks to get back on my feet completely.'

Her heart was beating so fast, it actually seemed to hurt. A voice within her cried, *He knows what happened to you*! Her shame grew worse by the moment. She had to say something. She blurted the first thought that came to mind:

'I thought you were dead—'

He grinned. 'Glad I'm not. Otherwise I'd have missed this chance to see you. Yesterday I happened to pick up a Philadelphia paper. I noticed the advertisement for the play, saw your name in the cast and caught a train. I was up in the family circle tonight. Out here, I outlasted three much more prosperous-looking gentlemen. I'm sure they thought I was waiting for someone else. I'm not dressed well enough to present myself to the prettiest woman in the company.'

Conflicting emotions raged through Eleanor then. She was immensely happy to see Martin, but in conflict with her pleasure was a frantic compulsion to break away; flee from him, and from the memory of what she'd confessed in that moment of hysteria.

She called on her acting ability to put a chill into her voice:

'I'm glad to know you're alive and well. And I'm very flattered that you came all the way from Altoona to watch the play.'

'Not the play, Mrs Goldman. You.'

'Yes. Well – I must go. I'm late for an engagement.'

'Can't you break it? I'd like to buy you supper.'

'No, that isn't possible.'

'You're dining with someone else?'

'No, but—'

Her shame destroyed the impression of cool reserve she wanted to create. Unexpectedly on the verge of tears, she found her voice breaking:

'Please leave me alone, Mr Martin.'

She hurried toward the hack. He came after her and caught her arm. The hack driver leaned down to ask if she needed help. She shook her head, confused, frightened, all at once unable to control her emotions.

She moved a few paces down the sidewalk so the driver couldn't eavesdrop. Casting a long shadow, Martin followed.

'I don't mean to intrude on your mourning,' he said.

915

'But you made a great impression on me in Johnstown. A great impression—'

She understood what he was saying behind the screen of polite language. Her cheeks grew warm again. He went on:

'If you can't see me this evening, tell me how soon you can and I'll come back. When I want something, I'm a very persistent fellow.'

'Mr Martin, you must understand my situation. I'm a widow—'

'I respect that. I'm only saying that after a suitable time, I'd like to call on—'

'It's *impossible*!'

'Why?'

'I – I can't tell you. And you mustn't ask.'

'If it's because you're embarrassed about what you admitted to me – quite by accident, I think – you should know it makes absolutely no difference – no, please. Let me finish. Flat on my back after they yanked that bullet out me, I had a lot of time to think. I kept recalling what you said that night, and I decided that it must be a cross you'd carried all your life. For one moment in Johnstown, the cross was too heavy. Now if you don't like me or want any part of me, now or ever, so be it. But if the reason you refuse to see me is that cross, I'm telling you it makes no difference.'

His craggy face lit with that brilliant smile. 'You'll have to forgive me for being so forward, Mrs Goldman. I probably ought to be horsewhipped for speaking so soon after your husband's death. But I fell in love with you the minute I saw you in Johnstown. The first time we spoke, I knew you were the only woman I wanted. The only one I ever would want. I have very little money, poor prospects – not much to offer except my feeling for you and a conviction that I don't dare waste time. Not all that much of it is given to us in this life. Your poor husband is proof of that.'

He drew a breath. 'Now may I take you to supper?'

Fear surged within her. She wanted to believe his assurances. She couldn't.

'No, Mr Martin, I don't think—'

'It doesn't *matter*,' he broke in gently. 'What happened is long in the past. But if it's still a burden, think of this. Two can carry a cross more easily than one.'

'This – this is absolutely insane—'

In a querulous voice, the hack driver called, 'Getting kind of late, ma'am. I've got a long drive to my place in Chester.'

Martin leaned down to her; whispered, 'Just supper. From there on we'll trust to luck.'

She formed the word *no*. But she couldn't utter it. Five seconds went by. Five more—

'Mrs Goldman?'

Then, incredibly, something loosened within her; loosened, broke free, and was swept away. She would always feel the shame. Yet its power suddenly seemed less potent, simply because the secret was no longer hers alone.

He didn't scorn her. He wanted her exactly as she was—

She was sure her face was red. She certainly felt foolish, surrendering to hope so quickly and eagerly. But she'd lived too long with grief. It was time that a little happiness – or at least a little hope – came her way—

'All right, Mr Martin.'

'You mean we'll go?'

'Yes. The truth is, I don't have an engagement, and I'm famished. I never eat dinner before a performance.'

Grinning, Martin sprang to the hack door. He handed it open and stood aside:

'After you.'

She bent to enter the hack, then paused to look at

917

him, 'Did you really expect I'd say yes to this kind of wild proposal?'

'Well, I had hopes. I told you I'm persistent. And while I'm not much for the formal ways of churches, I don't believe our lives are ruled purely by chance. After I survived that bullet in Johnstown, I figured I must have been spared for a reason. Let's trust to luck, Mrs Goldman. Maybe we'll find out the nature of that reason.'

She laughed.

'You are a very forward man.'

'That too. Want to get inside so the poor fellow on top can find us a restaurant and get on home to Chester?'

2

At the end of the Arch Street season, one week before Will's wedding in Hartford, Eleanor Kent Goldman and Cornelius Raphael Martin were married in a small family ceremony in the house on Beacon Street.

In private, Gideon told his daughter he was pleased with the match. He found Martin a smart, strong-minded fellow, with the kind of independence on which Gideon prided himself and admired in others. He wasn't the least put off by the fact that his daughter had fallen in love with a telegrapher:

'He's got more character and substance than hundreds with fancier occupations.'

'I agree,' she beamed, kissing her father's cheek. His expression grew sober:

'I'm also happy for another reason, Eleanor. You seem to be putting the past behind you successfully.'

He took her slight shrug and her small, quick smile as an assent. What she was thinking was far less positive.

Eleanor loved Rafe. She wanted to marry him. But she was terrified of failing again. How was it possible for a human being to be attracted and repelled by something at the same time?

But the attraction was stronger, and so they said their vows, and kissed, and outwardly no one suspected a thing – except perhaps the new bridegroom. Eleanor's anxiety persisted up to the very moment he placed the plain ring on her left hand. And the instant he did, anxiety became fear.

3

Like many American newlyweds, they wanted to see the Niagara Falls, which Eleanor had never visited even though she had played Buffalo several times. They didn't plan to reach their destination the first night, however. One of Gideon's carriages spirited them southward out of Boston, to a small country inn where they would spend the night. In the morning, the carriage would call for them and deliver them to a suburban rail station where they could catch a train for Albany.

The inn was small, quiet, and comfortable. There were only six rooms on the second floor. The largest had been reserved for the honeymooning couple. Rafe and Eleanor found a splendid old canopied bed, a fieldstone hearth with apple wood logs burning – the spring evening was cool – and a repast of champagne, caviar, cold salmon with capers, and other delicacies spread on big silver trays; an amenity arranged by the Kent family, they were sure. The innkeeper, cordial enough, didn't seem the sort to appreciate or regularly serve caviar.

The day, for all its joy, had been long and tiring.

Eleanor's mental state wasn't helped by her exhaustion. She tried to nibble a bit of dry toast with caviar and a dusting of golden egg yolk spooned over it, but she couldn't get it down. Rafe popped the cork of one of the three champagne bottles crowded into a bucket full of ice; the cork went ricocheting around the walls and the beamed ceiling like an oversized bullet. She ducked as it missed her and landed at his feet. With the foaming bottle wrapped in a white towel, he stood studying her. His grin faded.

'Not feeling like any of this, are you?'

'Rafe—'

'Not feeling like anything but rest.'

He put the bottle back in the bucket and bent to kiss her forehead. 'That's perfectly all right. Everything in its own time. We'll just curl up and sleep. I'm damn near worn out myself.'

His kindness touched her; prodded her to do what she knew she must, though she feared it.

'No,' she said softly, opening her lips a little as she kissed. 'We'll have a proper honeymoon. Just give me a few minutes.'

'Eleanor, believe me – you needn't flog yourself. I know how hard this is for you.' They had several times discussed the problems in her relationship with Leo. Yet all that candour and all his reassurances did nothing to slow her heartbeat or banish the dry, sour feel of her mouth. She hated herself; hated what she was. She hated the fact that he knew – and was incapable of believing his assurance that it didn't matter. Why had she consented to marry him? *Why?*

Panicked, she fled to the small dressing room. There, alone behind the closed door, she tried to compose herself. She unpinned her hair and changed from her travelling outfit to the fine Chantilly bed gown and matching robe Julia had given her. She wanted to be a good wife, but she'd wanted that with Leo, too, and she'd failed. Brushing her hair over and over, she told herself she would fail again tonight.

She delayed for twenty minutes; thirty. Then conscience temporarily won out over fear. She opened the door and walked back to the bedroom as if marching to her own execution.

Rafe had donned a smoking jacket of fine dark green crushed velvet. He looked monumentally uncomfortable in such finery. Barefoot, he sat with one ankle resting atop another on a hassock. He twirled a champagne glass nervously in his right hand. He, extinguished the lamps; the only light came from the dancing flames.

'My,' he breathed. 'Don't you look ravishing, Mrs Martin.'

She tried to smile. 'I am Mrs Martin, aren't I?'

'You certainly are – and I couldn't be happier.'

'But I'm afraid I'll never make a perfect wife.'

'Only fools ask for perfection in themselves or others.'

'Oh, Rafe – you are an incredibly kind man.'

'The hell I am,' he replied with that smile that charmed her so. 'I'm no saint. I'm just like those scientific fellows I've read about. The ones who go digging for old art treasures—'

'What on earth are you talking about?' she asked, diverted. He set his glass aside and walked to her.

'One of those fellows who digs around old Arabian ruins and turns up a beautiful, old lamp worth millions. You don't find them throwing away such a treasure just because it has a few nicks and dents.' He kissed the tip of her nose. 'We all have those, my love. Every man and woman God ever made.'

His voice was so gentle and reassuring, she almost forgot to be frightened. He leaned down and said, 'I know what's terrifying you. It needn't. We'll just sleep, that will be fine tonight – or any other night until you say otherwise. We're going to heal you, Eleanor—'

'*No!*' she cried softly, one arm flung round his neck. She brought her mouth up against his, and lost herself in the kiss and the embrace that accompanied it.

He kissed and caressed her in a tender way. It was her urging that took them to the bed. Yet as she slipped out of her robe and gown, she felt the tension tightening her loins, then her whole body.

He felt it too. His caresses stopped. Their naked bodies etched by the flickering fire, they sat on the edge on the bed with their hips and shoulders touching. He poured a glass of champagne and handed it to her.

'Drink a little of this. It might help.'

'Not as much as your kindness,' she murmured, bending to sip and wondering again whether she would fail him.

He put his left arm round her shoulder in a companionable way; he was, at that moment, as much her friend as her would-be lover. She finished the champagne and felt the tension lessen just a little. When he resumed his stroking and kissing, it was very slow; very gentle. He touched each part of her only after long minutes of careful preparation. Finally he lowered his body over hers – and the tension seized her again. Gazing down with concern and love, he quickly placed his right palm against her cheek:

'Don't worry, don't worry – I'll stop the moment you say. I don't want to hurt you.'

'You won't, darling,' she lied, drawing him to her. She couldn't help a pained cry as he entered.

She closed her eyes, cursing herself. He remained absolutely motionless. Moments passed. Then:

'Eleanor?'

Slowly the tension left her face. He was where he belonged – and she was enduring it. The first step had been taken.

She saw the imaginary door. One of its panels displayed a great raw opening, as if it had been chopped with an axe. She realized what the image meant. The door was breached; no longer capable of containing secrets—

'Yes,' she answered very softly. 'I'm all right. Love me Rafe. Please do—'

And he did, with consuming passion and tenderness. It hurt her a little, and he knew it, so he was careful and deliberate until the end when, with wondrous realization overcoming her disbelief, she was aware of an absence of pain, and next, just a faint stir of pleasure – gone so quickly she might have thought it hadn't happened at all.

But it had. *It had*.

Afterward, reliving the moment as she lay drowsing beside him, she was filled with a conviction that she might have escaped her yesterdays at long last. It might be that she could look forward to a chance of becoming a whole woman.

He alone made it possible because he loved her, and because he *knew* and said it didn't matter. Two could indeed bear a cross more easily than one.

Perhaps, she thought as his arm cradled her against his side, perhaps that was the secret of the survival of the Kents – and of all families that managed to withstand living in a world that was no better than its inhabitants: troubled, capricious, filled with error and contradiction.

Four hands lifting made a burden light. And the strength of those hands was love. She held that thought as she reached down to close her hand on his—

And cried.

She cried as she hadn't for months; perhaps years.

Anxious, he questioned her. She reassured him that it was only happiness that made her weep. Happiness, and freedom, and the final destruction of a door.

CHAPTER XIX

The Broken Promise

From Sacramento, Will telegraphed ahead to say that he and his new wife would be arriving via Pullman Palace Car. A note from Carter was waiting when they checked into an elegant suite at the Hope House, where they would be spending two weeks as guests of the owner. Carter's note said he'd meet them for luncheon next day, in the Grill Room of the Palace Hotel on Market Street.

Will was nervous about the coming encounter with his stepbrother, though he tried not to show it. He and Jo arrived at the Palace half an hour early and were already seated at a choice table in the mirror-paneled Grill Room when Carter walked in. Jo recognized him immediately from Will's descriptions.

Carter had stopped at the head waiter's podium and was chatting with two of the formally attired members of the staff. He whispered something – a joke, to judge from his smirk – and then all three men laughed unroariously.

He spied Will and Jo; grinned and waved. Will had to admit his stepbrother looked splendid. He was wearing a dark grey hopsack suit, obviously expensive, and a contrasting emerald-coloured waistcoat. He had a gold-headed stick tucked under his left arm. A heavy ring with a large white stone flashed on his right hand as he strolled toward them. Will was wearing a new suit and cravat, but he felt shabby by comparison.

Carter paused and bent over the gem-crusted hand of a double-chinned dowager, stopped again to exchange pleasantries with a couple of burly men who appeared to be both very wealthy and very coarse. He visited four other tables after that. There were no important-looking people in the room whom he didn't know. As for the rest, he ignored them.

When he reached Will and Jo, Carter grinned and said, 'Sorry to be late. Boss Buckley is encountering some trouble from a crowd of self-appointed reformers. It's taking extra effort to keep the faithful in line – so this is Jo!'

The transition from one thought to another was almost as swift and smooth as his move round the table. He lifted Jo out of her chair; clasped her in a brotherly hug. She blushed. Will saw that she enjoyed being the centre of attention – as did Carter.

'Marriage seems to be agreeing with you,' Carter said when he'd taken a chair. 'And it's Doctor Kent now, isn't it?'

'That's right. I managed to squeak through Harvard.'

Proudly, Jo said to Carter, 'He won't boast, but I will. He didn't squeak through. He was fifth from the top of his class.'

'Congratulations!' Carter exclaimed, beaming. 'Now all you have to do is sit back, peer at a few sore throats, and watch the gold roll in, eh?'

'Not quite,' Will answered with a guarded look. Even though his plans had been firm for more than a year, he hadn't shared them with his stepbrother. Each time he'd written to him, he'd avoided any mention of Jo's background and the practice waiting for him in the Bend. Even now, he was apprehensive about raising the subject of Drew and the Bend. But he wouldn't have a clear conscience until he did.

It had to be done privately, though. Jo knew nothing about the promise Carter had extracted during that walk on the Common so long ago.

A waiter offered elaborately printed menus. 'Thanks, Maurice,' Carter said without so much as a glance at the man. 'There ought to be something here to please you two. Kirkpatrick, the food manager, tries to satisfy everybody from the gourmand to the silver millionaire who ate his own shoe leather while he was making his pile. What looks good? Grizzly steak? Local venison? I'm told the grilled sand dabs are fine – I've never had them—'

'So much to choose from!' Jo said with an appreciative sigh. Will closed his menu and smiled at his stepbrother:

'Looks like your work's agreeing with you, too.'

'Absolutely. I love politics, and I love San Francisco. My old Harvard chum Willie Hearst is here. He publishes a morning paper.'

'Oh, yes, Hearst is very well known in the East,' Jo told him.

'Especially in the Kent household,' Will said. 'Papa keeps track of all the stunts he pulls. Like sending a couple up in a balloon to be married, or having a man jump off a ferryboat to see how long it takes the crew to rescue a passenger who falls overboard. He disapproves of things like that. He's getting pretty conservative in some ways. On the other hand, I think he's taken with the idea of hiring women to write about sensational subjects. What do they call reporters like that?'

'Sob sisters.'

Carter removed the wrapping from a long green cigar. He clipped one end of the cigar with small gold scissors. He rolled the cigar between his fingers, then clenched it between his teeth. 'Willie's sob sister is one of the best. Her name's Winifred Sweet, but she uses the byline Annie Laurie. She was a chorus girl whose show got stranded here. Hearst hired her – thanks, Maurice,' he said again as a flaring match appeared from over his right shoulder.

He bent to the match. When the cigar was lit Maurice

blew the match out and stepped back like a soldier at attention. Carter continued:

'Willie comes in for a lot of criticism because of his stunts. On the other hand, he makes no secret of the reason for them. The news is often hellishly dull. And there's one other problem with it. Rival papers can print it too. But manufactured material is exclusive. That's why Willie likes it. Right now, for instance, he and Annie are trying to figure out how a woman can get committed to the Home for Inebriates. Willie thinks there's a fine exposé lurking there.'

'You must see a lot of him,' Will said.

Carter's smile and nod said that was correct. 'Willie and I have a lot in common. Neither one of us could get through Harvard. He played one prank too many and they booted him out at the end of his junior year. He has a fine house over in Sausalito, and he found me one nearby. He keeps a jolly young lady named Tessie Powers who – oh, forgive me, Jo,' he said, pretending to be conscience-stricken. 'Shouldn't be saying such things in front of husband and wife.'

Will gazed at his stepbrother. 'Sounds like you really admire Hearst.'

'I do. He already influences public opinion and government policy in this part of California, and he thinks he can do it nationally, too. He's anxious to acquire a paper in New York. There's no limit to his ambition.' Carter puffed his cigar a moment. 'That's one of the ways we're alike. Shall we order?'

Carter opened his menu. For a moment he seemed a total stranger. In a sense he was. He was living in high style while working as a trusted aide of the city's Democratic boss – a man Gideon claimed was wholly corrupt. The paths and viewpoints of the stepbrothers had obviously diverged without either of them being fully aware of the changes brought about by time, circumstances, and differences in character.

Still, a bond remained. The bond of affection Will felt for the Carter Kent of yesterday; the Carter who'd given him confidence when he had none, and even fought his battles until he was old enough and clever enough to fight them for himself.

Carter chose a slab of venison with a side dish of salad that incorporated a generous portion of California artichokes. Will and Jo took the waiter's suggestion and ordered a Grill Room speciality, Pacific coast oysters baked into a savoury pie with a crackling light brown crust. Carter insisted on selecting the wine. Pouilly Fuissé for them; an expensive claret for himself. He finished a whole bottle while they were each drinking half of theirs.

As the meal progressed, Will grew increasingly ill at ease. The cause was partly what remained to be said, partly some things he was noticing which he'd overlooked in the first flush of the reunion. As always, Carter smiled a lot. But it struck Will that much of his spontaneity was gone, and that when he did smile, very little humour showed in his eyes. His behaviour seemd studied, every detail pointed toward creating a carefully calculated impression.

After they'd eaten, Carter lit another cigar. 'Jo, perhaps you'd like to refresh yourself while Will and I stroll off some of this food.'

'Fine,' Jo agreed, starting to rise. Carter leaped to pull her chair out. She smiled in appreciation.

'We'll meet you on the promenade of the grand court,' he said. She nodded and left. He followed her with admiring eyes.

'I applaud your choice, Will. She's a charming girl. Very bright, too.'

'A trifle overawed by you, I'm afraid,' Will said, folding his napkin.

'I must say I was surprised when you wrote to tell me you'd dumped the other girl. The one with the

928

pedigree who was going to make Ward McAllister forget you were Gideon Kent's son—'

They started out of the Grill Room. Carter added, 'I assume the social standing of Jo's family is equally good.'

'They have no social standing. They're shopkeepers in Hartford, Connecticut.'

'Oh.'

For a moment Carter seemed intensely interested in the glowing end of his cigar. A passing woman distracted him.

'Althea! What a treat to run into you again.'

'It's been too long, my dear,' the woman said, her tone faintly reproving. She was an attractive woman, buxom, expensively dressed, and obviously older than Carter. He kissed the hand on which she wore a wedding ring. Then, as she moved on, he returned his attention to Will, and said in a low voice:

'That woman has the most incredible body I've ever seen – and vast experience in using it. Otherwise, she's a stupid creature. Bitchy temper, too. I overlook it because of her – ah – professional expertise.'

Will forced a smile, but it was uneasy: 'You make her sound like a – like a thing, not a person.'

Carter gave him a puzzled stare. 'She's a woman. She has servants to cook and keep her eighteen-room house. With those feminine functions taken care of, what else is she good for except lying flat on her back? I was employing her a couple of times a week till her husband got back from a European business trip. It was doubly pleasant to cuckold him because he's a republican.'

They left the restaurant and made their way to the marble-floored promenade. The promenade overlooked a large interior court protected from the weather by a glass dome. Hacks and private carriages came and went through an arched portal leading to the street. The place had a lush smell. Plants grew in tubs, and there were trellises heavy with tropical flowers. In the distance, a string ensemble played a frothy waltz.

Will said nothing. He was assimilating his step-brother's last remarks, and finding that he didn't like them. Carter's unfeeling cynicism angered him; hurt him, too, somehow. Of course his stepbrother was showing off a little. But it was sadly evident that he'd changed.

'You said Jo's family isn't socially prominent,' Carter resumed. 'If that's the case, I assume they're at least respectably wealthy. It won't hurt to have one fortune added to another.'

Will turned to face his stepbrother. 'I didn't marry her for money. She doesn't have any.'

'Contacts in Hartford, then?' Carter responded with another smile. 'That's it, isn't it? She has the sort of contacts that enable you to practise successfully right away.'

Slowly, Will rubbed a palm across his mouth. He didn't want to provoke an argument. And yet he couldn't remain silent.

'Carter,' he said softly, 'try to understand something. I didn't marry Jo to use her. I married her because I love her. She's the most important thing in my life now.'

It was Carter's turn to look sadly puzzled:

'Surely not, little brother. A man's ambition comes ahead of everything. Or should. That's a fundamental lesson I learned long ago. Beyond that, if you care too much for a woman, you'll find it will distract you from your ambition.'

A sour, quirky smile spoiled his good looks for a second. 'You'll also find you've been a fool. Women should never be worshipped, or trusted. Just used.'

Will drew a long breath. 'I don't agree.'

'I see.' Carter's repertoire of smiles was a large one;

this variation was icily dismissive. 'Well, it's not my affair any longer.'

'Yes it is.'

'What's that?'

'It is your affair.'

'How so?'

'I made you a promise once.'

Carter responded with a slow, thoughtful nod. 'That's right. A promise that you'd be somebody and make sure everybody knew it.'

He drew smoke from the cigar, turned away, and sat down in one of the deep upholstered chairs with which the promenade was furnished. He crossed his legs, gazed up at his stepbrother, and finished his thought:

'I've never forgotten. But I was beginning to think you had.'

2

'This is very difficult for me—' Will began.

'Don't feel that way, little brother. I suspected something was on your mind. Whatever you came to say, say it. Let's not spoil our reunion any longer than absolutely necessary.'

The bitter note was unmistakable. What hurts had Carter suffered in all those years since Will had last seen him? What wounds was he trying to cover with the scar tissue of cynicism, mockery, indifference?

Noting Will's hesitation, Carter continued:

'Perhaps I can make it easier. I gather from what you've said about Jo that you don't think as you did at the time I left Boston. You don't think it's important to be successful – or recognized as successful.'

'It isn't important to me.'

'Then we no longer think the same way.'

Sadness overwhelmed Will when he saw the contempt in Carter's eyes. A moment later, though, he found himself growing annoyed with his stepbrother.

'No,' he said, 'I don't believe we do.'

Carter studied him. 'What happened, may I ask?'

A truthful answer would have been, *I started listening to my conscience instead of you.* But he couldn't say that.

The string ensemble was playing 'Tales from the Vienna Woods.' Further down the promenade, a woman laughed. With a ring of hooves and a rattle of traces, a splendid victoria arrived in the court. He could only hear his stepbrother's voice prompting him:

'What happend, Will?'

'I went my own way; that's all. Circumstances change as you grow up. You encounter new people. New ways of looking at things—'

'Granted. But only a fool loses sight of his goal. On my first night in San Francisco, I wandered the street. I was sick, feeling low, and wondering how the hell I'd ever get anywhere in life. But I never forgot where I *wanted* to go. That night I met a man who put me to work in politics, greased me into the local Democratic machine, and made it possible for me to hobnob with Willie on an equal footing again. The point is this. A chance meeting opened a door I hadn't seen before. But if it hadn't been the right kind of door, I'd have stepped back. No one's committed to poverty or obscurity except by his own choice.'

'I recall some letters you wrote when times were hard. You sounded a lot less positive then.'

Anger flickered on Carter's face before he looked away.

'Anyway, I disagree with you,' Will went on. 'I know people who will struggle all their lives, but they'll never be able to escape poverty and obscurity.'

With a scornful shrug, Carter said, 'Who are you talking about? People in the slums?'

'Exactly. I'm going to practise in a slum, as a matter of fact. Possibly the worst slum in New York.'

3

So there it was. Out at last. Carter couldn't maintain his derisive smile. His stunned disbelief was too strong:

'For your own good, I refuse to take you seriously.'

'Ask Jo. It's her brother's practice that I'm joining.'

'Good God. I can't believe this. Not after the promise you made me.'

'Carter, please – understand. It was the wrong kind of promise. Wrong for me, anyway.'

He hated to say that. He saw the glacial look it brought to his stepbrother's face. 'You really have changed,' Carter said.

'We all do.'

'Not I!' Carter blustered, as if he weren't quite sure of that statement. He stabbed his smouldering cigar into a sand urn near his chair, then rose. 'I still want what I wanted the day I left Boston. To give orders instead of taking them. I've found the way. I've learned a lot in a year's time. I've learned how to buy votes, and when and how to force others to do what I want. I've watched Willie use a newspaper to turn the public against the Southern Pacific or any other person or institution he dislikes. I've taken every one of those lessons to heart – and a lot of others that might shock you. And I'll tell you this. I won't be buried in a political grave in this town. The reformers are yapping after Buckley like hunting dogs, but they won't catch me.'

With uneasy admiration, Will said, 'You have it all planned, eh?'

'Indeed I do, little brother. Obviously you don't.'

Will thought of his wife, and his voice grew stronger:

'To the contrary. I know how I'm going to spend my life. I'm afraid it's a much less impressive plan than yours.'

'I agree.' Then the mockery was quickly replaced by an intense concern: 'Will, you had every chance – chances I never had – and you've thrown them all away. The slums, for Christ's sake!' He shook his head, starting to pace. 'Who's responsible? Is it your wife's doing? Apparently she's not as bright as I first thought—'

Will stiffened.

'Carter, please don't say any more.'

He didn't seem to hear: 'I'm afraid something must have beclouded your mind—'

'*Carter.*'

'—When you decided she was the person you should marry. You were certainly wrong about – *ah*!'

Afterward, Will could recall little about the moment except his sudden surge of rage. He'd lunged out of his chair, run at his stepbrother, and driven a clumsy punch into the green waistcoat.

Carter's midsection was solid. But Will had taken him by surprise. After his outcry, he doubled, dropping his stick. It rolled on the marble, clattering as he staggered away.

He braced himself against a pillar to keep from falling. Heads turned. A hotel bellman rushed toward them. Carter's slashing left hand ordered him back. The bellman hesitated, then walked off.

Will was still trembling. 'You can say anything you want about me. But never say a single word against Jo. Never.'

Carter straightened, composing his face. He dusted his waistcoat; retrieved his stick. Only then did he speak:

'If it were anyone else but you, little brother, I'd

probably send a couple of rockrollers to break your head for what you just did. This meeting has been a terrible disappointment. I always thought you'd amount to something. Obviously someone's filled your head with that pious garbage the Kent family has been purveying for several generations.'

A word about your duties—

'Yes, that's partly it.'

'Well – ' The cynical smile crept back. ' – it's very nice stuff for newspaper editorials. Unfortunately it has damn little relevance in the real world. If you've swallowed it, I'm sorry for you.'

Silence for a moment.

'Carter—'

'What is it?' he said without looking up. His gaze was fixed on his right sleeve, which he was carefully brushing with his other hand.

'I was feeling apologetic in the Grill Room. I don't feel that way any longer. What you say is wrong. I don't know what's made you so hard—'

Carter raised his stick as if it were a pointer. 'Practical, my boy. Practical!'

'—but I think you should be on notice.'

'About what?'

'If you ever do go to Washington—'

'You can count on it.'

'—and if I have anything to say about the policies of the *Union*, you'd better not expect automatic support from me, or the family. America has enough exploiters and manipulators already. We don't need more. Especially not in the government.'

Carter snickered. 'My God, how naïve you are. What do you think a government is – a city government, a county government, any government – except a pack of manipulators and exploiters? The game is to get all you can from the trough while convincing the rest of the hogs to be high-minded instead of hungry.'

935

Disgusted, Will turned away. He saw Jo watching from the entrance of the promenade. How long had she been there? Had she seen him strike his stepbrother?

The sight of her eradicated his anger. A weary sorrow overcame him again. 'I think we'd better call a halt to this.'

'I agree.'

'Look, I'm sorry I hit you. If we can't be friends, at least we needn't be enemies.'

Carter's hostile expression softened slightly. 'That isn't how you sounded a minute ago. Obviously the past no longer means much to you.'

'It means a great deal. It always will. You helped me stand on my own feet. I couldn't have done it alone. I can't begin to repay that debt—'

'You could by amounting to something. By refusing to swallow all that rot about Kent family responsibility – Kent family idealism. It's bullshit, Will. Pure sentimental bullshit. I tell you again – it has no application to the real world.'

Will shook his head. 'I think it's the only thing that makes the real world bearable. And maybe a little better year by year.'

'You're wrong. Forget it, I tell you!'

'I can't.' He drew another breath. 'And if that's the price you put on friendship—'

'Yes?'

'The price is too high.'

With a grieving look at his stepbrother, Carter said, 'You poor damn fool.'

'I'm going to pretend I didn't hear that,' Will managed to say. With great effort, he held out his right hand. 'Friends anyway?'

Carter looked at him; seemed on the point of shaking hands but then used his stick to tap Will's outstretched palm.

'I'm afraid not, little brother. Friendly enemies is the best I can do. Goodbye.'

Will watched him go. In the court, Carter approached a liveried doorman, his old, charming smile in place. As Will walked down the promenade to rejoin Jo, he heard his stepbrother call out cheerily:

'Whistle up my rig, will you, Trevor? I'm late for a meeting of the county committee, and someone's got to tell the simpletons how to vote.'

4

With an anxious look on her face, Jo came rushing to meet him.

'I stayed away because I saw you and Carter quarrelling. What went wrong? You were looking forward to this reunion so much—'

'Not as much as I pretended. I'll try to explain what happened, but I'm not sure I can.'

How do you explain that to live with yourself, you had to break a promise?

'Will we see him again while we're here?'

'No.' He realized he was immensely relieved.

'But you always thought so much of him—'

'That was a long time ago. We all grow up.'

He flexed the fingers of his right hand. He would feel a lasting regret about hitting his stepbrother. But Carter had, after all, invited it with his churlish remarks about Jo.

Well, they had served warning on each other. If there was friction in the future, so be it. The Carter Kent of yesterday was not the Carter Kent of today and, sad though that was, Will would accept it.

Jo would make it much easier. Looking into her eyes with boundless affection, he leaned forward and scandalized two elderly ladies by kissing her on the mouth.

'We all grow up,' he said again. 'Thank God.'

The following weekend, William Randolph Hearst's yacht *Aquila* left San Francisco harbour and steamed south toward Senator Hearst's 48,000-acre Piedra Blanca ranch. The ranch was an old Spanish grant in San Luis Obispo county; it had been raw land when the Senator purchased it, but now there was a spacious ranch house on a slope above the sea, and even a sturdy wharf jutting into San Simeon Bay.

Since the run down the coast was just about two hundred miles, Willie frequently took excursion parties there for long weekends. It could not be said that his guests were his friends. He had few; Carter was one of the chosen. Mostly – as on this occasion – those travelling aboard the superbly appointed yacht were associates and employees from the paper.

They had weighed anchor at eight in the morning. As the yacht steamed south in the light Pacific chop, a splendid breakfast including broiled trout, chicken in wine, and rum omelettes was served to the ladies and gentlemen in the main saloon. Competitors, and even the Senator, often called the free-spending young publisher Wasteful Willie, but when it came to generosity to his employees, their permanent mistresses, or temporary female friends, no one minded that he was extravagant.

After consuming a third glass of champagne, Carter rose from the table. Willie had told him earlier that he wanted to speak privately. As they left the saloon, the waspish Mr Bierce was explaining his employer's theories of journalism to a reporter from Seattle:

' – you see, Templeton, the differences between your indifferently successful paper and ours is Mr Hearst's understanding that stupefying news events do not happen every day. Yet what we wish to publish – every day – is stupefying news. We therefore create it.'

The guest looked sceptical, while a pretty, genteel and well-dressed girl seated near Bierce watched admiringly. She and Willie exchanged glances as the young publisher went out with Carter. Willie had found Tessie Powers waiting tables in a Cambridge restaurant. He had kept her during his undergraduate days. Following his dismissal from Harvard, he had brought her West and installed her in his fine house on a Sausalito hillside.

On deck, Willie swung his walking stick in a relaxed way. He had a whole collection of them, including a trick one which whistled. Carter had adopted the fashion for himself. Two elegant young gentlemen, they strolled forward to *Aquila*'s bow. Willie looked little different than he had at Harvard. More prosperous, perhaps, but physically, he had hardly changed.

Carter felt nervous. What was this all about? The flawless morning, the spectacularly beautiful California coast slipping by, the sense of being surrounded by fine, influential friends – all these paled because he knew something was on Willie's mind. At last Willie said:

'I don't want to spoil the trip with an endless discussion of the city we left behind, so let's conclude our business now and enjoy ourselves.'

Frowning, Carter said, 'I didn't know we had business to conduct.'

'Well, ah—' That shy, nervous smile. 'I have some.' He looked closely at his companion. 'Because we're friends I must issue a warning to you. I'm going to get the Boss.'

Carter chuckled, although in a nervous way. 'That's hardly news. You've been after Buckley for years. I think he got that idea when you helped defeat the city charter revision he and that Republican, Bill Higgins cooked up.'

'It was a fraud,' Willie said, squinting at the ocean. 'It would have resulted in even stronger boss rule – why are you smiling?'

'Because sometimes, I'm damned if I can figure you out. Willie the millionaire – Willie the aristocrat – Willie the workingman's friend. It doesn't fit together.'

'No, it doesn't,' Willie acknowledged with a slight smile. 'I don't know where I came by that streak of democracy. Probably my father picked it up wandering around the desert searching for a mother lode. You don't meet princes or plutocrats in the diggings, and you soon come to appreciate how hard most men work for the little they get. But you're quite right, I do stand with the gripman.' He was referring to the mythical San Francisco cable car worker who set the standards for what the paper would publish, and how it would publish it. Carter had frequently heard the litany: 'If it wouldn't amaze the gripman, don't print it. If he wouldn't understand it, rewrite it. If it's against his interests, I'm against it too.'

'In any case,' Willie went on, 'I'm compelled to tell you that powerful forces are forming an alliance against the Boss. It isn't merely a newspaper crusade.'

'Yes, I've caught hints of that.'

Willie bent forward, a queer, stork-like figure in the splendid sunshine; he seemed to be peering at his friend to make certain he understood:

'Buckley's going down, Carter. The machine will fly apart. Don't get hit by the pieces.'

Carter took a deep breath. 'I appreciate the warning. And I won't. First and foremost, I look after Carter Kent.'

Willie coughed. 'I really am not comfortable in this role—'

Carter frowned. 'What role?'

940

'Middle man. I was – asked to approach you.'

'By whom?'

'Certain gentlemen who must as yet remain anonymous. Certain influential people organizing a reform coalition whose object would be Buckley's ouster.'

He understood then. 'You're talking about Democrats. Members of the Boss's own party.'

After some deliberation, Willie said, 'I won't deny that assertion. These gentlemen are wondering how badly you want to protect yourself from a debacle that will surely destroy a great many careers. Enough to cooperate, perhaps? Pass along information if it's ever requested?' Hastily he raised his hands. 'This is all theoretical, you must appeciate—'

Carter gazed at the sunlit water and the wild, lonely coast running into the south. This was something new; something disturbing, and not at all clear cut. Democrats were conspiring against Democrats. Willie was clearly interested in seeing Carter save himself, yet at the same time was uncomfortable over the treachery that would be involved.

He thought of the past. Of all the hard lessons he'd learned. Would he ignore those lessons now? When the question was framed that way, it took him only an instant to make his decision.

'I'd be happy to have an exploratory discussion with these gentlemen, Willie. At some safe, confidential location, naturally. I'm not saying I would cooperate. But I'll discuss it.'

Wih a relieved smile, Willie whacked his stick on the rail. 'Splendid. That's all I need to know. You have a promising future, and I hate to see it cut short, though I was hesitant to make the overture. You've served old Chris Buckley well up to now.'

'He's gotten value for what he's paid,' Carter said. 'He's old enough to know that on a sinking ship, one man doesn't ask another for permission to jump into the lifeboat.'

Willie murmured something that sounded like, 'Mmm,' and leaned his elbows on the rail, scanning the sea.

Astern, members of the cruise party were coming out of the saloon, laughing and talking loudly. Carter tried to subdue the remorse he felt about his decision. Buckley had befriended and trusted him, and now he was preparing to betray that trust if it became necessary to save his own hide.

Well, what of it? The lifeboat analogy was valid. Even if it did make him feel guilty.

He fought the guilt, and ironically, just as he was beginning to overcome it, Willie caused it to flood back by saying:

'A shame your stepbrother couldn't join us.'

'Oh – ' This shrug was far too studied, Willie noticed. ' – he preferred to stay and see the sights. Besides, wives are never comfortable on these litle trips.

'You've seen very little of your stepbrother.'

'That's true.' Anger welled up, but Carter forced a brittle smile. 'We don't have much in common anymore.'

'I think you told me just before he arrived that he was a doctor.'

'That's right.'

'Quite ambitious, too.'

Carter's face hardened. Eyes fixed on the immensity of the Pacific, he said, 'I was wrong about that.'

Then the past, and the ties of blood obliterated cynicism and tore the next words from him.

'My stepbrother is the decent one one in our family. I'm afraid I'll have to be content being the successful one.'

Willie turned his head sharply, and started to speak.

But he didn't know how to answer such a strange remark; one so filled with pain.

As was Carter Kent's face.

EPILOGUE

. . . And Make a Mark

A few days before Christmas that same year, Gideon was moved to compose a year-end editorial for the *Union*.

On the evening he went into his office at home to work, the house on Beacon Street was already festively decorated. The rooms were fragrant with the smell of pine boughs, candle wax, popping corn, and the spiced apples Julia was preparing in the kitchen. A special effort to give the house a holiday air had seemed desirable since all three of the younger Kents would be arriving by train to spend the week between Christmas and New Year's. Carter was coming all the way from the West Coast.

While Gideon located paper and a pen, he tried to banish thoughts of his failing health. Of late the pains in his chest had become more frequent and more severe. Just the short walk from the dining room to the office left him winded.

He laid his writing materials on the desk, then warmed his hands at the fireplace. The office felt cosy. A heavy snow had fallen during the afternoon, settling in large, loaf-like mounds on the sills. The storm had passed rapidly out to sea and now the evening was clear and starry. Distantly, carollers sang.

It would be a treat to have the entire family together,

even though there were definite signs of strain. It was no secret that Will and Carter had quarrelled when Will and Jo were in San Francisco on their wedding trip. Will took all the blame. And he'd sent Carter a formal apology. Neither of them would go into detail about the cause of the quarrel – Julia had questioned Carter in several letters – but both young men let it be known that they had fundamental disagreements which would forever keep them from being as close as they once were.

Perhaps that kind of tension and separation was to be expected, Gideon thought as he walked slowly back to his desk. He and his brothers, Matt and Jeremiah, had taken separate paths. The country was becoming a sprawling, diverse place too – so why think it unusual for an American family to display some of that diversity?

The Kents were certainly doing so. Will, for example, showed every sign of becoming a reformer; the kind of man damned in public and feared in private by those he opposed. In the short time he'd been in practice in the Mulberry Bend, with his friend Drew as partner and his wife managing the office and serving as a visiting nurse, Will had become a friend and staunch ally of Jacob Riis. Riis's book on the New York slums had created a powerful movement for reform. Will helped that movement by writing to, and testifying before, any state or municipal agency responsible for enacting and enforcing health or real estate laws.

Once Gideon had feared that Will cared about nothing except personal security and prestige. How wrong he'd been. Will's decision to marry Jo Hastings had wrenched the young man round a full hundred and eighty degrees. Gideon was immensely proud of his son. Eventually, in his own way, Will would live up to the family tradition, and carry it on. He would make a lasting mark.

Carter was another matter. He was still working for Boss Buckley, but watching local developments very closely. In a recent note to Julia, he'd said that Buckley's enemies were trying to empanel a special grand jury in Sacramento. The jury's stated purpose was to investigate the activities of San Francisco's paid lobbyist. But that was only a diversion. Buckley, and the Buckley organization, were the true targets of reform elements in the Democratic party. Carter claimed the reformers really wanted Buckley's power for themselves.

The worsening situation, as well as Carter's own ambition, had prompted him to think of moving to a larger – and safer – arena. Washington. By means of his friendship with young Hearst, he thought it might be possible to gain the notice of Sentor Hearst and, through him, some kind of political appointment in the nation's capital. Once there, he'd have a whole range of new options available. But he had to protect himself until it all worked out. He'd hinted to Julia that he had made a secret overture to the San Francisco reform group.

He closed his letter by saying that some might consider his plans a betrayal of his employer, but he did not. It was a matter of survival. He was sure Buckley would have done the very same thing in his position.

In Gideon's opinion, Carter was not precisely dishonest, but he was a young man who savoured power, and wanted more. Whether that power would corrupt him completely, Gideon couldn't say. It corrupted many politicians – and Carter already showed signs of being tainted.

Yet politics might be the only arena in which Carter could accomplish anything even remotely worthwhile. He'd evidently made a good record in San Francisco. He'd risen rapidly in the local party organization.

Gideon suspected that his stepson would make a mark, though whether it would be an entirely admirable one remained to be seen. If he went to Washington – a pit of trimmers and privilege-seekers – the outlook was doubtful.

Make a mark. The words which came to mind so easily were a painful reminder of his own shortcomings.

Another constriction in his chest bent him over his desk for half a minute. After the pain passed, he took several deep breaths, nearly gasping to get them. When his breathing became more or less normal again, he glanced at the portrait of the family's founder.

As always, the determined set of the jaw and the faintly truculent expression in the painted eyes brought a smile to Gideon's face. How he wished he could have spent even five minutes with old Philip. He knew they would have liked and understood one another.

Yet thoughts of Philip, and Philip's remarkable life – so well summarized by the briquet, the tea bottle, and the Kentucky rifle – only served to reinforce Gideon's feeling of inadequacy. Soon he turned away from the painting.

Eleanor would be home for Christmas too, along with her husband. The remodelling of their theatre, which Eleanor had proudly named the Goldman, was going well. She was starting to plan her opening cycle of plays. Ibsen, mostly. She'd come in for a lot of criticism because of that choice. She seemed to be thriving on it.

The change in Eleanor was a distinct one. He'd realized it the last time he'd spent a few days in New York. His gamble that afternoon following the disastrous luncheon with the vice president had come out in his favour; Eleanor certainly wasn't locking out the world any longer. She'd joined the women's movement, and started organizing producers and performers to fight a threatened theatrical monopoly scheme.

Gideon was overjoyed to see a new, thoughtful, and militant Eleanor emerging.

Her only setback of late was a happy one. Just a few days ago, in a letter bubbling with good cheer, she'd revealed that she was expecting a baby – and eagerly looking forward to it, even though the pregnancy would keep her from performing on her own stage in the fall.

Gideon felt confident of the family's future now. Carter might not be a trustworthy steward of the Kent traditions, but Eleanor would be, and so would Will. At long last, both young people were developing an understanding and appreciation of those traditions. That turn of events would help make it a fine Christmas. Only one thing might taint the holiday—

Make a mark.

Not many days hence, it would be 1891. The year in which he would turn forty-eight; the start of a new decade.

Time was rushing on. The industrial nation was expanding and changing at a furious rate. The changes, the swift passage of time, and the certainty that his health was failing all heightened the gloomy feelings which had tormented him of late.

Inevitably, his eye was drawn back to the mementoes – those symbols of the family's strength, and the source of his desperate discontent. He studied the tea bottle. What could he leave that was truly his own contribution? The splinter from the mast of Old Ironsides was someone else's; he had merely rediscovered it. Matt could leave his paintings, and the Renoir cartoon. But everything Gideon thought of – a copy of the *Union*; a book from Kent and Son – struck him as too ordinary.

The problem still unsolved, he turned to the work which had brought him to the office.

He reached for the old Bible – his father's pulpit Bible – which he kept on the corner of his desk. He opened to the New Testament.

For his editorial he planned to write a few paragraphs on the decade just ahead, taking as his text Acts 2, the nineteenth verse, in which God said, *And I will shew wonders in heaven above, and signs in the earth beneath.* The signs referred to were dire ones. Blood; smoke and fire; the signs of the last days of mankind. Gideon meant to use the text in a more positive way, to characterize his vision of the coming ten-year period and the new century just beyond.

Of course his pessimism had not been removed overnight by the happy changes in the family. He still saw too much materialism in America; a materialism that threatened to corrupt too many of its citizens, as it had corrupted the Pennels. Last summer the patriarch of the Pennel family had been found hanging from a bedroom chandelier in his Westchester mansion. A day or two later it had become evident why he'd taken his own life. A shopgirl had gone to a West Side abortionist, been irreparably hurt, and had dragged herself to a charity hospital. Before she bled to death, she had summoned a reporter and named Thurman Pennel as the man who'd paid her to destroy his child.

Pennel's daughter was currently living in St Louis. Hester Davis of the *Union* had told Gideon that after Will had jilted her, the girl had been unable to find another suitor of quality. So she'd married a man of considerable wealth but no social standing; a Midwestern hardware merchant twice her age. Presumably she was now a ruler of whatever passed for Society in St Louis. Mrs Pennel was reportedly bedridden in a Long Island sanitarium for the nervously disturbed.

Gideon felt sorry for the Pennels now. Yet compassion didn't eradicate his feeling that they were worthless, venal people. People unmoved by principle, indifferent to corruption, driven by greed and concerned only with whether or not others admired and envied them.

In Gideon's opinion there were too many people like the Pennels in America. Perhaps it was merely part of a cycle which would reverse itself if the electorate again turned to leaders of substance; men who put principle above the kind of conventional thinking typical of party hacks. Among the Republicans, Gideon considered young Roosevelt such a man; a potential leader able to inspire people to heed their highest impulses instead of their lowest. On the other side of the political fence there was an impressive though rather shy professor of jurisprudence and political economy at Princetown. Gideon had met him recently. His name was Wilson.

Other things contributed to Gideon's hope. One was the country's incredible productivity. Year after year, America was setting records for industrial output – and doing it despite depression and political in-fighting.

Another strong point was the wondrous flood of inventions for which the American system provided a strong material incentive. A week earlier, he'd taken one of his infrequent forays as a working journalist and had visited the expanded West Orange, New Jersey laboratories of Thomas Edison.

Edison had showed off the machine with which he was currently tinkering. It was a device for rapidly projecting a series of still photographs so as to create the illusion of motion. Amazed and impressed, Gideon went on to New York with a valise full of notes which he turned into a report on the current activities of America's foremost mechanical genius.

Signs and wonders.

He glanced up, pen in hand, but the first word of his editorial was still unwritten. A dozen carollers had stopped beneath the office window. He listened to their song. 'Adeste Fideles,' the old, familiar hymn of praise and faith. He found himself softly singing a phrase or two. Inspired by the song, a sudden insight flashed into mind. Faith was not only the essence of the great

Christian holiday soon to be celebrated – the essence, indeed, of all the world's religions – it was the essence of America as well. What but faith in the goodness and uniqueness of its essential principles could unite and sustain a country as diverse as America? What but faith could have enabled the country to survive the trials of the Revolution, the chaos and grief of a civil war – or the rapacity of a small class of men such as Louis Kent and Thurman Pennel?

Faith was the essence of the family, too. Faith – its other name was hope – had brought young Philip from Auvergne to Boston. And now that the family was becoming diverse just like the nation, faith in commonly shared principles was all that could hold it together in the coming years.

Other Kents before him had left tangible symbols to show their faith in the family and in its future. That was what bothered Gideon most. For months, he'd been trying to think of what he could leave. He didn't know.

He looked from the portrait of Philip to the little bottle containing the thin layer of dried tea. He examined the other mementoes one by one, feeling a stab of jealousy when his eye came to rest on the box of earth from the Union Pacific. Even the Irishman Michael Boyle had contributed something, and he hadn't been born a Kent—

'Gideon?'

'Oh – Julia.'

He hadn't heard the door open. Smiling, she glided toward him, her skirts rustling. She bent over the desk:

'What are you writing, dear?'

With a rueful look, he held up the blank sheet. 'Nothing. It was to be an editorial, but I can't even get started.'

Her faint frown showed she knew something was wrong.

She walked to the window, gazing out at the snow-covered Common. As he followed, she said, 'I'm so looking forward to the children coming home. Even if Will and Carter find it hard to get along any more, I'll be glad to have them here. Sometimes I feel so – oh, so decrepit and worthless without them—'

She turned, her lovely dark eyes tinged with melancholy. She put her hands on his shoulders. 'We're old, you and I.'

He smiled. 'Getting there. Getting there. But the family's in good hands.'

'A little over a year ago, you didn't believe that.'

'True. But things are working out.'

She leaned back against him and gazed at the snow. 'How beautiful it is.' She heard him draw a quick, sharp breath, and turned. 'What's wrong? Is it the pain in your chest again?'

'No, there's nothing—'

'Gideon Kent, don't try to deceive me. This has gone on far too long. You must see someone! Your own son, preferably. He knows about the pain, by the way.'

'He does? How?'

'I should say he suspects. He told me so.'

'How did he find out, Julia?'

With a smile that didn't hide her concern, she said, 'Why, I suppose it has something to do with his being a doctor. He claims he's been aware of certain symptoms you've been exhibiting for months. I want you to speak to him the moment he arrives, Gideon. I won't hear of you saying no this time.'

Gideon laughed. 'Well – I know better than to argue with a determined woman. I'll let him look me over. But I assure you there's nothing wrong. I won't permit anything to be wrong.'

He slipped his arms round her from behind and pulled her gently against him as the fire crackled and filled the room with warmth. In his mind he heard bugles blowing; Stuart singing; cannon roaring. Quickly the sounds began to fade, just as the song of the carollers was fading—

'I'll be around ten years more at least,' he promised. 'I want to see the Kents safely into the twentieth century.'

'Spoken like a father. You forget your children are grown.'

'Yes, I do, don't I? Constantly.'

'They really don't need your protection any longer. They can get along very well on their own.'

'I know.' The sadness in those words was relieved by a smile. 'I will, however, fight to the end to keep them from guessing that I know.' He pivoted slowly to the mantel, the feelings of inadequacy overwhelming. 'I wonder what they'll add to that collection? I've added nothing.'

She turned to face him.

'Is that what you've been thinking about lately? At times you've seemed very troubled.'

He answered with a nod.

'But you've given the family a great deal, Gideon. Most particularly, three children to carry the Kents well into the next century. Even Carter will make his mark, though it probably won't be a spotless one. Your accomplishment is as real as any of those objects on the mantel. Don't you see that?'

'No.'

'A few years ago, you doubted there was anyone in the family to carry it on as you thought it should be carried on. You admit you've changed your mind—'

'Yes. Because the children have changed.'

'Changed and grown. With your guidance! They're strong, capable people. That's what you've put into this family. It may not be as visible as Philip's sword and gun, or the piece of mast you found. But it's every bit as substantial.'

He thought about that. Perhaps she was right. Perhaps she'd identified the best – the only thing – he could leave behind; the best that could be left behind by any man. Children who had been brought up to behave responsibly, and to believe in something beyond their own self-gratification.

A bit reassured, he squeezed her arm. A moment later he said:

'Would you mind if we walked a little?'

'It's very cold, dear.'

'We can bundle up. I'd like to go to the waterfront. I always feel closest to old Philip down there. A dock was the first piece of America he felt under his feet. I don't know whether you understand—'

'Certainly I do. But are you sure you're feeling up to it?'

'I'm perfectly fit. I tell you I intend to be around for a good many years yet. Count on it.'

'Oh, Gideon – I will. I love you so much.'

'I love you, Julia.'

They kissed, long and ardently, while the fire popped and a log broke and fell. Then the tall, bearded man and the lovely dark-haired woman left the room, and the watching eyes of the family's founder.

They donned old coats, scarves and gloves and overshoes, and stepped into a bright winter night that was surprisingly windless. Arm in arm, they strolled slowly through the melting snow, listening to sounds of Christmas merrymaking behind brightly lit windows, or catching the occasional music of carollers. Soon they reached the piers where dark vessels lay creaking in the cold. The harbour was not yet frozen. A rising moon glittered on the water that had been witness to so much history.

During the walk, Gideon had been turning Julia's remarks over and over in his mind. His children – and her son – were the legacy the two of them would leave

953

behind. Will's idealism, and Eleanor's – and whatever conscience he and Julia had managed to instil to temper Carter's opportunism – those were the mementoes they would add to the family's heritage.

It had taken Julia to make him see that, Lord, how he loved her. She was the one who always pulled him through the hardest times, and made him perceive light in the darkness. His sense of inadequacy began to fade, and he was able to fix his attention on the quiet sea stretching away eastward into moon-silvered darkness.

Out there lay Europe. Philip Kent's beginnings. The beginnings of the family. A feeling of tranquillity and confidence slowly fell over Gideon as he stared at the sea. The family was secure. It would go on, and it would thrive despite the inevitable reversals that were a part of life. Eleanor was already carrying still another generation. What signs and wonders would that child see? Many, he was sure.

How wisely old Philip had chosen. How wisely and how well. The Kents had grown up in a good land, and they had contributed in a small way to that growth and that goodness, Gideon thought as he gazed at the ocean separating the creaking pier from the great unseen land mass of Europe. All at once he was absolutely certain of one thing Julia had said. He was no longer necessary to the family's survival. There was a touch of sadness in knowing that, but there was also a release, and peace.

All at once a worm of pain began to gnaw the centre of his chest. He sat down on a bollard; drew a laboured breath. Then:

'You know, Julia, I never thought I'd live beyond my forty-seventh year, and now I've nearly made it. Only a few more days to go.'

'Forgive me, darling, but what's so special about forty-seven?'

He spoke with difficulty, the pain more intense all at

once. But he wasn't alarmed; it had been almost as intense many times before.

'That's an average man's lifetime. Ten years longer than it was the year I was born.'

'And you didn't think you'd make it?'

'No.'

'Well, I'm glad you did. But you should have known you would.'

The pain was crushing. He sat perfectly still.

'Should have known? Why?'

With her voice full of love, she said, 'You've never been an average man, Gideon. 'You've made a mark on this family that your children and their children will remember forever. Be proud of that. Be proud of them.'

He didn't answer, but he gave an almost imperceptible nod. In his mind he heard bugles blowing; Stuart singing; cannon roaring. How quickly it had all gone. Too quickly—

The lights on an outward bound steamer held Julia's attention for a moment or so. She didn't see Gideon stiffen briefly, then appear to relax. When she looked at him again, his good eye was closed.

He sat motionless. The wind stirred his gray hair and beard. She touched him and only then realized he wasn't asleep.

She clasped his shoulder to verify her suspicion. 'Oh, my dearest—' she whispered.

But as the first tears came to her eyes, she saw that he was smiling.

The Furies
John Jakes

Bestselling author of the *North and South* trilogy

Amanda de la Gura, survivor of the Alamo massacre, camp follower with the Mexican army, tavern owner in San Francisco, possesses true Kent family courage – and independence far beyond most women of her time.

An old enemy now owns the Boston publishing business founded by Philip Kent, and is producing sordid and racist books. Amanda is determined to regain the business that bears her name, to restore its honour. Her obsession leads to financial intrigue . . . to murder . . .

John Jakes' *The Furies*, the fourth of *The Kent Family Chronicles*, spans the violent political and social changes of the first half of the nineteenth century, through the life and loves of a remarkable and liberated woman.

FONTANA PAPERBACKS

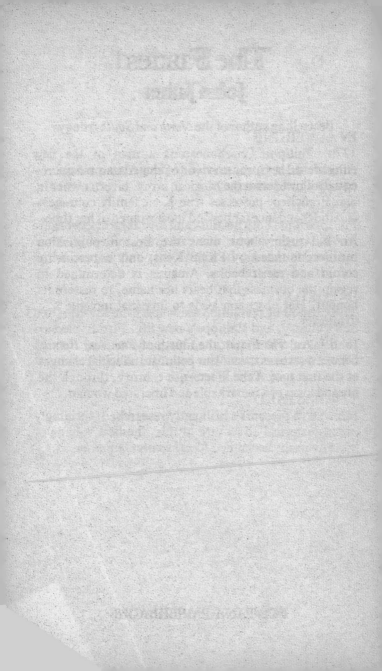

The Bastard
John Jakes

IN AUVERGNE
1770: Philippe Charboneau is a man of the new enlightened age, committed to dangerous principles – equality and democracy.

IN KENT
Philippe finds both hostility and love as he discovers the ironic truth about his ancestry. Fleeing from murderous threats, he knows that only escape to the colonies can save him.

IN BOSTON
The turmoil of revolution tears apart the loyalties of a new country, and Philippe's new life. Firmly pledged to the American patriots, his passions are divided between two women: the beautiful Alicia Parkhurst and headstrong Anne Ware.

THE BASTARD
John Jakes presents a brilliantly researched, thrillingly paced historical adventure in this, the first volume of his universally acclaimed *Kent Family Chronicles*.

FONTANA PAPERBACKS

Fontana Paperbacks: Fiction

Fontana is a leading paperback publisher of fiction. Below are some recent titles.

- ☐ JUSTICE Ian St James £4.50
- ☐ FIRST STRIKE Douglas Terman £3.99
- ☐ NOW AND THEN, AMEN Jon Cleary £3.50
- ☐ THE SHEIKH AND THE DUSTBIN
  George MacDonald Fraser £2.95
- ☐ FLASHMAN AT THE CHARGE
  George MacDonald Fraser £3.50
- ☐ BLACK WIDOW Bart Davis £3.50
- ☐ PAPER DOLL Jim Shephard £2.95
- ☐ TRAPP AND WORLD WAR III Brian Callison £2.95
- ☐ THE LAZARUS FILE Stuart Prebble £2.95

You can buy Fontana paperbacks at your local bookshop or newsagent. Or you can order them from Fontana Paperbacks, Cash Sales Department, Box 29, Douglas, Isle of Man. Please send a cheque, postal or money order (not currency) worth the purchase price plus 22p per book for postage (maximum postage required is £3.00 for orders within the UK).

NAME (Block letters)_____

ADDRESS_____

_____